READER'S DIGEST

CONDENSED BOOKS

FIRST EDITION

THE READER'S DIGEST ASSOCIATION LIMITED
25 Berkeley Square, London W1X 6AB

**THE READER'S DIGEST ASSOCIATION
SOUTH AFRICA (PTY) LTD**
Nedbank Centre, Strand Street, Cape Town

Printed in Great Britain by Petty & Sons Ltd, Leeds

Original cover design by Jeffery Matthews M.S.I.A.

For information as to ownership
of copyright in the material in this book see last page

ISBN 0 340 24481 X

Reader's Digest
CONDENSED BOOKS

THE MASTER MARINER
Nicholas Monsarrat

THE SNOW TIGER
Desmond Bagley

ALONE
IN THE WILDERNESS
Mike Tomkies

OVERLOAD
Arthur Hailey

COLLECTOR'S LIBRARY
EDITION

In this Volume:

THE

Master Mariner

by Nicholas Monsarrat (p. 9)

Nicholas Monsarrat's latest, and perhaps his greatest, novel is an epic of British sea-going adventure and achievement, a story to fire the imagination and fill the heart with pride.

The towering figures who shaped two hundred years of our maritime history are seen through the eyes of an ordinary seaman, Matthew Lawe, doomed to sail the seven seas until he has purged his guilt for a dreadful act of cowardice. Francis Drake pursuing the Armada, Samuel Pepys reforming the navy, Captain Cook exploring the world, Admiral Nelson routing the French: all play their part in a story full of vigour and excitement.

THE SNOW TIGER

by Desmond Bagley (p. 173)

For centuries the Maoris had recognized the threat of the mountainside looming over the little New Zealand town. Their name for it—Hukahoronui—meant "The Great Snow Slide", and recalled disasters of long ago. But the white men were eager for profit from the local mine and safety measures were costly, so they ignored the tiger of destruction sleeping under the mountain's deceptively soft white snow.

This is the exciting story of the appalling consequences of their apathy and greed, and of bitter rivalries which split the town in two.

ALONE in the Wilderness

by Mike Tomkies (p. 287)

Eagle and grizzly bear, cougar and caribou, squirrel and racoon: these were Mike Tomkies's neighbours when he threw up a successful career as a show-business journalist for a life in the log cabin he built for himself in the British Columbian wilderness.

He writes with humour and sensitivity of the rewards and hardships of solitude and self-sufficiency, of the homespun philosophy of old backwoodsmen and above all of the beauty and grandeur of one of the last wild places in the world.

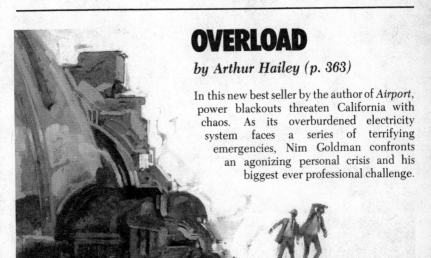

OVERLOAD

by Arthur Hailey (p. 363)

In this new best seller by the author of *Airport*, power blackouts threaten California with chaos. As its overburdened electricity system faces a series of terrifying emergencies, Nim Goldman confronts an agonizing personal crisis and his biggest ever professional challenge.

THE Master Mariner

Book One   Running Proud

A condensation of the book by

NICHOLAS MONSARRAT

Illustrations within the text
by Bruno Ellettori

PUBLISHED BY CASSELL

For over twenty years Nicholas Monsarrat has been planning what he sees as his lifetime's most important work, above even his legendary *The Cruel Sea*. It is nothing less than a two-part novel covering the whole proud history of British maritime achievement, from the days of the first Queen Elizabeth to those of the second. This first part takes us from the Armada to Trafalgar, more than two hundred years of adventure, battles and discovery.

One ordinary man spans the ages: Matthew Lawe, West Country seaman, doomed by a witch's curse endlessly to circle the globe until he has expiated a terrible act of cowardice. With Matthew we see Sir Francis Drake set his little ships against the might of the Spanish Armada; walk the teeming streets of seventeenth-century London with Samuel Pepys, secretary of the Admiralty; witness the epic voyages and shocking death of Captain Cook, the great navigator; observe at first-hand the private emotions and public triumphs of the most famous sailor of them all, Horatio Nelson.

In a novel of stunning breadth and power Nicholas Monsarrat brings vividly to life the great men who have shaped so much of our past—and our future—at sea. It is a story to stir the hearts of all of us.

Part One
1588

THE MAN at the edge of the tide mark stood a little apart from his fellows, not choosing to join the talk of the ship-boat's crew, wanting only to enjoy the hot July sun and the brief peace of the Plymouth shore. His ship-boat, bearing the vice-admiral and a half-score of his volunteer gentlemen, had grounded on the beach some way from the landing-steps to avoid the throng which pressed round their commander wherever he went. And now that he and the other great lords had gone about their business in Plymouth, the crew stood idling, glad of the sun, the firmness of the sand under their bare feet, and their shelter from the forcible wind which even now was whipping Plymouth Sound into a grey-white fury.

The man standing apart, by name Matthew Lawe, was of the middle height, broad, slow-moving, with the brown-grained skin and the spread stance of a West Country seaman. He was bravely

ABOVE: The Battle of the Armada, painted about 1600. Sir Francis Drake by Nicholas Hilliard.

dressed, like all his companions, as fitted the vice-admiral's own ship-boat's crew; his quilted coat was decked with bold Tudor ribbons of green and white. As chosen coxswain to the vice-admiral, he was a young man in earned authority. His crew were all trained men of his own making, and though he stood aloof he kept them within the corner of his eye, ready to check their talk if it grew rough or boisterous.

At his back lay Sutton Pool, the inner harbour of Plymouth; this Pool, and the whole Sound itself, was one forest of ships, a woven pattern of drying sails, steep oaken hulls, rocking masts, and banners streaming in the brisk southerly wind. Before him lay the town, clamorous and astir with men, and the slopes of the broad, green esplanade known as Plymouth Hoe. But Matthew Lawe was preoccupied with smaller things. His gaze rested on the tide mark: the rime of flotsam on the sand, the seaweed, the chippings of wood, the pale husks of shrimp and crab, the shells of periwinkle blue, blood red, dawn yellow. To him, this tide mark spelled peace —almost the sole peace in England on that day. For all elsewhere, in Plymouth, and indeed the whole realm, there was clamour, martial show, boasting, striving, and fear.

By now they had lain nearly eight weeks in harbour, and it had proved little enough time to make the *Revenge*, and all the other ships of the English fleet, ready to meet the might of Spain. Plymouth, finest of English harbours, could scarcely contain the men and ships that thronged about. Every young man within twenty miles, and every grandfather but lately dreaming by his chimney corner, was now labouring on ship's business. By day the ship-boats, barges, cock-boats, and pinnaces sped to and fro, bearing men and weapons; the fly-boats loaded with provisions went darting about; the powder hoys with their red flags of danger wove carefully through the fleet; on shore, the shipwrights and the sail-makers and the armourers toiled against the run of the clock, to fashion new spars, flaxen ropes, brass cannon, freshwater casks, shot for the cannon-royal.

By night these same men wandered ashore, drinking at the Turk's Head in St. Andrew's Street, and the Pope's Head in Looe Street, where the vice-admiral himself had his household. They drank deep, in courage or in fear, as sailors always do on the eve of battle; or they drew apart, and wrote crabbed letters to their wives; sometimes they would go wenching. But always, on the morrow, they returned to work, in their ships or at their forges; making the whole of Plymouth a cauldron of warlike preparation.

So it had been for the past two months or more; and now, with this spear-point of England thus sharpened and poised on the threshold of war, the ship-boat's crew was waiting, as they had waited on a hundred strands, from Plymouth to the Magellan Strait, for the greatest sailor in all the world.

They knew him as a man, yet saw him also as the gleaming pennant of achievement: Sir Francis Drake, vice-admiral of England, the first captain-general that ever sailed about the globe, knighted by the Queen's own hand on his return with staggering treasure. It was a name to enthral the common sort, and to inspire even the jealous among the glittering array of great lords who were his peers, they being seamen, men-at-arms, and venturers all—Raleigh, Frobisher, Humphrey Gilbert, Howard of Effingham, Richard Grenville, John Hawkins, designer of the English fleet—even among these, Sir Francis Drake was the nonpareil.

It was small wonder that, when he needed volunteers to man the ships against the threatening Armada of Spain, men and boys had flocked to his standard from every part of the West of England. There was one such among this very ship-boat's crew—young Jem, a farm lad who had walked a full hundred miles from Shepton Mallet in Somerset, and had taken to the oar like a Turk at the galleys. Indeed, Matthew Lawe himself, ten years earlier, as a runagate orphan boy from the Poor School at Barnstaple in Devon, had been cozened by the same magnet and had made the same translation from the plough to the sail. Drake, the great captain, drew men after him to the very end of the world.

There were some indeed who had striven to set up a quarrel when, by the Queen's command, almost on the eve of battle, Sir Francis had been supplanted in the rank of admiral by Lord Howard of Effingham. There were many who swore wounds and blood that this was a matter not of merit but of rank; and that merely because the Duke of Medina Sidonia was to lead the Spanish fleet, it was for this paltry reason thought necessary to oppose him with a man of noble family—as if one coat of arms could fight another. Clearly, Sir Francis's gifts and his exploits had entitled him to command the whole enterprise.

11

But Drake would have none of these rebellious mutterings: he led his squadron out to welcome the new lord admiral with an excellent grace, firing the salute to the *Ark Royal* and the other great Crown ships, sounding the trumpets and drums, lowering his own flag and putting in its place the vice-admiral's standard. Not for him the disobedience of lesser men. This had always been his quality, a faithful mirror of the obedience and self-command of the ancient Romans. And those who called him pirate and greedy freebooter were left to scratch their heads.

Suddenly there was a stir among the ship-boat's crew, a general pointing to seawards, and Matthew Lawe, preoccupied with a shell in the shape of a pearly breast-plate, was recalled to the world by one of his crew, shouting: "Matthew! The scouting pinnace!"

The crewman was John Waggoner, a man valued for his keen eye; it was he who, on that voyage round the globe, had ever been the first to spy their looked-for landfall, whether on the coast of Brazil or in the bleak latitudes of the Magellan Strait. Now John Waggoner was shading his eyes and pointing, and presently they saw what it was that had caught his attention at the very margin of Plymouth Sound—a small two-masted ship, coming on in hot haste, under full sail.

Matthew Lawe walked back a pace to the higher ground, to give him a longer range. "Is it truly she, John?"

"Aye . . . I can see his honour's banner at the foremast. . . . 'Tis the *Golden Hind*, come back again."

The *Golden Hind*—it was a name of omen; not the famous ship of Drake which had made the circumnavigation, but one of the same baptism, under Captain Thomas Fleming, dispatched these many days to scout for the coming of the Spanish Dons. They watched her bearing towards them, scudding before the frank wind; threading her way past the great ships of the fleet, lowering her flag to the admiral in the *Ark Royal*, dousing her taut sails one by one as she neared the confines of Sutton Pool.

She had a breathless air; as she drew near they saw that her mainsail was set high, and when she came up to her anchorage they could catch a flash of watery deck. Clearly she had news that would allow no delay. There was a creamy splash at her forefoot as the anchor plunged down; the last of her sails was loosely furled. Then, after some confusion and shouting, two small cock-boats were put over her side and drew away from the *Golden Hind*. The first buffeted its way out of the inner harbour again, making for the flagship lying in the Sound; the other, with a crew of four oars, and an officer sitting in the stern, was steering towards their own boat that bore the vice-admiral's standard, and presently grounded on the sand a few paces from them.

The officer jumped down in haste and strode towards them. He was a tall young man, with a weary face and yet a proud bearing. Matthew Lawe came forward, lifting his cap. "Sir!" he said, stiffly, as he had been schooled. "Coxswain to the vice-admiral!"

"Is his honour still ashore?"

"Aye, sir," Matthew answered. "Up to the Hoe this two hours."

"I'll go seek him. . . ." The officer turned towards his own boat, and called out, "Await me here!" Then he made as if to go.

Matthew Lawe summoned his courage. "Is there news, sir?"

The officer turned back, losing some of his haughtiness with his will to be the first to impart. "Yes, lad. The Spaniard is come at last."

"Where away, then?"

"Off the Lizard, when we left them. Nearer now, by God's blood!"

Lizard Point. Fewer than twenty leagues' distance from Plymouth. . . . As the young officer turned again towards the Hoe, Matthew felt, not for the first time in that year nor on that day, the mortal chill of fear.

2

FEAR. . . . It was something that a man must come to feel, who kept the company of Drake. No matter how bold one's spirit, nor how much a man confided in his captain's skill and fortune, fear crept in apace to confound judgment and turn the knees to water. For that famous skill must some time fail, that luck must run out.

For Matthew Lawe, fear had begun slowly, a single strand at a time. The sickly orphan boy of eleven years, who had run from the bleak and cruel Poor School in Barnstaple and taken to the sea, had followed his captain round the world, and now, when he was twice eleven years, and grown to broad manhood in the service of Sir Francis, he could not truly say at what moment he had felt himself more afraid than valiant.

Certainly it was not at the beginning, when the *Pelican*, with five other barks and pinnaces, and near one hundred and sixty men, had left Plymouth to try a course around the globe under a captain already renowned for his daring and good fortune. Then, it was all magic and young ecstasy, a voyage like a golden dream.

The *Pelican* and her train of pretty chickens—the barks *Marigold* and *Elizabeth*, the pinnaces *Christopher* and *Benedict*, the fly-boat *Swan*—had set sail from Plymouth in stormy seas. From thence forward, for the space of three years, not one day of that voyage was without its beauty, its strangeness, its excitement and its terror.

In Barbary on the coast of Africa they tasted the flesh of coconuts; on the line of the equator they ate dolphins, bonitos, and flying fish. Then they voyaged sixty-three days without sight of land, and when land came up, it was Brazil. Here the rude inhabitants, sighting their ships, lit fires and danced to conjure up shoals and storms; and presently they were struck by a gale. Here they killed three hundred seawolves with cudgels, and saw huge footprints ashore. Here they navigated, for a space, the great River del Plata.

Down south now for many days, and to Port St. Julian, where the treacherous Patagonians slew some of their company, and they found a gibbet used by Magellan near sixty years before to execute some of his rebellious crew. At its foot were their dry bones. Here also, Thomas Doughty, shipmaster in their own squadron, met a like fate. He had expressed the wish to return home, and had sought secretly to suborn others to this mutiny. Drake, learning of this, flew into a cold rage, damned them all for a clutch of caterpillars, had a public inquiry made, and asked for their verdict. Without delay, they pronounced Thomas Doughty the child of death and his head was struck from his body. When it was over, Drake took the head by the hair, shook it in the face of the company, and cried: "Long live the Queen of England!" Then he led them all in the holy Psalms.

Now (some said as a punishment for this murderous spite) came the dark part of their journey, the fearful passage through the Magellan Strait. Often it was as if a blind man were threading an endless forest of sailmaker's needles: every passage was stopped, and every lead that promised them progress grew narrow and came at last to a wall of rock. It seemed that they were doomed never to burst out into the Pacific Ocean, but would turn and twist till their ships fell to pieces and they themselves, grown gaunt, were food at last for the fish.

It was in this same Strait of Magellan that they changed the name of *Pelican* to that of *Golden Hind*, to honour the lord chancellor of England, Sir Christopher Hatton, whose coat of arms displayed a golden deer. Some hoped for better things from this change, and perhaps Sir Francis had mingled a good and a bad potion—for shortly they found a way through the Strait, and came out at last into the liberal sea of the Pacific, only to meet there a furious storm, which endured not five but fifty days.

In this storm, they lost the last of their consorts. The *Marigold* perished with all her souls aboard; the *Elizabeth* disgracefully turned her tail and fled back to England. (Of the others, the *Benedict* had parted company near Plymouth, the *Swan* and *Christopher* had grown leaky and been broken up for firewood.) Now the *Golden Hind* was alone, with half the world behind her, and half before.

It might have been thought that Sir Francis Drake would creep quietly homewards, having given ample proof of his valour. But such was not his mettle; he drew only strength and further ambition from adversity. He now embarked upon a fresh and glittering adventure. Perhaps it was now that the young Matthew Lawe, a lad rising thirteen years, felt his first foreboding.

Sir Francis hated Spain, with all his heart and mind; this hatred had pricked a spirit already rash enough. It grew partly from his devotion to his sovereign, Elizabeth, whom he wished to see queen without peer; partly from his loathing of the Spaniard's religion; and partly from misliking their cruelty and treachery. It enraged him that they showed neither honour nor mercy to their prisoners; his friend, John Oxenham, was after capture publicly hanged at Lima, and one of John Hawkins's men had been burnt alive in the marketplace of Seville.

Now was his time of revenge. He was loose in an ocean where

no Englishman had sailed before; no man knew him to be there; the rich plunder of Peru and New Spain was his for the fighting. He fell upon the Spaniard like a hawk unleashed.

They took ship after rich ship, they stormed ashore and wrought havoc, from Valparaiso to Panama. They took every kind of spoil—emeralds, gold, silks, china dishes, chests of *reals* of eight. They landed at Tarapaxa, and found by the seashore a Spaniard fast asleep, who had lying by him thirteen bars of silver, which weighed 4000 ducats Spanish; they took the silver, and left the man. To the north, they captured eight llamas, each carrying two leather bags of fifty pounds of silver. They seized 1700 jars of wine in one place; and in another, a falcon of gold, handsomely wrought, with a great emerald set in its breast.

Lastly they took a huge carrack of Spain, the *Cacafuego* (meaning Spit-Fire), boarding by stealth and killing their prey. She was the richest prize of all: her prime lading was twenty-six tons of pure silver, worth half a million English pounds. Then they quit the havoc they had wrought and sailed northwards again on their lawful way.

Now, as they voyaged northwards, seeking a passage which might trend east towards England and home, it grew cold—a nipping frost, which infected every part of the *Golden Hind*, and daily blighted their hopes. Presently, having reached the forty-eighth parallel north, they put back again; and venturing inshore they came to an entrance so broad and fair that Drake named it the Golden Gate.

They took possession of this land also, calling it Nova Albion. But the *Golden Hind* still stood at the crossroads of the world. Barred from a northeast passage home, Drake had choice of two pathways: to retrace the track by which he came, or to voyage onwards round the globe. Once again, he chose the unknown and the valiant path; and from then on their journey grew fantastic.

Seeking China, or a way past it, they sailed seven thousand miles across the Pacific, where no English ship had ever ventured; they were sixty-eight days without sight of land, divining their course by astrolabe, cross-staff, and compass, until they came to a confusion of islands: Mindanao, and the Moluccas, and Celebes, and Java. They found a strange land that had canoes full of savages with long nails, and blackened teeth, and holes in the lobes of their ears whence they hung their ornaments. For many months they wandered in that archipelago, seeking a way westwards. Free at last, they crossed another great ocean, and presently came up with the Cape of Good Hope, that which Diaz had first rounded, the fairest cape they saw in the whole circumference of the earth. But they passed by without a respite, and came home to Plymouth Sound again, having traversed the whole world and taken three years in the task.

It was a wondrous voyage for a boy, and for Sir Francis a resplendent feat of daring which resounded throughout the realm.

3

ABOVE them, on the pathway leading to the Hoe, there was a stir. The lieutenant from the cock-boat came into sight again. His brow was creased, and the silver-chased sword at his belt slapped his thigh angrily as he descended with resolute strides.

"Look closely," John Waggoner murmured, "and you will perceive the flea in his ear."

"How so?" Matthew Lawe said. "With such news of the coming of the Spaniard, he should have been received like a king!"

"Sir Francis is used to kings," Waggoner answered.

The lieutenant drew near them, his expression sour. His cock-boat's crew stood to their oars, waiting for his embarkation. Matthew Lawe doffed his cap afresh. "Did you find his honour, sir?"

"Aye," the lieutenant answered curtly.

"Does he come, then?"

"No. I found your *vice-admiral*," he said, with cutting emphasis, "playing at bowls, up on the Hoe. I told him that the Spaniard was near. He seemed to find it no greater matter. He said there was time to win the game, and thrash the Spaniards afterwards."

At that, there was a murmuring, and laughter among the two boats' crews. The cock-boat's men, who had driven far to bring their news, only to have it thus despised, were astonished, then full of derision; they jested that if some people were so slow into battle, they themselves must needs do the work of two.

Drake's own men were equally astonished, but staunch in their loyalty: if the vice-admiral had said this thing, then the thing was the truth. They bid the men of the *Golden Hind* go on ahead; the *Revenge* would follow shortly, to turn defeat into victory.

The lieutenant waited while the cock-boat was pushed to the waterline; then he and his crew were gone, with a flurry of oars, and Drake's men were left to wait at the tide mark, under the sun.

"Fools!" Waggoner said. "They do not know his honour. He will come when the time is ripe."

"If the Spaniards are up to the Lizard, it is ripe enough now," muttered James Weaver, an older man. "What was it he said—'win the game of bowls'? He trusts his luck too far."

"Luck!" Waggoner said. "Did luck bring us round the world? Skill, and preparation, and valour—those are his qualities. Luck is for children, and women!"

"Who talks of women?" another voice said. "Belike his honour plays his bowls between the sheets. . . . Shall he take time to finish *that* game? The Spaniards could be first in London town."

There was a roar of rough laughter.

"Curb your tongue!" Matthew said harshly to the man who had last spoken. "Are you looking for a lashing at the capstan?"

"Easy, Matthew," Waggoner interposed. "We did but jest."

"Then keep your jests. His honour does not roll in the same filth as you."

There was a wondering silence. They knew it was Matthew's duty to keep order, being the vice-admiral's coxswain—to command his crew, to see his boat trimmed with carpet and cushions, to cheer his gang with his silver whistle, and to steer his boat. Matthew had their respect; but he had never yet used his authority for so slight a reason.

Matthew turned away. He was uneasy, and secretly afraid, which was why he had rounded on one of his men for a careless joke. The talk of "winning the game of bowls" was what had moved him; it was just such a thing as Sir Francis would say, and it seemed to be forcing his famous luck too deep into peril. It could not be denied that their captain swallowed huge hazards in his appetite for conquest.

One such hazard, which might have been the ruin of them all, was the late attack on Cadiz. "Shall we squat like chickens, waiting for the fox?" Drake had demanded, when news of the great Armada's preparation reached England. "Do we drop an egg in terror, or thrust up a torch to smoke out the robber? By God's leave, I will take my torch and singe that Spanish king's beard!"

For this "singeing", he had chosen Cadiz, the heart of the enemy's might, thick with armed ships and warlike stores. He had sailed into their lair, sunk or burned thirty-three of the Spanish fleet, sailed forth again without a scratch, and so delayed their stroke that the Armada only set out now, a year late. But the chances they had faced in this enterprise. . . . Matthew Lawe could run with sweat at the mere remembrance.

And the offspring of this brazen insolence now towered above them all. A foe pricked to the raging fury of revenge, the Armada stood at the great door of England—while Drake, who had so boldly tempted them, delayed like a truant boy on Plymouth Hoe.

At his back Matthew Lawe heard young Jem, the farm lad who had learned his boasting in this same stable, say as he took a swig from the water keg, "Tomorrow we shall be quaffing Spanish blood!"; and Lawe, even as he smiled—for the boy was a favourite of them all—thought, with a sick heart: "This is the great Armada, not a harvest home. You will not be so bold, when you spill out your guts on the deck."

Matthew's private fear was the fear of all England: a country long convinced by rumour that she was to be invaded by a mighty foe, and long suspecting that cowards in high places, and Queen Elizabeth's miserly spirit, had left them defenceless. The royal coffers (it was said) were shrunk to nothing, and the fleets must make do with what they had.

The rumours grew like giants of despair. The Armada was to embark thirty thousand soldiers, under the Duke of Parma, at Dunkerque across the Channel. They would come in boats, in barges, in wicker coracles, and when they touched the coast of Kent they would sear it with flame and red-hot cannonballs, and set the whole downland afire, crops and villages and citizens alike. Then they would march inland and join hands with the Catholic north, and bring down the whole commonwealth. . . . England, like a starveling orphan, lay at their mercy already.

But Drake, who had great connections, and must have known his country's peril, would have none of it. The simple spur of anger was enough to spark him: to hear his Queen called "a poisonous strumpet" by the Dons of Spain doubled his loyalty—and his rashness. Sir Francis's loathing of the Catholic religion had become a byword, even among a nation split by the axe of this division. But could not such hatred lead a man too far? Could not courage itself?

Now warned by sudden noise and movement, Matthew Lawe looked up to the heights of Plymouth Hoe, and saw that he might soon discover his answer. A great press of people was advancing down the fair green slope which led to the beach. In the van was all the quality of Plymouth: ruffs and ribbons fluttering in the breeze, the sun gleaming on polished blades, silver buttons and buckles. At their back was a throng of townsfolk, less glittering but not less jaunty. High spirits were in the air; the man they escorted met only smiles and shining faces.

Matthew Lawe needed no second glance at this figure in the centre of the crowd. He rounded swiftly on his crew. "Launch your boat! Then stand to your oars!"

Their great captain drew near. He was forty-six, at the peak of manhood, with a countryman's stalwart body and a sailor's ruddy colour in his face. The red beard, which seemed to gape like a cavern when he was merry, and to jut like a rock when the mood —or the wind—turned contrary, was trimmed with as much care as one of his own sails. He was a man who could look the whole world in the face, and had indeed done as much, and either find it to his satisfaction, or make it so.

A fine friend, a foul enemy, he delighted to call his officers into conference when any doubt arose. He would listen. He would nod agreement, or tap his clay pipe-stem against his teeth. Then he would act just as he pleased, and neither man nor mouse would squeak thereafter. If they ever dared, the arrow-scar on his right cheek, the remembrance of an Indian skirmish ashore during that voyage around the world, would flame scarlet, like a pennant unfurling, and after that the tempest raged.

Sir Francis Drake was all energy now, as he strode resolutely down the hill at the van of his escort. His appearance was not brilliant, when set against the doublets slashed and laced, the velvet cloaks, the satin hose and feathered hats at his back. But his presence, like his humour, good or bad, was enough.

On the firm sand of the beach, with his boat rock-steady and waiting, he said his farewells. There were many flourishes of courtesy and much huzza-ing from the crowd. The lord mayor of Plymouth began a speech but was cut short. The freshening breeze, or the Dons, or Drake's own will, could not wait for windy civic pomp.

With no more delay the vice-admiral, and his small company, were borne on board their ship-boat. The throng on the beach gave a cheer; the quality saluted with their feathered hats, like an aviary disturbed. Then the boat's crew bent to their blades, and Matthew Lawe to his stern oar, and the sailors were alone on the business of the sea.

In the cushioned stern sheets, Drake sat frowning; but Matthew, who knew a frown from a scowl, was not put out. His honour was thinking deep, as well he might; and that was all. When at last the vice-admiral spoke, it was in one of those catch-thoughts which made men love him.

"Did you eat while you waited, Matthew?"

"Aye, your honour. They sent bread and beef from the inn."

"With a pretty wench to serve it?"

Matthew caught his humour. "Aye. Save she was a pot boy with a squint."

"Then praise God for the beef."

The scudding wind tugged at their clothing as they cleared the inner harbour, and set course for the great fleet of ships at anchor in the Sound. Matthew sighted his eye on the *Revenge*, their home, and bore down on his stern sweep to bring the boat on course. Presently, made bold by his captain's humour, he asked: "Did your honour win the game?"

Sir Francis Drake gave him a hard look. "What game?"

"Why, bowls, sir. Or so we heard."

"What else did you hear?"

On a sudden, it was no moment to be bold. "Naught else."

"You heard that I delayed." And as Matthew sat dumb, fearful that he had ventured too far, Drake continued: "Why do you think I delayed?"

"Sir, I do not know."

"The tide, lad, the tide!" Drake spoke loudly, as if to benefit his gentlemen who sat in the stern sheets with him. "The Spaniards are up to the Lizard. I could not prevent them if they were past Dover! Against this wind, we cannot leave harbour till the tide ebbs, and lets us go. We cannot sail; we can only pull ourselves out with hawsers and capstans, or tow with ship-boats. Our fleet will not move an inch towards the open Channel for four hours. So I stayed to finish the game. God save me from blockish fools who cannot tell a jest from the truth!"

"Sir, we did not know."

Instantly Drake smiled. "No matter, boy! Not a soul knows, seemingly. *But I know* . . . Now, tell your lads to pull, if it breaks their backs. We have work to do, and at last the time is right."

They rowed through the fleet right manfully, giving courage to those who spied the vice-admiral's standard and knew his squadron was now helmeted again. The mustered fleet was the bravest sight in England that day, each ship enough to give backbone to a butterfly. The tall hulls of blacked, oiled oak rose to glittering paintwork above: topping this were the shields with their gaudy heraldic badges—the Tudor rose, the cross of St. George, the fleur-de-lis; and at the very peak the noble flags and silken banners, that could be a hundred feet long, embroidered in silver and gold, streaming landwards as they were buffeted by the wind.

Their names were another banner of glory: *Ark Royal* the flagship, *Lion, Bear, Victory,* which was John Hawkins's own command, *Triumph, Centurion, Golden Hind, Dreadnought, Mayflower, Vanguard, Bonaventure* and *Delight.*

Now Matthew Lawe was steering his boat towards Drake's private squadron, set apart, since it had been ready and victualled for some days. Men crowded the bulwarks and sent up a cheer as the ship-boat with its golden standard passed by: men of the *Hope,* the *Nonpareil,* the *Swiftsure,* the *Advice,* and the *Aid.* But no ship in the fleet could match the welcome which waited for them as they drew alongside the *Revenge.* It was as if their vessel were dead when their captain was absent, and came to life when he set his foot upon the deck.

This Queen's galleon *Revenge* was a platform of courage in her own right. She sat squat in the water, because of the cauldron of weapons she bore; yet she could glide like a seagull, and ride an opposing sea like a war-horse mounting a parapet. From her sharp projecting beak, which carried the figurehead, to the tall sharp-cut stern, was one hundred and fifty feet. The high after-castle carried the gold-embossed stern gallery where the vice-admiral could walk at ease across the whole breadth of his ship. From this vantage he could, with a little craning of the neck, look across quarterdeck, maindeck, and forecastle, and the two tiers of guns which were the spitfire teeth of the *Revenge*.

While the rapture of welcome to the vice-admiral reached its height as he mounted to the quarterdeck, Matthew Lawe saw his ship-boat secure and then climbed the long swaying ladder to the oaken lair that was his home. Vaulting the bulwarks, he was met, as usual, by a fierce figure, Tuke the boatswain.

Tuke, whose body was monstrous, wore a leather jerkin, soaked in brine to harden it against the enemy, and a red woollen cap. He also carried his tool of office, the silver whistle which was one of the three allowed to the crew: to the master, to the boatswain, and to Matthew, as the captain's coxswain. But Tuke needed no whistle to confirm his rule over six hundred men. It was in his bulk, larded with fat, muscled like a plough horse: it was in his face, which bulged like a keg of ale, and in his manner, which proclaimed aloud: "I am below every officer, and above every man. *Do not let it slip your memory!*"

Now Tuke confronted Matthew Lawe, with his usual show of authority. "Is the ship-boat secure?"

"Aye."

"You were long enough returning."

"Aye."

It was best to deal with him so. The soft answer turned away wrath. Matthew could see why Tuke had grown such a merciless rogue; his duty was to stand between the men above—captain, lieutenant, master, sea-corporal, master gunner—and the men below: if he did not skin their backs, his own might be flayed. For through all this bombast there ran a gory thread of punishment: the harsh command which governed a Crown ship at sea. It was the Scale of Punishment for sailors who ran foul of the law. For stealing on board: PENALTY, ducking at the yardarms, and putting ashore, dead or alive. For sleeping on watch: PENALTY, once, a dousing: twice, a double dousing: thrice, bound to the mainmast for a day and a night: four times, hung at the bowsprit-end till he cut himself down, or starved to death. For drawing a weapon to strike the captain: PENALTY, loss of the right hand. For desertion: PENALTY, hanging or keel-raking, which was drawing underneath the ship. For murder: PENALTY, bound to the corpse, and thrown overboard. For mutiny: PENALTY, hanging overboard by the heels, till his brains be beaten out.

Penalties, penalties . . . were there no rewards, beyond beef and beer and the commander's glory? For if a man escaped the wrath of the great, or Tuke's fist, there was still death or maiming, on any tomorrow. Was it for this that a man went to sea?

It was. When Boatswain Tuke told Matthew with an oath to quit his airs as his honour's coxswain, and join the men hauling shot from the orlop deck, and to *jump!*, he knew that after a half-day's blessed peace on the tide mark, he was home. Down in the dungeon of the orlop deck, little more than a store-pit set above the bottom frames of the ship, it took time to grow accustomed to the gloom, lit by a single lantern. But after a moment or two, Matthew Lawe found his sight, and with it his friends.

Towards ten o'clock of the evening, the stubborn tide turned, and it was time to make their move. While the vice-admiral, as always, supped to the music of viols, the *Revenge* began her laborious journey out of Plymouth Sound, followed by her consorts. There was no space to sail, while the wind continued as stubborn against them as the tide had been. They must lift themselves out, as if by their own boot straps. They raised anchor and drew themselves inshore; then, with ropes and hawsers, capstan and brawny arm, they crept from quay to quay, and then from rock-face to rock-face, sending out new warps by carrying them ahead, making them secure to any ring-bolt, any projection of stone, and then hauling ever southwards towards the open Channel.

It took all the warm July night before they were clear, and into deep water; at anchor off Rame Head, with room to tack, waiting to see what the dawn would bring. But what a sight met their eyes as they looked landwards!

The whole coast of southern England, headland by headland, was aflame with giant beacons, spreading the alarm along the coast, and then marching inland as they were sighted from distant hamlets and villages, and the torch was taken up. England, with thanks to God, was at last awake.

Dawn came at four o'clock, as gentle as the birdsong which blessed it; and then, southwest beyond the Eddy Stones, they saw their enemy. The alarm raced round the ship as swiftly as the red glare of the beacons. Men, exhausted by their brutish work at the capstans, sprang up as other men called: "Come look—the great Armada!" Sailors ran to any vantage point in the rigging.

No man in England had ever set eyes on its like before. Matthew Lawe, astride the bowsprit which was his duty-place when handling sail, peered into the hazy morning; and as the brisk wind dispersed the mist, the amazing sight came up, in all its glory and terror. Away to the southwest, the Spanish fleet was running free up the Channel: a city of huge ships, with here and there a true cathedral afloat—one of the great galleons of Biscay or Seville or Tarragon—towering monstrously above its fellows. They were set in the form of a crescent, a demi-lune seven miles across, with the horns curving astern. It was like a single fist, clenched tight, aimed at the mouth or the heart or the guts, and nothing seemed more sure than that it must find its target, and pierce it, and bring it to bloody ruin.

Matthew, appalled and sick at heart, began to number them and then lost count—the distant mass of ships was too monstrous for a whirling brain. All he could think of, as he gripped the sprit with trembling knees, was the rumour of what lay within that mortal crescent of the Armada.

It was said that all these ships were larger, and stronger, than anything the English could put against them—and so it looked. It was said that they carried two thousand and five hundred pieces of ordnance, eight thousand sailors, and twenty thousand soldiers. It was said that they had within them people and things more wicked, cruel, and treacherous than any sailors or men-at-arms. There were ships with engines for storming castles, secret ships carrying women, who would poison men or infect their manhood, ships full of priests ready with branding irons, and scourges for heretic backs.

It was said—he came out of his dream of horror to find another of the sprit-sail men, Thomas Berry, grinning at him. "Wake up, Matthew! Do you want to fall in the sea before they send us a shot?"

Matthew smiled back wanly. "I do not want to fall in any fashion. . . ." He pointed towards the southwest. "Can you count them, Thomas? We need John Waggoner here, to number these vultures."

"John is sent back to the quarterdeck, helping his honour. He says, more than a hundred and twenty sail."

"And we have but eighty." Matthew shook his head, not hiding his discomfort. "What does his honour plan?—that we charge at them, like a pack of little hounds?"

Thomas Berry looked at him curiously. "What's your matter, Matthew? Cheerly, man! They are but Spaniards—women in armour. We have thrashed them round the world!"

"Not in these numbers."

"Then his honour will find a plan." Berry shaded his eyes, looking first at the crescent of the Armada, then landwards along the coast. "They have the wind of us, if we go out now. And there's little room to work between them and the land. If they choose to attack us here—"

The boatswain's whistle made its shrill call; then there was a shout, which rang the length of the *Revenge*. Tuke had lungs of brass, and did not spare them. "Heave up short to the anchor! Make sail!"

Lord Howard in the *Ark Royal* led the way; Drake's squadron followed. Then they divided: the *Ark Royal* to the south, round the farthest horn of the Spanish crescent, the *Revenge* to the west and north, to slip—if she could—between the land and the Armada, and so gain the weather gauge.

It was all done in a brilliant show of the sailor's art. All that day, and for most of a pitch-dark night, the *Revenge* led her consorts close inshore. These were Drake's own waters, where he had played in boyhood with rowboats; now he shepherded and put at risk Queen's galleons and men's lives. For hour after hour they tacked, and pinched the wind, and cheated rocks and shoals, and drove to exhaustion the men who must change sail a score of times in a single hour; and laboriously they drew ahead.

It was said later that if a few ships of the Armada had struck them then and there, Drake would have been destroyed, and Lord Howard's squadron overwhelmed at will. But the Duke of Medina Sidonia had his orders to take the Armada up the Channel and join with the Duke of Parma and his 30,000 invaders at Dunkerque; no other bait was to tempt him.

Thus the whole battleground was reversed. While the Armada bore onwards like a great travelling circus, Lord Howard and Sir

Francis joined hands behind it, with the wind at their backs and the enemy before. A pair of crouching sheepdogs could now turn themselves into wolves.

"Now we have them!" were Drake's constant words during the next few days, the confident boast of a sailor who had won the weather gauge on an enemy and was never to lose it till the last shot was fired. But there was no haste to engage closely; it was a time for darting in and out, for pouncing upon stragglers.

During this time Drake learned that his ships, smaller and lighter than the imposing foe, were better to manoeuvre; he also observed that a hurt Spanish ship was received into the centre of the crescent, like a sheep into the fold, while the huge protecting horns closed in on either side. But this could not always be done; and there came a day—the third day off the Race of Portland—when the English drew their first blood.

The unfortunate was a strong galleon, the *Nuestra Señora del Rosario*. She had been in collision with one of her consorts; she lost her bowsprit and her foremast; and though she was shepherded into the centre of the fleet, she soon became a nuisance to them. For she could not sail, and the Armada could not wait.

The laggard *Rosario* was left to fall behind; and when the *Revenge* came upon her, she was wallowing, dismasted, beyond control. Seeing that nothing stirred on board the wreck, and that no guns menaced the *Revenge*, Drake sent Matthew with an emissary by boat, to inquire if the *Rosario* surrendered.

When Matthew returned he bore a Spanish grandee representing the admiral of the *Rosario*, Don Pedro de Valdés.

"Well," Drake asked him curtly, "does he surrender?"

The noble Spaniard, exquisitely dressed in silk and gold-laced ruffles, answered with a polite question of his own. Might he know whom he had the honour of addressing?

Sir Francis Drake told him.

"Ah," the Spaniard answered. "That may well make this a different matter. I believe that Don Pedro de Valdés would think it an honour to surrender to such a valiant man."

And so it proved. The Spanish admiral, with a glance at the vanishing topsails of the Armada, struck his flag, and returned with Matthew in the ship-boat, to surrender to Sir Francis. The *Rosario*, with a prize crew aboard, sailed for Torbay. She carried chests of gold *escudos*, up to fifty thousand pieces, and other riches unusual in a ship of war, and Don Pedro de Valdés himself would fetch a fat ransom. The *Revenge* bore away, to take her station in the van.

"We will take twenty ships like her!" Drake said loudly, in the hearing of all on the quarterdeck, and they believed him. The vice-admiral's famous luck . . . privately, they said that his pirate's nose had led him to this prize. Now it could only lead him to glory.

4

THE PROMISE of glory was surely there. But who was to earn it, and who to pay for it, was something which vexed Matthew, who feared the answer, on both accounts, might be himself. While such humble fry as Matthew brooded on their chance of seeing the next dawn, Lord Howard of Effingham, admiral of this whole sea province, strove to make sure that every next dawn would glow more brightly than the last. There was no other way to prosper in battle. Now he divided his fleet into four squadrons, under himself, Drake, Frobisher, and Hawkins, and put his vice-admiral in the vanguard.

Now the true battle began, and it was the hottest work Drake's men had ever known. The Armada was not directly engaged; this cliff of huge galleons could not be scaled with the little ladders which were the English ships. But it could be worn down, undermined, sucked to disaster, piece by piece. It was hit-and-run-away, for the next four days and nights. Their ships proved quicker than the Spaniards' and their gunfire faster. Drake, the point of this burning spear, drove himself, and all his men, with a fury nearer to lust. The *Revenge*, darting in and out, was holed many times; the vice-admiral's own cabin was wrecked.

But though men were killed, no English vessels were forced from the fight, while ship after ship of the Armada was glad to limp into refuge. Sir Francis Drake could report to his Queen: "The feathers of the Spaniard are plucked one by one." It was a true account, though some fifty of his men were plucked at the same time. A Spanish galleon's broadside was like an evil mouth venting the breath of hell. Men were slain at their guns, men below were fired like torches, men on deck were swept to destruction in this iron hailstorm. Boatswain Tuke was one of those killed. Between one oath and the next, a cannonball took off his head, and laid it on the maindeck as neat as a duck on a platter. There was a bright side, it was thought, to every threatening cloud.

The *Revenge* and all the English squadrons pushed their enemy with relentless, pounding blows, until the proud crescent of the Armada lost all shape and became a formless rout. On the fifth day of this hot pursuit, they could only draw together and run for Calais Roads. There they anchored: to escape the foul weather and to make what repairs they could. They still maintained their last forlorn ambition, to embark the Duke of Parma's host of invaders, now camped round Dunkerque, for their vaunted "Enterprise of England".

Soon it was dusk on this last day. While the Spanish fleet lay crouched at anchor, the beacons still flamed along the English coast. Sir Francis and Lord Howard came together in council to plan their last stroke. They would "smoke them out!"

At the same hour of dusk, Matthew Lawe wanted sleep more than life itself. He lay face downwards in his hammock, slung in the stinking shelf which was the lowest tier of the forecastle: beset all about by men talking, men wolfing food, men groaning of their wounds; yet trying to shut out the *Revenge* and all else which stood between himself and his dream of hopeful life.

The past week's fighting, the long running battle up the Channel, the brazen uproar of cannon and counter-cannon, the hours of shifting sail and patching leaks, seemed to have sapped his strength beyond endurance. It had been crowned by the labour of today, when he and his crew had worked like dogs to prepare their fire ship, one of the eight vessels which were to be loosed into Calais Roads, on this evening's tide.

She was Drake's own property: the *Thomas*, of Plymouth, two hundred tons, a profitable ship which was now to be sacrificed to the fiery attack against the anchored Armada. They had sweated twelve hours to turn her into a torch: stuffing her with brushwood and tarry rope-ends; dousing the rigging with pitch; double-shotting the guns, which would explode when the heat of the fire reached them; setting up barrels of powder, and preparing the slow-match which would spark the ship into a volcano.

And this was the Sabbath day. . . . He turned on his back and stretched his weary limbs, and closed his eyes for the hundredth time, still sleepless, and tormented by it, yearning to be dead to this world but not yet ready for the next. His thoughts warred with his hunger for oblivion. The gory death of Boatswain Tuke had been no jest for Matthew Lawe. Tuke, a tyrant to the last, had been breathing fire down Matthew's neckerchief when a more frightful fire was loosed upon himself. The cannonball had missed Matthew by the span of a hand, and when he swung about, it was to see a great gout of blood erupting from a headless trunk, and the head itself spinning away like a scarlet dripping top before it settled on the deck.

If the *Revenge* had rolled to starboard a moment before, it would have been his own head. . . . This was the hazard of following the vice-admiral—the hazard which *must* claim him, perhaps within the next hour. . . . When presently he drifted into sweating sleep, it was only to dream that it *was* his own head, and as he advanced to claim his rightful property, the blood he slipped in was his own.

In his dream he crashed to the deck, bruising his shoulder—and he woke in abject terror to find his shoulder seized and shaken by a hand which would no more be denied than the hand of Death himself.

Would he never find sleep—even such evil sleep as this?

He turned over with a groan of despair, to meet the brave, cheerful face of young Jem the farm lad. "What is it, Jem?"

"You are called."

Matthew sat up. The hammock tipped, as every hammock had done since sailors were condemned to them, and he nearly fell. Jem, his strong arm ready, steadied him. "What is this, for Christ's love?" Matthew asked.

"A message from the master. The vice-admiral wishes to see his coxswain on the quarterdeck."

Matthew collected his wits. "Thank you, Jem." He straightened his rumpled clothes and managed a grin.

When Matthew topped the ladder and reached the quarterdeck, he found it thronged. From Drake himself to the pages of the volunteer gentlemen, all were dressed in their best finery, as if this were a palace audience rather than a pause in battle. He hesitated to advance, conscious of his rough clothes; but Sir Francis

sighted him, and beckoned. He approached and made his salute
with his cap. The company round the vice-admiral made place for
him and Drake's first words, as so often, were kind. "Have you
slept, Matthew?"

"Aye, your honour. Enough."

Drake smiled. "When a sailor admits enough sleep, it is the end
of the world." He waited for the laughter of those round him;
then he grew serious. First he pointed landwards, through the
dusk of evening, to the Spanish fleet at rest in Calais Roads. A
gleam from their beacon lights flamed red among their topsails.
"Mark the Spaniard," he said harshly, "whom we mean to burn!"
Then he swung about, and pointed towards the cluster of fire ships
prudently set apart from his own squadron. "What do you see
there?"

"The fire ships, your honour."

"And the nearest?"

"The *Thomas*, sir." Matthew was puzzled, and afraid, and even
a thought rebellious. Had he broken his sleep to answer children's
riddles? "Is aught wrong with her?"

"No—and nothing is going to be wrong! If I give my little ship
to the Queen, I will take care she is not wasted. *You* will take
care."

"Your honour?"

"When you see the *Thomas*, you see your new command."

There were smiles all round him at the words, which Drake's
companions must have been prepared for. But they could not
warm a sinking heart and spirit. Matthew wanted no new command such as this floating firebrand. He wanted to walk ashore,
and find peace. Any roadside ditch in Devon would serve.

The vice-admiral took up his instruction, the jutting red beard
flying all the signals of determination. "I want to make sure that
the *Thomas* keeps her true course, and strikes home. So she will
be manned and directed till the very last moment. Take the best
of your ship-boat's crew. Two will suffice, if they are lively and
determined. At my signal, cut the cable, and trim your sails. See
that she is well aimed for the greatest Spaniard at anchor. Then
light the brushwood in the lower hold. *Then* light the slow-match
for the powder kegs. But wait till the *Thomas* is full ablaze. Then
slip back into your boat, and leave her. . . . Is that clear?"

31

"Aye, your honour." Many things about it were clear. "Save, when are we to leave? How near to the Armada?"

"When you can smell their fear! When you are roasting yourselves!" But this was a joke, a merry jest before supper. "How near, is something in your own hands. That is why I send you, and not another man. And, Matthew—"

"Aye, sir?"

Drake was smiling now, a smile for a favourite, for the man he could trust. "I look to see you again."

It was a moment when Matthew knew, within his cold bones, that he would never see Drake again, in the living world.

As dusk· deepened into night, and the tide began to flood into Calais Roads, Matthew obeyed his orders with a sullen will. Work he must: work was all . . . if he paused to think, he began to tremble. . . . With the two men he had chosen to help him, John Waggoner and Jem the farm boy, he made ready the *Thomas* for her last voyage. The light working-sails were set. There was an axe handy to cut the cable. The ship-boat was moored under the stern, ready for their escape. Each man had a lantern for the firing, which would take the *Thomas* to her grave—and God-knew-what with her. Now they sat on the afterdeck, in the cold black of night; watchful for the signal from the *Revenge*. It had been a killing day, for work and sweat; now its fearful peak drew near.

John Waggoner looked up at the moon. "See how she swings. 'Tis a full flood tide already."

Matthew, whose teeth were desperately clenched, grunted his answer. But Jem's young spirits could never be quenched. He called out: "Give us the signal, your honour! We aim to fire the whole Armada for you!" Then, to Matthew at his side: "Shall they try a broadside at us, do you think?"

Matthew opened his mouth to answer, but his teeth chattered instead. "Curse this cold!" he mumbled. "A man cannot speak."

"We will be hot enough by and by!"

John Waggoner came suddenly to attention. "There it is!" he said. "They hoist the signal!" They looked towards the *Revenge*. Slowly a red light rose above the poop lantern. It was time to go.

Swiftly they moved. As Jem cut the anchor cable the bows fell off the wind, and one after another their topsails filled. Matthew tugged at the steering whip-staff and brought the *Thomas* onto her course. A glance astern showed that they had other black ghosts in company. But the *Thomas* led the way.

Steering down the wind, Matthew gazed fearfully at his target, the careless cluster of lights which the Spanish fleet was showing. They were still far off, but already there was something in his taut breast which could hardly wait a moment longer. He had only one clutching thought: never to approach too near the Armada, but to burn and begone! To John Waggoner, standing at his elbow, he said, "Set the fire below."

"So soon?" Waggoner objected, astonished. "We have a mile or more to go yet. If we—"

Matthew broke in roughly, "Light it, I say!"

Waggoner picked up his lantern, and went forward without a word.

Presently there was a burst of fire, then flickering flames within the forecastle. John Waggoner leapt up from below, and began to touch his lantern to the standing rigging in the bows, then to some bales of straw on deck. The fire crackled and spread while Matthew watched it, appalled. It was so huge and fierce. ... It was a signal to the whole world. ... His guilt began to match his fear. They had fired too early, and every man in the fleet would know it.

Standing at the whip-staff, he could almost feel the vice-admiral's bleak eyes on the back of his skull. Drake might even see him, outlined against the flames, and be cursing him already. For the *Thomas*, in full blaze, must be alerting the Armada, and betraying all the other fire ships, which had hoped to be dark as the night.

But "Burn and begone!" remained his craven watchword. Somewhere in that raging fight up-Channel, he had had enough of war, and all that now followed was the child of this sickness. He must continue to the end, wherever it lay. ... He called to Jem in the shadows, "Take your lantern down to the waist, lad, ready for the slow-match. I will tell you when."

"But Matthew. ... We are so far off! We can hardly see the Armada, but by God they can see us! What use to touch off the powder now?"

"I did not say *now!*" Matthew snarled at him. "I mean, go down and stand ready. Cannot you feel the wind? We are running in like a storm."

Jem turned to look at the fore-part of the ship. It was now beset by mounting flames: already the rigging dripped great gouts of blazing pitch onto the deck below. "It is a storm for us, not for the Dons. I say we are too early."

"And I say, do what I order!" Between shame and fear, Matthew's voice was almost a scream. "Do you want me to tell the vice-admiral, one of my crew refused to obey?"

"Tell him what you choose." From Jem, these were the boldest words of his life. He shrugged his shoulders, picked up his lantern, and was away. Like John Waggoner, another friend was lost.

The *Thomas* plunged onwards, a fiery beacon alone upon a tossing sea. It was not possible to see where they were headed. All was wasted, all was lost. Yet somehow a little mouse of profit —perhaps a single man's life—might be saved.

The ship heeled over suddenly to a lurching wave. A spar, loosed from the blazing foremast, came crashing down. A scream in the darkness told him that it had struck Jem. Perhaps it had pinned him down; but the lantern in his hand made its own wild arc in the air, and plunged into a stack of straw. On the instant, the dry kindling took fire. Matthew, distraught, left the whip-staff and advanced a step at a time towards this new sea of flame. "Jem?" he called out fearfully.

"I'm trapped!" Jem's voice was full of his agony. "Christ's sake, my leg is gone! Help me, Matt!"

Already, in the fiery glow, he could be seen, beating at the flames round him, like a man caught in a monstrous tide-rip. But Matthew knew only one thing: that the fire would be among the powder barrels in a moment. He began to back away again.

Within the circle of fire, Jem saw him retreat, and could still be astonished at his friend. "Matthew! You run away! Don't you hear me?"

There was another, far-off cry from the bows. John Waggoner was also trapped.

Matthew Lawe looked this way and that. The powder kegs would burst at any moment. Or the double-shotted cannon would spray the world with grief. There was no time, not even to loose the ship-boat and climb in. He ran for the ship's side.

Jem's wailing voice followed him. "Matthew! The flames! My leg! Curse you for a coward! *Do you want to live for ever?*"

But Matthew Lawe was deaf to all save his thudding heart, ready to crack from fear. Now an outcast beyond honour, beyond the sailor's creed, he took leave of his shipmates, vaulted the bulwarks, and threw himself into the sea.

5

THE PROUD galleon *San Vigilio*, finest daughter of the Biscayan squadron of the Armada, was now no more than a fugitive drab. Her commander, Don Iago de Olivarez, was shamed by it. But he could do nothing to mend it.

He sat alone in his day-cabin, forty feet above the waves, hungry and cold like all his crew, in a small harbour of an island in the Hebrides—did the English really prosper in these harsh northern airs?—and wondered, as all Spain would soon wonder, what had gone amiss with their enterprise.

They had started out with such high hopes. They would thrash El Draque, invade his pest house of a country, depose *that woman* who went by the name of Queen Elizabeth, and bring an erring nation back into the true fold of Christ, and of Spain. What had turned these high hopes to such starveling despair? It had been blamed on their failure to take Plymouth, when that city was bare of its defences. Others had questioned their fighting skill in the long battle up the Channel. As a last excuse, defeat had been assigned to the weather, which had been so fair for the English, so foul for Spain.

Don Iago de Olivarez drew his cloak about his thin shoulders. Certainly matters had gone amiss, in terrible measure, as soon as they had anchored in Calais Roads where they had thought themselves safe for the night. Fire ships were the only danger, so the Armada made ready for fire ships, with grappling pinnaces to drag them aside; and fire ships it was, but the plan with the pinnaces failed because of the foul dark weather, and the whole fleet had to cut their cables and scatter before the threatening burning.

True, no single one of these flaming attackers found its mark, thanks to one foolish fire ship which gave the alarm while they still had time to escape; but the escape did more harm than all the English fleet combined. Ships missed their course and ran aground;

ships bore down on other ships, and tangled in confusion, and were lost; cut cables became wrapped round rudders, so that a galleon, tethered like a cow at pasture, could make no escape when the next day dawned.

Olivarez, with his *San Vigilio*, was one of the fortunate. Having seen the errant fire ship while it was still distant, he cut his cable without waiting for his admiral's orders and laid a course north-eastwards up the Flemish coast. At dawn he found his flagship *San Martin*, joined her company with five others, and sent out scouting pinnaces to look for stragglers. By noon they were an Armada again, though shrunken and battered. Then the wind turned sour, blowing fiercely from the same southerly point. They could only forget the dreams of invasion from Dunkerque, and continue on northwards, wherever this might lead.

Before dusk the English, led by El Draque, were on their heels once more. The Armada formed into that demi-lune which had shown such strength before. There was a fine running battle all the way up the North Sea. But it was finer for the English. Ship after Spanish ship was holed, or its rigging shot away, while its luckless hulk sagged down the wind, to be lost. They could not get to grips with these nimble adversaries. Soon the English could close the range, and fire at will. For the Armada was the first to run out of shot. They might have been ruined altogether, if their attackers' guns had not also cooled for lack of powder. The English could only follow, dogged and silent, as far as Berwick Head; and there, having shown their foe the back door of England, they bore away for the Firth of Forth. The Armada, scattered but still numerous, vanished below a troubled horizon. First they had clung together, sixty ships and more. But in the weeks of wicked weather which beset them as they neared the top of Scotland, they were forced into scattering. And in this lonely wilderness ships began to die.

Olivarez, fighting his groaning ship through the worst seas in the world, between the Orcades and the Shetland Isles, watched men whom he loved, and stout ships, cast ashore as if they were sodden driftwood. Others drifted down the bitter wind, laden with doomed and starving men, to find their graves in Norway, or Russia, or the limitless ice of the Arctic.

The *San Vigilio*'s last consort, the galleon *San Josef*, they watched tossed ashore onto the rocks of the Orcades. Even as she struck, bands of murderous men dashed out of caves and began to kill her people as they crawled ashore. Sailors in the last extremity of terror fought for their lives in the surf; but no living man ever stood upright more than a few feet from the tide mark.

She was the last friend they ever saw. After her death, the *San Vigilio* was alone in a wilderness of howling seas, lacking any food save rotting meat and salt fish, and mouldy bread as hard as stone, the water in the casks foul beyond human bearing. Men were dying because they could only retch on this evil swill. Her rigging was tangled in ruins. Exhausted sailors who worked day and night at the pumps to keep her afloat, had no strength to repair it. Below decks there was a multitude of sick and wounded.

It was a month before the *San Vigilio* turned Cape Wrath, and there she faced the full force of the storm blowing ceaselessly against them, and mountainous seas which had crossed the whole Atlantic to vent their spite upon this last survivor. Whatever happened when he put ashore here, and no matter how murderous their welcome, Olivarez could not venture out into the wild Atlantic in an attempt to reach the coast of Spain before his crew had rested, and made their repairs, and loaded stores.

At dusk on a bitter September evening, his ship crept into a slit of harbour which the faded chart told him was part of the Isle of Mull, and there dropped anchor. There was only a coarse shingle beach, and stark cliffs and windswept trees. The few stone cottages were thatched with heather. Though there might have been many eyes watching them, not a face showed and not a dog barked.

Olivarez's servant Carlos, a pinched scarecrow like himself, woke him from a fitful dreaming doze. Stiff and cold, he stretched limbs which had been aching for as far back as his memory could reach. "What is the time, Carlos?"

"Near nine, my lord."

"And what of the day?"

"Cold as charity, my lord. There was even *snow* in the night. How people can live in such purgatory. . . . Man need not seek the end of the world. . . . It is here. . . . Will you eat now?"

"Yes. What have you for me?"

Carlos pursed his thin lips. "Mulled wine, my lord. Bread toasted with oil. The fish, you should not eat any more."

It was the same wretched fare as always, and after a night in shelter. "Is not the forage party back yet?"

"No, my lord. And what they will find here, God knows!"

"But what time did they put ashore?"

"Two hours past, or more."

"Bring the wine. Then call Don Alonzo to my cabin."

"He waits already, sir."

Don Alonzo, his nephew and secretary, had lost much of his fire and zeal since he first joined the *San Vigilio*, on the warm shores of Corunna. Nothing of his splendid garde-robe had weathered their voyage without ruin, and the soft leather thigh-boots which had once set off his manly legs now hung forlornly. He entered the great cabin, and made his salute.

"What news of the forage party?" Olivarez asked.

"Nothing, Uncle, to my knowledge."

"But they have been ashore since seven o'clock!"

"So they tell me. I've been waiting for news in my cabin. Fray Bernardo wishes to see you. He says there is a curse on us."

"Go tell him to wait on me," his uncle said, "and then make inquiry about the foraging."

Fray Bernardo, a black friar of the Dominicans, had been a thin man at home, in the sun-warmed castle on the slopes of the Sierra de Guadarrama, and he was the same thin man on board the *San Vigilio*, marooned in this icy hole in the Hebrides. And he never failed to wield the same rod, with the same fierce piety. On this cold grey morning, Fray Bernardo lacked nothing of his zeal. "Good morning, my son."

"Good morning, Fray Bernardo. I hope you are glad to be at rest, for a change."

"I am not at rest. Rest is sloth. Sloth is sinful."

Well, well, Olivarez thought, God pardon us sinners. . . . To bring relief to a severe subject, he said, "I am sorry we have not found fresh provisions yet. But perhaps our fortune will turn soon."

"Perhaps it will never turn."

Olivarez surveyed the bony face. "Why do you say that?"

"Because there is still a poison in your ship."

Olivarez sighed. So the chaplain still thirsted after his prey. . . . "Is the Englishman well?"

"Perhaps as well as he will ever be."

"What is it you want, then?"

"The just punishment of a heretic! What else?"

"Then why did you not let him die?"

"That is not punishment. It is escape."

Don Iago sighed again. These Dominicans were so strict! Why need they fatten up the sacrifice before the slaughter? Why must they yearn to tear to pieces a poor rabbit of an Englishman, who had fallen into their hands by chance?

"Has he spoken?"

"Many times. It is always the same story. But now it should have an end. I must do my duty and you must do yours."

"He is a prisoner of war."

"He is a heretic, an infection! Can you wonder we have been so punished? I would examine him formally, in your presence. I will establish his guilt before God, and you will punish him before the world. Only so can this ship be cleansed."

There would be no end to this until Fray Bernardo won his way. It was something they had carried with them for many weeks: the question of the man in the boat. "Very well." Don Iago was resigned. "Have him brought up."

Below, a guard woke Matthew Lawe from a miserable sleep with signs and gestures, and snarling noises, meaning, "Get up! Follow me!"

For the first time in weeks he was to travel elsewhere.

On trembling legs he followed his keeper up one ladder, and then another, and then a third. There he was left for a moment of peace till he regained his strength in the first feeble daylight he had seen since Calais Roads.

All that time he had been lying half senseless, sick and starved, in the black dungeon below, and suffering the fearful shocks of a sea battle as well. A sailor's instinct told him that the ship in which he lay was enormous; yet she was tossed about by mountainous waves, torn and holed by cannon shot, and turned into a hellish cauldron of noise and flame by her reply.

Then gradually the shocks receded, the cannonade died to nothing, and the only enemy was the sea. But this continued to beat furiously at their shattered hull, and by the suck of the pumps, day after day, the sea might prove the worst enemy of all.

His prison became the last frail ladder between life and death for the wounded and the sick. Countless men were laid down to die in his company. In such a cage of torment, buffeted by vile weather, sustained by food which a rat would have passed over in this plague pit of the damned, Matthew Lawe had time to consider his plight, and the guilt which had brought him to it. During these days of torture, certain Spanish sailors, learning his condition, had strength to curse him before they died. But none of these enemies could have matched Matthew's hatred of himself, nor salved his own shame.

After his coward's flight he had swum for his life towards the shore of Flanders, and swum into a kind of madness which had a fellowship with his own. In the darkness, a panic fear struck the great Armada as soon as the first fire ship was sighted. Borne on the wind were shouts of warning, and signal guns firing, and the thud of axe blows. Black shapes began to move between the sea and the land, while at his back the fire ships—the true fire ships, not the disgraced *Thomas* which had blown up in fiery ruin as soon as he quit her decks—bore down in flames upon the Spanish fleet. Matthew Lawe trod the water, half-drowned already, cold to the marrow of his bones. A vast bulk drew near him, and passed by, hissing its own desperation. The last effort he could recall was to grasp at a smaller shadow, a forgotten ship-boat still towing astern. He had hauled himself on board in frantic terror, and there collapsed. He had only wakened in the stinking hole which was now below him.

In the weeks that followed, only one man had been kind, a stern priest who asked questions, and scanned the answers as if his life might depend on it. But he seemed to wish Matthew to live. Matthew did not ask why. He could only love his only friend.

Yet he did not tell all of the truth in this noisome confessional. Need one be shamed before God as well as man. . . ? He had said that he had fallen overboard from one of the fire ships, that he was not a spy, but only a sailor in misfortune. He acknowledged his Protestant faith, but added with toadlike humility that he had had no chance to learn any other. Would he recant his sins? Matthew could answer, in the very garments of truth, that he wished that he could.

Now his prison guard gestured again. By another ladder, and yet another, he climbed painfully upwards. Was there no end to this wondrous ship? Its decks were huge, and there was tier after tier of them, mounting to the sky. As it grew lighter, and the pale gleam from the gunports became sunshine streaming through bayed windows, as if into some palace, Matthew could only be astonished that the *Revenge*, and the others, had dared to challenge this monster.

Presently he emerged into cold sunlight, and then into a cabin more splendid than two of Lord Howard's own in the *Ark Royal*. Here he found the priest whom he trusted, and a great lord with a proud face, whom he did not, and the questioning began.

Fray Bernardo's English was excellent, and Don Iago's serviceable enough; together they made brisk work of Matthew Lawe's condition. He was their prisoner of war: a hostage from the sea. He owed his life to the *San Vigilio*. What that life was worth now could hardly be measured in the cheapest coin of the realm.

Don Iago de Olivarez, whom great rank had not made arrogant or cruel, surveyed this bruised and wretched man with compassion. Then his sailor's eyes narrowed, and he asked sharply: "What is that circling your neck?"

"My whistle, your honour."

"So I thought. I also carry a silver whistle, as commander of this ship. Have you been lying to us? Are you an officer?"

"No, sir. A coxswain. I commanded a ship-boat. The whistle is the badge of office."

"What ship-boat is this?"

"The vice-admiral's. Sir Francis Drake."

A deadly silence fell. So here was a man with the fearsome taint of Drake, of treacherous evil, infecting the *San Vigilio*. . . . Olivarez, conscious of cold chill, came back to his questioning: "So. . . . We call him El Draque . . . we call him many things. . . . So you were his—how did you name it?—his coxswain. . . . But were you in command of a fire ship as well?"

Matthew was not strong enough, nor quick enough of wit, to dissemble. "It was his own fire ship, your honour. The leader."

"The leader? The one that gave the alarm?"

"Yes, sir."

Olivarez surveyed him grimly. "Why was your ship fired so early?"

"There was a mistake, your honour."

"But what sort of mistake? You set the fire by accident?"

"No, your honour. I thought—I thought we were close enough."

"And did not wish to come closer?"

Matthew looked down at the rich carpet on the cabin deck, unable to meet this man's eyes. "Yes, sir."

"And after that, you—fell?"

Wretchedly, Matthew knew that this lord, who had a sailor's mind, had divined the truth. And now he was urgent to confess it —to purge his guilt before such a witness.

"No, your honour. The *Thomas* was on fire. She was ready to burst! So—I jumped."

When Don Iago said, "We are grateful to you," Matthew's shame was complete.

Now Fray Bernardo took command, in the voice of a higher authority. "You have named El Draque," he began, bearing down on Matthew. "Tell me, what did El Draque think of the faith of Rome?"

Matthew still believed the priest to be a man who would honour the truth, even though it sounded harsh to his ear. "He hated it."

"Did he teach you to hate it?"

"He talked of such things."

"And you listened and believed?"

"Yes."

"So you hate Rome? You would destroy it?"

Aware of danger in this fierce tone, Matthew was growing doubtful of his friend. "Sir, I told you earlier, I know nothing save what I have been taught."

"I know what you have been *taught*. I wish to hear what you believe." And, as Matthew still hesitated, Fray Bernardo brought to his voice a silky menace: "Have you been *taught* that we have whips and pinching-irons, to make men tell the truth?"

Matthew mumbled, "Yes, sir."

"Well, you may believe it. Let us begin again, without deceit. Are you an enemy of the Roman faith?"

Matthew could only answer what he believed the priest wished to hear. Yes, he had hated Rome, as he had been taught. Yes, he must have been in error, because he was deceived by lies. Yes, he believed what Fray Bernardo was telling him now. He freely acknowledged his sins, and wished to repent them. He was ready ᴏ recant. He would accept this new faith, because it was the only true faith.

It was then that the fearful shock fell on his ears. Fray Bernardo sat back in his chair and nodded almost gently at the abject man before him. "That is well. You have now confessed all, recanted all, and found the truth at last. . . . By the infinite mercy of God, *you may die at peace.*"

A betrayed man could only stare back, confounded beyond belief. So it had all been a jest, a monstrous cruel game which he could never have won, whatever grovelling surrender he had made. So Sir Francis had taught them true: the Spaniards *did* torture and burn their prisoners, to the glory of their merciless God!

In spite of his peril, Matthew was about to protest when there were sudden shouts from outside, then a brisk rally of musket shots. Don Alonzo burst into the cabin. "Uncle, Uncle!" he cried. "The forage party! They must all be dead—*butchered* by these heathen rogues! We saw but two of our men left, running down to the beach, chased by men in skirts, who cut them down with great swords before they could reach the boat. We fired on the demons, but they were too far away."

"Tell Captain Barrameda to wait on me instantly," Olivarez commanded. He swung towards Matthew and the priest. "We must close our business," he said. "I cannot deal with such matters now."

"But your verdict, my son? The case is proved. This man is—"

"This man is nothing," Olivarez snapped. "We have our own fellows to save—or to bury. And we still lack stores, and stores I must have."

Matthew was led below.

Whatever sport the "men in skirts" thought they might have with a foraging party of fifteen sailors, they changed their minds on sighting a hundred armed men, led by a shining Hercules, Captain Barrameda, a soldier magnificently tall, the finest fighting man aboard the *San Vigilio.* When he returned, he made his report to Olivarez on the quarterdeck.

"My lord, we found no enemy—not a hair of their cursed heads —but we found our party. They were dead to a man, the last two near the boat on the beach. The others had been hacked to death as they were filling their water barrels. They had been stripped naked, with fingers cropped off for the worth of a ring or two. But their heads were taken first."

Olivarez, with savage thoughts of vengeance, asked: "Where were these murderers hiding?"

"I suppose in the hills, my lord. The huts, all save one where an old mad woman was hiding and spitting curses at us, were empty. We could have spent a week chasing the villains and found none. So I wasted no time on that. We buried our men, and turned to the water barrels and the forage. It will be worth sending again. There is good water, and a little game, but we will have to be strongly armed. We brought back sixteen barrels of water. We killed three deer, and found ten others smoked and hanging in the huts. There is fish in plenty. We also brought back the old mad woman. She has the look of a witch. But proud. . . . She might tell us something of account."

The old woman was hauled on board and set among her captors. But, as Captain Barrameda, who could tell the quality of a man at a glance, and perhaps half the quality of a woman, had said, she was proud—proud of something which they could not divine. A tiny woman in rags, her imperious eyes stared back at them as if she had the power of life or death on every soul who met her gaze.

She had a curved beak of a nose, an olive skin darker than their own, and a grey crest of matted hair, and a wild freedom of movement. She hopped rather than walked, and mouthed and grimaced continually, and snapped her crooked fingers, contemptuous of this world of men who had only a chance authority. Though proud, she was ugly beyond belief; and the Spanish sailors and soldiers, after a first astonishment, burst out in coarse laughter when she seemed to curse them, for her tongue was wild and unknown.

For reasons of heavenly guidance and earthly knowledge, Fray Bernardo seemed the most suited to communicate with this strange visitor. But when he had done his best, in his Latinate English, and a little French, he had to confess that he could make nothing of her answers.

"It is a sort of English," he told Olivarez. "There is a word here and there, but twisted out of shape. I heard her say that she could tell us the hour of our death, which is a matter only for God. But as to the rest. . . ."

Olivarez surveyed this wild, half-human, half-ape of a woman. Sane men, even sane men who had the ear of God, were only simple creatures; the mad might have not only God's ear, but perhaps His tongue as well. He thought of Fray Bernardo's disdainful phrase, "a sort of English", and he perceived a sort of answer, which was a sort of Englishman.

"Bring up the prisoner," he commanded, and Matthew Lawe was again lifted from his place below. Loosed once more into the light of day, he thought that he was going to his death; it would have amazed him less than the madhouse into which he was propelled. Round about him was a great array of lords and officers; in front was the multitude of the *San Vigilio*'s crew, greeting his appearance with a growling hiss which was the word *Ingles*. In the centre of this daunting audience, an old hag stood at bay: an outcast like himself.

Don Iago went straight to command. "We cannot understand this woman, who is a prisoner," he told Matthew. "Put questions to her. Discover what she is."

A man of Devon translating the Scottish tongue for Spanish ears?—it was no more mad than anything else in a world turned upside down. But it was more simple than he had thought. The weird old woman seemed moved by his presence, and answered him freely. Her speech was as rough as the crags which guarded their haven, yet it was—as Fray Bernardo had judged—a sort of English. Matthew found that he could recognize its lilt from the speech of an usher long ago at the Barnstaple Poor School, another sort of outcast far from his home in the north, who had breathed fire and brimstone on a clutch of orphan children, but who had mourned all the time his exile from a land he called "Scotland the Fair".

The tale which the old woman told Matthew, and the tale which he told Don Iago in his turn, was not to be believed, only passed on to wiser ears to make what they could of a riddle. She was a famous witch, he reported, by the name of Morag—the witch of Drumnin on the mainland, come over for the yearly fortune telling, and caught by foreign tyrants who did not know the vileness of their insult—nor their own ill luck.

45

She could prophesy—even among these barbarians, and God would curse them ten times ten, for laying hands on one of His anointed.

Olivarez, a man of inquiring mind, he did not shrink from any aspect of learning. "Let us put her to the test," he said, to those round him. "If she can prophesy, I would hear it."

But Fray Bernardo objected. "This is sinful. It is superstition. It is not seemly for you to give it countenance."

"Nothing is *seemly* in this hell-hole," Olivarez answered. "I have lost fifteen men murdered! I wish to know what is in store for the rest of us." And to Matthew: "Tell the old hag to prophesy concerning the Armada, the might of Spain. What is its fate?"

"Worse than the past." They could all hear a taunting in the

old woman's voice. "And *less* than the past. They say this great might of Spain has not taken as much as one little ship of the English. They have not burned one sheepcote in all the land. Such is this great Armada!"

"You put yourself in peril," Don Iago said sternly to Morag. "Yet we are not ashamed of our ill luck." Then, in a sudden bursting-out of spirit, he commanded: "Prophesy! Prophesy! I will have you hanged for silence, not for speech!"

She gazed at him with fiery eyes. "Are you sure, great lord?"

"Aye."

"Well, enough." She mumbled to herself, then she dealt a cruel blow to the side of her own face, and seemed to fall into a trance. Her voice grew deeper, coming from far away. She began to speak

of "we", as if crowded round with devilish spirits. "We see Spanish prisoners, bound with ropes, whipped homewards like little boys in disgrace."

Matthew fearfully repeated her words in a clearer tongue. Olivarez, controlling his anger, asked, "What is the fate of this ship?"

"Your ship is lying in Maclean's country. . . . We have a little chief here, Maclean of Deuart. But his family will be great lords and they will search for this ship through the ages."

"Search? How search? *Where* search?"

"In this very place," Morag answered. "In Tobermory."

"They will look here, in Tobermory, for this ship?"

"Till the end of time."

Olivarez relaxed, with a sigh. It had no sense to it. Perhaps the old witch was only mad, after all. But Fray Bernardo attacked with venom. "You are evil!" he cried. He turned to Matthew Lawe. "Both of you are evil! And you will pay God's price for it!"

After a silence, Morag called out in a high voice: "He is beyond your power."

Fray Bernardo, understanding her now, replied in anger, "My power is God's power. Nothing is beyond it!"

"We do not see with your foolish eyes. You are blind. We are not. We tell you, you will not kill this man. No mortal will kill him. Nations not yet in the womb will break their swords against the rock of his fortress." Her voice began to fade, and her ancient body to droop like a bird submissive to the snare. "Hear our last word," she said, in a cracked whisper. "He will not die. . . . He will wander . . . the wild waters . . . until. . . ."

"Until when?"

"Till all the seas run dry. . . ." Then, with a withered screech, the witch fell senseless to the deck, and no man on board the *San Vigilio* saw more than a crumpled bag of dead bones, nor heard a sound beyond the bleak mourning wind, sighing a little of life and a whole realm of death.

Though Don Olivarez could not believe the witch's words, all that he would say with all his cold authority was, "The Englishman shall be put to work like any other prisoner."

Eight days after the evil day of Morag, the galleon had been laden with water and deer's meat and made ready for her sailing.

They had all been evil days for Matthew Lawe, the man with the brand of death on his brow—or, worse still, the brand of life.

Morag the witch had signed the warrant of his execution. He had suffered a great enemy in the priest, but now all the world was his enemy on board the *San Vigilio*. To her sailors and soldiers alike, he was the object of fear and hatred; the word of his timeless salvation had gone the length and breadth of the ship, and he was cruelly taunted with it by men who, fearing their own miserable death, wished to share it liberally before it was too late. Matthew had expected to die at every nightfall, and when he woke to a new day in his dungeon, it was to the same terror. What had stood in the way he could not discover, save that it was not mercy. Meanwhile, he had been set to work ashore with the forage parties, guarding one of their boats, while the countryside was scoured for sustenance.

Now, on what proved to be the last morning of this easy captivity, he found that he had made one friend: Juan Batista, a poor witless boy who was also the butt of much cruelty. Against the crime of life, Juan had only one defence, a smile; and this morning he smiled on Matthew, and they drew together. Juan, it seemed, had something to impart. Since he could not speak, he drew pictures in the sand. Nudging Matthew to full attention as they lay by their boats, Juan took a splinter of driftwood, and drew the shape of a galleon. He pointed across the bay to the *San Vigilio*. Matthew nodded. Juan then outlined the sun, a circle in the sky. Then he scuffed this out, and drew another circle, farther on the larboard side. Then he smoothed away the picture of the *San Vigilio*, so that only the sun was left.

Matthew nodded vigorously. So far, the story was clear. On the morrow, the sun would still be in the sky, but the *San Vigilio* would not be in the bay.

Juan now ceased to smile. With the splinter of wood poised, he looked at Matthew, and shook his head dolefully. Then he drew a cross, tall and stark. He put the figure of a man against it, with small flourishes which Matthew swiftly divined were cords. Then wavering lines appeared, mounting upwards from the foot of the cross till they consumed the figure of the bound man. These could only be fire.

It was enough—but to make certain sure, Matthew pointed to

49

the picture, and touched his own breast. Juan nodded and laid his hand on Matthew's own. Now it was more than enough. Tonight or tomorrow, before the *San Vigilio* sailed, he was to die the cruel death which the priest had promised.

Wild thoughts assailed his brain, and then cool command, coming from God-knew-what remnant of spirit. Though he could not believe the old witch who had prophesied that he would live, he believed Juan when the boy assured him of his death. He was doomed, and he must act.

He had nothing to give this poor messenger, who might also be his saviour. Yet he had! Bending his neck, Matthew lifted from it his badge of office, the silver whistle of his command and put it in Juan's hand. The simple boy smiled his thanks. He fingered the whistle lovingly, then thrust it deep into the heel of his shoe. Then—oh wise young man—he lay down and feigned sleep.

Matthew looked carefully about him. Shouts and laughter came from the hillside. A musket shot rang out. The forage party was having some sport with a cornered hind, leaving another to go free. Matthew rose to his knees and first crept, then walked, and then ran for the shelter of the heather hills. He reached them panting, and not a sweet bird stirred, nor betrayed his flight.

His guards searched for him but briefly, arguing that they must not delay the ship's sailing. At evening the three boats began to ply back to the ship.

After a night of cold and terror, Matthew was trembling witness to the last act of all. From his cragside lair, burrowed within the coarse heather, he peeped out at the *San Vigilio*, a half-mile below him in the haven of Tobermory. He watched her sails loosed, and saw a brisk muster of sailors advance to the ledge below the forecastle, to lift her anchor. He was shivering and starved with cold, yet the sight was the happiest of his life. The *San Vigilio* was leaving at last, with all her company.

A trumpet sounded across the bay as the anchor broke surface. The sails filled; then the galleon set course for the harbour's mouth. She was a brave sight, this leviathan—which might be the last ship of Spain—to a man no longer captive on board.

Then all melted into horror.

While the *San Vigilio* was still within the arm of the bay, a cannon shot boomed out from her highest tier of guns. Whether this was a final thrust at the murderous foe, or a curse on Matthew Lawe, or the last gesture of bravado, only her commander could have told. But it *was* her last. There was a huge burst of noise and smoke, and on the instant she was engulfed in fire from end to end. Matthew watched appalled as this great torch erupted, but the ship split asunder, and heeled and sank so quickly that there was little time for horror; only for pity.

On the sea, all the flotsam of disaster began to break the surface: planks of wood, barrels rolling aimlessly, scorched sails. Then the heads of men appeared, men screaming, and struggling against the merciless suck of the water, and swimming wildly for the shore.

Even as they did so, other upright men with swords came out of their secret hiding places among the rocks, and stood waiting.

For Matthew Lawe it was the moment to move before the lust for blood marred the difference between a Spaniard and his poor captive. Stiffly he rose, and made for a hilltop on the farther side of the bay. Below the crest, so that he would not be outlined, he turned his face to the sun, and began to creep southwards, across the Isle of Mull towards the mainland. The long flight had begun.

Interlude

SAVE THAT she was more comely than most, and young and willing, the girl in the grimy bed was like any other girl shaped for the sport of sailors. Just as there was a price for this foul room under the eaves of the inn, so there was a price for her willingness; and Matthew Lawe had had to pay for both, cash on the barrel-head.

After their sport, the girl slept, like a log of driftwood lulled below the surface of life by the greater power of the sea, and Matthew was left to rule the kingdom of the land. It was no great heritage. While he swigged his cold ale in the darkness, the room itself grew colder; the girl stole the best portion of the blankets, as the candle wick flickered, begging piteously to be snuffed; even the ale had turned sour, needing courage in the swallowing.

He would have a fine thick head on the morrow, when he must

board ship again and take up the sweat and stink of life without the fourth part of a silver shilling to show for his pains. He savoured, as best he could, the last of the ale, the last of his purse, and the last of the land. If nothing could be counted on save spent drink, spent money, and spent manhood, then what a swinish couch had Christ their Saviour spread for the limbs of man!

Yet it was a bed he must lie on; he could not change it. He was doomed to the mariner's squalid calendar of life: doomed to make a harsh voyage, to come ashore rich (by the humble standards of his trade), and then to drink his fill, lay claim to a wench, spend on her a year's earnings in a few days or weeks, and ship out again without a groat in his pocket.

So, it seemed, he must go on and on, until—and now those dark thoughts came flooding in and drowning everything else in a swift nightmare of doubt and fear.

This was his doom, as proclaimed by the mad old witch of Drumnin so long ago. In all the vast peepshow of the world, all the pictures changed but one doomed man did not. His body had not moved with the years, nor had his face altered by a line, nor his hair by a single lock. *He was the same man.*

The chill wind sighed in the eaves; behind the wainscot the rats scuttled. No comfort there save cold and corruption. He lay back, and plucked at a string of courage. These fearful thoughts were part of his calendar, part of every last night ashore; and what he must do now, to defeat them, took hold on him again. Some divine or devil's spark came to his aid, reminding him of the sovereign cure for such despair.

Tomorrow he sailed, but tomorrow was not yet. Tonight still lay at his side. He turned towards the sleeping girl and pressed her to him until she wakened. When he slept at last, he dreamed of apes and peacocks, roaring seas and soft strands, and mermaids with gleaming breasts.

At dawn-light he awoke, and dressed and stowed his gear. The girl, snug beneath the blankets, did not stir. It was time to leave; Matthew hoisted his sea-chest on his shoulder and descended by the creaking stairway. Out in the pale sunlight, he tautened certain idle sinews and began to stride across the cobblestones. He must once again embrace the horrid press of his fellow man. He must sail on.

Part Two
1682

IT WAS A fair brave English day, and all of Portsmouth knew it. The sun shone as if by royal command, the flags fluttered like clapping hands. King Charles was here, and his comely mistress the Duchess of Portsmouth, and his more sober Papist brother James, Duke of York, and a throng of nobility to line the dockside.

There was a royal yacht to be launched, and free ale to be quaffed; and nothing for the common sort to do but gape and enjoy, and swallow their regal bounty. It was a Portsmouth holiday, with the honest smell of brine to sweeten it, and the goodly feeling that all men here, and women, too, and the children who

ABOVE: Seventeenth-century Greenwich by Hendrik Danckerts. Samuel Pepys by J. Hauls.

would be the next breed of sailors, were celebrants at the very shrine of the sea—the finest seaport in all England.

Matthew Lawe, who had landed not six hours before from a skinflint *barca longa* plying the Guinea trade, knew nothing save that it seemed to be a holiday, and there was a pretty ship enthroned on a launching cradle, and lords and ladies in the best vantage points. At first he only listened to talk around him of the Portsmouth citizens of high and low degree; and there was plenty to be heard. After five years in his African wilderness, he had need of such scholarship.

A pursy fellow standing next to him, and a townsman of some consequence, if his fine grey cloak and lofty nose could be judged aright, eyed Matthew's face, and then his outlandish breeches, which were from the ship's store and baggy as a pair of udders before milking, all he had in the world. "Such galligaskins!" he intoned. "We do not often see such a style hereabouts. Art 'ee from Portsmouth?"

"Nay. Barnstaple. I came ashore this morning. From the Western Sea—the Guinea trade. Our last touch was at Lisbon."

The ocean words were his passport and established his honourable rate.

"A sailor!" cried a little twisted fellow with a face as creased as a walnut. "Welcome ashore!"

Matthew grinned and looked about him happily. The focus of all this merry crowd was the yacht on the wheeled launching cradle, a lovesome thing, all curves and tapered spars and bright paintwork: ready rigged, her sails hoisted and drawing gently, her royal banners blessing the vulgar air, and the whole dainty conceit thirsting for the embrace of the sea. What it must be, to command such a ship! What it must be, to command the gold to build her!

Matthew gestured towards the treasure. "What is she to be called, the little yacht?"

"Why, the *Fubbs*, of course!" said his new friend with the walnut-creased face. "What else would the King's favourite vessel be called?"

"*Fubbs*?" The smirking round about Matthew declared the strange word to be part of an unknown jest. "There's a name! What does it mean?"

A wharfman turned at his question. "Where have you been, for the love of God? It is the King's pet name for his trollop."

Matthew was still lost, and did not mind confessing it. "What trollop is this? I have been away these five years. A man could lose count."

"The Duchess of Portsmouth," put in a man with a drunkard's flaming nose. "Mistress Fubbs." He raised an ale mug. "I drink to her! Good fellows all! I would drink to anyone who keeps us in ale." He raised his mug, and proclaimed with drunken gravity, "I give you the Duchess of Portsmouth, and the King's majesty, and the *Fubbs*, and all who sail in her, and God bless Sam Pepys who gives us the ships." He then lost his balance, and fell down, and, sitting squat like a broody hen, finally drank.

The throng all round them laughed, and then raised up the fallen warrior. The townsman looked coldly down a very cold nose. "You may jest," he told them, "but open sin is open sin, if the King himself gives it licence. He may call her Fubbs, if he wishes to. I would call her Bathsheba!"

"The jade does not matter," the wharfman said. "What sticks in my gullet is the yacht itself. What does the King want with another royal yacht? He has fifteen already, and all to play at racing games with his brother the Duke of York. Is this what we pay our taxes for? Royal toys, I call them!"

But the King had an ally in a larded citizen who sat fat on the world like a tun of Rhenish wine and who, it seemed, had once been a loyal sailor. "Royal yacht she may be," he wheezed, "but that is not all. She is navy-planned and navy-built. They do not carve toys. It is their chance to try new plans, new ships. This one is Phineas Pett's new dream. Ketch-rigged—the first ever to be so. Will she sail better? That is what we shall find out, and perhaps copy it later. She will serve with the fleet if need be. Or she will voyage round the coast, and plot the tides and the shallows. So talk not of royal toys! No ship of this quality is ever wasted."

Matthew plucked at a familiar name. "Phineas Pett? Him that built the old *Bear* for Sir Walter?"

"The *Bear*?" the fat man repeated, puzzled. "What *Bear* is that? And which Sir Walter?"

"Why, Raleigh, of course," Matthew answered—and stopped

appalled, before a gaping chasm. Then he managed a foolish smile. "Nay, that cannot be! My wits were wandering—"

Among the circle that looked at him in wonder, the townsman's eyes were the most searching. "What know you of Sir Phineas Pett that built the *Bear*?"

"I must have heard his name," Matthew said lamely.

"Then you have long ears. This one is his grandson."

It was a moment of confusion, but Matthew was rescued by chance and time. At the farther end of the quay, there was a sudden lively stir, the glint of steel on soldiers' breasts, and the glitter of halberds above the throng. Behind this, a burst of gleaming silks and frothing plumed hats caught the sunlight.

There was a roar of loyal huzzas as the tall handsome figure of King Charles strode through the parting crowd. The royal party mounted the bannered dais in front of the yacht. The great moment was at hand, and the greatest man in the realm was its spear-point.

If the King who had ruled for two-and-twenty years was, at fifty-two, past his lusty prime, as some whispered, he was still every inch a man and a monarch. His huge curled wig and foppish clothes might, on any other man, have earned him disrespect, and the outrageous petticoat breeches—tight to the knee-bone, then flouncing out into a full twelve inches of foamy lace—would have seemed fit only for ribaldry. But for Charles their King, all such frippery, being his own choice, was also theirs.

They loved him, and the full-throated roar came from full hearts as well. For a near quarter-century, he had shepherded them through countless hazards: the desolation of plague, the scourge of fire, war and the threat of war, plot and counter-plot, broil and ferment enough to topple a whole dynasty of kings.

But King Charles had lived, and endured, and prospered, and had fashioned Merry England out of the dull grey tyranny of Cromwell. A king who could do that, and rebuild a great city from its ashes, and turn back the Dutch from its very water gates, might bed ten mistresses and don all the petticoats he chose, if it kept him so supple and strong, so loving and so loved.

Portsmouth loved him especially as a friend of sailors. They knew that the King and his "little advocate" of the navy, Mr.

Secretary Pepys, had toiled for wearisome years to give England a fleet, and its seamen their bread. They loved above all the fact that, on this great occasion, the fat and fussy little man in his fine clothes now stood side by side with his tall monarch. He had earned his day of glory in the sunshine.

For Matthew Lawe's instruction the townsman had been pointing out the dignitaries, as one by one they took their place of privilege on the dais. "There is your Mistress Fubbs," he said disdainfully, when a small figure in the gayest clothes of all made its way to the forefront. Matthew found himself stirred at this glimpse of a lively shrine of sin. . . . "A bedfellow for twelve years, and now a duchess! And she came to court as a maid-of-honour! The gentleman in the black hat and cloak is the master shipwright, Sir Phineas Pett. Your *old* friend. And now you have a better sight of Samuel Pepys," the townsman went on, as the diminutive figure in shining pale blue moved to the front of the dais. Pepys suddenly stumbled, and would have fallen, if a royal arm had not come to his rescue.

"By God, the fellow is drunk!" the wharfman said.

"Have some pity, for pity's sake!" said the man with the flaming nose, from a companionable heart. "He is near blind, as we all know. He did no more than miss his step."

"Mr. Pepys is not so blind, when he *peeps* into the public purse!" the wharfman replied. "Look at those fine clothes! First he is secretary of the navy. Then suddenly he is a traitor, walled up in the Tower of London. Then he is near back in office again. In and out like a weathercock! But does he starve? Never! Now he has treasures in his house. Whence came such a mountain of money? We all know the stink of corruption that fouls every navy ship that was ever launched. There is a finger in every purse of guineas. Sam Pepys may be blind, but he can smell a profit, whenever he sees a hank of cordage or a stack of timber."

On a sudden, a cannon shot boomed out from the Portsmouth bastions above, and the chosen apprentice lad, beribboned like a little maypole, advanced towards the launching cradle, with a wooden sledgehammer as big as himself poised for the stroke. Then King Charles raised his hand. The sledge fell, with one fair stroke, and the chock beneath the hind wheel vanished. The well-greased chariot began to roll and rumble down the slipway, then took the water with a merry splash. First the forefoot dipped, then the whole shapely length of the hull—and the *Fubbs*, fluttering free of her cradle, swam at last!

There was a rousing cheer. Men concealed below ran out on deck and began to trim the yards and bear down on the helm. With all sails drawing, the *Fubbs* turned shorewards to face the dais, as if to curtsy to her King, and then began to cruise very prettily down the harbour. It was all done in a right seamanlike manner, and the crowds loved it.

"Now they christen her," said the townsman. "Look—there is the goblet now!"

There was a gleaming flash of gold from the dais, as a shapely chalice was passed from the King to the duchess, from the duchess to the Duke of York, from him to Sir Phineas Pett, and so on down the line of the royal party.

"By God's blood!" the drunkard said. "I wish I was younger. I would dive for it myself."

"Dive?" Matthew questioned him. "What dive is this?"

"Have you not seen the christening splash? When that golden goblet returns to the King, he will drain it, then throw it into the water. All the lads will dive in and try to fish it out."

"What then? Do they keep it?"

"Nay, they sell it back to the master shipwright."

"At what price?" Matthew asked.

"Whatever the old shark will pay. Perhaps twenty guineas."

It was riches beyond avarice. "By the Wounds, I will try it myself!" Matthew cried. "How do I set about it?"

"Canst swim well?" the fat man asked. "There are rogues who have been waiting for this chance since the keel was laid. They would rip off your parts, if they see you come near the gold."

"I can swim. And I have played water games before."

"Then make for the steps there. Mark where the goblet falls, and jump straightway, before they stir up the mud. With luck, you may dive and follow it down."

Matthew forced a way through the throng, and joined a band of suspicious, glowering ruffians at the head of the steps. Avoiding every eye, he watched the dais. Already the goblet had made its laughing circle of the great, and was back in the King's hands. His Majesty drained the last of it. The empty goblet dropped, then rose in the air and was launched in a generous arc, which bespoke a manly arm behind it. At this, Matthew Lawe stripped off his jerkin and dived head-first into the harbour. As he came to the surface, the golden target made its own dive, five yards beyond his head.

Violence followed. Angry cries, peals of drunken laughter were succeeded by splashes, bullet-heads butting, flailing limbs, bodies sinking like stones and rising like volcanoes, as the host of greedy or desperate men launched themselves upon their goal.

Though Matthew, with lungs well filled, was already submerged beneath this watery avalanche, he felt its weight, and some of its malice. A hand reached out to grasp his hair, and he clawed it loose. He had the goblet within his grasp when another pair of hands fastened on his throat. A backward kick found its mark, and he was free of enemies. He rose with his prize, thrust it down his breeches, and leaving behind the milling shoal of swimmers, dog-paddled gently ashore.

His hour of triumph began when he topped the steps once more, a bedraggled figure naked to the waist, below which the absurd galligaskins bulged monstrously. He retrieved his jerkin from a sympathetic onlooker, and, since he was the first to return from the battle, his movements were watched from the royal dais. He gripped the golden cup, and brandished it on high.

"By Holy Cross, he has it!" his coat-holder shouted, and the cry was taken up on every side, as the sunlight put fire in the goblet. His late circle of friends were jumping for joy. There had been no other moment in Matthew's life when his friends outnumbered his foes, by such a regiment. Yet the peak of that day was still to come. In the next hour, Matthew Lawe made a giant step forward. It could not last, but while it endured, it lit his private sky as the Northern Lights could set a whole icy world on fire.

As he mounted the steps of the dais with his prize, the first to meet him was the guardian of civic pomp, the mayor of Portsmouth himself: a small swill-tub of a man, red and sweating under the pressures of this day. "Well done, young man," he said, as his gaze rested with distaste on this dripping scarecrow. "Give me the goblet and I will see that you are properly rewarded."

Matthew might have said Yes on any other day. But he was

within sight, a brief glimpse told him, of greatness, and a real King crowned it. He would make his own mark, and be damned to all lackeys standing in his path. "I would deliver it myself," he answered firmly.

"Let him through to the master shipwright, if you please, Mr. Mayor," the voice of true majesty called.

Yet it was not to Sir Phineas Pett that Matthew steered his course. Vaguely he saw the tall figure of the monarch; clearly he spied the delicious armful which adorned his side. Without hesitation, he marched forward, bowed low, and offered the golden cup of *Fubbs* to Fubbs herself.

Louise de Kéroualle, Duchess of Portsmouth, was not one of the world's holy innocents; no woman who had made the progress from lady-in-waiting to King's mistress could be found wanting in such a circumstance as now presented itself. She had made an exact measure of Matthew Lawe before he had straightened his back. Her answer to this newcomer was feminine, and wise. She assumed a radiant face, took the cup, and then—wonder of wonders—curtsyed to her benefactor. Royal smiles, encouraging laughter, a burst of cheering, and lustful growls of approval from the commonality, showed that she had acquitted herself to perfection.

The strong, well-formed young man, in a humour beyond his station, lost his sauciness and became a pliant slave again. Yet he had enough of his wits about him to note a lesson of life—that people close by, whether high or low, scarcely matched their public portrait. The radiant Fubbs, though arch and elegant, was now a haggard beauty. In early middle age, she was hardly a meal for a lusty man. The lusty man himself, who now bent upon Matthew a pair of piercing eyes, was no more a king in this realm; at fifty-two, he had grown worn by care, so that the dashing monarch was a tall shrunken shell. No peacock display of finery could mask the gaunt crow within. Yet he could still play the king to all his loving subjects, and he did so now. "You swim like an otter," he said smiling. "Where did you learn such skills?"

"As a sailor, sire," Matthew answered, abashed.

"Sailors are the blood of this realm. Could I say less, in Portsmouth? Your name?"

"Matthew Lawe, sire."

"Well, Matthew Lawe, you have conquered more than the sea today." He gave an intimate glance towards his duchess. "I have never witnessed such gallantry, on either side. But you have earned more than a curtsy. . . . Mr. Mayor!"

The mayor of Portsmouth came to trembling attention.

"Pray remove your hat of office, and put it to profitable use. We are in honour bound to ransom this cup. Walk the length of the dais, Mr. Mayor, and say to all, 'Spare a guinea *or so*—for the swimmer.' I would direct your diligence towards my royal brother, to Mr. Pepys, and to all such great benefactors. . . . I will lead."

A gentle lift of a finger under the nose of a courtier close to him produced a silken purse, and the purse shed five golden guineas, dropped into the mayor's beaver hat. Others followed steadily as the collector made his rounds. At the end, the mayor's hat bore more weight of gold than it had ever held brains; and when it was all spilled out into Matthew's cupped hands, he was accorded the gracious smiles due to a victor. His head in a whirl, Matthew Lawe had never been so warmed and cherished in all the hungry years so far.

Now the *Fubbs* yacht was seen to be returning down the length of Portsmouth Harbour. Matthew, with his wealth safely tucked into his breeches, turned to take his leave, just as the noble assembly on the dais pressed forward to gain a vantage point.

The surging spilled out one small awkward figure, tumbled backwards by stronger bodies. It was Mr. Samuel Pepys, who would have fallen if Matthew had not stepped up to support him under his arms.

"Throngs, throngs!" Mr. Pepys said testily. "One might as well be set loose in Bedlam!" He peered upwards with clouded eyes. "Thank 'ee for a strong arm. Who are you, lad?"

"Matthew Lawe, sir. I brought back the christening cup."

"Ah, the sailor who can swim. That is a rare fish indeed!"

Matthew had made no judgment, as yet, of what such a great man, secretary of the navy board, should resemble, save that he *must* be a lordly tyrant, with his power of life or death over common sailors. Mr. Samuel Pepys was no such thing. He was tiny, barely up to Matthew's shoulder, and fat, and fussy, and decked out like a paunchy marionette whose master could afford silken strings.

Though the face was wise, it was not commanding. Subtract his rank, Matthew thought, and he might be an ageing lawyer's clerk, robbed of his eyesight by musty parchment and cramped penmanship. "You did well, Matthew Lawe. You sailed upon us like a true man-o'-war's man. The boarding of Mistress Fubbs was most valiant. I hope you did as well in profit."

"Sire, I have not yet counted."

"You must indeed be a sailor! But when you come to reckon it, you will find a gold piece from myself."

"Thank you kindly, sir."

"It was my duty and my pleasure," Mr. Pepys went on grandly. He caught a brief sight of the yacht, curvetting to a breeze like a frisking colt, and he exclaimed: "Now *there* is the prettiest thing that ever swam! And when the royal pleasure is slaked, we can use her as guard ship. Did you ever sail in one of the King's ships?"

"I—no, sir."

Pepys looked at him with sharper eyes. "You hesitated. What was it—did you run?"

"No, sir. I only meant that I have seen no special service. All the ships in the realm are the King's."

"Amen to that! Whether war or peace, they serve a common cause." He rubbed his plump hands one against the other. "Well —I to my desk, and you to your mariner's toil. Have you a berth waiting?"

"No, sir. We take what we can, or else go hungry."

Mr. Pepys gave another of his sharp glances, belying his fabled short sight. "How would you mend that, as a sailor?"

Matthew, emboldened, answered from an ancient experience which no man, great or small, could ever share: "Sir, treat us as men of worth, not to be cast off and cast on again, as the mood takes."

"But when there are no ships, and no places?"

"If that is true today, 'twill be a lie tomorrow."

"Well said! You are older than your years. . . . Believe me, for your comfort, there are men at work on such questions. And I am one."

When he was alone, Matthew counted his reward: forty-four

golden guineas. Now, for a space, he was rich in wordly goods—
and, he decided, rich in human kind. By this he was not remembering the King, nor his wayward duchess. But a small, funny old
fellow with great new thoughts of the sea: Mr. Secretary Pepys.

2

WHEN HIS store of guineas had dwindled to ten, Matthew
Lawe shipped out of Portsmouth on the *Grace & Favour*,
a humble collier with little grace and no favour, plying
from London to the far West Country and back again. It was in this
small stinkard of a ship, better than a year later, that he sailed into
the Pool of London. He had not sighted it for many years, and now,
in the spring of 1684, the prospect was astonishing.

This was a great new London, which had outdone the phoenix
in rising from the ashes of the old. After the most malevolent of
plagues, which in a single week had condemned seven thousand
citizens to death, and the searing of the greatest fire ever seen in
England, the city might have died. But Charles their King, and
Christopher Wren their architect, had other dreams, and a spirit
to fulfil them.

The brave reality now blessed the eye, with whole terraces of
lordly buildings; and all crowned at the eastern end by the
rising mass of the new cathedral of St. Paul's to lift the heart of
Everyman closer to heaven. At the other margin of the river's
great sweep, the towered Palace of Whitehall set a kingly stamp
upon a dream come true.

But in this vast metropolis, Matthew was a cast-off again, a
mere riverbank wanderer. Good sea berths were scarce, and poor
ones no better than starveling servitude. Then chance, the most
precious clove-spice in the whole pomander of life, came to his
aid, and set him on the high road.

On an April morning in 1684, he was wandering the quays
which flanked the water gate of Somerset House when he came
upon a liveried waterman, his choleric face as purple as his coat,
near to bursting with rage as he looked this way and that along the
river front. It needed no magician to divine that he was waiting
for someone, and could not wait much longer. Below him, his boat

63

lay idle on the lapping tideway: a handsome little barge, gilded like a coach, with two benches for the oarsmen, and stern sheets cushioned for half a dozen passengers. In it were two untended oars, an empty tiller, and a single oarsman in the same purple livery.

The waterman on the quay stamped and swore, then, as Matthew drew near, he barked out, "You! Can you pull an oar?"

"Aye, I can row. What is it you need? A bow-man? A man to keep stroke?"

"Well, you have the sound of a sailor, thanks be," the waterman said. "I am called to the Privy Stairs." He pointed towards White-hall Palace. "And no one to pull the second oar. My mate is sick or drunk!"

"How much will you pay me?" Matthew asked.

The waterman turned sly. "I'll see that you do well."

"*I* will see," said Matthew, who knew a man caught on a lee shore when he met one. "I must eat more than promises tonight."

Somewhere near at hand a church bell struck the hour, and the waterman jumped. "Well enough—the day's rate for the time you serve." And as Matthew nodded agreement, the waterman jumped down into his little barge. "Hurry!" he shouted. "And put on that boat-cloak, or you will scare his honour as well as the crows."

"His honour", when they had stemmed the tide and made fast at Whitehall Privy Stairs, was Mr. Samuel Pepys. The little man did not stand small this morning; his moment of leave-taking from the Palace water gate was attended by bowing courtiers, secretaries who preceded him with a chest of papers, and even the Duke of York bidding him farewell. Mr. Pepys was newly arrived from Windsor Castle where he had been named by royal appointment secretary of affairs of the Admiralty with power to refashion his beloved navy according to his own dream. In brief, he had returned after favour and disfavour, renown and venomous attack, not only to full favour but to the greatest glory of his life.

He was therefore in high good humour, laughing as he stepped on board and waving to the company. As soon as they were unloosed, he turned to the waterman. "Jem Belcher," he charged, with mock sternness, "you have delayed me!"

"Your pardon, sir. I have a man sick."

"I care not if he be hanged! If you delay me, then I delay the grooms of the antechamber who attend me, and they delay the King, and so the realm rots. . . ." But he did not seem to give a fig for any of this. Sitting on his cushioned throne, he was his own king, and could order everything in view.

Jem Belcher eased the tiller as the barge began to stem the ebbtide. "To the Westminster gate, your honour?"

"No. I have two hours of holiday this morning. Take me down-river to the Tower stairs. I will find a coach for the return. And do not break your backs. I would enjoy this journey."

In the bright sunshine, riding the swift tideway, they began their progress down the great blood artery of the Thames. There was all to admire in the fine buildings on their left hand, and the green meadows and rushbeds of Lambeth Marsh on the south bank. There was room to breathe also, and freedom from the narrow alleys and pressing crowds of the city. The best view of London was to be won thus.

"Better than my own coach," Mr. Pepys exclaimed presently. "There is only one way to travel through this town. Did you say you had a man sick?"

"Aye, sir. Doggett failed me. But I found another."

Mr. Pepys turned, and looked directly at Matthew for the first time. He frowned, in puzzlement. "I know you," he said.

Matthew looked up from his oar and nodded. "It was at Portsmouth, sir," he said. "The launching of the *Fubbs* yacht. I am—"

"Matthew Lawe the swimmer!" Mr. Pepys exclaimed. "The sailor also. . . . Do you follow me, Matthew?"

Matthew grinned. "No, sir. But I would do so."

"Would you now! You may be in luck, Matthew Lawe. I am like to say Yes to all the world this forenoon."

Two miles downstream, they shot the swirling tide of London Bridge, with its fifteen narrow arches and double rank of houses and shops; and so came to the Tower stairs, and the end of their journey. Mr. Pepys stood up as the boat was berthed. "I have a box," he declared, looking down at Matthew. "Full of state papers, which means that if you let it fall in the river you and I shall lose our heads. Can you carry such a box for me, and find a coach? Are you free?"

"Aye, sir."

Mr. Pepys stepped ashore, while Matthew shouldered the box and made to follow him.

"What are you at, you crow?" Jem Belcher growled at Matthew. "You are bound to me. I'll not pay—"

Matthew swung and faced him. A furious man was nothing new in his life, and nothing of consequence either. "There is no charge," he said grandly. "Thank you, waterman. You did well."

During the long rumbling coach journey through the new heart of the city, in which Mr. Pepys took continual delight—whether at the sight of a fine building rising high, a fishman crying his wares, or a pretty maid arching her breasts towards the spring sunlight—on all this homeward way, the great man chattered like a magpie. His journey from Whitehall Palace to the Tower had been a gulp of air, a sigh of purest pleasure, before he buckled on his armour.

Being mortal, being Mr. Pepys—old in sin as well as new in power—he could also spare a side glance towards his princely salary: two thousand a year, with house rent, travelling funds, and all the other perquisites of office, to match a peak of authority never yet bestowed on any servant of the Crown. But today his talk was of the past. He was fifty-one, and tomorrow was bright with hope. Yet he had taken that river ride to touch his roots again, sometimes with regretful hands.

"Seething Lane," Pepys announced to Matthew, peering out of the rattling coach window. "I came to live here in 1660, when I was first made a clerk. The old navy office was under the same roof. I was twenty-seven, and married five years. My wife was only twenty. In that house—" he pointed, "I lived for fourteen years. We were happy there—and then she died, and I was happy no more. They were cruel times, in any case."

Matthew could only ask: "How cruel, sir?"

"You must then have been a lad," Mr. Pepys told him, "and not a Londoner either. We saw the Great Plague of '65 from that house, the most evil scourge that ever struck. The Bills of Mortality rose every week, by tens, and hundreds, and thousands. But the worst evil of the Plague—forgetting the stench of the death pits where people dragged themselves to die—was what it did to living men. It made us more cruel to one another than if we were dogs. We barred our windows, and prayed to be spared, while pitiful wretches knocked at our doors pleading for help. . . . The Court removed from London, and my wife too, and I stayed working alone in Seething Lane. When all was done, I put on the airs of a brave archangel! But in truth, I never lived so merrily, nor got so much, as during that Plague time."

"Got so much?" Matthew repeated, puzzled. "In gold?"

"Women. They thought they heard the Last Trump, and it was the most desperate call to arms I ever knew."

Matthew, the country boy turned humble sailor, was conscious of a horrid shock. So this was Mr. Samuel Pepys, the great officer of state. He was no better than some low-born randy rascal. To go a-whoring in the midst of a plague, with his wife sent away for safety. . . . He sat silent in the tumbling coach, as it rolled along Cheapside into the holy shadow of St. Paul's, and wondered what respect should be paid to rank, if all were equal hogwash.

Then Mr. Pepys, whether nudged by an Almighty hand or divining the disapproval of this simple mind, sought to justify the occasion. "Well, I was punished. Or *began* to be punished; for it is a long business, and no man is quit of it until he dies. My reading eyes were starting to fail from too much close labour—print and writing were becoming mere torture. To discover a meaning, I had to peer down at a page, letter by letter, through a leather tube. My own precious diary could scarce be kept up, for fear of going blind. At work, all long communications must be read out to me."

Matthew was once more in thrall to a valiant man. "But sir, why did you not resign? So much of the work was done."

"It is never done!" Mr. Pepys said sharply. "I had navy business to finish, or to begin, and I still have. And I thought that my eyes might mend, if I plotted to spare them." Then he smiled, the man overtaking the paragon of duty. "And who gives up office when he can crawl to work?"

It was difficult to catch such a mood, or to answer it worthily. Did every man of stature melt into laughter at his own smallness? Perhaps Matthew would never know. He could only listen, and hope to learn.

"But before that, we were all punished, the year that followed the Plague," Mr. Pepys went on. "Where were you when the fire took London? At sea?"

"Aye. By turns. Did the fire touch here?" he asked, looking out at the rise of Fleet Street and the brave houses on either side.

"*Touch?* We drive through the very graveyard! There was not a house left standing, in all this mile. From the Tower to Temple Bar, from High Holborn to the river, all was burned to nothing."

"How long did it burn?"

"Six days. In that time, God made the great world, and in that time He destroyed this little one."

It had started, Mr. Pepys said as their coach voyaged onwards, on a fine September night, when he had been called from his bed to watch "a little fire in the city". It was near, in a neighbouring street behind Mark Lane. But there was a good easterly wind. The little fire would blow away, or blow out. He had gone back to his bed—and that was the last time he slept for four nights.

By mid-morning the flames had taken hold among numberless little wooden houses roofed and coated with pitch, as ready for the torch as a quick-match.

At noon the northern buildings on London Bridge were all in flames and the citizens of the riverside were already flinging their goods into barges and lighters, and making their escape. No one was doing a hand's turn to oppose the peril. Mr. Pepys, a sober citizen with access to authority, took boat to Whitehall, interrupted the King in conference, and gave him the news. He was sent back with a message to the Lord Mayor: "Pull down the houses. Make a fire-break."

"I found the Lord Mayor, and told him," said Pepys. "I might have been speaking to the fire itself. 'What can I do?' was his answer. 'No one will obey me!'"

It was true. Those who had been scorched were in terrified flight. Their laden carts were running over each other. At the water's edge, boats and barges crashed together as desperate men tried to claw away from the burning land. Pepys and his household, to escape the heat, had watched it from the south side of the river. At dusk, it was already enough to put terror into any heart.

"You know the sea," he said to Matthew broodingly. "This was a sea turned to a furnace—a horrid malicious bloody flame, near a mile across. It could only gain. . . . Next day, as it crept near the house, I sent our main goods away, by coach to the country. The whole world was on this same run—we fought for our space like animals."

Then he went back to Seething Lane and the navy office, to do his duty.

The fourth day was the worst. Though the King took direct command, with the Duke of York at his side and a whole regiment of troops to do their bidding, the fire spread ever westwards. Old St. Paul's went, sending a river of molten lead down from its roof as it fell. Flames leaped across the gap, nearly trapping the duke and his soldiers within a ring of fire.

To the east, it was Mr. Pepys's navy office which was in desperate need. On his own authority, Pepys sent a call for sailors and dockhands from the yards at Woolwich and Deptford, to pull down the houses near Seething Lane. "The sailors came running with ropes and axes, God bless them, to save the heart of their navy. But at two o'clock of another sleepless night, the fire reached the bottom of Seething Lane, and all was gone. So I gathered the last of the gold—mine and the navy's—and took boat to Woolwich. I was near dead with tiredness. . . . By morning, there could be nothing else to save."

But by morning, he returned to a miracle. The fire had stopped at the lower end of Seething Lane. Both house and navy office stood intact, thanks to those loyal sailors. Indeed, all the fire in the city had now been contained. With the help of king and duke, rope and powder, soldiers and seamen, the monster was tamed.

Walking the streets later, he trod on a grisly blackened skeleton, still hot enough to scorch his feet through the soles of his shoes. When the count was made, some 13,000 houses had been burnt, and 100,000 people rendered homeless.

"But I was proud of England that day. Where else in the world would a king, using his own hands, lead his men to save so much of his capital from ruin? And not all was a curse in '66," Mr. Pepys said, as their coach rolled downhill towards Charing Cross and the Palace of Whitehall. "The flame, at the least, cleansed the city from its infection. And it gave us this reborn city. My friend Mr. Evelyn used to say, the happiest sight after the fire was to see the King, with a great broadsheet in his lap, sketching out a new London."

Mr. Pepys, enjoying his tour of the city, stopped their coach at the margin of St. James's Park, which with its meadows and duck-ponds was as pastoral as the Garden of Eden. He looked across the spacious park, shading his weak eyes against the sun and the rippling gleam of water.

"In the old days I used to walk here every morning with his majesty, or his brother the duke, and by God I will do so again! We will talk, as we used to, of the navy—there is naught else of account. . . ." He turned towards Matthew once more. "Never forget—at the time I was speaking of, the plague year and the fire year, the Dutch were for ever tearing at our throats, without mercy. And all we had to oppose them was a shadow of a navy. You spoke something of it when we met at Portsmouth, and it was like hearing an old story from a young mouth. We starve our men,

and let our ships rot, and then we are surprised when we run into danger, and have to build again at speed. But what you cannot know of, is the enemy within."

"What enemy is this, sir?"

"Thieves!" Mr. Pepys answered promptly. "The navy has been a target of corruption since I was a young clerk, twenty-five years ago. I found it so then, and I will find it so again tomorrow morning. We were fair game for every cheat who ever bought a contract, every hog that smelled the public trough, *because we had to have the ships*. We were sold green wood, rusted iron, rotten meat, bread not fit for the swill tub. And if it cost a sailor his life, then sailors were simpletons, and deserved it."

This was strange hearing for Matthew Lawe, who thought he

must know more than most about following the sea, and now saw that he had glimpsed only a speck on that same ocean. There were greater villainies than using chain-shot, a worse scourge than a boatswain with a ready fist. There were pirates ashore in England:

"Oh, I put down plenty of villains," continued Mr. Pepys, "and so I knit it all together in time. But I made too many enemies on the road, so I was put down in my turn by the lord chancellor, who needed a stick to beat the King. That dog is dead a year and I live again. But while I was down, the navy was down. Though Parliament voted money by the million, it has all been swallowed up. There is no fleet worth the name today. . . . So I am recalled, and told to build again." But his face had grown melancholy, as though confidence had ebbed to the tide mark below his brave words. "It is the greatest chance of my life. But I am not young any more."

In all sympathy, Matthew could only declare that it happened to the best of men.

"What?" Mr. Pepys replied instantly. "Do you think the King would give employment to some old dotard with his senses gone? If you have any such thoughts, pray keep them private, or we may fall out. Now—answer me these questions."

They came thick and fast, sometimes in friendly guise, sometimes like little pincers. Could Matthew read and write? Had he worked as captain's clerk? As store-keeper? As anything better than tarry mariner? Could he judge honest timber? If some poor fellow's widow came to the office with a ticket for his last voyage, would Matthew honour it, or buy it at a fat discount? Or perhaps tear up the ticket, and take the woman?

"Well, you have the sea at your heart," Samuel Pepys said finally, as their coach turned back towards Buckingham Street, where they were bound. "So have I. Until we learn to flap our wings and fly, sailors are the world-makers. What I need now is another pair of young eyes. And two strong arms. And most of all, I need faithful hearts about me. I have had enough of traitors, great and small." When the coach stopped before the fine front door of his house, Mr. Pepys delivered a friendly verdict: "We shall see. . . . Now hand me down."

The house at No. 12, Buckingham Street, which Samuel Pepys shared with Will Hewer, his faithful clerk and valiant friend of twenty-four years, was elegant, busy, and of good repute. Evidence of wealth was everywhere: in the furnishings, the silverware, the polished wood of cupboard and chest of drawers, the gleaming candle brackets, the wine which stood ready for serving, the smell of linseed oil patiently rubbed upon every cherished surface. Samuel Pepys might have seen hard days. But he had prospered also.

Will Hewer was the anchor of this harbourage. A personable man of forty, strong, and fair-haired, it was he to whom all turned when Mr. Pepys was absent. He was not surprised by a new clerk, entering without notice under the wing of the secretary. A private discourse with Mr. Pepys, a close examination of Matthew himself, and the disposal was made, with every sign of good humour and concise direction.

"You will lodge in one of the garrets," said Will Hewer to Matthew, "and work at a desk near mine at Derby House. We are all one family here, and we all serve the same great man. And if there is need to turn his music pages, or usher a King's messenger to his room at midnight, or expel a stray cat from his garden, then the one nearest at hand will do it."

Talk of music pages and King's messengers did nothing to raise Matthew's confidence. He said: "I will do what I can. But I fear to make mistakes."

"Keep that fear, and you will prosper. If you fail, you will be told, and so you will learn. If you fail again, I shall peer into your ears to discover what makes a blockhead. Meantime, I have a good grey suit which will serve you for tonight, when there will be great company."

At that moment, Mr. Pepys himself appeared at the end of the long gallery where they stood, splendidly arrayed in laced finery, newly donned for the expected gathering. The little man, for all his awkward figure, looked as resplendent as his elegant house. Matthew sighed despondently. "It is all so rich," he murmured. "What must a man do, to earn such paradise?"

"He must work," said Will Hewer. "Like the man we watch. What you see, all around you, comes not from accident, or theft, or plotting in some dark corner. It is a reward for ceaseless service, and tomorrow he will earn it again. . . . Now he needs his footstool. Will you carry it?"

"Aye."

"Then put on your grey suit, and prepare for duty."

Mr. Pepys had extended himself to honour his well-wishers on the occasion of his Admiralty appointment, and his household had laboured mightily preparing a sumptuous meal. At one end of the table stood a neck and shoulder of mutton festooned with carrots, and at the other a leg of the same, with cauliflower steeped in the best Cheddar sauce. In between were a pair of rabbits, a breast of larded veal with wine, and six little chickens which nested among artichokes and peas. Bottles of claret for the quality, and beer for the humble, completed a repast which no common seaman could have dreamed of.

Matthew sat far down the table, a ghostly figure in candle shadow, among the nobodies. There were two other clerks who eyed him warily, some cousins of Will Hewer's, and a solemn man who said, "I am Sam Stallybrass from Deptford Dock," and uttered not a word more. But Matthew was greatly content. There was food in plenty, and plentifully more to watch.

At the head of the table, under the brightest of candles, Mr. Pepys held court among a brilliant company. At least one of them was a lord, because he was addressed as "my lord" with every drawing of breath, while his lady was flattered some decades beyond her true deserts. But she had the jewels to make the purchase. There was present a great admiral, before whom all others fell silent—save for Mr. Pepys. In a pause, their host was heard to ask: "What think you of my scheme to put a lighthouse on the Eddystone Rock?" To which the admiral replied: "My dear sir, I think whatever you think. There is no man better qualified to judge—as his majesty has today endorsed."

There was a rotund member of the Parliament who roundly condemned all public expenditure while he quaffed the choicest wine. But always there were women, to dispel every hint of argument, to add the harmony of desire to the cutting edge of rivalry.

The company grew merry. Mr. Pepys's good fortune was pledged. The candlelight fell warmly on silk and satin, ruffle and lace, craggy male brows and the more tender valleys of shoulder and breast. Matthew sat entranced. This was the life a man was born to—if only he could lean forward by twenty feet and embrace it.

He could even, for a space, forget the other life beneath the

stairs, to which he more properly belonged. On an earlier errand
to the kitchen he had found a dark hive of industry. There was a
cook in a foul temper and two menservants, who had much to do.
There were three serving-girls, treated as bond-slaves by the cook,
and as tempting halfwits by the men.

One of them was a sprightly child, pretty as a leaping lamb,
sweetly fleshed, innocent as snow. They had exchanged glances,
in the manner of the confederate young, and he had her name,
which was Lucy. He would not forget her!

After supper, and a walk upon the roof leads to drink the evening
air and the lights of London, music reigned. Samuel Pepys, it
seemed, was a musician of renown, and not reluctant to show it to
the world. He played with equal skill the flageolet, the lute, and
the bass viol: he sang a very fair baritone. His friends married
their skill with his, and added to it their own harmony. One could
be near to tears in witnessing this delight, while remembering its
occasion—that today a man of honour had his honour restored,
that he was safe among his friends, and that his only wish, by way
of celebration, was to make music in this loving company.

"Well, were we not merry?" Mr. Pepys exclaimed, when all at
last were gone and Matthew and his new master were left alone.
Pepys had cast himself into a chair, loosened his shoes and neck-
cloth, and now signed to Matthew to pour him a glass of wine.
Already mellow in liquor, he was wholly pleased with the world.
"I have not seen a finer supper table this year! And the music was
a delight." He looked up as Matthew set a goblet in his hand.
"Will you take wine, Matthew?"

Matthew still had a serviceable thirst. "Why sir, I—"

"You are wise," said Mr. Pepys. "It is best to know when one
has had enough." He drank heartily, and sat back at ease. "Music.
My love. I have thanked God for it all my life. There were times
when only song could take away the foul taste of men. When my
wife was alive—" A shadow came over his flushed face, and he
did not finish. Matthew divined that for all the pleasures of a
noble house, this might be a lonely man.

"It must have been a great sorrow," he ventured.

"She drove me mad!" said Mr. Pepys, instantly restored.
"Though I loved her always, she could bring me to rage. Money
for hats and ribbons, silken stockings, buckled shoes! If she saw

75

me even give a glance to a woman, she would roar until my ears burst! She was French. A jealous race."

"Were you not jealous, sir?" Matthew asked.

"Aye! And pray why not? She was very fair. But a man not jealous is a man out of love—and with her I was never out of love, even in the fiercest of storms."

Silence fell again, while all around them the timbers creaked, as if they too were settling for the night. Presently Mr. Pepys drew from his waistband his newest toy, a handsome watch of Switzerland, enamelled in blue and gold. "Ten o'clock. Time to make an end. We work tomorrow. I foresee a paper mountain already."

"I hope I may serve you, sir. I will need direction."

"You will receive it, never fear! You said in the barge, 'I will follow you.' I like willing men. Following is service, and service is life. I follow the King. . . . Whom have you followed, in your time?"

"None of note, sir. Some good captains, and some less good."

Mr. Pepys eyed him with a smile. "What makes a good captain?"

It was late, but Matthew did his best. "A strong will and a kind heart. And courage all the time."

"There are a few such men. Will Hewer is one. Follow him at the start—copy him—you could not do better. He was seventeen, and a young rogue, when I first took him in. But he went to work and prospered, and near twenty years later it was *he* that took *me* in—into this very house—when I was put down. You cannot buy such a man for gold, but you may win him with a smile."

Matthew Lawe, faced with such peaks of achievement, felt bound to admit his doubts. "But how can I take this road? I wish to, above all else. What is the first step?"

"You took it this morning," said Mr. Pepys. "Listen to me. You must never doubt that a man can rise in the world. Otherwise, we are no better than little ants that creep and crawl. You can rise, just as I have risen. I rose from a tailor's son, and fell from power, and rose again. . . . I was reviled by men—some of the greatest villains in the realm. Where are they now? Dead as crows. Where am I? Secretary of the Admiralty. *And I did not plot to win it.* I worked! With head up, head down, and head up again."

It was difficult not to take fire from such flights of oratory. "I would do the same, if I could," Matthew said.

"Then set a course, and hold to it. Do not steal. Do not cringe. Do not vaunt yourself. Do not neglect the great. But do not sell them your soul. And never forget, there is a larger scene than our cramped little lives. For some fortunates, it is the whole world. For us it is the sea, and in this cause we serve." He sided his goblet, and rose to stretch and to retrieve his shoes. "Sleep well, Matthew. But before you do so, go down, and send Lucy to help me undress.".

There was one more thread to the weaving of that strange day and night. It happened after his errand to the kitchens. After loitering below in search of a privy, he stole upstairs again, but softly, so as not to wake the household. It was this secrecy which gave him his last view of the secretary of the Admiralty preparing for slumber.

A shaft of candlelight from a door half open attracted his eye, and in all innocence he approached. On a chair within, Mr. Pepys sat at ease, with his coat shed, while pretty Lucy combed his hair. Presently he reached up, with a smile almost fatherly, and began to unbutton the throat of her bodice until it was wide and free, and the tender flesh peeped out as pretty as her yielding face.

It seemed that Mr. Secretary Pepys was unreformed—as his beloved wife might have been the first to tell him.

3

FROM THE first hour that Matthew reported for his duty and began to explore a whole library of bound volumes of navy letters, accounts, plans of the past and schemes for the future, he was amazed at this lifetime of industry, and its variety. Much of the past was astonishing, and Mr. Pepys's vision of the future was magical. Years before, he had instituted an examination for naval lieutenants, to promote knowledge of navigation. He had assisted at the founding of the Hudson's Bay Company, whereby roving adventurers, still searching for the Northwest Passage, were encouraged to remain in the New World to trade on a continent of fabulous riches.

At the Royal Observatory at Greenwich he had contrived to promote coastal lighting and buoyed channels for safe pilotage.

He took a special interest in shipbuilding and ship design. He had laboured for years to improve the lot of the common seaman, so that a faithful man who had served his country was not paid off at the end of a voyage with an almost worthless "ticket."

When Mr. Pepys returned to power on that April morning of 1684 of his meeting with Matthew, it was to find that the whole conduct of the Royal Navy, from the laying of a keel to the dismissal of a ship's company, had once more become a giant swindle. But it was not too much for Samuel Pepys. Within a few weeks he held it all in his hand again; and within six months, when he had removed the Admiralty itself to No. 12, Buckingham Street, he held it in his own house also. The years passed. . . .

THROUGH THE OPEN DOOR of his private office, Mr. Pepys kept an eye upon the Long Room where sat the copying clerks perched high on their stools. Even as he dictated to Matthew, he was watchful of all that went on. Matthew sat at the small table opposite the secretary, and with weary brain and cramped fingers pursued the third hour of his morning toil. The shorthand which he had now mastered could scarcely keep pace with the nimble tongue and searching intellect of this man who never rested, never flagged.

"New regulations of the guard ships," Mr. Pepys proclaimed in his slow, steady, relentless voice. "*One:* six months' stores to be kept handy at all times. *Two:* the captain is to sleep on board without fail. . . ."

The flow of words did not cease for another half hour. Then silence fell, save for the distant scratching of pens. Waiting for Mr. Pepys to continue, his pen poised over the paper, Matthew lapsed into a daydream in which life at sea, duty ashore, pulling an oar and pushing a pen were all tumbled together. He awoke, guiltily, to find the secretary's eyes fixed upon him. But the gaze was not fierce. "You look downcast, Matthew."

"No, sir."

"Very well—you look absent." With rare understanding, Mr. Pepys laid his finger upon it. "After two years, do you hanker for the sea again?"

"Aye, sir. On some days. I was thinking of duty on the guard ship, or of setting sail again. . . . Things I can master myself."

Mr. Pepys waved his hand, indicating all he could see from his desk. "You have mastered this. And very well."

Matthew took heart at the praise. "Sir, I have been proud to do so. But . . . it is a dry berth."

"You would rather live wet?"

"On some days," Matthew said again.

"Who knows—those days may come again? But land-sailors are necessary, and I hope you have come to know it. Behind every man at sea sits a man on land. We must feed that man at sea, and pay him, and care for him, and nurse him when he is sick. We must do the same for his ship—and first we must build that ship, and make it honest, and then keep it in trim, fit to voyage, fit to fight, fit to endure."

It was an old sermon—old and familiar, like bread and cheese, which sustained life yet did not glorify it. Matthew was indeed proud of his Admiralty service. Yet there remained these spring days of beckoning sunshine and briny promise, when a pen could not match a coil of rope, nor a staid office floor a heaving quarter-deck. Ships moved and jumped and lived. Desks only mouldered into dust.

Mr. Pepys was speaking again. "So take heart—and take these notes! I will need my credit and debit accounts by next Monday morning, for the money bill in Parliament. . . . Then tomorrow you and I will take a holiday."

"A holiday?" Matthew repeated, surprised.

"Well, a coachman's holiday. We will inspect a dockyard, and I shall dismiss a rogue. Then I will show you Bedlam."

The next morning neither the Deptford Dockyard, some seven miles down the river, nor the dismissible rogue, who was Sam Stallybrass, last met at Mr. Pepys's own supper party on that night when Matthew first joined the household, was ready for the onset of the secretary of the Admiralty.

"We will board them while they sleep," Mr. Pepys had said grimly as their coach rumbled eastwards. "It is the best way with knaves. . . . I judged Stallybrass honest, and I judged him wrong. Does he think because he put his feet under my table that he is licensed to steal from the King's own purse? Enough is enough!"

They found Stallybrass in an idle dockyard where not a man seemed to be giving a fair hour's work for his wage. Stallybrass—

feet on desk, flagon in hand—was caught: first by surprise, then by an array of bills of receipt and bills of payment—the matter of a thousand pounds spent on timber, which was spirited away on a dark night, then sold back to the Crown for another thousand, then found to be green, unseasoned stuff which any honest dockyard officer would have condemned.

Stallybrass blustered and then cringed and begged for mercy. "I made a mistake," he whined. "Any man can be forgiven for that. Give me another chance, Sam."

"It was one mistake too many," said Mr. Pepys. "There is a year's perjury and theft in this one transaction alone! There are twenty like it. I have warned you in the past. Now you are dismissed. You will leave the dockyard tonight—with empty hands, if you please. Captain Lysart of the guard ship will rule, until his majesty makes known his will."

Matthew Lawe, hovering in the background, was not the only man in Deptford Dockyard whose hearing had been at full stretch. As he and Mr. Pepys walked out, first to the guard ship where Captain Lysart received his orders, then to the main gate where their coach waited, men who had been playing at cards were suddenly dealing hammer-blows upon innocent irons. Other men tripped in their haste to carry coils of rope from one neglected corner to another. Axes were sharpened, nails driven into wormy wood, sailcloth folded and unfolded like a hopeful bride's best linen. Movement was all.

"Oh, they will act the angel for a space," said Mr. Pepys. "Then the poison will creep in again, and I will pay another doctor's visit and bleed them a little, and so it will go, till we are all dust. There are tides of endeavour, tides of honesty, as well as salt water. . . . Now let us forget all, and repair to Lloyd's Coffee House."

There the secretary had some private transaction to complete, and a modest dinner of cold fowl, cheese, and Rhenish wine to enjoy. Newly opened in Lombard Street by Edward Lloyd, a printer with a taste for company, Lloyd's Coffee House had quickly become the resort of men whose business was the sea.

There were shipowners, shipbuilders, and ship's captains, merchants discussing the sale of their cargoes, or planning new schemes which might thrive on good fortune or founder on the first rock in the English Channel. There were shipbrokers, who took their chance on the price of a cargo, whether it was wine or winkles, cloth of gold or Calicut, and on the skill of the sailor who carried it. There were other men who, ready to insure the whole worth of a ship, would make out a policy for the sum agreed, and write their names one under the other, till the cost was warranted in full. These "underwriters" would prosper in good times, and might face ruin in bad. It was a wager on the quality of ships and men, a gamester's paradise.

In this guarded backwater of the ocean, Mr. Pepys was received like a prince—which, in the sea world, he was. Men waited their turn to approach his table, to offer their services, and then to withdraw and give place to other courteous supplicants.

The merchant banker with whom he had particular business—one Mr. Mond—was the envy of all as Mr. Pepys was seen to peruse an offered paper, set his name to it, and shake hands upon the bargain: a loan from Mr. Pepys of £800, at one-half *per centum* a month. It was Mr. Pepys's private gold which kept the banker in credit.

A tall fellow of genial good humour but with a sharp eye for business, Mr. Edward Lloyd waited on them himself. He was full of schemes, and glad of an illustrious ear.

"A club is what I plan here," he told them. "For men whose interest is the commerce of the sea. I would collect all shipping news, all the daily intelligence of arriving and departing, the latest prices for the latest cargoes, and display them where they can be read in passing. Even a newspaper, Mr. Pepys: 'Lloyd's News of Shipping'." He gave Mr. Pepys a sharpish glance. "May I say that I have your patronage, sir?"

Mr. Pepys returned a glance equally sharp, then smiled. "I expect that you *will* say it, Lloyd. I would think it churlish to deny."

With that he nodded, rose, and took his leave. Preparing to step into his coach, he confided to Matthew: "Lloyd is on the right course. An honest place with honest company. A man's word is his bond there, or he would not prosper. Now I will match it with the foulest spot in London."

Bedlam proclaimed its repute to the very street outside, which was Moorfields; it puffed out the smell and sound of misery, and as Matthew and Mr. Pepys entered the gates and paid their two-pence to pass through, both noise and stench grew horrendous. From corridors far and near, shrieks of laughter, groans of pain, bellows of rage resounded. It was no better than the sound of an animal forest, the speechless uproar of the damned.

Near at hand the Bedlam hucksters cried their wares.

"Poking sticks! Poking sticks! Stir them up!"

"Tin trumpets! Make them start!"

"Pinching irons! Nip them as they reach out!"

Matthew was already confused. "Sir, what is this selling?" he asked Mr. Pepys.

"To bait the lunatics. Here is the greatest show in London, but it can be dull without a little sport. You would not think that this place was named for Bethlehem." They advanced into the place named for their Saviour's cradle.

The mad lay in iron cages, ten and twenty together, on straw fouled as if by cattle; or they stood plucking at the bars or fought bloodily among themselves. Between the cages the strollers and the drunkards and the family parties moved to and fro, laughing, taunting, tormenting, calling out to each other at some fresh delight.

"I wonder," said Mr. Pepys, "on which side of the bars are the madmen." He was watching a fat slattern of a woman, armed with a poking stick, prodding at a gaunt young man whose vacant eyes were ringed by a tortured face. The youth would not stir. The woman's friends encouraged her with cackles of laughter. Suddenly the young man flung out an arm, at lightning speed, and seized the stick. Then he thrust the point into his breast, and drove it home, as if to say: "There—have your way." As blood gushed from both breast and mouth, the transfixed youth fell insensible. The crowd, robbed of activity, moved on.

"God help us all," said Mr. Pepys. There was compassion in his tone. But Matthew, sickened at the sight, could not forget that he and his master were there as willing onlookers. On which side, indeed, were the mad?

There were many more souls in torment who caught his eye, as their Bedlam voyage continued. One was an ancient greybeard, dressed in filthy rags, who clung shrieking to the bars, shaking them and calling out: "I am John Baptist! Hear me before you perish!'' A frothing spittle fell from his lips. *"Prophesy! Prophesy!"* the crowd roared.

When the old man was silent, they poked at his wasted limbs, and made trumpet noises. But all he could do was to repeat: "I am John Baptist! Repent before too late!" There was one truly mad.

There was another captive, who looked no more mad than the holy mother of God: a piteous girl, gentle in her desolation, with three whey-faced children clinging to her skirts. She was watching the faces of the passers-by in a desperate search for help: it was to kindly Mr. Pepys and troubled Matthew Lawe that she addressed her appeal. "Good sirs," she called, advancing to the bars, dragging her children with her, "can you not help me? *I am not mad!"*

Mr. Pepys, to his honour, stopped to listen. The children whimpered, the young mother spoke in a torrent. Her idle husband had left her, penniless with three children to feed. She had stolen some bread. She was caught, and had been taken to the back room of the baker's shop. There the baker had offered to let her go free, if—if—. He had advanced upon her. She had struggled, and screamed, and tried to beat him about the head to defend herself. "You must be mad," said the baker venomously, nursing his wounds—and from that moment she was declared mad, a danger to herself and to all lawful citizens.

Stern justice, faced with such a fearsome assault on the very fabric of society, had decreed Bedlam for this miscreant, adding that if, as it appeared, there were children, it would be unnatural to part them from their mother. Thus did the hapless family come to this pass. They lacked bread, and after bread, freedom. Could not the kind gentleman help?

Was her tale true? Was it the child of a mind diseased? Or was it whining lies?

"I will make inquiry," said Mr. Pepys, and Matthew knew that he would. A coin changed hands though too many envious eyes must have caught the gleam of gold for its later safety. Meanwhile they were free to pass on, and the woman was not, and the children were not, and all the sour evil of mankind could be smelled in that distinction.

Matthew grew aware that there were other loiterers round about them who gave no more than a careless look to the cages. "Oh, there is more to Bedlam than its proper purpose," Mr. Pepys confirmed, when Matthew asked his question. "It is a good dry walk, to escape the rain. But there are, as you see, ladies of the town going about their business, and customers in plenty. This is a sure market for lechers."

Mr. Pepys consulted his pocket watch. "Would you wait to see the lunatics fed? It is a rare battle-piece." When Matthew answered, No, he had seen enough, Mr. Pepys declared: "Very well—so home." They passed out of the gates, into the gathering twilight, where their coach was waiting.

"Can you see to write?" Mr. Pepys asked, as they started off.

"Aye, sir."

"Some notes for the morrow." Mr. Pepys was dictating already, his tongue as apt as his brain. "*Item:* Convey to Mond eight hundred pounds in gold. *Item:* The King to approve dismissal of Sam Stallybrass. *Query:* Sir John Haydon, Governor of Bedlam Hospital: the favour of a report upon that woman and her children. . . . I hope I was not fooled," added Mr. Pepys. "And now for future business. There are still some sick and dying seamen unpaid. *We must honour our promises!* What I would propose to the Admiralty board is. . . ."

Their coach rolled and rumbled, and made steady progress through the streets, while the business of the navy advanced as steadily.

At Buckingham Street Mr. Pepys, tired with his many exertions, went early to bed; he did not even call on little Lucy to assist him. The girl, coming up the stairway, met Matthew coming down; their meeting owed something to his design.

"Does the master need me?" she whispered.

He shook his head, smiling in the dim light, staring at her. They were near enough for touching. "No," he said. "He sleeps already. But I am still wakeful."

She gave him a close glance, which melted into surprising softness. "That I can see. . . . Will you never have done with this?"

"Not this side of your bed."

He was bold, because the gentleness which surprised him was the first hint of her readiness. Little Lucy was a coltish child no longer, but a grown woman who had blossomed to full flower. Yet for years she had held him off: sometimes merrily, sometimes angrily, sometimes with shyness.

Now, on this night, she was different. She was looking up at him from the step below his on the stairway, with eyes glowing like stars at dusk; and his vantage point gave him a most quickening view of her bosom, now sprouted from shy maidenhood to a creamy fullness.

"Well," she said at last, "if you will not give up the chase, then I suppose I must, for weariness alone. . . . And I would not waste my errand."

She advanced a step upwards, until she was touching him, and their arms went out to each other at the same moment.

4

THE YEAR of 1688 brought turmoil to the English. Charles, their King, had died, and now there was revolution against his successor, James, who had become mad for Popery and his subjects equally mad against it.

Certain prudent or ambitious men ruled that this king must go. To replace English James they sent for a Dutchman.

William Prince of Orange was a good safe man, grandson of Charles the First, husband to King James's daughter, and a brave Protestant soldier. Receiving his secret invitation, he landed in Devon at the head of 14,000 soldiers, having first outwitted the whole English fleet, forged by Mr. Pepys into a great sea-weapon and now tossed away by a timid and irresolute Lord High Admiral.

As Dutch William stormed eastwards towards London, men rallied to his standard as if they were obedient subjects already. King James was allowed to escape to France and into limbo, as William of Orange drove down Piccadilly to Whitehall Palace and his throne.

It was enough for England: King Billy was their man! It was also enough for Mr. Secretary Pepys. He had done his loyal best, but now wind and tide must set against him, beyond any swimmer's strength. Mr. Pepys could sniff a wind as well as any in the land. Friend and servant of two kings, he knew that he would not suit this third.

It was known before all the world that he had laboured mightily to mobilize the fleet against the Dutch invasion, and supported King James, the navy's staunchest friend, to the very end, as his oath of office commanded him.

He was now bare to that biting wind, and defenceless. While others had trimmed their sails, or lain low, or entered into secret treason to support the invader, Pepys had remained steadfast at his desk. He could remain there no longer.

If a king could be toppled, any man smaller could be crushed in the mire.

There came a dreadful day, after a cold audience with his new sovereign, when he called Matthew into his sanctum and motioned him to close the door. He spent some time in sombre thought as Matthew waited. Then he began:

"A letter to the Lord High Admiral, the Right Honourable the Lord Dartmouth. My dear Lord: This is to commend to your gracious favour all the Crown servants at present working in the office of the Admiralty, and in particular one Matthew Lawe, who has served as my confidential clerk with a zeal and industry not less than those I have endeavoured to accord to your lordship and his late majesty. When you have time to consider, I pray that you will bear this name in mind. I have the honour to be, my dear lord, with every truth and regard, your lordship's most humble and obedient servant."

It was Samuel Pepys's way—a most moving way—of breaking the news to his friend.

Matthew was thunderstruck. He could scarcely complete his writing, which at the end scrawled and wandered like a child's.

"For God's sake, sir—what is this?"

"There is no need to tell you more. . . . I do not know if it will serve any purpose."

"But *why*? Are they all mad?"

"They are new, and strong. I am not."

Indeed, he did not look so. His face, in the pale light of a February day, seemed as grey as the London sky, and as ready to dissolve into misty tears.

Matthew, bitterly mourning already, could only think: The end of the world is not some awesome thunderbolt, it is a child's cry in a grown man's mouth.

Humbly Matthew asked: "Sir, must you go?"

Mr. Pepys stirred himself, as ready to deal with this question as with a thousand others. "I have not yet been told. But today there was proclaimed a cessation of all public offices until their holders are given new authority. I have it in mind that they will not give it to me."

"Then they are beyond reason!"

"No passion, Matthew," Mr. Pepys reproved him. "The world turns, and some are left behind. . . . It is better to walk away than to be led in chains."

"*Chains?* For God's sake—"

But gallant Mr. Pepys was gaining in spirit, even as Matthew Lawe gave way to despair. Suddenly he was busy with a paper which he had drawn from his breast pocket, and then with his laborious reading-tube.

"Think not of chains," he said. "Think of freedom and love." He tapped the page before him. "Here is a letter from Will Hewer I have carried next to my heart these two months, written at the first moment when he feared my downfall. I ask you to remember it—here speaks a tender spirit at a time of trial." He bent to his leather spy-glass, and read slowly: "'You may rest assured that I am wholly yours, and that you will never want the utmost of my constant, faithful and personal service. As all I have proceeded from you, so all I have and am is and shall be yours.'" Mr. Pepys raised his head, and his eyes were moist with more than painful streaming. "With such friends," he murmured, "who cares a fig for enemies?"

Now they were both near to tears. "I would write you such a letter at this very hour," Matthew said.

"That I know." Then Mr. Pepys recollected himself, and took command again. "Cheerily, Matthew! Our cause will survive. Make one last note of *why!*" His voice changed to the dry dictating tone. "Sum total of the figure for tonnage of the Royal Navy during my tenure of office. At the beginning: 62,600. At this end, 101,000." He caught his breath, and sat back. "Let them milk *that* from me!"

Then the first secretary of the Admiralty put his desk in order, and—a noble heart drained, within a man untarnished—walked ashore for ever.

Part Three
1759

IN THE YEAR 1759 the Old World and the New were alike in
ferment. On the ruins of the Mogul Empire, halfway across
the world in India, France had been striving to erect her own.
There she was uprooted and sent packing by a soldier-statesman,
"Clive of India". The same fate befell her in the Caribee, where
Guadeloupe, the richest jewel of the Leeward Islands, was lost to
her and won to British arms. France had chosen to be the enemy. Now
the enemy was on the run. She must be kept at it.

This mighty surge of power was the brainchild of William Pitt,
the "Great Commoner" and first minister of Parliament; and the
next part of his dream of empire was to drive the French from
Canada as well, before they could bind these harsh northern

ABOVE: *The Taking of Quebec, an engraving of 1797. Captain James Cook by Nathaniel Dance.*

possessions to their languid estates in Louisiana. Certainly, in English eyes, the colonies of America, growing apart from the motherland, were rebellious and should be disciplined. But first there was the French fortress of Quebec on the St. Lawrence River, the thorn which must be plucked out.

In the spring of that year, 1759, Matthew Lawe stood high on a hillside above the Newfoundland harbour of St. John's and stared long at the town below and the sea beyond.

"Deemed unwanted in the present state of the Admiralty service", he had long since escaped the land and found the sea again in the Portuguese schooner *Consuela* fishing the Grand Banks to the south of Newfoundland. It was a world of fish and fortitude, commerce and courage, rare skill and evil luck: navigation by guess and by God, storm by appointment: great catches of cod to match great hopes, bitter waste of time to poison past memories. It bred sailors, and it broke them—the eternal lesson of the sea, which ruled all and was indifferent to all save its own twin masters, the wind aloft and the raging tides below.

As the seasons and the years had reeled out, he had not lost his allegiance for this frontier-harbour of St. John's. He had spent other winters here, and starved, and lived; in soft-seeking years he had sailed south to Florida or the Bahamas, and passed a season among sun-warmed oranges instead of frozen whale-meat. But always in the spring of the year he returned to the Grand Banks, and commended his soul to cod. Freed from the Portuguese, he had taken British merchant service for a while, but now he was without a ship.

There was one hope of finding a new berth: and it was for this that Matthew was watching on the sunny hillside above St. John's.

The rumours of war had not passed Newfoundland by, set as it was at a crossroads of the western Atlantic where so much was stirring. There was talk among the schooner crews of a great English fleet carrying ten thousand soldiers—which was assembling at Halifax, the finest harbour of New Scotland. Would some of these ships put into St. John's to water or to send a press-gang ashore in search of useful seamen? Better to work under honest navy discipline than to languish here. Matthew now saw that this blessing might be at hand.

He had sighted the ship more than an hour before: a warship, as the tiers of her gunports proclaimed. Her southerly course had been planned to stem the tide, sluicing northwards at the top of its flood, and she was heading in for the harbour.

He watched in great admiration and great hope as she made her run for the entrance. This was a big ship, more than a frigate, and her broad bottom was subject to the pull of the current, while her towering sails were trimmed to push her in an opposite direction. It was all done to perfection, and not slowly, as some masters tried to make the passage of the Narrows.

At the very moment of balance she put her helm hard up and turned as if on a sixpence piece, while the royals and topsails were doused; then she made a dart for the entrance. Just as the thrust of the tide lost its power, the ship was pointed directly at the only safe channel: she lost half her speed, and glided inwards, knowing the water to be an ally instead of an enemy.

Then she began to weave through the inlet, while Matthew, who knew its hazards as he knew the scars on his sea-worn hands, could only say: "I swear to God, that fellow could thread a needle with his ship!"

The stranger threaded the needle, turning and twisting through rocks big and small, and sailed out smooth and serene into the broad harbour of St. John's. Her cannon boomed forth a salute of nine guns. Then she backed all sail, dropped her anchor, and lay at peace, with one last cannon shot to announce: "I am here."

As the booming echoed round the hills and valleys, Matthew Lawe marched resolutely downhill, into the arms of his unknown but already welcome friend, a press-master of the Royal Navy.

The ship was the *Pembroke*, detached from the main British fleet and sent north from Halifax to clear the coast of French supply convoys before the attack on Quebec. During her southerly return, she was to seize any likely sailors from their great breeding-ground of Newfoundland.

The *Pembroke* was a ship-of-the-line, a third-rate of 64 guns, 1250 tons, almost fire-new from Plymouth Dock, Captain John Simcoe in command. The gifted ship-handler who had threaded her through the Narrows with such swift dexterity was the master, one James Cook.

Aboard such warships the master bore the sole burden of navigation, pilotage, and any surveys required in uncharted waters. Under the captain, he set the courses and handled the ship; he was also concerned with stores, with masts and spars, sails and rigging, and the management of the crew. A good master was beyond price.

Being without commission, he wore no uniform. Always he was surrounded by glittering officers of superior rank and class: lieutenants, mates, even midshipmen. But he was the trained man among all of them, and his quarters showed his true rank: placed just forward of the captain's great cabin. He was the captain's right hand; and fortunate was the captain who could put all his trust in it.

James Cook, at thirty, was such a man. Born a Yorkshire farm boy he later became a shop-lad at Staithes, a fishing port, where the sea began to exert its pull, like the tide its power. Within a year the grocer's boy of eighteen had bound himself to a shipowner of Whitby, concerned with coastal commerce. Here he found his private heaven and learned navigation and seamanship. Step by step he rose, and at the age of twenty-seven was offered command of his own ship. Instead he took his giant step. As Matthew did this day, he turned his back on the past and volunteered into the Royal Navy as able seaman.

Such a man could only rise again. After four weeks in his first ship, he was rated master's mate; he was appointed master of his second, the *Solebay* frigate, in two years; and master once more, two months later, of his third. This third was the *Pembroke*, and the *Pembroke* was destined, like James Cook himself, for great enterprise.

She had spent the winter, before her burst upon St. John's, in Halifax harbour, trimming up for the task ahead—the conquest of Quebec on the uncharted St. Lawrence River. Captain Simcoe, a man of inquiring, open mind, had long been convinced that in science and mathematics lay the true secret of navigation, whether practised on the broad ocean or the inlets of such a river as the St. Lawrence. *Measurement*—that was his great word and his great dream: measurement of the infinite wheeling stars and the dependable sun: measurement of distance, depth, current, tidal height, angles of sight, length of shadow—and all locked within the most precious measurable element, time itself. In his great cabin, hard by Cook's quarters, he set up a small palace of navigation, and all that winter the two of them toiled together to perfect a plan which would take *Pembroke* and the fleet up the St. Lawrence River to their target, Quebec.

The river course was only a tiny miniature, when set against the massive surface of the globe: some five hundred miles in all. But if it could be extended to all the world. . . . James Cook was the eager pupil, set on fire by new visions so far beyond the lead-line, the dead-reckoning, the tired eyes of the lookout, that it opened up a whole fresh universe. This year would be Quebec's; next year, who but God Almighty could set a limit to it? For James Cook, this enlargement of mind was his captain's richest gift, and sadly his last. By springtime, *Pembroke* was poised, with her fleet in company, to lead the way to Quebec and conquest.

Matthew Lawe, when better acquainted, once ventured to ask the master of the *Pembroke* how he had so risen in the world.

Cook chanced to be at his ease, which was rare. He was a big man, lean, raw-boned, awkward, yet strong. Above a keen and hawkish face his piercing eyes were also at rest.

"I followed my star," James Cook answered. "There may come a day when I shall follow every star in the night sky. But that is promise, which lies in the future. Performance is for *now*—today and tomorrow. Life is divided small—one hour at a time, one *minute* at a time. Fill them all, put them together, and you have the whole of life. But forget one hour, forget one minute, and you may have nothing. You may have *failure!*" He pronounced it as the worst word in his private lexicon. "Think on it! If we run on a rock tomorrow, we lose all. Perhaps as much as twenty working years. If we avoid that rock, we have nineteen years of promise saved. *Do not run on that rock!*"

It for ever pleased Matthew that these simple cautionary words were of the same tune as had signalled his first link with James Cook, and his first mark in a new world of naval competence.

It happened on their passage southwards from St. John's to Halifax, when Matthew was standing his first trick at *Pembroke*'s wheel and they were approaching Sable Island.

Matthew, from long experience, knew Sable Island and its hazards, which had trapped a legion of ships: the banks of sand and silt and broken rock which changed with the seasons, receding here, stretching out new claws there, adding new perils within the space of any week. On one fearful night he had lain exhausted

92

on its beach, surrounded by dead men and the timbers of his old fishing schooner, the *Consuela*. He still feared it.

Now, planted four-square at the wheel below a billow of canvas, he knew that they were heading into danger.

James Cook, as always, was busy at his chart table, measuring this, measuring that. Meanwhile, the *Pembroke* ploughed on, with the low face of Sable to port. But Sable was moving closer than it should.

Matthew did not know what to say, nor whether to say it. The master was for him the greatest man on board; Matthew was nothing—a pair of sinewy hands, a pair of bare feet. Such walking objects did not speak to masters for any reason save "Aye, sir." Above everything, they did not correct his navigation.

But Matthew knew that he must. His hands on the wheel knew it, and his feet on the deck of a ship which was sliding up-wind as well as holding her course. At that moment, James Cook unbent from the chart table and walked back to his customary stance at the helmsman's back. Matthew summoned all his spirit, and said over his shoulder: "We are carried to port, sir."

Cook, whose mind had been intent on greater things, answered: "Aye. 'Tis the tide's pull." He turned his spy-glass onto Sable Island, lying flat and innocent some two miles ahead on their port hand, and studied it intently. Then he said: "We are set to clear it, by a long mile."

It was not true. They were set to clear what they could see, not what might lie underneath. Matthew drew one of the deepest breaths of many a year and said, "Sir, may I speak?"

James Cook, surprised, stepped forward. "Speak? Of course you may speak! We breathe the same air. What is it?"

Matthew dived headlong in. "Sir, I know this island. I was cast ashore there, one summer night when we were also set to clear. But there was a long spit of shoal water underneath, and there we grounded. It was a new arm of land."

Cook looked at him keenly. "A *new* arm?"

"Aye, sir. It happens every season. Every tide, for all I know. We had a saying, 'Sable is black!'"

"What, then?"

"Do you mean, what course?"

"Aye. And hurry."

"Come up-wind and leave it on the other hand. We have sea-room, and the tide will serve us better."

James Cook moved swiftly. "Down helm!" he ordered. "Bring her to port." Then he bawled: "Watch on deck. Brace your yards back—and jump!"

They jumped, being willing men under a master they trusted, and *Pembroke* stood out to seaward of Sable Island and presently passed it safely by. When all was clear, and she was back on course for Halifax, Cook growled to the boatswain: "Relieve the wheel," and then grimly to Matthew: "Come with me."

But he was not grim in anger, only hungry to learn and to record. At the chart table he drew a swift picture of Sable Island, which was in the shape of a bean pod, with its fat curve towards the southeast. Then the questions began: "Where did your ship strike?"

Matthew pointed. "The northerly end. The side we were set to pass today. The new shoal ran out northeast. We had coasted it a month before, and there was nothing to bring us harm."

"How far off was your course?"

"A half mile."

James Cook made a mark on his picture. "What ship was this?"

"A Banks schooner. Portuguese."

"What was her draught?"

"Some fifteen feet. No more."

Cook made another note. "What then?"

"The foremast went. Then the wind came up and we were rolled over. So we jumped and swam ashore. Eight men in all. Eight from thirty."

"How long were you left ashore?"

"No more than three days. The wind fell light, and friends put down a skiff and took us off."

"God bless all sailors," said James Cook. "They look after their own. How old are you?"

"Thirty years, sir."

"And long on the coast?"

"Ten years."

"Where have you voyaged, in this region?"

"The fishing grounds. New England. And south to Florida."

"Never in the St. Lawrence Gulf?"

"No, sir."

"Nor I, past Gaspé Point. Nor anyone. But we will make our way. . . . Well, thank 'ee." He smiled. "When next we are running on a rock, do not fear to speak out."

Matthew went forward with his head high. The hot press of St. John's had never captured a happier man.

2

IT WAS a fine advance guard which set sail from Halifax early in May, rounded Cape Breton, and laid course for the mouth of the St. Lawrence. They were thirteen ships-of-the-line, charged with one simple duty which was the core of the attack on Quebec: to find the way there in strength, whatever the hazards; to mark that highway, and to wait for the main fleet and the British army to follow them and take the city by storm.

The *Pembroke* led the way, since James Cook had voyaged farthest in the Gulf and, with Captain Simcoe, had toiled at those winter plans. As well as her crew, she carried an advance guard of one hundred red-coated soldiers and marines, to give teeth to the ship and see her past the enemies lying in wait on either side of the river.

These soldiers were as proud as Lucifer, and their greatest pride was in their regiment, the 47th Foot. When asked of this they would answer with the arrogance of acknowledged heroes: "We are Wolfe's Own." General James Wolfe, the darling of the British army, would be in command of all, as soon as battle was joined.

But first, for the *Pembroke*, there must be sad sacrifice to the gods of war. Captain John Simcoe, ship-bound for a hard winter and working without respite on the plans for the approach to Quebec, was now an exhausted man. He kept to his cabin from the moment the *Pembroke* cleared Halifax. He could eat nothing, nor rally his strength; and within ten days he took leave of life.

With the heartbreaking sailors' ceremony which could never fail to move, *Pembroke* buried her captain under the lee of Anticosti Island. As the marines beat their muffled drums, all ships in company struck their topsails. The guns began a mournful booming; twenty cannon shots tolled their salute, with a half-minute pause between each. Then the canvas packet dipped beneath the tide. At dusk a new captain, Wheelock of the *Squirrel*, took command.

It was a sea story, as old as the first ship that ever dared the ocean. A man died, another stepped forward to take his place.

James Cook's skill was now more precious than ever, as the *Pembroke* pressed on through tumbling ice floes which, though troublesome, were at least good springtime news. The river was opening to them.

But the good news faded swiftly. Beyond Gaspé Point, Cook knew nothing at firsthand of what lay in store. The charts which he and John Simcoe had drawn were based upon the hearsay of the coast, or on captured French maps which might have been doctored for the confusion of later invaders.

For the next two hundred miles the river narrowed inexorably, and their voyage became a multitude of puzzles. The St. Lawrence began to lapse into a very millstream: its currents ran all ways at once, its eddies were sudden and spiteful, its whirlpools fed by waterfalls plunging from the cliffs on either side. They could only make progress with an east wind at their back.

Cannon fire from the shore attended their passing. They sighted Algonquin scouts who kept pace with them, for mile after mile. Anchored from dusk until dawn within reach of these savages, the *Pembroke*'s soldiers mounted a guard, and changed it every hour. Yet still they made their slow progress up-river, probing for the deeps and the shallows, marking the channel as they passed. And on the twenty-third day, James Cook could say to his captain, and to Matthew standing near by: "Tomorrow the Traverse!"

That evening, Corporal Ned Pym, a large, ruddy grenadier who had become friendly with Matthew, asked him: "What is this Traverse? All are talking of it."

"'Tis the next piece of the river, and the last." Matthew could answer with certainty, since he had seen the great chart which might—or might not—give them their clue to what lay ahead. "From here we have one mile to go before we reach Quebec. But it is the worst mile of all. Not one big ship has ever passed through. It is a crossing, from one side of the river to the other, and then on through to the pool below the citadel. There were sea marks laid down by the French, but they have been cut away. Now we have to discover it for ourselves."

"But how do we discover it?" Corporal Pym asked.

"We row," Matthew answered, in the tone of a man who would be pulling an oar. "We take six longboats, and six men with lead-lines to sound the depths, and twenty buoys with flags, and some soldiers to drive off the Indians while we do the work. We find our way through, and we mark it so that the fleet can follow, and then we return."

"How long might this take?"

"The master says three days."

"And if there is a safe channel, what then?"

"The *Pembroke* and the rest of our ships sail through and anchor. Then we send a pinnace back, and she will signal 'All clear' to the main fleet, and they come up-river, and we are all knit together, and ready for the attack."

"It cannot be too soon for me!" said Corporal Pym. "But how do we engage?"

"We land with boats. We have them ready in the hold, in pieces. A carpenter sticks them together. . . . So we land. There will be a hill above us, or a cliff. We climb it. Or better, *you* climb it while we hold your coats. Then you climb down again, and tell us: 'Huzza! We have taken Quebec!'"

"That we will do—never fear! With General Wolfe to lead, we can take anything."

Matthew had heard this boasting talk before, and could not mock it. In his own life he had been fired with the same certainty. It was the one sure mark of leadership, that it could prompt such words. But the renowned General Wolfe was still a mystery to sailors. "Have you met this Wolfe?" he asked.

"Aye. Well—I have seen him, and followed him at Louisburg last year, when we trounced the French from eastern Canada. We know he has not been beaten in the field. So—"

The *Pembroke* rocked gently to the river's urge. Night was coming down like the curtain of the world. Jingling, stamping soldiers were marshalling in the waist of the ship, ready for the first hour of their vigil. For sailor and soldier alike, tomorrow might be the testing day.

Corporal Pym said suddenly: "He reads poems to his officers."

It was not the easiest recommendation to swallow. "Why would he do that?"

"God's blood, how can I tell? But they love him for it."

"Will he read poems to the French? Will he read them to sleep?"

Corporal Pym of Wolfe's Own said with proper regimental pride, "He will do what he chooses, and we will follow him."

Though the next two days were back-breaking work for common sailors, it was not Matthew's back which was broken. By the first dawn of this Traverse time, he found himself promoted to master's mate and he could sit beside James Cook in the longboat's thwarts, and had only to exercise his brain.

As the first longboat, the master's own, was about to be lowered over *Pembroke*'s broad bulwark, Cook had snapped his fingers at the boatswain and, indicating Matthew, told him, "I need this man at my side. Find another oarsman." To Matthew he said, "Carry these for me into the boat, and drop nothing, or we lose our labour."

"These" were a spy-glass, a precious chart, a set of pencils and an ancient backstaff which, cunningly altered to show the distance off shore, was the master's particular treasure. As Matthew gathered them, James Cook told him: "You are rated master's mate on our return. *If we do not run on a rock!*"

They did not meet any such disaster, though it was not for lack of rocks. As soon as the six longboats put out from the fleet and began to row upstream, they were caught in a swift current which harassed them for the rest of the day. James Cook's plan was to lead the procession, taking soundings with the lead-line as he went: at any chosen moment, when the water grew shallow and a turn might be necessary, the boat immediately astern dropped a flagged fair-way buoy, while the rest played leapfrog, passing ahead, and continuing on their course. It was as if they were threading one needle with six strands of awkward twine. The power of the broad river seemed determined to deny their progress, little whirlpools became engulfing tides, a boat could be swept sideways between one oar-stroke and another, and forced off its course into the riverbank, while the coxswain shouted: "Row, damn you! Bend your backs!"

All had to be done swiftly, there were other enemies beside a spiteful current and an unknown course. The boats, crawling in single file, were a ready target for those on shore. There was musket fire, and sometimes a volley of cannon shot which hissed over their heads before plunging into the river. As yet the gunners on the bank could not depress their weapons deep enough to find their target.

In the bows of Matthew's longboat, the spear-point of this enterprise, the leadsman called continually, as fast as he could lower his line and reel in: "Three fathom and shelving! By the deep, four! No bottom! Dry rock to starboard!" James Cook himself steered, nursing the tiller like the arm of a favourite child, while Matthew at his side marked the chart as he was ordered. The sailors gasped under the hot sun, and toiled without ceasing. They could not even see where they were going. They were simple brawn, and eyeless. Others were brain and sight.

Thus the whole day passed, with no respite from pulling and hauling, taking soundings exact enough to satisfy James Cook, heaving over the side the anchors which secured the buoys.

But it was deep bliss for exhausted men to turn for home at last, and to float downstream once more with scarcely a touch on the oars: especially to move past the evidence of their long toil—fifteen flagged buoys, securely set in a deep channel leading through the Traverse. Even the master, re-living a day's work which had borne such fruit, was satisfied. "We have done well," he said to Matthew, as he examined the chart against each buoy as it was passed. "That is more than half our course plotted. . . ."

Next day, new crews for the boats, new buoys for the second half of the journey, and—at Cook's request—more soldiers. "The French will wake up tomorrow, and see what we are after," he told Captain Wheelock. "They will not raise their hats as we pass by."

They raised instead an unholy rumpus. As the buoy-layers moved upstream again, the musket fire from the shore increased, and found its mark in wounded men and splintered oars. One French cannoneer discovered the range, scoring a hit on a long-boat. Its crew was sucked out of the ruined stern and rescued by the next boat in line. But by noon, the frail convoy came under the lee of Île d'Orléans, the last island to be passed before they reached the pool of Quebec, and they planted their final markers. Now the seaway was open.

It had been thought that the Île d'Orléans was deserted, and by the French it was, having moved across the river to the shelter of the Heights of Quebec. But they had left behind a fighting rear guard of their Algonquin allies. Matthew's boat, and two others with it, had scarcely grounded on the shallows of the island when their own leadsman toppled with an arrow through his throat. Cook shouted "On guard!" The corporal of marines who commanded their six marksmen bellowed: "Load and prime!" as the band of Indians in their fiercest war paint hurled themselves across the beach and into the shallows of the river.

It was swift and brutal. Though the marines fired a volley at the advancing foe, it could not stop such a weight of attack. Hands were laid upon the boats, to be chopped at with sailors' knives and soldiers' musket butts: tomahawks and clubs flailed down on bare heads and shoulders. Matthew laid about them with a heavy stern oar, his only weapon.

Then, as suddenly as it had begun, it ended. The marine corporal discharged a pistol at the leading warrior and carried off half his chest. He must have been their chief, for his men faltered. Then, cool as ever, the corporal lit two grenades, counted to five, and threw them into the mob. As they burst, screams of agony arose. Screams became panic, and the panic flight.

"Back away!" Cook commanded. The oars bit into the bloody froth of the river as the little fleet, separating from a treacherous land, drifted downstream into safety. They bore their dead and wounded home. But their work was done; the great Traverse was subdued.

On the morrow, the tenth day of June, the *Pembroke* and her squadron sailed majestically through, on a fine easterly wind which drove them surging past all hazards to an anchorage below Quebec. A pinnace was sent down to summon the main fleet; and within two weeks they were all assembled, without the loss of a single ship, or a trace of mud on a keel.

The newcomers were majestic also: nine ships-of-the-line, led by the *Neptune* of ninety guns, thirteen frigates, and one hundred and nineteen transports carrying the soldiery and the stores. With the first pathfinders, they all lay at anchor in the pool below Quebec, or behind the western tip of the Île d'Orléans. There they waited. Men and stores were landed on the island: the artillery set up their batteries; tented camps sprouted like mushrooms. Out of the holds came the pieces of landing craft, to be put together by ship's carpenters. The huge enterprise stood tiptoe on the brink of its launching.

But there they waited still, like blind men on a crossway. Presently it became clear that, for all this great huzza, the city of Quebec was unassailable.

It was a problem for the soldiers, as sceptic sailors were not slow to point out. The military had been carried to Quebec most tenderly, like children to a dame school; there they had been stood up on the shore, their beautiful scarlet coats had been dusted, the very sweat wiped from their brows. *Now* what did they lack? A change of napkins? And where was their famed General Wolfe, and what was he doing? Sucking a teat?

Corporal Ned Pym, met on shore when he was guarding a store party from the *Pembroke*, answered Matthew curtly when he asked why General Wolfe had not yet appeared. "He takes his time. He does not care to lose men. He is making his plans. When all is ready, he will move."

Certainly General James Wolfe was taking his time. But it was precious time, and running out. The weeks passed, and stretched to months. June turned to July, then to August, then to the first week of September. The summer season of attack was faltering to its close without a gainful stroke to show for it, and after that, ice would throttle the invaders where they impotently sat.

Wolfe delayed because he could not find an answer to a soldier's puzzle which had plagued him for eleven tormenting weeks. The citadel of Quebec sat upon a rampart of rock. It had been fortified by cunning French engineers. Its protective lines were alive with troops: its guns were sited to command east and west, north and south: it had food in plenty, and pure water springs. It had also a noble commander—Louis Joseph, Marquis de Montcalm de Saint-Véran—who would never submit to Anglo-Saxon rabble till his own head fell on the block. For James Wolfe, there was no way to scale these forbidding heights, called the Cliffs of Abraham. Troops thrust forward as a battering ram would be blunted in bloody chaos. . . . Then on the tenth of September, in a season of mortal doubt, General Wolfe, a remote figure, came touching-close, and remained so for ever.

The fifteen men who filtered through the trees onto the heights near Point Levis, on the other side of the river, directly opposite the western outskirts of Quebec, wore the dull grey working coats of private soldiers, so that, if sighted by spying eyes, they would pass for a patrol.

But under this drab disguise there were General Wolfe and five of his aides; Admiral Saunders, commander of the British fleet, and five of his; and Captain Wheelock of the *Pembroke*, his master, James Cook, and his master's mate.

Wolfe, at thirty-two, was slight, and undeniably frail. He had perhaps the strangest face ever worn by a major-general: chinless, meagre of forehead, coming to a little ferrety peak with the nose. For weeks he had been wretchedly ill, and still was. But none of this mattered a jot.

He was a commander to whom legends attached like ribbons round a maypole. The latest was that on his westward journey towards the French citadel, he had quoted a line from a newly published poem called *Elegy Written in a Country Churchyard*, by one Thomas Gray, to his officers gathered around him. "The paths of glory lead but to the grave," he had read aloud, then closed the book, looked around the silent company, and said: "Gentlemen, I would rather have written that than capture Quebec."

Now this small eggshell of a man stood on a windy height, gazing across at that same Quebec, and they all watched him, and when he spoke they all listened.

"We are here," he said, "to find the last way to Quebec, because *there*—" he pointed across the river "—is the city we must take unless we are to return in failure with our duty *not* done. We have tried all places else, and been rebuffed. If a way is not to be seen from here, then it is nowhere. Let us look."

He raised his spy-glass, and stared across the river. All followed his lead. What they were staring at was a great cliff of bush and rock leading to the heights of a bare plateau called the Plains of Abraham, a parade-ground for the military, a park for the bourgeois, and a wilderness in winter. Beyond it, more than a mile away, was the city, and below it, this giant staircase. Could it be scaled?

"Gentlemen, there seems to be a path," General Wolfe said suddenly. He commanded the searchers: "Take a line of sight from the church spire on the horizon. Come down to the cliff edge. A little to the left, there is a clump of trees. Below that there seems to be a track. At least it is worn bare. *It has been used by men.* Do you not see? It goes all the way down to the water's edge!" He lowered his spy-glass. "If that path has been used by men, even agile Indians climbing to the heights above, it can be used by us."

"It is a great climb," said the admiral. "Do we know how high?"

Captain Wheelock answered: "We can measure. Master Cook!"

James Cook signed to Matthew, who brought forward his treasured backstaff. Cook sighted it: one arm on the base of the cliff, the other on its peak. He knew already the exact breadth of the river. Swiftly he drew his triangle, and made his calculation. Then he said, "Sir, some three hundred and forty feet. No more."

There was silence as this harsh fact was digested. Three hundred and forty feet up a goat track clinging to a cliff might be no hindrance to an agile Indian. But for plodding foot soldiers with back packs and muskets? For ammunition and supplies? For cannon to cover their advance on the city?

Only one voice could break the silence. It came in the cool tones of command: "I have it in mind to scale that cliff."

Only one voice would dare to dissuade him. Admiral Saunders said: "It is a fearful risk."

"I agree." From private strength Wolfe could always listen; from greater vision he could answer. "But there is a worse risk in standing still—we lose the whole enterprise! Look again at the empty plains. Where is their defence? The clump of trees may hide a guard hut or a tent or two, but beyond that there is nothing. Once we are up there, we can stroll to Quebec for our Sunday promenade!"

"Once we are up." Admiral Saunders was not opposing for opposition's sake: he had his sums to do. "How many men?"

"Some five thousand. We must match the French."

"Five thousand means one hundred landing craft. Guns also?"

"Two batteries. Let us say, twenty cannon."

"Ten more boats. And supplies?"

"Supplies may wait. We are not setting up home for the winter —we are attacking!" Suddenly Wolfe was all afire. "Sir Charles," he told the admiral, "this is our only way. We have at most a

103

month before we must leave, or be iced in and starved. I tell you plainly—if *you* must leave in a month, *I* must climb now!"

"And the plan?"

"We cross in force, at night. We scale. We haul up our guns. At dawn we advance. We do or die!"

Every word of Wolfe's ringing challenge was to come true, save the last, which was translated by malignant fate into "Do *and* die."

The armada of small landing craft set out in the deepening dusk of the night of September 13. With sailors' skill and soldiers' discipline, both men and boats—5,000 of the one and 125 of the other—had been marshalled in darkness, and hidden by daylight behind the Île d'Orléans for three successive days. Each boat was driven by ten pairs of oars, muffled with cotton waste soaked in tallow: each boat carried two cannon, their polished snouts dulled by lamp-black, or fifty soldiers with muskets clasped between their knees, sitting in rows like men at a play. Silence was all, secrecy was paramount. If betrayed, this hair-raising assault, the like of which had never been attempted by British arms, would end at daybreak in blood and rout.

In the first boat, proudly styled *Pembroke*'s Number One, was a cargo equally proud: James Cook, the trusted pilot, Colonel Howard of Wolfe's Own, Captain Wheelock who would serve as beachmaster as soon as the fleet landed; and a pale figure in a boat-cloak, shivering with fever, who was the god of this enterprise. Wolfe would lead them, sick or well, in darkness or in daylight; and his armed guard of forty picked men loved him for it.

Hunched in the stern sheets, Matthew steered—to glory or to ruin—under the narrow eye of the master; in the bows Corporal Ned Pym crouched his great bulk and nursed his musket. He was to be the first man ashore, the first to find if there were guards posted at the water level, the first to try the unknown.

Following *Pembroke*'s Number One was a single long file of boats, stretching across the river like a snake closing in to strike: all rowing in utter silence towards the towering darkness of the cliff. There were no voices, no lights. The moon was down. Only the black river knew of their passing as they crept in under the shadow of the Cliffs of Abraham.

The moment his boat grounded, Ned Pym leaped ashore—and into silence. His footfall on the sand was the only sound, and his swift advance the only movement. After a long minute's doubt, the corporal—and with him a whole army—had their answer. The beach was not guarded, and the cliff above awaited them.

He returned to the boat, and whispered: "Out! Follow me! Not a sound!" As the forty men of the general's guard slid over the gunwale and waded ashore, the second boat came in alongside the first. Soon the whole beach was full of craft, and moving shadows, and well-drilled men forming their platoons. When the first five hundred soldiers were marshalled, with ten boats' crews laden with ropes for hauling the cannon, the climb began.

Corporal Pym and ten men led the way, with General Wolfe close at his back. It was pitiless work. Step by labouring step they lifted themselves skywards. Some noise now could not be avoided. Dislodged stones tumbled downwards, falling on other stones— and sometimes upon the heads of men who could not withhold a grunt of pain. The breathing of heavy-laden soldiers and sailors often came near to groaning. Their only guide was pricking starlight, and their only goal the sky itself, and the dark lip of the hill so far above them.

One hundred feet, two hundred, three hundred: they toiled for ever upwards. Each shared the same hazard, the same crushing labour, whether he was a dumb ox of a grenadier or a frail general with a dream of conquest within his thudding heart.

Matthew Lawe toiled: round his neck was ten fathom of coiled rope, and in each hand a pair of iron grappling hooks. It was a burden for a giant—or a master's mate. When he reached the top, astern of the advance guard, he was exhausted. But as he stood at last on the Plains of Abraham, among the trees which had been their marker for the climb, it was to find that a small battle had been joined and won already. The victor was Corporal Pym and his squadron of ten. At their feet were three French soldiers from the guard-post, surprised, overrun, dead to this and all other nights.

In the darkness, triumphant Ned Pym whispered: "Well met, Matthew! Now we show *you* the way!"

Matthew peered at his friend, and then at the crumpled bodies. He whispered back: "How did it go?"

"Easy as a butter slide. Two were asleep in the tent. One was eating his supper outside. His back was to the river, and to me.

A jealous woman could not have wished a better target! Then we scratched on the tent wall and called '*En garde!*' The other two came running out, and they were dead before they could say Bon Jew!"

An officer hissed "Silence!" Then silence it was, as men from below began to stumble towards the trees, in their tens and hundreds, and Wolfe's Own became an army massing on the field of battle.

Hauling up the guns was work for the sailors, who were better skilled than soldiers at lifting things aloft. There were twenty guns: they must be hoisted up three hundred feet, from the water's edge to the level plain above, a goat track which wandered through scrub and trees, round stony corners, past overhanging rocks, onwards and upwards.

Matthew Lawe, with his grappling irons and coils of rope, was the anchor man at the top; below him, James Cook—a master rigger—calculated the turns and twists of the path, the linked machinery which could draw a gun past one hazard, and be released, and lowered again for the next arrival.

Much of it was rope work, sweating pull and haul; all of it was groaning labour, with aching muscle set against stubborn weight, the law of gravity against the will to conquer it. The guns had wheels, but they could not run free on this rocky traverse; the wheels had spokes, and these could be turned by hands and arms. Matthew's realm of haulage was the last thirty feet, which could only be overcome by iron claws biting into trees, and ropes and pulleys on which the lives of the men toiling below depended. So one by one the guns went up, and topped the crest of the cliff, and took their place in twin batteries whose target was the fortress of Quebec and the enemy's protective lines outside.

Two hours before dawn the task was done. The guns stood in their ranks like dumb soldiers waiting for the wand of the sun to bring them to life. Matthew, his duty discharged, coiled his ropes, collected the grappling hooks of all the hoisting parties, counted them, and set them on one side. In the past, there had always been a harsh man who mustered such stores; now it was himself. He was dog-tired, but who could sleep, on the edge of such a battle, within touching distance of the dawn?

Silence fell on the camp. No fires could be lighted. Men dozed with their cold bellies to the hard earth, or stared wakeful at the stars, thinking of the battle which was almost upon them. They had all come so far, soldiers and sailors alike: three thousand miles across a salt ocean, two hundred miles up a river, one mile across it, and three hundred feet up the Cliffs of Abraham.

Now it was for the soldiers alone.

At the first hint of dawn, the soldiers stirred. The obliging sun, still fathoms deep below the eastern horizon, showed them their goal, the distant lofty towers of the city of Quebec. On the level ground between, a mist still lingered: an autumn morning mist, coming up from the river below, promising them cover and secrecy at the moment when it was most needed.

Under its shelter, they moved forward a full half mile, and their guns with them, drawn now not by horses or sailors, but by heavy dragoons who leaned against the traces to move their burdens. There they paused, and set up their batteries, and formed their ranks.

General Wolfe, pale as the dawn, eager and spirited as the youngest unblooded recruit, had a new plan of battle intended to add strength to his assault and to spare the lives of his men. It was to form up in two ranks, instead of a serried mass of infantry which no enemy marksmen could miss: two ranks only, the first shoulder to shoulder, the second spaced so that they could fire between the necks of their comrades. He had named it, to his officers, as his "thin red line", and now on the Plains of Abraham, it became real.

While these ranks formed in their six battalions, the light was growing: still misty, always mysterious, but firmly established. Presently it brought them a cold sunrise, that hardest moment for courage in all the world of fear. As daylight gained and the mist melted, the gunners sighted their cannon at the enemy lines before the city.

James Wolfe, a master of patience and perfection, waited until he was fully satisfied with the light and with his dispositions. Then he took his place, a fighting general, on the right of the line and in front of his troops. As the last of the mist vanished, he gave his signal. The battery commander called "Fire!" and Wolfe himself, raising his sword, called "Advance!"

As the cannon roared, the thin red line began to walk and then to trot. The city of Quebec awoke to its dawn of terror: the sight of five thousand red-coated men advancing on them, where no men ought to be. There was one short mile between them.

Soldiers started to fall, Wolfe's Own; yet more soldiers in blue started to run: Frenchmen, surprised, appalled by their danger. They fell back from their protecting lines and made for the open gate of the citadel. But they did not pass through. The Marquis de Montcalm, wakened from sleep by a wild alarm, summoned his undoubted bravery, and sallied out to stiffen his fleeing compatriots and to stem the foe. It was a mistake: better to have let the runners in, slammed the gate, and waited for winter itself to starve the British force and trap the British fleet.

But Montcalm was all noble courage and no clear thought. It was to cost him his life, for he fell mortally wounded that day. It was also the turn of the battle. Soon it was red coats everywhere, a curling wave which broke over the blue and tossed it back against the citadel walls. Now the city gate *was* shut—but caught outside were its main defenders, steadily harried and cut down. For them there was no escape.

Presently red-coated men began to drop from the battlefield. They straggled back, limping, swaying, holding on to each other, pausing to staunch their wounds or perhaps to die. They were the victors who had paid much, and sometimes all.

There was a litter coming slowly towards the men in the trees, with four bearers as tender as children. Ominously, it seemed to be set apart. Fatally it was preceded by a drum major who beat a slow, mournful roll: a sort of whisper on the drum head, then a single solid beat, then a whisper, then a beat, all repeated at a pace so dolorous that marchers could take eight steps between one thud and the next. It was a rhythm Matthew had never heard before.

It was Colonel Howard who broke a fearful silence. "Sweet Jesus!" he murmured—the soldier's oath was a prayer from a stricken heart. "He beats 'The Warrior Home'."

Wolfe's shattered body was laid gently down at the edge of the trees. His splendid uniform—a red coat lined with blue satin, and white knee breeches—was a torn ruin of grime and gore: three gross wounds to head and chest bespoke the agony to this frail remnant of man. His face was beyond paleness, sinking down to a greenish mask of death.

On the instant, Wolfe was surrounded by anguished, weeping men. They were all Wolfe's Own, and suddenly they were all orphaned of a loving father.

Colonel Howard, his face working, bent to the litter which could only be a funeral bier. "They run, sir!" he said—he almost shouted—striving to pierce the most terrible deafness of all. "See how they run!"

James Wolfe did not see how they ran. He had already closed his mortal eyes. But the soldier who spoke to him lived out his life in the holy belief that his general had heard.

When all was over, preparing to drop down-river in the dusk of the year, with the sailors' work done and the soldiers triumphant, James Cook told Matthew: "I am bound for a new ship." He spoke in the quiet of the quarterdeck, when the *Pembroke* was ready for the night. "She is the *Northumberland*, the squadron flagship. We winter in Halifax, and then I am set to survey the coast. They require every league and fathom, from Newfoundland to New England, examined and described. Admiral Saunders speaks of a commission. I might be captain soon!"

Fortunate man, Matthew thought, with envy and admiration: he follows his star, and it has only begun to climb the sky. The next words were an astonishment. "And you?" Cook asked. "What would you be, in a perfect world?"

Matthew was not proud. He chose the lowest rank of officer. "A midshipman?"

"Why not?" Cook echoed a phrase of long ago: "A man can rise if he wills." Who had first said that? Old Sam Pepys? All the turning universe was old. . . . "If you have that will, you should stay with me, Matthew. I shall not always be on this coast. I plan to survey the world!"

3

HE DID survey that world, from the cold Russian seas to the gentle South Pacific: from that North American coast to the ice line of the Antarctic: from Cape Horn to the Sandwich Islands, Bering Strait to Botany Bay, Plymouth Sound to the Great Barrier Reef.

He measured all, and charted it, and tied it to the sun and the moon and the stars, with exact bonds which were never to be matched in his own century. Orion's Belt was his girdle, Sirius, the Dog Star, his faithful guide, and the Southern Cross his altarpiece. Beneath their friendly gaze, land at last took shape on countless maps which were the faithful reflection of the land itself.

His instruments were mechanical, and marvellous. He got what he needed from the scientists, the mathematicians, the clockmakers. From one such gifted man he won a sextant for measuring the celestial sky, the great-grandchild of the ancient astrolabe itself. From another came tables of time and tide which could at last be trusted; and from a third a compass better by far than anything yet devised, whose bowl floated in a bath of whale oil to protect it against the shocks of the sea.

But the greatest gift of all was given by his Yorkshire friend John Harrison, the village carpenter turned clockmaker who laboured a lifetime to make, for mariners, a trustworthy seafaring clock. The worst enemy of such a timepiece, apart from the movement of the ship, was the variation of temperature as it was carried from the Arctic to the tropics, through the cold of night and the heat of the day. John Harrison's answer was to balance this variation by the use of different metals which would, in their sum, annul the rigours of heat and cold. He fashioned a large watch which could make such compensations, and it served to such effect that after a three-year voyage round the world, Cook found its error in longitude to be less than eight miles—or one-tenth of one second *per diem*.

This was triumph—and freedom at last. At sea, the measurement of latitude—the distance north or south of the equator—had been easy since the days of the first astrolabe. It was governed by the noonday sun. But longitude—the east and west measurement—had long eluded mariners. Now, with Harrison's clock, James Cook knew at any moment, by night or day, the exact time at the meridian line which ran through Greenwich Observatory in London: at that same moment, by star measurement, he knew the time in the place where he sat, whether ten miles or ten thousand from home. Then he put the two together, and made a simple calculation. Since twenty-four hours was the sun's circle of the earth, one hour of difference, east or west, measured fifteen degrees on the face of the globe. Fifteen degrees was some nine hundred sea miles at the equator, and less as the ship moved north or south of it. But by how much? The tables gave the answer—and here was longitude at last!

From that moment forward, each mile of surging sea was a measurable square on a chart. Man need no longer go in search of a coast, or in fear of it. Tapping his finger on such a chart, Cook could say: "I am *here*. The land is *there*. If God holds the wind, I shall reach that coast at noon on Christmas Day."

His other instruments were his marvellous eye, his brain, his fierce genius for challenging the sea and wringing victory from it. He was a sea commander first; if a ship would be safer in any other hands, then (his men believed) they could only be God's. He cared for his sailors and was determined to find ways of ridding his ships of those sea diseases which seemed to have settled on the navy like a curse. The bald and cruel truth was that every seventh man who joined one of His Majesty's ships-of-war could expect to die, not by any exertion of the enemy, but of ship fever (which was typhus), scurvy, or dysentery.

James Cook began to cleanse his ships and to keep them so. The middle decks were smoked out with gunpowder mixed with vinegar, the lower holds made sweeter by fire pots burning deep within the hull. He opened gunports whenever this was safe; he designed and installed vents which would admit air on one side of the ship and suck it out of the other. He rigged wind scoops of canvas to press a fresh breeze below. He gave his men the means of drying their clothes as soon as they came off watch—and made them do so.

Then he turned his attention to scurvy which was the primal curse, the Killer Maritime. The gums grew spongy and swollen. The teeth began to fall out. Legs grew ulcered. At the last, a raging fever consumed the sufferer's wits. This delirium was not to be survived by any living soul in any ship under the sun.

James Cook had long thought, in common with naval surgeons, that a constant supply of fresh fruit and vegetables, to counter the morbid salt beef and mouldy bread, must be the answer. If these rarities were not to be found, save when a ship touched a fertile coast, then something which ships could carry with them must take their place.

Summoning all the cunning and authority at his command, he

set to work. On his voyages, strange foods, mysterious liquors, crept into the innocent bill-of-fare. Words stranger still, such as "anti-scorbutic", were used to excuse sourcrout, which was cabbage pickled in vinegar; sticks of celery, tough enough to plug a leak in an old bucket; a marmalade of carrots which stained the teeth to a brilliance beyond the sunset; boiled weeds, christened "scurvy grass". Instead of honest ale, a concoction of malt and yeast, boiled to a thick syrup, then watered till it might be forced past the gullet, was the best to be had; or, on feast days, the rind and juice of lemons and oranges, mistreated in the same way. Or the milk of coconuts. *Coconuts!*

The sailors grumbled till the air grew thick. The hardest tussle of all concerned raw onions. The order had gone out at the beginning of Cook's second voyage around the world: each man was to eat twenty pounds of onions within a week, and half that amount later on.

Twenty pounds of onions? He must be jesting! Twenty pounds was likely to be eighty onions. Were they expected to work the ship, while stuffed with onions like a duck in an oven?

"Eat them," Cook commanded. "They are good for you." And a little later: "Eat them, or you will be lashed." He kept his word. One marine who refused his burden of onions, received twelve lashes. The grumbling, like the onions, disappeared promptly.

On Cook's second voyage, with all its hazards only one man out of two ships' companies died of disease—and he the cook!

The captain had the acclaim of countless grateful sailors, and his own were the foremost. He was awarded the prized gold Copley Medal by that most august and critical body of judges, the Royal Society of London, bespeaking his matchless exercise of a commander's care. His own men awarded their own medallion and thus engraved it in speech: that on board Cook's ships every day was a Sunday—the day of cleanliness and order.

And now, on his last round-the-world voyage, what wonders he had led those men to see! For Midshipman Lawe they surpassed all the ancient memories of his first great wandering with Drake in the very springtime of the world.

At the heart of this journey was still the search for that Northwest Passage which for ever eluded sailors. It took them from Plymouth round the Cape of Good Hope, across to Tasmania and

112

New Zealand, and through the islands of the Pacific Ocean—one third of the surface of the globe—to the west coast of North America. There the search led northwards, to the Bering Straits of Alaska; and there they were turned back, defeated as ever by the swirling fogs and the ice walls, and found a softer haven in Hawaii, that paradise of the Pacific, with its coral atolls and trustful people who welcomed Cook as a god.

To this world of gentle, abundant, innocent nature—God-given, sun-blessed, man-measured by gifted inquirers—voyaged Captain James Cook, skilful and benevolent explorer, prince of sailors; and here he came at last, in his ship the *Resolution*, to the place of his death.

By the time he anchored off Hawaii, with his consort-ship the *Discovery*, Cook was growing weary. He had held a world-encircling sea command, with all its burdens and cares, for nine long years without respite; and now his fine and feeling mind was becoming overwhelmed by a voyage which seemed to be stretching to infinity.

His tired *Resolution*, a Whitby cat of 462 tons, which he had chosen himself from that Northumbrian cradle of ships and men which had first nursed James Cook the apprentice-boy of long ago, was continually leaking, and for ever demanding new masts and patched-up sails. When at last he came to anchor in the fine harbour of Kealakekua Bay, Cook had little to sustain his spirit and much to bleed it away.

His men were full of discontent at the harshness of a captain who would not let them enjoy the women of this paradise and never ceased urging them to live cleanly. Cook was determined that they should not damage their innocent hosts. He had formed a special affection for these Hawaiian islands; when he had touched here earlier before the bitter northland foray, he had been moved by his reception as a divine king, the feasting and gifts which followed. Now, on his return, Cook knew in his heart that he could not repay them with the tainted gifts his men might provide. No woman was to be allowed on board. No man was to be left on shore at night. The men were scandalized. Had they sailed halfway round the world, to take Holy Orders at the end?

Their captain had other cares to plague him. Most damaging to his spirit was the thieving of the islanders, which he had noted before but which now grew bold and impudent: a deed of daring, and also a jest against these almighty gods whose powers, perhaps, were not absolute. The strangest objects were spirited away: a single oar, a nail. Midshipman Matthew Lawe lost the bronze cap of his spy-glass—useless to anyone but himself. A thwarted attempt was even made to tow away one of the *Resolution*'s boats.

James Cook grew angry, first for the affront to his pride, and then because he loved this ship of resolution which had carried him so far and so faithfully. He could not bear to see her robbed. His officers could not ignore a new severity in their commander as soon as the men of Kealakekua Bay returned to their old tricks. Thieves were triced up and flogged; others had their ears cropped off in brutal punishment. The James Cook of these harsh latter days was scarcely to be recognized. In the cramped mess-room, Midshipman Lawe, who had advanced among men and minds of great achievement in a world which could still astonish him, was astonished now to hear Lieutenant Williamson, the Irish fire-eater, much given to violence, thunder out: "Let him crop off their ears, I say! These natives understand only one language, and if they choose to rob us they should hear it, loud and clear!"

Matthew, knowing his shipmates, was ready to wager that Williamson alone held this harsh view, and that all others would disagree. By now it was enough for this Irish ranter to say "Aye" to anything, for every listener to answer "No"—and so it proved.

"Certainly we are not so stern on the *Discovery*," said a midshipman visitor from that ship. Matthew added his quiet verdict, which was his shipmates' own: "I think he has changed."

In the silence which followed below, the captain's firm voice sounded from the quarterdeck: "Turn up the hands."

When the ship's company was assembled, James Cook addressed his crew. A hard gaunt grey man, tall as an unbending tree, who had not eased his grip on ships or men, or courses sailed, for three long years, he was formidable in the captain's blue tail-coat with its blaze of gold braid and buttons, his tricorne hat and white knee-breeches, and his symbol of office—the brass-bound telescope with scarlet leather handpiece: a man dressed to suit his unquestioned authority, yet a man grown secret and solitary under the weight of command.

"We sail tomorrow," he announced sternly. "This is our last

night in these friendly islands. There will be a farewell feast ashore. Your conduct must do honour to your ship. If it does not the usual punishments will follow. . . . *And I will sail tomorrow with a full ship's company.* I want no deserters, I am leaving no man ashore for a soft life as a landsman!" The crew dispersed, murmuring of loves lost for ever, the officers went about their duties with faces suitably blank. No man dared question James Cook, their changed commander.

The feast of their second farewell must have cost the Hawaiian islanders dear. It seemed that they were glad to see the *Resolution* sail, and that this entertainment, by its very richness, signalled that it was to be the last. Once more the chief, Palea, who was Cook's special friend, led the ceremonies. Once more the presents poured out: the hogs, the green turtles, the sugarcane, the fish. Chief Palea's gift for Captain James Cook, their visiting god, outshone all others: a cloak beyond price, of orange, white and purple feathers, six feet long and a hundred years in the making. It was presented with the divine honours due to a departing deity.

In the morning they sailed away, attended for many miles by a great fleet of canoes, decked out with all the signals of peace and goodwill. They sailed away—and they returned.

Within two days, a violent squall sprung the *Resolution*'s foremast at the head; it also proved to be rotted at the heel. It must be replaced, or firmly fished with stout splints, before they could face any further voyaging. It could only be done at Kealakekua, where the timber was seasoned and the welcome warm; and there a week later, *Resolution* and her consort dropped their anchors, in a bay silent and deserted. Thus James Cook returned in need of help, which should not happen to a god.

The humour of the islanders had changed, was Matthew Lawe's mournful thought, after two days spent ashore overlooking the carpenters working on the *Resolution*'s foremast. The natives were sullen when spoken to, and insolent when checked for thieving. Were they perhaps asking: "Have we not given enough of our wood and water, enough of yams and hogs and fish and fruit? *Enough of our worship?*" If Cook were a god, and his ships magic in their potency, how could his fleet be damaged, and turned about? Perhaps these were false gods. Perhaps they were only frail men—even great Cook.

Then the throwing began: a coconut, then a stone, then many stones. The sailors had to retreat from their work on the foremast. Matthew, reporting this to Cook at noontime, found him fiercely calm, like a man who knows he must soon decide on some great step. But the captain only said: "Very well, I will go see for myself. . . . What think you of all these troubles, Mr. Lawe?"

Matthew, made confident, spoke from his heart: "Sir, I say, God damn the foremast!"

James Cook suddenly gave a rare sweet smile which none had seen for many months. "Matthew," he said, "you are all mariner!"

It was the last shaft of sunshine in all their fateful voyage.

Cook went ashore that same afternoon to inspect the carpenters' work. For the first time he was openly insulted and mocked, by a huge crowd which followed him to the water's edge and tried to lay hands on the pinnace. In the mêlée, Chief Palea was struck on the head by an oar, whereupon he seized it out of the oarsman's hand and, in a rage, snapped it in two across his own thigh.

It was possible that, at this moment of anger and tumult, Palea became an enemy instead of a friend. James Cook, returning with great difficulty to his ship, seemed to match this mood with fury. His first response was a curt order: "All marines and sentries on shore duty will load with ball."

There could be little doubt that someone must now be killed.

His officers—save for fierce Lieutenant Williamson—were appalled at the order and the risks attending it. Matthew, in mournful brooding on the quarterdeck as dusk fell on Kealakekua Bay, could only see it as a self-inflicted wound, by a man drawn fatally to his own destruction. He could even be envious at this movement of the finger of fate. What should a man do, who had worked hard enough, voyaged far enough, and lived long enough? What *did* a man do, who was weary of travel and thus of life?

Only one thing, which now needed one more signal.

It came that same night, with the theft of the *Discovery*'s cutter, seized and towed ashore in the darkest hour. She was the biggest and best of all the *Discovery*'s little chickens, and for reasons of both pride and plain good shipkeeping the loss must not be accepted.

At first light on that holy Sunday morn, which was the fourteenth day of February, 1779, Cook in a quiet rage set in train his counterblow. Three *Resolution* boats, manned and armed, would go ashore in force, and take as hostage a chief, greater than Palea, whom they knew as Kerreeoboo. He would be held in captivity against the return of the *Discovery*'s cutter. James Cook, with one Lieutenant Phillips and nine of his marines, would lead this foray himself in the pinnace. There was also a small cutter under Lieutenant King, and a launch with Lieutenant Williamson in command and Matthew Lawe to aid him.

Cook landed unopposed. The islanders knew well enough what he had come to recover. . . . The small cutter stood on guard at the head of the bay, while Williamson's launch waited in the shallows with enough water under her keel to give her freedom. Cook and his marines marched uphill to the house of Kerreeoboo.

The old man received Cook with every courtesy, and when invited to return with him to the *Resolution*, agreed readily. Presently Cook and the marines, and Kerreeoboo with his wife and two sons, began their return journey to the bay and the waiting pinnace. They were followed by an increasing throng. Many were armed: all were murmuring freely.

When they came in sight of those waiting in the pinnace and the launch, they seemed like a dark stream of lava flowing down to the sea. Tall Cook stood out, like a forest giant among bushes, the marines at his back, but all were becoming engulfed in a black tide, lapping and snarling at their heels. Matthew, sitting in the stern sheets of the launch, opposite Lieutenant Williamson, with four marines beside them, stared through his glass.

"They are armed!" he said suddenly. He had glimpsed spears and daggers, clubs and stones, all openly displayed. The iron daggers were gifts of friendship from Cook. "Sir, they are too close to him!"

Williamson, whose bold Irish colour seemed to have taken on a touch of pallor, said to his coxswain: "Back water! Come astern! We are too close. We must be ready to move."

The launch drew farther off, and then stopped. As if in answer to this shameless move, Cook and the great crowd at his heels started to cross the beach. Then there was played out the last act of tragedy.

Chief Kerreeoboo, with one of his sons already in the pinnace, began to falter. His wife was holding on to him, pleading, screaming at him, twining her arms around his neck. Suddenly he sat down on the sand. He would go no farther. Straightaway his islanders surged forward and surrounded him, so that he could not be reached by nine marines, nor ninety. Cook and his guard were now alone, near the water's edge, while close about them a vast throng began to shout and howl, and shake their weapons.

Making his last prudent decision, Cook ordered Lieutenant Phillips: "Into the pinnace! We shall never take him now without too much killing." But before any of the party could move, Cook was threatened with a dagger-thrust from behind, and he turned and raised his double-barrelled musket.

It was perhaps a measure of the changed man that before the landing he had loaded his piece with two different charges. One barrel held small-shot, a gentler persuasive. The other was charged ball, which inevitably killed.

He fired the small-shot barrel. His assailant, a bearded warrior near as tall as Cook, laughed as the pellets pattered harmlessly against his war-mat; and the laugh seemed to spur the crowd to furious assault. They fell upon the marines: Phillips was stabbed, others of his men were knocked down, and, with the line about to be overrun, Cook fired his second barrel, and killed his man.

Then he shouted again: "To the pinnace!" and at the same time lifted his long arm and waved to the launch.

The view from the launch was now so terrible that the men on board called out to Williamson for some action, and to the marines to use their muskets. But the Irishman ordered: "Hold your fire!" and to his coxswain: "Back water! Come astern again!"

"Astern" was cowardly retreat. Matthew could support this no longer. Were they to be mere spectators of this slaughter? He spoke his scandalized mind: "Sir, we *must* fire. We *must* go in! Look there! They will have the captain in a moment!"

Williamson turned and roared at him: "Not so. He meant that we should stand off and protect his pinnace when it is clear of the beach."

The great fire-eater was dribbling out fear. At this craven nonsense, Matthew beseeched him for the last time: "It will never be clear, if we sit here like dummies."

Suddenly, one of the bow-men, looking landwards towards the tumult, screamed out: "For God's sake, he is down!" and Matthew

could only watch with all the rest of a useless, spineless boat's crew, the murder of their captain.

Amid a breaking wave of dark bodies and flailing arms, Cook was struck from behind with a club, then stabbed in the neck with a dagger. He fell, and villainous hands held him face downwards in a rock pool, while he was repeatedly stabbed. Hauled high on a rock, the body suffered further wild mutilation as the pinnace and the launch retreated. They left behind their captain and four dead marines, on a beach swiftly deserted by the islanders, now struck with terror at what they had done.

The pinnace, full of wounded men, could do nothing to recover the dead. Williamson, with an unblemished launch, might easily have done so, but he would only mutter, as a crumpled braggart: "Later, later," while his men, in rage and contempt, laid back on their sick-hearted oars, and rowed to the ships; and on the ships a deathly silence fell.

The first wild grief was for James Cook their captain; and the first great outburst of anger broke against Lieutenant Williamson, who might have saved him, and did not, and might have recovered his honoured body, and did not do so either. Williamson could well have forfeited his own life, by some unfortunate night-time accident: men spat on the deck as he passed. He was a very quiet man, among friend and foe alike, for many days thereafter.

Captain George Clerke of the *Discovery*, now took command and—though exhausted with care, and carrying the seeds of his own death within his breast—played a cool hand. He dismissed any immediate idea of action against Williamson, though he took written depositions from witnesses. Such a Crowner's Quest could come later. For now, two things he must have: the foremast of his new ship *Resolution*, without which they could not sail, and the body of her captain, without which they should not. On these requirements he bent a mind calm beyond all common quality— and secured them both.

A strong, armed party was put ashore on the fatal beach, and the essential spar was recovered without trouble and towed back to the ship, where it was hoisted to the *Resolution*'s upper deck for the carpenters to complete their work.

Then began the bargaining over Cook's remains. Natives, creeping towards them fearfully, whispered that the body had been carried deep into the country, and been cut up and its parts distributed, as trophies of war, to all the island chiefs. Captain Clerke threatened fearful punishment if the remains were not returned.

After two days, a young priest delivered on board a piece of flesh, nine pounds in weight, from Cook's thigh. Then, five days later, with much ceremonial thudding of drums, a chief presented himself on the quarterdeck with a bundle wrapped and covered by a feathered cloak spotted black and white, and with prudent alacrity, withdrew.

The bundle was opened by Clerke, supported by his officers, in Cook's own cabin, and their horrified eyes saw: both the hands, salted and pickled; the skull, lacking jawbone and scalp; the scalp with ears adhering; and the longest bones of thigh, and leg and arm, which were the private trophies of Chief Kerreeoboo. Next day came the final accounting: the missing jawbone, the feet, the shoes, and the bruised barrels of that musket which had brought its owner to this pass.

These poor remains were decently coffined, and buried that evening in the deep of Kealakekua Bay; and on the morrow's morn the *Resolution* and the *Discovery* weighed their anchors, and quit the accursed place for ever.

It was the *Gazette*, long afterwards, which told Matthew Lawe, always mourning a cherished friend and patron, that there still dwelt in England a certain private grief far deeper than any that Cook's shipmates could know. It lay locked in the heart of their captain's wife. Mrs. Elizabeth Cook had borne him six children. Of these, three had died during his lifetime. She was thus left, on her widowhood, with her two eldest sons, who were both midshipmen, and her youngest.

Nathaniel, the second, perished within a year of his father, in a West Indian hurricane which sent his ship down with all hands. The youngest, Hugh, destined for the Church, died of a fever when he was seventeen, studying at Cambridge. One month later Commander James Cook, the darling namesake, the eldest, the last hostage, was drowned in an open boat off Plymouth when trying, in fierce weather, to rejoin his ship the *Spitfire* sloop.

Matthew Lawe, reading the cold print of the *Gazette*, could only think, in savage hatred of fate: "When God eats, He cleans the platter!"

Part Four
1790

MOVING TO and fro on his errands of service, the coffee-house waiter had begun to stare at Matthew's empty cup each time he passed the table. Matthew knew the signs, from long and mortifying experience. London was full of half-pay officers such as he, hoping for a berth, yearning to get to sea again, yet left high and dry on the beach by peacetime doldrums. Since they languished in genteel penury, they were no longer favoured customers in any house which lived by trade.

Lieutenant Matthew Lawe of the Royal Navy had been counting his pennies, day after day, for more than three years of threadbare idleness. For him it was tarnished braid on a jacket which

ABOVE: *The Battle of the Nile by Nicholas Pocock. Lord Nelson by L. F. Abbott.*

barely held together, poor lodgings, scant food, walking by the riverbank to while away the day, one cup of coffee in the morning and a second at night.

The waiter stopped before him and asked, in that tone halfway between deference and disdain: "Another cup, sir?"

Matthew looked up. "No, I think not." He made his retreat and walked slowly towards the river, and the Pool of London. It was better to watch ships than to brood over dry coffee grounds. But whether walking, or sitting, or staring, he needed money and he needed a friend with influence. He had neither.

He had owed his great promotion to lieutenant to the favour of James Cook, who had made written recommendation of him in the last shipboard report he ever penned. Promotion had served him well—and then not at all.

In the spring of 1782, two years after the sad return from Hawaii, he had made one voyage on convoy duty to Quebec, as third lieutenant under Captain Horatio Nelson in the frigate *Albermarle*, and thence southwards in search of Yankee prizes. Later he secured a berth in one of the guard ships at Portsmouth: a dull task, scarcely touching the sea. Then she was put out of commission. It was dreary peacetime again, with the French calling it quits for a space—and for Matthew, like a thousand others, there was now nothing at all.

This morning, as on every other morning, there were ships aplenty in the Pool: merchantmen loading and unloading, barges, ferrymen, store boats, water carriers, and those predatory skiffs which made their living by scouring the tideway for corpses. But there was nothing worthy of note for a competent navy officer. Matthew turned his eyes aside, and by chance sighted on the lip of the quay another such beachcomber: an officer of superior rank doing the very same as he—gazing nostalgically at anything that floated. In a moment of astonishment he recognized his old commander from the *Albermarle*: Captain Nelson himself. Captain Nelson had sighted Matthew's familiar uniform and drew closer to examine it. When he had established his man, his greeting was given without any air of surprise: "Lawe, is it not? Good morning to you."

"Good morning, sir," said Matthew, returning a salute of the finest formality for many years. "I hope I see you well, sir?"

Matthew did not see his captain well. Horatio Nelson, never distinguished in person, seemed to have shrunk down to the very minimum of man since they had met some eight years ago. He was drawn and thin: his keen eyes were the only lively feature in a yellowish face.

"You see me *alive!*" he answered tartly. "I have been wretchedly ill with fever since my cursed West Indies commission. And half-pay idleness in England is *not* the best physic."

He is the same as myself, Matthew thought, amazed that it should happen to captains and lieutenants alike. He is beached and dry. "Do you reside in London, sir?"

"Never!" Nelson said roundly. "It is like Babylon for expense! I am no more than a farmer now; three years ashore. It is bread and cheese and a humble cottage for me. *My* stone frigate is my own father's Norfolk rectory. Oh, I trudge up to London every quarter day, so that they will not forget my face at the Admiralty. But to what purpose? It is ten minutes with some polite fellow—they are excessively polite, like executioners who beg leave to strike off your head—and he says, 'Well, well, Captain Nelson! You look in the pink, sir!' I do not look in the pink, damn it. I look in the yellow, like a drop't leaf, and a cursed ugly colour it is. . . . Then this *fellow* tells me: 'To our regret, there are no wars to fight. *Ergo*, there are no ships to be manned. *Ergo*, no officers are wanted. But do not fail to keep touch with us.' And so on, and so forth. Well, I have no ship now—and that, I fancy, is your own case."

What a man this had become. The spark had shown in the *Albermarle*: now it was a working flame. Self-knowledge, energy constrained but readily on call, life abundant in the midst of dusty decay—they all shone out of him. Beyond all else, Matthew knew that he must somehow cling to this man: not for advancement, but for the secrets of valour and endurance, without which life was no more than a weary plod without end. He answered: "Certainly I lack employment, sir. I have had no berth for near four years."

"What was your last ship?"

"The *Medway*, sir. Guard ship at Portsmouth."

"Prison service! I would as soon go for a soldier!"

Matthew became aware that Captain Nelson had been examining him with some care. The sharp blue eyes must have already noted his woeful shortcomings in dress. Now they were busy on his face. Matthew answered as boldly as he could: "I had no better choice, sir, in those years. But I am ready for improvement now, within the hour!"

"Are you married, Mr. Lawe?"

"No, sir."

"I can recommend it," the captain said, with a shade more formality than fire. "I have been married these past three years. On the West Indies station—the only benefit that ever came out of it!"

"I offer my congratulations, sir. Have you children?"

"No . . . well, a stepson. My wife was a widow. So you are free to move?"

"Aye, sir."

"I need a man of all trades—secretarial, agricultural, companionable, confidential. In short, a sailor. But it will not be sailor's work. Are you willing?"

"With all my heart, sir."

"The place is Burnham Thorpe, thirty miles from Norwich. The time is not yet—we are painting the parlour, the kitchen, the passageways. Come at mid-summer, say . . . the twenty-first day of June. You may begin by helping me with the turnips. Now I bid you good morning."

Thus, on a certain summer's day in 1790, Lieutenant Matthew Lawe took a spectral oar in his hand, laid it across his shoulders, and walked inland to Norfolk.

The Parsonage House of Burnham Thorpe was two red-tiled houses put together in the shape of an anchor with one fluke, set in thirty acres of mixed gardens, lawns, vegetable plots, and trees, with a running stream to divide them. Beyond the trees the wind blew incessantly across bare flat fields, and the curling North Sea waves for ever attacked the coast. In this rural palace—as it was to Matthew Lawe after his cramped London lodgings—there dwelt a slender branch of the Nelson family: one man of God, one man of the sea, one wife, and one stepchild.

The Reverend Edmund Nelson, now sixty-eight, was an ageing churchman in whom piety, humility, and a certain contented indolence had combined to fashion a classic country parson, half-

125

way to heaven and resigned to the remainder of the journey. His son Horatio, not resigned to any aspect of idleness, was waiting for *his* heaven, which was in the hands of the Admiralty. His daughter-in-law, Frances, born Woolward, widowed as Nisbet, now to be known as Fanny Nelson, was thirty-two, as was her sailor husband: a girl who had blossomed early in the hot house of the Caribbean where her uncle had been president of Nevis Island, and whom this transplant to frigid Norfolk had rendered plain, dull, and ill. Her son Josiah Nisbet, a spoiled boy of ten, was happily at boarding school much of the year, and thought of for the navy.

To this tranquil household Lieutenant Lawe, "a valued sea-officer and friend" in Nelson's words of introduction, was presently admitted. His welcome was kindly from Nelson, who seemed to need a trusted male confidant, courteous from the rector, reserved from Mrs. Nelson. The Parsonage House was draughty in summer; in autumn cold and damp; in winter the biting northeast wind from the sea seemed to cut through the walls. Outdoors was a land of tossing branches, of laden air coarse with sand and salt, and of whirling windmills which ground the corn which kept men alive to endure this malice.

Mrs. Nelson would take to her bed for days, sustained by a log fire in the grate, a procession of warming-pans and hot stones wrapped in flannel, and beef tea spiced with cloves. Her father-in-law bore all with stoic Christianity, mufflers, and mittens. Nelson had rheumatic pinchings, like some relic from the Aged Sailors' Refuge.

Matthew's attic room, with no refinements to warm it, might have been the masthead in winter. . . . There were times when he slept in his boat-cloak. Yet he had come to anchor in a secure berth, and it was blissful ease to enjoy it and to earn it willingly. His duties were a morsel of everything, from letter writing to digging roots, from carrying prayer books in church to drenching a sick calf. But mostly he served as a companion for an achingly bored man, who talked avidly of his lost love, the sea: his Holy Grail, his most pure lust.

Slowly the seasons turned and turned again. Early in 1792 the Reverend Edmund Nelson, who was seventy and failing, left the household at Burnham Thorpe and removed to a nearby village, more convenient to his many tasks which he would fulfil to the end of his ministry. Before making his farewells, he talked with Matthew of his despairing son. "I know Horace to be unhappy," he said. It was "Horace" within the family circle: "Horatio" was for formal wear, in that great outside world which had forgotten him. "Yet he fared so well in the service. A post-captain at twenty-one—I was so proud of him on that day! Cannot he be content with it? He has this farm to keep him occupied, and his dear wife who is so attentive, and Josiah growing up."

Matthew could scarcely listen, so far from a sailor's world was this. "With respect, sir," he said, "Captain Nelson remains ambitious, which may be God's will."

"Yes, yes," the old man answered, suddenly fretful. "When one has tasted glory. . . . But do you, who know him well, believe that he can be truly happy here?"

"Not truly, no."

"What then?"

"He lives in hope, as I do."

It may have been that the rector, before he left the Parsonage House, spoke of this conversation with someone even more closely concerned. A few weeks afterwards, with the household shrunken and the daily round as quiet as a mouse with dropsy, Mrs. Nelson broached to Matthew the subject of a husband in limbo.

He had talked little with his hostess during his two years' sojourn, and nothing of any intimacy. Now, as they sat in the faded parlour, she with her tapestry frame and he with idle hands, he expected nothing more than an hour's civil exchange before dinner. But to his surprise she said: "Pray tell me, Mr. Lawe, is Captain Nelson content with his life ashore?"

He was startled, and looked at her with a closer attention than he had ever dared. He saw a woman withdrawn and silent, pale, suffering as ever from a winter cold: dressed in severest grey, as if she were widowed already: a woman apart who knew not why. He could do no more than feel his way. "I do not know, ma'am. Of course he would wish to be at sea. He is convinced that he should be. So he waits, with patience."

"And cannot be resigned?"

Matthew did not like the word. Why should a man be "resigned", if he still had the breath of life in him? It might serve for monks, and the feeble old. But for men? For sailors? For *Nelson?* "As to that, ma'am," he answered warily, "the captain must speak for himself."

Mrs. Nelson eyed him and sighed. It was clear that she had expected more, and was now herself "resigned"—to disappointment. At length she said: "We all wait with patience. I wait to return to the sunshine, but will not see it. So I do my best, loyally."

The ground was dangerous. It meant that her best was not good enough, and she was telling him so, with some resentment. But why no happy man at her side? Why no joy, no loving concord? *Why no children?* Not the bravest lieutenant would have ventured his toes into such private strife, which might be no small element in that land-sickness which made sailors yearn for the sea.

The seasons turned once more. All that year they worked in the garden, and watched men digging and ditching and hedging and harvesting—a poor yield in a barren time. In the autumn they walked among the bare trees. "Two thousand of these go to build a ship-of-the-line," Nelson would say, eyeing a broad stand of oak. "I *thirst* to see them cut down and put to use!"

Reading the political news from France in that tumultuous year of revolution, Nelson went to London once more, as did a thousand other hopeful officers, to offer service in the fleet. The fleet remained deaf and blind. Nelson returned despondent, and shivering, and took to his bed.

"Malaria," Matthew was informed, when at last the pale yellow ghost emerged from his sick room. "I have suffered from it since I was a midshipman in the Far East. When it strikes, I lie down and sweat awhile. Then it leaves me alone for a year or two."

"I did not know, sir."

"Oh, I have every disease in the pharmacopoeia," Nelson answered. "But they seem to forget me when I am afloat. . . ." He was standing at the study window, gazing out across a garden in the bleak grip of winter towards a farming flatland. "After these wretched bouts, I have a kind of curtain over my eyes, a pale film which comes and goes. Even now, I cannot see the far ten-acre." He turned about suddenly. "I do not wish to! I hate the land! Miserable grudging stuff that will not *give!* What am I doing here? What are we? Navy officers? I have not been a navy officer since the *Boreas* paid off in 1787. Five empty years! It drives me near to madness! We are sea animals, you and I. We came from it, and we must return to it. Either we swim, or we die. I must get back, even if I have to take service with the Russians!"

He had never been lower in his despair. After a silent, brooding supper, he went to bed shivering again, in desolation. The sea animal, trapped above the tide mark, had begun to gasp for that element which alone would keep it alive.

Then all changed.

2

IT CHANGED with the ultimate in gory signals: the severing of a man's head from his body, a great gout of royal blood and a falling trophy caught neatly in a wicker basket as the mob howled its triumph. King Louis XVI of France, guillotined, had more power to move hearts and minds than he ever enjoyed as a whole man.

The story was heard with horror in England, which had not beheaded a king for one hundred and forty-four years but which now seemed threatened by the fever in France. Revolutionary clubs were formed even in peaceable Norfolk, with tap room meetings for "Friends of the People", and "Resolution Men". Soon the mobs, the riots, the insolence of common men overblown with the promise of power, threatened to outstrip the magistrates.

Presently another king gave another signal. George III of England delivered himself of a speech to the House of Commons, stating in cold terms that England could no longer be neutral in continental affairs, since foreign persons were fomenting troubles within his own happy realm. It was the royal will that his military and naval forces be increased, to preserve internal stability and external strength. Within a week navy ships were being floated out of dock: their sailors were summoned, and came running. Among these was Captain Horatio Nelson, who did not wait for a sign which might never reach him. He posted to London; and took Matthew with him.

There Lieutenant Matthew Lawe, whose three-year employment had enabled him to purchase a dress uniform worthy of the name, and who now wore it with pride, waited in the park of St.

James for Captain Nelson to return from the Admiralty building near by. At last, Nelson came hasting towards him, almost running; Nelson, with a light in his eye, a smile on his lips, and colour in his cheeks which had not been seen for years. As he drew near, the gleam in his eye was bright enough to serve the masthead lantern at midnight.

"I have a ship!" he said as soon as he was within earshot. His meagre figure seemed to have grown tall and proud as a main-mast. "A ship-of-the-line! My first!"

Matthew, overjoyed, stepped forward. "That is wonderful news, sir. I beg leave to shake you by the hand."

The hand clasp was warm and fervent. "I am promised a sixty-four," Nelson said. "A seventy-four was offered, if I wished to wait some months, but I closed for the one most ready. Five years is long enough."

"What ship is it?"

"That is not yet decided. One of three, I believe. You are with me, Mr. Lawe, named for a berth already. And Josiah too, as a youngster—he will benefit, I hope, from midshipman's service under my direct eye. But *your* first task is to raise men in Norfolk. I fancy there are many who will come forward, and the fewer pressed men and gaolbirds in my ship, the better we shall be."

They waited nearly three weeks in pleasurable industry and ease for the name of Captain Nelson's new command. Then it was given: the *Agamemnon*, the promised 64-gun battleship, lying at Chatham in the last stage of dockyard care. She needed a crew, and that was all.

"She is one of the finest afloat," Nelson told Matthew, after he had seen her. "I would not exchange now, if I were offered the *Victory*. I must attend her at Chatham, and you are needed back in Norfolk. Spread the good news. Find me willing men. Post bills in the taverns, speak to the mayors. Promise nothing but hard work, fair treatment, the chance of action and prizes, and the utmost care as long as I command. If that is not enough, then the breed of English sailors is dead!"

The breed was not dead, however neglectful had been their treatment. In the time allowed him Matthew Lawe raised two hundred volunteers, ready to serve (as he was not ashamed to declare) "a leader worthy of love".

Thus, in the sixth year of his exile, leaving behind a proud father and an obstinately childless wife, Nelson went joyfully back to sea. He was to join Lord Hood's squadron in the Mediterranean: Lord Hood, an admiral friend from old days on the West Indies station, whose flag would be hoisted in the *Victory*.

By the time Lord Hood and his squadron of fourteen line-ships had spent a month cruising off the great French port of Toulon in the hope of enticing their fleet to come out, it had grown clear that the French ships were not to be drawn. Toulon was strong, well fortified, not to be breached from the sea. Let the British fleet waste their time on it.

There was only one alternative to assault: a taut blockade and the pinching hunger which must go with it, since a poor country-side in the turmoil of revolution could not sustain this crowded port. Hood put this in train in June. At the end of August the city, broken by starvation and internal strife, hung out its white flags and surrendered.

There was no time wasted in rejoicing, though extra gills of rum went round and the men lined the bulwarks, cheering, whenever they passed another British ship on blockade duty. Lord Hood knew that Toulon could only be held by soldiers, who must enter and take control before a French land force came to rescue it. The nearest troops, England's Neapolitan allies, were at Naples. They must be summoned to join.

For this commission, which might require a cool and persuasive man as well as a fast ship, he detached Captain Nelson and the *Agamemnon* which had now made a name for herself in speed and competence. Nelson was to deliver urgent dispatches to the British Ambassador, Sir William Hamilton; to supplement these writings with any explanation which Sir William Hamilton, who had negotiated the treaty of friendship, might need in his representations to the King of Naples; and to remain on that station for as long as was necessary.

It was blissful freedom and important service wrapped in the same enterprise, and Nelson had never been happier in his life. As soon as he set his prow eastwards into the gentle Mediterranean blue, he entered a sailor's heaven not glimpsed for six years, yet no more than a prelude to the noble music of his time.

When the *Agamemnon* had one more day of her voyage to

Naples to run, and all the world was fair, and all the sky was light blue, and all the sea dark, and all their billowing canvas rose tier by tier in triple towers of white strength, Captain Horatio Nelson made his customary appearance on deck.

He looked what he had speedily become in recent months: a small resplendent lion of energy. As soon as he was sighted, all his officers withdrew to the lee side, leaving their captain with half the breadth of the quarterdeck for his private use.

The withdrawal was a mark of respect, and a mark also of the loneliness of command on a big ship-of-the-line. There was a vast gulf separating this single man from the six hundred others on board, and no one in sight would dare to cross it unless beckoned.

Nelson waited his own good time before acknowledging the presence of his ship's company. Having glanced aloft at their taut sails, and astern at the helmsman, whose eyes were suddenly linked to the compass card as if by marine glue, he took a turn or two along the length of the quarterdeck. Then he turned and walked aft again, and stood still under the shadow of the wheel, his feet braced against the gentle roll which was the *Agamemnon*'s eternal dance when running proud before the wind.

Matthew, standing alert among a group which included John Wilson the master, Martin Hinton the first lieutenant, and Midshipman Josiah Nisbet, watched his captain as keenly as any. He continued to be astonished at the transformation which had been wrought in the man now enthroned. Less than a year previous, they had both been dull clodhoppers on a Norfolk farm, thirsting for that sea employment which never came. Now the one was captain—captain next to God—of a fine fighting ship, under his most exact command. Matthew Lawe had prospered well in the shade of this eminence, and, giving of his best, had found the best reward, which was trust.

Nelson turned to beckon to his first lieutenant. Martin Hinton came forward, saluted, uncovered his head, and waited in silence. He would no more have spoken first than an oyster would have opened its maw to cry, "I am a native of Whitstable! Do me honour!"

Nelson returned his salute. "Good morning, Mr. Hinton."

"Good morning, sir."

"Anything worth the reporting?"

"No, sir. Course, east-south-east. Distance made good since yesterday noon, one hundred thirty miles. No land in sight. No ships sighted. No men sick. One man to be reported to you."

"For why?"

"Sir, I report top man Adam Ratcliff, being slow to turn out, slow aloft, and slow off the yard. Second offence."

"In your opinion, Mr. Hinton, a flogging matter?"

"No, sir." Hinton, aware of a strict yet humane captain, tailored his advice in the same direction. "Better he were logged as incurable seasick, and put among the waisters."

"Seasick?" Nelson, after half a lifetime afloat, was still subject to this same sailor's curse, as all his officers knew. He might have been contemptuous of another's weakness, but he was not. He was Nelson. "Seasick? Forgive the poor cripple. See him taken off the topyards. Better a live cook's mate than a dead seaman. Now bring me Lieutenant Lawe, Doctor Roxburgh, Mr. Nisbet, the master, the master gunner, and the gunner's mate for gun drill."

When they were all assembled, and salutes exchanged, Nelson made known his orders without delay. "It is broadsides today, and broadsides until I am satisfied. We use blank cartridge. Broadsides, first to starboard, then to larboard. I wish to hear a true ripple-firing, from stem to stern—the shots close together, but *not* one great thunderbolt to shake the ship to matchwood. Is that understood?"

There was a murmur of assent, and Nelson proceeded: "Dr. Roxburgh, set up your tables, with instruments ready as if for action. I will send down wounded men for your attention. Master gunner, prepare the gun crews. Mr. Wilson, when we are finished with the starboard firing, come smartly about and lay a course opposite for the larboard guns to bear. Mr. Nisbet—" he stared at his stepson as if at a small stranger who might prove to be human, "attend me with your notebook. Go fetch it now, and do not lag behind." They began to disperse at a nod from their captain, who was left with Matthew and Martin Hinton. Nelson turned to Matthew. "Take station on the lower tier, Mr. Lawe. Ripple-fire broadsides, from both decks. It will go upper, lower, upper, lower, stem to stern; as swift as possible, but no two guns together. If any gun is early or late, I will have its number. Let the gunners listen out sharply, and they will learn the tune."

To Hinton, he said, "Now, in five minutes, beat to quarters. Let me hear old *Heart of Oak* thunder out! Report to me when all is ready."

Within a short space all was the bustle of simulated war. When the drummers beat out their rhythm of "Ta-ta-TON, Ta-ta-TON", on that foreboding note which could fire one man to courage and another to deathly fear, there came from below the rumble of guns running out, and the sharp slap of gunports raised and secured. The marine sharpshooters clambered up the rigging and took up their posts on the yards, while John Wilson, the master, mustered his force of top men and yard men and pull-haul men to steer the ship into action.

Lieutenant Hinton returned to Nelson's side, with the report: "Crew at quarters, sir, and ready."

"Hoist signal for close action," Nelson commanded, and the signal lieutenant ran to the halyards. To Lawe he said: "Below with you," and Matthew went swiftly down into another world. On his way to the lower gun deck he passed through the midshipmen's rough quarters which now became the surgeon's lair. The tables and chests had been ranged in rows, and covered with sailcloth, to serve as the surgeon's chopping blocks. Below them on the deck were buckets full of sponges and dressings, and larger empty mess kits for amputated limbs. At one side stood a rack of saws, another of knives and probes; and a barrel of rum for sufferers to quaff before they came to this encounter. Such was the *Agamemnon's* haven of mercy, to which, in action, a procession of groaning, screaming, silent, and bleeding men would be carried down, within moments of the first enemy fire: a hell below, to match the hell above.

Matthew found the head of the ladder and stepped down to the fiery heart of the ship. There was order here also. The guns were already run out, prepared for the first broadside, and their questing snouts seemed to sniff the air beyond the open ports, alert for the chase and the kill. On their blood-red carriages—a colour repeated all round the gun deck, to mask the morbid stains of battle—the lashings had been doubled, against that fearful recoil which could turn a gun into a mad bull, charging red hot across the deck through men and weapons till it finished up in gory chaos on the opposite side; or, since a 32-pounder weighed two tons, tore a hole in the ship's hull and disappeared into the sea.

The men stood to their guns, their tarry pigtails safely coiled, their head scarves tightly bound about their ears. Round them were ranged the shot racks, powder shovels, the sheepskin sponges for swabbing out the barrels, the rammers to force home the cannon shot, the hand-spikes for training their weapons towards a mortal wound.

All was as ready as human wit could devise. Success still lay, and always would, in the lap of chance. A gun might misfire, destroying the rhythm. A gun captain might be deafened by the monstrous noise bursting out upon him from a few feet away, and miss his turn. In true action a heavy-shotted gun might explode, or break its bonds and begin its rampage; or an enemy hit might fill the deck with huge flying splinters, which inflicted the most terrible wounds.

Nicholls, the master gunner at the centre of this iron tangle, greeted Matthew as if they were both guests at some sedate family breakfast. He had a face grey like his guns, weathered as the timbers surrounding them. This was his own small empire, and the emperor had it in his grasp as a shepherd his gentle flock.

Matthew asked if he were ready. "It is an important trial of our strength," he cautioned. "The captain is looking for perfection."

"So am I, sir. So am I. And *my* perfection is that I am still alive, after thirty-four years of service."

Then a stentorian voice from above relayed the order: "*Broadsides!*" and on the instant the brazen tongues began to roar. At the first test they did not roar so well. Guns misfired; other guns went unheard; when their ship turned on the larboard tack, a single shot was followed by a ghastly silence, since the next gun captain below had not the wit to fill the gap.

At mid-morning, a sulphurous inquest was held. "I do not know," Nelson told his assembled officers, "what effect our gunnery will have upon the enemy, but by God it terrifies me! Our next exercise, beginning in ten minutes, will be *broadsides*, and after the noon break it will be broadsides again, until I am satisfied. Dismiss!"

And so it went all the day until the guns spoke true.

Towards sunset the masthead lookout hailed the deck, and reported land ahead. Far to the southeast was a gilded crown of land, dark at its base, pearly pink at its peak; cropped off short. It was the distant crater of Vesuvius.

"Shorten sail!" Nelson ordered. "We will dawdle the night, and present our compliments at the godly hour of nine." He added, for the benefit of any within earshot: "*With exact gun salutes!*"

The next morning, precisely at nine, Master Gunner Nicholls strode to and fro between his two lines of saluting cannon set upon the foredeck, intoning the hallowed rhythm of a naval salute, which began with a secret murmur and ended in crisp command: "If I were not a gunner, I would not be here—FIRE ONE! If I were not a gunner, I would not be here—FIRE TWO! If I were not a gunner, I would not be here—"

The *Agamemnon*, gliding forward into the matchless beauty of the Bay of Naples, was paying due respects: fifty-one guns for the King of the Two Sicilies, and nine more for the British Ambassador to His Majesty's Court.

The arm of the bay, enclosing a shining bowl of blue-green water, a small armada of painted fishing boats, and terraces of sun-warmed buildings with noble hills beyond, was one of the most fair in the world. Poets had hymned it, lovers had languished in its embrace. Nelson, his telescope busy, felt all the satisfaction of a fine landfall. Who would not be proud of a handsome 64-gun ship of war, now dousing and furling her greater sails as their way fell off and anchors were lowered? Who would choose to be in Norfolk?

Then his eye was caught by a sudden splash of colour at the entrance to the inner harbour: a gilded barge decked with flags was headed in their direction. Nelson, standing on the quarter-deck with his immediate officers about him, said, "It is the British Ambassador. We are honoured . . . Mr. Nisbet! Pass the word to pipe the side!"

Sir William Hamilton, a veteran envoy of sixty-three, whose interests were finely balanced between archaeology, diplomacy, and elegant self-indulgence, had held his present post for nearly thirty years.

"It would please me greatly," he told Nelson after he came aboard, "if you would make your home ashore with me for as long as you choose. The Palazzo Sessa is tolerably comfortable, Lady Hamilton would be delighted, and you and I have much to discuss. I must tell you that we dine with his majesty tomorrow."

Nelson was especially welcome because Sir William wished to see a British ship-of-the-line at anchor in Naples harbour, as evidence of British goodwill, to buttress this Sicilian alliance which he had spent half a lifetime in fostering. It might also be that this strange-looking little fellow might amuse his wife, who at twenty-eight was thirty-five years his junior, and was, even after a bare two years of marriage, sometimes in need of distraction.

At the Palazzo Sessa, a town-dwelling set halfway up the hillside so that one might obtain matchless views of the bay, Nelson and his escorts, Matthew Lawe and Midshipman Nisbet, found sumptuous comfort such as none of them had ever known before. Marble corridors opened upon room after room of splendid proportion. A vast pillared portico led to a succession of gardens. Nelson, accorded the royal suite, was lost in its magnificence—and then emboldened. After this, it seemed that he need never be daunted again: not by display, not by hand-and-foot service, not by the touch of aristocratic luxury.

They dined privately, with Sir William presiding at one end of the oval walnut table, and his wife at the other. Emma Hamilton, gowned in shimmering blue, was at the peak of her beauty: a flame-haired charmer, perfect of skin, opulent of figure, natural and amiable in manner. She seemed, as the wine flowed and the sun slanted through the louvred shutters, to become all things to all men. To her husband she was attentive and dutiful, to Nelson full of subtle flattery, to Matthew Lawe companionable and reassuring. For the gangling young Josiah Nisbet she was half mother, half partner in the turbulent discontents of youth. Peace and good humour reigned supreme.

They retired early, on that first night, after Nelson's dispatches were closely discussed, and Lady Hamilton had sung to the piano, and—at the urging of her husband—had mysteriously promised that she would perform her "Attitudes" for their amusement some evening.

The next morning Matthew wakened to the bounteous comfort of a canopied feather bed, and a discreet knock at the door. An imposing figure entered. This was Gaetano Spedilo, the ambassador's valet, whom Sir William, on the previous evening had called "the true mainstay of this household"—tall, swarthy, wizened and bewhiskered, with the self-importance of a man who knew himself indispensable.

He advanced, bowed, and murmured: "*Buon giorno, signor tenente.*" He turned, and beckoned in a footman bearing an ambrosial dish of hot chocolate on a tray. Then he helped Matthew into a silk robe and poured his chocolate. He hoped the lieutenant had slept well. A man needed sleep after such a fearful voyage. Was there anything—anything in the *world*—he might do for the lieutenant before preparing his bath?

Sipping his chocolate, enjoying every element in this free and unaccustomed world, Matthew idly asked Gaetano about the "Attitudes" Lady Hamilton had spoken of.

The valet came to immediate attention. His fingers began to weave the air. Ah, the Attitudes . . . *bellissimo!* The *tenente* must understand that *la signora* had been of—of the theatrical persuasion, before she married the ambassador. It was said that she had the whole of London at her feet. The Attitudes were— well, the French would call them *tableaux*. She would dress in a certain way, and pose herself in a certain way, and the ambassador would hold up a candelabra so, to light the scene, and *ecco!* there arrived an Attitude! It might portray the goddess of love, or a warrior queen, or a girl of the streets. All Naples society was in raptures with the Attitudes. Well, perhaps not all the *women.*

"I look forward to this entertainment," said Matthew. "How long have they been married?"

"Two years, *tenente*. But she was residing here for five years before the matrimonials."

The ground seemed to be growing delicate. "She was, perhaps, a friend of the family?"

"*Exactly!*" Gaetano exclaimed. "It is said that the ambassador's nephew, Mr. Greville relinquished her to please his uncle. Thus she came here to improve her Italian. And here she stayed."

Gaetano now busied himself with the disposal of the pot of chocolate, the cup and the tray and then with making straight Matthew's uniform clothes and linen. Then the valet, with a bow, turned to go. "Thank you, Gaetano," Matthew said. "You have been most helpful."

Gaetano spread out his arms, miming a warm embrace. "There is only one reason for that, *tenente*. We love the English!"

"We love the English!" King Ferdinand declared to Captain Horatio Nelson at dinner that night. "They are the saviours of our nation! That is why I was so happy to see your brave ship enter my harbour."

Privately Nelson might have wished that the King of the Two Sicilies were not such a boorish peasant, huge and fiery of nose, scarlet of complexion, raucous of voice, and gross of appetite. But one must, Nelson thought, take kings as they came. He had not met so many of them that he could afford to be dainty. It was a vast and glittering throng which had been assembled at the Palazzo Reale to honour the naval guests. All of the *Agamemnon*'s officers who could be spared had come ashore for it: even Midshipman Nisbet had been found a place. The meal was prodigious, the red wine flowed in rivers, the noise was enough to shake the chandeliers.

"The fellow needs us," the ambassador had told Nelson earlier. "If not, it would be bread and macaroni for us, and the dregs of Naples fire water to wash it down. You will see his quality: a *popular* monarch whom the people love as long as their stomachs are full, but without any external strength except through our alliance. At dinner he will flatter you. You need do nothing much but smile, and agree on all matters, and stiffen him if he raises hands to heaven and tells you he cannot spare any troops for Toulon. He can spare them well enough."

Sir William might have been gifted with the devil's own second sight, even to the raising of the royal hands to heaven. But in the course of the meal, these had been lowered again. "Yesterday I thought it impossible for me to send the troops you ask," King Ferdinand was now declaring. He beckoned to his major-domo, who signalled to a wine butler, who refilled their glasses. "But I am ready to do so, to help an ally and a friend in need. . . . Tell me, what is the least that would satisfy your government?"

It was something new for Nelson to speak for his government, but having had the benefit of advice from Sir William, he was not a lonely gladiator. "Sire, I believe, six thousand."

"And what is the most?"

"Sire, I believe, six thousand."

Their eyes met, and suddenly the King burst out with a great

140

bellow of laughter. "*Gran Dio*, I like your spirit, Captain!" he said, spluttering, as all eyes turned towards them. "Very well—six thousand it shall be. Are you content?"

"Indeed, your majesty. And thank you kindly."

"There is one condition. I wish to see your ship."

"I should be deeply honoured. You will find us rough, I fear."

"I will find what I seek," the King answered grandly. "A British fighting ship with a friend on board to greet me. Tomorrow, then? Or Sunday?"

"Sunday," Captain Nelson answered. "At one o'clock, sire—if that will not interfere with your devotions."

The sailors quit Sir William's hospitable roof early next morning. There was much to be done on board, even though the ambassador had undertaken to provide plates, cutlery, food, and wine for the royal visit, from the resources of the Palazzo Sessa.

It was a thoughtful party, affected by excesses of indulgence and second thoughts on duty and pleasure, which sat in the stern sheets of the captain's barge and headed towards the *Agamemnon*. Young Josiah had the first queasy headache of his life; Nelson was musing loftily on certain battle plans if his ship were cornered by the French in Naples harbour, and, at a lower level, on the number of plates and spoons necessary for a royal visit; and Matthew, with fewer cares and longer hindsight, was wishing that he might be marooned in Naples for ever.

The oars thudded against the tholepins, the sun began to gain strength, and the *Agamemnon* to emerge, in all her towering majesty, from a drifting surface fog. Matthew, who had become a stranger to silence during the last two days, felt it his duty to bridge an unusual gap. He chose what was uppermost in his mind. "Sir, what did you think of our entertainment last night?"

Nelson was preoccupied. "What entertainment? At the royal palace?"

"I was referring to the Palazzo Sessa, sir. The later entertainment—the Attitudes."

"I thought," his captain answered austerely, "what we should all think: that they were tasteful and enjoyable. I have never seen so much done with a shawl and a tambourine. What did you think, Josiah? Did you enjoy Lady Hamilton's play-acting?"

Josiah answered with unaccustomed fervour: "I thought it the most beautiful thing I ever saw, sir."

"Did you so? Then we may be all in agreement."

"Her ladyship," Matthew said, "must have had a great vocation before her marriage."

Nelson seemed to see some slur in this. "And why not? It is *now* that we should think of. I believe that she is an amiable young woman, who does honour to the station to which she has been raised."

"Yes, indeed, sir."

"That should be enough for all." He then altered course, uncovering for a moment a whole mine of private thought. "I have said before, that once past Gibraltar every man is a bachelor. By which I mean, Mr. Lawe, that he is married only to his ship!"

On Sunday morning all was bustle on board the *Agamemnon*—bustle which Nelson hated: domestic, social, unseamanlike. It demanded that his first lieutenant must supervise the twining of coloured ribbons round the honest rope rail of their ladder; that Lieutenant Lawe muster wine glasses, and inspect them for fingermarks; that the master gunner fashion fireworks; the marine trumpeters practise courtly flourishes; and Midshipman Nisbet tie up nosegays for the ladies.

It was *war*—with macaroni for cutlasses, sun awnings for topsails! It was no more than Nelson's own Attitudes—and it was a damned imposition. Though this was what his career demanded, his manhood fiercely rebelled.

The company, which must assemble discreetly before the royal barge left the inner harbour, came on board in droves: the elite of Sicilian society and of the British colony, led by Sir William and his lady.

Then happily all was changed. The small pinnace which presently put out from Naples fish-quay bore an urgent message from a certain person ashore for the captain of the *Agamemnon*. It informed him that a French convoy of one man-of-war and three merchant sail was at anchor off Sardinia, and could be surprised, if his ship were ready for action.

First Lieutenant Hinton, who had read the message, stood waiting by Nelson's side. After a suitable pause he asked: "Your orders, sir?"

"Are we fit for sea, Mr. Hinton?"

"We can be, sir. Right promptly!"

"Then we sail," Nelson said. To Sir William Hamilton, some minutes later, he announced: "Sir, with great regret, I must forgo this occasion, and leave harbour instantly."

His resolve was clear, his motives strangely mixed. He wished to show this fashionable world that a British ship-of-the-line never forgot her prime purpose. He must remind himself that sailors were not born to indulge themselves ashore when duty beckoned. He must exorcize certain improprieties of conduct, or intention, or sensual ambition. There was only one way.

Brusquely he shed the burden of his guests, weighed anchor, and sailed within two hours; not to embrace the softer shores of life, nor see Sir William or his wife for five fateful years.

3

IN THE *Agamemnon*, his first love among his line ships, Nelson saw continuous action against the French. The battle honours came thick and fast. After two full actions, he was promoted commodore and given command of the larger *Captain*.

The *Captain* inspired him to his greatest exploit so far—and brought him his greatest reward: knighthood and promotion to rear-admiral. It happened at the Battle of Cape St. Vincent, when Britain's Mediterranean fleet met France's Spanish allies off the southwestern tip of Portugal. This "Valentine"—the battle was fought on the fourteenth day of February, 1797—brought Nelson to two acts of daring. The first was to leave the English line-of-battle one minute before the future Lord St. Vincent, his commander-in-chief, signalled him to do so, and to cut the Spanish squadron into two confused halves.

The second was to lay alongside the nearest enemy, the 80-gun *San Nicolas*, one of the largest of the Spaniards, and to lead a boarding party. She was quickly taken, but in the confusion she in turn fell foul of a consort even larger, the towering *San Josef* of 112 guns. Using the *San Nicolas* as a convenient gangway, Commodore Nelson led his men up and up to the deck of the *San Josef*, made a determined hand-to-hand assault—and a second Spanish ship surrendered to him, within the same hour.

It was a victory which resounded throughout the fleet, and

"Nelson's Patent Bridge for Boarding First-rates" swiftly became a legend, like the man himself.

In all this Nelson had been forced to surrender a little of his own private armament here and there. . . . At the assault on the French garrison at Calvi, in Corsica, he was struck by a splinter on the brow, and lost the sight of his right eye; ever afterwards he wore a protective green shade over his left, that sole survivor which must be cherished. Later, when leading the boats from his new ship *Theseus* to capture a Spanish treasure ship in Santa Cruz, Teneriffe, he forfeited his right arm.

This had seemed the worst blow of all, the crippledom of body and of hope. Sent home to England as an invalid, in constant and monstrous pain from a nerve imprisoned within the ligatured stump, he had resigned himself once again to bread-and-cheese and a labourer's cottage—all that a one-armed admiral could now expect.

But within half a year, with the nerve subdued and the stump miraculously healed, he was appointed to the *Vanguard*, of 74 guns, and sent to join Admiral St. Vincent off the Portuguese coast. There he was given a squadron of ships with a roving commission in the Mediterranean; and there this sailor with one eye, one arm, and one ambition began to forge a steel circle of friends, a band of brothers, fellow captains who were never to falter in their loyalty, until he, the fixed star in this firmament, fell from the sky.

Their names were all to become famous: Hardy, Fremantle, Ball, Blackwood, Foley, Hallowell, Berry, Troubridge, Collingwood, Saumarez, Hood. These were the men whom a small battered admiral led to glory. They were men he could trust, men who did not need the Nelson touch to make them brave, only to bind them together into a single sword. They were his, and he was theirs; and the harshest word, and the greatest tribute which ever came out of this brotherhood, was from one of them who growled, some minutes before the last battle of all: "How I wish that fellow Nelson would not crowd us with signals. *We all know what to do.*"

In the year 1798, Admiral Nelson's squadron, of *Vanguard*, *Alexander*, and *Orion*, with four frigates and a sloop, were intent on the chase of Napoleon's fleet, now loose in the Mediterranean.

The best intelligence was that it carried unnumbered troops, 12,000 cavalry, and Napoleon himself; and the best conjecture was that Napoleon, after looting Malta, was bound for Egypt, and then for the conquering of India. With reinforcements pressing in from England, which brought his strength to fourteen ships-of-the-line, among them the finest to be found afloat, Nelson came upon his quarry, on the first day of August, in Aboukir Bay at the mouth of the Nile.

The *Vanguard*'s signal-midshipman, perched high on the royal mainyard, hailed the deck. "From Captain Foley, the *Goliath*, sir." The voice through the speaking trumpet was piping high, both with youth and wild anticipation. "Enemy in sight. Moored in line of battle."

"*Moored!*" Nelson repeated. "By God, we might have them!" A shower of signals came cascading out, and were translated into hoists as fast as hardworked men could send them soaring upwards on the *Vanguard*. "Make to *Goliath* and Captain Hood on *Zealous*: 'Rejoin me and take station ahead'. Make to all others: 'Form up in line astern. Prepare for battle!'"

Then, with these signals acknowledged by a fleet suddenly in ferment, the admiral took a turn about the deck. The sound of guns running out, the bustle and the shouting, were all as they should be. There was nothing new here, but this time, this time it might turn at last to gold and glory. Rejoining his flag-captain, with Matthew Lawe standing by, he said: "Press on, Berry. We must make the most of daylight." Then, never at a loss for a phrase, Nelson said: "It is either a peerage, or Westminster Abbey."

A glorious victory, or noble death. . . . That was *his* estimate, *his* private portion on earth or in heaven. . . . But what of others? Was this man beginning, Matthew wondered, to believe himself set apart from the company of mortal men?

For the first time in years not to be measured, Matthew was once again beginning to be afraid. This was like following old Drake's star again. Then, his captain-general had soared to the skies, only to lead them too far out.

Soon the English fleet viewed in all its promise or peril thirteen French ships, anchored within Aboukir Bay in a curving column, a phantom of that old demi-lune of the Armada, some two hundred years before. In the centre of the French line was the towering bulk of their flagship, *L'Orient*, a monster of one hundred and twenty guns, against the seventy-four of the best English ships. The French line had been anchored as near as they dared to the shallow water of the bay behind them.

There looked to be no room nor depth enough to pass inside them. They had made themselves an embayed fortress, and at their back was a forest of French tricolour flags, on every house, on every hill, on every beached boat. Napoleon the conqueror had already landed, won his Battle of the Pyramids and made Egypt his own. But he had made it his own as a land animal. The English sailors and the ships remained, to dispute the claim.

Standing braced with his back against the quarterdeck rail, confident that Captain Berry had the *Vanguard* in his grasp, just as his own arm embraced the fleet, Nelson looked about him. Others might see the strength of the French battle array; Nelson saw its weakness. Already he was strangely elevated, like a giant about to spring.

"Let them flaunt their little flags," he told Matthew. "Here we have a line of their ships. A serpent of ships. The serpent of the Nile." He put a question which seemed idle. "Who was the serpent of the Nile?"

"Cleopatra, sir."

"And what do you do with Cleopatra?"

"Put another serpent to her bosom?"

"Such ingratitude! But you are right! Here is Cleopatra the sea-serpent, lying still, but watchful. You may tread on its head, and risk its poison, or you may aim lower, and break its back. I tell you, we will break this back by the time the moon is up!"

Matthew needed no reminder that this "breaking of the back" was the core of "Signal Book, Plan Four" for which Nelson's band of brother captains had been brilliantly schooled. Its purpose was to concentrate their fire on one point, whether it was one ship out of two, or one prime target out of twenty: to destroy *that*, and then to enlarge the scene of destruction. For this they had been constantly summoned on board the *Vanguard* for conference, for questions to and fro. All they need do now was to remember their lessons, never to lag behind, and never to fail a friend.

The English fleet ran on, backed by a sun already lowering in the west, and its leaders would soon begin to overlap the French

146

line of anchor. On board the *Vanguard* telescopes were busy, just as the enemy's signal flags now started to chatter like a flock of starlings at dusk, recall-signals for their men ashore.

Nelson pointed towards the great bulk of the French flagship *L'Orient*, far ahead and seventh of the line. "In that ship," he said, "is Admiral François Paul de Brueys. He thinks himself safe. He thinks he can out-gun us, ship for ship, and he is right. He thinks that no ship of ours can pass inshore, and engage his fleet from behind. *I believe he is wrong!* Capel!"

Signal-Lieutenant Capel sped across the deck to receive his orders. Swiftly the flags were hoisted, taken from the well-thumbed battle-plan: certain captains, according to their own judgment, had leave to quit the line and pass inshore of any anchored enemy, if the risk were acceptable. The risk was surely there; entering a strange bay cursed by rocks and shoals, with dubious charts, no pilots, and darkness coming on, was a formidable test of seamanship.

Six ships elected for it: the two leaders, Hood's *Zealous* and Foley's *Goliath*, followed by *Orion*, *Audacious*, *Theseus*, and *Culloden*. The last-named ran aground on an outlying spit, and, though serving as a useful buoy for some late arrivals, gave Captain Troubridge a desolate night. All the rest passed safely by, pressing between the French ships and the shoal water, firing broadsides as they went, then anchoring by the stern opposite their agreed adversary and letting loose, one by one, a most bloody hammering.

The enemy had been caught unawares: their landward guns were useless, the decks and gunports being cluttered with stores, furniture, bags, boxes, and lumber of all kinds. Some had been half-shorn of their crews, who were trapped ashore, storing and watering. The blind side was a gift from the gods.

The *Vanguard* led the seaward squadron, which anchored in its turn, so that most French ships had a foe menacing them on either side. After that, there was nothing but darkness, blood, and death.

Caught in a deadly cross-cannonade, ships began to lose their masts and take fire, ships began to sink, ships began to cut their cables and run for the beach. There was no lack of sublime French courage, but there was also murderous disadvantage in fire power.

Ships began to haul down their colours and surrender. The thunder and the glare of battle was so awesome that weaker men died of shock. Then, after two hours of this pitiless grappling, one small strong man was hit. Standing on the quarterdeck with Matthew Lawe and Berry, Nelson was struck on the brow by a piece of langrel shot, that evil charge of metal scraps, jagged iron, bolts, bars, and links of chain so beloved of the French. It cut to the bone the old wound above his sightless right eye, and carved out a flap of bleeding flesh which blinded the other. He fell to the deck. Matthew Lawe, whom all this monstrous uproar of torn ships, crashing spars, and men shambling down to their death had sickened and terrified, together with Captain Berry, assisted Nelson below. The ghastly figure, pale and drenched with blood, was laid in a cot and the surgeon summoned. He declared the injury to be a flesh wound only; stitched it up, bandaged it, ordered his patient to remain quiet, and went on to other, grosser mishaps.

Flag-Captain Berry returned many times, to report French ships sinking, burned, or surrendered. The total was hardly to be believed. Then Captain Berry reappeared, full of even greater good news: the French flagship, L'Orient, was afire, and like to sink or explode. Few of her consorts in the enemy fleet would survive.

"Help me on deck," Nelson said. "This is a last moment which I *must* see."

He saw it, as did twenty thousand other sailors, fearful or triumphant, on that hell-brew of a night. L'Orient had been painting ship, and paint buckets, oil jars, and wiping-rags had been allowed to accumulate on the upper deck. These had now caught fire, and so had the whole vast ship.

The flames spread greedily from spar to spar, sail to sail, deck to lower deck. The gunners on both sides, as if by agreement, grew silent as they watched the tongues of fire, the whirling sparks, reach up past new-tarred rigging to a black, smoke-laden sky. None had ever seen a mightier, more desolate funeral pyre. But there must be a last fearsome rage to come. As the fire ate downwards into her vitals, it would also devour her powder-magazine.

Matthew, supporting Nelson until he found his feet, watched in horror. He had never been more afraid of what he must soon

148

see. He could not purge this quailing spirit, the sickness of his doom. As one man's courage rose, so another's faded. *For him, fire had once more proved the greatest of all terrors.* Once again, the moment proclaimed the malediction of Francis Drake: anyone who stood near to a valiant man stood in danger of death.

At ten o'clock, *L'Orient* blew up, with a frightful gust of flame. The shattering roar might have been heard ten miles away. There was a pause, like a giant intake of breath, and then the bloody rain began. Torn spars soared upwards, then plunged back into the sea. Flaming timbers hissed as they reached the fouled water. Burning scraps of sail and rope, like fiery feathers, fell on other ships. Dead men dropped from the sky, as neglected, mistreated dolls.

Then the fire was quenched, and the flagship, with a gallant admiral and hundreds of his men, was engulfed for ever. On Aboukir Bay, silence came down like a pall.

Nelson himself was the first of their company to speak. Compassionate in victory, he said to Matthew: "If we have a floatable boat left, send off Lieutenant Galwey to search for survivors." But there was no answer, and when Nelson turned towards Matthew it was to find his trusted lieutenant in a dead faint.

At sunrise a guilty and ashamed Matthew Lawe, who had woken among wounded men, came furtively on deck. If only he had been struck, as Nelson had been struck; if only he had shed honest blood, gained one livid scar to advertise his valour. If only he had played the man, in place of the mouse.

Astonishingly, he reached the *Vanguard*'s tangled deck to find himself innocent. First Lieutenant Galwey greeted him with nothing in his voice save welcome. When he said: "Good morning, Matthew! Are you well?" it was as one triumphant survivor to another.

"Well enough," Matthew answered, feeling his way back to a world of repute. "I know not what put me down. All I remember is the French flagship bursting apart . . . I am sorry to have been of so little service."

"'Tis the luck of the lottery. There was a man at the foremast who was killed by the same shock. Not a mark on his body, but overboard he must go. . . . I may tell you, you were mourned. The admiral thought you dead."

"But how does he do?"

"Well enough, like yourself. It was a fair deep butcher's slice, but they heal, thank God. He is resting below. So is Captain Berry." Galwey flung one of his arms wide, encompassing the bay, the sunrise, the gory fruits of battle. "Look about you, Matthew. Victory! You will never see a finer scene, if you live to be a hundred!"

The scene was not "finer" than anything, save for a painter requiring the shores of hell for his canvas; but victory it was. Aboukir Bay was an utter, mournful, silent desolation. Most ships had surrendered, two had been destroyed or burned, some were to be spied ashore, as smoking hulks with no colours showing, and no life either. The bay was a soiled pond of charred wood, sodden canvas, spars—the refuse of defeat. For a long moment the two men surveyed the waste around them.

"We were out all night, fishing for swimmers," Galwey said, "But we lifted a poor crop. Perhaps eighty. . . . But think of it. *All* the French fleet is captured or burned! *All!* Well, two line-ships made their escape, and two frigates. But they will not make their fortunes by themselves. The tally is two ships sunk and nine surrendered. That is more than victory. It is *conquest!*"

All over the fleet, after twelve hours of fighting and slaving and enduring the thunder-crack of war, men had dropped asleep at their guns, at the capstan-bars, at the tail-end of a rope. They could not be driven more, nor was there need to drive. The Battle of the Nile was won, and peace after carnage, blessed peace, came swiftly upon them, while on the *Vanguard*, one weeping French survivor related to any one who would listen the most moving story of the night.

Some breeds of men catch fire of their own accord. Some others take marvellous heart from this example. A few may pass on the spark of valour to their children. The French flagship *L'Orient*, in her last moments, had given to mankind a magic, shining pattern of this chain of courage.

Admiral François Paul de Brueys, his body nearly severed in two, legless, with tourniquets on both his stumps, chose to die facing his foes in an armchair on his own quarterdeck. This he did. His flag-captain, Comte Louis de Casabianca, a fighting sailor set in the same mould of bravery, now in supreme and lonely command, fought his ship, eaten to the heart by flames, until shortly before her end. Then he was hit, and fell, and on his deck he died.

He was not, in death, so lonely. He was loved. He had with him his son Jacques, just old enough to be an *aspirant*, a midshipman. Ten years was never a great age, but great enough for love and valour mixed. Jacques de Casabianca cradled his father's body until the last, and then, drenched with the dearest blood of his life, stood up and looked about him. He found himself alone, within a roaring curtain of fire; alone save for the terrorized men now leaving their guns, and every other duty, and leaping into the sea.

He did not leap, he stayed. Thus, till the end of time, the boy stood on the burning deck, whence all but he had fled; and was ripped to immortality as the ship went up in fire.

ON HER SLOW JOURNEY back to Naples, the battered *Vanguard* was dismasted in a gale. Taken in tow by the frigate *Thalia*, she made harbour as a limping cripple. News of the greatest victory of British naval arms for a hundred years or more had preceded them. There were flags and fireworks and crowds everywhere. The bay was filled with hundreds of pleasure craft, some with bands trumpeting out a fair version of "Rule Britannia!" The saluting guns ashore did not wait for the *Vanguard*'s courtesy; they began to blaze away as soon as the ship was sighted, to make clear to the world where the honour lay—with Nelson, the Victor of the Nile. The French had been rendered shipless in the Mediterranean, at one glorious stroke, and Naples was to be the first city to celebrate it.

The anchor plunged down and the barge of His Britannic Majesty's Ambassador left the quay and ploughed towards them. It was "ladies first" up the ladder, and the first lady followed by Sir William Hamilton, was a sight for the weariest of eyes. When Nelson saw Emma Hamilton, after a lapse of five years, he could be in no doubt that a warm welcome was his.

At thirty-three, she had grown a little stouter—or, in accordance with taste, to a most noble armful. She wore a billowing blue gown, a scarf embroidered with gold anchors, and a spangled head-band inscribed "Nelson and Victory". What she saw so suddenly was what Matthew and all others who sailed with him saw, and had grown accustomed to for many years: a small ruin of a man, battle weary, with one empty sleeve, one shaded eye, and now a fresh bandage to mask yet another wound gained in the service of his country.

She might have been overcome by his appearance, or by the blast of saluting gunfire, or by real and deep feeling. She might have rehearsed a truly dramatic Attitude. It mattered nothing to either of them.

Emma Hamilton gasped: "Oh God, is it possible?" and tottered towards him. Then, as Sir William looked on with appropriate if controlled concern, she was taken by what seemed to be a fainting fit, fell upon Nelson's breast, and there remained for ever.

<hr>

4

IF BLESSED old Sam Pepys had been casting "The Accounts of Lord Nelson", Matthew Lawe's quick-writing fingers would, in July of 1800, have noted as follows:

ITEM: He is Rear-Admiral of the Red, Baron Nelson of the Nile, Duke of Bronte in Sicily, and Baron Crocodile to his mistress; Freeman of the City of London; possessor of a vast collection of tasselled swords of honour, gold medals, jewelled stars, diamond-studded boxes, gifts from Eastern potentates and Western men-of-business; recipient of a grant of £10,000 from the East India Company, and a parliamentary pension of £2,000 a year.

ITEM: His *amour* is the accepted scandal of the fleet, the grim reproach of established society, and the delight of the populace.

ITEM: He has lost arm and eye, health and spirits, in the most gallant public service; knit together a Mediterranean fleet which is paramount over six thousand square miles of blue water; earned the love of every sailor who comes near to him, and a grudging respect from disapproving masters at home.

ITEM: He is recalled to London, with Sir William Hamilton, both out of favour yet rapturously admired.

BALANCE: I swim against the stream with the Bard of Avon, and must declare: Take him for all in all, he is a Man, We shall not look upon his like again.

The trio of Nelsonians, as they were now named by shocked

or envious society, Lord Nelson, Lady Hamilton, and a contented Sir William, made an almost royal progress to Florence, Trieste, Vienna, Prague, Dresden, and Hamburg on their four months' journey home. At every significant pause, British ambassadors and ministers gave them hospitality.

Her ladyship had grown large in every particular; her voice was louder, her laughter more piercing, her appetite for liquor noticeable, and her figure opulent as a dream of Venus. She loved company, and could scarcely endure without it. Among many other pastimes, she had formed a passion for gambling. Thus, everywhere they travelled, everywhere they lodged, there must be concerts, dinner parties, balls, and card parties. Lord Nelson, it was remarked, shared no such taste for gaming, and would sometimes fall asleep at the table. But he seemed to dote upon her in all else.

Sometimes, it was further remarked, she was taken with sudden sickness, and had to leave the company. Sir William, with whom, by a natural equation, Matthew now spent more time than with anyone, dismissed it as of small concern. Indeed Emma Hamilton would always recover briskly, and regain her spirits, and with them her taste for feasting, loud laughter, and outrageous play.

They landed at Yarmouth, in the common mail-packet, no frigate (though requested) having been sent by a censorious Admiralty to accommodate the Hero of the Nile. But the good citizens of Norfolk, knowing well enough both the common gossip and the disapproval of authority, made an English decision that they liked a naughty admiral with victory tucked under his belt.

As church bells pealed, as fireworks pierced a gloomy November sky and lantern lights proclaimed the now universal motto, "Nelson and Victory", the Nelsonian coach was pulled upwards from the harbour by loyal and loving townfolk. The mayor gave their own hero the freedom of the town, and set him down to an honest English dinner.

Ale was flowing freely as a distinguished party advanced to show themselves on the balcony of their hotel. Lord Nelson delivered a modest speech of thanks; Emma Hamilton made a brief appearance to the roars of a lustful mob; Sir William bowed his thanks; and Nelson again, his glittering medals aflame under the lamplight, with Matthew Lawe holding his scarlet-lined boat-cloak, bowed and waved. The hero was home again. To the greatest storm of all his forty-two years.

What was sweet triumph in Norfolk was poison in London: poison to the court, to the Admiralty, to society in general. It was poison, of a particular kind, to a blameless, injured, Lady Nelson.

She had waited so long, in the dullness of a workaday world, in dry virtue, for the rewards of constancy and the fruits of a glittering career: hearing nothing meanwhile save tales of sunshine far away, splendid palaces, royal favours, victories, honours, and Lady Hamilton. Now the man was returned to her. But though they shared the same roof at last, she waited still for reassurance, for love, for anything.

Time and chance had stolen it away. He had been too long absent. It did not need an hour to discover that she was out of favour. As Emma Hamilton could do nothing wrong, Fanny Nelson could do nothing right.

Apart from his fascination with a beautiful woman, when set against his duty to share bed and board with a dull and sallow mate, he had a deep source of irritation, pricked by his own guilt, in their only remaining bond, Josiah Nisbet. Josiah, spoiled by great connections, had gone downhill like a shambling bullock. His stepfather had always advanced his career, begged pardon for his shortcomings, and stood him up again. But there seemed no means whereby an uncouth lout could be turned into an officer. Given command of the frigate *Thalia* at the age of nineteen, Captain Nisbet, with hardly any delay, was in dire disgrace, for drunkenness, incompetence, and insufferable conduct towards his officers.

His immediate commander, Admiral Duckworth, confessed to Nelson that he was unable to allow this useless fellow to remain on his station. He added a suggestion that Josiah should spend some months with Lady Nelson. There could have been no prescription more unfortunate in its undertones. Unfairly, with hatred and frustration mixed, it was something else against Fanny.

London was a disaster. Flaunting themselves at the theatre, Lord Nelson and Emma drew all eyes. But they were never a pair. Behind them in the box, were two others: a courteous, withdrawn Sir William, and a grey shadow who was the hero's wife. A frightful scene at an evening supper party, in surroundings of great consequence, finally brought down the curtain on a nuptial dance of the dead.

When Matthew Lawe presented himself at Lord Nelson's new house in Dover Street, with a hired carriage to convey his admiral's wife to the party at the home of a relenting Lord of the Admiralty, he knew the awkwardness of his arrival alone. "Good evening, your ladyship," he said as he was ushered into the drawing room. Lady Nelson was, as usual, pale and drawn; the purple satin and the strange jewelled turban which was now the foolish rage of London looked no more than hesitant play-acting. She could not match the most modest rival. . . . When she glanced beyond him in search of another figure who should have been there, Matthew knew that all excuses would seem lame.

"Good evening, Mr. Lawe. Is his lordship below?"

"No, my lady. He sent apologies for a change of plans, and asked me to escort you to Admiralty House. He will join you there."

Lady Nelson considered this. He saw the look in her face which he had seen so often: the look of disappointment, of resignation, of defeat. There had been many such slights in the past month. She said: "Where is he detained?"

"At Grosvenor Square. He had some business with Sir William."

She rose, a small sad figure in her absurd finery. "Very well," she said bitterly, "I am ready."

As they arrived before Admiralty House, there was the usual group of idlers waiting for their hero. They raised a stir as Matthew's dress uniform was sighted, and then fell silent when he was recognized to be a lesser man. For Fanny Nelson there was nothing at all.

The company which presently assembled upstairs had to wait almost an hour for the last three guests to make their appearance. Yet they were forgiven their tardiness. Sir William Hamilton was his usual quiet self; Emma came in under full sail, like a swan among sparrows; Lord Nelson, haggard, lean as a drumstick, was gold-braided from head to foot and bemedalled from arm to empty sleeve. They were applauded and led to the shining supper table. An hour later, all harmony was shattered as a cruel farce was played to its very end.

The distinguished guests at the supper party, some of them

still reserved, a few censorious, all agog, were no match for the Nelsonians. Nelson himself, seated between his hostess and Lady Hamilton, was resplendent. Emma Hamilton was at her best —or worst: blooming like the most overblown rose in the Garden of Eden, noisy, screeching with laughter at the smallest display of wit, flushed with wine, and above all fondly attentive to the hero of the hour.

She cut up his meat as he directed, and passed choice morsels to his opened lips, her eyes liquid with adoration. He received all this like a boy who had fallen among shepherdesses in some pastoral romp, and found one in particular who would satisfy every appetite.

It was scandalous, and touching, and beyond belief. This was the man, Matthew Lawe thought, from his safe station far down the table, who had boarded the *San Josef* and routed the French fleet at the Nile, and fought like a tiger wherever he was engaged. This was the hero, the admiral?

For Lady Nelson his wife, seated across the table with a full view of this charade, it was worse than rejection, it was public insult. But brave in her desolation, she decided to make a small fight of it. When dessert was served, she took a small handful of walnuts, cracked them, peeled them, and leant forward to offer this small tribute to her husband. It was irritably brushed aside, almost struck away, by a man who could not bear to have his attention disturbed. Guests and servants alike looked on aghast as the violence of the gesture sent a broken wine glass reeling across the table.

In an atmosphere electrical, Lady Nelson was seen to be in tears. She could only be an object of pity. But even now her moment was stolen from her. In the silence, Emma Hamilton announced that she must retire. She rose, and suddenly it was no charade: she was trembling, deathly pale, and near to fainting.

Nelson, glaring across the table, exerting a monstrous will, seemed to be directing his wife to support her and, after a moment, it was Fanny Nelson who helped her stricken rival from the room.

Time passed, conversation languished, save for the low voices of scandalized guests: the supper party seemed in suspense. Lord Nelson, with an empty place by his side, had turned glum and irritable. Presently, after an oppressive silence, he drank off his wine, and signalled Lieutenant Matthew Lawe with an imperious turn of his head, to go scouting ahead and see what was in the wind.

Followed by the stares of the company, Matthew rose, bowed to his hostess, and swiftly passed through the doorway, and out into the passage. He had not long to search. Emma Hamilton had not been able to reach the safety of a retiring room before she succumbed to violent sickness. She was, with Lady Nelson, in the partial seclusion of a side-closet, which was hung with coats and hats. Fortunately it also held a sofa, and a wash-hand-stand with ewer and basin. One small lady was still holding the head of one large one, to assist her in some last spasms of vomiting.

Aware of a shadow, Fanny Nelson looked up, met Matthew's eyes and nodded. Presently, in a sort of pale alliance they assisted Emma to the couch. Recumbent, her clothing in disarray, her recent stoutness was unmistakable in its origin. Even under the voluminous fashions, her pregnancy could be seen to be far advanced, perhaps as much as seven months.

Matthew in his commonsense heart had known of it; Fanny Nelson had not. At a stroke she perceived the degrading truth, and all its implications, and its insult to her own barren state. She ceased her ministrations as if her patient were already dead of the plague, and rose to her feet. Then Lady Nelson looked down, as Emma opened wan eyes, and spoke: "Your ladyship should really take more care." With this barbed comment Lady Nelson quit the room, and the house, and a world of treachery, and saw her lord no more.

Lord Nelson was shortly ordered away by the Admiralty, which could trust no other man, to prepare a new fleet for a new battle, and another matchless victory, this time against the Danes in Copenhagen.

Matthew, a man for all occasions, was left behind to settle his lordship's papers—in fact, to aid in the delivery of twins, the burial of one and the spiriting away of another. This was a live girl child, carried off to a trusted wetnurse. Sir William, after expressing hopes that his wife had recovered from her recent indisposition, retired to peaceful sleep: the most temperate of men, and surely the wisest human being of all.

HE MAN at the edge of the tide mark stood a little apart from the crewmen as the admiral's barge from the *Victory* waited at the foot of Southsea Steps, close by Portsmouth Harbour. He had his watch to keep, and they their tongues to wag: the admiral's coxswain would keep order enough, without any aid from Lieutenant Lawe. Thus Matthew waited alone—though no more than a few yards from the greatest Portsmouth throng he had ever seen.

Above him, the ramparts of the town were crowned with a huge press of people, come to bid farewell to the *Victory* and to her admiral, Lord Nelson, who was the darling of all England. These Portsmouth crowds had besieged his inn all morning. Since it was a Saturday—the fourteenth day of September, 1805—the holiday throng was immense. Thus he was delayed.

He had been delayed in the same fashion all over London, where he had spent his brief leave after two years of ceaseless shipboard life, ceaseless chasing of the French. People could not bear to let him pass without saying what they had to say, whether with words, or staring silence, or out-thrust arms. They said, or yearned to say: "You are England. You are us afloat. Go out to fight—but we beg you to *live!*"

They loved him, and must see him, and cheer him, and touch him if they could. It would always be so, in admiration and honour until the very end, which might have come at Cape St. Vincent, or Calvi, or the Nile, or Copenhagen: an end which must fall due one day—and by now, that "one day" was already late, in the envious calendar of chance. Every story in the world must have its stop, and every myth of greatness its reduction to the bare bones of truth.

The myths abounded. They had started long ago with Nelson's lost eye, and the lost arm, and the triumph of the Nile; and had grown even greater with the victory of Copenhagen.

There Nelson had been second-in-command to a hesitant admiral, Sir Hyde Parker, who in the heat of battle had hoisted a signal of recall. It was disobeyed. Nelson first pretended that it had not been reported to him; then, reminded by an anxious signal-midshipman as he walked to and fro on a blood-slippery deck, he put his telescope, supported on the shoulder of a grinning seaman, to his blind eye, searched the admiral's flagship, and remarked to his flag-captain, for all the world to hear: "I have only one eye, Foley. I have a right to be blind sometimes."

He had gone on to a victory complete and undeniable. The Board of Admiralty had replaced Hyde Parker as commander-in-chief—with Lord Nelson himself. The common people loved every moment of it, and another true myth was added to the packet of such delights.

There was, as always, some swinish radical comment. A cartoon of the day showed a huge Emma Hamilton surrounded by empty wine bottles, a tiny lecherous eye-patched Nelson leering in her direction, and a dotard labelled "Old Antiquity" dozing in an armchair. The caption to this masterpiece was singularly vile: "Which has the Copenhagen Eye?"

Old Antiquity himself had died at his house in Piccadilly some two years before, having moved there for the very purpose, from the estate called Merton Place in Surrey which the three had shared since Copenhagen. He died in Emma's arms, and holding Nelson's hand, in perfect peace, proclaiming to the end the honourable conduct, beyond any reproach, of a distinguished naval officer, and named him, in a last codicil to his will, as "my dearest friend, Lord Nelson, the most virtuous, loyal, and truly brave character I ever met with; God bless him, and shame fall on those who do not say Amen."

It was at Merton, extravagant, blessed, peaceful Merton, that Lord Nelson had spent his leave of twenty-five days, enjoying the company of his "wife in the eyes of God", and playing with his daughter, baptized Horatia, now nearing five years old.

This was the bliss which, with urgent news that the French fleet was at sea off Cadiz, he must now exchange for battle—and now, here he was to do so!

Far away along the ramparts of Portsmouth a distant roar of cheering swelled, heralding the man. Matthew, climbing half a dozen steps upwards for a better view, saw what he had been waiting for, and knew, and loved, and often feared for its close acquaintance with death: Horatio Nelson, a small figure, but gleaming, bright as the buttons on God's creation robe, walking along the shoreline, the fatal edge of the tide mark, before he took to the sea.

Matthew was quick to step down again, and send the barge's crew back to their stations—oars raised upright, caps off, legs crossed, backs straight—and to acquaint another man of rank with the news: Flag-Captain Hardy, who had been sitting in his admiral's barge, ready to welcome him back to the *Victory*.

Matthew announced: "He is sighted, sir." Huge Hardy, who could not walk upright in the *Victory's* great cabin for fear of breaking his skull on the massive beams above, also stepped ashore to greet his master.

Lord Nelson came into view. Huzza! was the cry as the greatest sailor in the world passed through the crowds. But many knelt as he passed, and kept silence, or wept. This great sailor was off to battle again. Battles wounded, battles killed. It was a time for prayer, not picnic jollity.

The Right Honourable the Viscount Nelson, Vice-Admiral of the White, shook a few urgent hands, and began to descend his last sixteen steps towards the sea. He was pale, infinitely composed, yet jaunty as a magpie on a bough. Taking his last step downwards, he acknowledged the salutes of his flag-captain, his lieutenant, and his colonel of marines. He smiled up at Hardy: "Are we ready for sea?"

"Aye, my lord."

There had never been any other answer.

To Hardy his lordship said: "God bless you." And to Matthew, with another intimate smile: "God bless us all. . . . Now—on board, and off to work!"

Five weeks later, and some twelve hundred sea-miles from Portsmouth, at noon on October the twenty-first, 1805, while the world checked its breath, the battle of Cape Trafalgar began off the southwest coast of Spain at the entrance of the Straits of Gibraltar. As the two fleets faced each other—27 English ships-of-the-line, 33 fine Frenchmen and Spaniards— Lord Nelson held the whole of Europe in his hand. One mistake, one change of wind, one wrong helm order, might deliver up the freedom of the seas, and a whole continent, to the strangling will of Napoleon. The invasion of England would result and would only precede a universal tyranny.

He knew it all, in his head and heart, and with his head he had made his dispositions. After skilful night-time manoeuvres, with plenty of false signals from rockets, guns, and Bengal lights for the enemy, and none but the truth for his fleet, dawn found him with his two lines of battle poised to strike, ten miles to windward of the enemy—a sailor's masterpiece planned a full year before. Now only the heart, with its courage, was needed.

At noon—the great scale of time was shrinking down to half a day—that plan was unfolding with a majestic slowness, the wind having fallen light. The two columns of the English fleet, one led by the *Victory* with twelve battleships, the other by Admiral Collingwood in the *Royal Sovereign* with fifteen, were moving to cut through the enemy lines, a massive bent bow five miles long. Once there, they would lay about them till the fight was over.

It was a perilous plan, since before the general action was joined the two leading ships would be unsupported, and must take their punishment. But all Nelson's captains had long been in accord with it, and all knew their duty, which was for ever governed by their admiral's final words: "If signals cannot be seen, no captain can do very wrong if he places his ship alongside that of an enemy."

Certainly he had noble ships in company: the *Téméraire*, the beloved *Agamemnon* under the command of Edward Berry; *Bellerophon* and *Spartiate*, old crocodiles of the Nile battle, *Polyphemus* and *Defiance* of Copenhagen, *Euryalus* his most faithful frigate, the *Orion*. To Nelson, it was all perfection. Old ships, old friends. . . . The wind fell lighter still as the two British lines in their livery of black and yellow, copied from the admired *Victory*, came slowly within range, and the thunder of the guns began.

Captain Blackwood, who as commander of the frigate squadron had remained on board the flagship to receive his last instructions, was bidden farewell when the first French shots were fired. He had spent some time in trying to persuade his admiral to transfer to the *Euryalus*, and direct the battle from a safer vantage point.

But Nelson would have none of it. "For the sake of example" he would not quit the *Victory*, where men were stripped bare-chested for action and gun-crews were itching to blast off, where bands were playing "Rule Britannia!" on the poop-deck.

Blackwood, taking his leave, was left to remember a foreboding goodbye, delivered in unmistakable words as he stepped down the ladder: "God bless you, Blackwood. I shall never speak to you again."

At half-past noon—the time scale of this sailor's world was now reduced to hours—the pell-mell battle was in full roar, with frightful carnage on both sides. It was close work, ship to ship, marksman to marksman, and presently hull to hull. Shots were seen to meet in mid-air as the gun duels became point blank. The *Victory*, which had taken a merciless battering from three of the enemy before she could bring her own guns to bear, at last engaged the *Bucentaure*, the flagship of Admiral Villeneuve, one of the two French captains to escape from the Nile, with a score to settle.

The *Victory*, a three-decker, had one hundred guns at her disposal, and a fearsome piece of ordnance on the foredeck to back them up: a 68-pound carronade which fired a round shot preceded by a keg of five hundred red-hot musket balls.

One single broadside, double-shotted, with the help of this foredeck monster, reduced the *Bucentaure* to disabled silence. Then, on the other side, the French *Redoutable* was seen to be approaching, and raking them with langrel shot. A moment later Mr. Scott, the admiral's secretary, standing close to Lord Nelson, and not five feet from the huge-framed Hardy, whose shoe-buckle had already been torn off, was cut in two by her second broadside.

It was Matthew Lawe, searched for diligently all over the ship, who must now take his place.

Since the first splintering shots had begun to assail the *Victory*, Matthew had been skulking—he could not, in his own soul, find any other word for it—in the dark cockpit, where the first wounded of the battle were beginning to be carried down. Summoned by a master's mate, he climbed up to a fearful scene. The rage of battle was the worst he had ever known. But first of all, as he peered out of the quarterdeck hatch, he was aghast at the brightness of his admiral.

Nelson was clad in no more than the blue and white of his working rig. Yet the gold braid caught the sun, the hat proclaimed his rank, the blaze of stars on his breast attested to four orders of knightly splendour. A cockatoo among crows could not have made a better target for a hunter.

Beyond him, the decks of the *Victory* had already been brought close to ruin. Though poor Scott's body, with many others, had been thrown overboard, much grim evidence remained. The smell of death was not honest powder, but the foulness of scattered entrails. Their topmasts were gone, and their sails in scorched tatters. On the quarterdeck, the wheel had been shot to splinters; the flagship was being steered from below, by ropes and tackles which needed the strong arms of forty men to turn the tiller.

Nelson, observant of this shambles remained cool to iciness, pale as a ghost, yet possessed by his own demon of courage: ready to die, aflame to live and conquer—and watchful of everything. He gave Matthew a keen glance as he drew near. "Mr. Lawe, what are you at?"

"I was helping the surgeon, my lord."

"Well. . . . Is Mr. Beatty busy?"

"Unhappily yes, my lord."

"He will be busier yet. This work is too warm to last. Scott is gone from us. So, transform yourself into a signal-lieutenant, and a secretary." Suddenly he smiled, in that fashion which made men, for ever after remember him as one to love. Matthew felt that his admiral had divined the truth and, as with little midshipmen at their first blood-taste of battle, or old comrades who faltered under a heavy load, was ready to place an instant comforting arm round their shoulders. "Transform yourself also to a friend."

"Willingly, my lord."

"It is all I need."

At one o'clock, amid a continuing, frightful uproar, Captain Hardy approached. He pointed to the *Bucentaure*, which was silent but not yet surrendered, to another ship of the second French line which seemed ready to engage, and last to the *Redoutable*, breathing fire and smoke.

"My lord," Hardy said, cool as his admiral, "we must lay alongside one of them. Which shall it be?"

"It does not matter," Nelson answered, and thus chose his death.

Hardy made straight for *Redoutable*, the fiercest Frenchman of them all. Within minutes they were grappled together, their rigging entangled, their sturdy hulls prepared to bruise each other to pieces and their men to board like tigers.

Redoutable fired langrel shot, poured out musket balls, dropped flaming torches, and tossed down hand-grenades upon the deck. Along the yards her marksmen took aim and fired, and laughed, and sometimes tumbled down to their death. The *Victory* also had her ardent sportsmen.

At forty minutes past one o'clock—the time scale had now shrunk down to such little segments of eternity—Matthew, attending his admiral and noting his orders, signals, and entries for a later battle-journal, saw a blue-coated French marine, perched in the mizzen-top of the *Redoutable* no more than fifteen yards away, take steady aim at himself—or at Nelson by his side. In pure terror, he could do nothing honourable, nor useful. He did not shout a warning, or try to draw his commander aside. Instead, as the *Victory* rolled to a chance bumping from her enemy, he stumbled away, took half a dozen steps, and found himself in safety behind the mainmast, to which Nelson had, long ago in peaceful Portsmouth, nailed a horseshoe. From this shameful lair he peeped out to see his admiral, the true target, fall in a poor heap upon the deck, and heard the gasp of his wounded words to Captain Hardy: "My backbone is shot through."

After many battles, many blows, many false alarms and glimpses of mortality, he was right.

Down and down to the cockpit, the great terminal of pain, was borne Lord Nelson, with a handkerchief spread over his face and across the starry orders of his breast: not in mourning but, at his own wish, in disguise. There were fifty other sufferers below, and bearers coming and leaving. There was enough grief in the ship, without the dread news of their admiral's wound.

Amid the muted noise of battle, the thud of cannonballs tearing at their ship's side, Mr. Beatty the surgeon, with his two assistants, were very busy. The arrival of another crumpled man was nothing; he must take his turn, in accord with Nelson's own fleet orders. So they hacked and sawed, bandaged and strapped, staunched gross wounds, let others take their fatal course. They did their swift best and prayed mercy for their forced transgressions. Surgeons, though angels, were only men.

Then their chief became aware of an extraordinary murmuring round about him. It grew stronger than the shrieks of men under his treatment, invading the cockpit like some unearthly music. The handkerchief had fallen from Nelson's face and chest as he was laid down, and the shocked words of the wounded, themselves sick with suffering, became clear. The music of pity could not, need not be denied. . . . Quickly and mercifully a new patient was stripped and carried to a cot, and Beatty, with great tenderness, made his examination. Though he began: "I will not hurt you more, my lord," he went on to do so, as a necessary probing pursued its course. In ten anguished minutes he had traced, as well as he could, the path of a musket ball, which had pierced the shoulder slightly from above, passed through the chest, struck the spine, and lodged in the muscles below the other arm.

But a surgeon must know more. "My lord, can you hear me?"

"Yes, Beatty."

"Pray tell me what you feel."

Nelson, rallying, spoke remarkably clear: "A gush of blood within the breast, every few minutes. . . . No feeling in my lower parts. . . . Pain—" he gasped suddenly, "much pain in the backbone. Send for Hardy."

"My lord, you must rest."

"I must die, and you know it. Send for Hardy."

While they waited, and Beatty was called away, and men died and others cried out, and the chaplain, fanning with torn strips of paper when the admiral panted for air, gave his lordship constant sips of lemonade, and rubbed the cold flesh of his chest, two watchers in the darkness of the cockpit kept a humble vigil.

They were Matthew Lawe, who had followed down, and a friend of long ago, Gaetano Spedilo, once Sir William's faithful valet and now by natural inheritance, the proud body-servant of Lord Nelson. But Gaetano was no longer proud. He was already reduced to bitter weeping. Matthew was not proud, nor ever would be so again.

Mostly they were silent together. When they talked, it was in whispers. If their cheeks were wet, they only foretold the tears of a world of sailors. "*Tenente,* my eyes are so poor, I cannot see." The tall, whiskered, merry-minded Neapolitan had surrendered to grief. "Is he gone?"

"No, no," Matthew answered, and wished to believe it. "He moves his head."

"But he must die?"

165

"By his look, yes."

"God curse them all! To kill an admiral!"

"They could not have chosen a better."

"And to think that I put such a polish on his stars and orders, not five hours back. And now, and now—sir, do you think that the medals were the mark?"

Matthew could only answer: "Yes."

"*Maledizione!*"

Then the two guilty servants of a great man began to witness his dissolution. It seemed to start with the arrival of Flag-Captain Thomas Masterman Hardy, who was at last freed from his urgent duty on deck to comfort a loved commander. With the greatest irony of all, it was accompanied by the sound of hearty cheering from above.

As Hardy bent over Nelson, the admiral opened his eyes and asked: "Is it Hardy? Thank God! What is the cheering?"

"Fresh surrenders, my lord."

"But none of ours, I hope."

"Not a stick."

"How many of the French?"

"Fourteen for certain, perhaps more. And Villeneuve has struck his flag, and is prisoner on board the *Mars*."

"I had hoped for twenty."

"Twenty will come. . . . How is your lordship?"

"They have done for me, Hardy."

Hardy, looking down on a face already beset with the ghostly pallor of death, could still answer: "Not so. Never so! I hope and pray you will reach London, to report a glorious victory." Then he became Hardy the work-horse sailor again. "My lord, I must leave you now. It is not yet over. There are prizes to be had, and the French may rally. There are brave men afloat today."

"Hardy, you are the best fellow in the world." But Nelson, exhausted by the exchange, now had to whisper: "Bend near."

"What is it, my lord?"

A distressed voice answered: "Do not throw me overboard."

"Never!"

"Let Lady Hamilton have my hair."

The tall flag-captain pressed his hand and left him; and ordinary care, the same for wounded seamen as for stricken

166

admirals, became the rule. An hour passed, as it passed for all, fanning his brow, wiping cold sweat from his forehead, putting a cup to his lips, trying to ease the bursting pain in his back and breast. Then Mr. Beatty, streaked with the blood of a hundred other men, came to his side once more. He had just taken an arm from the socket of a gunner who had immediately died; now he returned to what must certainly be another death: death by pale lantern light, in the heart of a rolling war-torn ship: death inevitable, piteous, and brave.

Nelson's anxious mind was still upon the battle. "Send for Hardy again," he told Beatty. "I have ordered him down four times. Why does he not come? He is killed—I know it!"

Beatty touched a fluttering heart, and then the lower half of a body which had lost all sensation. "My lord, do not concern yourself. I know him to be alive. But he cannot leave his command."

"I will die before he is here!"

"Indeed, my lord, I hope not."

The form of words must have pierced a cloudy brain. Nelson murmured: "Beatty, tell me the truth."

The surgeon answered: "My lord, unhappily for our country, nothing can be done for you," and then turned to hide his tears.

"Oh, God, he is weeping!" the man in the shadows said.

"Who is weeping?" Gaetano asked.

"The surgeon."

"Then the admiral is gone?"

"No. But soon."

"Christ have mercy."

Though he was not yet gone, the scale of time was now to be measured in mere seconds, by the beat of a faltering pulse. As Hardy returned to the cockpit, Lord Nelson began to die in all his three estates, as sailor, man, and lover.

To Captain Hardy he was an admiral, with the care of a fleet, and a beloved ship, still tormenting the brain. Under his poor back he had felt the *Victory* rising and falling to a westerly swell, the forerunner of a storm. He remembered the hungry shoals of Trafalgar, waiting to catch them if they drifted too far. "Anchor, Hardy. Signal to anchor!"

"My lord, do you intend that I should give the order to the fleet? Admiral Collingwood will—"

"While I live, I command! Do *you* anchor, Hardy!"

"Aye, sir."

"Use your judgment. . . . That, I trust for ever. . . . I am going soon. Kiss me, Hardy."

Hardy said: "Farewell, my lord," and kissed him twice, once as he had been ordered and once again, after a long watchful moment, as a strong man alive saluting one who could no longer be numbered in the same company. Then he climbed, as he must, back to his sea service.

To the chaplain, Dr. Scott, Lord Nelson made his last claim on heaven: "Doctor Scott, I have not been such a *great* sinner."

To any who might still hear him: "Take care of poor Lady Hamilton. Thank God I have done my duty."

At half-past four a noble heart cracked and ceased to beat; and to the sound of distant gunfire, after forty-seven years of faithful endeavour, time gave up its value.

With the coming of dusk on this dreadful day, Matthew crept out on deck to survey a scene sublime and tragic. It was a prospect too great for his own grief and shame, which must await another day, another age. All that he could bear to do, this night, was to gaze, and remember, and mourn.

Stillness had fallen on a mighty battlefield, though an eerie churchyard wind persisted, ruffling the water, making what remained of their shrouds and rigging sigh in protest. The westward Atlantic swell which presaged a storm was steadily building, and they must soon go. Sombrely he allowed his eyes to wander. Fifty wounded ships were riding, with little sign of life, on a sluggish, tainted sea. Ships still burning, ships with their sides beaten in. Ships which were mere hulks, with not a spar showing above their decks. Some ships with four hundred killed.

But twenty of the French and Spanish were prizes; and though the *Victory* had fallen cold and silent, there was near by the triumphant *Téméraire* with two captives, one of them the fatal *Redoutable*, lashed on either side.

Would ships be valued more precious than men?

When darkness came, and the far ships faded, the coldest words of all began to go round the fleet, with a midshipman's whispered report: "No admiral's lights on board the *Victory*."

Victory.

Nicholas Monsarrat

"*The Master Mariner* is the product of a 22-year think," says Nicholas Monsarrat. It began in 1956 when he had just finished writing his latest best seller. He was struggling to find a new subject for a book and, as a life-long lover of ships and the sea, he embarked on a trip to all the world's principal harbours, hoping for inspiration. Gradually an idea began to take hold: he would tell the story of what British sailors had done to open up the globe. "I wanted the book to have everything: fighting, exploring, charting, our vast trading pattern. . . ."

What emerged was a plan for an epic novel which would begin with the defeat of the Spanish Armada in 1588 and continue to the completion of the St. Lawrence Seaway in 1958. Ten years later Monsarrat had been twice round the world and had amassed four hundred pages of research notes. Several other books intervened and by the time he sat down to write *Running Proud* in 1974 he realized that he would have to read most of the reference books all over again.

Monsarrat is now at work on Matthew Lawe's second two hundred years. He and his wife Ann, also a writer, work at their home on Gozo, a small island off Malta. "I live in a little village where nothing happens," he says. "In the morning the flock of goats goes past. In the evening it comes back. It's ideal writing country."

Born in Liverpool in 1910, Monsarrat read Law at Cambridge, but after a brief stint in his uncle's legal firm in Nottingham ran off to a London garret, where he made a scant living as a freelance writer. During World War II he served with distinction in the Royal Navy, and later worked as a British Information Officer, first in South Africa, then in Canada. And all the while he kept on writing.

Monsarrat's twelfth book, *The Cruel Sea*, based on his wartime experiences, became a runaway best seller. Its success made it possible for him to devote all his energies to writing. "I love it," he says. "To make a living from writing is a miracle." He works seven days a week, producing exactly six hundred words a day. "I know it sounds a bit machine-like, but as long as one knows it's a good book, that's all that counts."

THE SNOW TIGER

A condensation of the book by
DESMOND BAGLEY

Illustrated by Walter Stackpool

PUBLISHED BY COLLINS

*Snow is not a wolf in sheep's clothing, it
is a tiger in lamb's clothing . . .*

Hukahoronui, a tiny New Zealand mountain
town, discovers the grim truth of this
statement when a "snow tiger" in the form of
an avalanche claws through the community
in a matter of minutes, destroying everything
in its path.

   The far-flung links of the past and the
present knit together at the ensuing Court
of Inquiry; Ian Ballard, the newly-appointed
manager of the local mine, and grandson of
the founder of the mining corporation, fights
to justify a decision of his which cost many
lives . . . and gave his enemies an
unparalleled opportunity to brand him
scapegoat.

PROLOGUE...

It was not a big avalanche, but it did not need to be very big to kill a man, and it was only because of Mike McGill's insistence on the Oertel cord that Ballard survived. Just as a man may survive in an ocean with the proper equipment and yet drown in a foot of water, so Ian Ballard may have perished in a minor slippage that would have gone unrecorded even in avalanche-conscious Switzerland.

McGill, a Canadian, was a good skier, and he had taken the novice under his wing. They had met during an après-ski session and had taken an immediate liking to each other. Although they were the same age McGill appeared to be the older man, possibly because of his more varied life as a meteorologist and expert on snow. He became interested because Ballard had much to teach of areas other than snow and ice. They complemented each other, which is not an uncommon basis for friendship.

One morning McGill proposed something new. "We've got to get you on to soft snow. There's nothing like cutting a first track."

They went up by the chair-lift, and after an hour arrived at the top of the clear slope McGill had chosen, following local advice. He unzipped a pocket of his anorak and produced two coils of red cord, one of which he handed to Ballard. "It looks all right, but we won't take chances. Tie one end around your waist."

"What for?"

"It's an Oertel cord—a simple device which has saved a lot of lives. If there's an avalanche and you get buried there'll be a bit of that red cord on the surface to show where you are so you can be dug out fast."

Ballard looked down the slope. "Is there likely to be an avalanche?"

"Not that I know of," said McGill cheerfully. "If I thought there was serious risk we wouldn't be going down at all. But *any* snow on *any* slope can be dangerous."

Ballard began to tie the cord. McGill said, "Do you know what to do if the snow does slide?"

"Start praying?"

McGill grinned. "The first thing is to throw the sticks away, then snap off the fastenings on your skis. When the snow hits, try to head up to the surface. Hold your breath and bring one arm in front of your face, but not too close—that will give you an air space to breathe, and maybe you can shout so that someone can hear you." He laughed at the expression on Ballard's face, and said lightly, "Let's go. I'll go first, not too fast, and you follow and do what I do."

He launched himself down the slope of virgin snow and Ballard followed and had the most exhilarating ride of his life. The cold wind keened past his ears, apart from that the only sound was the hiss of his skis. At the bottom of the slope he said enthusiastically, "That was great! Let's do it again."

THE LATE afternoon sun was sending long shadows across the snow as they reached the top of the slope. McGill said, "Keep to the centre in the sunlight; don't go into the shadowed areas."

Ballard took off and McGill followed, keeping an eye on Ballard for faults for future instructions. All went well until he noted that Ballard was swinging towards steeper ground where shadows lay. He increased speed, calling out, "Keep to the main slope, Ian."

Even as he shouted he saw Ballard trip. Then the whole slope started to slide, taking Ballard with it in a swirl of powder snow. A rumble filled the air with the noise of soft thunder.

Ballard found himself in a world of mad instability, upside

174

down and rotating violently. Suddenly he felt an excruciating pain in his left thigh, as though his leg was being unscrewed from the hip. The tumbling motion ceased and he remembered what McGill had said about making an air space about his mouth, so he brought up his left hand across his face. Then all motion stopped and Ballard was unconscious.

McGill waited until there was no further movement and then skied to the edge of the tumbled snow. It took him half an hour to explore the area and he found nothing. In his mind he could see a graph—the length of time buried plotted against the chance of survival. He reached the lower edge of the slide and looked up indecisively. He would make one five-minute pass and if he did not find anything he would head back to the ski lodge to find expert help—including an avalanche dog.

He went upwards slowly, his eyes flickering from side to side, and then he saw a tiny fleck of blood-red. It was less than the size of his little finger-nail but it was enough. He hauled on the red cord until he came up against resistance, then started to dig with his hands. The snow was soft, and he came across Ballard at a little more than three feet deep. When he cleared Ballard's body he knew that the left leg, from its impossible position, was broken.

He took off his anorak and tucked it closely around Ballard to keep him warm. Then he set off to the road below where he was lucky enough to stop a passing car.

Less than two hours later Ballard was in hospital.

SIX WEEKS later Ballard was still bed-ridden. His leg was a long time in healing because the muscles had been torn. He had been flown to London on a stretcher, whereupon his mother had swooped on him in his mews flat and carried him to her home.

One morning he heard raised voices coming from the floor below. The door opened and his mother came in, stormy in the brow. "Your grandfather insists on seeing you," she said curtly. "I told him you're not well but he's as unreasonable as ever."

"Bring him in Mother; there's nothing wrong with me besides a bad leg."

Ian had not seen old Ben Ballard for a year and a half and he was shocked at the transformation. His grandfather looked every day of his eighty-seven years. He came in slowly, leaning heavily upon a blackthorn stick, and lowered himself creakily into a chair. He surveyed Ian sardonically. "So you went skiing and you couldn't even do that right. Was it on company time?"

"No," said Ian equably. "And you know it. It was my first holiday for nearly three years."

"Humph! But you're lying in that bed on company time."

Ian's mother was outraged. "You're heartless!"

"Shut up Harriet," said the old man without turning his head. "And go away."

Ian caught his mother's eye and nodded slightly. She stormed out of the room.

"Your manners haven't improved," Ian said flatly.

Ben wheezed with laughter. "That's why I like you, boy; no one else would have said that to my face. I didn't mean what I said about you lying in bed on company time—because you're not. You've been replaced."

"Fired!"

"There'll be a job when you're fit enough. Nearly four years ago we opened a gold mine in New Zealand. Now that the price of gold has gone up, the prospects are good. The managing director is an old idiot called Fisher, but he's retiring next month."

Ian was cautious. "Would I have sole responsibility?"

"You know the managing director is responsible to the board."

"Yes, and I know the Ballard set-up. The board dances on strings pulled from London. I have no wish to be office boy to my revered uncles. I don't know why you let them get away with what they're doing."

"When I set up the Trust I relinquished control. What your uncles do is their business now."

"And yet you have a managing directorship in your gift?"

Ben offered a sharklike grin. "Your uncles are not the only ones who can pull strings from time to time."

Ian thought about it. "Where is this mine?"

"South Island." Ben's voice was studiedly casual. "Place called Hukahoronui."

176

"*No!*" It was torn from Ian involuntarily.

"What's the matter? Scared to go back?" Ben's upper lip drew back. "If you are then you're no blood of mine."

Ian took a deep breath. "Do you know what it means? To go back? You know how I loathe the place."

"So you were unhappy there—that was a long time ago. If you turn down this offer you'll never be happy again. For the rest of your life you'll wonder about it."

Ian stared at him. "You're an old devil!"

The old man chuckled. "That's as may be. Now listen. I had four sons and three of them aren't worth the powder to blow 'em to hell. They're crooked, and they're making Ballard Holdings into a stink in the City of London." Ben drew himself up. "God knows I was no angel in my time, but nobody ever accused Ben Ballard of being dishonest and nobody ever knew me to go back on my word." His voice became milder. "I had a fourth son and I hoped for a lot from him, but he was ruined by a whining, puling woman, just as she damned near ruined you before I had the wit to jerk you out of that valley in New Zealand."

Ian's voice was tight. "Let's leave my mother out of this."

Ben held up his hand. "I like your loyalty, Ian, even though it's misplaced. But did I do right to get you out of Hukahoronui?"

Ian's voice was low. "I've never thanked you for that."

"Oh, you have a good brain and I didn't like to see it wasted. Bread cast on the waters, boy. I've come for repayment."

"Do I have to make up my mind now?"

Ben's voice was sardonic. "Do you want to talk it over with your mother? You're a grown man of thirty-five. Make a decision of your own for once in your life."

Ian paused, then said, "All right. I'll go to Hukahoronui."

Ben said, "There's quite a town there now. The first mayor was John Peterson. A power in the community the Petersons are."

"Are they still there?"

"Of course. John, Eric and Charlie."

"But not Alec."

"No—not Alec," Ben agreed.

"You're really asking for something, aren't you? You know that putting a Ballard into Huka is like putting a detonator into a stick of dynamite."

Ben leaned forward. "The Petersons being the dynamite, I presume. It's a tough job I've handed you. I want you to run that mine better than it's been run up to now. Dobbs, the manager, is a chronic fence-sitter. Cameron, the engineer, is a has-been. You have to put some backbone into that lot."

He leaned back in his chair. "Of course, the Petersons won't welcome you. It's not likely, is it, when it's a family tradition of theirs that they were robbed of the mine?"

He made as if to rise, then paused. "If anything serious should happen—to Ballard Holdings or to me—get in touch with Bill Stenning." He thought awhile. "On second thoughts, don't bother. Bill will get in touch with you fast enough."

"What's this about?"

"Don't worry; it may never happen." Ben got slowly to his feet and made his way to the door. He stopped halfway and held up the blackthorn stick. "I doubt if I'll want this any more. I'll send it to you tomorrow. You'll need it."

He paused and raised his voice. "You can come in now, Harriet. No need to listen at the keyhole."

BALLARD was depressed as he drove west from Christchurch in a company Land-Rover. He was going back to his origins. Hukahoronui. He hated the place.

A deep valley in the mountains is entered by a narrow rock-split gap. A river runs through, cold from the ice water of the high peaks, and there is a scattering of houses up the valley, loosely centred about a church, a general store and a village school. His mother had once been the schoolteacher.

There had been heavy snowfalls and even with snow tyres Ballard now found the going tricky. After a lot of low gear work he reached the Gap and pulled off on to level ground overlooking the gorge.

Hukahoronui had certainly changed. In the distance was a little township where no township had been. Under the western slope of the valley was a cluster of industrial buildings, presumably

178

belonging to the mine. A streamer of black smoke from a tall chimney was a stain against the white hillside.

Beyond the township in the far distance Ballard saw Turi's house beneath the great rock called Kamakamaru. He wondered if Turi were still alive. He had been an old man even when Ballard left the valley, although age in a Maori is difficult to estimate, especially for a youth of sixteen.

But there was something else about the valley that was strange. The hill slope on the western side was now almost treeless. Gone were the stands of tall white pine and cedar, of kahikatea and kohekohe. The snows stretched from the high slopes to the base in one smooth, beautiful sweep. It looked good for skiing.

He switched on the engine and went down into the town. He was impressed by the way it had been laid out. He could see the areas which, in summer, would be pleasant open gardens and there was a children's playground, the swings and slides, the see-saws and the jungle gym, now stalactited with icicles.

There were houses built along the bluff that projected into the river; when Ballard was a child it was called the Big Bend and was where they had their swimming hole. Peterson's store used to be at the base of the bluff, and so it still was. In his day it had been single-storey with a corrugated iron roof. Now it was two-storey, and there were big plateglass windows brightly lit.

Across the street was a still-raw concrete building, the Hotel D'Archiac. The street was reasonably busy; private cars and industrial trucks passed by and women with shopping bags hurried before the shops closed. Ballard pulled into a parking space, reached for the blackthorn stick and crossed the road leaning on it. He supposed that Dobbs, the mine manager, would have arranged accommodation for him, but it was late in the day and he was quite prepared to spend a night in the hotel and introduce himself to the mine staff the following morning.

As he approached the hotel entrance a brawny man came out quickly and bumped his shoulder. The man made a mutter of annoyance and strode to a parked car. Ballard recognized Eric, the second of the three Peterson brothers.

Ballard turned to go into the hotel and encountered an elderly

179

woman who looked at him with slowly dawning recognition. "Why, it's Ian Ballard, isn't it?" she said.

He hunted through his memories to find a face to match hers. "Hello, Mrs Samson," he said.

"Ian Ballard, whatever are you doing here?"

He looked out of the corner of his eye and saw Eric Peterson staring at him, frozen in the act of unlocking his car.

"Right now I'm going into the hotel to book a room," he said. He was sharply aware that Eric Peterson was walking towards him.

"Ian Ballard." Peterson's voice was expressionless.

Mrs Samson said, "Do you two know each other? This is Eric Peters. . ." Her voice tailed away and the wary look came into her eyes of one who has almost committed a social gaffe.

There was little humour in Peterson's thin smile. "And what are you doing here?"

Ballard said, "I'm the new managing director of the mine."

"Well, well!" Peterson said in tones of synthetic wonder. "So the Ballards are coming out of hiding. Have you run out of phoney company names?"

"Not really," said Ballard. "We've got a computer that makes them up for us. How are you doing, Eric?"

Peterson looked at Ballard's stick. "A lot better than you, apparently. Hurt your leg? Nothing trivial, I hope."

Mrs Samson suddenly discovered reasons for not being there.

Peterson watched her go. "Did I hear you say you are booking a room in the hotel?" He took Ballard's arm. "Let me introduce you to the manager. Johnnie and I own half of this place."

He stopped at the reception desk. "Jeff Weston is manager here. Jeff, this is Ian Ballard, an old friend. Give him the best room we have." His eyes went flinty and his voice hardened. "For twenty-four hours. After that we're full. I wouldn't want you to get the wrong idea of your welcome here, Ballard."

He strode away. Ballard said lightly, "Eric always was a joker. Do I sign the register, Mr Weston?"

That night Ballard wrote to Mike McGill:

I remember you telling me that you'd be in New Zealand this year. Why don't you come out earlier as my guest? I'm in a place called Hukahoronui in South Island; there's a lot of snow and the skiing looks great. Let me know what you think of the idea—I'd like to meet your plane.

SIX WEEKS later Ballard met McGill at the airport in Auckland and they went down to Hukahoronui. Fifteen miles from Hukahoronui they came across a Volkswagen stuck in a drift. It contained two American skiers. They helped haul the car free and received effusive thanks from the two men, Miller and Newman.

"You're going to get stuck again," said Ballard. "You'd better go on ahead and I'll follow." They hauled the Volkswagen out of trouble five times before they reached Hukahoronui. Newman said, "It's real good of you guys to go to all this trouble."

Ballard smiled and pointed. "That's the Gap—the entrance to the valley. Once you're through, you're home and dry."

They watched the Volkswagen descend into the valley, then Ballard pulled off the road. "Well, there is the mine."

McGill surveyed the scene with a professional eye. Frowning slightly, he looked at the white sweep of the western slope. "What do you get out of it?"

"Gold in small quantities," said Ballard. "At present we're just breaking even—just servicing the capital investment of a couple of million pounds sterling. But the pickings are getting richer as we follow the reef."

McGill nodded abstractedly. He was peering at the rock walls on either side of the Gap. "Do you have much trouble in keeping the road clear just here?"

"We didn't seem to years ago when I used to live here. But we're having a fair amount now."

"It'll get worse," said McGill. "I did a check; there's a lot of precipitation this year and the forecast is for more."

"Good for skiers," said Ballard. "Bad for mining."

He drove down through the town to the mine office. "Come and meet the senior staff," he said. He led the way to an inner office where two men were discussing a plan laid on a desk.

Harry Dobbs, the mine manager, was a thin-faced New

Zealander with a dyspeptic expression. Cameron, the engineer, was a broad-shouldered American pushing sixty but not admitting it. They shook hands, and Ballard said, "Everything okay?"

Dobbs said in a thin voice, "The situation is deteriorating at the same rate."

Cameron chuckled. "What he means is that we're still having snow trouble. We had a truck stuck in the Gap yesterday; took two 'dozers to get it out."

"Mike, here, says things will get worse, and he ought to know —he's a snow expert," said Ballard.

"I've been known to be wrong," protested McGill. He looked through the window. "Is that the mine entrance?"

Cameron followed his gaze. "Yes, that's the portal. Most people think of a mine as having a vertical shaft, but we just drove into the mountainside. It slopes down inside as we follow the reef."

Ballard said, "Let's get you settled in, Mike. I'm going to be busy for maybe an hour. I'll get someone to take you to my house." They went into the outer office. "Betty here will show you where it is. The bedroom on the left at the back is yours."

NEARLY THREE hours later, when Ballard came into the house McGill had unpacked, taken a walk around town and returned to the house to make an urgent telephone call.

Ballard winced. "Oh, hell! I forgot to tell Mrs Evans we were coming back. There's no grub ready."

"Relax," said McGill. "There's something in the oven—McGill's Antarctic Burgoo, as served in all the best restaurants south of latitude sixty." They went into the living-room, and McGill said, "I used your phone. I hope you don't mind. Is there a chance of getting a parcel from Christchurch in for me?"

Ballard picked up the telephone. "Cameron has a truck coming from Christchurch. I might catch it before it leaves. Hello, Maureen, can you get me the Christchurch office?"

"I had a look round town. Is most of it mine property?"

"A lot of it. Houses for the married couples and single quarters and a club house for the bachelors. This is a mine house."

"How many mine employees?"

"At the last count it was a hundred and four—including office staff. The total population is a bit over eight hundred."

An electronic voice crackled in Ballard's ear, and he said, "Sam, Dr McGill wants to talk to you—hold on."

McGill took the telephone. "Do you know where Advanced Headquarters for Operation Deep Freeze is? Go to the Headquarters Building and ask Chief Petty Officer Finney there to give you the parcel for me . . . McGill. Right."

"What was all that about?" asked Ballard.

"I just thought I'd keep myself occupied while I'm here." McGill changed the subject. "What's with your Mr Dobbs? He looks as though he's swallowed a lemon."

Ballard smiled wearily. "He reckons he should have been put on the board of directors and given my job. To make it worse, the whole mine is owned by the Ballard family."

"There's a name for that kind of thing—nepotism. No wonder Dobbs is acid," McGill said.

"If it's nepotism it isn't doing me any good," said Ballard. There was a touch of savagery in his voice. "I don't have shares in this or any other Ballard company. I don't have a penny except my director's fees."

"What's the matter? Come from the wrong side of the family?"

"I have a grandfather who's an egotistical old monster and I had a father who wouldn't co-operate. Dad told the old boy to go to hell and he's never forgotten it. The Ballards control companies with a capital value of two hundred and twenty million pounds. Their own shareholdings are about forty-two million pounds. I have three rapacious old uncles and half a dozen cousins who follow the breed. They're only interested in loot and between them they're running the show into the ground."

He breathed heavily. "When I came here I went underground, and that night I prayed we wouldn't have a visit from the Inspector of Mines before I had time to straighten things out."

"Had someone been cutting corners?"

"I doubt any criminal intent, but negligence combined with parsimony has led to a situation in which the company could find itself in serious trouble."

183

"Why stick to a Ballard company if you feel like this?"

"Oh, I don't know—some remnants of family loyalty," said Ballard tiredly. "After all, my grandfather did pay for my education."

McGill noted Ballard's depression and decided to change the subject. "Let's eat, and I'll tell you about the ice worms in Alaska." He plunged into an improbable story.

THE NEXT morning was bright and sunny. When Ballard got up he found Mrs Evans in the kitchen.

She scolded him. "You should have let me know when you were coming back. I only learned by chance from Betty last night. Your friend has gone out already, but he'll be back for a late breakfast."

When he had dressed he found McGill in the living-room unwrapping a parcel which contained sections of aluminium tubing each nestling in an individual canvas pocket. "Your truck got through," said McGill. "These are the tools of my trade."

He wolfed a plateful of bacon and eggs, and pleased Mrs Evans by asking for more. Then he said, "You asked me here for the skiing, and there's no time like the present. How's your leg?"

Ballard shook his head. "The leg is all right, but sorry, Mike—not today. I'm a working man."

"You'd better come and see what I'm doing." Something in McGill's serious tone made Ballard look at him sharply. "I want an independent witness. I'm going to make a professional investigation. You're the boss man of the mine and you've got authority to close it down if need be. But that depends on what I find. I couldn't believe my eyes at what I saw yesterday. It looked like a recipe for instant disaster."

"Where?"

McGill walked to the window and pointed at the steep, blinding white snow slope above the mine. "Up there."

TWO HOURS later they were nearly three thousand feet above the mine and half way up the slope. McGill took off his skis and stuck them vertically into the snow. "Another safety measure," he said. "If there's a slide then the skis will tell someone that we've been swept away."

184

"The last time you talked about avalanches I was in one."

McGill grinned. "Don't fool yourself. You were in a trickle—a mere hundred feet. If this lot goes it'll be quite different." He began to take aluminium tubing from his pack and assemble it. "This is a penetrometer—a sort of pocket piledriver—it measures the resistance of the snow. It also gives us a core, and temperature readings at ten-centimetre intervals. All the data for a snow profile."

There was a sliding weight which dropped down a narrow rod before hitting the top of the aluminium tube and driving it into the snow. Each time the weight dropped McGill noted the distance of penetration and recorded it in a notebook. They added lengths of tubing and hit bottom at 158 centimetres—about five feet.

"There's a hard layer somewhere in the middle." McGill made a connection and plugged the end into a box with a dial on it. "Make a note of these temperatures." He erected a tripod and a miniature block and tackle and started to haul out the tube. As the sections came free he disconnected them carefully and then took a knife and sliced through the ice in the tube. He put the tubes back into the pack, complete with the snow cores they contained. "We'll have a look at those back at the house. Now we do four more in a line diagonally down the slope."

They had just finished the fourth boring when Ballard turned to see three skiers traversing down towards them. When the leader came around in a flashy stem christiana, stopped with a spray of snow and lifted blue-tinted goggles, Ballard recognized Charlie Peterson. The others were the Americans from the Volkswagen, Miller and Newman.

Peterson looked at Ballard with some astonishment. "Oh, it's you! Eric told me you were back." He looked curiously at the dismantled penetrometer. "What are you doing?"

McGill answered, "Testing the stresses on this snow slope."

Charlie grinned at Ballard. "Since when did you become interested in snow? Your Ma wouldn't let you out in it for fear you'd catch cold."

Ballard said evenly, "I've become interested in a lot of things since then, Charlie."

Newman said abruptly, "Let's go, Charlie. I don't know what

you have against this guy and I don't much care. All I know is he helped us yesterday."

Charlie swung around and pointed down the slope. "All right. We go down in traverses—that way first. This is a good slope for practising stem turns."

"Wait a minute," said McGill sharply. "I wouldn't do that. It could be dangerous."

"Crossing the road can be dangerous," Charlie said contemptuously and pushed off. Miller and Newman followed without a word. McGill and Ballard watched them. Nothing happened.

"Who's the jerk?" McGill asked.

"Charlie Peterson. He's set up as a ski instructor."

"I keep forgetting you were brought up here." McGill scratched his cheek reflectively. "I need information. I want to find someone in the valley whose family has lived here a long time."

Ballard thought for a moment, then pointed with his ski-stick. "See that rock down there? That's Kamakamaru, and a man called Turi Buck lives in a house just on the other side. I should have seen him before now but I've been too busy."

When Ballard knocked on the door of Turi Buck's house it was opened by a Maori girl of about fourteen. "I'm looking for Turi Buck," Ballard said, and the girl went away, calling "Grandpa, there's someone to see you."

Turi appeared and Ballard was a little shocked at what he saw; Turi's hair was a frizzled grey and his face was seamed like a water-eroded hillside. "Ian!" said Turi in delight. "I heard you were back. I thought you had forgotten me. Come in."

"Work, Turi; the work comes first—you taught me that. This is my friend, Mike McGill."

Turi led them into a room familiar to Ballard. Over the fieldstone fireplace was a *wapiti* deer head with its great spread of antlers, and a wood fire burned beneath it. On the walls were wood carvings inlaid with shimmering *paua* shell. The greenstone Maori war axe was still there and, in pride of place, Turi's *whakapapa* stick, intricately carved, which gave his ancestry.

"Did that beautiful young lady call you 'Grandpa'?"

"I am a grandfather five times now," Turi said.

"How is Tawhaki?" said Ballard. He had been Ballard's playmate as a child and a constant companion as he grew older.

"He does well," said Turi. "He went to the University of Otago and has a post in the Department of Finance in Auckland."

"I'll look him up when next I'm there." Ballard saw Turi regarding McGill with interest. "Mike is very interested in snow."

Turi's seamed face broke into a grim smile. "Then there's something for you here, Mike. We have more snow than I can remember since 1943."

Ballard went to the window. On the other side of the valley the cedar branches drooped heavily under the weight of snow. He said, "What happened to the trees on the west slope, Turi?"

McGill became alert. "That slope used to be timbered?"

"When they put in the mine they wanted props," Turi said. "The Petersons own that land; they made a good profit. Your mother shouldn't have sold it to them, Ian."

Ballard said, "Didn't anybody think of what would happen when the snow came?"

"Oh, yes," said Turi. "I objected very loudly. But who would listen to an old man?" His lips twisted. "Especially one with a brown skin."

McGill said slowly, "The stupid, greedy bastards. When did you come to the valley, Mr Buck?"

"I was born here. New Year's Day, 1900."

"Who built this house?"

"My father built it in about 1880, on the site of my grandfather's house. My people have lived here a long time."

McGill nodded. "Did your father give any reason for building on the same site? Under this big rock?"

"He said that anyone building in Hukahoronui must take precautions."

"He knew what he was talking about." McGill turned to Ballard. "I'd like to test those snow samples pretty quickly. May I come back to talk to you, Mr Buck?"

"You must both come back. Come to supper." Turi watched them put on their skis and, as they traversed the slope which led away from the house, he waved and called, "*Haere ra!*" (Farewell!)

187

GOVERNMENT OF NEW ZEALAND

The Hearing
of the
Commission of Inquiry
into the
Disaster at Hukahoronui

CHAIRMAN: Dr H. A. Harrison

ASSESSORS: Prof. J. W. Rolandson
Mr F. G. French

SECRETARY: Mr J. Reed

in the Canterbury Provincial Chamber

CHRISTCHURCH, SOUTH ISLAND

AT THE HEARING...

THE great hall in Christchurch, built in the mid-nineteenth century, was floridly magnificent, with a painted and carved ceiling, wood panelling and a lot of stained glass. Three highbacked chairs were set behind the rostrum, and before each chair was a new note-pad with two ball-point pens to the left and three newly sharpened pencils to the right. With the water carafes and the glasses, the whole looked like place settings at a dining table.

The public gallery at the end of the hall was already full. The hum of conversation died as three men took their places behind the rostrum. The man in the centre was elderly with a shock of white hair and deeply lined face. He spoke quietly in an even voice.

"In the winter of this year, on the eighteenth of July, a disaster occurred in the township of Hukahoronui on the South Island of New Zealand in which fifty-four people lost their lives. The New Zealand Government has appointed a Commission of Inquiry, of which I am Chairman. My name is Arthur Harrison and I am Rector of Canterbury University. With me are two assessors, Professor J. W. Rolandson of the Department of Scientific and Industrial Research and Mr F. G. French of the New Zealand Mines Department. The gentleman immediately below me is Mr John Reed, Secretary to the Commission."

Harrison surveyed the tables in the hall. "There are several interested parties present. John Rickman, barrister, representing the Hukahoronui Mining Company, Proprietary, Limited; Michael Gunn, barrister, representing the General Miners' Union of New Zealand and the relatives of its members who lost their lives in the disaster; Alfred Smithers, barrister, representing the Ministry of Civil Defence, and Peter Lyall, barrister, representing Charles Stewart Peterson and Eric Parnell Peterson."

Harrison paused and frowned. "I must warn the legal gentlemen that this is not a court of law," he went on. "It is a Commission of Inquiry, empowered to make its own rules of procedure. The object is to find the truth of what happened during the events which led up to the avalanche at Hukahoronui, during the avalanche itself, and afterwards." He leaned back in his chair.

"We wish to find the truth unimpeded by legal technicalities, and the reason we wish to find the truth is to make certain that such a disaster does not happen again. The force of this consideration is so great that the Commission hereby rules that evidence given here may not be used in any future legal action other than criminal which may eventuate as a result of the avalanche at Hukahoronui. The protection of lives in the future is of more importance than the punishment of those who may be felt to be guilty of acts of omission or commission arising out of the disaster. The Commission is legally empowered to make such a ruling and I hereby do so."

Gunn hastily rose to his feet. "Mr Chairman; do you not think that is an arbitrary decision? There will be matters of compensation arising. If interested parties are denied the use of evidence in a future legal action, surely an injustice will be done."

"Mr Gunn, I have no doubt that the government will appoint an arbitrator who will study the findings of this Commission and make the necessary dispositions. Does that satisfy you?"

Gunn bobbed his head, a pleased expression on his face. "Indeed it does, Mr Chairman."

Harrison put his hands together. "We are gathering information in chronological order. Because of this, any person giving evidence may be asked to step down before his evidence is wholly completed if we find it necessary to do some filling in. I gather that the appearance of Mr Ballard in Hukahoronui led to a series of events which may—or may not—have relevance to the disaster. The first witness should be Mr Ballard."

Reed, the secretary, said, "Will you come forward, Mr Ballard, and sit there?" He indicated an ornately carved chair. "Your name is Ian Dacre Ballard?"

"Yes, sir."

"And you are managing director of the Hukahoronui Mining Company, Proprietary, Limited?"

"No, sir. I was suspended from my duties a fortnight after the disaster."

190

"But at the time of the avalanche were you managing director of the company?" Harrison said.

"Yes, sir."

"Can the witness describe his qualifications for the position?"

Harrison jerked his head to identify the source of the interruption. "You will oblige me by not calling out in this hall, Mr Lyall. However, the question is relevant and the witness will answer."

"I have a degree in mining engineering from Birmingham University. I have done post-graduate studies in South Africa and the United States. I attended the Harvard Business School for two years."

Lyall had his hand in the air. "But no *practical* experience as a mining engineer?"

"As managing director my field was rather that of business administrator."

"A valid point," said Harrison. "A managing director need not have the technical expertise of the men he directs. If it were so, a large number of our managing directors would be immediately unemployed—and possibly unemployable."

He waited until the laughter died away, "Mr Ballard, at what point did you become aware of danger by avalanche?"

"Only a few days before the disaster. My attention was drawn to it by a friend, Mike McGill, who came to visit me."

Harrison consulted a document. "I see that Dr McGill has voluntarily consented to appear as a witness. I think it would be better if we heard his evidence from his own lips."

Ballard returned to his seat. McGill walked towards the rostrum carrying a slim leather satchel. Reed said, "Your name is Michael Howard McGill?"

"Yes, sir."

"It is very public-spirited of you to volunteer to stay and give evidence," Harrison said.

McGill smiled. "No trouble at all, sir. I have to be in Christchurch in any case. I leave for the Antarctic next month. As you may know, the Operation Deep Freeze flights leave from here."

"Will you tell us something about yourself, Dr McGill?" Harrison said.

191

"I took a B.Sc. in physics at the University of Vancouver, M.Sc. in meteorology at Columbia University and D.Sc. in glaciology at the California Institute of Technology. I have spent two seasons in the Antarctic, a year in Greenland at Camp Century, two years in Alaska and I have just completed a year's sabbatical in Switzerland doing theoretical studies.

"At present I work as a civilian scientist in the Cold Regions Research and Engineering Laboratory of the United States Army Terrestrial Science Centre."

Harrison gave a nervous cough. "For simplicity's sake, Dr McGill, how would you describe your employment at present?"

McGill grinned. "I have been described as a snowman." A ripple of laughter swept across the hall. "I should say that I am engaged on practical and theoretical studies of snow and ice which will give a better understanding of the movement of those materials, particularly in relation to avalanches."

McGill unzipped his satchel and took out a sheaf of papers. "I have written an entire report on the events that occurred at Hukahoronui—from the technical side, of course. I submit the report to the Commission. Part One consists of my findings on the first series of snow profiles which was submitted to the mine management and, later, to the municipal authorities of Hukahoronui."

Harrison flipped through the pages and frowned, then he passed the papers to one of the assessors, Professor Rolandson. They conferred in low voices, then Harrison said, "This is all very well, Dr McGill; but your report appears to be highly technical. Could you not describe your findings in a language that can be understood by others apart from yourself and Professor Rolandson?"

"Of course," said McGill. "Indeed, I did so to the people in Hukahoronui." McGill clasped his hands in front of him. "Snow is not so much a substance as a process; it changes in time. It begins with a snowflake falling to earth. It is a six-sided crystal which begins a sort of evaporation and becomes a small, rounded granule. This results in a higher density because the air is squeezed out. Because of the evaporative process, there is water vapour in the snow mass and, due to the low temperature, the separate granules tend to bond together by freezing."

"This bond is not particularly strong, is it?" asked Rolandson.

"Not when compared with other materials. The next thing to take into account is that the temperature through the snow cover is warmer at the bottom than the top. There is still a lot of air in the snow cover and the relatively warm air at the bottom begins to rise, carrying water vapour with it. The vapour precipitates on the colder granules above and a new kind of crystal begins to form —a cup crystal. It's a conical shape, with a hollow in the blunt end, and it's a quarter-inch long on average."

McGill paused, and when Rolandson remained silent, he said, "Graph Two shows the penetrometer readings—that is the resistance of the snow to stress. Half way down on all the samples there is a layer of surface hoar."

Harrison interrupted. "If it is not on the surface how can it be described as surface hoar?"

"It *was* on the surface. Normally, when the sun hits it in the morning it disappears. In this case, I imagine that clouds came over before sunrise and it began to snow again quite heavily. The layer of hoar was covered and preserved."

"With what significance?" queried Rolandson.

"Several things could happen. The layer is quite hard and smooth and could form a sliding surface for the snow above it. The most likely place for cup crystals to form would be just under the hoar layer."

"You emphasize cup crystals. In what way are they dangerous?"

"Because of their rounded shape and because there is very little bonding between one crystal and another. As a rough analogy I would suggest that it would be difficult for a man to walk on a floor loosely packed with billiard balls."

"Was there any evidence of cup crystals forming at this time?"

"They had begun to form in sample one, the highest up the slope. I had reason to believe that the process would continue which would result in a marked decline in stability. The weather forecast indicated more snow—more weight—on that slope. I came to the conclusion that the snow cover on the western slope of the valley was relatively unstable and thus formed a potential avalanche hazard. I informed the mine management.

"The problem was to explain the evidence and to get them to accept it. Mr Ballard had already accepted it. Mr Cameron wanted to go through the figures in detail, but he came around in the end. The others weren't as convinced. It went like this . . ."

AS IT WAS...

I̶T̶ HAD been Cameron, as an engineer, who had seen the true significance of the cup crystals. "Could you draw a picture of one of those, Mike?"

"Sure." McGill made a drawing. Cameron stared at it.

"What you've sketched here is a pretty good picture of a tapered roller bearing. If you get a lot of weight on top the whole hillside could come down on ready-made bearings." He passed the drawing to Dobbs who looked at it with Quentin, the union representative, peering over his shoulder.

Dobbs said, "Are you seriously telling us that there'll be an avalanche which will fall on this mine?"

"Not exactly," said McGill carefully. "What I'm saying is that there is a potential hazard that must be watched. Future snow precipitation and an appreciable rise in wind speed wouldn't help much. You have to take precautions. Protecting the mine portal, for instance. There's a steel construction called Wonder Arch which comes in useful. It's used a lot in the Antarctic."

"Is it expensive?" asked Dobbs. The mine manager's voice was clouded with doubt.

McGill shrugged. "It depends on how much you put money against lives on the balance sheet."

Ballard said, "I'll put it to the board of directors."

"That's not all," said McGill. "That slope is dangerous mostly because it's been stripped of timber. It will have to be stabilized again, and that means building snow rakes. Good snow rakes cost sixty dollars a foot run—I doubt if you'd get away with under a million dollars."

The sound of Dobbs' indrawn breath was harsh. "Then there's the snow deflection walls at the bottom," went on McGill inexorably. "That's more—maybe even half a million."

"The board won't stand for it," said Dobbs. "They're not going to put in that extra capital for no increase in production."

Quentin stirred. "Would you want to close down the mine? My people would have something to say about that. There's a lot at stake. I'm protecting the men's jobs. That's what they put me in here for." Quentin looked at McGill hostilely. "He comes busting in here with his tale of doom, but who the hell is he, anyway?"

Ballard said, "As of yesterday Dr McGill became a professional consultant employed by this company to give us advice on certain problems. Tell them what's really worrying you, Mike."

McGill said, "I'm worried about the town."

There was a silence and then Cameron cleared his throat. "It's snowing again," he said.

AT THE HEARING...

"THAT just about finished the meeting," said McGill. "It was decided that the mine management should consult with the town council. But three of the councillors were absent from town that day and it was impossible to find a quorum. The meeting was held next morning—the Saturday. There was one other person present at my request—Mr Turi Buck. I asked him because he knew more about the history of Hukahoronui than anyone else I'd met."

Gunn had his hand up, and Harrison said, "Yes, Mr Gunn?"

"May I question the witness, Mr Chairman? Dr McGill, the meeting took place on the fifth of July. It is now December, nearly five months later. You have given evidence that Mr Quentin, the elected union leader at Hukahoronui mine, seemed to be more intent on filling the pockets of his comrades than in preserving their lives. Now Mr Quentin is not here to defend himself—he was killed in the disaster. Since I represent the union I must defend him. I put it to you that your recollection of this meeting so long ago may be incorrect."

"No, sir; it is not incorrect."

"If it is your claim to have a memory so much better than other men then I must accept it, I suppose."

"I am a scientist and I am accustomed to taking notes. I wrote up my diary half an hour after the meeting finished."

"Do you know how Mr Quentin died?"

"I know very well how Mr Quentin died."

"No more questions," said Gunn with an air of disgust. "I am quite finished with this witness."

"May I add something?" McGill glanced at Harrison. "The reason the death roll in the Hukahoronui disaster was higher than it need have been lies in the actions, reactions and inactions of many men who were confronted with an unprecedented situation beyond their understanding. Mr Quentin was one such man. I know that he died in the disaster and I know he died heroically. Nevertheless, the truth must be told so that other men, in the future, when faced with a similar situation will *know* the right thing to do."

"*Mr Chairman!*" Rickman was on his feet, finger upraised. "This is monstrous! Must a witness make speeches and tell us our duty? Must..."

Harrison's gavel cracked down. "Mr Rickman, may I again remind you that this is *not* a court of law and that procedure is at my sole discretion. Dr McGill has just restated the nature and intention of this Commission of Inquiry in words more well chosen and acute than I myself used in the opening proceedings . . . Mr Buck, you will replace Dr McGill in the witness chair."

Harrison drew his note-pad towards him. "Now Mr Buck, can you tell us who was present at the town council meeting?" he said.

"There was Ia. . . Mr Ballard and Mr Cameron and Mr Quentin from the mine. Dr McGill was there. And there was Mr Houghton, the mayor, and Mr John Peterson and Eric Peterson, Mr Warrick and Mrs Samson, the last five being members of the council."

"Well, perhaps you can tell us what went on at the meeting."

"Dr McGill told them there was a danger of avalanche and he told them why, and they didn't believe him."

Lyall put up his hand. "Mr Chairman, it is incumbent on me to point out that of the five council members only Mr Eric Peterson is able to be here."

"Does Mr Peterson wish to be a witness?"

"He does."

"Then he will have his chance later. At present we are hearing the evidence of Mr Buck."

"With respect, Mr Chairman, it is well known in Hukahoronui that Mr Ballard and Mr Buck are friends of many years standing. It may be thought that the evidence given here is too one-sided."

Harrison leaned back in his chair. "It is evident, Mr Lyall, that you are doing at least one of two things. You are impugning the integrity of this Commission, or you are questioning the honesty of Mr Buck. Do I understand you correctly?"

"I do not question the integrity of the Commission, sir."

Turi Buck's face was stricken as he half rose from his chair. Ian dug his elbow into Rickman's ribs, and said, "The bastard! Intervene and get on with that line of questioning I gave you."

Rickman shook his head. "It would be most unwise. It wouldn't be in the interests of the company." He twisted his head and looked at Lyall. "See how he's stirring things up."

"But, damn it, he's making us into some sort of conspiracy."

Rickman stared at him unwinkingly. "But not involving the company," he snapped.

Ballard raised his hand. "Mr Chairman, I would like to question Mr Buck."

Harrison frowned. "I thought you had representation, Mr Ballard?"

Ballard said, "As of thirty seconds ago Mr Rickman ceased to represent me. He will, of course, continue to represent the company."

Amid the wave of uproar that washed across the hall Rickman said, "You young fool! What the devil do you think you're doing?"

"You're fired," said Ballard briefly.

Harrison waited for silence before he addressed Ballard. "Are

197

you asking for an adjournment so that you may obtain a new legal adviser?"

"No, sir. For today I am content to represent myself. I do not wish to waste the time of the Commission."

"Most laudable. And you wish to interrogate Mr Buck?"

"I object," said Rickman. "Apart from the personal insult in being dismissed so cavalierly and in public, I consider this to be most irregular."

Harrison sighed. "Even in a law court it has not been unknown for a person to represent himself, choosing not to enlist the aid— or otherwise—of a lawyer. Therefore I will allow it. Proceed, Mr Ballard."

Ballard smiled at Turi. "Mr Buck, at the meeting with the council was a map produced and were you asked to point out various places on that map?"

"Yes, sir."

"Can you give us a translation from Maori into English of the name Hukahoronui?"

"Yes, sir; it means 'The Great Snow Slide'."

There was a subdued murmur from behind Ballard. "There is a great rock between your house and the mountainside, is there not? What is the name of that rock?"

"Kamakamaru. It means 'The Rock of Shelter'."

Again came that quickly suppressed sound in the hall. Ballard consulted a paper. At last he raised his head and asked quietly, "Did your family name the valley and the rock?"

"No, they were already named when my grandfather came from North Island. His house was rebuilt by my father in 1880."

"Did your father replace the house because it had been damaged by an avalanche?"

"No, sir. He replaced it because it was in bad condition and because the family was growing larger."

"Do you know of any avalanches in the valley of Hukahoronui?"

"Yes, there was an avalanche in 1912 when I was a boy. A family called Bailey had built a house quite close to ours but not protected by Kamakamaru. My father warned the Baileys but they took no notice of him. The Bailey house was swept away and the whole family of seven died. I helped dig out the bodies."

"So the rock—Kamakamaru—acted as a splitting wedge?"

"The snow flowed around Kamakamaru, and our house was safe."

"Any more avalanches?"

"There was one in 1918. There were no lives lost nor damage to property."

"A six-year gap. Any more?"

"There was the avalanche of 1943—a very large one. It broke a lot of trees on the west slope."

"Were there any fatalities in the avalanche of 1943?"

Turi's eyes opened wide. "Why, yes, Ian. Your father was killed. You saw it happen—you were maybe four years old."

There was a gust of pent-up emotion let loose in the hall.

Ballard said, "Would you be able to point out the place where my father was killed?"

"Just where the mine office is now."

"Mr Buck, you have given us a lot of information. Was the same information given to the councillors at the meeting?"

"Yes, it was."

Ballard leaned back and glanced at Lyall who already had his hand up. "I would like to ask Mr Buck one or two questions."

Harrison nodded. "Very well, Mr Lyall."

"How far down the slope did the avalanche of 1943 come? Did it go anywhere near the Peterson supermarket?"

"It didn't go anywhere near the Peterson store."

"Remarkable. Now tell me, if the store was not destroyed by the big avalanche of 1943, why then was it destroyed this year?"

Ballard let out a sigh, and let Lyall dig his own pit.

Turi looked blank. "The trees, of course. They started cutting them when the mine opened four years ago. The cutting went on for two years and by that time the slope was just about stripped."

Asked if he had further questions Lyall warily said he had none.

Ballard raised his hand, "I would like to ask Mr Buck one more question. Mr Buck, what was the immediate reaction of the councillors towards your revelations about the incidence of avalanches in Hukahoronui?"

Turi Buck froze. "I would rather not say."

The hall was very quiet when someone said, "I can answer that question." McGill stepped forward holding a notebook. "As is my habit, I took notes immediately after the meeting. Mr Eric Peterson's exact words were, 'Turi Buck is an ignorant old black man. He knows nothing—he never has and he never will.'"

The hall erupted in a babble of noise and when at last Harrison could make himself heard, he said in anger, "This hearing is adjourned until further notice."

AS IT WAS...

"TURI BUCK is an ignorant old black man . . ."

The words had hung heavily in an embarrassed silence in the residents' lounge of the Hotel D'Archiac which did duty as a council chamber. At last the mayor, Matthew Houghton, coughed nervously and said, "There's no call for that sort of talk, Eric."

Eric went red but said nothing. John Peterson addressed himself to McGill. "So you've come up with past avalanches, and now you say there's going to be another."

"I have *not* said that."

"Then what *are* you saying?" demanded Houghton.

McGill spread his hands. "You have a potential hazard here."

Peterson said, "It seems pretty flimsy to me. From the line you're shooting it seems to me that you want us to spend a lot of money because of something that may never happen."

"There's something I don't understand," said Houghton. "If there have been avalanches in the past, why weren't the houses knocked down? My house was the second one built in the valley; my grandfather built it in 1850."

"My bet is that houses survived because the builders were lucky or knew what they were about," McGill said. "But now you've got a whole township here—built when the mine started—not just a few scattered houses."

"So what are you asking us to do?" asked John Peterson.

200

"You must notify the appropriate authority outside the valley that a hazard exists. You must have rescue gear stored in safe places where it can be got at in case of disaster. You'll have to have men trained to use that equipment. And you'll have to have planning in case it becomes necessary to evacuate the town."

John Peterson stared. "What foolish talk is this?"

Eric Peterson said, "If we have to train men we have to pay them; if we have to have equipment we have to pay for it. Where do we get the money?"

Quentin laughed bitterly. "You haven't heard anything yet. Ask McGill how much it will cost to protect the mine. Wait till you hear the long-term precautions."

"Not to protect the mine," snapped Ballard. "To protect the town. In a case like this you'll get a government grant."

Eric Peterson looked at his brother. "Everyone knows that government grants don't cover everything. Guess how much the town rates will be next year if this damn silly caper carries on."

Ballard said, "How much is your life worth, Eric?"

"According to McGill, I'm safe. My building is one of the survivors."

"The only reason the store survived in 1943 was because of the trees," said Ballard. "Now they're gone there's nothing between you and the snow. You made a bad bargain there."

Eric stood up. "Too right I made a bad bargain, or rather, my old man did. You know that when your mother sold him the property she cheated him of the mineral rights. She even kept hold of the land at the bottom where the mine is now—just enough land to put up the crushing mill to work the ore she gets out of *our* land."

Ballard rubbed his eyes. "That's not the way it was, Eric," he said. "She doesn't hold the mineral rights. My father separated them from the property. He did it in his will. Your father didn't buy the land till five years after my father died."

"I don't know what this is all about," said McGill. "But I don't think it has anything to do with snow on a hillside. Those missing trees do; there's nothing left to bind the snow."

Eric shrugged and sat down again. "It's a lousy piece of land,

201

anyway. Too steep for cattle, and I couldn't even get in the hay crop this year."

McGill's head jerked up. "What happened to your hay crop?"

John Peterson rolled his eyes towards the ceiling. "For God's sake, Eric! Indulge his curiosity. Then perhaps we can get this meeting over. I've got things to do."

Eric shrugged. "It was the rain—the crop was sodden, so I gave it up."

"So you cut down the trees, which is bad enough. Then you leave uncut grass, which is worse," said McGill. "Long, wet grass on a hillside is just about the slipperiest stuff there is. The chances of an avalanche have just gone up considerably."

"Dr McGill is right," said Ballard.

Eric Peterson lunged to his feet. "Am I some sort of public enemy? And anyone called Ballard is the last one to accuse me of anything at all. Anyone with a yellow . . ."

Matt Houghton looked bleak. "That's old history and nothing to do with the subject here."

McGill stood up. "Gentlemen, I can do nothing more. I shall leave you to your deliberations."

"Where can we get hold of you if we need further information?" asked Houghton.

"At Mr Ballard's house," said McGill. "Or up near the west slope—it needs further investigation. But don't send anyone up there to find me. In fact, no one should be allowed on that slope from now on. It's dangerous." He left the meeting.

AT THE HEARING...

THE press gallery was jammed after the adjournment. Harrison led Eric Peterson through his evidence.

"So we arrive at the point when Dr McGill delivered his bad news. What happened then, Mr Peterson?"

"Well, the meeting went on for a long time. My brother argued that even if McGill was anywhere near right, we didn't want to

202

start a panic. You must realize that any decision concerning the town had to be made by the council. It wasn't up to the mine management to tell the town what to do."

"I appreciate your position," said Harrison. "What happened then?"

"Matt Houghton said he'd telephone the Department of Civil Defence in Christchurch and get a second opinion. Mr Cameron suggested he also talk to someone in the Forestry Department. Then it was decided we'd meet at eleven the next morning, even though it was Sunday."

"I see." Harrison looked around. "Has anyone any further questions to ask Mr Peterson?"

Smithers raised his hand. "I represent the Ministry of Civil Defence. Was a telephone call in fact made to the Civil Defence authorities?"

"Not to my knowledge. Matt Houghton said after the meeting he'd do what he always did before making a decision—sleep on it."

"And the police—were they notified?"

"Our policeman, Arthur Pye, was away up at the head of the valley investigating a case of sheep worrying."

"So *nobody* outside Hukahoronui knew of the situation?" said Smithers incredulously. "And *in* Hukahoronui the knowledge was confined to a handful of people?"

"Yes, sir."

"Mr Peterson, you were a responsible official. Would you not agree that preparations for a crisis in your community were conspicuous by their absence? I am not speaking of avalanches only —we do live in an earthquake prone country, a major reason for the existence of the Ministry of Civil Defence. Did no one on the council read the directives sent out by my Ministry?"

"We get a lot of stuff from the government." Peterson shrugged.

"Have you any further questions, Mr Smithers?" asked Harrison.

"None I care to ask this witness," said Smithers curtly.

"Then you may step down, Mr Peterson."

Peterson left the witness chair with an air of relief. Harrison said, "Mr Cameron, the engineer of the Hukahoronui Mining Company, has been hospitalized for many months due to the injuries he received in the disaster. However, he now feels well enough to give evidence. Will you come forward, Mr Cameron?"

Cameron limped to the witness chair leaning heavily on the arm of a male nurse. He had lost a lot of weight; his cheeks were sunken and his hair, pepper and salt at the time of the avalanche, was now white. He looked an old man.

Harrison said, "Joseph McNeil Cameron, I understand that you have evidence to give about the events of the evening of the Saturday you had the meeting with the council."

"Yes, sir," said Cameron. "There was a dinner-dance at the Hotel D'Archiac that night. I had invited Mr Ballard and Dr McGill to be my guests. My daughter, Stacey, was also present. She was on vacation from the States. During dinner I learned that the mayor had not made the telephone calls. That, combined with a new and most disturbing report from Dr McGill, worried all of us very much."

"Could you go into that in more detail?" said Harrison.

"Why, yes. We were just starting dinner . . ."

AS IT WAS...

McGill had inspected the menu. "Colonial goose," he said. "That sounds good."

Ballard chuckled. "Don't expect poultry. It's stuffed hogget. Midway between lamb and mutton."

"I was going to order that," said Stacey Cameron. She was a tall, dark girl with typical American svelte good looks.

"A trap for the unwary tourist," commented McGill. "Talking of that, when are you going back to the States, Stacey?"

"Just ten days left," she said with a sigh.

Over dinner Cameron yarned about some of the practical difficulties they had run into when getting the mine going. "The folks around here weren't very enthusiastic at first. All except old man Peterson, of course, who saw the possibilities."

"That reminds me," said McGill. "What's with the Petersons?"

204

Cameron said, "John has the brains, Eric has the drive, and Charlie has the muscle and precious little else. Old Peterson died last year."

"You forgot Liz," said Stacey. "She's sitting over there."

Ballard turned his head. He had not seen Liz Peterson since his return to the valley and his image was still of a freckled, gawky girl with pigtails and skinned knees. What he saw was something quite different and he drew in his breath.

Liz Peterson, a tall redhead, was a rarity—a really beautiful girl whose loveliness lay deep in the structure of her skull, and in the smooth sheen of health and youth.

"Any of the Petersons married yet?" Ballard asked.

"Not Charlie, but John is—and Eric's engaged. Liz should have been married long ago but Charlie has a way of scaring her young men."

McGill said, "The Petersons don't like you, Ian. What was all that about this morning?"

"An old quarrel," said Ballard shortly. "My father had a row with my grandfather and emigrated to New Zealand. When he found gold on his land he was still enough of a Ballard to leave the land to my mother, and the mineral rights to my grandfather.

"My mother sold most of the land to old Peterson, who neglected to check if he had the mineral rights. But when my grandfather started to exploit the rights then all hell broke loose. Accusations of bad faith were tossed around like confetti."

"But the mine brought prosperity to the valley, and those who made a profit from it were the Petersons with their store. The Ballards certainly aren't: the company is just breaking even. I don't know what's going to happen if we have to put in avalanche protection."

"I've got some figures for you on that, Joe," said McGill. "When you design the avalanche gallery over the mine portal allow for an impact pressure of ten tons a square foot."

"*That much?*" Cameron asked incredulously.

"From all accounts the 1943 slide was an airborne powder avalanche, and so was the 1912 slide, according to Turi Buck. Airborne powder snow is fast and it packs a hell of a wallop."

Ballard said, "The 1943 avalanche turned a hundred acres of big trees into firewood."

"Now I *know* why you're worried about the town," Cameron put down his fork. "Here comes Matt Houghton. If you tell him what you've just told me maybe he'll become as scared as I am." As Houghton came up, his bald head gleaming, Cameron said, "What did the Civil Defence people have to say?"

Houghton sat down heavily. "I haven't had time to talk to them yet. We'll be posting signs on the slope tomorrow."

Ballard leaned forward. "What do you mean, Matt—you didn't have time?"

Houghton flapped his hand. "It's *Saturday*, Ian," he said plaintively.

"Do you really think that Civil Defence Headquarters closes down at weekends? All you have to do is to lift up a telephone."

"Take it easy, Ian. I have enough trouble with the Petersons. Charlie takes the line that no one can prevent him from walking— or skiing—on his own land."

"Is he out of his mind?"

Houghton sighed. "You know Charlie. It's that old feud getting in the way."

"I don't want any ancient history—what matters is that snow on the slope above this town. I'm going to make sure the right thing is done."

McGill said, "Mr Houghton, I've taken more samples from the slope and the stability is deteriorating. I've just notified Mr Cameron to prepare for something hitting the mine very hard indeed. I have to tell you that also applies to the town."

Houghton was affronted. "Why the hell didn't you talk like this at the meeting this morning instead of pussyfooting around with scientific quibbles? You said the hazard was potential."

McGill was exasperated. "I sometimes wonder if we speak the same language. The hazard still *is* potential and will be until something happens. Then it'll be too late to do anything about it."

Ballard said, "Go back to your council and tell them that if they don't do something constructive by midday tomorrow I'll call a public meeting and put it to the people direct."

206

"And telephone Civil Defence as soon as you can," added McGill. "I'm going out to check the weather again."

Houghton took a deep breath and stood up. His face was red and shiny with sweat. "I'll do the best I can," he said, and walked away.

Cameron talked with Ballard for some time and then they were joined by Stacey Cameron.

Later, when the night-club shuffle had replaced rock rhythms Ballard cocked an ear towards the dance floor. "Dance?" he suggested to Stacey.

She grimaced. "Thanks all the same, but I've been danced off my feet tonight." She sat down and flexed her toes. "Liz Peterson seems to think that you're ignoring her. Why don't you ask her for a dance?"

"Well, why not?" He headed for the dance floor.

Stacey looked past her father. "Here's Mike back. How's the weather, Mike?"

"Heavy snow setting in." McGill checked his watch. "Nearly midnight. How long do these shindigs go on?"

"The dancing will stop dead on midnight," said Cameron. "Very religious guys, these New Zealanders. No dancing on Sunday."

McGill nodded. "I won't be sorry to get to bed." He stretched. "What did the Civil Defence crowd have to say?"

"Houghton didn't call. He said a few hours wouldn't make any difference and he wasn't going to ring in the middle of the night and make a fool of himself."

"He *didn't!*" McGill grabbed Cameron by the arm. "What have you done about it? Did Ian try?" Cameron shook his head. "Then he's a fool—and so are you. Where's the telephone?"

"In the lobby," said Cameron. "Look, Mike, there'll be no one there at this time of night qualified to tell you anything."

"Tell me—hell!" said McGill. "I'm going to tell them! I'm going to raise the alarm."

He walked away rapidly with Cameron on his heels. As they skirted the dance floor there was a shout and a sudden disturbance. Ballard had been dancing with Liz Peterson when Charlie's meaty hand fell on his shoulder and spun him around. Charlie's face was sweaty and alcohol fumes came from him as he whispered hoarsely, "Stay away from my sister, Ballard!"

"Take your hand off me," said Ballard.

"Stop this nonsense," said Liz. "You get crazier every day, Charlie."

Ballard's arms hung down in front of him, crossed at the wrists, and suddenly he brought them up sharply, hitting Charlie's arm at the elbow with considerable force and thus breaking free.

McGill and Cameron crossed the floor to where the two men bristled at each other and when Charlie lunged forward Cameron grabbed one arm and expertly twisted it behind Charlie's back.

"Break it up," said McGill. "This is a dance floor."

"All right, Ballard," said Charlie. "I'll see you outside when you don't have your friends to help you."

In the distance a voice was raised. "Mr Ballard's wanted on the telephone." Ballard walked past Charlie without so much as looking at him.

"What's going on here?" someone demanded.

McGill turned to find Eric Peterson at his elbow. "Your kid brother has gone off his rocker."

Eric said to Charlie, coldly, "I've told you about this before."

Charlie jerked his arm free. "But it's Ballard!" he pleaded.

Eric frowned. "I don't care who it is. You don't make these scenes again. Not in public."

McGill caught Cameron's eye and they moved off to the lobby and found Ballard at the reception desk.

"The call will be from Crowell, if I'm lucky—chairman of the company. He lives in Auckland."

"After you with the phone—I want to ring Christchurch," McGill said.

Ballard picked up the telephone. A testy voice said, "I have half a dozen message slips here asking me to ring you. It had better be important."

Ballard said grimly. "We have reason to suppose that the mine—and the town—is in danger of destruction by avalanche."

There was silence broken only by a surge of music from the dance floor. Crowell said, "Are you serious?"

208

"I don't joke about things like this. I want you to get on to the Ministry of Civil Defence. We may need help fast."

McGill saw Charlie Peterson run past heading for Ballard. Charlie grabbed Ballard by the shoulder.

"I'm going to break you in half," he shouted.

Lost in the uproar was a soft rumble of distant thunder. Ballard punched at Charlie, hampered by the telephone he held. McGill laid hands on Charlie and hauled him away.

Ballard, breathing heavily, again put the telephone to his ear. Crowell said, ". . . going on there?" The line went dead.

McGill spun Charlie around and laid him cold with a right cross to the jaw as all the lights went out.

AT THE HEARING...

"After the lights went out things got pretty confused," said Cameron in a low voice. The nurse poured him a glass of water, and Cameron took it, his hand shaking.

Harrison watched him carefully. "You've been giving evidence for quite a long time, Mr Cameron, and I think you should stand down for the moment. Since we are taking evidence chronologically the next witness should be Mr Crowell."

A short, stout man walked up to the rostrum with some reluctance. As he sat down he turned his head to look at Rickman, who nodded reassuringly. Reed said, "What is your full name?"

Crowell licked his lips nervously. "Henry James Crowell."

"And your occupation?"

"I'm the chairman of several companies, including the Huka-horonui Mining Company."

Harrison said, "You have been listening to evidence relating to a telephone call which you made to Mr Ballard. Did you, in fact, make that call?"

"Yes, I arrived home late on Saturday night. There were messages from Mr Ballard that I should telephone him immediately. Something about an avalanche. I didn't quite understand."

"Didn't you ask him to explain further?"

"Yes." Crowell's hands twitched. "But he wasn't very coherent."

"Can the witness state whether or not Mr Ballard asked him to contact the Ministry of Civil Defence to warn them of impending danger to Hukahoronui?" asked the representative of the Ministry.

"He did say something along those lines, but there was a lot of music and screaming on the line. Then I was cut off."

"What did you do then?" asked Harrison.

"I talked it over with my wife."

A ripple of amusement passed over the hall. Harrison knocked sharply with his gavel. "*Did* you contact the Ministry of Civil Defence?"

Crowell hesitated. "No, sir."

"Why not?"

"I thought it was some sort of joke. With that music and uproar on the line . . . well, I thought Mr Ballard was drunk."

John Rickman, barrister for the Hukahoronui Mining Company, had his hand up. Harrison nodded. "Who appointed Mr Ballard as managing director?" Rickman asked.

"The instruction came from London—from a majority shareholder."

"You had nothing to do with his appointment, then? Could we say that Mr Ballard was foisted upon you?"

"As a minority shareholder I didn't have much say in the matter."

"That is all," said Rickman.

"It has been suggested that Mr Ballard was 'foisted' upon you." Harrison uttered the word as though it had a nasty taste. "Upon his appointment, did you make any complaint?"

Crowell shrugged. "No. I thought he was a personable enough young man—perhaps a little too young for the job."

Harrison shook his head slowly as he regarded this most unsatisfactory witness. "Very well. I have no further questions." He looked down from the rostrum. "Yes, Mr Ballard?"

"I would like to ask some questions. Mr Crowell, two weeks after the disaster the board suspended me from my duties. Why?"

Rickman's hand shot up. "Objection! What happened two weeks after the incident does not come within the scope of this Inquiry."

"Mr Rickman has a point," said Harrison. "I cannot really see that this is helpful."

Ballard smiled. "May I argue the point?"

"Certainly."

"Mr Chairman, this Inquiry is being widely reported in the press, not only in New Zealand but also in the United Kingdom. Regardless of your findings, the public is going to blame someone for those unnecessary deaths. Now, certain imputations have been made about my character, my drinking habits and a supposed propensity for practical joking which, in my own interests, I cannot allow to pass unchallenged. I ask to be allowed to question Mr Crowell about these matters, and the fact that I was suspended from my duties a fortnight after the disaster certainly seems to me to be a legitimate reason for inquiry."

Harrison conferred briefly with his two assessors, then said, "It is not the wish of this Commission that a man's reputation be put lightly at stake. You may continue your questioning, Mr Ballard."

"Why was I suspended from duties, Mr Crowell?"

"It was a unanimous decision of the board."

"That is not answering my question. The instructions to appoint me came from a majority shareholder in London. Is that shareholder a member of the board?"

Crowell twitched nervously. "No, he is not."

"Then is it not a fact that your board of directors has no real power and is thus a democratic sham? Is it not a fact that the power to control the company lies in the City of London?"

"That is a misreading of the situation," said Crowell sullenly.

"Did the instruction to suspend me also come from London?"

"It may have done."

"Is it not a fact that a suggestion was made—by you—that the company was in danger of being in bad odour because of evidence to be given at this Inquiry? And is it not a fact that you intimated that I, as a Johnny-come-lately, was an ideal person to shuffle the responsibility onto, and that it was then that the

211

instruction was given—from London—that I be suspended?"

"Objection!" cried Rickman. "Mr Ballard cannot lead the witness in this way."

"I tend to agree," said Harrison.

"I withdraw the question." Ballard knew from the rustle in the press gallery that he had made his point where it mattered. "I shall return to the telephone conversation. When you were cut off, did you attempt to replace the call?"

"No."

"Why not?"

"You heard my evidence. I thought you were drunk."

"How long did you think I'd been drunk, Mr Crowell? You said in evidence that messages had been left by me. The first message I left was at eleven-thirty that morning.''

"I didn't give it a thought."

"And you did not communicate with the Ministry of Civil Defence. As a matter of interest, Mr Crowell, what *did* you do?"

"I went to bed."

"You went to bed," repeated Ballard slowly. He waited until Crowell was rising from the chair in a half crouch. "Oh, one further thing. Did you come forward voluntarily to give evidence here, or were you subpoena'd?"

"I object," said Rickman.

"I agree, Mr Rickman," said Harrison smoothly. "This Commission need not be instructed that Mr Crowell was subpoena'd—it already knows." He ignored the indescribable noise that came from Rickman and continued blandly, "You may step down, Mr Crowell. Now I think it is time to get back to what happened in Hukahoronui after the lights were extinguished. Dr McGill, you were present in the Hotel D'Archiac when the lights went out. What happened then?"

McGill rose and walked to the witness chair. "The management of the hotel provided candles and kerosene lanterns. I was told that a breakdown of electricity supply was not uncommon. The dance was over, anyway, so everybody went home."

"Including you?"

"Yes. I went home with Mr Ballard and went to bed."

212

MᴄGɪʟʟ had been woken from a sound sleep by Ballard. Nothing happened when he flicked the lamp switch and then he remembered the power failure. "What time is it?"

"Five-thirty. Cameron just rang up—luckily the local exchange has batteries as an auxiliary for emergencies. It seems one of his men left early this morning to go to Christchurch to see his mother. He says he can't get out of the valley; the Gap is closed off with a wall of snow so high he can't see the top."

"I think I'd better go and look at it," said McGill.

Ballard said, "I'll come with you." He left to put on ski pants and an anorak and then joined McGill in the Land-Rover. He pushed the self-starter; it whined but the engine did not fire.

"You've flooded her," said McGill. "Wait a couple of minutes." He pulled on gloves. "What's between you and Charlie Peterson?"

"It's an old story," said Ballard. "Not worth repeating."

"If an old quarrel is getting in the way of co-operation with the council I'd better know about it. Charlie did enough damage last night."

"It goes back a long way," said Ballard. "I was born in 1939 in England, and brought here as a baby. My father had split with old Ben and decided to farm here. Then the war came and he joined the army. I didn't see him until he came back in 1943. I was four years old. Then he was killed in the avalanche here. It hit my mother hard and she turned a bit neurotic."

"What form did it take?"

"She became over-protective as far as I was concerned."

"'Don't go near the water until you've learned to swim'," quoted McGill.

"You don't know how true that was, Mike. All the kids could swim well except me. I was twelve when it happened."

He took out a packet of cigarettes and offered one to McGill. "It was in the spring and Alec Peterson and I were down by the river. Alec was the fourth of the Peterson brothers—and Charlie's twin.

213

There was a lot of melt water coming down from the mountains—the river was full, cold and flowing fast. All I could do was dog-paddle in the shallows, but Alec was tough for a ten-year-old, and a strong swimmer."

"Don't tell me," said McGill. "He got into trouble."

"I think he got cramp," said Ballard. "Anyway, he let out a yell as he was swept out into the main stream. I knew I wouldn't have a hope of getting him out, but I knew that the river swirled around the bluff and on the other side there was an eddy where anything floating usually came ashore. So I belted across the bluff, past the Peterson store as fast as I could run.

"I was right. Alec came inshore and I was able to wade in and grab him. But on his way around the bluff he'd bashed his head on a rock. His skull was cracked and he was stone dead."

"Nasty! But I don't see how you could be blamed for anything."

"Two other people heard Alec when he yelled. Afterwards they said they'd seen me running away and leaving Alec. The two witnesses were Alec's brothers—Charlie and Eric."

McGill whistled. "Now I'm beginning to see."

"They made my life a misery for the next four years. They set all the other kids against me. I think I'd have gone nuts if it hadn't been for Turi's son, Tawhaki. Anyway, when I was sixteen my grandfather, old Ben, appeared in the valley as though he'd dropped from the sky. He listened to the gossip, took one look at me and another at my mother, and then they had a flaming row. The upshot of it was that I went to England with him. My mother stayed on for a few years, then she went back to England, too."

McGill said, "I still don't get it. Grown men don't behave like Charlie's behaving because of something that happened when they were kids."

"While you can't call Charlie retarded, he's never really grown up . . . But there's nothing much we can do about it." Ballard prodded at the starter again and the engine caught with a steady throb. "Let's go up to the Gap."

They drove up the road which paralleled the river. As the head-lights' beam swept across the ravine that the river had cut McGill said, "Have you ever seen the river as full as that?"

214

Ballard stopped the car. "Never so high. The ravine is more than thirty feet deep here." He drove on into town, and as they were passing the supermarket McGill pointed to a car just pulling out. "Looks as though he's leaving, too."

McGill wound down the side window. "Going far, Mr Peterson?"

John Peterson said, "I've an early business appointment in Christchurch tomorrow."

"You may be disappointed," said McGill. "Our information is that the Gap is blocked."

"Impossible!"

"We're just going to have a look. Maybe you'd like to tag along behind."

Ballard drove until he was stopped by a cliff which had no right to be there. "My God!" he said. "Just look at it!"

McGill got out and walked towards the wall of snow. He prodded at it and then looked upwards, shaking his head.

Ballard got out of the car just as John Peterson drew alongside. McGill said blandly, "What you are seeing, Mr Peterson, is the end result of an avalanche. Nobody will be leaving Hukahoronui for quite some time—at least, not in a car." He thrust a handful of snow under Peterson's nose. "Soft, harmless stuff, isn't it? Just like lamb's wool." His fingers closed on the snow, making a fist. "There was a man in my line of business called Zdarsky," he said. "An Austrian and a pioneer in snow studies. Zdarsky said, 'Snow is not a wolf in sheep's clothing—it is a tiger in lamb's clothing.'"

He opened his fist. "Look at that, Mr Peterson. What is it?"

In the palm of his gloved hand lay a lump of hard ice.

AT THE HEARING...

"So THAT was the first avalanche," said Harrison, "and it meant that no vehicles could leave or enter the valley?"

"That is correct," McGill said. "It had been my intention to persuade the town council to evacuate the population of the valley until the danger had receded. This was now impossible."

"Surely the obstacle could be climbed?"

"By the fit and active, of course; but what of the elderly, the handicapped and the children? But at least one member of the town council, Mr John Peterson, was now convinced that avalanches were something to be reckoned with in Hukahoronui. We went back to the town to get some action going."

Harrison nodded and made a note. "What was the name of the man you quoted to Mr Peterson?"

"Matthias Zdarsky. I have an anecdote which may have some bearing on what I quoted to Mr Peterson."

"Proceed," said Harrison. "As long as it does not take us too far from our purpose here."

"A couple of years ago I was in Western Canada as a technical adviser on avalanche protection. There was a cartographic draughtsman who had been given the job of drawing a map of the area showing all the sites of avalanche hazard. It was a long job but he had nearly finished when one day he found that some joker had written in medieval lettering on each avalanche site the words, 'Here be Tygers,' just as on an old map. The draughtsman didn't think much of it as a joke, but the boss of his department took the map, had it framed, and hung it on the wall of his office. You see, everyone in the game knows about Matthias Zdarsky and what happened to him."

"An interesting anecdote," said Harrison. "And perfectly relevant. What did happen to Zdarsky?"

"He was in the Austrian Army during the First World War. At that time both sides—Austrians and Italians—were using avalanches as weapons in the Dolomites and the Tyrol. It's said that eighty thousand men died in avalanches during the war. In 1916 Zdarsky was going to the rescue of twenty-five Austrian soldiers who had been caught in an avalanche when he himself was caught in one. He had eighty broken bones and dislocations, and it was eleven years before he could ski again."

The hall was hushed.

Presently Harrison said, "Thank you, Dr McGill. I think we will now adjourn. This hearing will recommence at ten in the morning on Monday."

THE participants of the hearing flooded on to the pavement and began to disperse. Mike McGill, driving Ballard to the hotel, slanted an eye at him. "Fifty-four people died, and the public want a scapegoat. If your company can get out from under by sacrificing you, that's what they'll do."

"Save it, Mike," said Ballard shortly, "I'm too tired."

At the hotel McGill took two beers to a table. He drank and gasped with pleasure. "God, how I needed that!"

Ballard took out his wallet and extracted a piece of paper. "I was leaving the hotel this morning when I got this." He passed it to McGill. "My grandfather's dead."

McGill read the cablegram. "Ian, I'm sorry. Your mother wants you to go home? But you're not going back, are you?"

"No. It's just moral blackmail." He shook his head. "You know, Mike, it hit me harder than I thought it would."

"Judging by the way you talked about him, I'm surprised you feel anything at all."

"Oh, he was a cantankerous old devil but there was something about him . . ."

"What happens to Ballard Holdings now?"

"The old man established a Trust. I never really got the hang of it because I knew I wouldn't figure in it. I imagine my uncles will run things pretty much as they are now. Which is to say badly."

He drained his glass. "I feel sticky. I'm going for a swim."

BALLARD SWAM another length of the hotel pool and then climbed out and began to rub himself down. McGill came sauntering across the lawn followed by the man from the hotel office who said, "A telegram, Mr Ballard."

"Thanks." Ballard scanned it rapidly, frowned and handed it to McGill. "It's from England. The last time I saw him old Ben said something about Stenning. Why should a man suddenly fly half way across the world to see me?"

217

"Who is Stenning?"

"A friend of my grandfather's."

McGill began calculating. "He says he's leaving on the night flight. That means he'll be here tomorrow. Who is he, apart from being your grandfather's friend?"

"A lawyer. He specializes in taxes. He's a tough old bird, about as ruthless as old Ben was himself."

McGill chuckled. "He's probably come to confess that he slipped up on sorting out the death duties, and instead of three million from the old man you're just going to get three thousand."

Ballard grinned. "I'm not going to get three cents. He said that he'd educate me and I'd have to stand on my own feet as he'd done at my age . . . Well, I've decided to leave the Ballard Group."

"What will you do?"

"Haven't made up my mind yet."

"An old guy flying half way across the world," mused McGill. "Could be important, Ian." He looked up. "Hi, Liz." He drew up a chair for her. She had an Alsatian dog with her and Ballard rubbed it behind the ears. "How's the boy, Victor?" The Alsatian lolled his tongue and his tail wagged vigorously.

Liz said, "I nearly gave Charlie a heart attack just now. I said that if anyone else implied that Ian was drunk I'd offer my services as your witness. I can tell when the man I'm dancing with is drunk, and Ian wasn't, but Charlie certainly was."

"I'd be careful, Liz," said Ballard. "Charlie can be violent."

"Don't I know it! But I can handle him."

"Thanks for the support, Liz. I've made a couple of decisions and now the way ahead seems a lot clearer. You've had a lot to do with it."

She looked at her watch. "I think I'll sit with my brothers this afternoon. I might learn something that will help you. Come on, Victor."

As she walked away McGill said, "The prettiest spy I ever did see. By the way, what are these decisions you've made?"

"You've heard one—I'm leaving the Ballard Group."

"And the other?"

"I'm getting married," said Ballard placidly.

218

"Well, congratulations. Who's the lucky girl?"

"Liz Peterson—if she'll have me."

"You must be insane," said McGill. "Who'd want Charlie as a brother-in-law?"

NEXT MORNING Ballard went to the hospital to visit Cameron, to cheer him up. McGill said, "I'll go see him tomorrow. I have things to do at Deep Freeze Headquarters."

"I'll be out that way this afternoon," said Ballard. "I'm picking up Stenning at Harewood. Want a lift back?"

"Thanks," said McGill. "Ask for me in the office."

Ballard found Cameron talking to Liz Peterson. They stayed until Cameron sent them off, saying that young people must have something better to do than to sit around in hospitals. Outside, in the sunshine, Ballard said, "What about having lunch with me?"

She hesitated fractionally, but said, "I'd like that. It'll cost you lunch for two, though. I can't leave Victor in my car." She laughed. "Love me—love my dog."

As Ballard started the engine of his car, she said, "I've been thinking about leaving New Zealand."

"Where would you go?"

"England, I suppose. Then perhaps America. You've travelled around a bit, haven't you? I've always wanted to travel—to see things."

He drove out of the hospital grounds. "Yes, I've been places, but they've always been working trips. I'll tell you one thing—I certainly never expected to come back to New Zealand."

"Then why did you?"

Ballard sighed. "My grandfather wanted me to. He was a forceful old bird."

"He was! I didn't know he was dead."

"He died a few days ago."

"Oh, Ian! I am sorry."

"So am I, in a way. We didn't always see eye to eye, but I'll miss him. Now that he's gone I won't be staying with the Ballard Group. In fact, I've just about made that impossible."

"It's like Mike says—neither of us get on with our relatives."

220

Liz laughed. "I had a row with Charlie last night. Someone saw us together yesterday and split to Charlie."

"Don't get into trouble because of me, Liz."

"I'm tired of Charlie's tantrums. I'm a grown woman and I'll meet whoever I like. I told him so last night." She rubbed the side of her face reflectively.

Ballard glanced sideways and caught the action. "He *hit* you?"

"Not for the first time, but it's going to be the last." She saw the expression on Ballard's face. "Not to worry, Ian. I can defend myself. I'm reckoned to be a pretty aggressive tennis player and those smash services develop the muscles."

"So you hit him back. I doubt if that would make much of an impression on Charlie."

She grinned impishly. "I happened to be holding a plateful of spaghetti at the time." When Ballard burst out laughing she added, "Eric socked him, too. We're quite a happy family."

He turned the car into the hotel car park.

As they walked into the hotel foyer he said, "The grub's not bad here . . ." Suddenly he halted in his stride. "It's Cousin Francis. Now where the devil did he spring from?"

A youngish man in a business suit stepped in front of them, unsmiling. "Good morning, Frank," said Ballard. "Miss Peterson, this is my cousin, Frank Ballard."

Frank Ballard gave her a curt nod. "I want to talk to you, Ian. In private."

"All right. After lunch, then."

"No, I'm catching a plane back to Sydney almost immediately. It'll have to be now."

"I'll wait for you by the pool, Ian. Come on, Victor." Liz walked away without waiting for an answer.

Frank said, "What about your room?"

"All right." Ballard led the way. As he closed the door he said, "What brings you from Australia, Frank?"

Frank swung around. "Why did you put your local chairman— old Crowell—through the hoops the way you did yesterday? He was on the phone to me, crying on my shoulder."

"Aren't you forgetting that Crowell suspended me from duty?"

221

"You flaming idiot! The suspension was only until the Inquiry was over. If you'd kept quiet everything would have been all right, and you'd be back in the saddle next week. As it is, I'm not so sure."

Ian sat on the bed. "If I'd kept quiet I'd be a dead duck, and you know it. Between the company and the Petersons I wouldn't stand a chance."

"This is a *Ballard* company," Frank said furiously. "Have you no family feeling? When the Inquiry starts again you'd better keep quiet. If you do that maybe there's still a job for you in the Group."

"You know what I think of the Group—I've never made a secret of it," Ian said ironically.

"You know how big we are," Frank burst out. "We just have to pass the word around and you'll never get a job in mining again. You don't even have to *do* anything—just stop asking damn fool questions in public."

Ian stood up. "Don't push me, Frank," he warned.

"For God's sake, be reasonable, Ian. You know we're going to float a new issue of Hukahoronui shares. What chance do you think we'll have if you continue to hold up the chairman of the board as a bloody fool?"

Ian said, "Any more pressure from you and I'll start asking questions about conditions in that mine. I don't like being manipulated, Frank. And another thing: the day before I was fired I saw the result of the latest assay. Rich pickings, Frank, my boy. But can you tell me why those results haven't been given to the shareholders?"

"That's none of your business."

"That mine is going to make a fortune, but the way you'll set it up I don't think the ordinary shareholders will see much of it."

"*Nobody* will make anything if you get on your hind legs and start asking questions about avalanche defences. Do you know how much it will cost us if this Commission goes the wrong way?"

Ian stared at him. "What do you mean—the wrong way? Were you thinking of *not* putting in avalanche defences?"

"Hell, there's only an avalanche every thirty years or so. By the time the next one comes the mine will be worked out."

Ian took a deep breath. "I thought you lot were bad enough but now I know the depth of your greed." His voice was hard. "And I suggest we bring this conversation to a sudden halt." He crossed to the door and threw it open. "Out!"

Frank paused outside the door. "You're finished, Ian. I hope you know that."

Ian closed the door in his face.

As HE DROVE Liz back to the hospital to pick up her car he said, "Sorry about the gloomy lunch, Liz. I have a few things on my mind."

"What's the matter? You were all right until you saw your cousin."

He pulled the car off the road, parked and turned to face her. "I'll also be going to England as soon as the Inquiry is over," he said. "Why don't we go together?"

"Is this by way of being a proposal, Ian?" She smiled. "Or do I go as your mistress?"

"That's up to you."

Liz laughed. "Shakespeare didn't write this script. I know we're like the Montagues and Capulets, but Romeo never made an offer like that." She put her hand on his. "I like you, Ian, but I'm not sure I love you."

"That's the problem," he said. "We haven't known each other long enough. Just two or three days at Huka, rudely interrupted by a disaster, and a week here."

"Don't you believe in love at first sight?"

"I do," said Ballard. "It happened to me at the dance on the night everything started."

Pensively she said, "If I do go to England with you there'll be no strings. I'm my own woman, Ian. And if after a while I leave you, it will be my choice again. Do you understand?"

He nodded. "I understand."

"And let me tell you something else just to clear up something which may have been on your mind. Eric is against the Ballards on principle—it's not just you. But with Charlie it definitely is you. Now, I was only two when Alec died; I never knew him.

And you were twelve then, and now you're thirty-five. I don't know the rights and wrongs of Alec's death—and I don't care. I'll be going to England with a man, not a twelve-year-old.''

BALLARD dropped Liz at the hospital and went on to Deep Freeze Headquarters. "Old Stenning's due in fifteen minutes," he told McGill. They drove to Harewood Airport, two minutes away, and waited on the concourse. As the passengers streamed through the terminal Ballard said, "There he is," and McGill saw a tall, old man with white hair and the face of an ascetic.

Ballard stepped forward. "Good afternoon, Mr Stenning." They shook hands. "This is Mike McGill, a friend."

"I'm looking forward to discussing the disaster with you, Dr McGill," Stenning said.

"Any time I'm not in court, Mr Stenning."

At the hotel McGill made himself scarce while Ballard showed Stenning his room. Stenning said, "I'm not as resilient as I used to be, Ian. I'm going to bed. Your grandfather would have said a thing or two about that, were he here. At my age he was an assiduous globe-trotter." He shook his head, "I'm sorry he's gone."

"So am I," said Ballard.

Stenning regarded him curiously. "Are you? In my opinion he didn't treat you very well. Now, if you'll excuse a tired old man ... I'll see you tomorrow, Ian."

Stenning was absent from breakfast next morning. McGill buttered a slice of toast. "He doesn't seem to be in much of a hurry. Just like a lawyer; they work to a different sort of time from the rest of us."

"I had a visit from one of my relatives yesterday," said Ballard. "My cousin Frank." He told McGill what had happened.

McGill whistled. "How come Frank was in Sydney? Very convenient, wasn't it?"

"The Ballard Group has interests in many countries, including Australia."

They talked desultorily until McGill had finished his coffee. "I'm going to the hospital to see Joe. If Stenning has anything important to say he won't want me around."

Ballard read the Sunday papers by the pool, concentrating on the account of the Inquiry. It was eleven-thirty before Stenning appeared, carrying newspaper clippings. "You're having quite a time at this Inquiry," he said as he sat down. "I don't think your family is going to like the things you've been saying."

"I know. I had a visit from Frank yesterday," said Ballard. "He wants me to shut up. I showed him the door."

Stenning did not comment but he looked pleased. "You know, I was more than your grandfather's lawyer. I was also his friend."

"I know he placed a lot of trust in you."

"Trust—that's what I want to talk about," said Stenning, and smiled. "Do you know anything about estate duties in the United Kingdom?"

"Death duties? Nothing much."

"A man may give his money away—to his family usually, or to a charitable foundation, as Ben did. However, if he dies within seven years of the transaction having taken place then his gift is assessed for estate duty just as if he hadn't made it at all. If he dies after seven years have elapsed then the gift escapes the tax. Ben died after the seven-year period."

"Therefore the Foundation doesn't have to pay the tax."

"Precisely. The Ballard Foundation got a lot of money. The interest on it supports several laboratories working mostly in the fields of mining safety and health."

"My God!" said Ballard in astonishment. "Do the trustees know how the Ballard Group works? Every safety regulation is broken if they think they can get away with it. That's like giving with one hand and taking with the other."

Stenning nodded. "That perturbed Ben, but there was nothing he could do about it, for reasons you shall see. Now let us take a look at the trustees. There are five—your uncle Edward, your cousin Frank, and three old friends of Ben's—Lord Brockhurst, Sir William Bendell and myself. I am the chairman of the Board of Trustees."

"I'm surprised that two of the family are trustees. Ben had no great regard for them."

"He had no great regard for any of his grandchildren, either,

225

except one." Stenning jabbed forward a thin forefinger. "You."

"He had funny ways of showing it," said Ballard wryly.

"He saw to your education and left you alone. Seven years ago, when you were twenty-eight, he thought you were immature for your years. He thought your mother had something to do with that.

"He couldn't see himself putting so much money and power into the hands of one so young. So he set up the Ballard Foundation. And he watched you like a hawk because he wanted to see how you turned out."

Ballard grimaced. "Did I come up to expectations?"

"He never found out," said Stenning. "He died before the Hukahoronui experiment was completed."

Ballard stared at him. "What experiment?"

"You were being tested," said Stenning. "You were now thirty-five; you were more than competent at any job you'd been given and you knew how to handle men. But Ben had a feeling that you have a soft centre, and he discovered a way to find out if this was indeed so. He told me that the Petersons had walked all over you when you were a boy. He sent you to Hukahoronui to see if the same thing would happen."

Ballard was suddenly angry. "Who did he think he was? God? And what was it all for?"

Stenning said evenly, "You can't be as naive as that. Ben wanted you on the Board of Trustees. Brockhurst, Billy Bendell and myself are all old friends of Ben. We had to have two of the family on the board so they wouldn't smell a rat. If they had suspected what Ben was up to they'd have found a way to wreck his plan. The board is self-perpetuating. If a member retires there is a vote to elect his replacement and—this is important—the retiring member has a vote. Brockhurst is nearly eighty. When he retires you'll have his vote, you'll have Billy Bendell's vote, and you'll have my vote—and that's a majority and there's nothing the Ballards can do about it."

Ian said, "This is all very well, but I'm not an administrator, not of the trustee kind. I suppose there'd be an honorarium, but I have a living to earn."

Stenning shook his head sadly. "You still don't get the point.

Ben set up the Foundation for one reason only—to prevent his fortune from being dissipated and to keep the Ballard Group intact but out of the hands of his sons. The total value of the shares in the Ballard Group is two hundred and thirty-two million pounds. The holdings of your uncles and all your cousins is about fourteen million pounds. Whoever controls the Foundation controls the Ballard Group of companies. For seven years we've been waiting for you to come into your inheritance."

Ballard felt as though the wind had been knocked from him. That wonderful, egotistical, crazy old man! He rubbed his eyes and was aware of wetness. Stenning had been saying something. "What was that?"

"I said there's a snag," said Stenning. "Two days before he died Ben extracted a promise from me to come out here to see if the Petersons were still walking over you. I've been reading the newspaper accounts of the Inquiry with great interest, though I'm too much of a lawyer to believe all I read. You've been putting up a good fight, Ian, but it seems to me that the Petersons are still walking over you. Ben considered that the man who cannot defend himself is not the man to control the Ballard Group."

"And you are to be my sole judge?"

Stenning inclined his head. "The last task Ben set me is the hardest."

"That's the second shock you've handed me today," said Ballard. "I'd like to go away and think about this for a while."

"Very understandable," said Stenning.

AT THE HEARING...

At ten minutes to ten on Monday Ballard was in his seat and running through his notes. He saw Stenning ushered to a seat in the distinguished visitors' section. Stenning's eyes passed Ballard without a flicker.

A shadow fell athwart the table and Ballard looked up to see Rickman. "Mr Ballard, Mr Crowell was most annoyed on Friday

227

at your treatment of him on the witness stand, but he's had the weekend to think it over and now he's in a more considerate frame of mind," Rickman said.

"I'm glad to hear it." Ballard kept his face straight.

"You may not know it but Mr Crowell is taking the chairmanship of New Zealand Mineral Holdings, the parent company of the Hukahoronui Mining Company. He feels that to do the double job—chairmanship of both companies—would be too much for him. Consequently the chairmanship of the mining company will fall vacant."

"Interesting," said Ballard neutrally.

"You know that assays at the mine before the avalanche showed a highly enhanced gold enrichment, and the board decided to float a share issue. A considerable number of stock options will go with the job of chairman. When the news of the increased gold values is released the share prices will inevitably go up. Anyone with options will be in a position to make a lot of money."

"Isn't that illegal? Inside deals are frowned on."

"I assure you that the way it will be done will be perfectly legal," said Rickman smoothly. "Mr Crowell feels that you have qualities that make you suitable for the position of chairman should you wish to be considered as a candidate."

"For what consideration?" Ballard asked bluntly.

"Come now, Mr Ballard. We're both men of the world and we both know what we're talking about. It's a position few young men would turn down—especially in view of the evidence which may be forthcoming presently at this Inquiry—evidence particularly damaging to yourself. The effect of that evidence *could* be minimized." He paused. "Or vice versa."

Ian said, "I wouldn't want to be a man of your world, Mr Rickman. I'm a plain-speaking man and I'll tell you what I think. First you attempt to bribe me, and now you threaten me. I told Frank Ballard that neither would work. Get lost, Mr Rickman."

Rickman made an ejaculation of disgust, turned his back and walked to his seat.

Ballard turned his attention to the seat reserved for witnesses. Mike McGill raised his eyebrows in silent interrogation, and

228

Ballard winked at him. He had told Mike in confidence why Stenning had flown to New Zealand in such a hurry, and McGill had choked over his beer. "Two hundred and thirty-two million pounds . . . !"

"It's not mine," Ballard had said dryly. "It belongs to the shareholders."

"That may be, but you'll control it."

"I'm not a trustee yet. It's Stenning's decision."

"No, it isn't," McGill said sharply. "It's your decision. All you have to do is to steamroller the Petersons, and you have to do it publicly at the Inquiry."

"Steamroller the Petersons," repeated Ballard. "Liz might not think a lot of that."

"The world well lost for a woman—is that what you think?" McGill snorted. "Well, Stenning has made the issue quite clear. That's your last chance . . ."

Now Eric Peterson was giving evidence. "It must have been seven o'clock on the Sunday morning when my brother, John, woke me. With him were Mr Ballard and Dr McGill. They said there'd been an avalanche, that the Gap was blocked and that no one could get in or out. At first I didn't believe them. My brother got busy on the telephone and called an emergency council meeting at the supermarket."

AS IT WAS...

There had been no cold glare from the overhead fluorescent tubes that early Sunday morning. Two oil lamps gave a warmer glow which paled as the sky grew brighter.

Eric Peterson stoked the old-fashioned pot-bellied stove with billets of wood, and commented, "I'm glad we didn't get rid of this relic."

Matt Houghton walked up the aisle towards the group around the stove. "I know we agreed to meet this morning, but this is beyond a joke. Do you know the time?"

John Peterson said, "There's been an avalanche in the Gap, Matt. It's blocked completely. When there's been one avalanche there can be another." He added, "I suggest we apologize to Dr McGill and listen to his suggestions."

"No apology needed—and here's my first suggestion," McGill said. "There aren't enough of us here. I want more men brought in; strong men who don't scare easy. And women, too; but no shrinking violets—I want the bossy kind. Mrs Samson, will you act as secretary? Take down the names of those who are suggested."

Ten minutes later McGill said, "That ought to be enough. Mrs Samson, will you go out immediately, round up all those people and see they get here as soon as possible."

He looked out at the thin light. "The first thing that should be done is to let outside know what's happening here. As soon as it gets light enough I want men to climb out. If what comes down the hill is a powder avalanche then this store is going to go. I want all these shelves stripped and the food taken to a safe place —Turi Buck's house for a starter."

Houghton said, "We can't put the whole population in Turi Buck's house. I think we all ought to go up the east slope."

"That's out," said McGill. He leaned forward. "I hope it doesn't happen, Mr Houghton, but if a powder avalanche comes down the west slope it will cross the valley bottom and go clean across the river. I don't know how far it will go up the east slope."

Houghton looked sceptical, and McGill tapped him on the knee. "It will be moving very fast, Mr Houghton. Not only faster than you can run, but faster than you can drive a car."

"Is that your guess, McGill?" asked Eric.

"That's my estimate. The snow at the Gap was too dry for my liking. The drier it is the more likely it is to form a powder avalanche, and the more the temperature drops the drier it will get. And the temperature is dropping very quickly."

Eric said, "What about the mine? It would be a perfect place to put the people. It's like an air raid shelter right inside the mountain."

"I'm not sure it's a good thought," McGill said. "The portal is

230

right at the bottom of the slope and any avalanche is going to go right over it."

"But if, as you said, most of the snow will go right across the valley, then there'll be no trouble in getting out when it's over," said Houghton.

"That's when I was talking about a powder avalanche," said McGill. "But supposing the temperature rises, then it won't be a powder avalanche. It will be slower and wetter and a lot of snow will pile up at the bottom of the slope. And that will block the mine portal. Wet snow sets like concrete after an avalanche."

"The mine has the equipment," said John Peterson. "If they can mine rock, they can mine snow—or ice. They could be out an hour after it's over."

McGill stared at him. "I don't think we're on the same wavelength. Do you know how much snow there is on the west slope? My estimate is a million tons—plus."

Houghton said flatly, "Impossible!"

"You've got nearly two thousand acres up there covered with over six feet of snow," McGill said. "And it's been snowing like crazy for the last thirty-six hours, so I'm likely to be underestimating." He rubbed his jaw. "What do you think, Ian?"

"If you have fluid flowing past the portal at speeds you've been describing you'll also get some weird effects inside the mine. It'll be like blowing across the top of a bottle, but more so."

"Suction," said McGill. "It might pull all the air right out. I hadn't thought of that."

Someone walked along the aisle from the entrance. Ballard turned and saw a uniformed policeman. A sudden inspiration hit him and he smote McGill on the back. "Radio!" he said. "Pye must have a transmitter."

Arthur Pye stopped. "Morning, John. What's the trouble? Ma Samson said you wanted to see me on the double."

Ballard cut in. "Arthur, you have a radio transmitter, don't you?"

"Normally I do, Mr Ballard, but it's been acting up a bit, so it went in for servicing on Friday. I'll have it back tomorrow."

McGill groaned. John Peterson put up his hand and explained

231

the problem concisely. Pye said, "What's being done about this?"

John indicated the growing crowd at the entrance. "We're getting together some of the steadier people."

"You'd better tell them the bad news quickly," advised Pye. "They're getting a bit restive."

McGill nodded in appreciation.

AT THE HEARING...

Eric Peterson said, "Those people took a lot of convincing that the town was in danger."

Harrison said, "How was this situation finally resolved?"

"Arthur Pye said it was time to cut the cackle. He was very forceful about it."

Harrison addressed the hall. "Constable Pye, as you may know, was killed after the avalanche in a most valiant rescue attempt. Yesterday I was informed that Constable Pye and Mr William Quentin, the union representative at the mine, have been posthumously awarded the George Cross by Her Majesty."

There was a storm of applause. When the hall quietened, Harrison said to Eric Peterson, "Can you tell us what Mr Ballard was doing at this time?"

"He used the telephone, and then talked to Mr Cameron."

"You did not hear what they said?"

"No, sir."

Harrison looked at Ballard. "In view of a certain decision that was made about this time, I would like to hear what was said in that conversation. Will you step forward, Mr Ballard?"

Ballard was tense. In Hukahoronui he had made a decision, and now he was called upon to justify it. Because of that decision fifty-four people had died who might now be alive and the knowledge lay heavily upon him. He clasped his hands tightly to prevent his fingers trembling.

Harrison said, "Can you give us the gist of the conversation you had with Mr Cameron at that time?"

232

Ballard's voice was steady. "We talked about Mr Eric Peterson's proposal that the mine be used as a shelter. Dr McGill had said that powder avalanches were very fast—anything up to two hundred and eighty miles an hour." He paused. "But inside the snow mass there would be considerable turbulence resulting in gusts in excess of five hundred miles an hour. As the avalanche swept past the portal of the mine the suction would be tremendous."

"And what of the second type of avalanche?"

"The wet snow avalanche would come down possibly at a speed of thirty to forty miles an hour. As snow of that nature sets hard into ice immediately, we were faced with the possibility of having several hundred thousand tons of ice of an unknown thickness between hundreds of people in the mine and the outside world. These were the problems discussed by myself and Mr Cameron."

"And what were Mr Cameron's views?" asked Harrison.

AS IT WAS...

CAMERON had been pungent. "You want to put the whole population into a hole in a mountain because of something that may never happen? How long are they going to sit in there just waiting? They might stand it a day then they'll want out. Do you think you can stop them?"

"The town council might."

Cameron said, "To tell the truth, I'm not too happy about *anyone* being in the mine if there's going to be a fall. A million tons of snow falling an average vertical height of three thousand feet must set up *some* vibrations."

Ballard narrowed his eyes. "What are you getting at, Joe?"

"Well, you know we've been cutting a few corners."

"Why, in the name of God, did you let them get away with it?"

"My immediate boss is that spineless lump of jelly, Dobbs," snapped Cameron. "And the men were as bad. That production bonus the company has been handing out is near criminal. The guys are only human and if they can earn a fast buck by ignoring

233

a regulation they'll go for the dough every time. And Dobbs looked the other way because he got a piece of the cake, too."

"And you?"

Cameron looked at the floor. "I did my best. I pleaded for more money to go into safety, to go into supporting structures. All I got was the one answer—'Make do.'"

"All that's water under the bridge. What's worrying you?"

"If that lot falls off the mountain—wet snow or dry, it doesn't matter—it's going to make a hell of a big thump. I don't think the supporting structures will take it."

Ballard drew in his breath. "Anyone in the mine now?"

"Sunday maintenance crew. Some engineers and electricians."

"Get them out now. And bloody well jump, Joe."

Ballard turned and went to the noisy argumentative crowd near the door. Arthur Pye raised his voice in a bull bellow. "Quiet! Let's hear what McGill has to say."

McGill turned as Ballard arrived at his elbow. "We've been discussing Eric Peterson's idea of using the mine as a shelter. I think it's not such a bad idea if Joe Cameron can put a stopper at the entrance. And it will easily hold everyone."

"No," said Ballard. "Nobody is going in. I've just ordered the men who are already in the mine to come out. I don't think the mine is safe."

Pye frowned. "Not safe?"

"As soon as the men are out I'm having the entrance sealed," said Ballard.

AT THE HEARING...

"And that's how it was," said Ballard.

Harrison said to the assessor on his left, "Do you have any questions, Mr French?"

"Indeed I have." French drew his chair around so that he could get a good view of Ballard. "You know that I am from the Department of Mines, Mr Ballard. I have followed your evidence with

234

great care. Because of the peculiar nature of this country the mining regulations are framed in such a way as to take account of earthquakes.

"After the disaster the mine was unsealed and the supporting structures had proved to be equal to the shock. Nothing had collapsed. If the whole population of Hukahoronui had sheltered in the mine, as was proposed by Mr Eric Peterson, they would all have been safe. What do you say to that, Mr Ballard?"

Ballard looked troubled. "It has weighed heavily on my mind ever since the avalanche. It is now evident that I made the wrong decision, but were I placed in the same position again I would not vary my decision."

There was an uneasy rustle from the public gallery. Harrison said gently, "But the mine *should* have been safe, Mr Ballard." He looked at French. "Was the mine unsealed by a member of the Inspectorate of Mines, Mr French?"

"Yes, it was. His report was unfavourable."

Ballard said, "I made a similar report to the board of the company. I request that it be introduced as evidence."

Harrison leaned forward. "Mr Rickman, can that report be produced?"

Rickman whispered with Crowell for a few minutes, then he looked up. "No such report has been received from Mr Ballard."

Ballard was pale. He said, "I can provide the Commission with a copy of that report."

"With respect, Mr Chairman," said Rickman. "The fact that Mr Ballard can provide a copy of a report does not necessarily mean that a report was sent to the board of the company."

Harrison looked interested. "Are you seriously suggesting that the report Mr Ballard has offered to me has been fraudulently written after the event?"

Ballard looked at Rickman who looked back at him blandly. "Mr Rickman is imputing that I am a liar."

"Oh no!" said Rickman with an ingenuous air. "Only that you very well could be."

"I would delight in answering any questions concerning the safety of the mine from Mr French, from Mr Gunn, who represents the General Mining Union, or from any other interested person," said Ballard.

The smile disappeared from Rickman's face as Gunn seized upon the offer. "Mr Ballard, apart from this disputed report did you mention the matter to anyone else at the time?"

"I talked about it to Mr Dobbs, Mr Cameron, and Dr McGill, both before and after the avalanche."

"Had you taken steps to right matters?"

"I wrote the report and was preparing to follow it up."

"How long was it before the disaster that you took up your position with the company?"

"Six weeks."

"Only six weeks!" echoed Gunn in well-simulated surprise. "Then Mr Rickman, or even Mr Lyall, can hardly suggest that you were responsible for the state of affairs in the mine."

Rickman remained silent.

"But someone must have been responsible," pursued Gunn. "What was the reason for this scandalous state of affairs?"

"The mine was teetering on the verge of loss. All margins had to be shaved. Anything that did not conduce towards productivity went to the wall—and that included safety margins." Ballard looked towards Rickman. "Now that a rich vein of conglomerate ore has been struck one hopes that more money will go to safety."

Rickman leaped to his feet. "Mr Chairman, I must protest. The witness is giving away the very secrets of the company. Is this the conduct of a responsible managing director?"

Pandemonium broke out. Harrison hammered on the rostrum.

"The hearing is adjourned until those present can control themselves."

WHEN THE Commission of Inquiry re-convened in the afternoon the late sun poured through the stained glass windows of the hall. Patches of colour lay across the tables; the carafe of water in front of Ballard looked as though it was filled with blood.

Harrison said acidly, "I hope we do not have a recurrence of the behaviour which led to the adjournment of this morning's session." He consulted his notes. "I would like to ask one further question, Mr Ballard. I have looked through your evidence and I find that Mr Dobbs, the mine manager and Mr Cameron's superior, has figured little. Where was Mr Dobbs all this time?"

Ballard hesitated. "I don't really know. He seemed to retreat into himself. He relinquished all his duties into my hands. I was perturbed and I sent Dr Scott to see if he could discover what was the matter."

Harrison consulted his notes again. "I will call Dr Scott later, if it proves necessary. Dr McGill seems to have taken charge at this time. We had better hear his testimony. Dr McGill, what was then the prime consideration in your mind?"

McGill took his seat, and said, "The safety of the people. And I had a great deal of co-operation. Mr Ballard and John Peterson were very able joint chiefs-of-staff. Mr Ballard provided the resources of the mine, while Mr Peterson did the same for the town. I would like especially at this time to commend John Peterson. It was important to communicate with outside. Two teams were sent to climb out of the valley as soon as light permitted. One team was to climb the avalanche debris blocking the Gap, the other took a more circuitous route. There was a thick mist—almost a fog."

Professor Rolandson looked up, "I'd like to know about that."

"The first avalanche blocked the river as well as the road. The river had been frozen but the water flowed freely under the ice. When the river was blocked the water rose and broke the ice. The water was relatively warm and on contact with the cold air produced a mist."

"An ingenious theory," said Rolandson.

"The fog hampered our operations considerably," said McGill. "The main thing was to convince the town people we were serious and this is why the telephone system was so important. The council members spoke by telephone with every household in the valley, and it was at this time I became worried about the telephone exchange. It was right in the open and sure to be hit. One of the mine electricians volunteered to man the board. However, Mrs Maureen Scanlon said that it was her board and that no one else was going to touch it."

McGill lowered his voice. "The telephone system worked perfectly right up to the time of the avalanche, when the exchange was destroyed and Mrs Scanlon was killed. Mr John Peterson was also killed at that time in an effort to save Mrs Scanlon."

Professor Rolandson said, "How certain were you, at this time, that there would be another avalanche?"

"Avalanches are notoriously unpredictable. But based upon my investigation of the slope I put the chance of an avalanche at about seventy per cent—and rising as the temperature fell."

"I take it that the people were advised to go to safe places. Who determined those places?" Harrison asked.

"I did, sir," McGill hesitated. "I looked at as much of the actual ground as I could and tried to take advantage of topographical features; anything to put something between the people and the snow. The difficulty was no one wanted to leave a warm house to stay in the open in the snow. And I had to think of what to do *after* the avalanche hit. To find a person buried in snow is exceptionally difficult. Speed is essential. Swiss experience shows that it takes a trained team of twenty men twenty hours to thoroughly probe an area of one hectare of snow after an avalanche.

"Well, we had no trained men and no equipment. We had to improvise with what we had. We stripped TV antennae from the houses; these provided aluminium tubing to make probes for the rescue teams. Mr Cameron, at the mine workshop, made them up into lengths of ten feet. I organized three teams, a total of sixty men, and tried to give a crash course in avalanche rescue . . ."

AS IT WAS...

THE MIST had been clammy against the skin. It wreathed in coils as the slight breeze shifted. A large group of men, bulky in cold weather clothing, milled about aimlessly, stamping their feet, beating their arms across their chests.

"All right, you guys," yelled McGill. "Those who have probes step forward and line up. Feet about ten inches apart."

Holding a ball of string, he gave the end to the man on the extreme left of the line. "Hold that." He walked along the line, unreeling string, until he was at the extreme right then he cut the string and gave it to the man on the end. "Now, you two guys bend down and stretch that string tight on the snow. Everyone else put the toes of their boots against the string.

"Pretend that in front of you is an area in which you think someone is buried, but you don't know exactly where. You put the probe in front of the toe of your left boot, and push down."

All the men probed. "Okay, now you do the same at the toe of your right boot."

Someone called out. "How do we know when we've found a body?"

"You'll know. It's unmistakable," McGill said. "We call this a fine search, and there's a ninety-five per cent chance of finding a body if there's one there. If you do hit a body go easy on the pressure—don't use that probe as a spear. Call your team leader, who will mark the spot for the digging team. Right, now you markers take a step forward—not more than a foot—and stretch that string again. All you others put your toes against it and probe again the same way as before."

"Here comes Cameron with more probes now," someone called.

McGill swung around to see a truck halt and Cameron come towards them.

"How are you doing, Mike?" Cameron asked.

McGill looked about to make sure he was out of earshot of the men. "Not good. These guys are enthusiastic enough, but when it comes to the crunch they'll not be much use. Some of them might be under the snow instead of on top and the rest will be good for nothing. A million tons of snow—or anything else, for that matter—dropping close by takes the pith out of a man. It's known as disaster shock. We'll need outside help, and I hope they have dogs. Half the victims of avalanches in Switzerland are found by dogs."

Cameron watched the line of men probing into the snow. "Then what are you doing all this for?"

"Just to keep up morale. How many probes did you bring?"

"Twenty. There'll be another twenty in under an hour." He looked back at the truck. "I'll be on my way."

As Cameron drove away a Land-Rover swept up. Two men got out, one of them Ballard. Ballard hurried over.

"Mike, this is Jack MacAllister. He's an electrical engineer. He came over the Gap after discovering the power breakdown."

"We met a couple of your people on top," said MacAllister. "They've gone on to get to a telephone. They told us what was happening so I came on down to see for myself."

"Thank God!" said McGill. "What are the chances of evacuating the valley—all the people?"

MacAllister shook his head. "Not a chance. It took me all my time getting over. That snow has set solid—it's more like ice now. In places it's a vertical climb."

"At least now we've got through to outside."

"They knew last night," said MacAllister unexpectedly. "I telephoned the police after I'd been to the scene of the break in the cable. There's a whole gang of them on the other side of the Gap right now. Hush! What's that?"

There was a faint drone from overhead, growing louder. "An airplane," said McGill, straining his eyes against the mist.

They listened while the aircraft droned for about ten minutes and then went away, only to return five minutes later.

"AND THAT'S it," said McGill. He looked at Harrison. "That's when the avalance hit us . . ."

AVALANCHE...

HIGH ON the western slope and deep in the snow the processes of disaster were well advanced. Air, slightly warmed from the ground, rose through the snow laden with water vapour until it reached the impenetrable layer of hoar frost half way through the snow mass. Here it cooled to create tapered cup crystals.

The heavy snow-fall of the past two days had increased the

240

weight operating against the cup crystals. A man may take an orange pip, hold it gently between forefinger and thumb and squeeze ever so gently—and the orange pip will be propelled with considerable velocity. So it was on the western slope. A heavy-footed hawk alighting on the snow could provide that little extra pressure and set the cup crystals in motion.

Something like that did occur and a small slippage started. The new-fallen snow, very dry and powdery, was lifted by the sudden movement and a white plume arose like a puff of smoke. But underneath chaos had begun. The fragile ice plate of the hoar layer cracked, jostling the cup crystals beneath which began to roll. Cracks spread wide, zig-zagging at high speed from the point of original breakage.

It was a lightning chain reaction; one event followed another and suddenly a section of the snow fifty feet across slumped forward. Presently the whole of the higher slope across a front of a hundred yards was plunging downwards.

Five seconds after the first slippage an agile man two hundred yards down the slope could have avoided death by running aside. The speed of the young avalanche was not much more than ten miles an hour. But the air resistance caused the feathery surface snow to rise and, as the speed increased, more of the snow powder became airborne.

The powder mixed turbulently with the air to form a gas with a density ten times that of air. The gas cloud picked up speed and moved ahead of the main slide. Twenty seconds after the first slippage it was moving at fifty miles an hour, hammering gustily at the snow slope and smashing the delicate balance of forces that held the snow in place.

The avalanche fed hungrily on the snow lower down the slope. Already the whole of the upper slope was seething across a front of four hundred yards, and clouds of snow rose like the thunder-heads of a summer's day, but incredibly faster.

At seventy miles an hour the avalanche cloud began to pull the surrounding air into itself, increasing its volume. At a hundred miles an hour the turbulence in its entrails was causing blasts of two hundred miles an hour. At a hundred and thirty miles an hour whirlwinds began to form along its edges with internal velocities of more than three hundred miles an hour.

By this time the mature avalanche was moving so fast that the air in front did not have time to get out of the way. An air blast began to develop in front of the rapidly moving snow, a travelling shock wave which could destroy a building as effectively as a bomb.

A million tons of snow and a hundred thousand tons of air were on the move at over two hundred miles an hour, with much greater internal gusting. The air blast hit the mist at the bottom of the valley and squirted it aside violently to reveal momentarily a few buildings. A fraction of a second later the main body of the avalanche hit the valley bottom.

The white death had come to Hukahoronui.

DR ROBERT SCOTT regarded Harold Dobbs with a clinical eye. Dobbs had not shaved for a couple of days and the stubble was dirty grey on his cheeks and chin. His eyes were bloodshot and his fingers twitched in his lap as he sat in an armchair, his face averted.

Scott noted the nearly empty gin bottle and the half full glass on the table and said, "Mr Ballard asked me to call in. He's worried that you might be ill."

"There's nothing wrong with me," said Dobbs. "Go away."

Scott said, "There must be something wrong, Harry. Why haven't you been working for the past couple of days? The company is entitled to some sort of explanation. After all, you *are* the mine manager. You know what's going on out there, don't you?"

"Let Ian Ballard handle it," snarled Dobbs. "He took my job, didn't he? Crowell said I'd be managing director when Fisher went. But oh no! This young Pommy sprout gets the job because he's called Ballard. The Ballards not only took my job but they expect me to serve under a Ballard. Well, they can damn well think again."

Scott said gently, "Even so, that's no excuse for pulling out now without a word. Not when there's trouble."

"Trouble!" Dobbs ground out the word. "The man's an idiot.

He's talking of spending millions to stop a few flakes of snow falling off a hillside. Where's the money to come from?"

Scott stood up. It had not taken him long to come to the conclusion that Dobbs was unbalanced. "I think we'd better get you to a safer place. If anything happens out there this house will be one of the first hit."

"Poppycock!" jeered Dobbs.

Scott shrugged and picked up his bag. "Suit yourself."

When he heard Scott's car start up Dobbs picked up his drink and went to the window. In the mist he could just make out the outline of the office block. He shook his head sorrowfully. "Closed down!" he whispered.

Suddenly the mist cleared and he felt a strange vibration through the soles of his feet. The office block lifted off its foundations and floated through the air towards him. He looked at it, mouth gaping, as it soared right over his house.

Then the window smashed before his eyes and a sliver of glass drove through his throat before the house exploded around him.

Harry Dobbs was the first man to be killed in Hukahoronui.

The poor devil, thought Dr Scott as he started his car. *A retreat from reality*.

He had gone three hundred yards when he found that the car would not answer to the wheel and he had an eerie sensation of floating. Then he saw, to his astonishment, that the car wheels were a good three feet from the ground. Before he had time to blink the car was flipped on to its back and he was knocked unconscious.

When he came round he found the car was again upright. Wincing, his fingers exploring the bump on his head, he looked about him. At first he could not recognize where he was, and when he did recognize his position his mind refused to believe it.

"I've been carried right across the river!" he whispered. He looked to where the township of Hukahoronui should have been. There was nothing but a jumble of snow.

Afterwards he measured the distance he had been taken by the avalanche. His car had been carried nearly three-quarters of a mile horizontally, across the river, and lifted nearly three hundred feet vertically to be deposited a fair distance up the east slope. The engine had stopped but when he turned on the ignition it purred away as sweetly as ever.

Dr Scott got out of the car and trudged through the snow, carrying his black bag, to where the supermarket had been, and he was still unable to take in the enormity of the disaster.

RALPH W. NEWMAN, the American tourist, had come to Hukahoronui for the skiing. He had certainly never expected to find himself in a line of twenty men, holding a long aluminium pole and driving it into the snow at the toe of each boot to the rasped commands of a Canadian scientist.

The man next to him nodded at McGill. "That joker would make a good sergeant-major."

"Think he's right about this avalanche?"

"He seems to know what he's doing." The other man leaned on his probe. "My name's Jack Haslam. I work at the mine. Where's your friend?"

"Miller? I don't know. He went out early this morning."

The probes went in methodically. Drive down . . . haul out . . . until a sudden yell from McGill stopped Newman. There was something in the quality of the shout which made his hair prickle.

"Take cover! You've got less than thirty seconds."

Newman ran towards the cluster of rocks that had been allotted to him in case of emergency. Haslam was at his elbow and as they reached the rocks he grabbed Newman by the arm. "This way! Used to play in here when I was a kid."

More men jammed into the small cave. One of them was Brewer, the probe team leader, who said, "Quiet, everyone!"

Suddenly there was a violent howl and the air was sucked out of the cave. Newman fought for breath. The rock underneath quivered and there was a thunderous drumming noise overhead. The air in the cave filled with fine particles of snow which began to build up thickly about the tangle of huddled bodies.

The men nearest the entrance scrabbled with their hands but the snow came swirling much more quickly than they could cope

244

with. "Cover your mouths!" shouted Brewer, and with difficulty
Newman brought his arm across his face. He felt the snow build
up about him, cold but dry. Finally, the space in the cave not
occupied by bodies was filled completely with snow. The noise
stopped. Newman found by pushing he could compress the snow
and make an air space. He remembered that Brewer had been
nearest to the cave entrance. "Can you get out?" he yelled.

From what seemed a hundred miles he heard a faint voice.
"Not a chance! There's a lot of snow outside!"

Newman was aware of the dead weight of Haslam next to him.
"There's a guy called Haslam here," he yelled. "He's unconscious."

Brewer said, "Wait a minute. I'm trying to get my torch from
my pocket." There were gasping sounds and the wriggling of
bodies, then a beam of light shot out over Haslam, and Brewer
crawled forward. Newman felt for Haslam's wrist pulse but could
detect no movement. "I think the guy's dead."

"There's snow in his mouth," said Brewer.

Newman put his finger in Haslam's mouth. "Not enough to stop
him breathing. Give me room—I'm going to try the kiss of life."

Room was made with difficulty, the men pushing the powdery
snow away, plastering it to the wall of the cave. "Maybe he died
of shock," someone suggested.

Newman breathed air into Haslam's lungs and then pumped
his chest. After fifteen minutes he stopped. "No good. He's gone."

Brewer snapped off the light and there was darkness and silence.
At last Newman said, "Nobody is going to find us with probes in
this cave. It looks as though we'll have to save ourselves."

Newman groped about and found Haslam's hat which he placed
over the dead man's face. It was a futile but human gesture.

There were six men jammed in that narrow cleft in the rock;
Brewer asked them to call out their names: Newman, Brewer,
Anderson, Jenkins, Fowler and Castle.

And the dead man—Haslam.

Turi Buck, Ruihi, his daughter-in-law, and his grand-daughter
were coping well with the influx of children. The house under the
great rock of Kamakamaru was too large now that his family

had grown up and gone and he welcomed the bustle and clamour. He relished less the glacial eye of Miss Frobisher, the schoolteacher who accompanied the children. Miss Frobisher's comments had a high acid content.

Dave Scanlon arrived with a truckload of canned goods and drums of fuel. Turi showed him where to put the oil and then supervised the unloading of the food by some of the older children. He then went to the back of the house where Jock McLean, the Scots engineer from the mine, was installing the generator.

McLean had drilled holes in the rock and inserted bolts. Now he was lowering the generator by means of a block and tackle.

Ruihi came out with a laden tray. "Will you have some tea, Mr McLean? There are homemade cakes."

"Thanks, I'll be glad o' that." McLean's eyes lit up as he bit into a cake. "Good," he said, rather indistinctly. "An old widower like me doesn't often get the chance o' real home cookin'."

Turi cocked his head on one side. He had heard a noise and for a moment thought it was an airplane. Then he recognized the eerie bass hum and a higher whistling sound.

He grabbed McLean's arm. "Into the house—quick! The snow is coming!" Looking at the old man's contorted face, McLean believed him instantly.

Turi slammed and locked the back door as soon as they were inside. "The children . . ." Then the avalanche hit.

The fundamental note was deep in the bass—a sound which grabbed his stomach as though he was being squeezed by a giant hand. He opened his mouth and air was expelled forcibly from his lungs as his diaphragm kicked sickeningly. Superimposed on the bass was a series of high-pitched whistles of ear-piercing intensity. The light had suddenly gone as though by an eclipse of the sun, and all he saw through the window was a dirty grey blur. The house lurched as it received two swift buffets. The window smashed inwards and fine snow dust jetted through the broken panes as though squirted from a great hose pipe. Then there was an opposite reaction. Air was sucked from the room.

The avalanche swept by the rock of Kamakamaru in under twenty seconds. When it was over McLean stood still, his ears

246

ringing, covered from head to foot with fine snow powder which gave him the appearance of a ghost.

Turi Buck stirred and shook his head, his hands to his ears. He said, "It is over." His voice reverberated in the cavities of his skull. "It is over." Every child in the house was screaming. "We must see to the children," said Turi.

"Yes," said McLean. His eyes were glazed and staring, his voice came out creakily. He frowned and deep cracks appeared in the powdering of snow that covered his lean face. He looked at Turi. "You're bleeding," he said.

The cut on Turi Buck's face, caused by a fragment of flying glass, was the only physical wound suffered by anyone in the house. Psychic wounds were something else.

Other houses in the valley were not as lucky.

MATT HOUGHTON's house was built on the other side of the river and a considerable way up the east slope, and to his mind the commanding view from his front porch added two thousand dollars to the value of the property. Houghton had a streak of vanity and, since his election as mayor of Hukahoronui, liked to think he was overlooking his kingdom.

This Sunday his wife, Mamie, was making tea and cutting piles of sandwiches, and he was playing the genial host to a number of unexpected visitors, the old people from the valley.

"It's so very good of you to have us here," said Mrs Jarvis tremulously. At eighty-two she was the oldest person in Hukahoronui. "Do you think we're safe here?"

"This house has not been knocked down by an avalanche yet, so I can't see it happening now." Houghton laughed jovially.

A tall, stringy woman carrying a clipboard walked over to Houghton. "Well, how are things, Mrs Fawcett?" he asked heartily.

She consulted the list. "All here except for Jack Baxter. Jim Hatherley is bringing him." She held her head on one side and looked up at the ceiling. "That airplane is here again."

"Doesn't that fool of a pilot know that any sound can start an avalanche?" said Houghton irritably. He went out on to the porch where he stared at the sky. There was nothing to be seen.

He was about to go back inside when Jim Hatherley ran up. "I've got trouble, Mr Houghton. Jack Baxter slipped when he was getting out of the car. I'm pretty sure he's bust his leg."

"Better telephone the doctor; the phone's in the hall. I'll go down and see to Jack."

"Okay," Hatherley went into the house and got Maureen Scanlon at the exchange. He said, "Maureen, do you think you can find Dr Scott . . .?"

"I'll try." The line clicked as she broke connection.

THE AVALANCHE eventually came to a halt a hundred yards from the Houghton house. There was no danger of it being overwhelmed with snow. But the air blast came up the hill at about one hundred and fifty miles an hour. It ripped off the roof and the house exploded as though hit by a bomb. Twenty-eight people died, some immediately, others in hospitals a few days later.

When the house was hit Houghton was bending over Baxter. He was protected by the car, and the car was protected by a hillock. When the air blast roared up the hill the car did nothing more than rock heavily on its springs. Houghton was mystified, but not alarmed. He looked under the car, then walked around to where he could see into the valley. His gaze shifted and he rubbed the back of his neck perplexedly. He could not see the town of which he was mayor.

Baxter moaned and Houghton turned to go up to the house, and then stopped dead. *There was no house!*

A strangled noise and froth came from his lips. Stiffly he toppled forward and never knew when he hit the ground.

Presently a querulous voice said, "Matt! Where is everybody?" Jack Baxter, his leg broken, but untouched by the avalanche was still very much alive. He did not understand then, or ever after, how lucky he was to have broken his leg at the moment he did.

STACEY CAMERON drove to Dr Scott's house. Because she had first-aid training she had volunteered to help on the medical side. Liz Peterson was there.

"Dr Scott wants us to round up medical supplies," Liz said.

They drove to the chemist's shop where Liz knocked angrily on the locked door. "Rawson promised to be here," she said.

She looked past Stacey at a truck coming down the street, and waved it down. "Dave, have you seen Rawson anywhere?" she called.

Dave Scanlon said, "I saw him going into the hotel about half an hour ago."

At the Hotel D'Archiac, a rumble of male voices came from the crowded bar and the dining-room was being prepared for lunch as though it was any other Sunday of the year.

Liz saw Eric standing at the entrance to the bar and brought him across the lobby with a jerk of her head. "Is Rawson in there?"

"Yes, I saw him talking to—"

"Get him out. We need medical supplies."

Presently he came back with Rawson, a tall, gaunt man who wore thick-lensed spectacles. "I suppose I'd better come," he said.

When he unlocked his shop he said fussily, "I don't know that I'm not breaking the law by doing this." He scanned Liz's list with maddening deliberation. "My!" he said at last. "Who is going to pay for all this?"

Liz slammed her hand on the counter. "If you're worried about the money put it on Johnnie's account."

"Wait a minute. All this morphine. I can't issue that without a prescription. This is most irregular."

"If you turn to the last page you'll find Dr Scott's signature."

"That's not good enough . . ."

"Now look here: if you don't get moving and produce everything on that list I'll have Arthur Pye confiscate your whole stock. Stacey, use that telephone and find Arthur Pye."

"Oh, very well, let's begin," Rawson said hastily. "Bandages —ten dozen boxes of two-inch, ten dozen boxes of three-inch, the same of six . . ." He broke off. "We'll have to go into the stock room for those." He unlocked the door. "All the bandages are on those shelves to the right. I'll be in the dispensary getting the drugs together."

The two girls marched past him and, shaking his head at the impetuosity of modern youth, he went into the dispensary and unlocked the cupboard in which he kept the registered drugs. He began filling a box with ampoules, keeping careful count and making a note every so often in the Poisons Register. He was a most meticulous man.

He was not to know it but the combination of his broken promise and his scrupulosity meant that he was a dead man. He was still in the dispensary when the avalanche hit.

When the front of the shop caved in, the shock caused a half-gallon bottle to leap off a shelf and smash on the table before him. It was full of hydrochloric acid which splashed over his face and body. Fortunately, when he opened his mouth to scream it filled with soft snow and he died quickly of asphyxia.

Liz was hurled against stacked boxes of bandages which cushioned the shock, although the edge of a shelf broke two of her ribs. The whole mass, shelving, boxes, and the bodies of Liz and Stacey, was forced against the rear wall which gave, and Liz was precipitated through the air in a tangle of streaming bandages.

She fell onto snow, and more snow covered her, clamping her arms and legs. She was quite conscious and wondered if she were about to die.

She did not know that Stacey Cameron was in much the same position not more than ten feet away. Both girls lost consciousness at about the same time.

THE HOTEL D'Archiac was speedily demolished. Most of the men who were drinking in the bar were killed by flying bottles. Alice Harper, the waitress who had served McGill with colonial goose on the previous evening, was killed by a heavy suitcase which fell from the bedroom above.

A lot of miners, holding a protest meeting in the dining-room about the mine being closed, died when the roof fell in. Bill Quentin, who had stirred the miners up, had left the hotel with Eric Peterson only moments before it was destroyed.

"Where are you going?" he asked Eric.

"To join Johnnie in the cellar of the old Fisher house."

"Don't tell me you believe in Doomsday?"

Eric stopped on the opposite pavement. His back was to the Fisher house and so he did not see his brother run across the road towards the telephone exchange. "Johnnie's no fool and he believes in it," he said. "And I'm beginning to."

"I think I'll come with you," said Quentin. The two men were just going down the steps into the basement when the house was hit. Eric tumbled the rest of the way. Bill Quentin fell on top of Eric and broke Eric's arm; he himself was quite unhurt.

AFTER SHOUTING his warning, McGill dropped into his own selected shelter, jostled by Ballard. He grabbed the telephone which had been installed by a mine electrician and rang the exchange. "Plug me into John Peterson, Mrs Scanlon, and then get out of there—fast!"

"I understand." The ringing tone came into his ear.

"John Peterson here."

"McGill. Get your people under cover. It's coming down."

"What about Maureen Scanlon?"

"I've told her to get out. Keep an eye open for her."

Mrs Scanlon took off the headset, stood up, and lifted her coat from a hook. Peterson had earlier told her to join him in the old Fisher building in case of an emergency. The switchboard buzzed. She turned back and lifted the headset. "What number do you want?"

"Maureen, do you think you can find Dr Scott? This is Jim Hatherley at Matt Houghton's house. Old Jack Baxter took a bad fall and we think he's broken his leg."

"I'll try." She rang Scott's house.

In the Fisher house Peterson ran into the hall. A freckled-faced fourteen-year-old girl was standing in the doorway, and he said, "Into the basement, Mary. On the double."

But she said, "Where are you going?"

"To fetch Mrs Scanlon." He ran up the empty street, reached the corner where a road ran towards the mine, cast a glance along it, and skidded to a frantic halt. The mine office block was flying through the air directly at him, disintegrating as it came. It fell squarely on to the telephone exchange, obliterating it.

The wind gusted at him and he felt a tremendous pain in his chest. *Heart attack!* he thought dimly. He lost consciousness and died very soon thereafter.

In the basement of the Fisher house no-one died but there were several serious injuries.

IN THE supermarket, Councillor Phil Warrick said, "I hope Dr McGill knows what he's doing about this avalanche. I swear my arms have lengthened two inches because of lugging around all this food. We've just about got it cleared." He lifted the lid of the stove and dropped in some chunks of wood. It was nearly red-hot.

Maureen Scanlon's husband, Dave, said, "I'm worried about Maureen. Someone said the exchange is too exposed. I'll just pop along and see her." He turned to go, and froze in mid-stride.

A three-ton truck parked outside was picked up bodily and thrown through the plateglass windows of the supermarket like a monstrous projectile. Even as it came the building was collapsing around them, the showy false front shearing through the roof. Dave Scanlon died instantly, hit by the truck and mashed to a bloody pulp.

The cast-iron stove was ripped from its concrete plinth. It was driven through the rear wall of the store and hit a fuel oil tank, which ruptured. Phil Warrick went flying after the stove and fell on top of it. The lid came off and a stream of hot embers shot out, igniting the oil which streamed from the tank. The fire could not last long because of the snow which drove over the area, but it lasted long enough to kill Phil Warrick. Embracing the hot stove, he was burned alive under six feet of snow.

JOE CAMERON, driving a truck back to the mine after delivering snow probes, was caught in the open. The air blast slammed at the truck broadside on and it rocked violently; then the snow cloud toppled it over and it began to roll.

In the cabin of the truck Cameron was getting a mauling.

His right foot was trapped between the accelerator and clutch pedals and his body flopped helplessly from side to side. When his arm went through the spokes of the wheel it broke with a dry crack.

The truck came to rest upside down under fifteen feet of snow. Cameron was also upside down, his head resting against the cabin roof and his foot still trapped. There was much snow in the cabin, stained bright red from a gash on his cheek. He was unconscious, but presently he stirred and groaned.

He had the eerie impression that his head was bulging with the pressure of blood and he had a headache of nauseating intensity. He shouted, but even to him it sounded weak.

There was no way of knowing how much snow there was above him. He detected a little stuffiness in the air of the cabin and that made him afraid. It would be hell to die slowly of lack of oxygen.

There was something else Cameron did not know, and it was better for him that he should not. The truck was upside down in the river bed, and the snow which had dammed the flow of water was being eaten into upstream of him. Inexorably the river was coming to him.

First came the air blast and then the heavy hammer fist of the snow cloud.

Following these came the sliding surface snow, moving in a flowing tide across Hukahoronui. It washed around the church and the spire shuddered; it obliterated the wreckage of the hotel and swept over the remnants of Mr Rawson's shop; it reached the supermarket and covered the burned body of Phil Warrick; then it went on across the bluff to the river where it spilled over the edge and filled the river bed with snow.

Across the river it slowed until it was moving at no more than the speed of a man running fast. A little later, when it encountered the rising ground of the east slope, it stopped entirely, having clothed destruction in immaculate whiteness.

The avalanche had finished. The disaster had not.

AFTERMATH...

McGILL climbed to the top of a small mound of snow, looked down the valley, and said softly, "Oh my God!"

The only building he could see was the church, which looked as though it had been given a coat of whitewash. For the rest, there was just a hummocky expanse of snow.

He went back to Ballard and bent over him. "Come on, Ian. It's over now and we have work to do."

Ballard raised his head slowly. His eyes were dark smudges in a white face and showed no comprehension. He was suffering from disaster shock. His lips worked before he said, "What?"

McGill was not feeling too good himself, but because he had known what would happen he had been able to ward off the worst effects. A lot of people must have died and, if the rest of the survivors were like Ballard, then a lot more would die from want of help. He slapped Ballard across the face very hard. "Get up, Ian," he said harshly.

Ballard heaved himself up, rubbing his stinging cheek, and McGill led him to the viewpoint. "Take a look."

Ballard's face crumpled. "There's nothing left," he breathed.

"There's plenty left," contradicted McGill. "But we have to find it. We have to get some sort of organization going."

Fifteen minutes later they had grown from two to twenty. The stunned survivors were ruthlessly extracted from the holes where they were hiding. They were all shocked in varying degrees and all showed a marked aversion to looking up at the slope from which disaster had come. They stood around apathetically with their backs to the west.

McGill selected the brightest of them and set them searching in their turn, and more survivors came to light. To Ballard he said, "Take three men and go to Turi Buck's house. Find out how they're shaping." He himself set off for the town. His last command was: "If anyone finds Dr Scott, he's to report to me. We'll use the church as a base."

WHEN BALLARD and his team arrived at the house he was thankful to hear voices and even laughter. Turi was sitting in a big armchair surrounded by a flock of children, looking like a biblical patriarch.

"Thank God!" Ian said. "Are you all right, Turi?"

"We're all fine." Turi nodded to where Ruihi was supporting Miss Frobisher and administering tea. Miss Frobisher had been of no use at all. She had curled into a foetal ball and whimpered from time to time. "She was shaken up a bit."

From behind the house came a whine which settled into a steady throb. Startled, Ballard said, "What's that?"

"I think Jock McLean will be testing the generator." Turi stood up. "Would you like some tea?" he asked. Ballard nodded dumbly. When the tea, laced liberally with brandy, and the sandwiches arrived Ballard ate as hungrily as though he had not eaten for a week.

"We have plenty of food," Turi said.

"We'll take some back to town. It will be a load to carry but we'll have to manage."

Ruihi said, "The car's in the garage, isn't it?"

Ballard sat upright. "You have a *car?*"

The car proved to be an elderly station-wagon and he ignored it because of the Ferguson tractor standing next to it. Fifteen minutes later the tractor was loaded with canned goods and on its way to town.

When Ballard arrived at the church he found more people than he had expected, with McGill at an improvised desk by the altar, the centre of a growing organization. In one corner Dr Scott was very busy aided by three women. Most of his patients had broken bones and two men were breaking up a pew to make splints. Ballard saw that Eric Peterson was in line for attention, so he strode over to him. "Is Liz all right?"

Eric's face was white. "I don't know. She and that American girl were at Rawson's shop, I think, when we were hit." His eyes were bleak. "The shop's gone." There was hysteria in his voice.

"I'll check," said Ballard.

He went over to McGill. "Turi's place is okay," he said. "They've got a generator working and I have a load of food outside—with a tractor."

McGill gave a long sigh. "Thank God the kids are safe." He nodded. "Good work, Ian." Ballard turned away and McGill said, "Where are you going?"

"To look for Liz and Stacey."

"You'll do nothing of the kind," snapped McGill. "If you go tramping out there you'll ruin the scent for a dog, and a dog can do better work than a hundred men."

Ballard was about to reply hotly but someone pushed past him and said quickly, "I've just come from Houghton's house and it's like a butcher's shop. I found Jack Baxter and Matt Houghton outside the house. Jack's as chirpy as a cricket, but his leg's broken. There's something funny about Matt; he can hardly speak and he's paralysed all down one side."

"Could be a stroke," said Scott.

"I put them both in a car and brought them down as far as I could. I didn't dare cross the river on that soft snow so I left them on the other side."

"And the house?"

"I didn't stop to count the bodies. Some are still alive."

They had not been conscious of the distant vibration in the air but now it burst upon them with a bellow. Ballard ducked his head, thinking it was another avalanche about to hit them but McGill looked up at the roof. "A plane—and a big one!"

They ran to the church door. The aircraft had gone down the valley and was now banking to come back. It was a big transport marked with United States Navy insignia. A ragged cheer broke out and there was a beatific smile on McGill's face.

"A Navy Hercules," he said. "The Marines have arrived in the nick of time. It's the outfit that does all the flying in the Antarctic in support of our Operation Deep Freeze."

The Hercules steadied, flying straight down the valley. From its stern, black specks dropped and then the parachutes opened and blossomed like multi-coloured flowers. McGill counted: ". . . seven . . . eight . . . nine . . . ten. And those are just the experts we need."

256

Lieut-Commander Jesse Rusch, United States Navy, smothered his parachute and snapped the quick release button.

It had become a much prized tradition that the Antarctic Development Squadron Six doubled up on rescue operations, particularly those involving air transport, and to Rusch's knowledge no rescue flight had ever run short of volunteers. Now he checked the others as they came down, then turned to meet the group of men stumbling towards him across the snow. As McGill approached Rusch stepped forward. "You've cut yourself a slice of trouble, Mike. Are you in charge?"

"No!" Ballard came forward, his hand gripping Peterson's good arm. "This is Eric Peterson, a town councillor—the only one around. He represents civil authority."

"Me!" Peterson said to Ballard. "What about Matt Houghton?"

"He seems to have had a stroke."

Peterson's face worked. "I can't fly fast on a broken wing. You'd better be co-opted, Ian. You and McGill."

"Right!" Ballard turned to Rusch. "We need medical supplies," he said.

"Those we've got." Rusch swung around and yelled, "Hey, Chief, I want the medical sled—on the double."

Ballard said, "Dr Scott will take charge of that. What about communications, Lieutenant?"

"We have five walkie-talkies, so we can set up a network. There's a bigger transmitter in one of the sleds for outside communication. We ought to be able to raise Christchurch."

"I'd like to talk to somebody at Civil Defence as soon as possible," Ballard said.

On the way back to the church McGill fell in step with Ballard. "What did Turi feed you on at the house? Raw meat? What's the idea of pushing Peterson forward like that?"

"Strategy. He abdicated—didn't you hear him? Look, Mike: I'm a trained administrator and I'd be wasted doing anything else. You're a snowman and you'd be wasted doing anything else. Let's get our priorities right."

"Makes sense." McGill grinned. "And legal too. We're now town councillors, you and me both."

They went into the church. Rusch stopped and frowned. The pews were full of white-faced, lethargic men and women with lustreless eyes. They sat or lay in abandoned attitudes, still and silent, gazing back in horror at the closeness of death.

"We'll need blankets," said Ballard. "And what else, Mike?"

"Trained men—in quantity. They can come in by helicopter and light planes equipped with skis. Rescue dogs, too. And they can get these people out on the return trip," said McGill.

"There are no dogs in the country as far as I know," said Rusch, "but try Mount Cook and Coronet Peak."

Ballard nodded. Those were popular skiing and climbing areas. "There should be trained men there, too." He raised his voice. "Arthur, come here for a minute."

Arthur Pye walked to the desk. His face was haggard and his movements stiff, but there was that spark of intelligence in his eyes which was missing from most of the others.

"How many missing, Arthur?" Ballard said.

"It's hard getting anything out of anybody." Pye hesitated. "Of course I'm not sure—they're still drifting in, one or two at a time. Say three hundred and fifty."

Rusch stiffened. *"That many!"*

McGill said, "The ones who are coming in now are the lucky ones. There'll be others who are buried."

"Come on, Mike," said Rusch. "Let's start looking."

One of the Americans stopped in front of Ballard. "CPO Laird, sir. I've got the radio set up outside. But I have a portable handset you can use here. It's two-way—use it like an ordinary telephone." He put the handset down.

Ballard looked down. "Who will I be talking to?"

"Communications Centre, Operation Deep Freeze."

Ballard took a deep breath and stretched out his hand.

"Hello, this is Ballard. Can you put me through to Civil Defence Headquarters?"

RUSCH, McGill and two of the American servicemen crunched across the snow over the desolation that was Hukahoronui. McGill took off his glove and bent to feel the texture of the snow.

258

"It's hardening," he said. "I was training some guys in snow rescue before we got hit. I said then they'd be no good, and I was right. What's worrying me is that we're going to get several hundred people flying in here." McGill nodded to the west slope. "There's still a lot of snow up there, so I think only half of it came down, sliding on a hoar frost surface. I'm worried that she'll come down again. I'd like to take a look."

The man behind Rusch touched his arm, "Look at that dog, sir. It's sniffing at something in the snow."

An Alsatian was pawing at the snow and whining. As they approached, the dog looked up and wagged its tail and then scraped at the snow with its forepaw. "Maybe it's not trained," said McGill. "But it's the best we've got."

They found the body beneath three feet of snow and Rusch said, "What happened to his face? Do you know him, Mike?"

"His wife wouldn't know him," said McGill bleakly. His face was pale.

The dog wagged its tail and trotted off across the snow, where it stopped and began to sniff and scratch again. "Round up some men and dig wherever that dog scratches," Rusch said.

McGill heard skis hissing on snow and turned to see two men approaching. The one in the lead pushed up his goggles. "What can I do to help?" said Charlie Peterson. Miller was behind him.

McGill said, "You can lend me your skis. I'm going up the mountain."

Charlie looked down at the body. "It's Rawson!"

"How do you know?" asked Rusch. "The guy's got no face."

Charlie pointed. "He lost the first joint of the little finger of his left hand." He looked at McGill. "Take Miller's skis. I'll come with you."

"That slope's not the safest place in the world, Charlie."

Charlie grinned crookedly. "You can get killed crossing the road. I said that before, didn't I?"

Rusch watched them go. It wasn't a job he would fancy. "Sir!" one of his men called. "We've got another one—alive and female."

Rusch strode over. "Be careful with that shovel."

Liz Peterson was lifted on to a sled and covered with a blanket.

259

Rusch looked down at her. "Lovely girl," he commented. "We've just started to earn our pay."

The dog in the next hour found two more victims, both alive. Then he lost interest. The snow was very deep and hard to get through, and the scent was failing. His name, Rusch learned, was Victor and he belonged to the Scanlons. They did not survive and he found a good home with Liz Peterson.

AT FIRST there was just a handful of rescuers but the number swelled hour by hour, brought in by helicopter and ski plane. Mountain rangers came from Mount Cook, Coronet Peak, Mount Egmont, Tongariro—men skilled in snow rescue. Doctors came in Air Force and US Navy helicopters, which took out the children and the badly injured. The mass of snow which blocked the Gap was attacked fiercely. Steps were cut and guide ropes laid so that within hours it was possible to enter or leave the valley. Volunteers from the mountain clubs who had come in dozens from as far as North Island also formed teams to probe the snow foot by foot, over four hundred acres of it.

Ballard was glad to be relieved by a professional Civil Defence man flown in from Christchurch. He stayed on at his desk in the church to help Arthur Pye with the identification of the survivors and the dead and the listing of those still missing. There was pain in his eyes as he saw the name of Stacey Cameron on the list of the dead. He said, "Any news of Joe Cameron?"

Pye shook his head. "Not a sign. He must be buried out there somewhere. They've found Dobbs dead. Funny thing about that: the chap who dug him out said that Dobbs had cut his throat."

Ballard walked over to a pew where Liz Peterson was lying swathed in blankets. He knelt beside her, and said, "How are you feeling, Liz?"

"A bit better now. Have you found Johnnie yet?"

He said gently, "He's dead, Liz." She closed her eyes. "He died well, trying to get Mrs Scanlon out of the exchange."

Liz opened her eyes. "And Stacey?" Ballard shook his head.

"But she was standing right next to me. How can she be dead when I'm not?"

"Stacey was only a few feet from you but nobody knew that. When there were enough men to make a proper search it was too late for Stacey. And her father is missing."

"Poor Stacey. She was on holiday, you know." Liz leaned up on one elbow. "I've seen Eric, but where's Charlie?"

"He volunteered to go up the mountain. Mike is afraid there'll be another fall so he's gone to check."

"Oh my God!" said Liz. "It would be terrible if it happened again." She began to shiver uncontrollably.

"Don't worry. Mike wouldn't be on the mountain if he thought it was that dangerous." He pressed her back, then tucked the blankets about her. "I think you'll be going out on the next flight. I must leave now, but I'll see you before you go."

The American, Miller, wandered up. His face was pasty white and his eyes looked like two burnt holes in a blanket. "Any news of Ralph Newman yet?"

"I'm sorry, Mr Miller. Nothing yet."

Miller moved away again, mumbling to himself as he went. He had been asking that same question at ten-minute intervals.

SEVEN MEN—one dead—locked in a cave by snow and ice.

"How long has it been?" asked Brewer.

Newman peered at his watch. "Nearly six hours. What about another try?"

"It's useless and dangerous. You dig into the snow and it falls in from the top. You're safer here in the cave. They'll be coming for us pretty soon."

"If there's anyone left up there. Like to bet on it, Brewer?"

"I'm not a rich Yank," said Brewer. "I don't have the money to bet with."

"Just your life," said Newman. "If we stay here we'll die anyway."

"If you can't be more cheerful you'd better keep quiet," said Brewer sharply.

Newman was boiling with frustration. "There might be only six feet of snow above us. That's nothing."

Newman was entirely wrong. The rock immediately above the

cave was high, which was why the place had been chosen as offering good shelter from the avalanche. And so it was—but the hollow in front of the rock had filled with snow as a housewife fills a cup with flour. The depth of snow above the cave entrance was sixty feet.

HIGH ON the west slope McGill paused for breath and leaned on his ski-poles. He glanced at Charlie Peterson. "We want no bouncing about. Try to imagine you're walking on custard and don't want to break the skin."

He turned his ski-pole over. "This is eyeball science," he said wryly. "I lost my kit." He pushed the stick into the snow and when it hit bottom he marked the depth with his thumb and withdrew the stick. "Under three feet—that's not too bad. I wish to hell I knew what was down there."

"Why don't we dig and find out?"

"That's just what I'm going to do. You stand up-slope about ten yards. Keep your eyes on me. If anything gives, mark the place where you last saw me."

McGill was gentle but he worked quickly. Finally he thrust his arm down and came up clutching some brown strands. "Long grass. That's not too good." He straightened. "We'll go across diagonally and upward. I have an idea the avalanche broke up there by those exposed rocks. I'd like to have a look at the place."

Charlie showed signs of nervousness. "I think we should get off the slope," he said.

"Not far to go now," said McGill equably. "We'll head straight up. Why the sudden jitters?"

"I don't like standing out here. I saw what happened before."

An aircraft went overhead very low and McGill saw the white blur of a face behind a window. Whoever it was seemed to be taking photographs. There was a splintering noise from the valley behind him and he turned around. On the white floor of the valley the black specks which were men began to converge on one point like ants intent on dismembering a dead beetle.

They watched for a while but could not distinguish the cause of the sudden activity. Then Charlie said, "Oh, God! Look!"

In the valley there was a blossom of red fire, and a coil of oily black smoke grew upwards like a giant tree.

Breath whistled from McGill. "Let's get down there."

"Sure thing," said Charlie.

JESSE RUSCH was going towards the church but turned aside sharply as someone yelled, "I've found somebody." He had to smile as someone else said disgustedly, "It's a flaming cow."

Rusch said, "Dig it out anyway. There might be someone under it." Privately he thought it unlikely, so he said, "Three men to the cow—the rest can carry on probing."

A group of men was standing twenty yards away, their hands in their pockets. "You lot," he called. "Come and give a hand." They stared at him with blank eyes, turned their backs and shuffled away slowly.

One man digging flung down his shovel. "God Almighty!" he said passionately. "I've flown four hundred miles to help these bastards, and the lead-swingers won't even help themselves."

"Leave them be," said Rusch quietly. "They're not themselves. Regard them as dead men, if that's any help." He went on his way.

Outside the church he encountered a helicopter pilot called Harry Baker, and saw that Baker was angry. Baker jerked his thumb at the sky. "If it gets any worse there'll be trouble. Some maniac buzzed me up there as I was coming in. He was taking photographs."

"All right, Harry. I'll see the Civil Defence people here and see what we can do about tightening up air control."

A stretcher bearing Mrs Haslam was being loaded into the helicopter by Arthur Pye and Bill Quentin. She moaned feebly, "Where's Jack? I want my Jack."

Harry Baker adjusted his helmet and said to the ground controller, "When I take off I want this crowd to stand back." He jerked his thumb at the sky. "It's bad enough being crowded up there." He climbed into the cockpit, and the ground controller shouted, "All right, stand back, everybody."

The helicopter looked ungainly as it rose from the ground. Quentin was not watching when the crash happened, but Pye saw

263

it. The helicopter rose directly into the path of a low-flying light plane which appeared from nowhere. There was a splintering crash and, locked together, the two machines dropped into the snow.

Everyone began to run, with Pye and Quentin in the lead. They heaved on the sliding door of the helicopter which slid half open creakingly, then jammed.

Two children were strapped into a seat, their bodies lolling forward. Arthur Pye did not know whether they were living or dead as he fumbled at the straps, and he had no time to find out. He freed the first and passed her back to Quentin, and then tackled the second. From far away he heard a bellow from the ground controller—"You guys in there had better be quick. She might go up."

He passed the child into waiting hands then turned to a stretcher. "Is that you, Jack?" Mrs Haslam's eyes stared at him unwinkingly.

"Yes, that's right. I've come to take you home."

At that moment Pye saw a white flash and felt searing heat, and when he inhaled he drew flaming petrol vapour into his lungs. He felt no pain and was dead before he knew it, and so were Bill Quentin, Mrs Haslam, Harry Baker and his co-pilot.

TWENTY-FOUR hours after the avalanche the number of those still missing had been cut down to seventeen. All the others had been accounted for—dead and alive. Ballard said glumly, "There's still no sign of Joe Cameron."

"We'll be able to get bulldozers in this afternoon," said Rusch. "That should speed things up."

"A bulldozer blade could chop a man in half," said Ballard.

"We'll be careful," said Rusch. "But speed is important now. If anyone buried is still alive now they can't last much longer."

CAMERON, trapped in the truck, was almost totally exhausted, his body racked with pain. He had been sick during the night and had been afraid of choking. Now he became aware of a sound and, at first, thought it was human. It sounded as though someone was

264

chuckling quietly. Then he thought he was going mad—who would be laughing in the middle of a snowdrift?

His senses swam and he passed out for a few minutes. When he awoke the sound had subtly changed and it was now more of a gurgle, such as might be made by a contented baby in its cot. After listening for a long time he knew what it was and again became afraid. He was listening to the sound of water.

Presently a trickle of water entered the cabin and swirled about his scalp as he hung upside down, and now he knew that he would drown.

On the surface two young men were piloting a bulldozer through hummocky snow alongside the river. The driver was John Skinner, a construction worker from Auckland, and a member of the Alpine Sports Club. His companion was a university lecturer and a member of the Canterbury University Ski Club called Roger Halliwell.

Skinner stopped the bulldozer by the river. A section of snow in the river bed slumped as it was undercut by water and Halliwell said, "I think I saw something down there."

He dropped from the bulldozer and walked to the edge of the river and suddenly sank up to his waist in slushy snow. He had a nightmare vision of going right down, but found himself standing on something. He put his hand down into the snow. It was a wheel with a tyre on it. "There's a car in here," he yelled.

Skinner unclipped a wire rope from the rear of the bulldozer. There was a big snap-shackle on each end, one of which he clipped to a stout bar on the bulldozer. Halliwell caught the rope on the second cast.

In the cabin Cameron was close to drowning. The water covered his nose even though he withdrew his head into his shoulders like a tortoise trying to retreat into its shell. The truck lurched and was hauled bodily from the river bed. Cameron screamed at the pain and thought his back was being broken.

"There's someone in here," Halliwell said in wonder. "And he's alive, by God!"

Within the hour Cameron was in a helicopter on his way to Christchurch. But he was a broken man.

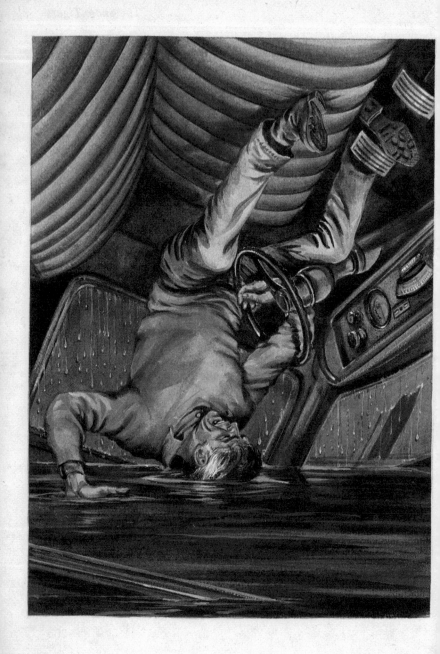

ALL NIGHT Newman had been digging upwards in total darkness. He had to dig a hole at least two feet in diameter to accommodate the shoulders of a broad man. His most useful tool was a ballpoint pen which he jabbed repeatedly into the snow, breaking it out, chunk by chunk. Often the snow dropped into his eyes.

He did not know how far he had to dig and had he known it was as much as sixty feet it is doubtful if he would have begun. He dug alone; the others in the cave had lapsed into total apathy.

Fifty-two hours after the avalanche the sky was darkening and Sam Foster, a ranger from Tongariro, debated with himself whether it was worth while having his team continue the search. He strode into a sloping hollow and the snow gave under his feet.

Newman had dug to within a foot of the surface, and when Foster's weight broke through one of Foster's boots slammed into his head. Newman fell down the hole he had made. It was not a long fall because the bottom of the hole was packed with the debris of his digging. But it was enough to break his neck.

The others, of course, were rescued, excepting Haslam who was dead already. Newman was the last person to die in the valley.

AT THE HEARING...

HARRISON drew in a long breath. "And so we come to the avalanche itself. It has been suggested in the press that the sound of an airplane, sent to investigate by Civil Defence, was the trigger which set the avalanche in motion. What are your views on that, Dr McGill?"

"That's utter nonsense, sir," said McGill. "The idea that sound can trigger an avalanche is a myth. In Montana experiments were made by F-106 aircraft making aimed dives and pulling out at supersonic speeds. Those did cause avalanche release. But the plane I heard flying over Hukahoronui could not in any way have triggered that avalanche."

Harrison smiled. "The pilot of that aircraft will be very glad to hear that. I believe it has been on his conscience."

267

"It needn't be," said McGill. "That snow was ready to come down, and it came down without his assistance."

"It appears that the pilot and observer of that aircraft were the only people to see the avalanche as it began to fall. You are excused, Dr McGill. Call Flying Officer Charles Howard Hatry."

Hatry was a fresh-faced young man of about twenty, wearing the uniform of the Royal New Zealand Air Force.

Harrison said, "Mr Hatry, how was it that you came to be flying over Hukahoronui at that time?"

"Sir, I had orders to fly from Christchurch to Hukahoronui, take some photographs, to land if possible, find out the situation and radio back. I believe the orders originated with Civil Defence. Flight-Lieutenant Storey was the pilot and I was the observer. When we got to Hukahoronui landing was out the question. There was a thick layer of cloud or mist on the valley floor. We radioed Christchurch and were told to fly around for a while in case the mist lifted."

"What were the weather conditions—other than the low mist?"

"The sky was clear and the sun very strong. The clarity of the air was good for photography. I took two spools of the area around the valley—seventy-two exposures."

Harrison shook some glossy black-and-whites from an envelope and began to hold them up one at a time. Hatry leaned forward. "Yes, sir, those are the official photographs."

"Are we to understand that there are some *unofficial* photographs?"

Hatry shifted in his seat. "I'm keen on cine photography and I happened to have my camera along. I decided to shoot off a reel."

"And while you were shooting this film the avalanche began and you managed to film it?"

"Some of it, sir. It's not a very good film, I'm afraid."

"But when you had it developed you realized its importance and offered it to this Commission. I think it will be the best evidence available. Please have the screen set up, Mr Reed."

The hall buzzed with voices as the ushers set up the screen and projector. Curtains were drawn over the windows. There was a click and a whirr, and the screen lit up. Suddenly a recognizable scene appeared—white mountains and blue sky. It was replaced by a shot of the ground. "That's the valley," said Hatry.

The film could have been any amateur travelogue—hand-held and unsteady. But the tension in the hall grew as the seconds went by. Presently Hatry said, "That's when it started. I think it's coming along about now. I asked Lieutenant Storey to fly north along the Hukahoronui valley."

"How high were you flying?" asked Rolandson.

"A little over two thousand feet above the valley floor."

"So the west slope of the valley actually stretched above you."

"Yes, sir. Afterwards I found the slope was six thousand feet from crest to valley. Here it is now."

It was a shot showing a little blue sky at the top of the screen, and a few scattered rocks jutting from snow so white as to make the eyes ache. The scene suddenly jogged and blurred, then steadied. A faint plume of grey appeared which grew larger as it moved down the slope. It disappeared sideways as though the camera had panned away. "We had trouble in positioning the aircraft," said Hatry apologetically. "I suppose we were excited."

There came another shot of a boiling, growing cloud of whiteness which plunged down the mountainside. It could be seen that the whole of the upper slope was in motion. Almost near the bottom the bank of mist which covered the valley floor was driven back as though an invisible jet was playing on it, and buildings could be seen briefly. Then the snow swept over everything.

The tail of the film slapped. "That's when the film ran out," said Hatry. "We were then ordered to return to Christchurch."

"Thank you, Mr Hatry. You may step down. Have you any comments on what you have just seen, Dr McGill?"

"Most interesting. One of the features is that it showed something we knew but could not prove. Because of the mist we could see that there was an air blast in advance of the moving mass of snow. Such a blast could cause considerable damage. I think the film should be preserved. I wouldn't mind having a copy of it myself for study."

Harrison looked at the clock. "The time has come for our adjournment." His gavel tapped on the rostrum.

McGILL left the hall with Flying Officer Hatry, talking fast and making gestures with his hands. When they made off in different directions someone caught McGill's elbow and he turned to find the Peterson brothers just behind him. Eric said, "I'd like to thank you for what you said about Johnnie."

"No need," said McGill. "Credit given where it's due."

"All the same," said Eric a little awkwardly, "it was good of you —especially when you're on the other side, so to speak."

"Now hold on a minute," said McGill sharply. "I'm a neutral around here. This is an Inquiry, not a court battle."

Charlie looked unimpressed. "Everybody knows that Ballard and you are in each other's pockets."

"Give it a rest," said Eric exasperatedly.

"Why the hell should I?" said Charlie. "I used to have three brothers and now I've got one—and that bastard killed two of them. You're Ballard's friend—you tell him that if he so much as looks at Liz again I'll kill him."

Eric pulled Charlie away. "Charlie, sometimes I think you're going out of your mind." He shook his head wearily. "Sorry about that, McGill."

Charlie allowed himself to be led away, but twisted his head and shouted to McGill, "Don't forget to tell Ballard."

AT THE hotel Stenning went to his room to clean up. His suit was too heavy for the New Zealand summer and he felt uncomfortably sticky. He sat for a while in his dressing-gown while he made notes of the events at the Inquiry. He shook his head over the evidence and thought that young Ballard was not in a favourable position; the business of the safety of the mine might go heavily against him should someone try to push the point.

After a while he dressed and went outside to find Ballard sitting at a table near the pool with an extraordinarily beautiful young woman. Ballard caught sight of him and stood up. "Miss Peterson, this is Mr Stenning, a visitor from England."

Stenning's white eyebrows lifted as he heard the name, but he merely said, "Good evening, Miss Peterson." He sat down and watched Ballard and Liz with curious eyes.

Ballard said, "Here's Mike. What kept you?"

"A run-in with Liz's charming brothers. Hi, Liz."

"What about my brothers?" Liz asked. She fondled the ears of her dog Victor, sitting by her chair.

"Eric's all right, but have you ever wondered about Charlie? If I were a psychiatrist I'd tend to diagnose paranoia. He threatened to kill Ian if he ever meets him."

Stenning broke in, "He used the word 'kill'?"

"The very word."

Liz said, "I'll have a talk with Master Charlie. But let's not talk about the Petersons. How's your tennis, Ian?"

"Not bad," said Ballard.

"Let's go," she said.

McGill watched them as they walked towards the tennis courts with Victor trotting behind, then he turned back to Stenning.

"Tell me—if Ian marries a Peterson, does that count in your Peterson Bashing Contest?"

Stenning slanted his eyes at McGill. "So he told you about that. Your question is hard to answer. I doubt if it is what Ben had in mind." He stood up. "I think I'll take a short nap."

AT THE hotel desk the receptionist said, "There's a letter for you, Dr McGill."

As McGill opened the letter a cheque slipped out and his eyes widened as he saw the amount it was made out for. His brows drew together as he read the first page of the letter.

When Ballard arrived back from tennis McGill was waiting for him and steered him into the bar. McGill crooked his finger at the bartender. "Two doubles. We're celebrating, Ian. In my pocket, I have a steamroller. It arrived air mail from Los Angeles." He took the letter from his breast pocket and waved it under Ballard's nose. "Read it, my friend. It's the saving of you."

Ballard opened the envelope, glanced at the cheque and said, "What the hell is this? A bribe?"

"Read," urged McGill. The letter was from the American, Miller. Its contents were appalling.

Dear Dr McGill,

I have been wanting to write this letter for a long time but I have been putting it off because I guess I was scared. What happened has been on my conscience ever since the avalanche which caused so many deaths, including that of my good friend, Ralph Newman.

Early on the morning of that dreadful Sunday I went skiing with Charlie Peterson. We went into the hills at the head of the valley but the slopes were not very good there, and Charlie suggested we go nearer Hukahoronui. We finally arrived at the top of the west slope above the town and saw a sign there saying that no skiing was allowed. But Charlie said it was Peterson land and that no one could stop him doing what he wanted on his own land. He stood there laughing, and went on with a lot of real wild talk.

He said that an avalanche might be a good thing, and anything that could get rid of Mr Ballard couldn't be all bad. He said that Ballard had killed his brother and stolen the mine from his father. He said the mine wouldn't do Ballard much good if it wasn't there.

I told him he was talking crazy and asked him how he could make a whole gold mine disappear. Suddenly he shouted, 'I'll show you!' and took off down the hill. He wasn't going fast and he kept jumping up and down very heavily. I went after him to try to stop him, but suddenly there was a crackling noise like French fries in the pan and Charlie gave a shout. I saw him jumping sideways up the hill.

Then the slide started. Charlie and I were safe because we were above the fall. We just stood there and watched it happen and I've never seen a more awful sight. I started to cry. I'm not ashamed of that. Charlie shook me and said to keep my mouth shut. He said if I told anybody he would kill me. I believed him when he said that—he was crazy enough for anything.

He said it was just a lot of feathery stuff that had gone and it had probably just given the people a good scare, though he hoped it had done for the mine. He laughed as he said that. So we went into the town and saw the dreadful thing that had happened, and Charlie threatened me again. I am deeply ashamed of my silence and I hope this letter will go towards making amends. I suppose there will be a public fund for the families of the victims. I enclose a check for $10,000. This is nearly all my savings.

BALLARD looked up. "For God's sake! We can't use *this*."

"Why not? Stenning would just love you."

"Mike, we *expected* an avalanche, didn't we? You exonerated the pilot of that plane. Does this really make any difference? Besides . . ."

McGill sighed. "Lovers' Lane must run straight and narrow? Ian, you have the Ballard Trust in the palm of your hand. That son of a bitch killed fifty-four people. If Miller had claimed it was accidental I might have gone along, but he says Charlie did it deliberately. You *can't* suppress it. It's my responsibility. The letter is addressed to me." He took it from Ballard and put it back in his pocket.

"Liz will never believe I didn't go along with you," said Ballard gloomily. "When are you going to give the letter to Harrison?"

"Tomorrow, of course."

"Hold off for a bit," said Ballard urgently. "I'd like to get straightened out with Liz first. I wouldn't want her to get this slammed at her cold at the Inquiry. She wouldn't be the woman I want to marry if she didn't have some family loyalty."

McGill pondered. "Okay, I'll save it for twenty-four hours." He twisted on his stool and watched Ballard walk out of the bar, then he turned back to the bartender. "Two more doubles."

"Then the gentleman is coming back?"

"No, he's not coming back," said McGill absently. "But you're right about one thing. He *is* a gentleman—and there are damned few of them around these days."

BALLARD and Stenning dined together that night. Ballard was abstracted and in no mood for small talk. Stenning noted this and was quiet, but over coffee he asked, "Ian, what is your relationship with Miss Peterson?"

Ballard jerked his head, a little startled by the intrusive question. "I don't see that's any of your business."

"Don't you?" Stenning stirred his coffee. "You forget the matter of the Ballard Trust. It is still very much on *my* mind. I have to interpret Ben's wishes and he didn't tell me about Liz Peterson."

"Don't tell me you want me to walk over her, too." Ballard's lip curled. "He didn't tell you about Liz because for him women didn't exist. The old man only lived for business."

Stenning nodded. "I think you are right. This therefore has a strong bearing on how I intend to interpret his wishes. You may marry Miss Peterson or you may not. Whatever you do will have no bearing on my decision regarding your suitability as a trustee."

"Thanks," said Ballard hollowly.

"Of course, the problem still remains with her brothers."

"Do you really believe that if I walk over the Petersons, as you so delicately put it, I would stand a chance with Liz?"

"Yes, you would appear to have quite a problem."

Ballard stood up. "Then to hell with you, Mr Stenning." He threw down his napkin. "And to hell with the Ballard Trust."

Stenning watched him walk away, his face expressionless.

Ballard telephoned Liz at her hotel and asked to see her. "You'd better not come here," she said. "Charlie wouldn't like it. I'll come to your hotel."

At nine-thirty when Liz had not shown up he was pacing the floor in his room. At nine-forty the telephone rang and he grabbed it. "A guest for you, Mr Ballard."

In the lounge he saw Stenning reading a newspaper in a corner but there was no sign of Liz. From behind him a voice said, "I'll bet you didn't expect *me*, Ballard."

Charlie Peterson swayed slightly on his feet. His face was red-dened and a tic worked convulsively under his left eye. "Liz won't be here," he said. "I've made sure of that. I've told you before— stay away from my sister."

Ballard said, "I asked Liz to come here because I had something important to tell her. Since she isn't here I'll tell you."

Something in his tone of voice caught Charlie's attention. He narrowed his eyes, and said, "All right, say your piece."

"You're in bad trouble. We know what you did on top of the west slope before the avalanche."

274

"I wasn't on the west slope. Who says I was?"

"Miller says so," said Ballard quietly. "We have a letter. It will be given to Harrison tomorrow morning."

Charlie swallowed. "And what am I supposed to have done?"

"Miller says you deliberately started the avalanche."

The tic on Charlie's face twitched. "Lies!" he shouted. "He's a bloody liar!"

"Now listen to me. I'm giving you a chance, Charlie, to get in your version to Harrison before the letter is produced. And don't think I'm doing it for you. I'm doing this for Liz. I didn't want her to hear it for the first time in court."

"Some chance," sneered Charlie. "You and McGill cooked this up." He stood up and jabbed out his finger. "I tell you, if I catch you anywhere I can get at you, you'll wish you'd never heard of the Peterson family." He walked abruptly from the lounge.

McGill worked late that night in a photographic darkroom at Deep Freeze Advanced Headquarters. It was long after midnight before he finished and all he had to show was some eight by ten glossies and a few transparencies.

He drove back to the hotel and parked his car next to Ballard's, which was empty and locked. He was about to go into the hotel when he heard a thread of sound. He walked to the other side of Ballard's car and stepped on something soft in the darkness.

The night porter looked up in alarm as McGill burst into the foyer. "Phone for a doctor and an ambulance," said McGill breathlessly. "There's a seriously injured man in the car park."

A minute later McGill was hammering on Stenning's door. Stenning's white hair was tousled and his eyes still sleep-filled. McGill was curt. "You'd better come with me and see the result of your goddamn meddling."

"And what do you mean by that?" McGill didn't answer. They hastened across the car park which was now brightly lit.

A startled exclamation was torn from Stenning as he looked down at the bloody body of Ballard. "Oh, my God! It looks like a car accident. He could have crawled in here."

"Then where's the trail of blood he left? What you're looking at, Stenning, is a man who has almost been beaten to death. It's what happens when a man gets *walked over*, Stenning." McGill's voice was harsh and accusing. "You sit in your plush offices in the City of London and you manipulate men. This is the reality . . ."

Stenning swallowed. "There was no intention of . . ."

"No intention of murder? What else do you expect to happen when you interfere with a maniac like Charlie Peterson?"

"Do you *know* it was Peterson?"

"Yes," said McGill bluntly.

"How do you know?"

McGill paused. He suddenly realized he was still holding the photographs and his mind worked fast. "I know," he said, lying deliberately. "Because Ian told me before he passed out."

AT THE HEARING...

At ten o'clock the following morning Harrison walked into the hall, waited until the rustling had stopped, then said, "I have to report that Mr Ian Ballard was seriously injured in a car accident in the early hours of this morning and is at present in Princess Margaret Hospital. How is Mr Ballard, Dr McGill?"

"He's still unconscious, Mr Chairman."

"I'm sorry to hear it. It's good of you to return, but not really necessary under the circumstances."

"Mr Chairman, I am in possession of fresh evidence," McGill took an envelope from his pocket. "I received this letter and discussed the contents with Mr Ballard. We agreed it was too important to conceal, even though it could destroy a man's reputation."

He handed the letter to Harrison. It took him a long time to read and the lines of his face deepened as he read. At last he raised his head, and said, "Yes, it would have been wrong to withhold this. I see that each page is signed and counter-signed, and has the seal of a notary public. Would that be the American equivalent of our own Commissioner for Oaths?"

"It is almost the exact equivalent, Mr Chairman."

Harrison's eyes roved about the room. "Mr Lyall, would you

mind stepping over here? This concerns one of your clients. I think you'd better read it." He held out the letter.

A few minutes later Lyall said nervously, "I don't really know what to say, Mr Chairman." His face was pale. "I feel inclined to withdraw from this case."

"Do you?" Harrison's voice was grim. "This is not a *case*, Mr Lyall; it is a Commission of Inquiry."

Red spots now burned in Lyall's cheeks. "Very well," he said abruptly. "But is it admissible evidence?"

McGill said, "I have other supporting evidence."

"No evidence can be brought to support it if the letter itself is not admissible," said Lyall. "And if you admit the letter there will certainly be grounds for appeal."

"There'll be no appeal," said McGill. "And you know it."

"You are not here to argue a lawyer's case, Dr McGill," said Harrison in tones of freezing rebuke. He took the letter from Lyall and passed it to the Secretary to the Commission. "Read that aloud, please."

When Reed had finished all eyes turned in one direction.

Charlie Peterson was slumped in his chair, his eyes staring. Eric was looking at him with a baffled expression. Liz was sitting upright, her brow contracted, her lips compressed.

Charlie's eyes flicked from side to side and he jumped to his feet. "Miller is a liar! He started the avalanche, not me."

"Sit down, Mr Peterson," Harrison said icily. "Dr McGill, you mentioned that you have other evidence. We will hear it."

"It is photographic evidence, Mr Chairman," said McGill. "I have taken the liberty of having a cine-projector made available. I would like to operate it myself. I have here the original film taken of the avalanche by Flying Officer Hatry. The film he submitted to the Commission was a copy; the original is a better print."

It took a few minutes for the apparatus to be set up, then an unsteady picture appeared on the screen and McGill switched off the projector to freeze the action. "As you can see, the avalanche started here, just by these rocks. I have here a greatly enlarged portion of that scene which I am going to put in this special projector. It is called a comparator." He switched it on.

"Here are the rocks and there is the plume of snow powder which is the start of the avalanche. The next slide you will see is a similar shot but taken thirty-six frames later. That is, there is a two-second difference between the taking of the two photographs." He went back to the comparator and inserted the second slide.

"There is not much difference, as you can see. The plume of snow powder is marginally greater." He paused. "But if we alternate the slides rapidly, as this machine is designed to do, you will see something curious." The image on the screen began to flicker rapidly and the snow plume oscillated. "Two of what I thought to be rocks—those two specks there—are obviously moving. I submit that the speck at the top is Miller, and the one beneath is Peterson climbing up to him after the avalanche was triggered."

"Can you prove this, Dr McGill?" asked Harrison.

McGill was silent for a moment. "No," he admitted, "but I have more evidence." He returned to the projector. "After the avalanche I went up on the west slope to see if there was further hazard. Charlie Peterson volunteered to accompany me. We made an examination of the slope and Mr Peterson showed no sign of nerves. It was only after I had indicated my intention to examine the site where the avalanche had begun that he showed signs of nervousness, and suggested we go down. In the event we never reached the site. There was the air accident in the valley and we went down the slope immediately."

"Interesting," said Harrison. "But I don't see the point."

"This is the point," said McGill. "While we were on the slope an aircraft flew over us at very low altitude and I saw someone taking photographs. I discovered afterwards that the plane had been chartered by a newspaper here in Christchurch. I went to the newspaper office early last night and went through all the photographs that had been taken. Here are some of them."

The projector clicked and flashed again, and a black-and-white photograph appeared on the screen. McGill said, "In the bottom-right-hand corner you can see Peterson and me. In the top left corner you see exposed rocks. By the rocks there are ski tracks, here—and here. I think that Peterson didn't want me to see those tracks; that's why he was nervous."

McGill put another picture on the screen. "Here is an enlargement of the breakaway point of the avalanche. There is a ski track going into it, and this ragged line, and another here, is where a man jumped up the slope. It had been snowing heavily that night, and all these tracks could only have been made on the morning of the avalanche." He switched off the projector. "I further state on oath that the first time I saw Miller and Peterson on that Sunday they were both on skis."

"Turn on the lights," said Harrison. Sunlight flooded the room as an usher pulled aside a curtain. Charlie was on his feet.

"Damn you all!" he cried. "It was Ballard who killed my brother —everyone knows that! Nobody would have died if they'd gone into the mine as Eric wanted. And Alec wouldn't have drowned if it hadn't been for Ballard." Froth flecked his lips, his throat worked convulsively. "He started the avalanche—him and Miller between them! Ballard didn't like Huka or anyone in it." He threw his arms wide. "He wanted to *destroy* it—and he *did!*"

Eric grabbed Charlie's arm, but Charlie tossed him aside effortlessly. "And McGill was in on the whole thing and I'm going to kill the bastard!" He plunged towards McGill but Eric had recovered and was on his back.

There was a brief flurry, then Charlie ran for the door. It opened before he got there and he ran into the arms of two policemen. They put an armlock on him and he was marched out of sight.

Harrison thumped his gavel in vain. Into the uproar he said quietly, "This hearing is adjourned."

EPILOGUE...

HALF-AN-HOUR later McGill, still in the hall, was besieged by reporters. "No comment," he kept repeating.

He broke free, went into the first room he saw, and slammed the door behind him. He turned and saw Harrison and Stenning.

"You've caused quite a stir, Dr McGill," said Harrison.

McGill grimaced. "Not as much as Charlie. How is he?"

"Under sedation. I think there's a case for a court order for psychiatric treatment," Harrison said. "Oh, this is Mr Stenning, a visitor from England. He's here to see how we conduct our administrative justice. I've been telling him that not all our Inquiries are so rowdy." He picked up his briefcase. "It will be safe to leave by the back way, gentlemen."

Stenning said, "Could I have a word with you, Dr McGill?"

When they were alone Stenning remarked, "That letter was not admissible, because Miller was not there to be cross-examined. I think the Inquiry will be adjourned while Harrison takes legal advice. It shows the inadvisability of setting a layman to do a lawyer's job."

McGill shrugged. "Does it matter now? We've seen that Charlie is as crazy as a loon."

Stenning regarded him speculatively. "It's strange that Ian had agreed that the letter should be produced. At the end of our last conversation Ian told me and the Ballard Trust to go to hell. It would be interesting to know exactly when he changed his mind."

"I think when Charlie Peterson started beating the hell out of him."

"You think it *was* Peterson?"

"You've just seen Charlie in action. He tossed Eric around as though he was a rag doll, and Eric's no midget. And I got a good look at his hands this afternoon. His knuckles were raw."

"Is that the only reason you think it was Peterson? I have to be sure, Dr McGill."

"Of course not," said McGill, lying bravely with a frank open face. "Ian told me himself when I found him in the car park. He said, 'It was Charlie. Use the letter and smash him.' Then he passed out."

"I see," Stenning smiled, and said obliquely, "I think Ian is lucky to have you for a friend."

"I'd do the same for anyone who was getting the raw end of a deal, Mr Stenning. He was getting it from both sides, you know. Your hands are not entirely clean in this matter."

Abruptly he turned his back on Stenning and left the room. As he went into the vestibule he ran into Liz Peterson. She slapped his face with all the force she could muster.

His head rocked and he grabbed her wrist. "Steady, Liz."

"How could you do that to Charlie?" she said passionately.

"Someone had to stop him."

"You needn't have crucified him in public."

"How would you suggest? He was going insane. He was eaten up by guilt and he wanted to pour it all out on Ian."

"Ian!" Liz said contemptuously. "That man wanted to marry me. I never want to see him again. He could have suppressed that letter."

"He wanted to," said McGill. "But I talked him out of it. He was supposed to see you last night. Did he?"

She shook her head. "Charlie got me into his car on some excuse, then drove out of town going like a maniac." She swallowed. "Anyway, he dumped me on a country road. It was nearly midnight when I got back into town. I phoned Ian but he wasn't in."

"Did Charlie know you were going to see Ian?"

"Not unless Eric told him."

"So you told Eric, and Eric mentioned it to Charlie. That was a fool thing to do." He took her arm. "You need talking to, my girl, and you'd better have a drink while you listen."

Five minutes later in a hotel lounge McGill said, "It's a bit of a convoluted story. When Miller's letter came, Ian read it and asked me just one question. He wanted to know if the avalanche would have happened anyway, regardless of what Charlie had done. I had to say it would have come down. Once Ian heard that he wanted me to suppress the letter. I talked him out of that, but then he said he wanted to clear things with you."

"And I didn't turn up," Liz said dully.

"The next time I saw him he was a hospital case, and I was lying like a flat fish to a man called Stenning—you've met him."

He told her about old Ben Ballard, the Ballard Trust and the task that had been laid upon Stenning. It took quite a while. He wound up by saying, "Even when Ian knew about Miller's letter he told Stenning to go to hell."

"He was prepared to give all that up?" said Liz slowly.

281

"Not because he didn't want to hurt Charlie, but because he didn't want to hurt you. Anyway, it doesn't matter any more. Stenning has evidence that Ian did walk over the Petersons in the end. Though I think old Ben was wrong. He said a man must have steel in him to run the Ballard Group but what the Group needs now is a man-manager, an administrator, a diplomat—and Ian is all of those. And if he needs any steel he'll have it if he has a Peterson next to him."

Liz put her hand on McGill's. "I'm torn, Mike. The police have taken Charlie away because of the avalanche . . ."

"No!" said McGill sharply. "Not because of the avalanche. That hasn't been proved—and may never be. Ian intended to meet you last night but, instead, he got Charlie. And Charlie beat Ian half to death. The police were waiting to arrest Charlie for assault as soon as he came out of the hall."

Liz was as pale as she had been when McGill had first seen her in the church after the avalanche. He said gently, "He had to be stopped, Liz. I've often wondered what would have happened if he and I had gone that extra two hundred feet up the west slope after the avalanche and I'd seen those ski tracks . . ."

Liz sighed shudderingly. "I knew he was violent and had his strange ways, and I knew they were becoming worse. But not as bad as this. What will become of him, Mike?"

"There'll be people to look after him. I don't think he'll stand trial for anything. He's beyond that, Liz."

She nodded. "So it's all over."

"It's over," he agreed. "My masters want me to go south to the Pole." McGill leaned back in his chair and picked up his glass. He said casually, "Ian is in the Princess Margaret Hospital—third floor. The Ward Sister is a tough old bird but if you say you are Ian's fiancée she might let you . . ."

He became aware he was talking to thin air. "Hey, you haven't finished your drink!"

But Liz was halfway across the room on her way and beside her Victor trotted, his tail waving in a proud plume.

Desmond Bagley

"I want to write—Galsworthy's dead and there's only Maugham left, so there's a chance for me," the fourteen-year-old Desmond Bagley told his mother when she asked him what he planned to do in life. Today, forty years on, Bagley has long held a place in the top bracket of the world's thriller writers. He has notched up sales of over five million copies, and editions of his books have appeared in thirteen different countries . . .

Meticulous research; strong action; sharply differentiated characters; violence, but without the sadism that too often accompanies it: this is the Bagley recipe. Add to this his conviction that an author should be an entertainer and not a pedagogue, plus a rather endearing habit of falling in love with the countries in which he sets his plots, and one begins to understand the compulsive grip his tough, literate, fast-paced stories exert on the reader.

Desmond Bagley averages a novel a year. He makes almost no notes, writes his first draft straight onto the typewriter, and carries his vast store of technical and geographical information in his head. But query his facts and he is likely to show you an article from some obscure mining journal; ask him how he gets his plots and he will produce a newspaper cutting or his pocket notebook, in which he occasionally jots down an idea.

Bagley was born and bred in Westmorland. In 1946, tired of austerity England, he decided to emigrate to South Africa. Here he tried his hand at freelance journalism. Then, with the help of his wife, director of a bookshop, he set to work systematically to see what kind of book sold well and who published it. The result was that he decided to write a thriller for the English publishers, Collins. After analysing many thrillers to isolate what seemed to him the ingredients of success, he produced *The Golden Keel*, which was about gold-smuggling. Collins accepted it at once and Bagley was on the way to realizing his dream of becoming a best-selling author.

The Bagleys now live in Guernsey, and Bagley has plenty of time to indulge his hobbies: sailing, motor-boating, reading and what he calls "just plain loafing".

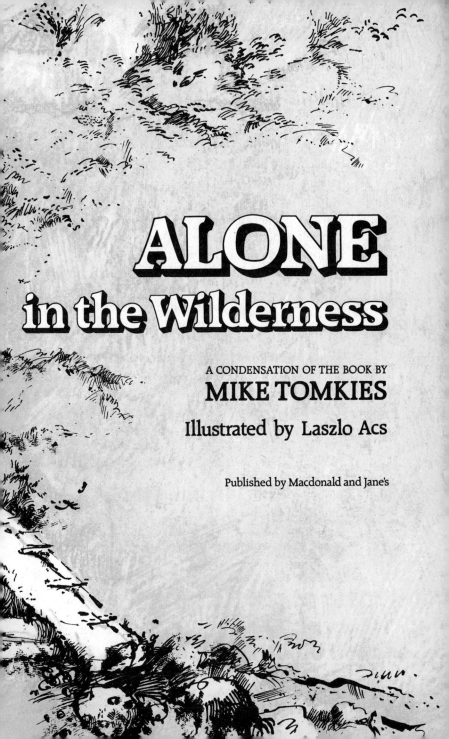

ALONE
in the Wilderness

A CONDENSATION OF THE BOOK BY
MIKE TOMKIES

Illustrated by Laszlo Acs

Published by Macdonald and Jane's

Mike Tomkies is one of those rare people who have transformed dreams into reality. In his late thirties he abandoned his glamorous career as a show-business journalist and carved out for himself a totally different existence in the solitude of the Canadian wilderness.

It was hard, lonely and often dangerous, but he not only survived, he triumphed; for in the wisdom of the old backwoodsmen he discovered a serenity and a love of animals that was to change his life. He found himself sharing his food and shelter with skunks, racoons and squirrels. He was adopted by Booto, the wild dog of the woods. He travelled by boat and foot miles into areas almost unknown to man to see some of the world's endangered species: the caribou and cougars, and those near-legendary giants of the wilderness, the grizzly bears. He returned to become one of the world's most eloquent campaigners for the wildlife we are in danger of destroying for ever.

A memorable story by a man of extraordinary determination, vividly observed, often humorous, always fascinating.

Chapter 1

Pausing from my four-mile row, I lay back in the leaky boat and looked over the Pacific Ocean at a wilderness view I could hardly believe was now mine. The sun bridled a liquid track of gold across the sea. In the distance flowering arbutus trees fringed the lone firs on grey granite islands, while around me in the green waters a school of salmon swam. Mesmerized, I watched a rainbow form from a sea mist and touch the nearest island, like a finger from the sky. Drifting gently on the sea, I turned from the islands to look at the rocky two acres of my homestead claim of the mainland of British Columbia. Was it possible this small bay, this cliff, these trees, this incredible view—the good place for which I'd searched so long— was *really* now my own?

At nearly forty, a thoroughly urbanized man and former journalist whose life in the big cities of Europe had become stale and pointless, I had fled from London and all we loosely call civilization to emigrate to Canada to write in the ancient silence of the wilderness what I hoped would be a successful novel.

There, where one faced only the simple physical challenges of the elements, I felt I would be freed, that just by living close to nature away from all I'd known, I might somehow begin my life over again.

BRITISH COLUMBIA has a stark grandeur that at first flays the mind of a city-conditioned man. This vast province, almost as large as central Europe, is the last free frontier left in the western world. Untamed forests clothe colossal mountains in areas half the size of England. Bounded in the east by the Rockies and licked and battered in the west by the mighty Pacific, it is a gargantuan, indifferent land with waterfalls higher than Niagara, log-jams that can dam up lakes for six miles, cataclysmic forest fires that can clear fifty miles of high timber in a week, a land in whose great fastness grizzly bears and cougars, the last of the great North American carnivores, find their only real stronghold.

When I first left the ferryboat heading north from Vancouver and began looking for a cabin, I felt an immediate instinct to rush back to the sheltered life I'd known. I felt utterly alien, scared, sure there could be little compromise for a man living there alone.

To start with I tried hard to fit in with the typical work of the coast, as a logger and as a deckhand on a salmon boat. Then, hearing about a piece of land that *might* be free for a homestead site, I rowed down to it, took a brief walk about it, and rushed off to the government agent's office in Vancouver to stake my claim.

The agent pointed out there was no water, gas, electricity, telephone line, and no road within a mile of the place.

"I know," I said with a grin. "But the view is unbelievable!" He promised that the Lands Branch would let me know in a few months.

That day I bought an old milk truck for three hundred dollars in whose cavernous interior I built a caravan home. Then donning my creaking journalistic harness I set off on the 1,672-mile trip to Hollywood to do some writing to restore my finances. And when my mail finally brought a British Columbia Lands Branch letter saying that for one hundred and ten dollars a year I could lease the two wild acres, I packed my belongings and drove the truck north. I rented again the cabin and boat I'd used on my first visit to the coast and rowed the four miles down to my new land.

So here I was once more. As I sat there in the sun watching an otter ribboning over the rocks on my beach, I felt I was adrift in an enchanted world, sitting upon a painted ocean created by Turner.

But now there was work to do. I had less than a month to erect a shelter on my cliff before I had to leave the rented cabin. I rowed to my beach and unloaded the initial equipment I'd bought—a four-foot bucksaw, an axe, a sledgehammer, and two alloy tree wedges.

I was strapping the saw to my belt so I'd have two hands free to climb up when I heard a shrieking commotion far away to the left. Over the northern land spit of the next-door bay a bald eagle had been wheeling in circles. Now two gulls launched themselves from a cliff where they had their eggs. Calling loudly, they banked, turned, and dived at the huge bird. I couldn't quite see how it happened, but there was a sudden explosion of white feathers, and then the eagle came beating towards my beach, one of the gulls held lightly in a huge talon. The sea bird looked puny in death, its head dangling and bright blood seeping from its side. As the great eagle passed above, its white-feathered head turned momentarily, its baleful yellow eye glaring down at me.

Chastened, I climbed the cliff. The land went upwards at forty degrees in a hill of large rocks and gullies. There was no level spot on which to build—and the only way to transport materials was by sea. Apart from the superb view, there was little but rocky ground covered with wiry brush, shore pines, alder, a few cedars and some firs. Building a home here now appeared a daunting if not crazy prospect for a man alone.

Clearly my biggest problem would be how to get heavy logs up to the site. The cliff was over twenty feet high but there was already one large tree trunk forming a bridge between the top of it and the beach. Twenty-five yards up my hill, but leaning too far to the south, stood a seventy-foot fir some two feet thick. It was my only hope. Somehow I had to fell that tree and manoeuvre it so it dropped side by side with the tree already there. I could then cut steps across both trunks to make a log staircase.

I sawed the wedge-like undercut facing the way I wanted the tree to fall. With frequent rests I cut into the back of the tree until the saw nearly met the undercut, but still the tree gave no sign of which way it would go. Drawing on my short logging experience, I drove wedges in with the sledgehammer.

Suddenly it started. I leaped back behind another tree in case my amateur calculations had been wrong. The fir went down, fibres tearing with pistol-like cracks, hit the cliff top, bounced up, tipped over, then slid with a tearing noise and an earth-shaking thump right next to the tree already there.

I now had two trees going down the cliff exactly side by side, not more than three inches apart all the way down. I stared in total disbelief. Surely some mighty beginner's luck had come to my aid. That log staircase would cut my labours by half and it seemed a fine omen for the future.

It was only later, back in the rented cabin, as I ate my stew by flickering candlelight, that I felt a twinge of fear. All my London friends had told me I was crazy to live out this primitive dream at my age—and maybe they were right. I knew little of the sea that would now have to be my main source of food as well as transport, and both bear and cougar were said to inhabit the mountainous terrain behind my land.

Sleep came hard that night, and as the logs spat, the cabin filled with the perfume of burning resin, mosquitoes whined, and mice charged about the floor. But at least I had my schedule planned: I'd rise at dawn, write for a few hours, then go down the coast to work on my new homesite for the rest of each day. Thus mind and body would be exercised in harmony together, the beauties of the wilderness acting naturally as a spur to both.

This naive idea soon went awry. Next morning, as I shuffled through my notes, a most almighty hammering broke out from above the cabin. I rushed out, climbed up the track, and there, before a tiny, dilapidated shack I'd been told would be empty, an old man was levelling a log with an axe. I felt unreasonable resentment—as the noise rang starkly against the silent trees, it seemed worse than being back in a city.

"Well, hello there! So you har my new neighbour!" he said heartily, oddly putting h's before some of his vowels. "Come hup, come hup. Hi hope my noise doesn't bother you!" And he stared at me quizzically, his blue eyes ringed with the grey of age. He was a square, chunky man of average height, his body old but tanned and honed to fitness by hard work. He said his name was Ed Louette and he was a retired log carpenter from the northern interior. It was impossible to remain annoyed before that cheerful face, and after the introductions I told him my problem.

"So, you build with words and hi build with logs! Hi've never met a writer before," he continued. "Hi was due to leave here last week but hi wrote to the landlord hi'd stay and rebuilt this old cabin. Well, hi've nothing better to do! But your work *is* important, so hi won't start hammering until one o'clock, how's that?"

After such hearty bonhomie, I said that was fine. Ed then tapped the log.

"That's yellow cedar. Nothing like it for cabin walls, y'know. Hit's hard as iron—and warm. Hi brought it up from the beach."

I laughed and stared at the big log. "Ho, they're not too heavy," he said. "Hi only bring three up a day. If hi was a young man hi'd carry them hall day, but now I'm sixty-seven and have a weak heart so hi take life easy!" I bent down and, staggering, managed to get the log onto my shoulder. Yet this old man had carried it up the steep hill path and a hundred yards along the road! I dropped the log, staring at Ed Louette in amazement. Sixty-seven and a weak heart?

Feeling guilty that I'd silenced Ed, I tried to start work on my book, but I couldn't concentrate—the land down the coast was calling. I gave up and, snatching my tools, went to my "property".

Until now I'd only seen the place from the beach. This time I decided to find it through the maze of old logging tracks that had not been used since the start of the century. The tracks petered out at the top of the hill. Leaving the truck I threaded my way through rocks and alders for a further half an hour before I stood again on the cliff above the beach of my little half-moon bay. Yet again I had the feeling I must be mad. It would clearly be as much as I could do in the month available to build a log *platform* on which I could put a tent, never mind a whole cabin.

Chapter 2

At dawn next day I was awakened by a loud crash. Ed Louette had dumped a sackful of oysters on my veranda. "There you har, neighbour!" he cried. "Some fine hoysters from the hisland for you!" It was his peace offering.

"Hoysters are good for you," he said emphatically. "All that phosphorus! Do you know what I eat? Hoysters, heggs, and honions!"

Ed never ate raw oysters but had his own recipes. And he breathlessly gave them to me right then. I could dip them in egg white, roll them in breadcrumbs dried in the sun, and fry them lightly in butter. I could make oyster stew by mixing them with fried onions, rice, peas, and a tin of mushroom soup. Or I could fry them in bacon fat and eat them with oat or wheat cakes. There were enough oysters in his sack to have stacked a city oyster bar for a week. And all free. Touched in spite of the rude awakening, I thanked him and told him not to worry about his hammering. I had more important things to do than to write.

For the next few days I cut a trail through the thick brush and alder to the rear of my two acres. As I'd have to carry things on my back, I wanted to make the route as easy as possible, yet not make it obvious to any occasional passer-by. So I left the first twenty-five yards of alder wood almost as it was.

On the third day it began to rain. I'd never seen rain to equal the torrential downpours on the British Columbian coast. It beat into my eyes, sneaked down my back, and even crept through the ventilation holes of my rain jacket and trickled down my armpits.

After six days I had a passable trail. The next two weeks were spent assaulting the rocky site on which I was to build. I dug out the loose rocks with pick and crowbar and rolled them over the cliff. This had a treble effect: it made the forty-degree slope level, raised the height of the beach below, and trimmed a good deal of useless fat from my waist. Once the site was ready, I dug holes through thick fir roots down to bedrock to anchor the two front log pillars of the platform.

At the back of the site I hacked holes in the exposed bedrock into which I could hook and cement the rear foundation logs so the cabin wouldn't fall into the sea. As I hacked away at the granite with a rapidly blunting pick and crowbar, a chip flew out and embedded itself half an inch below my right eye. I was lucky not to have lost the eye, and from then on I wore an old pair of swimming goggles for that work.

The next day I searched my beach for logs for the cabin's foundations. The beach was stacked high with drift logs of all kinds—fir, hemlock, spruce, with a few yellow and red cedar spars here and there. I cut the first two eight-foot logs from a straight yellow cedar, drove nails into their tops and with quadrupled nylon rope around the nails, painfully dragged them over the rocks, and up the fir tree "staircase".

Finally I had the logs in place as the front pillars. There were no others straight enough on my beach for the rest of my foundation, so I rowed half a mile to another beach, where I found two the right thickness. It took me the rest of the afternoon to cut them up, tow them back, and drag them to the foot of the cliff. They were too heavy for me to haul up the staircase.

It was time for more hard thinking, for many problems were looming. I sat on a mossy boulder watching some cream-pated wigeon drakes crowding around two dowdier grey-brown ducks, and made a mental note that I needed four of these fourteen-footers for the cabin base, eight more for the rafters, four logs for the corner posts. To haul them up the cliff I'd need a block and tackle. In a few days I would have to leave the rented cabin and its little boat, so I needed a boat of my own. And while I liked rowing, I wasn't sure I wanted to tow the basics of an entire cabin with a mere pair of oars when the only place I could put loads into the water was a dilapidated government wharf some four miles away. So I'd hire an outboard engine for a few days. Above all, I needed a good strong tent in which to live for the rest of the summer.

Next day I drove south to Vancouver, hired an old five-and-one-half-horsepower outboard, and found a secondhand ten-foot plywood dinghy for fifty-six dollars. I bought a heavy nine-foot-square tent, and block, tackle, and rope. I could now haul up the big logs for the foundations, curve-notch and nail them into place, and cut in slots for the floor joists. I used thick plywood for the floor and to box in a pie-shaped kitchen and toilet between the cabin floor and the sloping bedrock of the cliff.

One evening, when I came back to the rented cabin, Ed was waiting.

"Ho, so you have a new boat," he said heartily. "Hi thought you were hup to something! Are you staying here now?"

I couldn't hide it from him any longer. I told him about my land and the platform I was building for a tent. He laughed, surprised.

"Well, good for you, professor, good for you! Hi wondered what you were doing, leaving early hevery morning."

He looked into my boat and noticed I still had the oars from the rented cabin. "Ho, you'll need some hoars. Hi'll make some for you."

Two days later he handed me two perfect oars, copperbound at the ends, that he'd carved from spruce. And he refused to take any payment for them.

On my last day in the rented cabin I ferried out all my belongings. As I was loading up my boat, Ed came down the cliff path and offered me his. It was a calm day and by towing his boat astern of mine, I took everything at once. I set up the cooker in the kitchen and hung the pans from nails in the floor joists above. While I had cursed when making this basement to find that the bedrock ended in a jagged series of shelves, I now had cause to be thankful. I stowed all the unwanted relics of my life in civilization on these rough stone tiers, even placing a gilt mirror in such a way that when I sat down to eat meals from a small driftwood table (which saved me carrying my food up to the tent above) the mirror reflected the superb view over the islands, an idyllic scene of which I was sure I would never tire.

On my fortieth birthday I took up residence. It was a proud moment. The piping *whee-oos* of the male wigeon came up now from the placid gold and blue waters of my bay, and I looked down possessively from the sun-drenched platform at a small courting party. A grey-brown female was swimming around closely followed by three urgent drakes. What superb creations they were, for their finery would have graced any admiral of the fleet. Their greyish backs, finely pencilled with black, were broken by broad wing patches of startling white, and their secondary wing feathers overlay their primaries like black epaulettes.

As they crowded around the lady, they raised their creamy headcrests and sometimes lifted their wings. Not for them the squawking, squabbly notes one usually associates with ducks, for their soothing *whee-oos* sounded so plaintive and sweet they seemed the very embodiment of peace on that spring evening. Occasionally they jostled each other to get nearer to her, like men at a bar when a beautiful girl comes in alone, but there was no fighting. She plodded solemnly along, making an odd purring note, but her bright eyes betrayed her air of studied unawareness. She seemed to be sizing them up, for after a few minutes she quietly moved away, followed by only one drake. The other two stared mournfully but, accepting the situation like gentlemen, they paddled slowly towards the rest of the flock, now diving for eel grass and weed titbits near a small island away to the south.

Relaxing sleepily on my platform as the sun winked and dipped with golden flashes between the firs on the islands, I opened the bottle of cheap pink champagne I had bought for the occasion. It tasted like nectar.

Chapter 3

Each morning dawned in a silent primrose sky, the early light filtering through the firs and pines, etching the tangled, twisted shapes of the arbutus trees against the canvas above my head, turning the tent into a warm cauldron of green. Rising early, I'd see a salmon swirl against the placid water as it headed down the coast, or I'd see one of the lordly eagles passing by in lazy flight, though its glassy marigold eye missed no likely prey.

At first I tried unsuccessfully to begin work on the novel after only a hasty breakfast. Only hard work makes an honest man, my generation had been taught. So for weeks I suffered an obscure pressure, the guilt that I was not shaping up to "responsibility".

Nature solved the problem, for along with the fine, dazzling days came rainy ones. I learned these could be used for writing, while on the others I could work on my shelter, explore, or merely relax. There was no real hurry. I had no deadlines to meet.

Fishing daily from the tiny rowing boat with Ed's homemade oars became more than a hunt for food or even a day's sport—it became my way of life. To be able to row out into the superb tree-fringed bays and sit fishing in the sun seemed the finest freedom I had ever known.

I learned to live almost entirely from the sea. Apart from the oysters that lay two feet deep in a bay on one of the islands, I found clams and mussels, and I fished for rock cod, as well as occasional coho salmon. Many were the devious recipes cooked on the little stove. And occasionally, for a special treat, I bought meat at the nearest store—some twenty miles to the south. With care I could live easily on five dollars a week.

Rowing back one evening, I almost banged into Ed, who was returning from a trip behind Oyster Island. "Ho there, professor! What have you there?" Proudly I showed him my catch as we pulled ashore. His face dropped. "Rock cod and a dogfish. What are you going to do with *them?*"

"Eat them, of course."

"Heat them?" He stared at me in disbelief. "You can't heat fish like that. Well, rock cod are hall right if you've nothing else, but a dogfish! Dogfish are vermin. . . ."

"Well, we eat them in England," I said defensively. "We call them rock salmon, and eat them with chips."

"Vermin!" he repeated. "Scavengers! Just bang them on the head and throw them back, that's what we do with dogfish!" He turned back the wet sacking in his boat to reveal fat vermilion fish with bulging golden eyes. "Red snapper. Those are the best eating fish, next to salmon. Here!" He flicked a nine-pound fish into my boat. "Try that. Fry it in breadcrumbs and corn hoil and when you eat it, dip it in malt vinegar!"

Usually, however, I saw little of Ed, and it was three weeks before I met him again. I had mislaid an axe head and was sure I'd left it under the rented cabin. I drove back along the forest road in the truck and just as I found the axe head, Ed's chunky figure blocked out the evening light. He held a bottle of rye in his hand.

"Hello, neighbour! Hi thought that axe head was yours, so I sharpened it up but put it back there." He had, too. "Well, hi'll be leaving here soon, so would you care for a drink?" It was the first time I'd ever been invited into his cabin. The whole place smelled of linseed oil. His floor was covered with wood shavings and his tools lay everywhere, the symbols of his passion for creating in wood. He walked over to a kitchen corner, rubbed two red snapper fillets in his sun-dried breadcrumbs, and popped them into sizzling oil in a skillet on his wood stove.

As we ate the crisp fish in the flickering candlelight—mere hors d'oeuvres Ed explained as he heaved a vast pot of oyster stew onto the stove—we started on the rye. I noticed there was small spiders' webs in some of the cabin's window frames and high log corners.

"Hi always leave spiders alone," he told me. "They are good friends of man, y'know. They kill mosquitoes and hall the flies that get on the food. No, I never harm the spiders. They're more than welcome!" I felt guilty. I had hated spiders since childhood and always whacked them to death when I saw them. From that evening on, like Ed, I left them alone.

Shyly at first, and then with growing confidence as the rye warmed him, Ed showed me some of his work. Most impressive were the natural "art works"—a giraffe's head from a burl of fir, a chunk of hemlock that looked like a seaman's head complete with cap and beard, and a fir root carved into an abstract running rooster. He had only carved them enough to bring out their natural lines, then to preserve them he had dipped them into boiling linseed oil. He thrust the rooster into my hands, waved away any protests, and insisted I keep it. It is my talisman to this day.

Ed was a gifted creator. He had no artistic pretension and sought no recognition. As a youth, just after the era of the bullock and horse teams, he had toiled in Canada's great forests as a logger. Approaching forty, knowing he would soon be too old to climb and top the big trees, Ed had turned to carpentry and cabin and bunkhouse building. As his skill had grown, so had his reputation. And now I saw in the faded, yellowing pictures that he held out the great log ranchhouses, standing as mute testimony to the life of this man, one of the last of the North American log craftsmen.

Ed loved the wild and free creatures with a passion that matched mine, and kept many wildlife books on his shelves, checking the birds he saw each day with the pages at night. He dropped a hint once about a wild grizzly bear trek he had made when younger, but withstood my queries with, "Well, professor, I may tell you about that one day when you've been here a bit longer. But hi'll be leaving here tomorrow." He was going to one of the southern gulf islands for the rest of the summer. But he would be back on the coast around September. I hoped he would be back then. I did not intend to face winter in that exposed place in a tent, and if any man could teach me how to build a good cabin it would be Ed Louette.

I woke before dawn with a raging thirst and as I climbed down the rocks from the tent platform to my kitchen, I heard a thumping, scraping sound. I shone my torch and there on the log rafters sat a pack rat as big as a beaver, with a long bushy tail and eyes glowing red in the sudden beam. I shouted and followed its flight down the rocks with hefty swipes from my broom. I didn't relish the thought of a rat that size rummaging around my tent as I lay sleeping. Following it from above, I saw it disappear into a crevice. Later I examined the area. There seemed to be at least two nests in the crevice which ran back into a small tunnel between the rocks. The rats had hauled in sticks as thick as a man's thumb and lined the nests with leaves and shredded plant fibres. Outside was a small store of fruit seeds, mouldy cheese rinds, meat scraps and vegetable peelings, all purloined from my rubbish bin. I resisted the temptation to burn out the nests. After all, if the rats could put my rubbish to good use it was as good as my burying it. They had as much right to be there as I had and they were not doing me any harm. In a way they were company.

The decision not to burn out the pack rats was perhaps the unconscious start of my desire to fit in *with* nature as far as possible. In my years there, I never built a boundary fence or cut any live trees apart from topping a couple of overcrowded pine that blocked sunlight from the platform. Even my little trail wound in and out around trees. Stumbling over root clusters seemed a fair enough price to pay for just having the trees that went with them still around the place. Then I found myself making friends with the animal life around me.

One day when I was cleaning codfish and throwing the entrails to gathering crabs, a group of seagulls landed. Straight away two big males began dominating the flock. There was a strict pecking order and, with wings up and beaks outstretched, they screamed at the others to stand back while they first ate their fill. Suddenly I felt a dab on my boot, a young brown-and-white speckled gull had waddled over the rocks until it was right under the fish I was gutting, and was gulping down cod's tails, fins, skins as fast as he could. I noticed his left foot was all bunched and twisted inward. As gulls are lucky if one chick survives to maturity from a nest each year, the chances against this odd runt's surviving must have been fifty to one. I never· saw its parents feed it although it peeped plaintively at any gull flying near. Clearly desperation had forced him to come to me to pick up food the others dared not reach.

I named him Bert because he looked like my concept of a Bert. After that first visit he took to hanging around the bottom of my staircase. My monthly fire to burn what little refuse I had left after the bushy-tailed rats had delved into my garbage almost ceased. I had little rubbish to burn when Bert was around.

Ugly and stunted though he was, nature had compensated Bert in one way—he had magnificent wings. They seemed almost a quarter larger than those of the other fledglings. Already he flew more easily than they and soared with less wing action.

No sooner was I used to having Bert around than another guest arrived, also without a visiting card, and while he overstayed his welcome, he was the sort of guest one hardly asks to leave. Sitting at supper one night, I was astonished when a small black-and-white striped animal wandered straight into the kitchen, blinked at me in the candlelight, decided I was no danger, and promptly toddled over both my feet, and started rummaging among the empty cans in my rubbish bin. I was so astonished I didn't move—which was just as well, for my new friend was a striped skunk. All I knew about skunks was that if you scared them they promptly discharged twin barrels of acrid oil at you that smelled so obnoxious the only way to get rid of it was to burn everything it touched. I sat there petrified, not moving a muscle, while His Lordship ambled about good-naturedly, ignoring me as if I were some lowly tenant on his estate and he was just making sure I was keeping everything in good order.

The skunk is the true king of the animals, for his stench glands have won him a unique respect and he knows it. Not even the coyote or cougar dares assail his dignity, unless they're nearly starving in a harsh winter. Only the great horned owl and the golden eagle, who probably have little or no sense of smell, regard the skunk as a tasty dish. As my forceful guest retired behind my filing cabinet with some boiled fish scraps, I quietly sneaked up to bed. Halfway through the night I was awakened by loud snoring noises that seemed to come from right beneath me. The skunk was sleeping off his meal. I wasn't going to disturb him, so I stuffed bits of handkerchief in my ears and went back to sleep.

For four more nights the skunk shared my home and was the epitome of good manners, apart from his nightly snoring. He was easy-going, amiable, and his motto seemed clear: "You mind yours and I'll mind mine. If you don't, look out!" Then he disappeared.

Two weeks later an old retired logger complained at the store that a couple of skunks had set up home beneath his cabin three miles north of me. I said nothing. His Lordship had clearly decided my dwelling was substandard—or his wife had.

Occasionally, usually in the early morning, I saw the bald eagle flying low over the tent. I often wonder what inspired the name bald eagle, for bald it certainly is not. Its strong, wedge-shaped head is covered with magnificent glossy white feathers, rightful apparel for the king of birds. Sometimes I'd hear the high-pitched *kri-kri-kri* first, and I'd rush to the mosquito netting to catch a pre-breakfast glimpse as he set off on his regular hunting trip around his territory. It never occurred to me there might be more than one eagle in my area until one morning in May I was awakened by an odd drumming sound.

I hurried outside to see an extraordinary sight. High above the bay two eagles, their giant talons interlocked as if in a fight to the

death, were whirling down in a great spiral, tumbling over and over for several hundred feet. Their wing and snow-white tail feathers were being beaten backwards and forwards by the rushing air, sounding like flapping sails. Just as I thought they must fall to their deaths, they let go, and the smaller bird pulled out in a beautiful curve and effortlessly banked upwards again, while the larger eagle flapped away to the south, also gaining height. As I watched spellbound, the smaller eagle angled towards the other and as it flashed down from the windless sky, great talons extended, the other performed a perfect somersault and presented its claws. Once more interlocked, they fell until again, just above the surface, they separated and the larger female set off to the north, with the male beating along, seeming calmer and more content now, in her wake. What I had seen was not a fight at all but a rare part of their courtship display, the most impressive sight I had witnessed in the wild. I suddenly felt as if I were back in the magical days of childhood.

Chapter 4

Unconsciously, since Ed had left, I'd been turning more and more to the animals around me for a kind of companionship. After the unforgettable air dance of the eagles, I felt my keen curiosity about nature expanding even more. I knew bald eagles had been declining in recent years and it was strangely important that I now find out more about them.

It wasn't until June that I first thought their nest could be near by. I noticed the male was flying south over my tent early each morning, returning around midday, and also flying over again before dusk. Such a regular pattern made it seem likely he was feeding his mate and one or even two youngsters. Yet it appeared an impossible task to try and find the nest, for this great bird soars so effortlessly on its broad wings—which can span nearly eight feet—that it will cover twenty miles in a few minutes.

Then, at dusk one evening, an extraordinary thing happened. I was sitting idly in a clump of alders on the cliff edge watching my pack rats' nesting crevice. It was an oddly mosquito-free evening, probably between hatches, and I'd been there half an hour. One rat had already been out and had toured two tidal pools in the rocks below, and I wanted to see what it was up to. After another ten minutes, my perch was becoming uncomfortable and I was about to go when the rat came out again, sniffed the air cautiously, and walked off with its odd tottery gait towards the pools. Then a movement in the sky above the northerly land spit caught my eye. The male eagle had skimmed the fir trees and was coming towards me in a long glide. When halfway across the bay it banked and landed in a tree on the shore. It appeared to be staring hard in my direction. The pack rat, short-sighted as are all rodents, had seen nothing, of course, and was sniffing slowly along under a small rocky ridge that must have shielded it from the eagle's view.

The next moment the eagle had launched itself from the tree. It gave a few quick wing beats as it dropped low and came beating along the surface of the sea, it came straight towards me, swooped over the ridge at the last moment, dropped down with a rush of feathers and snatched my former raider in its talons, and flapped away transferring the rat to one foot and retracting the other like a jet leaving a runway. Eagles rarely use their beaks when killing small prey and one gripping stab of those two-inch talons had crushed the life from the big rat.

The most extraordinary thing about the attack, apart from my actually seeing it, was how the eagle had apparently planned it. It had clearly sat up in that tree and worked out that if it flew down low, keeping the rocky ridge between itself and its victim, the rat had little chance of escape.

Often now the eagles flew directly over my boat, sometimes quite low and without even looking down, as if I had become if not a friend at least a familiar and clearly harmless figure. They saw me long before I could see them, for their eyesight is at least three times as fine as a man's, and where a man might see a mere buff patch on a mossy escarpment half a mile away, the eagle would see three rock rabbits and even which way they were looking.

On another day I was astonished to see the male eagle stoop at a salmon rolling on the surface—and promptly disappear as the big fish dived in an effort to get away. The eagle did not let go, however, and presently both eagle and fish came up some five yards farther on. The eagle seemed to row itself and its prey ashore, half flying at first in a frantic effort to rise, then hunching itself along, swimming with half-folded wings. In the shallows it succeeded in dragging the salmon onto the stony shore where it left it, and flew to a low branch where it sunned its great wings. Eagles do not have oiled feathers like ducks or gulls, and on the rare occasions that they get waterlogged, they have to dry out their wings.

By now I had noticed that the eagles always seemed to be around one small island, and that it was dead in line with their frequent flights over the northern spit of land as seen from my tent.

It was on June 16 that I finally located the nest. I rowed out to the island, watched the big trees carefully, and after a few minutes, one of the eagles launched itself from a tall fir with an unusually flat top and began to soar to and fro. It was the female, and just below the top of the tree I could see a dark mass of sticks.

Next day in the low dawn light I rowed back to the island, landed out of sight, and quietly stole through the forest until, some two hundred yards from the shore, the splashings of white droppings beneath a giant fir gave the unmistakable clues. The tree was a good five feet thick at the base and, as I looked up, the massive nest spanned a V-fork between two branches some one hundred and twenty feet above my head. If the mother eagle was brooding right now I could not see, for despite her three-and-one-quarter-foot length, neither her beak nor her tail projected over the edges of her immense home.

The rocky ground rose steeply from the shore, and some fifty yards away I started to climb a small cedar and was only a few feet above the ground when the female eagle dropped down from her nest and glided out to sea. I hadn't climbed a tree since boyhood so I took my time, surprised to find I had to fight against a slight vertigo.

At twenty-five feet, clasping the trunk with one hand for dear life, I took out my old pocket telescope and steadied it against the trunk.

There were *two* young eaglets in the nest. One was partly fledged, with wing and tail quills just starting to sprout, but the smaller one was still in the white downy stage. It was an exciting discovery. Since World War II, bald eagles and some other birds of prey have been declining drastically, largely due to agricultural pesticides that are absorbed by the rodents the birds eat and that, washed into rivers by rainstorms, enter the tissues of their fish prey too. The build-up of poison induces sterility, and also causes them to lay more fragile, thin-shelled eggs which break easily in the nest. So finding this nest with two young was a stroke of luck.

I was just wondering how to build a small hide in the tree so I could occasionally watch their progress without upsetting them when I heard a rushing noise. I looked up—the mother eagle had seen me, had swung around in a large arc to come from behind, and was making great power dives over my tree. She banked, and dived down, roaring past me with what seemed hurricane speed. Although she never came closer than seven or eight yards, I got down that tree as fast as I could.

Four days later I returned, and set up a hide with sacking walls. The beauty of a sacking hide, apart from its lightness, is that while you can see out easily through the walls (I also made a small view hole for my fieldglass), the bird or animal cannot see in. Twice the inquisitive female landed on a branch a mere few feet away. I was afraid she would try to tear the hide to pieces, but she didn't. She just perched there, great gnarled talons looking as if they were strangling the branch, and glared. Gazing into that mad dandelion eye, so fierce it seemed to peer into your very soul, its iris expanding and contracting like some magical camera lens as the bird changed focus on objects near and far, was awe inspiring.

In early July I became worried about the smaller eaglet. It was not growing as fast as its companion and twice almost fell off the nest rim, only regaining its balance by weakly flapping its embryo wings and grabbing for dear life onto sticks with its beak. Also occasionally when the mother was not present, the bigger bird would peck at the smaller, sit on its head or harry it around the nest, keeping the centre spot for itself. I decided to leave them alone a whole week.

On my next visit though, sadly only the feathered eaglet was in the nest, asleep. Of the smaller one there was no sign. Clearly it had been unable to compete for food any longer and had suffered a harsh but common fate.

Half an hour later the remaining eaglet woke, stood up, flapped its blunt wings a few times, then started peering anxiously at the sky. But its mother did not appear in the hour I remained. Instead the eaglet picked at some rabbit remains and, to my delight, once trapped them awkwardly with one foot as it tugged at the tendons. Its foot didn't hold too well, the rabbit slipped out, and the eaglet fell over backwards, but it tried again and again, finally pulling off a morsel to swallow.

After another ten days I returned. The nest was empty. I looked round the area and saw the eaglet, now fully fledged, sitting on a thick branch close to the trunk of a big fir. It must have made its first short flight and now it stood there for over an hour as if afraid to move. When the mother returned to the empty nest, she landed there and stood with an oddly lost look, like the parent of an only child who has just left home for the first time. The eaglet lifted each foot slowly and moved inch by inch along the bough towards its home. It looked at the sky, down at the ground, then started to flap its wings, harder and harder, jumping up and down on the bough, until suddenly it leaped up into the slight wind and flapped without any difficulty straight back to the nest, landing so awkwardly it cannoned into its mother. The eaglet was now three months old and was ready to face the world.

A MAN LIVING ALONE in the wilds soon finds the "harmony of nature" is a mere myth, and the "divine plan" is rather a callous system in which each species struggles to survive against others. In nature the individual life is of little account.

The inexperienced man in the wilderness must learn fast, for there are few second chances. He needs monumental patience, for he cannot hurry the seasons nor change the weather. He is forced to capitulate to nature's forces, to bend with the gales, to shelter from the rains, to learn to make the most of calmer periods.

The astonishing thing about living wild and free by the sea is that eventually nearly everything one needs comes drifting up onto the beaches. On most fine days, after mornings working at the book, I wandered along the shore lines looking for any new drift lumber or useful logs for when I built my cabin.

Among the bountiful handouts delivered to me by the sea were a complete window frame, a pot of white paint, tins of motor oil, an antique whisky barrel, and half a mahogany boat from whose boards I made good shelves and a superb natural desk top. Although I now had the window frame I did not have a sill, which had to be L-shaped to prevent rainwater flooding in. Sure enough, a few weeks later, up drifted the right piece.

My biggest problem, though, remained fresh water, as important in the wild as food and shelter. Every time I left the tent for supplies I hung a gallon container from what I called my "water finger". I filled it from a creek about half a mile away as I carried other stores along the trail. But when this third finger of my left hand seemed to be getting a permanent crook, I decided to dig a well. In two whole days I had pick-axed and shovelled four separate holes without finding a trace of moisture. So I wrote to Ed. In a few days his terse reply came, written in a neat, open hand. "Find a big alder or willow where the roots are thick and go straight down, and dig there. . . ." Next day I did so and after hacking around and through small rocks, at six feet the ground grew mushy. Another two feet down and I had water pouring in. With two plastic hoses joined together I got a siphon system working. I stood in my kitchen and twisted the hose nozzle, and the water spurted ten feet—beautiful, crystal-clear cold water.

Chapter 5

One night I returned late from a fishing trip and was sitting on my veranda in the moonlight when I heard a scratching below. Instantly thinking "cougar!" I reached for my newly purchased spirit lamp, whose bright glare I was sure would scare off almost any animal, and looked cautiously over the edge.

307

There, sitting up in a begging position like a dog and waving its long-clawed hands like a shadow boxer, was a racoon. Its black-masked face looked owlishly up at me, blinking in the strong light. I'd heard that coons sometimes come around houses in the evening looking for scraps. This one had clearly smelled my fish, so I gently threw him a piece. To my delight he instantly dropped on all fours, went with a wobbly, catlike gait to the fish, and cautiously reached out for it, then hurried furtively into the undergrowth where he ate it with an audible smacking of lips. Then back he came with much more confidence. Lonesome as I was since Ed had left, I encouraged him and before long he was prowling around almost every night. I looked forward to his visits, hearing his scratch on the logs if the kitchen door was shut, seeing the strange red glow from his eyes in the lamplight as he sat, waiting patiently for scraps. Apart from knowing he would hardly wander abroad with such impunity if there was still a cougar within striking distance, I was glad of his company.

I nicknamed him Spooks because he always came at night, appearing so quietly if the door was open it seemed he had materialized out of the air. Although he was heftily built and some three feet long, a foot of which was bushy, black-ringed tail, he was a comical-looking character. He seemed half dog and half cat, with long sharp claws on all four feet. He was covered in grey fur and his face, with bright button eyes, erect ears, and sharp nose, looked alternately owlish or foxy. The black band across his eyes gave him the air of a brigand, a highwayman, which, I soon found out, also coincided with his nature.

The racoon is a redoubtable beast, for it combines the qualities of so many animals in one—the near-nocturnal sight of an owl, the fighting abilities of both cat and dog, the climbing speed of a monkey, and the cunning of a fox. It dens in old woodpeckers' holes, in hollow or broken parts of trees, in rocky ground crevices, even sometimes in old enlarged rabbit burrows.

It was first named *arakun* by the Algonquin Indians, but the early British settlers mispronounced the name, turning it to racoon. Although the craze for coonskin coats in the 1920s reduced its numbers, it soon reasserted itself, and even the 1955 craze for Davy Crockett hats failed to dent its populations. Today the coon positively thrives on man's encroachment and, like the persecuted

European foxes, it has learned to live near urban man, raiding his rubbish bins and stealing his chickens.

Within a couple of weeks Spooks was semi-tame. He even began following me up to the tent after his meal and while he refused to step over the threshold, he often sat licking his claws near where the spirit lamp warmed the side of the tent. Once he got used to me his movements were quite slow and he sat still for minutes at a time. If I held out food and said things like, "Here you are, Spooks, come along and eat it up," in a soft, soothing voice, he approached cautiously, extended both hands at full reach, took the morsel with great delicacy, then hastily retreated a few feet and ate it.

One evening when I'd forgotten to close the tent flap, I found Spooks inside. His curiosity finally had got the better of him, for everything on my shelves had been pulled onto the bed. Wrapping paper from my few chocolates was strewn about and Spooks himself was sitting oddly upright in a corner, like an old drunk asleep outside a restaurant kitchen's doorway, his fluffy tail held between his forepaws. Charming though he looked at that moment, I didn't want him moving in as an unpaid guest, and so I shooed him out with the broom. With a rasping snarl he scurried out and up the nearest tree.

When two nights later he began scratching at the tent as if to claw his way in, I felt he was becoming too much of a good thing. He puzzled me too, now, by sometimes taking the fish, bread or other food, and dashing off into the night with it. I thought he was probably storing it somewhere for future use. But one evening the problem was solved. As he waited outside the kitchen where I was now feeding him, I was aware of several pairs of redly glowing eyes watching us from the trees. Four more coons! One, far larger than the others, a female, was clearly Spooks's wife, and the other three small ones, who hissed and squabbled with each other, were the three surviving members of their brood, probably born in May.

Five coons, while not likely to gang up on a man, could soon reduce my tent to strips of canvas while searching for food when I was fishing or on a supply trip.

For the next few nights I threw scraps well away from the platform into the bushes, and I cut down on the fish dish. But shortly afterwards, about two a.m. one morning, the problem was solved for me.

I was awakened by a fearful racket—a cacophony of hisses, spits and barks and growls. I rushed out with my spirit lamp and there in its glow, cornered between the rocks and the log ends of the platform, was Spooks, his teeth bared in a snarl, slashing away with his claws at a large blackish-brown animal that promptly shot away from the light and disappeared into the forest before I could see it clearly. It must have been a dog, but I'd never seen a dog in the area before. As it fled crashing through the brush, Spooks glared up as I stood on the platform, then with a reproachful look he scrambled up the sheer face of the rock, and disappeared into the branches of an old fir. I never saw him again and the slight loneliness I'd felt before his arrival returned. Occasionally I still fed Bert, but even he was more wary now that he had learned the full use of his large wings.

Now it was time to think seriously about my cabin. Winter was on its way. The few poplars higher up were turning yellow, and alder leaves, the first to fall, swirled around the platform. The birch were losing their rich greens. There were gaps appearing in the trees to the north so now I could see the tiny bay next door that formerly had been hidden by the foliage. As I walked the trail, the falling leaves were opening up the landscape. Although the temperature drop was gradual, I now noticed my feet were cold until well after midday unless I was doing strenuous outdoor work. And to complicate things, the boat had begun to leak. However, I patched it up as best I could with plywood and thick paint.

One day at the store as I was picking up bolts, hinges, nails, a stove pipe, and paraphernalia for my cabin, I recognized a familiar chunky figure. It was Ed Louette, all neat in city clothes. He had just arrived on the bus with his inevitable bag of tools. He came back with me and we walked down together to my tent. As he looked at my platform, the log work of which I was so proud, Ed hid a smile and said I was doing all right—for a beginner.

"You know something," he said, "you should have built a cabin on this platform. Winter will soon be here." I said that had been my idea too, and that I'd been gathering materials.

He looked directly at me, staring intently for a few seconds as if summing me up.

"Well," he said, "*We'll* build you a cabin, professor. Yessir, we'll build you a nice little house and we'll start tomorrow!"

Ed Louette was one of the world's finest and last-surviving log craftsmen. I could only blurt out some awkward words of thanks. It was the start of an extraordinary nine days. That man, sixty-eight years old, worked at a pace I could barely match. He refused all short cuts, insisting we mortise-joint the corner posts and use plumb line and level. He taught me how to measure and cut the wall studs, stagger the wall bridging, notch the roof beams, make a template, how to cut roof shakes—roof tiles—from the red cedar spar, and even how to scribe logs so each fitted into the other, a most complicated procedure.

As I watched Ed's tough old hands working with such apparent ease, I felt a mounting envy. For him, none of the introspection of the writer. Those hands were proof of years of healthy creative endeavour that had made Ed a happy man.

"So many people seem unhappy because they're not doing something *himportant,*" Ed said once. "But what does it matter what a man does, provided he gives, contributes? You must make yourself love what you do, and do it as best you can. What other reason for life can we ever really know for sure?"

For lunch each day Ed devoured sandwiches made of brown bread, honey and molasses, sprinkled with wheat germ. They looked almost as atrocious as another dark red mixture that he munched with great enjoyment. I asked him what that was.

"Bull's hearts!" he answered. "By God, they're good for you! You know, a few years ago I began to feel bad. Hi went to a doctor and he examined me and said I had a weak heart. Hi had always to walk hup steps, not run. Well, hi came out of there and hi ran hup the first steps I saw! The heart is a muscle and can be made strong. But hi changed my diet, yessir, I changed my diet. A man is what he heats, I'm sure of that.

"Now the heart is the centre of an animal. No fat and hall the good blood! So hi cut the heart into strips and shove a strip into a small grinder. Then a carrot, then another strip of heart, then a carrot. That way it doesn't need much cooking and most of the goodness is left."

311

He broke off a piece and handed it to me. To my surprise it tasted delicious.

One thing Ed never ate was salt. He shrank in horror when he saw me putting some on my food one day and I asked him why.

"When hi was a child back in New Brunswick, in winter we almost *lived* on salted fish. At six years old, eating those fish was the same as sticking me in the guts with a knife. At fifteen they were pulling my teeth out and hi've worn false ever since. Every kid at school had a runny nose, heven the Indians, and coughed from fall to spring. What other reason could there be? I'm sure too much salt poisons the brains, makes people stupid. Well, I haven't touched a grain of salt for twenty years now—and I'm getting younger all the time!"

If Ed was a crank, he was the strongest, healthiest, happiest crank I ever met! At the end of each day I was ready for my bunk. But Ed refused ever to let me run him home by boat or truck. He preferred to walk the trail, then hitch, and if no one came along, he ambled the five miles to his hut.

One day I tried to bring up how I was to pay him for his help for I had little money to spare. Could I pay in instalments?

"Ho, I don't want to be paid!" he said, almost in disgust. "Hif you have money, pay the rate. If not, and I believe in you, hi work for nothing."

It was Ed's approach to the wonders of nature that attracted me most. His view seemed that of a marvelling child. Yet his knowledge of animal, bird and insect life was considerable. In his cabin I'd noticed books about animals and birds; so I mentioned my days with the bald eagles. He knew the nest well, had known it for several years, but he had not told me about it because he wanted the great birds to remain undisturbed. "We are killing hall the eagles," he said then with a trace of anger. "When hi first came here, you could see an eagle every hour of the day, but that pair are the honly ones I've seen here for three years, apart from that young one. It's the farmers and forest men with all their pesticides, you know."

I was surprised that an old man like Ed Louette felt so concerned about such matters. For several lunchtimes, in breaks from strenuous work, we talked of our wild, lovely places. We both agreed that in this last truly abundant wilderness of the northern

312

hemisphere, the superb scenery would soon pall if the glories of the wildlife all around us were not there too.

When I asked how he knew so much he told me how as a younger man he had trekked alone into wild mountains south of Bella Coola, nearly halfway up the British Columbian coast. Once he had trekked with a pal named Pappy Tihoni to a place they called their secret valley. What little he told me of that adventure sounded incredible—they had seen more than two dozen grizzly bears in three days—but when I pressed him for exact information about the secret valley he suddenly laughed, as if to disguise the fact he didn't want to tell me more.

"Listen, hi've come here to help build your house," he said. "So let's get hon with it. We don't want to waste good weather sitting here just jawing."

As we began work again, I asked how old he had been when he made his treks into the wilderness. "I set out on the first on my fortieth birthday," he said.

"I moved into this tent on mine," I returned.

He laughed. "You know, professor, you should go on a trek like that, maybe hin the spring. Yessir, a man like you should go and live in those mountains awhile, go through that wild place. You'll learn a lot, especially about yourself. But it will age you, mind. It'll sure age you!" And with a strange quizzical look at me, a look I never forgot, he went back to work.

By noon on the ninth day the entire cabin frame was up, including a beautifully finished golden-shake roof that, from the sea a mile away, glowed like an amber jewel amid the forest green. And it had cost me little but the price of nails. Ed ate his lunch, brushed the crumbs of his homemade bread from his knees, and stood up.

"Well, hi think I'll go and do some fishing now." He looked up at the sky. "Not many good days left. You get the sides on. Get your sides up while it's still dry!" And off he went, knowing I could see to the rest myself.

The plywood walls took me another week. For a bed I nailed four planks onto crosspieces and set them across my two saw-horses in a rear corner. I put my desk below the front window, giving me a view over the islands that I hoped would be an inspiration as I wrote throughout the winter. Dragging the solid

313

two-foot-six-inch mahogany door, given to me by a friend in Vancouver, from its storage place in the kitchen, I hung it from the rear southeast pillar, then nailed felt strips around its frame to make it draughtproof. I was surprised at how much room there was in the twelve-foot-square cabin.

Proudly I descended the log staircase and walked down to take a good look. There, in the midst of the virgin forest green, rose my new home. With its single window in the front, it looked like a quaint wooden garage on stilts.

As I lay on my bed that night, with the candlelight playing on the golden walls, the air heavy with wood fragrance, and with my superb view framed by the window, I felt an extraordinary exhilaration. Nothing had ever given me more pleasure than working with Ed and making this simple home in the wilds.

My joy was short-lived. Overnight, as if it had co-operated only until the moment I was safely inside, the weather broke. A cold wind, bringing big blobs of rain spattering onto the new roof, came in from the northwest probing its fingers into every gap. There's nothing like a blast or two of wind to show you your galeproof cabin is not! I spent hours blocking warps in the roof boards and holes around the inner sides of the log rafters.

Next day I hauled an old oil barrel, in which I'd already cut a stoking door and smoke outlet, into the cabin. This combined heater, cooking stove, and incinerator was a great idea, I thought. I was hammering away when I heard shrill chatters and squeaks coming from outside. Sitting on the curving fir's branch a mere four yards above my head was a cheeky Douglas squirrel, jerkily flirting his bushy, yellow-tipped tail, and scolding me for all he was worth. I wanted to be friendly, so I tossed a crust of bread onto the cabin roof, went back to work, and forgot him.

A few minutes later there was a clonk on my roof, a patter of clawed feet, then nothing. Slowly I inched out and sneaked a look over the roof. He was sitting on his little haunches, his long bushy tail curved like an S above his head, and in his delicate hands he held my bread up to his mouth, nibbling away with his buck teeth. "Hi, Douglas," I said softly. Instantly he bounded about six feet, hit the edge of the roof, and shot up the fir, then turned and cursed me roundly for disturbing his meal. Next day he was back. Around dawn he thudded on my roof and scampered around looking for an easy breakfast. He came for lunch, tea, and dinner, too—for he was hard at work. All day he gathered fir and pine cones, standing on one branch and reaching up on tiptoe to the one above. Then he'd bounce down to the forest floor and hare off with his booty—where to I never knew. He must have been stuffing them in his nest for his winter hoard. Douglas worked even harder than Ed Louette. It really clinched our relationship, however, when I found him drinking rainwater from a dish I'd accidentally left out near the kitchen. From then on I filled it each morning and put it on a projecting beam on the leeward side of the cabin. He became tamer and tamer, going hoppity-hoppity over my roof, scrabbling down the log pillars, stopping every now and then to give a little warbling song.

Chapter 6

By now I reckoned I had it all figured out—my survival in the wilderness winter. My biggest problem would be loneliness. I could combat that by escaping into my novel—the characters would be company of a sort, and weaving incidents together would help take me out of myself. But I had two other basic needs—food and firewood. I'd been alarmed by how much wood my oil-barrel stove could burn up—a whole tree of one-foot logs would roar away in a day if I wasn't careful. Well, the moment I felt writer's cramp I could row out a few miles and tow back drift logs from the beaches. And I could fish at the same time.

This part of my fine plan soon came unstuck, though. In the rough seas my rickety little boat sprang several new leaks and was soon beyond any patch-up jobs for winter use. I could not buy a bigger one because I needed to conserve finances. So I laid night fishing lines. But as the days grew colder and the fish deserted the shore for deeper and warmer water, I often caught nothing at all.

One day in October I met Ed on his beach. He told me he was

leaving in a few days to spend the winter in Vancouver, where he could read for hours in the fine new library or observe the foibles of his fellow man in the public gallery of the courthouse. And then, on my way to the store a few days later, I saw Ed's cabin ominously deserted. The red cotton curtains were drawn and it stood forlornly in the rain, a padlock on its door.

I felt horribly lonely as I walked back down the trail, the white-capped sea crunching into granite hollows, dragging rocks back into the deeper waters with a loud cracking sound. The tall alders near my well had lost nearly all their leaves and their slender grey-green trunks swayed rhythmically in the wind. The dogwood bush was now bereft, its lovely white flowers a mere memory. Here and there twisted arbutus trees stood in clusters, their red bark peeling and fluttering in ribbons, revealing bright green skin beneath, their long, dark leathery leaves rattling against each other as if reluctant to let go and die.

Shelter and warmth and food, though, were now my prime concern. For days I wandered the beaches and forests carrying and stacking drift and fallen wood for my primitive stove. I pickled oysters and mussels in vinegar. I boiled the free berries of autumn in sugar syrup, then bottled them in old honey jars with screw top lids. I brined beans, tomatoes, and carrots with salt. And I stacked apples and root vegetables in layers of hay and sawdust under my bed.

Until now the wilderness life had been largely idyllic, but in the early winter I began to find that land untamed or uninhabited flays the mind, throws it back upon itself. Alone when the great eagles, ducks, gulls and other birds have flown south, when animal friends are partly hibernating or have moved nearer civilized centres for the urban spoils, when the sun hides behind dark cloud on the low horizon day after day, one is left face to face with no one but oneself, and it can be an unnerving experience.

Until now consciousness of my complete isolation had been allayed by all the joys of outdoor summer life, by fascinating experiences with the animals around me, by building my platform, by meeting Ed and building my cabin with him. But now, imprisoned by bad weather, immersed in my book, I felt the real pangs of solitude.

Rain does more than wet you, somehow. It rains on your heart, your spirit. As I rose each morning and cooked and ate breakfast in the half-dark, and heard the ceaseless pounding of the waves against the cliff, I wished I had built the cabin farther up the slope. At times it felt the great rollers were battering into my very foundations. Then back up to my living room I scrambled, a spare log under each arm to dry by the smoky stove, shut the door fast and worked on my book for another eight- or ten-hour stint.

I found myself becoming more and more reliant upon the mail as a kind of emotional anchor. About once a fortnight I returned down the trail clutching what few letters I received, relishing the thought of reading them. Then I hoarded them for hours. Putting them on the desk, I'd find jobs to do, prepare supper, *anything* rather than actually read them and have nothing more to look forward to. Then as the simple meal bubbled away, I'd sip a glass or three of homemade wine, arrange the letters with the least interesting at the top and the more intimate ones at the bottom, and start to read.

It seemed ironic when I received one from a friend in London. "What on earth are you doing, still out there on that rock alone, dodging reality?" he wrote. I . . . dodging reality?

By late November loneliness had become a powerful enemy. I needed human company now, if only for a short while. Twice I tried walking up the trail and driving to a beer parlour near the town. I knew some of the men from my previous fishing and logging work—good, mad, simple characters. Struggling as I then was with my book, I felt little kinship with the raucous talk of big fish and trees, or the tough horseplay. I sat in the smoky haze, the lost emigrant with little to contribute.

For the whole of that winter, my novel now became what no book should ever be—a prop, the last and only prop, against an increasing spiritual as well as physical isolation. I persevered, though, because to give up would have meant surrendering to the pangs of loneliness.

"About time you suffered a bit, lad," I told the white face and black-ringed eyes in the piece of broken mirror. "You had your fun, so get back to your desk and *work!*" I said it aloud for I had now started talking to myself. It's said when a man talks to himself he is nearing madness. I think that I would have gone mad if I had not.

I did have some companionship, however. No sooner had I climbed into bed most nights than I would be disturbed by the mice, twice the size of British mice, who had discovered in the kitchen a perfect labyrinth of posts, shelves, and rock ledges along which they could run, jump, slide, and leap until they reached the food. Once full of my food, they sneaked up through tiny hidden gaps into the living room to play in the warmth from the embers of my stove.

Like a convict in solitary, I began to cultivate their friendship. I put all my dry stores into a tin box and at suppertime doled out their rations along with mine on the cabin floor. What beautiful little animals they were, with their black sparkling eyes, long whiskers, soft white bellies, and engaging, timorous habits! Rats and mice carry germs, say folks with horror. Yet these mice, far from human sewage and habitation, were for ever grooming and washing themselves like little cats. They were not house mice, they were deer mice, with spotless white boots on their feet. If they ever had to walk across mud or wet ground, they raised themselves up high, sort of on tiptoe, hurrying across into the dry again. At our little dinner parties they all sat around my circle of crumbs and cheese, nibbling away and wiping their long whiskers clear of crumbs, snatching titbits from each other like children at a party when left to their own devices.

One fine morning in early December as I wandered through the forest before visiting the store down the coast, I realized how much I was dreading the coming of Christmas. All my little ploys to stave off loneliness—talking to myself, dinner parties with the mice, hard physical exertion, losing myself in work—were losing their effectiveness. Day after day the low sky seemed to lean heavily upon the earth and upon my spirit. Some days were mere grey hushes—scarcely noticeably different from the long nights as I sat huddled in three sweaters, two pairs of trousers, and three pairs of socks in my boots—and the flickering candlelight made the typed words jump and twitch before my red-rimmed eyes.

A strange inner sadness grew as Christmas loomed nearer. I seemed to stand apart from myself, and, as I looked at everything around me, having been so long without social intercourse with fellow humans, I unconsciously began to invest the inanimate objects with thoughts and feelings. It no longer seemed odd to touch the trunks of the great firs and cedars and speak to them, promise I could never cut them down and would protect them if they would shelter me. As I lay in bed at night the face of Leonardo da Vinci in a painting I'd bought in Florence, now lit by the moonlight through the window, broke into a sardonic smile, and the eyes looked into mine with a fathomless yet critical stare.

Two days before Christmas I'd had enough. Now the feeling of utter isolation, the sense of deserting and being deserted by all we call normal life made me fear for my reason. That night I stopped work, had several glasses of wine, and set out to look for people—any company would do.

It was a fitful night, full of a stormy hell, with the moon emerging now and again from behind the dark, scudding clouds. I walked up the trail by torchlight and as I reached the truck I found a note tucked under the windscreen wiper. Some friends had come on the ferryboat from Vancouver for the three-day holiday and, looking for me, had eventually found the truck but, faced with the thick alder thicket in the dark, had not known where to go next. The note they left said they would be in the beer parlour. How wonderful!

I climbed into the truck, started it, and set out to drive fast along what seemed to be the old logging track where it ran along the top of a steep inland cliff. There was a loud bang, the front of the truck went down, then dropped sideways over the cliff. It hit the slope with its side, then its roof, then went on down. I thought, *This is it, God help me, and what a foolish way to go, rolling down a cliff.*

Instinctively I put my hands on the roof, my feet spread-eagled so I was like a starfish pressing back against my seat waiting for the one big final bang when I would know no more. But it never came. The truck suddenly stopped, hitting a tree and a huge rock simultaneously, the right way up, on a mossy bank. Not until I got out did I feel the pain in my neck, a wrenched arm from clinging to the wheel, and a bump on top of my head where I'd hit the roof on the first bounce. I climbed up the cliff, curiously elated at my escape, loudly and defiantly singing a tune I'd never heard before.

The next two days remain a blur in my memory. I walked out and met my pals from Vancouver and other people. We visited several beer parlours, were in and out of strange houses and in and out of brawls, and I had a great deal to drink.

My first normal memory after those strange three days was of sitting alone at my primitive desk, knowing only a desire to finish the book. I swore, as a man will at such times, that I'd never touch alcohol again, and with trembling hands emptied every bottle I had over the cliff. Then I hiked out and apologized for my behaviour to all and sundry.

A few nights later I awoke suddenly from a deep sleep and the whole cabin was filled with a strange new light. Grey shadows flitted across the now white walls. The unearthly silence was only broken now and again by a barely discernible hissing sound. At first I wondered if I was dreaming, but finding I was truly awake I got up and looked through the side window. Great snowflakes were falling, blanketing everything with a white shawl, while to the east wisps scudded across the face of a rising moon. I shivered and climbed back into bed.

Well before dawn I woke again. The moon was now at its height in a clear sky and the snow had stopped falling. I dressed and took a walk as I was sure another fall would be on its way and I had a sudden desire to see the white-mantled woods before the snow became unpleasantly deep. After crunching through the powdery new carpet for a quarter of a mile I found myself deep in a cedar grove. Delicately the long green sprays of the cedar branches flowed from one tree trunk to the other, as if to form naves in some giant cathedral. Through an opening in the screen canopy, shafts of moonlight filtered down as if coming through a stained-glass window. From the near distance came a faint musical sound as the creek, now fed by melting snow along its banks, hastened through its pebbly course to reach the sea. I stood for some moments in silent awe, healed by the balm of this wondrous scene. Then I heard faint footsteps scurrying along—some small creature scuffing through the snow. It was a racoon. Was it Spooks, I wondered, but I only saw a flash of its black mask and striped tail, then it was gone again. I stole over to where it had vanished. There in the snow were the tracks of a grouse, and behind, partly obliterating them in places, were the footsteps of the coon, like those of a tiny baby. Why had I never come out like this before, at night in the moonlight? The forest, the world about me, was not dead after all. I had

320

been so caught up in my work, living inside myself, I just hadn't looked hard enough, or at the right times.

That moonlight walk gave a great lift to my morale and revived my interest in nature. Now I resolved to finish the book as soon as possible so I'd be ready to seek fresh adventures in the spring.

Chapter 7

It was a raging February night. And as I sat at my desk, the rain beating drenching tattoos on the cabin roof, a movement made me look out of the side window. Two large, green eyes glared in from the darkness, moving from side to side. Suddenly I remembered an old man living alone down the coast who had been attacked by a cougar that came through his window one winter night.

Slowly I backed to the rear of the cabin for my torch and axe. At least I'd try and get one good chop at it if it came for me. Keeping well away from the window, I shone the torch—to find myself looking at a large dog! And the reason its eyes were moving from side to side was because its tail was wagging wildly with desperate hope. So I opened the door slightly and let him in.

He came slithering into the cabin in pools of water, wagging his tail so hard his hind legs skittered from beneath him. Despite his wide head, he was as thin as any dog I'd ever seen. I gave him the scraps from my supper and two tins of the best chunky steak— and he wolfed it all down as if he thought it the last meal he'd ever eat. As I wiped him dry with a towel, I realized this was probably the animal that had scared away Spooks in the summer. But now, every time I looked up from my work, I found his deep brown eyes upon me, and his tail thumped the floor to signify friendship.

So Booto, the wild dog from the forests, came into my life.

Over the next few weeks on visits to the store, I tried to find out more about him. It seemed he was everyone's yet no one's dog. He had come from the north as a pup with a couple who had abandoned him. Mostly he was fed by some folks who were start-ing a café near the fishing village, and a retired bulldozer driver and his wife three miles from me. Booto's early history, as far as I could piece it together, was that he was part Alsatian, part Labrador (which explained his thick jaws and gentleness with people), and one-quarter wolf, shown in his low hindquarters and long curved bushy tail.

To win scraps from the loggers and fishermen, he employed a number of cute performances designed to melt the flintiest heart. He used them all with me. He would scratch at a door and when it was opened, he'd sit up and beg in the most endearing way, crossing his white-booted paws with an appealing look. Or he'd roll on the ground and cover his eyes with a paw. The first time he treated me to his little act I roared with laughter, and as I did my face felt strange and I realized it was my first smile for many months. What a difference a smile makes, I thought, as I gratefully stroked his thick chestnut ruff and spoiled him with two fried eggs. I smiled again—at the sea, the islands, the trees—and soon every-thing around seemed to become a smile. I went back to my book that afternoon with renewed optimism.

One of my fears in adopting him was that he would, if only by his scent and presence, keep away all the wildlife friends I hoped to have back in the spring. But if the mice were any indication, it seemed I'd have no problem. One rainy night as I was working towards the end of the book, Booto lay with head on paws, glaring disconsolately at the downpour through the windows, when the mice came up through their entrance hole into the cabin. They certainly weren't put off by his scent and soon began skittering around as usual. To my surprise Booto just lay there, dead still, his eyes darting as the mice ran about like skaters on a pond.

Booto soon became a fine wilderness companion and I learned much forest lore from being with him. On long treks he would sniff out interesting items I'd have missed, like a squirrel's hoard, a vole's burrow, fish remains left by otter or mink on the shore. He could follow deer trails over rocky ground, trails that no human eye could detect. He never ran about wildly as some dogs do upon being let outside, disturbing every creature within hearing. Several times, miles inland, he led me upwind to small groups of black-tail deer, browsing the low hanging balsam fir branches.

It is hard to explain the pleasure I derived from such successful stalks of wild animals. Maybe it had to do with the hunting instinct that lies latent in most men, though I prefer to think it was more the sheer pleasure of seeing such creatures in their own kingdoms. Booto would stand, his floppy-tip ears cocked forward, obedient to my restraining hand and the whispered command, "Keep back."

I had always respected animals in their natural state more than any domestic pet, so it came as a slight shock to me to realize I now loved my new companion so much that he came first in my affections. Booto became more an equal than a pet, and certainly one of the best friends I ever had. True, he could offer no intellectual opinions, but the last thing I wanted now was a pal who broached such topics. His affection was unlimited and without strings. When I was unhappy, *he* was unhappy. When I was glad, he wagged his tail, begged, jumped, or rolled on the floor with a big, white-toothed grin.

Occasionally he let me know he disapproved of my behaviour, too—like on the day in March when I finally finished my novel. As I put the last page in my typewriter and pounded out the last words of what I hoped was a romantic yet realistic ending to the book, I felt a curious euphoria, almost tearful. I was elated that I'd now completed the long haul, yet sad that I would have to bid all my characters goodbye. But I'd long ago planned that final day.

First, I would break my resolve about drinking and celebrate. Second, I'd start looking for a job. And to achieve both I'd go to the beer parlour. This wasn't as odd as it sounds. On my first arrival in Canada, I'd got two outdoor jobs from beer parlours— one as a salmon-boat deckhand, the other as an assistant blaster helping to dynamite old stumps from the route of a new road.

Now I tried the beer parlour again, leaving Booto tied up outside. That night, with only a halfhearted offer of a job as a second joiner on two plywood cabins "sometime next month" and having imbibed a little too much, I came out with some noisy loggers and was about to climb into their car for a party at one of their homes when I felt a sharp tug on my jacket. I looked down, Booto had clamped his jaws firmly into my jacket hem and, growling slightly, refused to let go. The loggers roared with laughter.

"Looks like old Butch reckons you've had enough!" shouted one. Booto's grave disapproval was clear in his eyes.

"I reckon he's right," I said. "Good night, lads." And with that Booto and I walked the long, dark miles home. I'd forgotten my torch and instead, because like all dogs he could see far better in the dark than any human, I held onto Booto's tail and within an hour we were safely home. As I ate some bread and cheese, too tired to cook, I recalled the long talks with Ed Louette when he told me I should go on a trek into the mountains, into the world of the grizzly, moose, and caribou before I died. I remembered his piercing, challenging look as he had said, "You'll learn a lot, especially about yourself. But it will age you, mind. It'll sure age you."

There and then, I decided I *would* make that lonely trek this year. I only needed to raise some money.

That week as I read through the book, I really felt I'd got it right, that the lonely nine-months' slog had been worth while. I punch-holed it all together, wrote a covering letter, and with a fervent prayer mailed my baby to a leading literary agent.

Then came the best idea of all—there in the cabin I had files stacked with unsold material. Surely I could sell some to magazines here, and use the money to finance a deeper experience of the wilds. Within a week I had rewritten and mailed two stories. And as I typed away, Booto occasionally pushed his head onto my lap and wagged his tail, as if he approved of the idea too.

FROM HIGH ABOVE, the shrill, metallic *kri-kri-kri* sounded through the still air of the April morning, and as I hurried to the cabin door I thought, "They're back, they're back!" I looked out and saw the huge female eagle soaring aloft on her spread pinions, the sun peeping from behind the mountains to the east blazing her white tail and neck feathers into golden flames. With a few lazy flaps she glided again, far over the northern land spit and towards her old nesting place.

As I turned back, a new spider's web in the arbutus branches hung spangled with dew like a lacy necklace of diamonds, while beneath the umbrella of a dark leaf the little pirate sat, his feet on his master thread, waiting for the sun to dry the droplets. Now as I looked out over the motionless Pacific a small flight of mallards was winging in from the south, the females in front quacking faintly to each other as they slooshed into the water near the oyster island. Soon they would be pairing off, then away they would all go again, flying to inland lakes to nest and rear their young.

It was a good day, the first real spring morning, a time to be out amid the new-stirring life. I would go to the post office and see if the agent had sent word of my book. But first I'd go fishing, for it was too fine a morning to waste. As I went down the log staircase I saw a squirrel leap from the top of a pine to a fir branch, only a glimpse, but I was sure it was Douglas, and as he chattered away I knew I'd now be awakened fine and early in the mornings. I heaved the little old boat into the sea for the first time that year and as I rowed away from the shore Booto ran down the staircase and up and down over the rocky beach, whining with distress, perhaps thinking I was deserting him. At the same time I noticed tiny rivulets of water seeping in through the cracks in the boards. All right, for both reasons I'd not go out too far.

Four hundred yards from shore I let down my bright jigger, jerked it up and down, and within two minutes caught a four-pound green ling cod. Then suddenly water was gushing up through the opening cracks, the boat was rapidly filling. By frantic rowing I managed to get back to shore before it sank. But as I bailed out the boat and hauled it up the beach, a sharp rock gashed a hole where one of the boards had become completely rotten. As it lay on its side like a stranded grey fish, I knew my dinghy had come to the end of its days.

After lunch we walked along the forest road and there at the post office was the airmail letter I'd both hoped for and dreaded. At least he hadn't sent the book back, I thought, as I took the thin envelope and walked back in the watery sunshine, unable to read it until I reached home. At my desk I opened the letter with trembling hands. The words stared up at me starkly: "... you have attempted too much. ... The tone of the writing is also too strident for present day tastes. ..." He did not want to handle my book.

It is said trouble comes in threes. The final loss of my boat had been one blow, the rejection of my book the second, so when I hiked to the post office the next day and was handed a letter from the magazine to which I'd sent my stories, I had little doubt it would be the third. I was now so broke I would soon be in real trouble. As I walked back up the forest road under cloudless skies, I decided to take a long time to return to the empty cabin before reading yet more bad news. My trek to the north now seemed doomed, at least for this year.

Well, I had the whole day before me. We live only a day at a time, rich or poor. If I couldn't make the big trek, I could at least go for a really long walk right now. I decided to make a good ten-mile semi-circle across the mountain slopes then back down to the cabin.

I called Booto and we climbed a rocky face and headed into the dark forest. By the time we were a mile inland, the morning sun had cleared the mountain tops. Alder branches clicked in the warmth and here and there pushed out tiny sticky green buds. Yellow fronds of new needles adorned the drooping tips of hemlocks. From atop a bush a robin sang its first sweet song of spring and by my feet I saw a crumb of dark brown earth fall from a fern sprout as it shouldered its way into the light.

Within three hours I judged we were high above the area of the cabin and as I broke through the forest into a clearer space ahead I heard the faint rushing of a creek, its waters babbling now, swelled by the first melting of the high snow. Behind me, as if it had waited until I'd passed through, I heard the faint drumming of a woodpecker's beak on a rotten pine snag as it sought to find the softer places where beetle grubs tunnelled under the old damp bark.

Suddenly I was conscious of a reeking odour, rather like iodine. There was a crashing in the thick bushes near by, and a small brown bear cub with a curious wobbly baggy-trousered look stumbled across the track in front of me, just as the head and shoulders of a mother black bear emerged like some vast golliwog from the underbush near some upended tree roots. She saw us and began making strange *offa offa* aggressive grunting sounds. Terrified, my eyes instantly taking in the power of her shoulders, the sharp black claws of her heavy forefeet, I stood rooted to the spot. I remembered Ed's advice, "A black bear will never attack you unless you get between a mother and her cub. Even then she'll probably make a mock attack, then dodge around you. Keep still, don't show fear, and above all, don't run." Paralyzed, my heart pounding, I somehow kept still. But I was never more conscious of my own puniness than in the second or two that that powerful, sharp-eyed animal and I looked at each other.

She first seemed undecided between going for me or following her cub, then she dropped down and started to run in my direction. Booto took charge and barked at her, and she appeared to change her mind and go for him. He was far faster on his feet than the bear and, making strange, half-whining barks, he dodged about in front of her, luring her away from me. As I heard them crashing through the brush seawards, I quickly gathered my wits and hurried back towards the cabin.

After twenty minutes Booto caught up with me, looking not at all frightened but extremely pleased with himself. That night I gave my rescuer the best supper he'd ever had.

So excited was I by the incident with the bear I completely forgot the envelope in my breast pocket until after supper. I took it out, resigned myself to the inevitable contents, and opened it. I could hardly believe it when I read: ". . . your first story we are buying for $600. But for your second story we could pay a fee of $825. Would you please let us know if this is satisfactory? As for your third idea, we would also like to commission this and, again, it would command the full fee. . . ."

My whoop of joy and leap into the air startled Booto, who dashed to the door with a gruff bark, thinking there must be something outside. I grabbed him for one of our playful wrestles on the floor, but he was tired and groaned as he often did when he thought I was making a fool of myself. No matter. I got up again and hammered out a reply to the magazine editor. I was free! Now I could make the big trek I'd promised myself.

To carry equipment to a starting point, I needed my truck back, if it could be salvaged. I was also sick of having to walk to the store and back for supplies, for I was limited to what I could carry on my back (Booto's tins of dog food seemed to weigh heaviest!).

The next morning, therefore, I climbed down the inland cliff over which I'd crashed for a new look at my truck. The body was wrecked but the engine and wheels seemed undamaged. On previous trips to the small town to the south I'd noticed a grey truck

like mine, which had been parked ever since I'd come to the coast. I hitched down to see the owner, who after warning me the engine and two of its tyres were about finished, sold it to me for $180. Reluctantly admitting the task of retrieving my old truck was one I couldn't perform alone, I hired a garage owner with a winch crane. Towing my new truck, we somehow manoeuvred down the old logging tracks, and after much cursing, we managed to haul my battered old ruin up from its mossy grotto with his fifty-yard cable. To my great relief, although shaky on its mountings, the engine worked fine.

Over the next few weeks I manoeuvred both trucks into a forest clearing and laboured to make one good vehicle from the two semi-wrecks. Naturally it rained most of the time. Booto hated the entire operation and wouldn't look at me for hours. Mostly he sat under the truck in the dry, the thumping as he scratched himself the only reminder he was still there.

After the fourth day he'd had enough. Totally bored, he would sneak off for several hours when I wasn't looking. I wondered where he went, for neither the old bulldozer driver nor the café folk had seen him. By now Booto was deep into my affections and there were still moments now when the loneliness of the depths of winter, before he'd come into my life, returned.

Once the "new" patch-up truck was finished I thought of my trek in earnest. I quelled rising fears by deciding that as I had to go to Vancouver to buy a boat and equipment anyway, I'd find Ed and somehow persuade him to come with me.

On the drive down south Booto suddenly ran to the back of the truck and started whining and scratching at the door. Remembering his sneaking off, I stopped. He immediately ran up to a small cabin, the home of two elderly pensioners, who greeted Booto affectionately, called him Prince and told me they fed him whenever he turned up. I looked at Booto in surprise: apparently he thought little of trotting the seven miles between our homes if he felt bored. I told the couple of my impending trip and they agreed to look after Booto if I didn't wish to take him with me. Then we headed for the ferry.

We spent three days in Vancouver, buying supplies and sleeping in the truck. When I'd located a fine inflatable boat and second-hand five-horse-power outboard, I bought a light nylon pup tent and green shower suit, both of which would keep off rain and reduce my scent. With my trusty pocket telescope and staple foods like lentils, dried peas, barley, dried meat, flour, and oatmeal, I worked out I could carry all I needed on my back for up to ten days in a pack weighing less than forty pounds.

On the third night I finally located Ed at the beer parlour he'd once named. But after the first surprised greeting he said he would not come with me.

"No, no, I'm too old now," he protested. "Good God, a man is safe enough alone in that country, if he doesn't do anything foolish."

Back in his small room in a lodging house not far from Stanley Park, Ed drew me a map of the tidal flats and creeks on the coast opposite the northern tip of Vancouver Island where he thought bears could still be found. He checked my supply list, added suggestions, then reached for the rough map he'd drawn, and inserted a dot. "Look, if you get to the end of this hinlet, visit a friend of mine, Pappy Tihoni. Heck, if you are definitely going up, I'll write to him. He's about, ho, five or six miles hup river, on the north bank."

He laughed suddenly at a memory. "What gun are you taking with you?" I said I wasn't, that I didn't own one.

He reached down under his bed. "You'd better take this," he said, thrusting a stocky old World War I Mauser at me, and a box of fewer than a dozen shells. "We bought this old gun years ago at the cattle hauctions. Beautiful old thing—went through the First World War. Good gun, but you hold it real tight!"

I was astonished he possessed such a thing. "I'm not sure I want to take a gun," I said.

"You take it, professor. You may need it! It's Tihoni's gun, really. You can give it back to him when you get there. But don't use it unless you really have to. And you haim for the brain if it's close and sideways, or else the heart—right behind the front shoulder. Nothing else will stop a grizzly." He thought for a moment. "Don't take the dog. The only guy I know got killed by a grizzly was through his dog barking at it."

I took all the advice Ed had to offer and as I prepared to leave, he said, "Ho, one more thing."

"What's that?"

"Hif you find grizzly, you tell no one else. Too many men come here honly to kill."

I agreed, thanked him, and left.

Back at the cabin I spent many days ironing out problems I was loath to wrestle with for the first time on the actual trek: breaking in the new back-pack, practising with its full weight on rocky, treed slopes.

On the day before I left, Booto watched me haul the boat to the truck's roof with reproach in his eyes. He whined moodily when he saw my food and equipment. Next day I drove him to his friends down the coast. Reckoning it might help establish my claim to him, I brought ten dollars' worth of his favourite dog food and, laughing away the couple's protests that they'd be happy to feed him themselves, I put the food on their veranda and promised to pick him up in about a month. Then I drove on down to Vancouver.

Chapter 8

From Vancouver I crossed by ferry to Vancouver Island, and as I drove on up to the northeast coast, it rained steadily and heavily. It rained all the following day too, so that I was unwilling to launch the boat. But when the third morning dawned in a dead calm, with a low cloud mass shrouding the distant mountain peaks in mist, I decided to set off. By noon the next day I had crossed the strait, covered well over forty miles and entered the wild inlet. The waters here were a jade green colour. The mountains dwarfed me, their almost sheer slopes falling precipitously into the water. There were hardly any beaches on which to land, and if a storm had hit me I would have been in real trouble. For I was now an insignificant speck in a harsh and inhospitable landscape, and I had never felt so puny in my life.

As dusk began to fall I had covered another fifteen miles and I noted a huge rock slide on the north bank as I rounded a right-hand bend formed by the promontory of a high conical mountain.

Both signs coincided with the area where Ed's rough map indicated I might find bear. I pulled into a small bay below a cleft in the mountains, heaved the boat over wet branches, and set up camp by a small creek mouth.

Inside the pup tent I made a mattress of parallel rows of spruce branches, and cooked my bannocks and mush-stew supper. But I found it hard to sleep that night. This was the domain of the bear and the cougar, where *man* was the interloper, and I felt as much a greenhorn as when I'd first arrived in Canada. I woke several times to hear curious bumping noises, but I finally concluded the noises came from the creek waters tumbling over rocks and not from big bears clumping around the tent. My imagination would have to be severely controlled if I was going to complete this trek.

Progress was slow next day and heavy rain made life miserable. But by adapting an ancient Viking idea I passed the night comfortably enough. On their long voyages, the Vikings turned their boats upside down at night and sheltered beneath them. So I hauled the rubber boat onto a tiny gravel beach and tied it upside down from the wind, bridging it across some rocks and bushes. Then, erecting my pup tent beneath it, and with the rain hammering along its inflated keel, I cooked my meal and slept, remaining reasonably dry.

In the morning I hid two cans of fuel in the bushes for the return trip and rechecked my stores. I felt Pappy Tihoni would be pleased by my contribution, especially with the three flat half-bottles of rye I hoped would help lubricate our meeting. I slipped one into my jacket pocket, lashed everything else tight into my two packs, and strapped the rifle to one of them. Then I covered the last eighteen miles to the inlet's head.

As I approached I had to check my map, for I was confronted by three river mouths. The lie of the mountains indicated that the central river must be my true way. Even so, it constantly diverged around islands and I had to make split-second decisions as to which was the correct course. The water was lower than I'd anticipated and its pace in the narrower currents was fast. After some five or six miles the ravine sides became steeper and the lofty mountains began to rear higher into the sky. Three times I came to shale reefs and had to carry the engine and tank a few hundred yards, return for the supplies and rifle, then carry the boat on my back.

By the time I'd covered an estimated seven or eight miles, I'd seen no sign of Tihoni's cabin, which Ed had said was some six miles up. I throttled the engine down while debating whether to go ashore and walk back, when without warning it cut out. Four quick pulls refused to start it although the tank was half full. There was no alternative but to drift down river until I could manoeuvre to a bank. Not until then did I realize how strong the current really was.

With increasing fright I saw great jagged rocks flash by as I sought to steer between them and half-submerged trees in the small whirlpools. For about five minutes the dinghy shot and whirled about alarmingly as I tried to stave off disaster, then I saw the fork around the rocks where I'd made my third portage. The left fork went over some sharp rocks while the right flashed through a twenty-foot gorge in some deep, turbulent rapids. My only hope was to dash through there and try to reach the quieter water beyond. I managed to straighten the boat up but when I was halfway through, the dinghy twisted violently, capsized sideways, and I was thrown out. A whirlpool at the far end sucked me down about twelve feet until my ears popped, and when I came up I saw a trapped tree with other logs against it moving up and down in the swirl. Gasping in the icy water, hampered by my heavy wool lumberjacket, I instinctively struck out against the current for the log, came up beneath it, and felt the way to the surface blocked by other logs.

Desperately I threw myself backwards, praying for enough strength to get to the log again. As I surfaced, gulping in air, I heard a voice shouting, "Don't go against the river, go *with* it. Swim *across*—here!" A huge man had leaped into the river from the north bank on a bend below me and had somehow grabbed my boat and packs as they hit into the bend on their way down river. With a last strength born of terror, I managed to work my way obliquely across to where the man was clutching my dinghy with one hand and a tree on the bank with his other. As I drifted past I clutched the side of the dinghy so hard my fingers met in the rubber.

As I hung there with both hands, gasping for breath and terrified, the man smiled gently. "Tomkies, I presume?" he said. This was my introduction to Pappy Tihoni.

He heaved both boat and me ashore with one powerful sweep and said, "The first rule of falling from a rubber boat is never lose hold of it!" I managed a weak smile as, white with shock, I sank down on the bank and watched him haul up the water-logged engine, which was tied to the boat by cord.

"How on earth were you *here?*" I asked.

"Oh, I heard your engine popping away half a mile back," he said laconically. "Ed wrote me. I figured it might be you." Then he undid the rifle from the wet pack, shook the water from it, handling it fondly, and as he shook hands, said, "Hell, I'd pull ye out all over again to get this old beauty back! Are you OK? Come on, let's clean her up and dry off in the cabin. An' you can tell me how that old buzzard Ed is gettin' along."

I stood up shivering, felt the heaviness in my pocket, reached down and, with a faintly theatrical gesture, whipped the top off the unbroken bottle of rye and handed it to him. Pappy took a long swig, shot me a quizzical look, and as I followed suit, said, "Reckon you'll do."

That night as we draped my sodden clothes before his red-hot stove and I sat hunched in one of his outsize jackets, I learned a little about Pappy. At sixty-four he resembled a grizzly bear with his square head, almost romantically heroic, set upon massive shoulders. His paternal grandfather's parents had been Highlanders who had emigrated to the Yukon. Pappy had been born on a sledge and somewhere along the line Indian blood had been mixed into his strain, making him three-quarters Scots, one-quarter Indian, and one hundred per cent Canadian. Pappy had a deep respect for and an affinity with the Indian way of life, and in recent years had adopted the name Tihoni.

He seemed a curious mixture. Although he sometimes spoke in the slang of the Canadian bush with a trace of Scots, he often injected long obscure words into his conversation, attractively mispronounced, and it was clear they'd come from years of lonely reading. He said: "I always reckoned I was a lucky son of a gun. The Highland blood gets me up these damn mountains. The Indian gives me . . . heck, love I guess. Sure, love and a sort of reverence for this land, for the animals, birds, trees, rivers." He paused handing me a cup of his tea, spiced with pine needles for extra flavour. "When we European hordes brought our so-called civilization over here, lured the Indians with whisky, mirrors, knick-knacks and guns in return for millions of furs, we called 'em savages. Guess they were in some ways, but by God they know how to live in this land without wrecking it, without killing everything in sight. And I tell you this, that kind of instinct and feeling for the land the Indians were born with has to be taught again or modern society will destroy everythin' natural that's left."

As he talked I had the impression Pappy was deliberately acquainting me with his views and sounding out mine. He described the unspoiled Indian social life: how they cared for and respected the aged, how they seldom punished children but brought them up by careful instruction and most of all by good example.

He then likened the Indians' religious concepts to ours, showing that in spite of superstition and witchcraft, they bore much in common with the white man's belief in the Judaeo-Christian God. He retold the story of Tarenyawago (Hiawatha), a direct emissary of the Great Spirit who came to earth performing miracles and teaching the Indian nations art, wisdom, and knowledge—and how closely allied it seemed to him to the basic story of Christ, even to the ascent into heaven.

Finally, he told me how the Indians brought hunting to its golden age. They held the animals in reverence, never killing for sport or enjoyment but purely for sustenance, using every portion of meat, bone, and gut and wasting nothing.

"What few skills I possess in these woods in tracking animals," he finished, "were all learned from the old Indian ways. I guess I was lucky, meetin' some of the last old teachers."

Pappy Tihoni was far different from the hermit trapper I had expected to meet. His years of isolation, quiet study, and contemplation had produced his unusually whole, almost universal view of life. He'd remained simple in expression and often earthy in language, and instantly commanded my respect. He impressed me with his knowledge of North American animals, of which his natural favourite was the grizzly. He knew the Latin names of many of the seventy-eight species and sub-species.

"The grizzly wasn't officially seen by white men until the early 1800's about the time my great-grandpaw was born. For years the grizzly was the ferocious tyrant of the woods, a symbol of terror and romantic adventure. You know, there've been more lies told about the poor old grizzly than any animal we have. Mind you, I'm sure the grizzly those days *was* a fiercer animal. But after years of bein' shot, civilization destroyin' its lands, fear of man has been *bred* right into its instincts. In my years here I've only once been chased by a grizzly—had to shoot it unfortunately. Mostly they just stamp about and snarl, warnin' you not to do anything stupid."

I asked Pappy why he lived here all alone.

"Simple enough. Ever since I was a kid and read all those old adventure tales about the explorers and trappers I wanted to live in remote bits of the caribou country. But I married, had some kids. We worked the log camps all round here. Finally Louise, my wife, got tired movin' around, so we went down to what's now West Vancouver—real primitive in those days. We made ourselves a wooden house and I started a tree business of my own. Well, the kids grew up and left. Then Louise died. One day I thought, What the hell am I hangin' round here for? I'd never forgotten this place—this is where Ed and I ended up after our little walk through the mountains from Bella Coola."

"He told me about that trek."

Pappy laughed. "Ed's a wanderer. At first he was going to live here, too. But he gets itchy feet, never likes spending two summers in the same place. After we put up this cabin a few years back he took off—takin' my good gun for protection. Haven't seen him from that day to this."

I told him Ed had asked me to apologize for his not returning the gun.

"Hell, I wasn't bothered. I got a smaller one. Anyway, apart from a deer or two I don't kill any more. Ah, a man grows up! I figured after all the work Ed did on this cabin, he was entitled to the gun if he wanted it. Just take a look around. I doubt there's a man alive who can work logs like Ed."

I walked around the two-room cabin, unable to feel the faintest draught between the cedar logs in spite of the cool autumn winds. The whole place reflected Pappy's existence—a life honed down to essentials. The big pot-belly stove sat on a flat rock in the room's centre, throwing out its heat all around. An iron plate on top was his cooker. Inside the stove, a small iron box with a door gave him a tiny oven. Above it wire racks held layers of

berries drying on paper and deer sinews hung from the roof, ready
for splitting with a razor into threads.

Every corner of the room had its own function. One had a rough
wood table for eating and reading, with bookshelves above.
Another was his "kitchen", with dishes, cutlery, mugs, food boxes,
and a washbowl fed by a gravity pipe from the creek. A third
corner housed a bed and a clothes cupboard made of hand-hewn
boards. Above the bed dozens of musty old volumes, mostly classic
literature, lay in friendly attitudes against each other on three
rough shelves. In the other room, a wooden bunk huddled against
the wall away from a tangle of axes, sledges, toolboxes, brooms,
shovels, hoes and other outdoor bric-a-brac that threatened to
engulf it.

As I browsed around, Pappy's voice came through the door. "I
often told Ed he was crazy. He spends his life building beautiful
things for other folks, movin' on and never taking a cent for his
work. Know what he says? 'When I build for my own pleasure I
remain my own man.' You were lucky meetin' him."

"I know it," I said. "He helped me build my place, too."

"He's a real strange guy. Never got married, you know. He had
a girl once. Beautiful lass, younger'n him. She loved him all right
but . . . you know how it is with really good-lookin' women—she
wanted more, the big city life. Her beauty took her away, went off
to Hollywood. Never did hear how she made out. Poor Ed was
real shook up. Never looked at another woman. How about you?
You been married?"

At this revelation of a love affair Ed had never once mentioned,
I found myself telling Tihoni more about my life than I would
otherwise have done. We talked on into the evening and it was
after midnight when we prepared to turn in. Pappy said he was as
keen to start up country as I was. "I haven't been up in the real
grizzly and cougar country for a while myself," he said. "It'll be
good to have company. So if it's OK with you we'll leave early.
The caribou should be headin' through the high plateaux to the
valley before too long, so with any luck we'll catch 'em too, maybe
see a wolf or two."

I asked how far we'd need to go before we were likely to meet
grizzlies.

"There's a good bear fishin' ground about sixteen miles up river.

We'll head there first. And we won't take a boat either. Too much hassle packin' the damn thing." He slapped his huge thigh suddenly. "We'll just use the transport God gave us. Think yours will hold out? It's real tough country up there."

"Well, I am twenty years younger," I said jokingly, instantly regretting what might appear impertinence.

Pappy Tihoni paused at the door, his eyes twinkling in their large deep sockets. "That may not turn out to your advantage," he said.

Chapter 9

Not until the afternoon of the second day did we find our first grizzly tracks. As Pappy had predicted, it had been really tough going. Packing our heavy loads along the steep canyon sides had been hell, a hard test for a man's feet and knees, for there had been no relief for over ten miles from the precipitous inclines. And the small spruces were massed so thickly that at times we literally had to force our way between them.

Pappy went ahead, moving for all his bulk and age like some stealthy gorilla, and I soon realized his slow pace was the right one. He spoke little and only then in whispers, occasionally showing slight irritability if I didn't at once catch onto his meanings.

We found the first tracks, some nine and one-half inches long, in a small marshy area. They were the marks of a big grizzly. Pappy bent down for closer examination. "I don't know if I can track this bear," he said. "He's a good five miles, mebbe a day up on us. Want to try?" I nodded and we set off.

For about half a mile we stumbled through the trees on the grizzly's trail, working our way up the lower mountain slopes. Pappy found traces where I would have seen nothing—an up-turned pebble, a snapped twig, berry bushes whose sappy twigs showed they'd recently been denuded of remaining fruit, scrapings under logs and small holes where the bear had looked for grubs or mice. When the trail seemed to peter out completely on the higher, rockier land, Pappy suddenly sat down.

"Now, what do we know for sure?" I'd heard Ed say that.

"Maybe it's turned off?"

"Could be," said Pappy thoughtfully. "Well . . . I reckon it's a male. Broad tracks, toes spaced out: Middle-aged too, the claw marks aren't as sharp as a young bear's." Like some detective of the wilds, Pappy now put together the evidence, drawing inferences that never would have occurred to me. The grizzly had slowed down, deciding to look for food as he went, because his stride had lessened. He had moved yesterday afternoon or early this morning, by day anyhow, for if he'd walked at night he probably would have brushed against bushes, leaving hair on twigs, and we'd seen none. He had some definite place in mind because, although feeding sporadically, he was travelling fairly straight, not meandering about aimlessly. But he wasn't in any hurry. Nor had he been suddenly frightened or he'd have left droppings.

"Let's backtrack him and double check."

Not knowing exactly how far he was ahead, Pappy insisted we tread lightly. "Grizzlies often press their noses into the ground to feel if there's anything heavy approaching 'em, just like elk do."

After two more difficult miles of losing the tracks, re-checking and finding them again, Pappy stopped. "Hell, he's closer than I thought and gettin' suspicious," he whispered. He made a tight semi-circle until we came back on the bear's track. "Just as I thought. The old bear *is* checking his back trail." He chuckled. "We got a real smart son of a bitch here." He bent down, picked up some white-tipped hairs from the rocks. "See? He made this detour to the left, then sat down sniffin' the air and lookin' back to make sure he wasn't being followed. Grizzlies often do this."

He sat down for a while by some rocks above a river to think and I was grateful for the rest. At that moment two whisky-jacks began fluttering through the branches above our heads and squawking harshly. Immediately we heard a splashing sound below. "There he goes!" hissed Pappy, pointing down. It was as if part of the mountain itself had suddenly shifted. A huge grizzly was heaving its great body across the current. He was like some huge, hairy tuskless rhinoceros, with a back so broad behind its menacing hump that it looked almost flat. In fearful fascination I watched the behemoth reach the opposite bank and shake the water from its coat in a cascading rainbow spray. Then the grizzly cast us a brief look, almost of reproach it seemed, before vanishing into the trees. Pappy cursed under his breath. "My friend, we have just been outwitted by a very smart old grizzly." Then he removed his pack, stretched, and as he lay back in the last of the evening sun, he sighed and said, "Well, at least we *saw* him. That's all we wanted, right?"

We ate some of Pappy's oatcakes with cold fried eggs and cheese between and then lay in silence for half an hour, letting the blood restore some energy into our tired limbs. I removed my boots and found to my annoyance a small blister forming on the edge of one of my big toes. Pappy reached into his pack, pulled out a small soft pliable piece of buckskin. "Don't burst it. Put that in your boot," he said. "It's a sure cure, been dressed down with the buck's brains. You'll find the blister's gone by tomorrow." It was.

"You know the best sock of all? A fresh rabbit skin! Skin the rabbit, mould the wet skin, fur side out, round the foot, and shove it back in your boot. They last a week but are better than any woollen sock." As the sun faded behind a cleft in the mountains and the air grew colder, Pappy said the bear fishing ground was still some four miles farther upstream.

"We'll make camp soon so we'll be there before dawn," he said, slinging on his pack and heading back down the river. My legs and shoulders were stiff but if his were he gave little sign. Tracking animals under the old laws, he said, brought a man nearer to the animal state himself. Normal fatigue and pain could be healed by inner belief and the natural rhythms of the trek. I was astonished at his resource and energy, as if he drew a mystical strength from the very earth.

As we walked along the river bank and came to an eddy caused by some jammed logs, Pappy sneaked up and peered over. "Hmm, we'll take a fish or two," he said, extracting a three-pronged fish spear from his pack. "Cut me a willow pole, will you, about seven foot. Oh, and soak some barley mixture in a can." I cut and handed him the pole, and he bound his spear to it with some of his nylon fishing line.

"One of civilization's greatest boons—nylon line," he said with a laugh. "Holds tighter than any sinew!" He crouched on the logs and, after several deep jabs, impaled a salmon of about five pounds. In a trice he'd whacked it on the head, gutted it, and chopped it into steaks with the machete. As I poured the excess water from my can of barley and lentils and replaced the lid, Pappy wrapped the fish pieces in a plastic bag, handed them to me to put in my pack with the can, then set off upstream again. Within an hour we had made our campfire, feasted royally on pemmican hors d'œuvres and salmon steaks, and were in our sleeping bags.

In the morning we found a good position from which to observe the fishing ground. We lay hidden among small alder by a thicket of willow some ninety yards from the ground. Our faces were covered with small camouflage nets—one of the few items I'd brought of which Pappy totally approved.

From the shallow riffles in the river below us came a constant chattering, splashing noise as the salmon tried to batter their way through these natural ladders into the deeper pools above. For many this would be the end of their long, valiant haul from the ocean to reach their spawning grounds in the gravelly pools above. They lay barely moving on the bottom, like tatterdemalion scarecrows, their fins worn almost bare from their battles through the rocky beds below. These were the fish the bears caught, and in the first heavy spate, many would be washed away downstream.

Above us now an eagle and some ravens were gathering, circling in the wind. Suddenly the ravens began a loud squawking commotion and the metallic *kri-kri-kri* of the eagle sounded. Pappy cautiously raised his head. "We're in luck," he murmured.

I too looked up carefully. Two young grizzlies were shuffling slowly along the opposite bank. Both were in superb condition, their fur sleek and shiny with what appeared to be a grey wash on their humped backs and flanks. They had light-coloured ruffs around the backs and sides of their heads. "Three-year-olds, what we used to call grey backs," muttered Pappy. "Must be from the same litter." They appeared to be in no hurry, walking along with a rolling gait, their heads held low, swinging from side to side ponderously as though they were thinking out some problem.

As we watched the first came to a huge dead fir that lay

341

partly submerged across the creek bed. It sniffed the air, then cautiously crept out, as if testing whether the log would take its weight. Its short ears pricked forwards and its head darted from side to side as it followed the flashing movements of the fish below. Then, with stealthy movements, it flattened itself slightly and, followed by the other grizzly, moved out to the end of the trunk. Once there, it hooked the claws of its left forepaw into the log to give itself an anchor, then thrust its right paw into the water, stirring among the crowded salmon like a cat trying to hook a goldfish in its bowl. After a few convulsive darts it hooked a salmon to the surface, but the big fish wriggled free at the last moment. This happened several times.

The quieter bear on the far end of the log was having better luck. It had hooked under a fish of some six pounds and was holding it against the rough edge of the log with its claws. Twice it lowered its head to grab the salmon in its jaws but seemed unable to make it without losing its balance. Eventually it scraped the fish up the side of the log, seized it in its teeth, backed off the log, then loped into a marshy area of the bank, dropped the fish, and began to eat.

There was a sudden flurry in the water below. The first grizzly had hooked under a smaller fish, and with a deft flip had sent it sailing through a shower of spray to land some twenty feet back in the brush at the river's edge. As the salmon tried to wriggle its way back to the water, the bear ran to it, held it down with both paws and began chomping it up.

While the two bears were eating, there was a slight disturbance among a patch of willows and alders across the creek to our right, and a large bear, lighter coloured than the first two, emerged and began sauntering towards the fishing ground, with a cub scuffing by her side. The two bears who were already there eating quietly picked up their fish and discreetly retreated about thirty yards, where they continued their meal.

"This should be real interesting," whispered Pappy.

Without appearing even to glance at the two young bears, the mother continued towards the bank, occasionally giving little grunts and whines as if she were talking to her cub. She reached the river's edge where the cub sat down obediently and watched as its mother waded quietly into the shallow water. There she stood still, up to her chest in water, looking straight down into it. For a full minute she remained like this, then she plunged her head below the surface and emerged with a large fish in her jaws. With three slow bounds she galloped up onto the bank, shook herself vigorously, then took the fish onto a flat grassy patch, followed by her cub. As she seemed about to tear the fish into smaller pieces to give to the cub, she suddenly stopped, alert, made an odd coughing blast, snatched the fish in her jaws and bounded towards the forest edge, closely followed by her scampering youngster. In the same instant the two other bears also turned tail and loped away. As the ravens swooped down onto the remains of the fish they'd left, a deep-throated roar and a crashing in the brush to our right made them fly up again, squawking with terror. A huge black boar grizzly burst into the marsh clearing, covered the entire forty yards with some half-dozen long bounds, huffing loudly with each leap, and just as it seemed about to pursue the others, it brought itself up short with a great tearing of earth clods, like some runaway bulldozer suddenly applying its brakes.

"Holy crow!" I heard Pappy mutter beside me as he reached instinctively for the rifle. "Look at that mean old son of a bitch move!"

I stared at this animal with fearful awe. The old boar must have weighed over a thousand pounds, its forelegs like thick, bristly tree trunks. It cantered ponderously around the edge of the clearing as if making sure it had driven all the other bears from its own private reserve. Then it headed back to the river. Its fur seemed blackish-brown, with some fifth of its hairs tipped with silver. But the short hair around its huge square muzzle and ears was a light buff grey.

It paused as it reached the half-submerged log, sniffing the scent of the two earlier bears. Then it moved slowly to the shallow water running down the rocky bed of the riffles and crouched there as deathly still as a heron. It seemed to fade into the background like some ancient slab of granite.

The sky had gone dark and suddenly the surface of the pools in the river was wrinkled and a tinkling musical noise sounded all around us. It was raining. The grizzly remained motionless except for the occasional flick of an ear. A medium-sized salmon suddenly shot from the pool and landed five feet up the riffle, gave a tentative wriggle or two, then was washed back again. The grizzly appeared to take no notice. Another half minute ticked by, then the head of a large salmon appeared momentarily above the surface as if actually taking a look at the obstacle ahead. There was a pause as it disappeared again, then with a surge it was out of the pool, sending up a shower of spray as it tried to drive against the shallow, onrushing water. The grizzly waited till the fish was almost halfway through, then made a quick surging dash, pinned the fish down with the first stab of its great paw, snatched it up in its jaws, then casually wandered across the riffle, up on to the far bank, and continued on to a large cedar. There it dropped the fish in some long grasses and started on its way back to the river.

"Why didn't he eat the fish?" I asked in a whisper.

"He's real cunning," replied Pappy. "He knows the rain will soon swell the river. He's just catching 'em and caching 'em till later."

He was right. For the next half hour the bear concentrated on his fishing. After catching three more, each of which he carried flapping to the cedar, the grizzly settled down to his meal. Even at that distance we saw occasional flashes of huge canine teeth that must have been over two inches long. After eating two fish, he carefully piled the other fish together and started to dig.

Anyone who doubts the grizzly is the most powerful creature alive in all the Americas should have seen that animal at work. It tore into the rocky ground with the apparent ease of a bull-dozer. It buried the fish, raked the earth, roots, and leaves back over its cache, the whole operation taking a mere few minutes. Then, with a last look backwards and a few sniffs at the air, it sauntered off into the forest.

For the first time I became aware that my back was soaked from the heavy drips of rain that had fallen on us from the trees above.

"Satisfied?" asked Pappy. I told him if I'd seen nothing else during my years in Canada, the last hours would have made it all worth while.

"Well, the show's over," he said. "That old bear will be lyin' up now till evening. So will all the others. No self-respecting bear is about between nine and three in the afternoon. Let's go and dry off."

We stood up, stretching our wet cramped limbs. I kept glancing to where the grizzly had disappeared. Pappy grinned. "We're OK," he said, guessing my thoughts. "We're darn lucky the wind hasn't changed, I can tell you. Now, you want to try to find some cougar?"

He made it sound as if we were tourists in a zoo. I said I did, if he didn't mind going on. He pointed up to a valley between the distant mountains. "You see that last line of cedars on the right below those high bluffs? We go up through there, down the other side, then head around again to the river valley. There's a big lake in there and it's real good cougar country. We'll start up there in the morning."

We retraced our steps to our last camp site. Blasé though it may seem, we were a little tired of salmon and on the way back Pappy shot a small coast deer that ran, then stopped and looked back, as deer often do. As we butchered it on the spot, I remarked this was something I could never do without a feeling of distaste.

Pappy laughed and said, "Yeah, we should all be vegetarians! But hell, a man couldn't live in these forests without meat once in a while. There's a protein in it comes right from the very land we tread with these animals, maybe things scientists haven't yet measured."

Back at the camp we piled rocks in a square and made a roaring fire, helped by the resin-solid centre spear from a broken-off fir stump. For future use we boiled the shoulders in brine, then hung them from a pole frame to smoke awhile.

For our meal Pappy roasted a haunch on the red-hot windward side of the fire. Then he cut out a chunk of the delicious-smelling venison. After a few mouthfuls he looked at me and said, "I reckon it'll take us a couple of days to get up these little hills and down into that cougar country. It's real nice up there, alpine flowers and all. And there's a big lake with a slough in the valley there that is plumb full of muskrats. If we don't find cougar there, I'll...."

"You'll what?"

"I'll burn down the old cabin and go back to live in the towns," he said, winking, as if it was the worst thing that could happen to a man.

Chapter 10

Towards the end of the second day, we reached the gentler slopes leading to the first of the alpine plateaux. With the wind now veering through the high snowy peaks, it was much colder.

On the third afternoon the brush thinned out and we came to broad, parklike areas studded with small lodgepole pines. Here in the more fertile stretches of the peaty plateaux a few alpine flowers were blooming. Pappy identified arnica, yellow mimulus, and willowherb. There seemed to be creeks every half mile, some of them dropping down in beautiful and spectacular waterfalls framed by ferns and bright red and pink flowers. Above us, between the cloud traceries, we saw the permanent snow line.

As we walked along Pappy suddenly stopped. At first I thought he'd found some cougar tracks but as I followed his pointing finger to the high bluffs, I saw some large brown-and-grey animals with white underparts, long legs, and huge curving horns looking down nervously.

"Bighorn sheep," he said with surprise. "Well, I'm derned. Didn't know there were any bighorn around here. They're gettin' real scarce now. Come on, let's try some fun. Did you know sheep can fly?"

He ducked down behind a small outcrop, then started stalking upwards. When we'd covered over half a mile he crawled behind a large rock on a high promontory, with a big grin on his face. "OK," he whispered. "Let's jump 'em. Now!"

We both jumped out, showing ourselves. Three of the ewes had remained near where we'd first seen them. As soon as they saw us they shot away, leaping down the almost sheer face of the rocks with incredible agility. At times their feet just touched down, as if to maintain balance only, as they hurtled forwards at a break-neck speed, their hair rippling in the wind of their rapid descent. Within seconds they had covered about a quarter-mile of almost

346

perpendicular rock face, that no man could have negotiated without climbing irons, and disappeared.

"Now," said Pappy, "you *know* that sheep can fly, and none fly better than the bighorn."

He admired the bighorn because of their rugged independence. They lived the true spartan life, their kingdom on barren peaks at the very roof of the world. They disdained easier life in the lowlands, could scratch away snow with their forefeet to get at food, and if winters were really severe, could subsist on browsing scrub bushes or even balsam and fir. Once there had been a million or more, but now he doubted that twenty thousand had survived, so coveted by hunters were the large horn trophies of the rams.

Occasionally now we came across tracks of black bears and a fox or two. But it wasn't until we were heading down the far side of the mountains that we found the first pug marks of a cougar. We had now swung round from the high passes and were above the large slough before the lake in the long valley.

Several creeks fed into the slough, which spread out to a large lake some four miles long. The placid surface was alive with ducks and waterfowl. Along its banks the conifers gave way to clumps of alder, golden birch, and willow trees. As we stood in the forest we heard the sound of flashing pinions above us. A flock of huge, rare trumpeter swans had circled the lake and were homing their long necks onto its far end. Angelic white, their wings beat against the air with a strange whistling sound as they vanished below the tops of the trees ahead. The needles beneath our feet were yielding, like a cushion, and our nostrils were caressed by the gentle scent of resin, pine, and earth. "God's country," said Pappy under his breath.

As we neared the lake itself I noticed some V-shaped ripples in the water that were being made by the heads of swimming animals. At first I thought they were otters or beavers, but they were muskrats. "Otters usually swim in a sort of zigzag as they are on the lookout for fish. But muskrats an' beavers go straight for where they're heading," Pappy said. "Beavers have broader noses too, so they make a wider V." As we walked along the marshy banks, a slight mist rising among the reeds, we found some muskrat lodges. Two or three feet high and about three feet

347

across, they were made of chewed plants, mostly broad-leaved cat-tail or bullrush, and were built on old fallen logs, banks of mud, or in clumps of weed, using the stems like stilts.

We sat down in a thicket and stayed quiet for a few minutes. As we watched, a muskrat came swimming along, whiskers high above the ripples, and in its mouth it carried a thick piece of freshly cut root. It paddled up to a lodge, climbed out of the water, and vanished into one of the two entrance holes. "They often store bulbs and roots in there," Pappy said. "They can go in the top or through little underwater tunnels."

The muskrat community extended thirty yards along the edge of the lake, and as we were nearing its end Pappy stopped, pointing to the tracks of a small cougar. Then he started examining the alders on the bank. Eventually he indicated two torn shelters in the weeds of a mudbank far out. They looked as if a miniature tornado had hit them, with dents in the muddy debris a few yards from each muskrat home. Pappy pulled me closer to the trees. "See the rips in the bark—the cougar clawed its way through the trees, keepin' itself out of the bog. Could've been last night." He pointed to the dents by the lodges. "See those marks—that's where the old cat flailed out at the poor little devils as they tried to escape."

We struck off at a tangent to make early camp away from the lakeshore, walking through the birches into the higher, dry, more open forest of spruce and pine.

As we cut wood for our fire Pappy explained that in the winter muskrats were much safer from cougar or lynx attacks. When the lake froze over they would build a third kind of house—"push-ups". These were made on the actual surface of the ice, usually from the roots and stems of water plants, and became tiny frozen igloos. The muskrats would swim along until they found a pocket of air trapped below thinner ice, then using the air like a swimmer uses an oxygen tank, would gnaw through the ice and build the push-up. The relative warmth of the vegetation, with its later insulation of snow, plus the constant comings and goings of the animals, usually stopped the water freezing under the little house again. These push-ups weren't strictly homes but places where the muskrats could eat in safety and to which they could flee under water from danger.

Next day we breakfasted on boiled rice and a seven-pound lake trout. That morning we noticed that after a couple of miles the banks of the lake petered out, and by early afternoon we had reached the far end of the lake. We negotiated the rocky beds of the river and were clambering down through some tree arbours towards the grassland when I noticed some curved white objects lying in the grasses under some stunted birch. As we walked over an astonishing sight greeted us. Two skeletons lay side by side, locked in an eternal combat. The larger one, Pappy said, was of a mountain caribou, while the smaller, more streamlined one was that of a cougar. The caribou's head was twisted to one side and one of its antlers was embedded in the cougar's rib cage, its tip just a fraction away from the spinal column. Pappy lifted the cougar's skull which had a fracture above the right eye socket.

"Must've been a hell of a battle," Pappy surmised as he let the cougar's skull fall back to the ground. "This old cat must've stalked the caribou till it got in here, then it climbed onto that rock up there and came at it from above. Hard to say which died first. The cat probably raked its throat out but the bull must've smashed the cat against the rock and fractured its skull. Reckon its horns must've gone clean through the lungs, maybe hit the heart, too." For a few more moments we looked down at the remains of the two animals, an inevitable result of the relentless laws of nature.

The grasslands extended farther than was apparent from the other side of the lake. We hid ourselves in the scrubby bush at the edge of the pasture, hoping some caribou might come down from the treed slopes to graze on the far side. It was cold lying there and we were grateful when the sun came out from behind the high clouds and warmed us briefly. But it wasn't until late evening that our patience was rewarded. "There they are," whispered Pappy, touching my arm.

Just under a mile away we saw the brown forms of grazing caribou, looking exactly like reindeer, their close relations. As far as we could estimate, it was a small herd of about twenty-five animals with two smaller groups behind, each seeming to be attended by a large bull. The adult cows with calves or yearlings were leading the foraging for grass, sedges and mosses, and browsing on the willow and birch bushes.

"Well, that's just fine," said Pappy with a satisfied air. "They're hungry so they'll still be around tomorrow. Come on, time to make camp."

As we cooked our supper of rice, lentils and trout remains, and Pappy browned some bannocks in his little aluminium pan, I looked at his grizzled white head bent low over the fire and thought what an extraordinary character he was. This was a man who knew the wilds, the rivers, trees, and mountains, not merely in mind, but as though they were part of his soul. Alone, I knew I would have seen little of what we had witnessed.

As we talked later I asked him what he thought of the theories that animals had a sixth sense, and that that sense made them more scared when humans in their territories carried guns.

"I don't know," he replied honestly. "Sure, I see more bear and deer now when I walk about *not* meanin' 'em harm than I did when I was young and lookin' for something to shoot. But then I go slower now, with more care. I guess I learned a few things."

He laughed then, explaining he hadn't waited to shoot a young caribou buck because he wanted us to spend all next day watching the big deer. One shot might have sent them swimming across the lake. "Caribou swim far more readily than other deer," he said. "Heck, a caribou can swim up to six miles an hour. I've had a hard time tryin' to catch up to 'em in my canoe! Also, they have dense fur with hollow hairs and a thick coating of fat that acts like a built-in life jacket."

Next day we awoke in the pre-dawn twilight and crept back to the shallow depression where we'd spent the previous afternoon. The caribou were already grazing, almost directly in front of us, the nearest cows less than four hundred yards away. For an hour we watched them. Then as I was resting my head down on my hands, easing my aching neck, I felt Pappy tug my arm. "Wolf!" he hissed. Slowly I looked up through the grasses and at first saw nothing. Then, after straining my eyes, I saw three wolves gliding along through the birch glades on the far side of the pasture. They slunk at a furtive trot like silver-brown ghosts in that early light, their thick wavy fur blending perfectly into the background. Their behaviour seemed quite unaggressive and the caribou cows nearest them, apart from momentarily looking up and moving a few steps away, just carried on. Two of the bulls, without showing the slightest signs of panic and seemingly by instinct, slowly stationed themselves between the cows and where the wolves had vanished into the trees. At any moment I expected to see the wolves re-emerge and make a dash at the herd, or single out one caribou, but nothing happened and we didn't see them again.

During the noonday hours most of the caribou lay down, chewing the cud, and with nothing to do we dozed in the pale sun. By late afternoon they were back on their feet and three-quarters of the loosely grouped herd had passed us and were grazing on the pasture nearer the lake. Some of the cows were so close we could distinctly hear the cropping sound their flat teeth made on the herbage, and the odd clicking sound of their foot tendons as they put their weight on their hoofs—a noise that is said to alert the calf that its mother is moving.

After another hour my legs were numb from being so long in the same position, my neck and shoulders were aching from the effort of holding my head still, and I was about to disturb Pappy and urge him to think of our supper when a sudden disturbance in the grass behind the rocky outcrop to our right made me reach for Pappy's arm. He raised his head slowly and we saw the flattened form of a cougar sneaking along between the rocks—its underbelly brushing the earth, its jaws slightly apart. In the sun, its amber eyes reduced to slits, it glared balefully at a young buck grazing a few yards from the rocks and moved forwards in little trembling crouches. At the end of each stealthy run it gathered itself for the next, its leg joints protruding above each corner of its tawny body like the round wheel covers of an old-fashioned racing car. When it neared the end of the natural rock and grass cover it stopped, sinews and muscles bunching for its final leaping charge.

Everything happened at once. A moment before the mountain lion charged, the nearest group of caribou became aware of it, jumped into the air in confusion, looked at each other for a lead, then hoisted their tails and bolted at a high trot. As the cougar streaked with bouncing, tail-high bounds, the buck shot away in a semi-circle and thus the big cat missed with its first lunge at the throat. Suddenly the alarm became general and the whole herd began to run. The nearest bull lowered its antlers but it seemed more a symbolic or instinctive movement for it did not move to intercept. The cougar ignored it completely, and in two more bounds almost caught up to the fleeing buck, then swiped at its hindquarters, knocking it momentarily sideways and raking great welts of blood with its claws.

In a trice Pappy was up on one knee, took aim, fired, and brought down the buck. In the same split second the cougar bounded onto the fallen body, then heard the rifle's crack, leaped off again and, with flattened ears, shot behind a rocky outcrop and disappeared. The last thing we saw was the upraised tails of the caribou herd as they fled at great speed to the lake. "Holy crow! What luck!" cried Pappy, whacking me hard on the back. "I doubt there've been more'n a dozen men in the whole history of the world who've seen a cougar attack!"

I was so excited I could hardly speak. I felt my heart thudding under my ribs and as we walked out to the body of the young buck my legs trembled slightly. The buck was quite dead. The bullet from Pappy's superb shot had hit behind its right lower ribs, passed through its lungs and heart and out of the left shoulder.

The animal was bigger than I'd thought, weighing around 180 pounds. Pappy pointed to the long slashes caused by the cougar's claws on its flanks and hindquarters.

"It must've been a real young lion," he said, "to tackle an animal nearly twice its size in near daylight." He pulled out his knife and smiled at my nervous looks at the rocks. "Don't worry. It won't be back, not after that shot, not before nightfall anyway." He plunged his knife into the buck's neck, slashed the carotids to let the blood, and left it there. "Ah, well," he added, "I doubt it would have lived. These wounds would weaken it, go poisonous, make it easy prey for other cougars or wolves. Let's go get our packs and let it bleed awhile."

We walked back for our packs then returned, lifted the buck's rear quarters onto a rock to help the blood flow, then sat by some bushes. Pappy's knife projected from the buck's neck like some territorial marker establishing his claim. While waiting for the blood to let fully we talked.

Pappy was disappointed we had not seen any moose around the lake, especially as they had recently been growing in numbers. "You haven't lived till you've seen a big bull moose on the rampage," he said. "They go up to eighteen hundred pounds in Alaska, and can stand eight feet high at the shoulder. Most of the year they're pretty timid but when the bulls are ready to mate in the fall, they reckon they're the gods of the forests. They charge through, flattening small alders and willows like bulldozers, as if they weren't even there. They have only one cow at a time but mate with several, and if a rival appears—look out! I saw two fighting once. The old bull went beserk, battered his antlers against rocks, tramped on trees, and charged with a run that shook the earth. They hit so hard the smaller one was knocked into the lake, and he sure didn't come back, just swam off to find a cow of his own. If you're up a good tree and have found some antlers—elks', or caribou's will do, too—you can have some fun if there's a bull moose around. Just clatter the antlers against the branches an' he'll soon come a-runnin'."

He grinned. "When I was up here three years back I saw this old fellow standin' up to his shoulders in the swamp back there, wavin' his antlers about and splashing his head in the water, havin' a rare old time. I kept well out of the way. There's an old joke about moose, you know—they stand for hours in swamps not to escape flies but to hide their awful knobbly knees because they're ashamed of 'em!" He shook his head. "No, the moose is real smart. He can dodge all the summer flies while gettin' under-water roots. I've seen 'em submerge completely, tryin' to get the juicy roots on the bottom. They can stay under nearly a minute. I tell you, a man can get a hell of a shock walking out of the trees by a quiet lake when suddenly a huge moose emerges from the water like some prehistoric monster."

Later Pappy partly skinned, then butchered the caribou buck with the machete. We wrapped the heart, liver, shoulders, and part of the ribs in the last of our plastic bags to stop the blood seeping over our packs too much, then carried the big haunches in our hands to the lakeshore where we were going to camp for the last night. Before leaving Pappy cut off a long length of hide. "It's the only leather I know that shrinks when wet," he explained. "It's ideal for snow shoes and bindin' canoes."

354

Ravenous as we were, Pappy insisted that tonight we'd have the best meal of the whole trek. First he took out his extra bag of salt, sliced a haunch into three heavy strips, and put them to soak in a brine solution so thick an egg would probably have bounced right out of it. "Takes out some of the gamy tang," he explained. Following his instructions, I built our biggest fire so far between three upended rocks, while he fetched a thin slab of rock and some mud from the lakeside, and made an "oven" which he set across the rocks around the fire. This took almost an hour. As we appeased our hunger slightly with bannocks, he took the meat from the brine, set slices of liver between the strips, sprinkling it all with herbs, then with slices of two onions he'd kept in his pack and a liberal dressing of oil and fat, he wrapped the whole delicious package in tinfoil and set it in his oven.

As it cooked, the smudge from the fire helping to keep away the mosquitoes and black flies, we made a birch-pole frame and hung the remaining salt-dipped meat from it to smoke a bit, as well as the piece of hide that Pappy had scraped.

That evening as we ate, I learned that in the last one hundred years the march of man's civilization and hunting has reduced the total population of cougar to less than 13,000. Perhaps in a North America now claiming to be conservation minded, this largest and most beautiful of its wild cats ought to be given complete protection, along with the grizzly, except where *individual* animals of these breeds are proved to be a nuisance.

Pappy also told me mother cougars actually train their young to hunt and kill, though he'd never seen it himself. At first she leaves the cubs behind to go and make a kill, but at six weeks when the cubs weigh only about nine pounds, they can follow their mother on short forays. At four months they're running with her while she's hunting, and after she's produced the kill they all eat at leisure, laying up around the carcass until it's all gone. Often cubs run with their mother until two years old—when a male cub can be almost as big as she is. Pappy thought this habit made some naturalists believe that male and female cougars run and hunt together with her previous year's cubs.

"It might happen with a young male," he said. "But I reckon it's rare. When a new male arrives on the scene in her breeding period, he drives the kits away from his girl friend. And she knows it's right. The kits should now be able to take care of themselves, so she lets them go. Often this is the toughest part of a cougar's life. Suddenly it's alone and if it hasn't learned to hunt right, it can die."

Next morning it was time to return home. After Pappy had checked his bearings from various mountain landmarks, we set off on the long trek back. We now both looked like wild men—our beards were over an inch long, we had lost a good deal of weight, our clothing was tattered and frayed. But as we traversed those mountains tramping one of the loneliest places left on earth, I felt an extraordinary vigour. It was more than mere euphoria, more of an absolute certainty that I was now feeling entirely *myself*. And that this is how we all ought to feel all our lives. It seemed tragic that most of us never reach this peak in a lifetime, this natural harmony of mind and body and spirit. It came to me then that of all animals, only the weak, immature or unhealthy man is vicious for no reason. Hating himself and unable to admit it, he seeks to revenge himself upon others.

Towards evening we came out on a marshy ravine a few miles above the river that would guide us home, and Pappy stopped and pointed. Out there in the soft mud between willows and alders on the banks of a broad creek was a large area that had been threshed flat. It looked as if a couple of elephants had engaged in battle. Pappy quickly unstrapped his rifle.

"There's been a big grizzly here all right," he said. "Look," and he pointed to rear-foot tracks some seven inches wide and ten inches long. The tracks went in the direction of a rocky hill two hundred yards from the creek, each track preceded by a deep gouge mark.

"It was draggin' something real heavy," said Pappy, holding the gun in both hands, his eyes darting warily into the trees on each side. "Keep your eyes skinned, laddie, and keep behind me."

We had gone only a few more yards up the slope when we found the remains of a huge leg. The thigh bone was crushed and what little flesh remained smelled faintly of recent decay.

"Goddam," whispered Pappy. "He was haulin' a whole damn moose by the look of it. He must've found it dead, maybe after another bull killed it. He got as far as this, then stopped for a quick feed. Look at that leg, will you?" The powerful jaws of the grizzly, trying to get at the succulent marrow, had chomped the great bone up like spaghetti.

"Let's get out of here," I whispered. I had a distinct feeling we'd taken enough risks and were now pushing our luck too far. After a quick look around, Pappy turned to me, his blue eyes holding an amused twinkle. How he looked at that moment is a memory I shall always treasure—he stood there silhouetted against the treed skyline of that remote fastness, his huge horny hands gripping the old rifle, his great chest heaving slightly, his nostrils dilating like some old wilderness war horse—staunch, secure, powerful and loving. "You're right," he said softly. "We don't want to have to kill that old bear, do we?"

We reached his canoe two mornings later and I spent two more nights with him before saying farewell. In that time he shared more of his extraordinary wilderness lore, laughingly turned away my expressions of gratitude, but made me promise never to reveal his true name or the exact place of our adventures.

As we stood above my boat in the river, neither of us knew how to say goodbye. Suddenly a gnarled hand shot out. "We'll meet again," he said, and we both turned away.

Blessed with calm weather, I negotiated the river waters and the inlet without mishap and returned home. At the retired couple's cabin, Booto just stood there, stared, turned away as if he didn't believe it, then looked back again. Then he ran around in wild circles, yipping, and leaped up to lick my face.

Epilogue

As the last months of my stay in Canada passed by, a strange sense of anti-climax seemed to pervade my life, as if in some mysterious way I had served my time in my remote clifftop retreat and ought now to move on.

For one last evening I sat silently between the rocks in the rippling gold and blue of the sunset, feeling the wilderness had not only taught me many lessons but provided a meaning. Here the bodily rhythms had become one with the eternal rhythms of the sea, the sky and the wind. Mere reason alone had died and become reborn. I looked at my little cabin, at the logs I had laboured to haul up the log staircase, at the sea that had provided most of my food for more than three years, at the northern land spit over which the eagles always flew. I thought of Ed and Pappy Tihoni again, and the days with the caribou, the cougar and the grizzlies. I looked at Booto, panting contently in the late sunshine, and I suddenly felt an enormous gratitude. Canada had been good to me, good for me. It had shaken me from my city rut and had shown me a finer and fuller life. Here on this lonely cliff, five thousand miles from all I had previously known, my mind had been freed, I felt as if a new self had been formed. In the last moments of that golden dying day I felt strangely outside of time and space, suspended in a celestial limbo, shorn at last of doubt. I had lived close to nature, seen both its beauty and its callousness, and had been shown a path, a way that led beyond hope or fear, success or failure.

I did not know where I would go, only that my life, minor and of little account though it was, would be bound up somehow in the future between man and the last wild places.

High above me a skein of geese was heading south. Away to the west two doves were flying into the limitless horizon, like two tiny souls emblazoned on the sky as they migrated to their new and blessed home. Oh, there was time enough to think about the future, time enough to decide.

Mike Tomkies

True to the determination that came to him in the Canadian wilderness, Mike Tomkies is still to be found today in the last wild places. He lives in an old cottage beside a Scottish loch in the Western Highlands. No roads lead to it: there's only a six-mile path across the heather or an even longer journey by rowing boat. His only companions are an Alsatian called Moobli who helps him track the wildlife he studies, and Liane, the wildcat he has tamed, which lives in the woodshed beside the cottage.

Mike Tomkies's mother died when he was four and he was brought up by his father and grandmother. A city boy, he discovered the magic of the countryside at twelve during a holiday in a Sussex cottage, and his first job was as a gamekeeper. He served in the Coldstream Guards in the Middle East, worked as cook on a yacht, and was an extremely successful journalist and Hollywood columnist before he emigrated to Canada in 1966.

Today life moves at the pace he wishes, amid the rhythms of the seasons and the wildlife about his home. He fishes for food and keeps an ample vegetable garden. His larder is stocked with home-dried edible fungus, pickled fish and bottled wild fruits. Electricity for his record player he generates by a windmill outside his window. "Nothing in nature survives without a struggle," he says. "No one has the right to a good life: it has to be earned." His living comes from writing about the natural world, which he believes needs far stronger protection, not only for the wildlife it contains, but for man's own sake. His latest books, *My Wilderness Wildcats* and *Liane*, describe his experiences in breeding, releasing to the wild and taming these fascinating but rarely-seen animals.

Mike Tomkies values the life he has built for himself, and seldom leaves it. He did however return once to Canada to see his old friend Ed Louette. Strangely enough, a nephew of Ed's lives a few miles from him in Scotland and they have become friends. This odd coincidence helped confirm for him the rightness of his move to the Highlands. He has come to terms with one of the last wild places. He is a contented man.

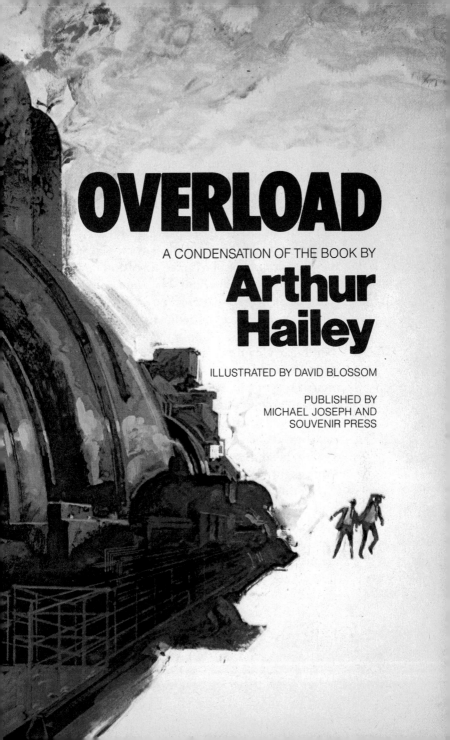

OVERLOAD

A CONDENSATION OF THE BOOK BY

Arthur Hailey

ILLUSTRATED BY DAVID BLOSSOM

PUBLISHED BY
MICHAEL JOSEPH AND
SOUVENIR PRESS

Overload! A massive power failure at a giant Californian electricity plant plunges a heavily populated area into darkness.

For Nim Goldman, a top executive of Golden State Power, this is only a preview of the electrical famine ahead. Unless a complacent power-guzzling public is restrained and new generating plants are built, blackouts could become an everyday occurrence.

Controversy rages as dedicated environmentalists, a determined reporter and a bomb-carrying terrorist try to thwart Goldman's plans. With his career in jeopardy and his marriage strained, he desperately seeks a solution to this demanding problem. Its urgency is dramatized for him when he meets a beautiful and sensitive woman whose every breath depends on life-sustaining electrical equipment.

Once again Arthur Hailey (author of *Airport* and *The Moneychangers*) has woven a fascinating story—one that lays bare the appalling possibilities for disaster which abound in our energy crisis.

ONE

Heat! Oppressive and enervating, it enveloped California from the Mexican border in the south to majestic Klamath Forest, elbowing northward into Oregon. Four days ago a dry thermal trough a thousand miles long, three hundred wide, had settled over the state. Now, at 1:00 p.m. on a Wednesday in July, Californians sweltered in temperatures from ninety degrees to well over a hundred, with no relief in sight.

Throughout cities and suburbs, in factories, offices, stores and homes, six million air conditioners hummed. On thousands of farms in the fertile Central Valley, armies of electric pumps gulped water from deep wells, directing it to thirsty cattle and parched crops—grain, grapes, citrus fruits, alfalfa, a hundred more. California had survived other heat waves. But in none had demands for electric power been so great.

"THAT'S it, then," the chief electric dispatcher said. "There goes the last of our spinning reserve."

Everyone within hearing already knew it—the regular staff and company executives crowding the energy control center of Golden State Power & Light. GSP&L was a giant among public utilities, the wellspring which produced and distributed two-thirds of California's electric power and natural gas. GSP&L was also rich, strong and—according to itself—efficient.

The energy control center was a security-restricted underground command post, centered by a communications console where the chief dispatcher and six assistants worked. Keyboards of two computer terminals were nearby. The walls housed banks of switches, diagrams of transmission lines and substations, with instruments monitoring the utility's two hundred and five electrical generating units in ninety-four plants around the state.

"You're positive there's no more power we can buy?" The question came from a tallish, muscularly built, shirt-sleeved figure standing at the dispatch console. Nim Goldman, vice-president of planning and assistant to the chairman of GSP&L, had a strong face, big-boned and ruddy, with eyes that looked out with directness and—most times, though not today—with a hint of humor. In his late forties, his hair black and curly with a few flecks of gray, Nim Goldman usually appeared younger, but not at the moment, because of strain. For days he had stayed at work until midnight and been up at 4:00 a.m. Like others in the control center, Nim was sweating, partly from tension, partly from the fact that the air conditioning had been turned off in deference to an urgent plea to the public to use less electric power because of the crisis. An appeal, however, that had gone mostly unheeded.

The chief dispatcher, a white-haired veteran, looked offended as he answered Nim's question. For two days dispatch aides had been continually on phones, shopping for surplus power. "We're pulling in every bit we can get from Oregon and Nevada, Mr. Goldman. Arizona's helping a little, but they've got problems too. Tomorrow they're asking to buy from *us*."

"Can we make it through this afternoon?" J. Eric Humphrey, chairman of the board, spoke in a cultured voice, in keeping with his old-Boston aplomb though he had lived in California for thirty years. He was a small, neat person who, despite the heat, wore a dark suit.

"Doesn't look good, sir," the chief dispatcher said.

As the dispatcher had pointed out moments earlier, GSP&L's last spinning reserve had been brought to full load. Golden State had two kinds of reserve—"spinning" and "ready." The spinning reserve comprised generators running below full capacity, though their output could be increased immediately. The ready reserve included plants not operating but prepared to start up and generate full load in ten to fifteen minutes.

An hour ago the last ready reserve—a gas-powered plant near Fresno—had had its status raised to spinning. Now the gas turbines were going to maximum output, leaving no more reserves.

A slightly stooped bulky man with a toby-jug face and beetling brows, spoke up harshly. "Damn it! If we'd had a correct weather forecast for today, we wouldn't be in this bind now." This was Ray Paulsen, executive vice-president of power supply.

"Every other forecaster made the same error as ours," Nim objected. "I read in last night's paper we'd have cooler air today."

"That's probably exactly where our forecaster got it—from some newspaper!" Paulsen glared at Nim, who shrugged. It was no secret that the two detested each other.

"Come on, Ray," Nim protested. "This isn't getting us anywhere. Let's deal with the crisis."

The big question was, Would demands for electric power exceed the supply available? If the answer proved to be yes, entire banks of substation switches would necessarily be opened, leaving whole communities without power, creating chaos.

An emergency brownout had been in effect since 10:00 a.m., reducing the voltage supplied to consumers by eight percent. The lower voltages made everything less efficient, from hair dryers to major appliances, and an eight percent brownout was the limit. Beyond that, motors would overheat or burn out. The last resort was load shedding—committing large areas to total blackout.

If GSP&L could somehow hold on past midafternoon, the time of peak demand on hot days, the load would ease. Then, assuming tomorrow was a cooler day—no problem. But if the present load increased, the worst could happen.

Ray Paulsen did not give up easily. "If the weather forecast had been accurate," he growled, "Magalia wouldn't have been released." Magalia Number 2, part of a plant north of Sacramento, was a big steam-driven generator capable of putting out six hundred thousand kilowatts. However, serious malfunctions kept it frequently out of service. Last night, after reading the forecast of lower temperatures, Paulsen had approved shutting down the unit to repair boiler leaks. Though desperately needed once again, Magalia Number 2 could not be back on line for two more days.

Nim Goldman had been conferring at the dispatch console. Now he said, "There's no longer any doubt. Load shedding will have to begin in half an hour." He glanced at the chairman. "We should alert the media. TV and radio can still get warnings out."

"Do it," Humphrey said.

Faces were grim. Intentional disruption of service had never occurred in the utility's century-and-a-quarter history. Nim Goldman was already telephoning instructions to public relations. It had been decided that the cuts would be known as rolling blackouts, a PR ploy to emphasize their temporary nature.

The chairman now asked, "Does anyone know where the chief is?" The "chief" was the chief engineer, Walter Talbot, a quiet, unflappable Scot whose wisdom in tight situations was legendary.

"Yes," Nim said. "He drove out to look at Big Lil."

The chairman frowned. "I hope nothing's wrong out there."

All eyes swung to an instrument panel with the legend above it: LA MISSION NUMBER 5. This was Big Lil, the newest and largest generator at La Mission plant, fifty miles outside the city.

Big Lil—built by Lilien Industries of Pennsylvania—was a monster delivering a million and a quarter kilowatts. It was fueled by oil in enormous quantities which created superheated steam to drive the giant turbine. Today, in the energy control center, a strip chart recorder showed that Big Lil was running at maximum, shouldering a massive six percent of the utility's total load.

"There was some turbine vibration reported this morning," Ray Paulsen explained. "The chief thought he should take a look."

It was then that it happened. Under the sign LA MISSION NUMBER 5 a buzzer sounded a series of short, sharp notes. Simultaneously, amber and red warning lights began blinking. The inked needle of Number 5's chart recorder faltered, then slid to zero.

"My God!" someone said. "Big Lil's tripped off the line."

A high-speed typewriter came to life, spewing out status reports as hundreds of high-voltage circuit breakers at switching centers and substations sprang open at computer command. The opening of the circuit breakers would save the system and protect other generators from harm. But the action had already plunged huge segments of the state into total electric blackout.

THE explosion at La Mission plant occurred entirely without warning. Half an hour earlier the chief engineer, Walter Talbot, had arrived to inspect La Mission Number 5—Big Lil. The chief was a slight, spindly man with a puckish sense of humor who talked in a broad Scottish accent. He was accompanied by the plant superintendent, a scholarly engineer named Danieli.

A slight vibration differing from the turbine's steady whine was audible to the trained ears of the chief and superintendent. But after tests, the chief pronounced, "It's naething tae worry over, and what's necessary we'll see to when the panic's bye."

The two, wearing hard hats, were standing close to Big Lil on metal gratings which formed the floor of the cathedral-like turbine hall. The monstrous turbine generator, a city block in length, sat perched on concrete pedestals. Immediately beneath was a massive steam chest with high-pressure steam lines going in from the boiler and out to the turbine. The explosion occurred an instant after Talbot spoke. It was a dynamite blast, which breached a three-foot-diameter steam line and a smaller lubricating-oil line. There was a deep, thunderous noise, and steam, at a temperature of a thousand degrees Fahrenheit and under a pressure of twenty-four hundred pounds per square inch, rushed through the gratings on which the two men were standing.

Talbot and Danieli died instantly. A few seconds later the entire scene was obscured by dense black smoke. Two plant workers, painting on a scaffold high above the turbine-room floor, blinded by the rising smoke, tried to clamber to a walkway some fifteen feet higher. They failed, and fell to their deaths below.

In the plant control room, total disaster was averted by the fast reactions of a technician at Number 5's control panel, who, aided by automatic devices, ensured that Big Lil was shut down without damage to the turbine generator's vital components.

It would take several days of inquiry and painstaking sifting of evidence to discover the explosion's cause.

At 11:40 that morning a white male of medium build, clean-shaven, sallow-complexioned, wearing steel-rimmed glasses and in the uniform of a Salvation Army officer, had approached La Mission's main gate on foot. He was carrying a briefcase.

Questioned by the security guard, the visitor produced a letter, apparently on GSP&L stationery, authorizing him to visit La Mission to solicit funds from employees for a Salvation Army program—a free lunch for needy children.

The guard directed the visitor to the plant superintendent's office, and the man left in the direction indicated. The guard saw no more of him until he walked out of the main gate twenty minutes later—an hour before the explosion.

If security had been tighter, such a visitor would not have been allowed inside unescorted. But GSP&L, like public utilities everywhere, faced special security problems. With hundreds of generating plants and other widely scattered facilities, complete security would have cost a fortune. For these reasons much of the utility's security program was cosmetic, based on calculated risk.

Police inquiries established that the supposed Salvation Army officer was an imposter. The letter he presented, while it may have been on GSP&L stationery—not difficult to come by—was a fake.

It was established that the man, once inside the powerhouse, did not go to the superintendent's office. He probably descended a stairway to the service floor beneath the main turbine hall. From this floor the lower portions of the generators could be clearly seen through the metal grating above. Big Lil would have been unmistakable because of its size.

The intruder might have known that La Mission was highly automated, with only a small work force; therefore his chances of being unobserved were good. Almost certainly, then, he moved directly under Big Lil, where he opened his briefcase containing a dynamite bomb. After actuating a timing mechanism, undoubtedly he reached up and placed the bomb on a metal flange near the junction of two steam lines. The saboteur could then walk unaccosted to the gate and out of the plant.

But all this came later. At La Mission, for some ninety minutes after the explosion, chaos reigned. Fire fighters had difficulty extinguishing the blazing oil. When the four bodies were removed, they were scarcely recognizable—"like boiled lobsters," a horrified employee said, from exposure to superheated steam.

Damage to Big Lil was slight. Repairs would take only a week.

NIM GOLDMAN was in an observation gallery, separated by glass from the energy control center, trying to answer questions from newspaper, TV and radio reporters. The utility's public relations vice-president, Teresa Van Buren, had appealed to Nim to be the spokesman at the impromptu press conference now in progress. Already some of the press people were antagonistic.

"Oh, for God's sake!" a reporter from the *California Examiner,* Nancy Molineaux, shouted. "Tell us what we came to find out. What went wrong? Who's responsible? When will the power be back on?"

Ms. Molineaux was intense, attractive—high cheekbones made her face seem haughty—and her usual expression was a mixture of curiosity and skepticism bordering on disdain. She was also chic, wore good clothes well on a willowy body, and was black. She had a reputation for investigating, then exposing, venality in public places. Nim regarded her as he would a needle-sharp icicle.

"What went wrong was an explosion at La Mission," Nim explained. "Four of our people have been killed."

Someone asked, "Do you know the cause of the explosion?"

"No."

Ms. Molineaux injected, "What about the power?"

"Some is back now. Everything should be normal by tonight."

Normal, Nim thought, except for Walter Talbot. Word of the chief's death had reached the energy control center with shattering suddenness. Nim had not yet grasped the reality of the news. In his eleven years with Golden State, he and the chief engineer had shared a mutual liking and habitually confided in each other.

"Will there be another blackout tomorrow?"

"Not if the heat wave ends."

As questioning continued, Mrs. Van Buren, a short, plump, bustling woman in her mid-forties, came into the gallery. "I have an announcement," she said. Her voice was emotional. "I'm authorized to say that sabotage is suspected in the explosion."

Amid the fusillade of questions which followed, Nim eased his way out of the observation gallery and back to energy control.

STEP by step, directed by energy control, the disrupted distribution system was returning to a state of order.

At the console the chief dispatcher leaned back in his gray swivel chair and said, "We're halfway home, Mr. Goldman."

It meant, Nim realized, that nearly half the area affected by blackout had full power restored. A computer could, and did, shut down the system faster than any human. But it took direct switching by technicians to put the system back together.

Cities and towns had priority and, district by district, were coming electrically alive once more. Suburbs, particularly those with industrial plants, were next. Rural areas would be last. Hospitals, water and sewage-treatment plants and phone-company installations rated special preference. Although these essential institutions usually had standby generators, which carried a partial load, outside power was necessary for normal functioning. There were also individuals who received special consideration.

The chief dispatcher had transferred his attention to an unusual circuitry map which had colored circles dotted over it.

Nim asked, "What's that?"

"That's life-sustaining equipment in private homes. Those red circles are iron lungs—respiratory equipment they call it now. Green is kidney dialysis machines. This orange circle is an oxygen-generating unit for an infant. We've got maps for every division."

"You've just filled a gap in my education," Nim acknowledged.

"Most people relying on life-sustaining equipment have the kind that switches over to batteries in emergency," the dispatcher continued. "Just the same, when outside power fails, we check quickly. If there's any problem, we rush in a portable generator."

"But we don't have that many portables—surely not enough for a widespread outage like today's."

"No. But today we were lucky." He indicated the map. "We have power back on in all these spots."

Nim studied the map, fascinated. One of the red circles marked an apartment house he had driven by many times—at Lakewood and Balboa. A name beside it read Sloan—presumably the respirator user. Who was Sloan? Nim wondered. What was he like?

TWO

"Nim." Eric Humphrey was calling from La Mission, where he had gone with Ray Paulsen immediately after first reports of the explosion. "I know you were personally well acquainted with Walter Talbot. How well do you know his wife?"

"Ardythe. Very well. How is it out there?"

"Grim. I never saw bodies of men burned by superheated steam before. I hope I never do again." The chairman's composure wavered briefly. "I'd like you to go to Mrs. Talbot as soon as possible. I understand she's taking it badly. Maybe you can help."

"All right," Nim said. "I'll do it."

"Thank you. And please convey to Mrs. Talbot my deep personal sympathy."

HIS substantial frame jammed into his Fiat X1/9 two-seater, Nim wove through downtown streets, headed toward San Roque, the suburb where Walter and Ardythe Talbot lived. It was early evening. The heat of the day had diminished, but not much.

As Nim saw it, today's brief power curtailment was merely a preview of far graver, dislocating shortages, perhaps only a year or two distant. The trouble was, almost no one seemed to care. Even within GSP&L there existed a complacency, translatable as: *Don't worry. Everything will come out all right. We shall manage. Meanwhile, don't let's rock the boat by creating public alarm.*

In recent months only three people in the GSP&L hierarchy—Walter Talbot, Teresa Van Buren and Nim—had pleaded for more directness. They favored blunt, immediate warnings to the public, press and politicians that a calamitous electrical famine was ahead and only a crash program of more generating plants and conservation measures could lessen its effect. But no change had been sanctioned. Now, one of the trio, Walter Talbot, was dead.

A resurgence of grief swept over Nim. Suddenly he realized he had neglected to tell Ruth he would be home late. He reached for the mobile phone below the instrument panel and dialed. Moments later a small voice said, "Goldman residence, Benjy Goldman speaking." Nim smiled. That was his son, Benjy, all right—even at ten, precise and systematized, in contrast to his sister, Leah, four years older and perennially disorganized.

"It's Dad," Nim said. "I'm on mobile." He had taught the family to wait when they heard that, because on a radiotelephone, conversations couldn't overlap. "Is everything all right?"

"Yes, Dad, it is now. The electricity went off. But I guess you knew. And, Dad, I reset all the clocks."

"That's good, and yes, I knew. Let me talk to your mother."

Another pause. Then, "Nim?" Ruth's soft voice. "We heard about Walter and the others on the news; it's really terrible. I'm truly sorry."

He knew that Ruth was aware of how close he and the chief had been. That kind of understanding was typical of Ruth, even though in other ways she and Nim seemed to have less and less rapport these days, compared with how it used to be. Not that there was any open hostility. Ruth would never let it come to that, Nim reasoned. He could visualize her now—composed and competent, her soft gray eyes sympathetic. She had a Madonna quality, he had often thought; even without her good looks, character alone would have made her beautiful.

Nim never ceased to respect Ruth. It was simply that their marriage had become uninteresting, even dull. There was something else too. Recently Ruth seemed to have developed interests of her own. Several times Nim had called home when normally she would have been there; instead, she appeared to have been out all day and later dodged explaining, which was unlike her. Had Ruth taken a lover? It seemed hardly possible.

"We're all shaken up," he acknowledged. "Eric has asked me to go to Ardythe. I expect I'll be very late. Don't wait up."

That was nothing new. On most evenings Nim worked late, and dinner at home was delayed or he missed it entirely. It also meant he saw little of Leah and Benjy, who were often asleep when Nim arrived. He felt guilty about the meager amount of time he spent with the children and he knew it troubled Ruth, though she rarely said so. Sometimes he wished she would complain more.

But tonight's absence needed no explanations or excuses.

"Poor Ardythe," Ruth said. "And that announcement on the news just now makes it even worse."

"What announcement?"

"The people who planted the bomb sent a message to a radio station. Boasting about what they'd done. Can you imagine?"

"Listen," Nim told Ruth, "it's important I hear the news. I'm going to hang up now. If I can, I'll call you later."

He replaced the phone and snapped on the radio to an all-news station. A trumpet blast announced a bulletin:

"A group calling itself Friends of Freedom has claimed responsibility for an explosion today at a Golden State Power & Light generating plant. The blast claimed four lives and caused a widespread failure of electric power.

"The disclosure was in a tape recording delivered to a local radio station late this afternoon. A man's voice on the tape—so far unidentified—stated, quote, Friends of Freedom are dedicated to a people's revolution and protest the greedy capitalist monopoly of power which belongs rightfully to the people. End quote."

Nim snapped off the radio. The news depressed him with its sickening futility.

In the growing dusk he parked outside the Talbots' modest two-story house and walked up the driveway. The front door was open and Nim went inside. Voices were coming from the living room. He could hear Ardythe. She sounded hysterical. He caught disconnected words: "Those murderers . . . good and kind, wouldn't harm anyone." Interspersed were other voices, attempting to bring calm.

Walter Talbot, Jr., met him in the hallway and shook his hand. "Thanks for coming, Nim."

There were perhaps ten people, mostly neighbors, in the living room as Nim and Wally went in. Ardythe Talbot was on a sofa, surrounded by several women, one of whom was Mary, Wally Jr.'s wife. Though Ardythe was sixty, she remained a strikingly handsome woman in radiant health. Today, though, her poise had crumbled. Her tearstained face appeared drawn and old.

"Oh, Nim." She put out her arms, and the others made way as he went to sit beside her. "You heard the terrible thing that happened to Walter?" she said.

"Yes, dear," he replied gently. "I heard."

Nim observed Wally take his wife aside; then the two of them approached the others, thanking them, ushering them out one by one. Soon the house was quiet, and Wally and Mary were busying themselves with glasses and ashtrays, tidying up the kitchen.

Ardythe mused. "Did you know we were married thirty-six years?" She began crying softly.

Nim put his arm around her and cradled her head on his shoulder. Holding her, he became aware of her fragrant and pleasing perfume. She stirred. She had stopped crying and moved closer. Then, to Nim's consternation, he discovered he was becoming increasingly aware of Ardythe as a woman. He had a stirring of conscience and a sudden realization that Wally Jr. and Mary would return momentarily. He gently kissed Ardythe on the forehead and got to his feet.

She gave him a shy smile, and shortly afterward he said his good-bys to the others and, inwardly shaken, he left.

In the car, driving home, Nim pondered his personal life. After his marriage fifteen years ago, he had resolutely stayed a one-woman man—for about four years. Then an opportunity for extra-curricular sex occurred and he hadn't fought it. Afterward there had been more opportunities. At first Nim assumed he could keep his philandering a secret. Then common sense told him that Ruth must realize what was happening. The extraordinary thing was that she never protested. Illogically this galled him. She should have reacted, perhaps shed angry tears. True, it might have made no difference, but Nim had often asked himself, Wasn't his defection at least worth *that* much?

"WE ARE agreed, then." J. Eric Humphrey's gaze swept over the nine men and two women—GSP&L's management committee—around the conference-room table. "We'll press for immediate approval of three projects—the Tunipah coal-burning plant, Devil's Gate pumped storage and Fincastle geothermal field."

Nods and murmured assent greeted the chairman's summation.

It was Monday afternoon. Five days had passed since the disastrous explosion at La Mission and the subsequent power failure. Because of cooler weather and some luck, no further blackouts had occurred. But one conclusion was inescapable. There *would* be other blackouts, far more serious, unless GSP&L began building greater generating capacity within a year. There could still be serious shortages; since a fossil-fueled power plant took five years to design and build, a nuclear plant six—preceded, in each case, by the four to six years it took to obtain the needed licenses.

"In addition," Oscar O'Brien, the general counsel, said, "I assume we will still press on with our nuclear license applications." O'Brien was a former government lawyer from Washington, a burly man, shaped like a bass fiddle, who smoked cigars continuously.

"Naturally," Humphrey responded, "we shall continue our nuclear program. But in terms of public psychology we'll be better off, I believe, to let nuclear stand alone and not be linked with the other plans. The route to nuclear is strewn with opposition."

The chairman continued. "I have arranged a meeting with the governor—in Sacramento the day after tomorrow. I intend to urge him to bring pressure on all regulatory agencies to start hearings on Tunipah next month."

"We'll never have a better time to press for action," Ray Paulsen added. "The power failure last week showed clearly that a crisis can·happen. Even in Sacramento I think they'll see that."

"In Sacramento," Oscar O'Brien said, "all they see is politics. And let's face it—our opponents will use politics to the hilt, with Tunipah at the top of their hate list."

Tunipah was, in several ways, the most vital of their plans. This wilderness area near the Nevada border had been chosen carefully. It held little interest for sportsmen or naturalists. It was difficult to get to, and only a few trails traversed it. What Golden State Power & Light proposed to build there was an enormous generating plant, big enough to supply six cities the size of San Francisco. The fuel to be used was coal.

Coal could be North America's answer to Arab oil. Coal deposits within the coterminous United States represented a third of the entire world's known supply and were more than enough to satisfy U.S. energy needs for three centuries. Admittedly, coal presented problems. Mining was one, air pollution another, though modern technologies were at work on both.

At Tunipah, what pollution there was would be far removed from inhabited or recreation areas. Something else Tunipah would do was permit the closing of some of GSP&L's older, oil-burning plants. This would further reduce dependence on imported oil and produce big cost savings.

Logic favored the Tunipah project. But, as all public utilities had learned, logic didn't rule if a handful of determined objectors decided otherwise.

"Is there more discussion?" J. Eric Humphrey asked.

"Yes," Teresa Van Buren said. "I'd like a nickel's worth."

Heads turned toward the public relations vice-president, who produced two newspapers, which she spread on the table. "This is this afternoon's *California Examiner* and this one, this morning's *Chronicle-West*. There's not a word in either about last week's power outage. For one day the subject was big news, the next day minor news; after that it disappeared."

"So what?" Paulsen said. "People lose interest."

"The general public thinks of a power shortage as a passing problem," Van Buren went on. "Almost no one is considering the effects of extended power shortages—drastically lower living standards, dislocation of industry, unemployment. And nothing will change that thinking unless we *make* it change."

Sharlett Underhill, vice-president of finance, asked, "How do you *make* anybody think anything?"

"I'll answer that," Nim said. "One way is to shout the truth and go on shouting loud and clear. We all know that in three years we'll be short on reserves, in four years we'll have none. Any fool can see what's coming—three years from now, blackouts every time it's hot; and in six years, blackouts almost every summer day. We have *got* to get new units built and we have to tell the public the consequences of not building them."

"I agree," Van Buren said. "Frankness is likely to improve our chances."

Sharlett Underhill shook her head. "I'm not so sure. And something else—I believe that the kind of statements we're talking about should come from the chairman."

"For the record," Humphrey put in mildly, "I was asked to appear on 'The Good Evening Show' and I deputed Nim. He does that kind of thing quite well."

"He'd do a whole lot better," the PR vice-president said, "if we gave him carte blanche to issue some plain, ugly warnings instead of insisting on the moderate line."

"I'm still in favor of a moderate line." This time the speaker was Fraser Fenton, thin and balding, who held the title of president, though his main responsibility was for gas operations. "Not all of us," he continued, "accept this gloomy view. I've been thirty-five years with this utility and I've seen problems come and go. I believe we'll get around the capacity shortage somehow—"

Nim Goldman interjected, "How?"

"Let me finish," Fenton said. "Right now we encounter organized opposition to everything we are trying to do, whether it's build more plants or increase rates. But I believe most of those in the opposition will eventually become tired, and then we'll go back to the way things used to be, when this utility and others did pretty much what they wanted. That's why we should continue taking a moderate line and not stir up trouble."

"I agree with all that," Ray Paulsen said.

Nim's eyes met Teresa Van Buren's and he knew their thoughts were the same. Fenton and Paulsen, and others like them, represented the majority of entrenched public utility executives, who had grown up in their jobs during easier times and refused to acknowledge that these were gone forever.

There were reasons for this attitude. Utilities, through most of their history, had been in a strong seller's market, able to sell as much of their product as they could produce, the process helped along by abundant sources of cheap power. Only in recent years, as power sources became scarcer, had utility executives needed to face hard, unpopular decisions. Nor, in older days, were they locked in combat with skillfully-led opposition groups.

"I'll admit to being ambivalent," Humphrey told the group, "on this question of should we or shouldn't we bore in harder with our public statements. Let's vote on it. A show of hands, please, for the harder approach."

Three hands went up—Teresa Van Buren's, Nim's and that of Oscar O'Brien, the general counsel.

"Against," the chairman called.

This time the raised hands numbered eight.

Humphrey nodded. "I'll go with the majority, which means we continue what someone called our moderate line."

"Come in," Humphrey said to Nim as they neared their adjoining offices down the hallway from the conference room. "There's something I want you to handle." He stopped to pick up a file from his desk, and they proceeded to the comfortable chairs in the lounge area of his suite.

"I presume you've seen the latest report in here." Humphrey indicated the file, which was labeled:

PROPERTY PROTECTION DEPARTMENT
SUBJECT: THEFT OF POWER

"Yes, I have."

The report, by a department head named Harry London,

described ways in which stealing of electric power and gas through tampering with meters had become epidemic.

Humphrey mused, "We lose an estimated twelve million dollars a year through theft of power—perhaps more."

"That estimate is conservative," Nim assured him.

The chairman drummed fingers on his chair arm. "We can't just sit back and let it happen. We must intensify our measures, if necessary increase our budget for investigation. I want you to tell Harry London that. And emphasize that I expect results."

HARRY LONDON was a short, craggy man—a former master sergeant of Marines and later a Los Angeles police detective. He had joined Golden State five years ago as assistant chief of security. For the past six months he had headed a new department—property protection—set up to deal with thefts of power. Now he and Nim were in London's office, a cramped glass cubicle.

"You read my report?" London asked.

"Yes. So did the chairman." Nim repeated J. Eric Humphrey's decision about intensified action and his demand for results.

London nodded. "You'll get results. Maybe this week. D day in Brookside is the day after tomorrow—Thursday."

Brookside was an affluent suburb some twenty miles from the city center. A pattern of power-theft cases had been discovered there, and now a more thorough investigation was planned. The "raid" would be spearheaded by London, his deputy Art Romeo, and three assistants. There would also be thirty meter readers plus half a dozen service engineers and two photographers.

On arrival at Brookside, the meter readers would begin house-to-house checks of electric and gas meters, searching for signs of tampering. They would also go to specific buildings, selected because of known theft patterns. When anything suspicious was located, the service engineers, backed up by Harry London's property protection men, would move in.

"I'd like to be in on this operation," Nim said.

"Be my guest on Thursday," London replied.

After that they talked about the sabotage at La Mission plant which had killed Walter Talbot and the others. London's background as a police detective had given him contacts with law-enforcement agencies. "The county sheriff is working with the

FBI and our own city police," he informed Nim. "But so far all leads have run up against a brick wall. The FBI believe they're looking for a new batch of kooks without police records—fanatics, crazy-smart in some ways, stupid in others. Because they aren't rational, it makes them harder to catch. But you never can tell. If I hear any rumbles, I'll let you know."

"Thanks, Harry," Nim said. "See you on Thursday."

THREE

The D day force arrived at Brookside at 8:00 a.m. and set up a communications center in the parking lot of a shopping plaza. Immediately the thirty meter readers were driven to areas where they would search for signs of power theft.

Nim reached Brookside at 9:00 a.m., to be met by Harry London, who wore a military-style shirt and smartly creased tan slacks. His shoes were brightly shined. Nim tossed his own suit coat into his Fiat. The sun had begun to bake the parking lot.

"Five clear fraud cases already," London said. "Four residential, one business, and that's a lulu. Do you want to see?"

"Sure."

As they drove away, Harry told Nim, "I've already got two feelings. One, what we'll be seeing today is the tip of an iceberg. Two, in some cases we may be up against professionals."

Harry stopped at a gas station and garage complex which included a tunnel-type car wash. Both men got out. A GSP&L service truck was parked there. "We've called a photographer," London said. "Meanwhile, the service guy is guarding the evidence."

A man in gray coveralls, with a foxlike face, walked toward them. London turned to Nim. "This is Mr. Jackson. He gave us permission to enter his premises to inspect the meters."

"Listen, like I told you," Jackson said, "I'm just the lessee here. It's another outfit owns the building." He appeared worried.

"But you own the business," London said. "And the gas and electric accounts are in your name. Right?"

"The way things are, the bank owns the damn business."

"But the bank didn't interfere with your meters."

"I'm tellin' the truth. I dunno who done it."

London preceded Nim into the gas station office, then to a small room beyond. On the far wall were switches, circuit breakers and meters for gas and electricity. A young man in GSP&L service uniform looked up as they came in. London introduced Nim, then said, "Tell Mr. Goldman what you found."

"Well, the electric meter was put in upside down, which makes it run backward or stop." Nim nodded, well aware of that simple but effective way to get free power. "The job on gas was fancier," the serviceman went on. "Take a look."

Nim watched as the man knelt and traced a pipe which emerged from a wall, then connected to a gas meter. "This is the line coming in from the company main." The serviceman's hand moved to the far side of the meter. "Over here is a line to the customer's outlets. They use gas here for a big water heater and hot-air car dryers. That's a lot of gas. Now look at this." He fingered what appeared to be pipe joints where the two pipes he had pointed to disappeared into the wall. Around each the cement had been loosened, some of it now in a small pile on the floor.

"I did that," the serviceman volunteered, "to get a better look. Those aren't ordinary joints. They're T-joints, connected to each other by another pipe, buried inside the wall."

"An old-fashioned cheater's bypass," London said. "Most of the gas used goes directly from the street to the appliances."

"There's enough still goes through the meter to keep it operating," the serviceman explained. "But gas flows where there's least resistance. There's some resistance in the meter, so most gas goes through that extra pipe—the freebie route."

A pert young woman carrying cameras and equipment came in. She inquired cheerfully, "Somebody here want pictures?"

"Sure do." London indicated the gas meter. "That setup first." He told Nim, "When we get a shot the way it is, we'll chip out the rest of the cement and expose the illegal pipe."

The garageman had been hovering in the rear. He protested, "Hey, you guys can't break up no wall. This's my place."

"I'll remind you, Mr. Jackson, you gave us permission to come in and check our equipment," Harry said. "Tampering with meters is a criminal offense, and the photos we take can be evidence. If you want to review your rights, I suggest you call your lawyer."

"I don't need no lawyer."

"That will be up to you, sir. But when we've finished here, we'll be disconnecting your gas and electricity. They'll stay disconnected until the amount owing is paid."

Outside, London said to Nim, "Ten to one he's in hock too deep to pay. Doubt if he'll tell us who did the work either."

As they got into the car, Nim asked, "Can we prosecute and make it stick?"

The ex-policeman shook his head. "I'll try. But most likely a court will insist we prove that Jackson did the rigging or knew about it. No way we can. Word will get around though, and that will scare a lot of other would-be Jacksons."

BY NOON there were already more than forty cases of meter tampering either proved or suspected. During the late morning Nim and Harry had gone to a trim house in a subdivision. One of the property protection staffers, a serviceman and the same photographer as before were clustered around an exterior electric meter near the side door.

"Nobody's home," London said. "The guy who lives here is a tool-and-die maker. It figures. Look at this." He pointed to a tiny hole in the glass cover of the meter. A small, stiff wire protruded through it. Inside the meter the wire extended to a metal disk, which normally revolved as electricity was consumed.

"That wire stops the disk from turning," London said, "so the meter doesn't record. When the wire's removed, everything's back the way it should be."

"Except for that little hole."

"You'd never notice it," the serviceman said, "unless you were looking hard. Clever."

"He won't feel so clever when he gets his next bill," London said.

At the communications center, reports of other discoveries continued to flow in. In one instance an ingenious customer had obtained an extra meter and substituted it for the GSP&L meter for part of each month, during which any electricity used was "free." Another offender had removed his gas meter entirely, filling the gap with a length of rubber hose—a dangerous method, but effective.

"Why do people do it?" Nim posed the question to London.

He had seen enough power thievery to grasp the size and hydra-headed nature of the beast.

"There's lots of reasons," London answered. "Some of it's crooked tradesmen—they're the ones I really want to catch. They put the word around that they'll do the meter fixing—at a price. It sounds easy, and people go along."

Nim nodded. "And most public utilities are so huge and impersonal, people don't equate power theft with stealing."

"AT THE risk of inflating your ego," Ruth Goldman said across the breakfast table, "you were pretty good on 'The Good Evening Show' last night."

It was Wednesday. Almost a week had passed since D day at Brookside. Leah and Benjy had left for an all-day recreation program, and Nim was having a leisurely breakfast with his wife.

Ruth had on an attractive green housecoat in vivid contrast to her neatly combed black hair and her milk-and-roses complexion. No matter how early it was, she always looked impeccable. Why was it, Nim speculated guiltily, that a man could lose sexual interest in his own attractive wife, yet desire other women? He supposed the answer was familiarity.

"Leah stayed up to watch you on TV," Ruth said. "Benjy wanted to, but fell asleep. They're both quite proud of you, you know. In fact, they idolize you." Ruth paused, then continued. "By the way, a couple of times you looked angry, ready to blow."

"But I didn't. I remembered management's stupid moderate line."

"Birdsong was baiting you, wasn't he?"

"The bastard tried." Nim scowled. "It didn't work."

Davey Birdsong headed an activist group called "power & light for people." The lowercase initials were, in Birdsong's words, "to emphasize we are not capitalists." He had been on the talk show too, where he ascribed the basest motives to everything GSP&L did. He had also attacked the company's latest application for an increase in rates. Despite the provocations, Nim had kept his cool.

"This morning's *Chronicle* says Birdsong's group, as well as the Sequoia Club, will oppose the plan to develop Tunipah." Ruth passed Nim the paper. "It's on page seven."

That was something else about Ruth. Somehow she managed to

stay one jump ahead of most others in keeping herself informed.

The brief item told Nim no more than Ruth had already. But it gave him the idea for a course of action which made him impatient to be at his desk. He gulped his coffee and stood up.

"Will you be home for dinner tonight?" Ruth asked.

"I'll try to be." Nim remembered how many times he had said the same thing, then failed to show.

"Oh, there is one thing," Ruth said. "Mother and Dad would like us all to go over for dinner a week from Friday."

Inwardly Nim groaned. Recently his relationship with his in-laws had become strained. Probably, he thought, because they had heard rumors of his philandering. But Nim knew there was no valid reason not to go to Ruth's parents', as she asked. It didn't happen often. And Ruth demanded very little of him, ever.

"Okay," he said. "Next week's pretty clear. When I get to the office, I'll make sure about Friday and phone you."

Ruth hesitated, then said, "Just tell me tonight. I'm leaving right after you've gone. I'll be out all day."

"Where are you going?"

"Oh, here and there. Do you tell *me* everywhere you go?"

So there it was again. The mystery. Nim felt a stab of jealousy, then rationalized: There was plenty he didn't tell Ruth.

NIM DROVE DOWNTOWN at a leisurely pace, employing the time to think about the Sequoia Club, mentioned in this morning's paper. Though it frequently opposed GSP&L, Nim admired the California-based Sequoia Club. History showed that giant industrial concerns, when left to their own devices, paid little heed to protecting the environment. Therefore a responsible restraining force was needed. The Sequoia Club filled that role. It had a national reputation for dedication in fights to preserve what remained of the natural unspoiled beauty of America. Its methods were ethical, its arguments judicious, and its leadership of the highest caliber.

Nim decided to make a personal appeal to the Sequoia Club's chairman, Laura Bo Carmichael, concerning Tunipah and two other power plants which Golden State proposed to build. Perhaps if he argued convincingly enough, the club might not oppose the projects.

Nim had been driving automatically, paying little attention to street names. Now he noticed he was in front of a stucco apartment building at the intersection of Lakewood and Balboa. It reminded him of something. . . . Suddenly he remembered. The day of the explosion and power failure two weeks ago, the chief dispatcher had produced a map showing life-sustaining equipment in private homes. At Lakewood and Balboa a red circle had warned of a person dependent on a powered respirator. For some reason the user's name had stayed with Nim—Sloan.

On impulse, Nim parked his car and got out. Above a series of mailboxes at the building entrance was a score of names, among them K. Sloan. Nim pressed a button beside the name.

The front door opened and a wizened old man, wearing baggy trousers and a windbreaker, peered at Nim. "You ring Sloan?"

"Yes, I did."

"I'm the janitor. Rings down my place too."

"Can I see Mr. Sloan?"

"Ain't no Mr. Sloan. Miss Sloan. Karen. Who're you?"

"Goldman." Nim showed a GSP&L identification card. "Am I correct in believing Miss Sloan is an invalid?"

"You could be. Except she don't like being called that. She's a quadriplegic. Do you know the difference between that and para?"

"I think so. A paraplegic is paralyzed from the waist down, a quadriplegic through the whole body."

"That's our Karen," the old man said. "You want to see her?"

"Do you know if it's convenient?"

"Soon find out." The janitor led the way into an elevator and took Nim up to the sixth floor. He led the way again and stopped before a door while he selected a key from a large bunch. He opened the door, then called out, "It's Jiminy. Brung a visitor."

"Come in," a new voice said, and Nim found himself in a vestibule, facing a short, dark-skinned woman with Hispanic features. She wore a pink smock similar to a nurse's uniform. From an inside room a pleasant voice called, "Come in—whoever you are."

"Leave you now," the janitor said from behind Nim.

As the outer door closed, Nim stepped into the living room.

"Hello," the same voice said. "What do you know that's new and exciting?"

Long afterward Nim would remember this moment—the first in which he ever saw Karen Sloan—in vivid detail. She was a mature woman, but appeared young and was extraordinarily beautiful. Nim guessed her age as thirty-six; later he would learn she was three years older. Her face was long—with sensuous lips opened in a smile, wide blue eyes appraising Nim, and a pert nose. Her skin was flawless and seemed opalescent. Long blond hair, parted in the middle, fell to her shoulders. Her hands were on a padded lapboard, the long nails manicured. She wore an attractive blue dress.

And she was in a wheelchair. A bulge in her dress showed that a respirator was beneath it, breathing for her. A tube, emerging below the dress hemline, was connected to a suitcaselike device secured to the rear of the chair. The chair's electric components were connected by a cord to a wall power outlet.

"Hello, Miss Sloan," Nim said. "I'm the electric man."

The smile widened. "Do you work on batteries, or are you plugged in too?"

Nim had a moment's nervousness. Whatever he had expected it was not this exquisite woman. He said, "I'll explain."

"Please do. And won't you sit down?"

"Thank you." He chose an armchair. Karen Sloan moved her head slightly and blew softly into a plastic tube extending on a gooseneck. At once her wheelchair swung around so she faced him directly.

"Hey!" he said. "That's a neat trick."

"I can do lots more. If I sip instead of blow, the chair moves backward." She showed him while he watched, fascinated. "My head is the only part of me I can move," Karen said matter-of-factly. "But you were going to tell me something."

"Yes," Nim said. "It all began two weeks ago, the day of the power failure. I saw you on a map." He told her about GSP&L's watchfulness over power users with life-sustaining equipment. "To be honest, I was curious. That's why I dropped in today."

"That's nice," Karen said. "To be thought about, I mean. I do remember that day—well. Suddenly my reading light went off and other electrical things stopped. Not the respirator, though. That switches over to battery right away."

The battery, Nim observed, was a twelve-volt type, such as those used in automobiles. It rested on a tray, also fixed to the wheelchair at the rear, below the respirator mechanism.

"What you always wonder," Karen said, "is how long the power will be off, and how long the battery will last."

"It ought to be good for several hours."

"Six and a half when fully charged—that's if I use the respirator only, without moving the chair. But when I go out, as happens most days, the battery gets run down."

"So if a power cut happened, then—"

"Josie—who you met coming in—would have to do something fast."

They went on chatting, and Nim learned that Karen had been stricken with polio when she was fifteen, just one year before the Salk vaccine went into widespread use in North America and, with Sabin vaccine a few years later, wiped polio from the landscape.

Nim asked, "Do you think about that one year much?"

"I used to—a lot. I'd ask, Why did *I* have to be one of the last few? Then I got to telling myself, What happened, happened. It can't be undone. So I started making the best of what there was, and when you do that, if something unexpected happens, you're grateful. Today *you* came. I don't even know your name."

When he told her, she asked, "Is Nim for Nimrod?"

"Yes."

"Isn't there something in the Bible . . . ?"

"In Genesis." Nim quoted, "*He was a mighty hunter by the grace of the Lord.* My religious grandfather chose the name."

"Are *you* a hunter, Nim?"

Was he? Perhaps, he thought, if circumstances had been different, he would have hunted this beautiful woman. Selfishly he, too, felt sad about that year-too-late vaccine.

He shook his head. "I'm no hunter."

Karen went on to explain that for twelve years she had been cared for in hospitals, much of that time in an old-fashioned iron lung. When more modern, portable equipment was developed it was possible for her to live away from an institution. At first she had gone back with her parents, but that hadn't worked. "It was too much of a strain on all of us." Then she moved to this apartment, where she had been for nearly eleven years.

"There are government allowances which pay the costs. Mostly I manage." Her father had a small plumbing business and her mother was a salesclerk in a department store, she told him. At the moment they were trying to accumulate money to buy Karen a van, which would increase her mobility. The van, which her aide Josie would drive, would be adapted to contain the wheelchair.

Although Karen could do almost nothing for herself, she told Nim she had learned to use a typewriter. "It's electric and I work it with a stick in my teeth. Sometimes I write poetry. Would you like me to send you some?"

"Yes, please. I'd like that." He got up to go and was amazed to discover that he had been with Karen more than an hour.

She asked him, "Will you come again?"

"If you'd like me to."

"Of course I would—Nim." Again that bewitching smile.

Josie showed him out.

THE IMAGE OF Karen, her breathtaking beauty, was still with Nim when he reached his office. His secretary, Victoria Davis, a young, competent black woman, looked up as he entered his two-room suite.

"Hi, Vicki," he said. "Is there much in the mail?"

"Nothing urgent. But there is a 'private and confidential' on your desk." She followed him to his inner office. At the same moment a dull thud caused a water carafe and glasses and the window to rattle.

Nim halted, listening. "What's that?"

"I've no idea. There was the same noise a few minutes ago."

Nim shrugged. Absently he began to open the buff manila envelope on his desk. As he did, the office door flew open and Harry London raced in, his face red from exertion. "No!" he screamed at Nim. "No!" He hurled himself across the room, seized the envelope, and put it down. "Out of here! Fast!"

They hurried out to the corridor, London pausing only long enough to slam both doors behind them.

Nim began an angry protest. "What the hell—"

From the inner office came the boom of an explosion. The walls shook. A nearby picture fell to the floor, its glass shattering. A second later another thud, clearly an explosion, came from somewhere beneath their feet.

"Letter bombs," London said. "That was the fourth. Fraser Fenton's dead, others injured."

FOUR

With a short stub of pencil Georgos Winslow Archambault (Yale, Class of '72) wrote in his journal:

> Yesterday, a successful foray against the fascist-capitalistic forces of oppression! An enemy leader—Fenton, president of Golden State Piss & Lickspittle—is dead!
>
> In the honored name of Friends of Freedom, the headquarters bastion of the ruthless exploiters of the people's energy resources was successfully attacked.

Georgos paused, his thin, ascetic face mirroring an intensity of thought. As always, he took considerable pains over his journal, believing that one day it would be an important historical document, ranking alongside such works as *Das Kapital* and *Quotations from Chairman Mao Tse-tung*.

He began a new train of thought:

> The demands of Friends of Freedom will be announced in a war communiqué today. They are:
>
> —Free supply of electricity and gas to the unemployed, those on welfare, and old people.
>
> —An immediate 25 percent reduction in charges for electric power and gas supplied to small homes and apartments.
>
> —Abandonment of plans to build more nuclear power plants. Existing nuclear plants to be closed immediately.
>
> Failure to accept and obey these demands will result in a stepped-up program of attacks.

That would do for starters. And the threat of intensified action was a real one. Georgos glanced around the cluttered basement workroom in which he was writing. The supplies of gunpowder, fuses, blasting caps, pipe casing, glycerine, acids and other chemicals were ample. And he knew how to use them, as did the other three young freedom fighters who lived in the house and accepted his leadership—Wayde, a scholar like Georgos and a disciple of Marx and Engels; Ute, an American Indian who nursed a burning hatred of the institutions which eclipsed his people's nationhood; and Felix, a product of Detroit's inner-city ghetto, whose philosophy was to burn, kill or otherwise destroy.

Georgos smiled, remembering yesterday's deadly letter bombs.

> Obviously our demands are awaited, because already the press and its docile ally television have begun echoing the Golden State Piss & Lickspittle line that no policies will be changed "as a result of terrorism."
>
> Garbage! Of course terrorism will cause changes. It always has, and always will. History abounds with examples.

Georgos considered some of the examples drilled into him during his training as a revolutionary. That was a few years after getting his doctorate. At Yale his major had been physics, and later he parlayed that degree into a doctorate in chemistry. Later still, the chemistry knowledge proved useful when he studied explosives—among other things—in Cuba. And all along the way he had been increasingly consumed by hatred for what he saw as the decadent tyrannical country of his birth.

Georgos' general disenchantment had not been helped by news that his father, a New York playboy, had gone through his eighth divorce and remarriage and that his mother, an internationally adored Greek movie actress, was again between husbands, having shed *her* sixth. Georgos loathed both his parents, even though he had neither seen nor heard from them since he was nine years old. His costs of living and schooling were paid impersonally through an Athens law firm.

So terrorism wouldn't change anything, eh?

> Terrorism is an instrument of social war. It permits a few enlightened individuals (such as Friends of Freedom) to weaken the iron grip of reactionary forces which hold, and abuse, power.
>
> Terrorism began the Russian Revolution. Algeria won independence from France through terrorism. The PLO, now represented at international conferences and the UN, used terrorism to gain worldwide attention.

Georgos Winslow Archambault stopped writing. He stood up and stretched. Glancing in a small, cracked wall mirror, he fingered his bushy mustache. He had grown it immediately after the attack on La Mission generating plant when he had posed as a Salvation Army officer. According to news reports, a plant security guard had described him as clean-shaven, so the mustache might at least confuse identification.

One thing he had *not* done was grow a beard. People expected revolutionaries to be bearded and unkempt; Georgos was careful to be precisely the reverse. Whenever he left the modest house he had rented, he could be mistaken for a stockbroker or banker.

Only one factor contradicted the cultivated bourgeois image. Georgos' hands were scarred and discolored. In the early days of his interest in explosives he had worked without gloves. He was more careful now, but the damage was done.

The agreeable odor of lunch—stuffed bell peppers—drifted down to him from above. His woman, Yvette, was an accomplished cook who knew what he liked and tried to please him. She was also in awe of his learning, having had a minimum of schooling herself.

As Georgos headed upstairs, he smiled and reminded himself that the war communiqué, with its just demands, must arrive at one of the city's radio stations later today.

LAURA BO CARMICHAEL and Nim Goldman were in the elegant Squire Room of the Fairhill Hotel, where they had met for lunch. It was a week later than Nim had intended, but the turmoil which followed the letter bombing at GSP&L had kept him occupied, helping to plan elaborate new security measures.

The Sequoia Club chairman—a former atomic scientist and an old friend of Nim's—was a small woman in her late sixties with a brisk manner and alert, penetrating eyes. She dressed severely, wore flat-heeled shoes, and did her hair in an old-fashioned bun.

"I'm glad to see you, Laura," Nim said. "I thought that over a meal was a good way to talk about some plans."

"I'll listen to you anytime, Nim, and I'm happy to have lunch. But don't think you can influence me."

Nim sipped a Bloody Mary. "It's about Tunipah mostly."

"I rather thought it would be."

Nim chose his next words carefully. "What I'd like you to consider, Laura, is not just Golden State Power & Light, or the Sequoia Club, or even the environment, but a whole wider spectrum. You could call it basic civilized values."

"Actually, I think about those things a good deal."

"Most of us do, but not realistically enough. Because every one of those values is in peril. Our entire system is in danger."

"That isn't a new argument, Nim. I usually hear it in conjunction with a line like, 'If this particular application'—to build a polluting this or that—'is not approved by tomorrow at the latest, then disaster will be swift and sure.'"

Their waiter appeared and presented two ornate menus. Mrs. Carmichael ignored hers. "An avocado and grapefruit salad."

Nim handed back his menu. "I'll have the same. . . . What seems impossible for most people to grasp," he continued, "is that North America is almost out of natural gas. All that remains is seven or eight years' supply, and even if new gas reserves are found, the best we can hope for is to serve existing users."

"And the reason we're running out of natural gas is because the big utility companies put profits ahead of conservation, and squandered a resource which could have lasted half a century more."

Nim grimaced. "We responded to public demand, but never mind. *How* all that natural gas got used is history. It can't be undone. Now, oil. There are still big supplies untapped, but the way oil is being guzzled, the world could be scraping the bottom of its wells by the turn of the century—*which isn't far away.*"

He stopped, then added, "All right, so much for natural gas and oil. Next, consider nuclear power."

At the mention of nuclear Laura's face had tightened. It always did. She was an impassioned foe of nuclear power plants.

She had been associated with the World War II Manhattan Project. After the first atomic bomb had been dropped, she was horrified. What gave her greatest guilt, however, was that she had not protested the dropping of the second bomb on Nagasaki, and her guilt was unallayed.

Their lunch had arrived, and she paused until the waiter had gone before saying, "You know, I still see the mushroom cloud."

"I think I understand," Nim said gently. "But should what happened then really be a factor in building nuclear plants today?"

"To me the two things are inseparable."

Nim shrugged. "In one way you and your people have won the nuclear battle," he declared. "You've won because you imposed a stalemate by legal ruses and delay. Some of the restraints you insisted on were good; others are absurd. But you made the outcome of any nuclear proposal so uncertain that most utilities simply can't commit themselves anymore."

Nim paused, then added, "Therefore at every point in planning we need a clear alternative route. That's coal."

"Coal and air pollution go together," Laura said. "Any coal-burning plant must be sited with extreme care."

"Which is why we chose Tunipah."

"That choice is wrong for ecological reasons. Certain species of plants and wildlife are found almost nowhere else but Tunipah. Your project would endanger them."

"Is one of the endangered plant species the Furbish lousewort?"

"Yes."

He sighed. Rumors about Furbish lousewort, a wild snapdragon, had reached GSP&L. "You know, of course," he said, "that botanists admit the Furbish lousewort has no ecological value."

Laura smiled. "Perhaps, for the public hearings, we'll find a scientist who takes an opposite view. Then there's the other Tunipah inhabitant, *Microdipodops*—sometimes known as a kangaroo mouse."

"Oh, my God!" Before their meeting, Nim had cautioned himself to stay cool, but he found his resolve slipping. "You'd let a mouse prohibit a project which will benefit millions of people?"

"I expect," Laura said calmly, "those relative benefits are something we'll be discussing in the months ahead."

"You're damn right we will! And I suppose you'll have the same kind of objections to the Fincastle geothermal plant and Devil's Gate pumped storage, both of which are the *cleanest* type of operation known to man or nature."

"You really can't expect me to give away all our reasons for opposition."

There was a silence between them, then Nim said, "Let me come back to where I started. If Golden State Power is blocked in *everything*, the result can only be catastrophic in ten years or less. Long daily blackouts will mean industry dislocation and massive unemployment, maybe as high as fifty percent. There'll be crop failures because of limited irrigation, resulting in food shortages. I tell you, people will go hungry. *It isn't imagination.* It's hard, cold fact. Don't you and your people care?"

"All right," Laura said. "Now it's my turn. Your thinking, Nim, is near-term. Environmentalists are looking at the long-range future. We intend to halt three centuries of spoliation of this earth. If we let ourselves be seduced by voices of expediency—voices like yours—even the little we've achieved will be undone."

"All that I'm pleading for is moderation."

"What you call moderation I see as a step backward. And taking it won't preserve a habitable world."

Nim said scornfully, "How habitable do you think the world I just described will be—with less and less electric power?"

"It might be better than you think," Laura answered. "We'd be moving toward a less materialistic standard of living."

She paused, then continued. "In what was once America the Beautiful we've created an ugly wasteland, belching ashes and acid into what used to be clean air, destroying life—human, animal and vegetable. We've turned sparkling rivers into sewers; now, along with the rest of the world, we're fouling the seas. What we environmentalists have done is dedicate ourselves to preserving something of what's left for generations not yet born, instead of squandering everything here and now."

"I agree with some of what you've said," Nim acknowledged. "But, Laura, you're part of a tiny group which thinks it knows what's best for everyone. You're prepared to ignore practicalities while you have your way like spoiled children. In the end, you may destroy us all."

Laura Bo Carmichael said coldly, "I don't believe we have anything more to say to each other."

FIVE

The earth underfoot vibrated. A great roaring, like a covey of jet airplanes taking off, shattered the silence and a fat plume of steam shot violently skyward. Instinctively those in the small group standing on a knoll pressed their hands over their ears.

Teresa Van Buren, uncovering her own ears, waved her arms and shouted, urging a return to the chartered bus in which the group had arrived. Hastily the twenty or so reporters on the press tour moved toward the bus parked fifty yards away.

Inside the air-conditioned vehicle, with doors closed tightly, the noise from outside was less intense. "We just got lucky," the GSP&L public relations director told the group. "Folks, you had the privilege of seeing a new geothermal well come in."

Through the bus windows the reporters looked back at the drill rig they had been watching when the eruption occurred—a tower-topped mechanism similar to that used in an oil field. Not far away were other wellheads, their natural pressurized steam deflected into a plumber's nightmare of huge pipes, conveying the steam to turbine generators in a dozen buildings.

The press party was in the rugged mountains of California's Sevilla County, site of Golden State Power's geothermal generating plants. Later they would move on to neighboring Fincastle Valley, where the utility hoped to create a further geothermal power complex. Tomorrow they would visit a subterranean hydroelectric plant and the intended site of another. Both proposed developments were soon to be the subject of public hearings. The excursion was intended as a media preview.

"If everyone's ready, we'll move on to lunch," Van Buren said. She motioned to the bus driver. "Let's go."

The bus traveled about a mile within the geothermal field, winding between wellheads, generator buildings and the maze of hissing pipes. It halted finally on an asphalted plateau, beside several house trailers which served as offices and living quarters for crews. Teresa Van Buren led the way into a trailer, where drinks had been set out on tables, and said, "Everybody help yourselves."

Most were on their second drink when a small helicopter, painted in GSP&L's orange and white, alighted nearby. Nim Goldman clambered out and moments later joined the press group.

"My, my!" Nancy Molineaux observed. "Aren't you the important one, to come by helicopter when the rest of us rated a bus!"

Nim regarded the young, attractive black woman cagily. "I had some other work to do this morning," he said, "which is why I left later than you and came the way I did."

Nancy Molineaux was not deterred. "Do all the utility executives use helicopters when they feel like it?"

"Nancy," Van Buren said sharply, "you know they don't."

"Our company," Nim volunteered, "owns half a dozen small

aircraft. Mainly they are used for patrolling transmission lines, checking mountain snow levels, and conveying urgent supplies. Occasionally one will convey a company executive if the reason is important. I was *told* this session was."

"Are you implying that now you're not so sure?"

"Hey, knock it off, Nancy!" a voice called from the rear. "The rest of us are not interested in this."

Ms. Molineaux wheeled on her colleagues. "Well, I *am*. I'm concerned about how the public's money is being squandered."

The conversation was cut short by the arrival of lunch—a capacious platter of hot meat pies and, in large earthenware dishes, mashed potatoes and zucchini. As the group helped themselves to the food, appetites sharpened by mountain air, the tensions of a moment earlier eased.

"I'm sated," Los Angeles *Times* announced at length. He leaned back from the table and sighed. "Better talk some shop, Tess, while we're still awake. How many years are these geysers good for?"

"I'll answer that," Nim said. "But first, what we're talking about are fumaroles, not geysers. Geysers send up boiling water with steam; fumaroles, steam only—much better for driving turbines. As to how long the steam will last, we can only guess. Thirty years minimum. Maybe twice that. Maybe more."

New West said, "Tell us what's going on down there in that crazy teakettle."

Nim nodded. "The earth was once a molten mass. When it cooled, a crust formed. Down inside, though—twenty miles down —it's as damned hot as ever and that residual heat sends up steam through thin places in the crust. Like here."

Sacramento *Bee* asked, "How thin is thin?"

"We're probably five miles above the hot mass now. In that five miles are surface fractures where the bulk of the steam has collected. When we drill a well, we try to hit such a fracture."

"How many other plants like this produce electricity?"

"Only a handful. The oldest is in Italy. There are others in New Zealand, in Japan, Iceland, Russia. None as big as California's. And there's a lot more potential in this country."

"It's also one of the cleanest, safest forms of energy," Van Buren interjected. "And—as costs go nowadays—cheap."

"Two questions," Nancy Molineaux said. "Number one: Tess used the word safe. But there have been accidents here. Right?"

"Right," Nim conceded. "Two serious accidents, when well-heads blew. That is, the steam got out of control. One well we managed to cap. The other—Old Desperado—we never have entirely."

He crossed to a window and pointed to a fenced-in area a quarter mile away. "It's over there."

Inside the fence, steam rose sporadically through bubbling mud at a dozen points. Outside, large red signs warned: EXTREME DANGER—KEEP AWAY.

"When Old Desperado blew," Nim said, "for a mile around it rained hot mud and rocks. Fortunately it happened at night, when few people were at work, and there were only two injuries, no deaths. The second blowout was less severe. No casualties."

"Could Old Desperado ever blow again?" the stringer for a group of small-town papers inquired.

"We believe not," Nim said tersely. "But there's no guarantee. What's your second question, Nancy?"

"It's this: Assuming everything the two of you have said is true, why isn't geothermal more developed?"

"The reason is politicians. Specifically, the U.S. Congress. Most of the land which should have been explored, long ago, for geothermal potential is federal government property. It took ten years of congressional double-talk before legislation was passed to authorize geothermal leasing on public lands—and after that, three more years while environmental regulations got written."

Teresa Van Buren broke in firmly. "That's enough! Let's talk about Fincastle Valley. We'll all be driving there soon."

Nim grinned. "Okay. Fincastle is unoccupied land and we *know* it's a geothermal area, with spectacular possibilities—for perhaps twice the electric power being generated here. Right now our geothermal setup saves ten million barrels of oil a year. We can triple that if . . ."

The briefing, with its information and cross-examination leavened by badinage, rolled on.

The day after the press tour Nim was pilloried in the *California Examiner*. Nancy Molineaux's story about the helicopter was in a box facing the editorial page:

Ever wonder what it would be like to have a private helicopter whisk you wherever you wanted?

Most of us will never experience that exotic pleasure.

Those who do fall into certain categories—the President of the United States, the late Howard Hughes, and, oh yes, executives of your friendly public utility, Golden State Power & Light. For example—Mr. Nimrod Goldman.

Why Goldman? you might ask.

Well, it seems that Mr. Goldman, who is a GSP&L vice-president, is too important to ride on a bus, even though one—privately chartered by Golden State Power—was going his way the other day and had plenty of spare seats. Instead, he chose a helicopter.

Especially damaging was a paragraph which read:

Electricity and gas consumers, already beset by high utility bills, may wonder about the way their money is being spent by this quasi-public company. Perhaps if executives like Goldman were to travel less glamorously, the resultant savings, along with other economies, could help hold down those persistent increases.

It had been a bad day, Nim realized, as he left his office. The combination of recent events—the lunch with Laura Bo Carmichael, the press tour, and now Nancy Molineaux's article—had left him exhausted and melancholy.

DAVEY BIRDSONG, who had been inspecting the Sequoia Club's impressive headquarters in a stately Cable Hill mansion, inquired cheekily, "Where's the chairman's private sauna?"

"We don't have one," Laura Bo Carmichael said a trifle stiffly. She was not entirely at ease with the bearded, portly Birdsong, who, though a naturalized American for many years, still exhibited some of the rough outback manners of his native Australia.

Laura had met Birdsong a few times at outside meetings, and although he seemed to make a point of sounding uncultured and dressed the same way—today he wore shabby jeans and running shoes—the Sequoia Club chairman was well aware he held a master's degree in sociology and was a part-time lecturer at the University of California in Berkeley. He had also put together the coalition of consumer, Church and left-wing political groups which called itself p&lfp—power & light for people.

The declared aim of p&lfp was "to fight the profit-bloated monster GSP&L on all fronts." So far p&lfp had opposed rate increases and the licensing of a nuclear power plant and had urged a take-over of the power company by municipalities. Now Birdsong's movement was seeking to join forces with the prestigious Sequoia Club in opposing the latest GSP&L expansion plans. A meeting with top club officials was to begin shortly.

"Geez, Laura baby," Birdsong observed, his gaze roaming the imposing paneled boardroom where they were talking, "I guess it's real soul inspiring to work in a ritzy layout like this."

She told him, "I'd prefer you not to call me Laura baby."

Grinning, Birdsong said, "I'll make a note of that."

At that moment a door opened and a small, neat man with iron-gray hair and rimless glasses entered the boardroom.

Laura said, "Mr. Birdsong, I believe you know our manager-secretary, Mr. Pritchett."

Birdsong put out a large, meaty hand. "We met on the battle-field a time or two. Hiya, Pritchy!"

When his hand had been pumped vigorously, the newcomer said dryly, "I hadn't considered environmental hearings to be battlefields, though I suppose they could be construed that way."

"Damn right, Pritchy! And when *I* go into battle, I fire every big gun and keep on firing. Oh, I'm not saying there isn't a place for your kind of opposition—you people bring a touch of class. I'm the one, though, who makes headlines."

"Perhaps," the manager-secretary said, "there is a place for *your* kind of opposition. Possibly, even, we need each other."

"Attaboy, Pritchy!"

While they were talking the two remaining members of the Sequoia Club executive committee came in—Irwin Saunders and Priscilla Quinn. Saunders was a balding, gravel-voiced lawyer who handled big-name divorce cases, Mrs. Quinn, a fashionably-dressed socialite. She accepted Birdsong's outstretched hand with reluctance, regarding him with a mixture of curiosity and distaste.

The five grouped themselves near one end of a long mahogany

table, with Laura at the head. "The Sequoia Club is concerned," she said, "about recent proposals of Golden State Power & Light which would be harmful to the environment. We will oppose them at forthcoming hearings."

Birdsong thumped the table. "Three bloody cheers for the Sequoia mob!"

The chairman raised her eyebrows. She continued. "What Mr. Birdsong has suggested in connection with that opposition are certain liaison arrangements between our organization and his."

Attention swung to Birdsong, who eyed the other four amiably, one by one, then plunged into his presentation. "The kind of opposition all of us are talking about is a war—with GSP&L the enemy. Therefore, just as in a war, an attack must be mounted on several fronts. No opportunity should be lost to snipe at GSP&L."

"Really," Mrs. Quinn injected, "I find this talk of war distasteful."

"Causes are often lost, Mrs. Quinn," Birdsong declared, "because of too much softness, an unwillingness to face reality."

"Let's get to specifics," Pritchett urged. "Mr. Birdsong, you referred to several fronts. . . ."

"Right! Fronts one, two and three—the public hearings on Tunipah, Fincastle Valley and Devil's Gate. You people will fight all those projects. So will my gallant p&lfp."

"On what grounds will you oppose?" Laura inquired.

"Not sure yet, but don't worry. We'll think of something."

Mrs. Quinn seemed shocked. The lawyer, Saunders, smiled.

"The fourth front," Birdsong went on, "is the annual meeting of GSP&L, two and a half weeks from now. I have some plans for that, though I'd be glad if you didn't ask me too much about them."

"You're implying," Saunders said, "that we'd be better off not knowing."

"Exactly, counselor."

"Then what," Laura asked, "is this talk of liaison about?"

Birdsong grinned. "Money. And something else about our working together—it would be better if it was confidential, *entre nous*."

"Then in what possible way," Mrs. Quinn asked, "would the Sequoia Club benefit?"

Irwin Saunders said, "I can answer that. The fact is, Priscilla,

400

anything which damages the image of GSP&L in any area is likely to diminish their strength and success in others."

"Why do you need money?" Pritchett asked Birdsong.

"We need it because p&lfp alone cannot afford all the preparations which are necessary if our combined opposition is to be effective. The amount I'm suggesting the Sequoia Club contribute is fifty thousand dollars, in two installments."

"What bothers me in all of this," Mrs. Quinn observed, "are certain implications of gutter fighting which I do not care for."

Mrs. Carmichael nodded. "I have precisely the same feeling."

Saunders interceded again. "In opposing Tunipah, Fincastle and Devil's Gate we shall present reasoned arguments. However, remembering the climate of the times, reason is not certain to prevail. We could use an ally that is more flamboyant, more calculated to excite public attention, which in turn will influence the regulators. Birdsong might add that aggressive element."

"TV and the press love me," Birdsong said. "I give them a show."

"That's true," Pritchett affirmed. "The media has used some outrageous statements of his while they've omitted our comments."

The chairman asked him, "Am I to assume you are in favor of what's proposed?"

"Yes, I am," Pritchett said. "There is one assurance, though, I'd like from Mr. Birdsong—namely, no violence by his group."

"Assurance given! My group despises violence *of any kind.*"

"I'm glad to hear it," Pritchett acknowledged. "By the way, I presume everyone has heard about the latest bombing at GSP&L."

The others nodded. Several days earlier a substation had been sabotaged, though damage was slight. The underground Friends of Freedom had claimed responsibility.

At this point Laura Bo Carmichael announced, "Mr. Birdsong, I'll ask you to leave us now so that we can discuss your proposal privately. We will be in touch with you soon."

Birdsong stood, beaming. "Well, cobbers all, it's been a privilege and pleasure. For now—so long!"

When the boardroom door had closed behind him, Mrs. Quinn spoke. "All my instincts are against trusting that man. I'm totally opposed to any linkage with his group."

"I'm sorry to hear that," Irwin Saunders said, "because I believe his diversionary tactics are exactly what we need to beat these new GSP&L proposals, which is the important thing."

"I must say, Mrs. Quinn," Pritchett remarked, "I agree with Irwin's view."

Priscilla Quinn shook her head decisively. "Nothing any of you say will make me change my mind."

The lawyer sighed. "Priscilla, you're being too prim."

"Possibly that's true." Mrs. Quinn flushed red. "But I also have principles, something which that disgusting man appears to lack."

"Madam Chairman," Saunders broke in smoothly, "the way I count the voting so far is two in favor, one against, which leaves the swing vote up to you."

"Yes," Laura acknowledged. "And I'll admit to ambivalence."

For another twenty minutes the debate went back and forth. Laura Bo Carmichael was weighing mentally the way her vote should go. If she followed her inclination and cast a no, there would be a two-to-two stalemate, which would have the same effect as outright rejection. If she voted for, it would be a decisive three to one.

Laura's instincts about Birdsong paralleled Priscilla Quinn's. The trouble was, she didn't particularly *want* to be linked with Priscilla Quinn—an undoubted snob, a society do-gooder. Something else: if she sided with Priscilla, it would look like a clear case of the women versus the men.

The eyes of the other three were focused on Laura. She hesitated, then she said decisively, "I vote yes."

"That does it!" Irwin Saunders rubbed his hands together. "Priscilla, why not be a good loser and make it unanimous?"

Tight-lipped, Mrs. Quinn said, "I think you will all regret that vote. I wish my dissent to be recorded."

DAVEY BIRDSONG left the Sequoia Club humming a jaunty tune. He had no doubt that the fifty thousand smackeroos was in the bag. He drove his beat-up Chevrolet through the city's center, stopping on a nondescript street, where he locked the car, then walked to a busy thoroughfare and took a westbound bus.

Before leaving the car, he had donned a hat and horn-rimmed glasses. After riding the bus for ten minutes, Birdsong got off and hailed a taxi, which he directed to drive north. A few minutes later he paid off the taxi and boarded another bus, going east.

Birdsong left the second bus, walked briskly for about five minutes, then stopped at a small row house. Almost at once the door opened and he went inside.

In the basement workroom of the Friends of Freedom hideaway, Georgos Archambault asked, "Were you careful in coming here?"

Birdsong growled, "Of course I was careful. I always am." Then he said accusingly, "You botched the substation job."

"There were reasons," Georgos said. "I'll explain."

On a makeshift couch against one wall a girl lay stretched out. She appeared to be in her twenties. Her small, round face, which in other circumstances might have been pretty, was waxen pale, her stringy blond hair in need of combing. Her right hand was heavily bandaged, the bandage stained with dried blood.

Birdsong looked at her and exploded. "Why is *she* here?"

"I was going to explain," Georgos said. "She was helping me at the substation and a blasting cap went off. It took off two of her fingers. She was bleeding like a pig. It was dark; I wasn't sure if we'd been heard. I did the job in a hurry."

"And where you put the bomb was stupid and useless," Birdsong said. "A firecracker would have done as much damage."

Georgos flushed. Before he could answer, the girl said, "I ought to go to a hospital."

"You can't and you won't." Birdsong exhibited none of the affability which was his trademark. He told Georgos angrily, "You know our arrangement. Get her out of here!"

Georgos motioned with his head, and the girl got off the couch and went upstairs. The arrangement Birdsong had mentioned was that no one else should be present when he and Georgos met. The real trouble, Georgos realized, was that he had become soft about Yvette. He had been more concerned about her injuries than the job to be done. Wanting to get her away safely was the real reason he had hurried—and botched.

When the girl had gone, Birdsong said, low-voiced, "Just make sure—no hospital, no doctor. There'd be questions, she knows too much. If you have to, get rid of her. There are easy ways."

Georgos was uncomfortable under Birdsong's scrutiny, but he needed him. For Georgos' source of money had abruptly dried

up. His mother, the Greek movie actress, had hit hard times, her young goddess looks gone forever. Georgos was delighted and hoped things would get worse for her. Just the same, a notification from her lawyers that no more payments from her would be made into his Chicago bank account had come at an awkward time.

Georgos told Birdsong, "We need some long green. Now."

"You'll get it." Birdsong permitted himself a wide smile. "And plenty. I found another money tree."

NIM was shaving. It was shortly after 7:00 a.m. on a Thursday in late August.

Ruth appeared at the bathroom door. She hesitated, then said, "I may be going away." In her quiet voice she corrected herself. "I *am* going away. For a week, perhaps longer."

Nim stared at her. "Why? Where?"

"Mother will have Leah and Benjy while I'm gone, and Mrs. Blair will come in as usual to clean. So it will just mean your having dinner out, and I'm sure you can arrange that."

Nim ignored the barb. He insisted, his voice rising, "You didn't answer my question. Where are you going, and why?"

"There's no need to shout." He sensed an uncharacteristic hardness. "I heard your question, but the way things are between us, I don't believe I should have to answer. Do you?"

Nim was silent, knowing precisely what Ruth meant. If he chose to have a succession of affairs, why shouldn't Ruth exercise similar freedom? Just the same, he felt a stab of jealousy. He now was convinced that Ruth was involved with another man.

"We both know," Ruth said, interrupting his thoughts, "that for a long time you and I have only been going through the motions of being married. We haven't talked about it. But I think we should." This time there was a tremor in her voice.

He asked, "Do you want to talk now?"

Ruth shook her head. "Perhaps when I come back."

Nim said dully, "All right."

THOUGH the exchange with Ruth—jolting in its suddenness—pre-occupied Nim during his drive downtown, activity at GSP&L headquarters quickly eclipsed personal thoughts.

The Public Utilities Commission had just turned down GSP&L's

application for a thirteen percent increase in gas and electricity rates. All morning Nim was involved in conferences in the chairman's office with a procession of executives from the financial and legal departments. The question was: Without the rate increase how could the utility carry on needed construction and stay solvent? The consensus: Without drastic cutbacks it wasn't possible.

Humphrey asked, "Does anyone have a theory about why *everything* we sought was rejected? Did we misjudge the profiles? Where was our strategy wrong?"

"I'm not sure our strategy *was* wrong," Oscar O'Brien, the general counsel, said. "And we sure as hell studied the profiles, and acted on them."

Behind the question and answer was a common practice of utility companies. Whenever a public utility commissioner was appointed, the companies made a detailed undercover study of the individual, including a psychiatric profile. The material was pored over by experts, who searched for weaknesses to be exploited. Later an executive of the utility would strike up a friendship and the commissioner would be entertained modestly at the executive's home or a private resort. No direct favors were asked. Often the tactic worked in a utility's favor. Occasionally it didn't.

Humphrey addressed the finance vice-president. "Sharlett, financially speaking, how do we get through next year?"

Sharlett Underhill, a trim brunette in her forties, normally unruffled, today appeared harried. "The options are limited," she said, "but I'll go over them."

She spread out several sheets of complex calculations. It soon became evident that there were two choices only. One was to cut back on construction and customer service. The other was to cease paying dividends to shareholders. It was affirmed that the first was unthinkable; the second could be disastrous, because it would send GSP&L's stock plummeting and place the company's future in jeopardy.

In the end, J. Eric Humphrey, tired and downcast, pronounced the verdict which the small top-level coterie had known from the beginning to be inevitable. "Management will recommend to the board of directors that payment of all dividends on the company's common stock be suspended immediately."

Never in its history had Golden State Power & Light failed to pay a dividend. As a result, GSP&L was known among investors as Old Faithful. Retirees, relying on regular dividends as their means of support, put their life savings confidently into GSP&L shares. Cautious trustees of other people's money did the same. Thus the omission of dividends would have widespread effect.

A regular board of directors meeting was already scheduled for 10:00 a.m. the following Monday. Presumably at that meeting the management decision would be confirmed, after which an immediate public statement would be made. Meanwhile, precautions were necessary to guard against information leaks.

"Outside this room," Sharlett Underhill reminded the others, "there must be no whisper of what is intended. Also, I must caution everyone that because of the inside information the four of us possess, any personal trading in the company's shares prior to Monday's announcement would be a criminal offense."

"I presume," Nim observed, "that everyone has remembered the annual meeting is in two weeks. We're going to face a lot of angry shareholders."

"Angry!" O'Brien grunted. "They'll be foaming at the mouth."

THE DOOR of Nim's office opened and Harry London walked in.

"Just read about that no-dividend deal," the property protection chief said, settling into a chair. "Thought you could stand a bit of good news for a change."

Announcement the preceding day of the dividend's cancellation, reluctantly agreed to by the board of directors, had caused incredulity in the financial world. Stockholder protests were flooding in, and panic selling had depressed GSP&L stock a devastating nine dollars a share, a third of its preannouncement value.

"Remember D day in Brookside?" London asked.

"Of course."

"We just got four court convictions."

Nim ran his mind over the meter-tampering incidents he had seen personally that day. "Which ones?"

"The guy with the gas station and car wash was one. Another was the tool-and-die maker. In both those cases, and two others you didn't see, the court handed down five-hundred-dollar fines. I got some other news too."

"Such as?"

"All along I've said that in a lot of these theft cases we're dealing with professionals. Remember?"

Nim nodded.

"Well, my deputy, Art Romeo, had a tip-off about a big office building downtown, the Zaco Building, where current transformers have been tampered with and the gas heating system has a massive illegal shunt. We recruited a janitor—we paid him to keep watch—and acting on his report, we were able to make three arrests."

London continued. "The firm that did the illegal work is a company called Quayle Electrical & Gas Contracting. It seems that Quayle has a good-size legitimate business. They also have a string of subcontractors to whom they farm out work. The way it looks now is that Quayle has used the legitimate side of its business as a cover-up for power stealing, which they've been into in a big way." London's voice reflected mounting enthusiasm. "I'm telling you, Nim, we've uncovered an enormous rat's nest."

"It all sounds promising," Nim said. "Keep me informed."

Harry London gave a wide, cheerful grin. "Yessir!"

Nim had the feeling that he was restraining himself from snapping off a smart salute.

SIX

Traditionally the annual meeting of Golden State Power & Light was a sedate proceeding, attended by two hundred or so of the more than five hundred thousand shareholders. But not this year.

At 12:00 noon, two hours before the meeting was due to begin, a trickle of shareholders began presenting credentials at the ballroom of the St. Charles Hotel, where seating had been provided for about two thousand. By 12:15 the trickle had become a flow. At 12.30 it was a flood tide.

Among those arriving, more than half were elderly people, and the mood of most varied between resentment and anger. Only still photographers were allowed inside the meeting hall. Two TV crews, encamped in the hotel lobby, had protested their exclusion to Teresa Van Buren. She told them, "It was decided that if we let television cameras in, it would turn the meeting into a circus."

A TV technician grumbled, "It already looks like a circus."

Soon after 12:30 it became evident that the space would be totally inadequate. At a hastily called conference between GSP&L and hotel officials, it was agreed to open another hall, where an overflow crowd of fifteen hundred could be accommodated. But at 1:40 there was standing room only in the second hall.

"I'm worried as hell," Harry London confided to Nim Goldman. The two were midway between the ballroom and overflow room where the din from both made it hard to hear each other. "Have you been outside?" London asked.

Nim shook his head, then, as the other motioned, followed him through the hotel lobby. Outside the St. Charles Hotel there was a crowd of several hundred placard-waving, shouting demonstrators. The TV crews had come out to film the action.

Some signs being held aloft read:

p&lfp DEMAND
LOWER GAS/ELECTRIC
RATES

KILL THE CAPITALIST
MONSTER
GSP&L

PUT PEOPLE
AHEAD OF PROFITS

Stockholders were still arriving indignant. A small man with a hearing-aid cried at the demonstrators, "I'm just as much people as you are, and I worked hard all my life to buy a few shares—"

He was drowned out by shouts of "Bloodsucking capitalist!" "Power belongs to the people!" and "Public ownership of GSP&L!"

Harry London observed quietly to Nim, "You see your friend Davey Birdsong over there, masterminding this?"

"No friend of mine," Nim said. "But yes, I see him." Birdsong's bulky figure was visible at the demonstration's rear. As the two watched, he raised a walkie-talkie to his lips.

"He's probably talking to someone inside," London said. "He has one share of stock in his name. I checked."

"One share is enough," Nim pointed out. "It gives anyone a right to be at the annual meeting."

"I know. And he has something else planned. I'm sure of it."

IN A small room behind the ballroom stage J. Eric Humphrey was reviewing the latest draft of the speech he would shortly make. As he read silently, turning pages, he would pause occasionally to pencil in a change. Out of deference to the chairman's concentration, the others present—Sharlett Underhill, Oscar O'Brien, Ray Paulsen, half a dozen directors—had fallen silent.

Then their heads turned as a security guard admitted Nim to the room.

"There's an angry mob out there," Nim announced.

"They have a right to be angry," the chairman said. "What *can* you tell people who put their money where they believed it was safe, and suddenly find it isn't, after all?"

"You could try telling them the truth," Sharlett Underhill said, her face flushing with emotion. "The truth that there isn't *anyplace* in this country where the thrifty and hardworking can put their money with an assurance of preserving its value. Not in companies like ours anymore—good, decent, efficient companies, forced into doing what we've done and taking the blame unfairly. And you certainly can't put money in savings accounts or bonds, where the interest doesn't keep pace with government-provoked inflation. Not since those charlatans in Washington debased the dollar and keep right on doing it."

The chairman said thoughtfully, "Sharlett, everything you say is true. Unfortunately most citizens aren't ready to listen yet."

Nim was looking at his watch. "Time to go."

"Now I know," Humphrey said as he led the way out, "how the Christians felt when they had to face the lions."

THE MANAGEMENT representatives filed onto the platform. As they did so the hubbub in the ballroom stilled briefly. Then a few voices shouted, "Boo!" Instantly the cry was taken up until a cacophony of boos and catcalls thundered through the hall.

When the disapproving chorus lessened slightly, Eric Humphrey leaned forward to the microphone in front of him. "Ladies and gentlemen, my opening remarks will be brief."

His next words were drowned out by cries of "You're damned right!" "Take questions now!" "Talk dividend."

When he could make himself heard again, Humphrey countered, "I certainly do intend to talk about dividends, but first—"

A woman stood up and yelled, "You should all resign! You can't even organize an annual meeting."

Other voices echoed, "Yes, resign! Resign!"

Eric Humphrey tried again. "Today's attendance, as many of you know, is unprecedented."

A strident voice: "So was cutting off our dividends!"

"I can only tell you that omission of our dividend was an action which was taken with great reluctance—"

The voice again: "Did you try cutting your own fat salary?"

Several things then happened simultaneously. A large tomato struck the chairman in the face. It was followed by more tomatoes and several eggs. Many in the audience jumped to their feet; a few were laughing, but others appeared disapproving.

Nim, on his feet, near the center of the ballroom, was searching for the source of the fusillade. Almost at once he saw Davey Birdsong speaking into a walkie-talkie. Nim guessed that he was giving orders, and tried to push his way toward Birdsong but found it impossible. The scene was one of total confusion.

Abruptly Nim found himself face to face with Nancy Molineaux. His anger flared. "I suppose you're loving all of this so you can write about us as viciously as usual."

"I just try to be factual, Mr. Goldman. I do investigative reporting where I think it's needed."

Impulsively he pointed across the room to Birdsong. "Why not investigate *him?* He's the one who's creating the disturbance."

"Do you *know* he is?"

Nim admitted, "No."

"Then let me tell *you* something. Whether he helped or not, this disturbance happened because a lot of people believe that Golden State Power & Light isn't being run the way it should be." With a contemptuous glance at Nim she moved away.

What had happened—as Nim suspected—was that Davey Birdsong had orchestrated all movements by issuing commands through the walkie-talkie. As well as arranging the demonstration in front of the hotel, the p&lfp had infiltrated the shareholders meeting by the device of having a dozen of its members, including Birdsong, purchase single shares of GSP&L stock several months earlier.

In the turmoil only a few heard Humphrey announce, "This meeting stands recessed. It will resume in half an hour."

TWICE since calling at Karen Sloan's apartment, Nim had talked to her on the telephone. He had promised to visit her again, but other events had crowded in and the visit had been postponed.

Now he was back in her living room and she bestowed on him the same radiant smile he remembered so well. Then she said, "I know this week has been difficult for you. I read about your company's annual meeting."

Instinctively Nim grimaced. The press coverage had concentrated on riotous aspects. But during the half-hour recess, order had been restored. In the marathon business session that ensued, nothing had changed, but much that needed to be said had been brought into the open. To Nim's surprise the most comprehensive and balanced view of the proceedings appeared in the *California Examiner* under Nancy Molineaux's by-line.

"If you don't mind," he told Karen, "our annual meeting is something I'd like to blot out for a while."

"Consider it blotted, Nimrod. *What* annual meeting?"

Kitchen sounds were audible from the adjoining room. When Nim had telephoned this morning, Karen invited him for lunch. Now Josie was preparing the meal.

"By the way," Karen said, "I hope you don't mind, but my parents are dropping in after lunch. It's my mother's day off and my father is working on a plumbing job not far from here."

Her parents, Karen explained, were originally from Austria and, in their teens during the mid-1930s, were brought to the United States as immigrants while war clouds gathered over Europe. In California they met, married and had two children—Cynthia and, three years later, Karen.

Josie appeared, wheeling a loaded tea cart. She set a small table in front of Nim and fitted a tray to Karen's wheelchair. From the cart she served cold salmon with a salad and warm French bread. Then, after pouring chilled white wine into two glasses, she asked Karen, "Shall I feed you or will Mr. Goldman?"

"Nimrod," Karen asked, "would you like to?"

Nim hesitated, but only for a moment. Then he said, "Yes, but if I do anything wrong, you'll have to tell me."

"It's easy. When I open my mouth, you pop some food in."

Near the end of the meal Karen said, "I've told you a lot about me. Now tell me more about you."

Nim began casually, speaking of his work, his marriage to Ruth, his children. Then, prompted by questioning from Karen, he spoke of his doubts—about where his own life was headed, the future of his marriage. But he was interrupted by the sharp note of a buzzer followed by voices—Josie's and others.

Karen called, "Come in!" and a moment later said, "Nimrod, I'd like you to meet my parents."

An elderly, dignified man with a thatch of graying hair and a weather-beaten face, extended his hand. "I'm Luther Sloan, Mr. Goldman. This is my wife, Henrietta. Karen told us about you."

Karen's mother shook hands. "It's good of you, Mr. Goldman, to visit our daughter." She was a small, neat woman. Once, Nim thought, she was probably beautiful, but now her face was aged, while her eyes betrayed strain and weariness.

As the Sloans sat down, Josie brought in a pot of coffee and four cups. Mrs. Sloan poured and helped Karen with hers.

"Daddy," Karen said, "how's your business going?"

"Not as good as it might. Materials cost so much. When I add labor, people think I'm cheating." Luther Sloan sighed. "Some days, I tell you, it's scarcely worth the trouble."

"Anyway, Karen," Henrietta said, "your father's business problems won't make the slightest difference to our getting you a van. We have almost enough money for a down payment."

"Mother," Karen protested, "I've said before, there isn't any urgency. I'm managing to get outdoors. Josie goes with me."

"But not as far as you could go." The mother's mouth set firmly. "I promise you, there *will* be a van. Soon."

"I've been thinking about that too," Nim said. "Last time I was here, Karen mentioned it. You know, my company often has small vans which are sold off after they've been used a year or two. If you like, I could ask our people to look out for something."

Luther Sloan brightened. "That would be a large help. Of course, any van will need adapting so the wheelchair can go in."

"Maybe we can help with that as well." Nim said.

They went on talking until, glancing at his watch, Nim announced, "I have to go."

"So do we," Luther Sloan said. "I am renewing some gas lines in an old building near here—for *your* gas, Mr. Goldman."

Karen's parents took their leave affectionately. Nim followed them out. With a smile Karen told him, "Come again soon."

In the elevator, all three were briefly silent, then Henrietta said, "We try to do the best we can for Karen. We wish it could be more."

Nim said, "I don't believe Karen feels that way. From what she's told me, she appreciates everything you've done for her."

Henrietta shook her head emphatically. "Whatever we do is the *least* we can do. Even then, it is a poor way to make up for what happened to Karen—because of what *we* did."

Luther put a hand gently on his wife's arm. "*Liebchen*, do not do this to yourself. It does no good." He sighed, then abruptly queried Nim. "Did Karen tell you how she contracted polio?"

"No. Well, not exactly."

They reached the street floor, and went outside, pausing as Henrietta said, "Karen was fifteen. She was a straight A student; she took part in school athletics. Everything ahead seemed good."

"The point my wife is making," Luther said, "is that that summer the two of us had arranged to go to Europe, with others from our Lutheran church. We had arranged, while we were gone, that Karen should go to summer camp. We told ourselves that some time in the country would be good for her—"

"The real truth is," Henrietta said, "we were thinking more of ourselves than Karen."

Her husband went on as if he had not been interrupted. "But Karen did not want to go to camp. There was a boy she was seeing. She wanted to stay home and be near him. But Cynthia was away; Karen would have been alone."

"Karen argued and argued," Henrietta said. "She said being alone did not matter and, as to the boy, that we could trust her. She even talked about having a premonition that if she went as we wished, something would go wrong. I will never forget that."

Once more Luther took up the narrative. "The upshot was, we insisted Karen go to camp. While she was there, a polio outbreak happened. Karen was one of the victims."

"If only she had stayed home—" Henrietta began.

"That's enough!" her husband broke in. "I'm sure Mr. Goldman has the picture."

"Yes," Nim said softly. "I do." Then he added, "I don't see why you should go on blaming yourselves for circumstances . . ." A glance from Luther silenced him. Nim realized that there was nothing else to say.

"Henrietta's right," Luther said. "I *do* think the same way she does. Both of us will take the guilt with us to our graves."

His wife put in, "So you see what I mean when I say that whatever we do for Karen is really nothing."

"It's a lot more than nothing," Nim said. "And thank you for telling me. I'll try to do something about the van soon."

J. ERIC HUMPHREY, Ray Paulsen, Teresa Van Buren, Oscar O'Brien and Nim were seated informally in the chairman's office suite. In less than two weeks public hearings on the proposed coal-burning, high-capacity generating plant at Tunipah would begin.

"About the upcoming hearings," Humphrey said incisively. "I want our own participation to be of the highest caliber. Our presentation must be factual, dignified. The opposition will try to provoke us. We must resist."

The moderate line, Nim realized, was still in effect.

At the Tunipah hearings Nim would present the broad sweep of the project, while others would testify on technical matters. Oscar O'Brien would lead all the GSP&L witnesses through interrogation. Nim and O'Brien already had had several rehearsals, in which Ray Paulsen shared.

During their work with O'Brien, Paulsen and Nim had suppressed their normal antagonism. Taking advantage of this quasi amiability, Nim had raised the subject of a used van for Karen Sloan because transportation was a department under power supply. To Nim's surprise, Paulsen was helpful. He had located a van and more than that, he was personally designing some modifications that would facilitate loading Karen's wheelchair into it. Karen telephoned Nim to say that a GSP&L mechanic had visited her to measure her chair and check on electrical connections.

"One of the best things that's ever happened to me," she said, "was your seeing that red circle on the map that day and afterward coming here. Speaking of that, when are you coming again, dear Nimrod? Soon, I hope."

He had promised he would.

SEVEN

It was the second day of hearings on the license application for Tunipah. J. Eric Humphrey had been summoned as the utility's first witness. O'Brien had led him quickly through a recital of the need for Tunipah and the site's advantages. Then there had been a more lengthy questioning by the counsel for the commission, who was followed by Roderick Pritchett of the Sequoia Club.

Davey Birdsong, appearing for p&lfp, was now cross-examining Humphrey, who sat red-faced and uncomfortable in the witness chair. Birdsong asked, "How much do you get paid each year?"

The GSP&L chairman glanced at O'Brien, at counsel's table, then answered, "Two hundred and forty-five thousand dollars."

Birdsong waved a hand airily. "No, sport, you misunderstand me. I didn't ask the capitalization of Golden State Power & Light. I asked how much bread *you* earn."

Humphrey, unamused, replied, "That is the figure I gave."

Someone in the audience called out, "Too damn much! We consumers are the ones who pay it!"

On the bench above, the presiding commissioner tapped his gavel and commanded, "Order!" The commissioner, in his midthirties and with a pink, boyish face, had been appointed to his post a year ago after service in the ruling political party. He was an accountant by training.

Now he regarded Birdsong, who was wearing his uniform of shabby jeans and running shoes. "You asked your question and you received an answer, Mr. Birdsong. Proceed, please."

"Certainly, Mr. Chairman." Birdsong swung back to Humphrey. "Are there other compensations which go with being the big cheese—" laughter from the spectators "—excuse me—the chairman of a public utility? A chauffeur-driven limousine, perhaps?"

"Yes."

"Plus a fat expense account?"

416

Humphrey said huffily, "I would not refer to it as fat."

"How about enormous?"

Humphrey was ill-equipped to handle Birdsong's flashy show-manship. He responded coldly. "My duties involve certain expenses which I am permitted to charge to our company."

"I'll bet! Now then, Eric baby, do you feel that to justify that enormous salary, you have to keep dreaming up schemes—like this Tunipah deal—which will make huge profits for your company?"

Seated in the public section, Nim fumed. Why didn't Humphrey answer bluntly, aggressively, as he could and should? *My salary, Mr. Birdsong, is a matter of public record. I am certain that you knew it before asking the question. Furthermore, the salary is not out of line for the chairman and chief executive of one of the nation's largest corporations; industrial organizations like GSP&L must be competitive in recruiting and retaining executive talent. To be specific: my experience and qualifications would certainly earn me an equal or larger salary elsewhere. And, Mr. Birdsong, if the company's directors and shareholders are dissatisfied with my performance, they have power to remove me. . . .*

But no! Nim thought glumly. The soft approach, excessive worrying about public image, pussyfooting, never standing up to the Birdsongs of the world—all these were the order of the day.

The hearings were being conducted in an oak-paneled chamber in a twelve-story building near the city's center, occupied by the California Energy Resources Conservation & Development Commission (California Energy Commission, for short). Directly across the street was the California Public Utilities Commission. The PUC (for short) would later conduct its own hearings on Tunipah, in large part repetitious, in this same room. Two additional public bodies would conduct hearings: the California Water Quality Resources Board and the Air Pollution Control District.

From his spectator's seat Nim could see the black reporter Nancy Molineaux among the press group. She had been watching Birdsong intently, as if appreciating his performance.

Birdsong was still questioning. "Tell me, Eric old pal, are you aware that projects like Tunipah would not be needed if you got behind conservation seriously? I mean *sold* it—with the same hard sell you're using right now in trying for permission to build more plants to make fatter and fatter profits?"

"In the first place," Humphrey responded, "the objective of Tunipah is to provide service to the community by anticipating increased demands for electricity. Profit is secondary. Furthermore, at Golden State Power & Light we do *not* try to sell more electricity; we urge conservation—*very* seriously. But conservation will never eliminate steady growth in electrical demand."

Birdsong prompted, "And that's your opinion?"

"Naturally it's my opinion."

"The same kind of prejudiced opinion that would like us to believe you don't care whether Tunipah makes a profit or not, when we know that *all* of you at Golden State care about profits—big, fat, *extortionate* profits at the expense of decent working people."

The rest of the words were drowned in cheers. Amid it all the commissioner banged his gavel, calling, "Order! Order!"

Nim realized that if this were a regular court proceeding, the chances were that Birdsong would long since have been cited for contempt. But hearings of this kind were allowed, deliberately, to operate loosely to be sure that all and sundry said their piece.

For another half an hour the p&lfp leader continued his interrogation, hammering home his contention that profits from Tunipah would be excessive and were the utility's major motivation. Nim conceded mentally that, while the charge was false, it would undoubtedly receive prominence in the media.

After two more days of uneventful testimony, the hearing was adjourned until the following Monday.

THREE WEEKS ago Ruth Goldman had startled Nim by announcing her intention to leave home for a while. Now, on Friday evening, during the weekend recess of the Tunipah hearings, Nim found himself alone in their house, Leah and Benjy having been taken by Ruth to their grandparents, with whom they would remain until Ruth's return, whenever that might be. Ruth had been vague about that, just as she had declined to say where she was going or with whom.

But there was nothing vague about her attitude toward him; it had been cool and definite—as if she had reached decisions within herself. What the decisions were, and how he would be affected, Nim had no idea. At first he told himself he should care, but was saddened to find he didn't. At least, not much.

Nim was accustomed to making decisions promptly and planning ahead. But where his marriage was concerned he had a curious reluctance to move, perhaps to face reality. If Ruth chose to seek a divorce, he would be disinclined to try to dissuade her. However, he would not take the step himself. Not yet.

But any discussion would have to await Ruth's return, he reflected, as he roamed the empty house.

Nim mixed himself a Scotch and water, and while doing so he caught sight of a portrait of Ruth painted several years ago. The artist had captured her beauty and serenity. For the sittings Ruth had worn a strapless evening gown, and the flesh tones of her graceful shoulders were uncannily real. There was even, on one shoulder, the small dark mole which she had had removed soon after the portrait was done.

Damn it! Where on earth had Ruth gone and who was the man?

Nim was restless, alone in the silent house. How about some work to occupy his mind? What could he do to prepare himself for his debut Monday as a witness at the Tunipah hearings?

An idea jumped into his mind from out of nowhere. *Coal!*

Tunipah *was* coal. Without coal no Tunipah electric generating plant was feasible. And yet, while Nim's technical expertise on coal was considerable, his practical experience was limited. There was a simple reason. As yet, no coal-burning electric generating plant existed inside California. Tunipah would be the first.

Somehow between now and Monday he must go to a coal-fueled plant. And he would return to the hearings a stronger witness with the sight, sound, taste and smell of coal fresh in his senses.

But a coal-burning plant where?

When the answer occurred to him, he sat at the telephone and dialed Denver, Colorado.

AT DENVER'S Stapleton International Airport, Thurston Jones shook Nim's hand warmly, then led the way to his car.

Thurston and Nim had been roommates at Stanford University. The friendship had endured, though they met only occasionally. Thurston was quiet, good-looking in a boyish way, and brilliant. Coincidentally he had followed the same career route as Nim and now was vice-president of planning for Public Service Company of Colorado, one of the nation's most respected producers of electricity and natural gas. Thurston also had what Nim lacked—wide practical experience in power generation by coal.

As they climbed into the car, a Ford Pinto, Thurston said, "It's really good to have you here, Nim." He added with a smile, "Even if you did just come for a taste of coal." He threaded the little car through Saturday morning traffic. "We'll go directly to our Cherokee plant, north of the city," he announced. "It's our biggest. Gobbles up coal like a starving brontosaurus."

"WE BURN seven and a half thousand tons a day here." The Cherokee plant superintendent shouted the information at Nim above the roar of pulverizer mills, fans and pumps. He was a sandy-haired young man whose surname—Folger—was stenciled on the red hard hat he wore. Nim had on a white hard hat labeled VISITOR. Thurston Jones had brought his own.

They were standing on a steel-plate floor near a gargantuan boiler into which coal—which had just been pulverized to a fine dust—was being air blown in enormous quantities. Inside the boiler the coal ignited instantly and became white hot. This heat transferred itself to a latticework of boiler tubes containing water, which promptly became high-pressure steam and ripsnorted to a separate superheater section, emerging at a thousand degrees Fahrenheit. The steam, in turn, rotated a turbine generator which —along with other boilers and turbines at Cherokee—supplied almost three-quarters of a million kilowatts to Denver and environs.

A fine gravel of black dust was underfoot. Already Nim was conscious of a grittiness in his mouth and nostrils.

"We clean up as often as we can," Superintendent Folger volunteered. "But coal is dirty."

For another hour Nim, Thurston and Folger explored Cherokee. A lengthy stop was at the enormous electrostatic dust collectors, whose purpose was to remove fly ash, which otherwise would belch from smokestacks as a pollutant. At length they emerged from the interior onto a walkway near the building's peak, two hundred feet above the ground. The walkway, linked to a maze of others beneath it by steep steel stairways, was actually a metal grating, with everything below visible. Though the day was sunny, the wind up here was cold and biting and Nim shivered. There was a sense of loneliness, he thought, of isolation and of danger.

"If you have your way, there's what you'll see at Tunipah," Thurston said. He was pointing to a gigantic coal pile directly ahead, an area of about fifteen acres. "You're looking at four months' supply for the plant."

"And underneath it all is what was once a meadow," Folger added. "Now it's an eyesore; but we need the coal."

There would be strong objections, Nim knew, to transferring this scene to the unspoiled wilderness of Tunipah.

They descended a metal stairway to a lower level. "Something else you'll find when you work with coal," the plant superintendent was saying, "is that . . ."

Nim wasn't listening. Some fifty feet ahead of him, and behind the backs of the other two, who were facing him, a coal conveyor belt was in operation. The belt carried coal to crushers, which pulverized it for instant burning. Now a portion of the conveyor belt, because of some large coal lumps, was blocked and overflowing. Above the moving belt a solitary workman, perched precariously on an overhead grating, was probing with a steel rod, attempting to clear the blockage.

Later Nim would learn that safety regulations required that the conveyor belt be shut down before a blockage was cleared. But plant workers sometimes ignored the regulation.

Within seconds the workman slipped and fell onto the belt below. Nim saw the man's mouth open as he cried out, but the sound was lost. Clearly he was hurt. The belt was carrying him higher, nearer the point where the coal crusher would cut him to pieces.

Only Nim had seen the accident happen. All he had time for was to leap forward, run, and shout as he went, "Stop the belt!"

Thurston and Folger spun around and raced after Nim.

Nim leaped onto the conveyor belt, landing clumsily, and scrambled forward over shifting coal, toward the dazed workman. The man was less than three feet from the deadly machinery.

Nim reached the workman and grabbed him to pull him back. He heard cloth rip and felt resistance. The man's clothing was caught in the moving belt. The clanking machinery was barely a foot away. Nim tugged desperately, knowing it was the last chance. The workman's right arm, which was ahead of his body, entered the machinery. Bone crushed and blood spurted as the belt moved on. Then, with unbelieving horror, Nim realized his own clothing was caught. It was too late even to save himself.

At that moment the belt stopped, reversed, then stopped again. Hands reached out, helping Nim return to the walkway, lifting down the semiconscious workman. An alarm bell was ringing. Thurston Jones had opened a metal box and was telephoning: "Get an ambulance and a doctor—fast!"

"I MAY not be a hero like you, Nim," Thurston declared cheerfully, "but in this town I do have a little pull." They were in Thurston's living room, Nim wearing a borrowed bathrobe and nursing a stiff Scotch and water. Thurston continued, "Your suit is being cleaned—no mean feat on a Saturday afternoon."

"Thanks."

Just then Thurston's wife, Ursula, came in accompanied by her younger sister, Daphne, a recent divorcée on a get-away-from-it-all visit from Britain. Neither woman was conventionally pretty; both were big-boned and tall. But their breezy personalities were attractive. Nim had known Ursula for eight years. He had met Daphne half an hour ago and liked her immediately.

"There is some other news," Thurston informed Nim. "The guy whose life you saved won't lose his arm. The surgeons say they can piece it together, and while it may not be strong enough to use in a coal plant anymore, at least he can put it around his wife and three small kids. That couple of feet you pulled the guy back made all the difference!"

Just then a reporter from the Denver *Post* arrived, wanting an interview and photographs of Nim. Reluctantly he obliged.

Soon after, Nim's suit was delivered from the cleaners, seeming none the worse for its sojourn on the coal conveyor, and then, with Nim and Daphne wedged tightly into the back of Thurston's Pinto, the four set out for dinner at the Brown Palace.

During dinner Nim and Daphne danced with each other several times, with an increasing closeness. Once, when they were at the table together, she squeezed Nim's arm. "I think you're rather super." And later, on the way home, Daphne murmured in Nim's ear, "Did I tell you I rather fancy you?"

His arms tightened around her in response.

"Leave your door ajar tonight," she said. "Your room's just down the hall from mine."

THEY HAD RETURNED an hour ago. Nim was fast asleep when a sound aroused him—the creak of the bedroom door opening fully. It was followed by another creak, then the click of the latch.

He heard a soft pad of feet and the rustle of a garment. Then she slid in beside him. Arms reached out. In the darkness lips found his own. The kiss was long, passionate.

"Daphne, darling," Nim whispered, "all day I've been wanting this to happen."

EIGHT

The presiding commissioner tapped lightly with his gavel. "Before the examination of this witness begins, I would like to commend him for his courage two days ago when he saved the life of a public utility employee in another state."

In the hearing room there was scattered applause.

Nim had assumed that news reports of the drama on the conveyor belt would be confined to Denver. Therefore he had been surprised to find himself the subject of a story featured prominently in that day's *Chronicle-West*. The report drew attention to his visit to the coal-burning generating plant, and Nim wondered what use, if any, the opposition would make of that.

Among those in the hearing room Nim recognized Laura Bo Carmichael and Roderick Pritchett, representing the Sequoia Club; Davey Birdsong of p&lfp; and, at the press table, Nancy Molineaux.

The utility's portly general counsel, Oscar O'Brien, was on his feet, facing the bench, ready to lead Nim through his testimony. "Mr. Goldman," O'Brien began, "please describe the circumstances which lead you to believe that the proposal being submitted to this commission is necessary and in the public interest."

"The studies of Golden State Power & Light," Nim replied, "supplemented by those of government agencies, estimate that by the middle of the next decade California's demand for electric power will be greater by far than present generating capacities. . . ." Nim strove to keep his tone conversational, to hold the interest of those listening. All in all he remained in the witness chair for a total of seven hours. However, he knew that his real ordeal—a succession of cross-examinations—was still to come.

CROSS-EXAMINATIONS began the next day. The commission counsel, a dry-as-dust lawyer named Holyoak, was first.

Roderick Pritchett, manager-secretary of the Sequoia Club, was next and the interrogation moved into higher gear. "Mr. Goldman, I have here a photograph. I'd like you to examine it, then tell me if what you see is familiar to you."

While Nim studied the eight-by-ten glossy print, a clerk handed out additional copies. Nim was puzzled. Most of the photo was black. Then he knew. It was the Cherokee plant coal pile. Mentally he cursed the publicity on his weekend journey.

"Well," he said, "I suppose it's a picture of coal."

Pritchett was smiling. "What coal and where?"

Reluctantly Nim said, "It's stored coal for use by a Public Service Company of Colorado plant near Denver."

"Precisely," Pritchett said. "Not a pretty picture, is it?"

"No. But the point is—"

"You have already answered my question, Mr. Goldman. Now let's move on. I have a second photograph for you to look at."

Pritchett handed him a color photo. Although Nim failed to recognize the specific scene—a breathtaking, rugged wilderness captured under a clear azure sky—he knew it had to be Tunipah.

Pritchett prompted, "Truly beautiful, is it not?"

"Yes, it is."

"Do you have any idea where that photograph was taken?"

"Tunipah, I presume." There was no point in playing games.

"Your presumption is correct, sir. Now I have a further question." Pritchett's tone sharpened. "Does it disturb you that what you and your company propose to do is superimpose *this hideous ugliness*"—he waved the coal pile picture in the air—"upon this *glorious beauty?*" Now he held up the color photo. "One of the few unspoiled nature sanctuaries in our state?"

Nim answered quietly, "Yes, of course it disturbs me. But I see it as a necessary compromise. Besides—"

"That's *sufficient*. The record will show your answer as yes."

Pritchett continued with other questions, but they were anticlimactic. At length he resumed his seat. The Sequoia Club, through shrewd use of the photographs, had scored heavily.

Next, Davey Birdsong lumbered to his feet. The big man wasted no time. He asked, "How did you get here?"

Nim looked surprised. "Well . . . I came in a taxi."

"In a *taxi?* You mean you *didn't* use your personal helicopter?"

It was obvious what kind of interrogation this would be. Nim answered, "*I* don't have a personal helicopter. Our *company* has several, which—"

"*Several!* You mean you get a choice—like between a Lincoln and a Cadillac?"

Nim said impatiently, "They are mainly for operational use."

"Which doesn't stop you using one when you need it personally, right?" Birdsong reached into a pocket and produced Nancy Molineaux's article published after the press tour.

"It says, 'Mr. Goldman . . . is too important to ride on a bus . . . he chose a helicopter.'" Birdsong looked up. "Is that true?"

"That is a prejudiced report," Nim said, "but—more or less true."

Birdsong pressed on, "Mr. Chairman, I would like this courageous newspaper report entered into evidence to demonstrate the rich living which officials like Goldman here accustom themselves to at the expense of poor consumers. Also it shows why expensive boondoggles like Tunipah, aimed at supporting this kind of habit as well as making extortionate profits, are foisted on an unsuspecting public."

The commissioner consulted with the administrative law judge, then announced, "The document will be admitted as an exhibit."

"Thank *you*, sir," Birdsong said.

It went on and on. What angered Nim was that not once were the important issues—future power requirements based on growth, industry economics, maintenance of living standards—touched on.

Birdsong finally concluded his questioning. After a short recess Laura Bo Carmichael was on the stand.

Despite her slight figure, the Sequoia Club chairman occupied the witness chair with the demeanor of a *grande dame*. Her voice, as she responded to questions put to her by Roderick Pritchett, was crisp and authoritative.

"Will you explain to the commissioners your reasons, and those of the Sequoia Club," Pritchett began, "for opposing the construction of a coal-powered generating plant in the Tunipah area?"

"Tunipah is one of the *very* few remaining natural wilderness areas in California. To despoil it with a huge, ugly, high-polluting industrial plant should be a blasphemy against God and nature."

"Are there," Pritchett continued, "any strains of natural life at Tunipah that have become extinct elsewhere?"

"There are two: a wild flower, the Furbish lousewort; and the *Microdipodops*, otherwise known as the kangaroo mouse."

Nim remembered his argument with Laura over lunch two months ago when he had objected: *You'd let a mouse prohibit a project which will benefit millions of people?*

Evidently the same possibility had occurred to Roderick Pritchett, because his next question was, "Do you expect people to say that human beings are more important than the Furbish lousewort and the *Microdipodops?*"

"I expect a great deal of that kind of criticism," Laura said. "But nothing changes the shortsightedness and folly of reducing, or eliminating, *any* endangered species."

"Would you explain that a little more?"

"Yes. As modern society has developed—urban sprawl, industry— we have upset the balance of nature, banished wild creatures from their habitat, or slaughtered them *en masse*, all the while forgetting that every part of nature depends on all the other parts for continuance and health." Laura paused. Already during her short time on the witness stand, Nim decided, she had raised the level of debate far above Birdsong's gallery-playing pettiness.

She continued. "In the past, environmental decisions were based on short-term expediency, almost never a larger view. At the same time, modern science—and I speak as a scientist—has ignored the truth that progress in one area may be harmful to nature as a whole. Automobile emissions are a huge example. Another is the excessive use of pesticides, which, in preserving certain life forms, have wiped out many more. It is a long list. Meanwhile, we are moving toward environmental suicide."

Her voice rose for the first time. "It is *all expediency*. If the process continues, I foresee the day when a single industrial project—like this monstrous Tunipah development—will be ruled as more important than the last remaining stand of daffodils."

The concluding words brought an outburst of applause. Nim thought angrily, Laura was using her stature as a scientist to make a *non-scientific*, emotional appeal.

He went on seething for another hour as the questions and responses, in similar vein, continued.

Davey Birdsong declined to cross-examine, stating grandiosely, "power & light for people supports the Sequoia Club view, so well expressed by Mrs. Carmichael."

NIM was back in the witness chair, giving new testimony and undergoing additional cross-examination. His tormentor, once again, was Davey Birdsong, who was saying, "Isn't it true, Goldman, that Golden State Power doesn't *want* conservation because conservation interferes with profits?"

"No, it isn't the truth, and it would take a twisted mind—like yours—to suggest or believe it." Nim knew he was being baited, and was rising to the bait, probably just as Birdsong intended.

"I'll ignore that nasty remark," Birdsong said, "and ask another question. Isn't the real reason you people aren't working hard at developing solar energy and wind power, which are available now, is because those are cheap power sources, and you wouldn't make the huge profits you expect from Tunipah?"

"The answer is no. Solar electricity is *not* available in sizable amounts, and won't be until the turn of the century at the earliest. Costs of collecting solar power are far higher than electricity from coal. As to wind power—forget it, except for small applications."

Undaunted, Birdsong resumed his attack. "Let's get back to that phony crisis you keep talking about."

"When it happens," Nim told him heatedly, "you can read those words back and eat them."

Birdsong's face reddened. "*I* won't be eating any words. *You* will! You'll *choke* on words—you and that capitalist gang at Golden State Power. Words from these hearings, which those of us who stand against you will keep going as long as we can. We'll tie you up with every legal blockage in the book. If we have to, we'll go on for twenty years. The *people* will stop your profiteering schemes, *Mister* Goldman. And the people will win!"

The p&lfp leader paused, breathing heavily. At the same moment Nim leaped to his feet, eyes blazing.

"Maybe you *will* stop those plants being built—Tunipah and others—just the way you say. And *if* you do it, it will be because this crazy, self-defeating system gives limitless power to egomaniacs and kooks and charlatans like you."

The room had fallen silent. Nim continued. "But spare us any sanctimonious drivel, Birdsong, about *you* representing the people. You don't. *We* represent the people—ordinary, decent people who rely on companies like ours to light and heat their homes, and keep factories working, and do the million other things *you'll* cut people off from if you and your kind have their way.

"What *you'll* do for people in the end is make them suffer. From desperate shortages, massive unemployment. And where will you be then, Birdsong? In hiding, probably, from the *people* who'll have found out what you really are—a cheat and a faker."

Nim knew he had gone too far. Yet *someone* had to speak out, whatever consequences came. As he paused for breath, the commissioner inquired coolly, "Have you finished, Mr. Goldman?"

Nim swung to face the bench. "No, Mr. Chairman, I haven't."

Having gone this far, Nim decided he was damned if he would get fainthearted. "Hearings like this, Mr. Chairman, are a time-wasting, costly charade. It's time wasting because it takes years to accomplish what ought to be done in weeks. And it's outrageously costly because taxpayers and power users pay millions for this crazy counterproductive system. It's a charade because we pretend that what we are doing makes sense when we know it doesn't."

The commissioner's face flushed crimson. Glaring at Nim, he pronounced, "That is *all* I will allow on that subject, Mr. Goldman." Then he slammed down his gavel. "This hearing is adjourned."

THERE was a buzz of excited conversation as the hearing room emptied. Nancy Molineaux remained at the press table reviewing her notes. Her head came up as Nim passed by. She said softly, "Baby, oh *baby!* Did you ever blow it!"

"If I did," he said, "I'm sure you'll make the most of it."

She shook her head and smiled lazily. "Don't need to make any-thing. You laid it out, ready for use. Man, oh man! *Wait* till you see tomorrow's papers."

He didn't answer and left Ms. Molineaux working on her notes, no doubt seeking the sharpest quotes with which to impale him.

"FROM this moment on," J. Eric Humphrey said, his voice like steel, "you will cease to be a spokesman for this company about *anything*. You will not appear on TV or radio. You will not give interviews to the press. Is that clear?"

"Yes," Nim said. "It's clear."

It was the afternoon of the day following Nim's outburst at the California Energy Commission hearing.

"As to public hearings," Humphrey went on, "you will, of course, no longer appear at any. Other arrangements will have to be made. For the time being, Teresa Van Buren will take your place."

"If you want my resignation, Eric, you can have it."

"No one said anything about resigning," the chairman stated.

Nim resisted an impulse to smile. He knew that he was valuable to Humphrey in a host of ways apart from public appearances. His planning role was one. For the moment he would do nothing rash.

"That is all for now," Humphrey said coldly. It was clear that the chairman would need time to get over his displeasure.

When Nim returned to his office, Teresa Van Buren was waiting. "If you want the truth," the PR director said, "I think you'll be vindicated eventually."

"Thanks, Tess." Nim dropped into a chair. He felt exhausted. "In the meantime," he said, "I'm gagged."

Without making a comment, Van Buren produced a *California Examiner* containing a front-page story by Nancy Molineaux:

GSP&L DISCIPLINES GOLDMAN AND DISAVOWS HIS OUTBURST

Nimrod Goldman, former fair-haired boy at Golden State Power & Light, today stands in disgrace, his future with the giant utility uncertain because of a temper tantrum yesterday, which created turmoil at a public hearing called to consider a proposed new generating plant at Tunipah. Meanwhile, his GSP&L bosses have dissociated themselves from Goldman's vitriolic attack on . . .

Van Buren said apologetically, "There was no way to stop the news being told about your being cut off as a spokesman."

Nim sighed. He still did not regret having spoken out. But it was depressing to be so totally alone, an outcast among his colleagues, which was what it amounted to.

Van Buren said, "Ms. Molineaux goes for the jugular as a habit. You two don't seem to like each other."

"I'd gladly cut that woman's heart out. If she has one."

He thought, It was Nancy Molineaux's description, "Nimrod Goldman . . . today stands in disgrace," which had really hurt. Not least, he realized, because he knew it to be true.

<h1 style="text-align:center">NINE</h1>

"Daddy," Leah said, addressing Nim across the dinner table, "will you get to spend more nights at home now?"

Nim was aware that Benjy was watching him intently, silently endorsing his sister's question. "I might," he said.

Benjy brightened. "And at weekends, too—will you get more time with us, Dad?"

"Maybe."

Ruth intervened. "I think you are being given a message." She smiled, something she had done infrequently since her return home several days ago. She was more serious, Nim was aware, at times preoccupied. The two of them still had not had their heart-to-heart talk; Ruth seemed to be avoiding it, and Nim, depressed from his recent experiences, had not made the effort on his own.

Now they were having an evening meal together—the third in three days, which in itself was unusual. Nim noticed something about Benjy and leaned forward. "What happened to your face?"

There was a bruise on Benjy's left cheek and a cut beneath the lower lip. "Oh, just something at school, Dad."

"What kind of something? Were you in a fight?"

"Yes, he was," Leah said. "Todd Thornton said you're a fink because you don't care about the environment. So Benjy hit him."

Nim said severely to Benjy, "No matter what anyone says about *anything*, it's wrong and stupid to hit people."

His son looked crestfallen. "Yes, Dad."

Nim was shocked that criticism directed at himself would find a target in his family also. He said softly, "I'm truly sorry, if anything that happened to me has hurt any of you."

"Oh, that's all right, Dad," Leah replied. "Mommy explained that you had more guts than all the others put together."

"It's true, isn't it?" Benjy asked eagerly.

"Of course it's true," Ruth said. "But your father can't say it about himself, can he? Which is why *I* told you."

Later, while Nim and Ruth were still at the table sipping coffee, and the children had left to watch TV, he said, "I'd like you to know that I appreciate what you told Leah and Benjy."

"If I hadn't believed it, I wouldn't have told them. Just because you and I aren't Romeo and Juliet anymore doesn't mean I've stopped thinking objectively about outside things."

So there it was, out in the open. He said, with the sadness that he felt, "What on earth has happened to us?"

Ruth answered sharply, "You should be best able to answer that. I'm curious about one thing, though—just how many other women have there been in our fifteen years of marriage?"

Having trouble in meeting Ruth's eyes, he said unhappily, "It was never serious. None of it. Not with any of them."

"That I *do* believe." Ruth's cheeks were flushed with anger. "For that matter, you were never serious about me."

"That isn't true! But if you feel that way, why did you wait until now to bring it up? Why have we never had this kind of talk before?"

"I suppose it was because I kept on hoping that you'd grow out of wanting every attractive woman you set eyes on. But you haven't changed. Also, since we're being honest, there was another reason. I was afraid of being on my own, of what it could do to Leah and Benjy. And I was too proud to admit that *my* marriage, like so many others, wasn't working." Ruth's voice broke for the first time. "Well, I'm not afraid, or proud, anymore. I just want out."

A spark of resistance flared in Nim. Weren't there two sides to everything, including this? "How about *your* love affair?" he asked. "Will your man friend move in as soon as I step out?"

"What man?"

"The one you've been seeing. The one you went away with."

Ruth had dried her eyes. "Do you really believe that? That I went with a man?"

"Well, didn't you?"

She shook her head slowly. "No."

"But I thought . . . ."

"I know you did. And I let you go on thinking it. I decided, spitefully, to let you have a taste of what I'd been feeling."

Nim winced, but persisted. "Then what were you doing . . . ?"

"That's my private business. But it wasn't a man."

432

He believed her. Absolutely.

He thought, Everything was coming apart at once. He wasn't sure if he wanted their marriage to go on or not. Most of what he had done and said recently had turned out to be wrong. "So where do we go from here?" he asked almost plaintively.

"I suppose"—Ruth's voice had gone cold again—"we each get a lawyer and begin staking out positions."

He pleaded, "But do we have to do it *now?*"

"Give me one valid reason for waiting. We both know that nothing is going to change between us, don't we?"

He said bleakly, "I suppose so." There was no point in promising to revise his own attitudes when he wasn't sure he could.

"Well, then . . ."

"Look . . . would you wait a month? Maybe two?" Instinct told him that Ruth, too, was reluctant to take the irrevocable step.

"All right," she said. "Because of what's just happened to you, I'll wait a little while."

"Thank you." He had a sense of relief that there would be an interval, however brief.

GEORGOS Winslow Archambault shivered. The October night was cold and a strong wind knifed around crags and boulders of the dark, lonely hill above the suburb of Millfield, where he was crawling on his belly toward a chain link fence protecting a GSP&L substation. Glancing back, Georgos saw that his woman, Yvette, was just a few yards behind. It was important that she keep up. She had the wire and detonators for tonight's operation, which involved the destruction of three substations by the entire Friends of Freedom force. At one of the other sites, Ute and Felix were working together; at the third, Wayde was operating alone. Their plan called for all three explosions to occur simultaneously.

When he reached the fence, Georgos detached a pair of heavy wire shears from his belt and began cutting a hole. He could see the lights of Millfield below him. All of them would be out soon.

The large substations that were the targets of tonight's triple strike had been chosen carefully. The damage done, if all went well, would cause a widespread blackout. It could be weeks before everything was switched back on. Maybe, after this, more people would take the Friends of Freedom seriously.

Click! The last strand of wire was severed and the cut portion of the fence fell away. Georgos, who was carrying three packets of plastic explosive, wriggled through.

Yvette, who was close behind, followed without difficulty. Her hand had healed—after a fashion—since her loss of two fingers a couple of months ago. However, the stumps were ugly, not sewn up neatly, as would have happened if a surgeon had attended her.

Inside the fence they moved forward. Cautiously avoiding high-voltage lines, Georgos taped plastic explosive to the three large transformers the substation housed. Yvette handed him detonators and played out wire to be connected to timing devices. After all three charges were in place, Yvette passed him, one by one, the clockwork fuse mechanisms with attached batteries. Handling each one gingerly, Georgos connected the wires from the detonators. He glanced at the luminous dial of his watch.

The three explosions would occur in eleven minutes. It barely gave them time to make it back down the hill to their car, hidden in a stand of trees. He commanded Yvette, "Get going!" This time she preceded him through the fence.

It was while Georgos himself was crawling out that he heard the sound of a car. Unmistakably it was using the private gravel road, owned by GSP&L, which provided access to the substation. A security patrol! Georgos stood up. He could see the reflection of headlights on some trees below.

He motioned to Yvette and snarled, "Over here!" He ran across the gravel road, then into a clump of bushes, where he dropped and flattened himself, Yvette beside him doing the same.

The car was approaching, and now the headlights were illuminating the entire area. Still, their chances of remaining concealed were good. Georgos checked his watch. Eight minutes to go.

The car stopped only a few feet from Georgos and Yvette, and a security guard got out. He had a flashlight with a powerful beam, which he moved from side to side as he began making a circuit of the fence. The driver seemed to be staying in the car. The first man had gone partway around when he found the cut fence, and shouted. "Jake! Call in an alarm! Something's funny here."

Georgos knew there was no alternative to what had to be done. He leaped to his feet, reaching to his belt for a hunting knife he carried in a sheath. It was a long, sharp, vicious knife. The leap

434

had carried Georgos almost to the car. One more pace and he wrenched open the driver's door. The startled occupant, an elderly guard, turned. He held a radio mike to his lips.

Georgos lunged. With a powerful upward thrust he buried the knife in the man's chest. The victim began a scream which subsided to a gurgle. Then he fell forward. Pulling hard, Georgos retrieved the knife and returned it to the sheath. He had seen a .38 in the guard's holster. Now he grabbed it and cocked it.

The first guard had heard something and was returning to the car. He called out, "Jake! You okay?" His gun was drawn.

Georgos fired three times, but the second and third shots were probably unnecessary. When the first bullet hit his chest, the guard pitched backward without a sound.

Georgos grabbed Yvette, who had risen to her feet at the sound of the shots. Not knowing if the guard in the car had radioed a message or not, they began running.

They were a third of the way down the hill when the sound of an explosion reached them. Seconds later there was another explosion and the sky lighted up with yellow-blue flashes. Then the reflection of flames from the fiercely burning oil lighted the sky. Rounding a bend, Georgos sensed that something was different. Then he realized: his objective had been fulfilled. All the lights of Millfield were out.

Georgos found their car where they had left it. Minutes later they were on their way, with blacked-out Millfield behind them.

Yvette's voice was hysterical. "You killed those men! You murdered them!"

"I had to," Georgos answered tersely. He was driving carefully; the last thing he wanted was to be stopped by the highway patrol. There was blood, he knew, on his clothing from the man he had knifed, and there would be blood on the knife also.

Yvette whined, "You didn't have to *kill* them!"

He shouted at her fiercely, "Shut up! Or I'll kill *you*."

Yvette continued sniveling. "That one in the car. *He was an old man!* I saw him!"

"He was a dirty fascist pig!" Georgos said it forcefully, in part to convince himself, for despite his anarchist training and the bombings since, he had not killed anyone at close quarters before, and the experience sickened him.

"You could go to prison for murder!"

He snarled back, "So could you. You're in this as much as I am. You were there, a part of it all. Whatever happens to me happens to you. And don't ever forget it!"

She was sobbing now, burbling something incoherent about wishing she hadn't gotten into this.

They were well beyond Millfield when he realized that the area they were passing through, normally brightly lighted, was also in total darkness. This meant that the other freedom fighters had succeeded in their objectives. *The entire glorious battle, fought under his generalship, had been won!*

"WHEN the power failed," Karen Sloan said from her wheelchair, "Josie and I were on our way home in Humperdinck."

"Humperdinck?" Nim was puzzled.

Karen gave him one of her glowing smiles. "Humperdinck is my beautiful van. I love it so much I gave it a name."

They were in the living room of Karen's apartment, and it was early evening in the first week of November. Nim had accepted an invitation from Karen to join her for dinner.

"About the power failure," Karen resumed. "I'd been to a movie—I can do so many things now that I couldn't before—and on the way home all the streetlights went out."

"Almost one hundred square miles." Nim sighed. "Everything."

"We could see it was widespread, so Josie drove directly to Redwood Grove Hospital, which is where I go if I ever have problems. They have an emergency generator. I stayed there for three days until the power was back on.

"It was an awful thing, Nimrod," Karen went on. "Not just the blackout, but those two security guards murdered. Whoever did it hasn't been caught yet?"

Nim shook his head. "It's a group—Friends of Freedom—which the police have been looking for for a long time. They believe the group is small, probably half a dozen people, and that one man is the brains. Whoever he is, he's a homicidal maniac."

Nim spoke feelingly. The effect of the latest bombing on the GSP&L system had been far worse than of any other preceding it. Equally depressing was the absence of usable clues. The police had obtained another voiceprint, matching earlier ones, from the bombastic tape recording received by a radio station the day after the bombings. But, as a detective told Nim, "those voiceprints can only be useful when we have someone to match them with."

"Nimrod," Karen said, interrupting his thoughts. "It's been a difficult time for you. I know because I read what the newspapers said about you, and saw reports on television."

Nim grimaced. "The hearings. I've been told I disgraced myself."

Karen said sharply, "What you said was sensible." She hesitated a moment. "After it happened I wrote some poetry for you. It's over there." She motioned with her head. "On the bureau."

Nim rose from his seat and crossed to a bureau beneath bookshelves. On top he saw a sheet of blue stationery. He read:

> *The moving finger sometimes does go back,*
> *Not to rewrite but to reread;*
> *And what was once dismissed, derided, mocked,*
> *May, in the fullness of a moon or two,*
> *Or even years,*
> *Be hailed as wisdom,*
> *Spoken forthrightly at that earlier time,*
> *And having needed courage*
> *To face the obloquy of others less perceptive,*
> *Though burdened with invective.*

> *Dear Nimrod!*
> *Remind yourself: A prophet's seldom praised*
> *Before sunset*
> *Of the day on which he first proclaimed*
> *Unpalatable truths.*
> *But if and when your truths*
> *In time become self-evident,*
> *Their author vindicated,*
> *Be, at that harvest moment, forgiving, gracious,*
> *Broad of mind, large-purposed,*
> *Amused by life's contrariness.*

> *For not to all, only the few,*
> *Are presbyopic gifts: long vision, clarity, sagacity,*
> *By chance, through lottery at birth,*
> *Bestowed by busy nature.*

Nim read the words a second time. At length he said, "Karen, you never cease to surprise me. I'm moved and grateful."

At that moment Josie marched in with a loaded dinner tray. The food was simple but tasty: a Waldorf salad, followed by a chicken casserole, then lemon sherbet. Nim had brought wine, and during their meal they talked, easily and leisurely.

The subject of Humperdinck, Karen's van, came up again.

"I'm worried," Karen told Nim, "about Daddy borrowing the money to pay for Humperdinck. His bank said no, so he went to a loan company and they agreed, but at higher interest. I know it will be hard for him to make the loan payments, because his business is not doing well, and he and Mother already help me with money when my allowances won't stretch."

Nim said thoughtfully, "Could I contribute a little?"

"No! Absolutely not! Our friendship is wonderful and I cherish it, but I won't take money from you—ever. Besides, you've already helped us enough with Humperdinck." Her voice softened. "I'm a proud and independent person. I hope you understand."

"Yes," he said. "I understand, and I respect you."

"Good! Now, dear Nimrod, you'll only believe what a difference Humperdinck has made to my life if you let me show you. So could we perhaps go to the symphony together?"

"Why not? I'll arrange it."

"I'm so happy," Karen said, "if I knew how, I'd purr!"

Nim heard a discreet cough and turned to see Josie standing at the doorway.

"Oh, Josie," Karen said. "Are you ready to go?" For Nim's benefit she added, "Josie's visiting her family tonight."

"Yes, I'm ready," the other woman acknowledged. "But will you be all right?"

"Well, I suppose so." Karen turned to Nim and said, "Josie won't be back until tomorrow morning. Normally I have a relief aide-housekeeper, but she's not well, so my sister is coming for the night." She glanced at a wall clock. "Cynthia will be here in an hour. Can you stay until then?"

"Of course."

"Well, then," Josie said. "I'll be going, and good night."

A few minutes later they heard the outer door closing.

"I'm glad you're here," Karen said. "I love talking to you."

Their conversation turned again to the Friends of Freedom.

"Why do those people do what they do?" Karen asked.

"A few of us at the company have done some thinking about that," Nim told her. "Remember the police theory I told you about—that the Friends of Freedom group was small, with one man the brains? Well, assuming that to be true, we thought that if we could get, even partially, inside the mind of the leader—we call him X—we'd improve our chances of catching him."

What Nim did not say was that the idea had occurred to him after the latest bombings when the security guards were murdered. Since then he, Harry London, Teresa Van Buren and Oscar O'Brien had met three times for lengthy brainstorming sessions, and while nothing positive had developed, all four felt they were moving closer to an understanding of the unknown saboteurs and X.

"You've assumed your X is a man," Karen said. "Have you considered the possibility of a woman?"

"Yes, but the odds favor a man, mainly because those tape recordings, received after every bombing, are of a man's voice. Also, in history almost all revolutions have been led by men; psychologists say women's minds are too logical and the details of revolution seldom make sense. Joan of Arc was an exception."

Karen smiled. "What other theories do you have?"

"Well, even though the leader isn't a woman, we're convinced there is a woman in the Friends of Freedom. For one thing, X is extremely vain—the tape recordings show that clearly. And he's strongly masculine. We listened to the tone, the choice of words. The description we all came up with was 'a young, robust male.'"

Karen had been listening intently. Now she said, "So your X is *macho*. Where does that lead you?"

"To a woman, because a man like X would need to have a woman around. Also, she has to be a confidante, because his vanity demands it. Look at it this way: the tapes show that X sees himself as a heroic figure. Therefore he would want his woman to view him the same way. So she has to know what he's doing."

"You certainly have an abundance of theories," Karen said.

Nim was silent for a moment, going over in his mind the remainder of the think group's conclusions.

Because of the *modus operandi* and a hint in the latest tape, they were convinced that X was the actual murderer of the guards. Furthermore, they now believed that X's woman was at the murder site.

Their reasoning: the project was X's most ambitious to date and he would want her to see him in action. Which made her not only a witness but an accessory to murder.

So how did that knowledge—or, rather, supposition—put them closer to learning the identity of X?

The answer: it didn't. But it revealed a vulnerability of X to be exploited. How to exploit it, if at all, was something unresolved.

Nim's thoughts were interrupted by the arrival of Karen's sister, Cynthia, who used her own key to let herself into the apartment. She was a tall brunette with a more forceful personality than Karen's, but possessing a similar charm. She was three years older than Karen, which made her forty-two, although she appeared younger.

Karen was tired. It was time for her to go to sleep, so after a brief introduction, Nim said good night to the sisters and left.

IT WAS five days before Christmas, and Nim was with J. Eric Humphrey, discussing several matters that were weighing heavily on the chairman's mind.

One was Tunipah. Hearings on GSP&L's license application were proceeding even more slowly than anticipated. As to other proposed generating plants, including Devil's Gate pumped storage and Fincastle geothermal, progress was equally slow.

Water was another reason for the chairman's concern. Despite two winter storms, seasonal precipitation in California had been alarmingly small. And winter snow was like money in the bank for a huge public utility. When the snow melted in spring, great rivers and streams cascaded downward, filling reservoirs which would fuel a vast network of hydroelectric power stations during the summer ahead. Now, according to estimates, hydroelectric power next year might be reduced by twenty-five percent because of the lack of runoff water.

Over and above this, however, was the chairman's biggest worry of all—oil.

Only that morning, in the *Chronicle-West*, a syndicated business columnist had summed up the situation:

The problem about oil has been creeping up on us like a tiger in the grass. It began with the decline of the U.S. dollar several years ago—our once respected greenback, but no longer good as gold because the dollar's gold backing has been canceled out.

Then, as the dollar plunged because of ineptitude and politics, the oil-exporting nations of the Middle East, North and West Africa, Indonesia and Venezuela raised their dollar prices in an attempt to stay even.

That didn't work. The dollar continued sinking because the U.S. has paid far more for imported oil than it earns from exports. And as more dollars departed for Saudi Arabia, Iran and elsewhere, more were printed by the U.S. Treasury, depleting the dollar's value even further. Finally the oil nations demanded payment in the only money which has never failed to keep its value—gold.

The United States refused to pay in gold. The U.S. doesn't *have* that much gold left, having squandered enormous amounts in futile attempts to demonetize gold. In fact, there's only sufficient in Fort Knox and the Federal Reserve banks to pay one year's oil bill with a bit left over.

Instead, the U.S. Treasury has offered to run the printing presses faster and produce more paper dollars.

But this time the oil nations have been adamant. They have said, in effect, "If we want paper money, we can print our own—without giving away our oil to get it." They now threaten, "No gold, no oil."

Meanwhile, discussions between governments are continuing so a compromise is possible. We'll wait and see.

The uncertainty about oil was an ominous, overhanging cloud. Nearly half of GSP&L's generating capacity was dependent on oil fuel, the bulk of it imported. With natural gas, which had once been available to generate electricity, now in short supply, the prospect of an oil, gas and water shortage simultaneously was something which Humphrey, Nim and other executives preferred not to think about. Humphrey, speculating on the oil crisis, told Nim, "If I were an Arab, I believe that *I'd* refuse paper dollars for my oil. I wonder if the United States will give in and use some of our gold, even though it would not last long?"

Then Humphrey sighed. "As if we didn't have enough to worry about—Tunipah, coal, water, gas, oil—now gold."

TEN

In her office in the Sequoia Club's headquarters, Laura Bo Carmichael hesitated, her pen poised over a check in front of her. It was for twenty-five thousand dollars, payable to power & light for people. The money would be the second installment of the fifty thousand dollars pledged to Davey Birdsong's organization last August, five months ago.

Laura's signature would make the check official. Yet the decision to ally the Sequoia Club with p&lfp had immediately plagued her with doubts. And the doubts had been reinforced by Davey Birdsong's behavior at the Tunipah hearings.

She asked herself again, Had the respected Sequoia Club dishonored itself by the association? She put her pen down, the check still unsigned, and reached for an intercom handset. When Roderick Pritchett answered, she said, "Roderick, could you come in please?"

"It occurs to me," she told the manager-secretary a few minutes later, "that we might reconsider making this second payment. If the first was a mistake, we need not compound it."

Pritchett, dapper as usual, seemed surprised, then ill at ease as he considered how to handle this tricky situation. "Has it occurred to you, Madam Chairman," he said, "that if we withheld those funds, we would be violating an agreement, honorably entered into, and fulfilled—so far—by the other side?"

"But *has* it been fulfilled? What did we get for the first twenty-five thousand—Birdsong's cheap, shoddy tactics?"

"I'd say," Pritchett said picking his way carefully among the words, "that Birdsong's tactics, while rough, have been shrewd. He has caused most of the media's attention to be focused on *opposition* to Tunipah, while the arguments of Golden State Power have received only trifling attention. He also succeeded in demolishing their key witness, Goldman, by provoking him first, then standing back while Goldman antagonized everyone in sight, including his own company."

"I felt sorry for him," Laura said. "I've known Nim Goldman for a long time and while he may be misguided, he's honest and sincere. He did not deserve what happened."

Pritchett said primly, "In these kinds of contests some reputations are apt to get bruised. The important thing, from the point of view of the Sequoia Club, is to win. Where Tunipah is concerned I believe we will."

"And *I've* never believed in winning *at all costs.*"

Nimbly backtracking, the manager-secretary assured her, "What I should have said is that the agreement with Birdsong will help attain our objectives, which are admirable, as we both know."

"But *where* is all that money going?"

"Some of it to Birdsong himself, of course. After all, he's still attending hearings every day, cross-examining witnesses. Then there are his supporters. He's managed to pack the hearings with them continuously."

"Are you suggesting that Birdsong pays those people?"

"Not all." Pritchett chose his words warily. "Let's say some of them have to be absent from work. Also, those same supporters, or others, staged demonstrations at the GSP&L annual meeting."

Laura Bo Carmichael appeared shocked. "A *paid* disruption of an annual meeting! With *our* money. I *do not like it.*"

"May I remind you, Madam Chairman," Pritchett remonstrated, "that we entered into this arrangement with our eyes open. We were aware that Birdsong's methods might be unorthodox, and we agreed there could be things we'd be better off not knowing. Those, incidentally, were Mr. Saunders' exact words."

"But did Irwin, at that time, understand Birdsong's methods?"

"I think," Pritchett said dryly, "he had a good idea."

The point was valid. Irwin Saunders was a rough-and-tumble fighter in the courts and was not noted for ethical niceties.

Laura asked, "And have you heard from Priscilla Quinn?"

"No." He smiled. "But, of course, Mrs. Quinn would be elated if we refused to make that second payment. She would go around telling everyone she was right and you were wrong."

It was a shrewd thrust. If the original decision were reversed at this late stage, it would be remembered that Laura Bo Carmichael had cast the pivotal vote; therefore her embarrassment would be acute, not least because of the accompanying admission that twenty-five thousand dollars of the club's money had been spent unwisely. And Priscilla Quinn would make the most of *that.*

Woman versus woman. For all her determination not to let her sex influence her decisions, in the end it was Laura's womanly pride which proved persuasive. Picking up her pen, she signed the p&lfp check and handed it to a smiling Roderick Pritchett.

"WE NEED MORE violence!" Davey Birdsong thumped a clenched fist angrily. "*And* a lot of bloody, messy deaths. It's the *only way* to stir up the dumb stupid public and get some action."

Across the wooden table which divided them, Georgos Winslow Archambault insisted, "I realize that. But what you are talking about requires organization and time. I'm doing my best, but we can't take on a target *every* night."

"And why not?" The big bearded man glared at Georgos.

Their argument was taking place in the basement workshop of the Friends of Freedom. "I told you before, there's enough bread for whatever you need," Birdsong continued. "And I just got more."

Georgos resented the increasing dominance of Birdsong since Georgos' own source of funds had dried up. "The last attack on the enemy," he declared stiffly, "was our most successful. We caused a power failure over one hundred square miles."

"Sure. And were any of our demands met?" Contemptuously Birdsong answered his own question. "No! And they *won't* be met! Not until there are piles of bodies in the streets. That's the lesson of *every revolution!* It's the only message the docile, moronic bourgeois understand."

"I know all that. Perhaps you have some better ideas?"

"You're damn right I do. Now listen to me." Birdsong lowered his voice. "First," he said, "we ask ourselves, Why are we doing what we are? And the answer is, Because the corrupt, spiritually bankrupt, grind-the-poor capitalist system has to be destroyed to allow *us*—the true believers, we who love our fellow men—to build anew and decently. The destruction, piece by piece, is what Friends of Freedom is beginning to do."

Davey Birdsong continued. "So where does the destruction begin? Ideally, everywhere. But because, so far, we are few in numbers, we choose a common denominator—electricity. It affects all the populace. It makes the bloated rich more bloated still. It allows minor comforts to the proletariat, deluding the masses into believing they are free. It is capitalism's tool, an opiate. Cut

444

off the electricity and you thrust a dagger in capitalism's heart! But more is required than disruption of electricity alone. We must draw greater attention to our objectives by disrupting—destroying —electricity's *people*."

"We already did some of that," Georgos pointed out. "We killed their chief engineer, their president—"

"Piddling numbers! I mean something big, where the killing will be in hundreds. That's when fear will set in, followed by panic. When *everyone* will be scurrying to do *exactly what we want!* And the opportunity we need is coming soon."

He produced a folded newspaper page on which a single-paragraph item had been ringed in red crayon:

POWER GROUP TO MEET

Possible nationwide shortages of electric power will be discussed next month when the National Electric Institute holds a four-day convention in the city's Christopher Columbus Hotel. A thousand delegates from public utilities and electrical manufacturers are expected to attend.

Georgos' eyes were agleam, his earlier resentment forgotten. "All those big wheels! We can mail letter bombs—"

"No! At best you'd kill half a dozen. I have a much better idea." Birdsong permitted himself a grim smile. "During the second day of that convention, when everybody has arrived, your people will plant two series of bombs in the hotel. The first set will be timed to go off at three a.m. That stage will concentrate on the main floor and mezzanine. The objective will be to block or destroy all exits as well as every stairway and elevator. So no one can escape when the second stage begins."

Georgos nodded as Birdsong continued. "After the first bombs have exploded, firebombs—exactly timed—will go off on the floors above, to set the hotel on fire and keep it burning."

A wide anticipatory smile spread over Georgos' face. He said breathlessly, "It's magnificent! And we can do it."

"*If* you do it right," Birdsong said, "not one person on those upper floors will leave that building alive."

"I'll need more explosives—a whole lot." Georgos' mind was working fast. "I know where to get them. And I must have a floor plan of the hotel—at least the main floor and mezzanine."

"We'll draw our own layout. Anyone can walk in there."

"We'll need something else," Georgos said. "Several dozen fire extinguishers—the kind that stand on their own base."

"Fire *extinguishers?* We want to start a fire, not put one out."

Georgos smiled slyly. "The fire extinguishers will be emptied and our time bombs put inside them. You can set down a fire extinguisher anywhere in a hotel without it being suspect."

Birdsong leaned forward and thumped Georgos on the shoulders. "That's diabolical! *Beautifully* diabolical!"

With mounting enthusiasm they continued planning.

RUTH and Nim were on their way to a dinner party being given by Ruth's parents, the Neubergers. Nim had noticed earlier that Ruth was in an easy, cheerful humor—a contrast to her moodiness, and sometimes outright depression, in recent weeks.

It was now mid-January, and even though three months had passed since their talk about divorce, neither had raised the subject again. Basically their relationship remained unchanged. Nim, however, had been spending increased time at home, and perhaps Leah's and Benjy's obvious enjoyment of their father had caused Ruth to hold back from a final confrontation. Nim was still unsure how he wanted their dilemma to be resolved.

At the Neubergers' apartment they received a warm welcome. Aaron Neuberger, short, stocky and totally bald, pumped his son-in-law's hand enthusiastically. Rachel, Ruth's mother, a voluminous woman, clasped Nim in her arms, then held him back appraisingly. "Nimrod, is my daughter not feeding you? All that I feel is bones. But we will put some meat on them tonight."

Nim was amused, yet touched. Word must have reached the Neubergers that his and Ruth's marriage was in jeopardy, and they were making an attempt to hold the family together. Nim glanced at Ruth, who was smiling at the demonstrative reception.

She was wearing a softly draped dress of blue-gray silk, with pearl earrings of the same shade. As always, her black hair was elegant, her skin soft and unblemished, though paler than normal.

As Nim and Ruth moved forward to meet those who had arrived earlier, he whispered, "You look beautiful tonight."

She looked at him sharply and said, low-voiced, "Have you any idea how long it is since you told me that?"

446

There was no time for more. They were surrounded by faces, going through introductions, shaking hands, and eventually they became separated. Among the two dozen or so guests, Nim recognized Dr. Levin, an internist who sometimes attended the Neubergers—an elderly gnomish man with a cherubic, cheerful face beneath a cloud of white hair.

"How are you, Nim?" Dr. Levin said. "Don't see you often. You look well, and Ruth looks especially beautiful tonight."

"Yes," Nim said. "I told her that as we came in."

The doctor nodded. "She conceals her problem, and her anxiety, well." He stopped, then added, "My anxiety too."

Nim regarded him, puzzled. "You're speaking of Ruth?"

"Of course." Levin sighed. "Sometimes I wish I didn't have to treat patients I care about as much as I do your wife. I've known her since she was a little girl, Nim. I hope you realize that everything possible is being done. Everything."

"Doctor," Nim said with a sudden sense of alarm, "I don't have the slightest idea what you are talking about."

"You don't?" An expression of confusion crossed the older man's face. "Ruth hasn't told you?"

"Told me *what?*"

"My friend." Dr. Levin put a hand on Nim's shoulder. "A patient is entitled to be protected against a gabby doctor. But you're Ruth's husband. I assumed—"

Nim protested. "For God's sake, what's the mystery?"

"I'm sorry." Dr. Levin shook his head. "You'll have to ask Ruth. When you do, tell her I regret my indiscretion. But tell her also— I think you ought to know."

With some embarrassment the doctor moved quickly away.

For Nim the next two hours were agony. Twice he eased his way through talkative groups to be beside Ruth, only to find that private conversation was impossible. At last the guests began to leave. Nim and Ruth joined the exodus.

A few minutes later, when they were in the car, Ruth turned to Nim. She said quietly, "I saw you talking with Dr. Levin."

Nim's hands tightened on the steering wheel. "Yes. Is there anything you want to tell me?"

"Such as?"

His pent-up frustration poured out. "Such as why you've been

447

going to Dr. Levin, what you are anxious about, and why you've kept it from me. And, oh yes, your doctor said he was sorry for being indiscreet, but that I ought to know—whatever *that* means."

"Yes," Ruth said. "I suppose it's time you did." Her voice was flat. "I'll tell you when we get home."

They drove the rest of the way in silence.

IT WAS 1:00 a.m. Nim sat facing Ruth in their cozy living room. The lights were low. "All right," Nim said. "Now give!"

Ruth took a deep breath, then began. "You remember that mole I had removed—six years ago?"

"Yes, I do." Nim had recalled it the night he had made the decision to visit Denver, when he had noticed the mole in the oil painting of Ruth which hung in this room. Nim glanced at the portrait now. There was the small, dark mole, on the left shoulder.

"It was a mole which might have had cancer cells. That's why Dr. Mittelman—you remember, he took care of me then—advised me to have it removed. I agreed, and afterward both he and the surgeon said there was no sign of anything having spread."

"Yes, I do remember Mittelman saying that."

"Both doctors were wrong." Ruth's voice dropped to a whisper. "There *were* cancer—melanoma—cells. They *had* spread. Now they're . . . all through my body." She barely managed to get the last words out before her body shook with violent sobbing.

For moments Nim sat numb, unable to comprehend. Then reality penetrated. With a whirlwind jumble of emotions—horror, guilt, anguish, pity, love—he went to his wife and took her in his arms.

He held her tightly, her face pressed hard against his own. "My darling, my dearest love, why have you never told me? *Why?*"

Her voice came weakly, muffled by tears. "We weren't close . . . not loving anymore. I didn't want just pity."

A wave of shame and self-disgust swept over him. Releasing Ruth, he took her hands, pleading, "It's late to ask forgiveness, but I do. I've been a fool—blind, selfish. . . ."

Ruth shook her head. "You don't have to say all that!"

"I want to say it because it's true. I see it now."

"I already told you I don't want . . . only pity."

He urged, "Look at me!" When she lifted her head, he said softly, "I love you, *and I mean it!* I always have, I guess, except I got mixed up and stupid. *Is* it too late?"

"No." Ruth gave the ghost of a smile. "I never did stop loving you, even though you've been a bastard."

"I admit it."

"Well," she said, "maybe we owe Dr. Levin something."

"Listen, dearest, we'll fight this thing together. And there'll be no more talk of separation or divorce."

She said loudly, strongly, "I never wanted either. Oh, Nim darling, hold me! Kiss me!"

He did. Then, as if it had never been, the gulf between them disappeared. For another hour they talked.

About eight months ago Ruth had become aware of a small lump on the left side of her neck. Dr. Mittelman had retired, so she went to Dr. Levin, who ordered extensive tests, including chest X-ray, liver scan and bone scan. The tests were performed over two weeks, which explained Ruth's daytime disappearances. Results showed that melanoma cells, after lying dormant for six years, had suddenly spread throughout her body.

"Whatever else was wrong between us," Nim protested, "you should have told me."

"You had so much on your mind. It was about the time Walter was killed. Anyway, I decided to keep it to myself."

"Your parents don't know?"

"No."

After the test results, Ruth explained, she had begun going to a local hospital once a week, as an outpatient, for chemotherapy. She suffered occasional nausea and some weight loss because of the treatments, but managed to conceal both. Nim's repeated absences from home had made it easier.

Nim put his head in his hands, his shame deepening. He had assumed Ruth was meeting another man, while all the time . . .

Later, Ruth went on, Dr. Levin informed her of a new treatment for melanoma at the Sloan-Kettering Institute in New York. Ruth went there for a two-week stay and a battery of tests.

Now Nim asked the question he had been dreading. "What do they say about the future—the prognosis?"

450

"There is no cure, and it's too late for surgery. But I could have a lot of years left." Ruth smiled wanly. "Also, I don't know whether I'll be better off taking the Sloan-Kettering treatment or not. But immunotherapy, which is what the doctors are working on, is supposed to excite antibodies so they act as a defense against what they call the invading melanoma."

"I'd like to talk to Dr. Levin," Nim said. "Do you mind?"

"Mind?" Ruth sighed. "No, I don't mind. It's so wonderful to have someone to lean on. Oh, Nim, I've needed you so much!"

He held her again. Soon afterward he led the way upstairs. For the first time in many months Nim and Ruth shared a bed, and in the early morning, as dawn was breaking, they made love.

THE following Monday Nim had a talk with Dr. Levin, whose attitude was neither defeatist nor reassuring. "Your wife may have many years of normal life," he told Nim. "But you must also know that her condition could deteriorate rapidly. Treatment, though, whether it's chemotherapy or immunotherapy, will tilt the odds in her favor.

"The only advice I can give," Dr. Levin added, "is what I've told your wife already: live one day at a time, and use it to the full. Don't let her put things off that she wants to do, and can. Come to think of it, that's good counsel for us all."

ELEVEN

Instinct told Nancy Molineaux she was on to something, possibly a major story, though so far she didn't know what she was looking for. She had decided not to confide in anyone yet, particularly the paper's city editor, who was always in a rush for results and could never understand that finesse and patience could be important tools of a good reporter. Nancy had both. And she had been using them since the GSP&L annual meeting when Nim Goldman had suggested angrily, "Why not investigate *him?*"

"Him" was Davey Birdsong.

Goldman, of course, did not expect her to take the suggestion seriously. But after thinking about it, Nancy had.

She had been curious about Birdsong before. She mistrusted

people who were always on the side of righteousness. Her experience was that those kinds of populist do-gooders were usually looking out for number one. She had seen a lot of that at first hand, especially in black communities.

Milo Molineaux, Nancy's father, was *not* a liberal do-gooder. He was a building contractor who, throughout his life, had pursued one forthright objective: to transform himself from a poor black boy from rural Louisiana into a rich man. He had succeeded, and done it honestly, and Mr. Molineaux was very rich indeed.

Yet her father, Nancy had observed, had done more for people of his own race—by providing steady employment, fair wages and human dignity—than a thousand political activists and their kind, who (as the saying went) "had never had to meet a payroll."

She despised the white liberals who acted as if they were trying to atone personally for three hundred years of slavery by behaving as if a black person could do nothing wrong—ever.

She did not despise Nim Goldman. In fact she had come to like and respect him. He had guts and was honest, which was more than you could say for most of those sleazy pontificators at the hearing where Goldman had blown his cool and spoken his mind.

After that hearing, Nancy had written the story she had because she prided herself in being a good journalist. Which meant·being ruthless, putting emotions, personal feelings, second. But none of it had stopped her feeling sorry for Goldman.

So there was a certain justice, Nancy thought, in that having abandoned Goldman as a target, she had switched attention to Birdsong. Birdsong she most assuredly did *not* admire, being already certain that he was a phony and probably a crook.

She had begun by quietly investigating p&lfp. Birdsong, she discovered, had founded p&lfp four years earlier, at a time when inflation, plus increased oil prices, had forced electricity and gas rates substantially higher. Without question the increases caused hardship to lower- and middle-income families, and Birdsong had proclaimed himself the people's champion.

His flamboyance earned him instant media attention, and he capitalized on it by recruiting thousands of members into p&lfp. To accomplish this, Birdsong employed a small army of university students as canvassers. Nancy had managed to locate several who

452

had worked for him. All, without exception, were soured by the experience. "We thought we were helping the underprivileged," one former student, now an architect, told Nancy. "But we discovered we were mostly helping Davey Birdsong."

The canvassers went door to door with petitions addressed to the governor and other state officials, which urged reduced utility rates for hard-pressed residential users. When they had a signature, they solicited a donation of three dollars "to help the campaign," which included a year's membership in p&lfp. "Birdsong promised us," a young woman said, "one dollar out of every three collected, but we only got a fourth of that."

Nancy learned that Birdsong had recruited probably thirty-five thousand members the first year. Over and above the amount paid out to canvassers, Nancy figured that the receipts of p&lfp were probably close to a hundred thousand dollars—cash. And the collection of money by p&lfp was continuing. Then there was Birdsong's other income, from university lecturing and writing.

What did Birdsong do with all that money? True, p&lfp *did* provide an active, vocal opposition to Golden State Power & Light. But even allowing generous expenses and a personal salary for Birdsong, there was *no way* he could have spent more than half of what was coming in. So how about the remainder? The best guess was that Birdsong was siphoning it off.

Nancy couldn't prove it, though. Not yet.

There was a rumor that Birdsong had appealed to the Sequoia Club for financial support. Nancy was certain the wealthy and prestigious Sequoia Club would have no truck with Davey Birdsong. Just the same, she had put out feelers. So far, no results.

The most intriguing question of all came up one day in January when Nancy happened to see Davey Birdsong on a downtown street. Without reasoning why, she decided to follow him. What came next was like something out of an espionage novel.

Although Nancy was positive Birdsong had not seen her, he behaved as if he was determined to shake off pursuit. First, he walked into the busy lobby of a hotel, ducked into a men's room, and a few minutes later came out wearing dark glasses and a soft felt hat. He left the hotel by a side door. Nancy followed.

She almost lost him when he boarded a bus, which promptly closed its doors. Luckily a taxi was approaching. Nancy hailed it, flashed a twenty-dollar bill, and told the driver, a young black, "Keep that bus in sight, but don't make it obvious we're following it. Every time it stops, though, I want to see who gets off."

"Will do, lady! Just sit back. Leave the action to me." The driver was smart and resourceful. Whenever the bus stopped, he managed to position the taxi so she could see clearly. Finally, about four miles from his point of boarding, Birdsong got off.

"That's the one—with the beard," she told her driver.

"Right on!" The cabby accelerated past without glancing in Birdsong's direction, then eased into a curb. "I got him in the mirror, lady. Now he's crossing the street." After a minute or two, "Be damned if he ain't getting on another bus."

They followed the second bus too. This time Birdsong got off after a few blocks and hailed a taxi. As it pulled away, Nancy could see his face peering through the rear window.

Nancy reasoned: there was no sense in pushing her luck. "Let him go. Take me back downtown," she told the cabby. She hoped Birdsong had not detected her taxi trailing him, but if she persisted, he undoubtedly would. Solving the mystery of where he went, and why, would have to be done some other way.

"Geez, lady, kinda hard to figure you out," the cabby complained. "First you wanna tail the guy, then you quit."

Because he had done his best, she explained why she didn't want to be that close and possibly be seen.

"Gotcha," the young driver said. Then he turned his head. "You still wanna find out where the beard goes?"

"Yes." Birdsong's elaborate precautions had convinced Nancy that something important was happening.

"Maybe we could work a deal," the driver said. "Me and two buddies who ain't working. We all got cars with CB radios, and we could take turns following the beard, pulling a switcheroo so he don't keep seeing the same heap. We'd use the radios."

"How much would it cost?" Nancy asked.

"Have to figure that out, lady."

"When you've done your figuring, call me." She scribbled her home phone number on the back of a business card.

He called late that night. By then she had looked up Birdsong's address in the phone book. "Two hunnert and fifty a week," he said. "That's for me and the other two."

She hesitated. But her instincts told her yes.

Should she ask the *Examiner* for the money? Nancy was doubtful. If she did, she would have to disclose what she had uncovered about p&lfp, and she was certain the paper would want to publish the material immediately. But Nancy believed that there was more to come, so she decided to go ahead on her own.

She would pay the money herself and hope to get it back later. If she didn't, it would be no great disaster, for by most standards, Nancy Molineaux was wealthy. Several years ago her father had established a trust fund which provided her with a regular, comfortable income.

Nancy heard nothing from the cabdriver, whose name was Vickery, for six days. At the end of that time he brought her a neatly written report. All of Birdsong's movements were described; they were innocuous. At no point had he shown awareness of being followed or made an attempt to throw any follower off.

"One week ain't enough," Vickery said. "Wanna try another?"

Nancy thought, Why not?

In another seven days he was back with similarly negative results. Disappointed, she told him, "Okay, that's all."

The young man regarded her with unconcealed contempt. "You gonna give up now? Look whatcha got invested!" When he sensed her wavering, he urged, "Go for broke! Try one more week."

She thought about it. She had proof that Birdsong was a fraud. Was he a crook? And would finding where he went so mysteriously help the story she intended to write? Finally, should she cut her losses or—as the kid put it—go for broke? Her instincts told her the answer should be yes.

"Okay, hotshot," she told Vickery. "One week. But no more."

They hit pay dirt on the fourth day. Vickery phoned, then came to her apartment that night. "This aft the beard tried to shake anybody off, the way he did that first day. But we beat the bastard."

The young cabby's report showed that Birdsong had driven his own car from his apartment garage and parked it on the opposite side of the city. Before leaving the car, he had put on dark glasses and a hat. Then he had taken a taxi back across town, followed by two bus rides in differing directions, and finally, a roundabout walk to a block of drab, run-down houses on the city's east side. He went into a house and stayed for two hours, Vickery said. The address was 117 Crocker Street.

After that, the report continued, Birdsong took a taxi to a point a few blocks from where his car was parked. From there he walked to the car and drove home.

Vickery asked, "Wannus to watch the beard some more?"

Nancy shook her head. "No more."

Two days later Nancy was seated in her Mercedes 250SL, observing the house which Birdsong had visited. She had brought binoculars and parked a block and a half away, where she had a clear view but would not be observed herself.

She had been there nearly two hours. It was approaching noon, and there had been no activity at number 117. She was wondering if she should leave when a beat-up brown Volkswagen van stopped in front of the house.

A man got out. Through the binoculars Nancy saw that he was lean, with close-cropped hair and a bushy mustache. He opened the rear door of the vehicle and lifted out two red cylinders, then carried them toward the house. Nancy realized they were fire extinguishers.

The man made two more journeys between the VW and the house, each time carrying in two more fire extinguishers. Six altogether. After the final pair he drove away.

Nancy sat wondering. Why would so small a house need so much fire protection? Suddenly she exclaimed, "Damn!" She had not noted the VW's license number. She was chiding herself when she realized that a young woman had come out of 117. She was slight in build and carelessly dressed in jeans and a pea coat.

Nancy did not hesitate. She started the car and warily followed the girl until she saw her enter a supermarket. Nancy drove into the adjacent parking lot, locked the car, and followed inside.

The girl was at the end of an aisle, putting cans into a shopping cart. Nancy got a cart herself and moved casually toward the girl, who was holding a bottle of vegetable oil in her left hand. Then Nancy noticed on the girl's right hand what looked like an improvised glove. Clearly it shielded a deformity or an injury.

Nancy maneuvered her cart past, then turned, smiled and said brightly, "Hi! Don't we know each other?" She added, "I think we have a mutual acquaintance, Davey Birdsong."

The girl's face went ashen white and the glass bottle fell from her hand, shattering on the floor.

Nancy took the girl's arm. "Let's get out of here," she said. Unresisting, the girl allowed Nancy to steer her toward the Mercedes. As the passenger door was opened, she became alert.

"I have to get back!" She looked at Nancy wildly. "Who *are* you?"

"I'm a friend. Look, there's a bar around the block. Why don't we go there, have a drink? You look as if you could use one."

"I tell you I can't!"

"Yes, you can, and you will," Nancy said. "Because if you don't, I'm going to phone Davey Birdsong and tell him—" She had no idea how she would have finished the sentence, but its effect was electric. The girl got into the car.

A few minutes later they entered the bar. Its interior smelled of mildew. As they sat down, Nancy added, "What's your name?"

"Yvette."

A waiter appeared and Yvette ordered a beer, Nancy a daiquiri. Then the girl asked again, "Who are you?"

"My name is Nancy Molineaux. I'm a newspaper reporter."

"What do you want from me?" the girl whispered.

"Some information. Like who lives in that house you came out of. What goes on there? Why does Davey Birdsong visit?"

"It's none of your business."

Nancy tried a random shot. "Okay, I guess I should have gone to the police in the first place and—"

"No!" Yvette put her face in her hands and began to sob.

Nancy reached across the table. "I know you're in some kind of trouble. If you'll let me, I'll help."

Through the sobbing: "Nobody can help."

"Listen," Nancy said. "I'll make a deal. If you'll agree to meet me again, I won't say or do anything in the meantime."

"When?" Again the mix of doubt and fear.

"A week from today, next Wednesday—same time, same place."

With a nod of agreement Yvette left.

Driving away, Nancy wondered, Where did Davey Birdsong and Yvette fit in? The girl's sobbing at Nancy's remark about the police suggested that something illegal was going on. If so, what? It was like trying to assemble a jigsaw puzzle without the slightest notion of the end result.

ANOTHER piece of the jigsaw fell into place next day.

A mailroom employee of the Sequoia Club, an elderly black woman named Grace, had once asked Nancy Molineaux's help in obtaining city-subsidized housing. All it had taken was a telephone call and use of the *California Examiner*'s influence to get her near the top of the list, but Grace had insisted that if she could ever return the favor, she would.

Several weeks ago Nancy had called her at home and mentioned the rumor that p&lfp was seeking financial help from the Sequoia Club. Would she try to discover, Nancy asked, whether there was any substance to it? Today Grace had visited Nancy at the *Examiner*. They went into a soundproof glass cubicle, and Grace reached into her bag and pulled out a copy of a Sequoia Club memo.

Grace explained. Three envelopes, all marked private and confidential, had come through the mailroom. One was unsealed— probably through a secretary's carelessness—and Grace had slipped it aside. Later, when she was unobserved, she read it and made a Xerox copy. Nancy read the confidential memo carefully:

From: Roderick Pritchett
To: Members of Special Executive Committee

 The second donation to B's organization from the contingency fund, and agreed to at our August 22 meeting, has now been paid.

Nancy asked, "Who were the envelopes addressed to?"

"One to Irwin Saunders, the lawyer. One to Mrs. Carmichael, our chairman, and the other was addressed to Priscilla Quinn, a board member. Is it what you wanted?" Grace asked anxiously.

"I'm not sure." Nancy read the memo again. "It might be."

"You won't let on where that came from?" Grace said.

"I don't even know you," Nancy assured her.

The older woman smiled and stood up.

Wondering if the B in the memo referred to Birdsong, Nancy returned to her desk. She telephoned Irwin Saunders. When he came on the line, she said, "I'd like to discuss the Sequoia Club's donation to Mr. Birdsong's power & light for people."

Saunders laughed. "Nancy, that kind of I-already-know-but-would-like-some-confirmation statement is the oldest ploy in the book. I'm a wily old fish who doesn't take those baits."

She persisted. "But it is our understanding that there's a linkup between the Sequoia Club and p&lfp."

"That's a subject about which I'm unlikely to know anything."

Score *one* for me, she thought. He had not said I don't know.

"My information," she said, "is that a Sequoia Club committee decided—"

"Tell me about that alleged committee, Nancy. Who was on it?"

If she mentioned the names she knew—Carmichael, Quinn—he would be on the phone immediately to caution them. Nancy wanted to get there first. She lied. "I don't have any names."

"In other words, you don't have a damn thing." He was suddenly less friendly. "You're wasting my time, Miss Molineaux."

Even before he hung up, Nancy had been leafing through a phone directory. . . . There it was: Quinn, Dempster W. R. She dialed, and when after the second ring a cool female voice came on the line, Nancy identified herself.

"What is it you want?" Priscilla Quinn asked.

"Mrs. Quinn, when the Sequoia Club executive committee decided to team up with Davey Birdsong's p&lfp, what was—"

Priscilla Quinn said sharply, "That committee meeting, and the entire arrangement, are supposed to be confidential."

Bingo! "Well," Nancy said, "maybe Birdsong talked."

"Very likely. I would never trust that man."

"Then may I ask why you agreed to support his—"

"I didn't. I voted against the idea." A note of alarm entered Priscilla Quinn's voice. "I hope you're not planning to quote me."

"Mrs. Quinn," Nancy pointed out, "you said nothing about our conversation being off the record."

The other woman said indignantly, "Well, I do now."

"It's too late." Nancy paused, considering. "What I *will* do is make a deal."

"What kind of deal?"

"I won't mention that I spoke to you *if* you'll tell me how much money was paid by the Sequoia Club to p&lfp," Nancy answered.

A pause. Then, very quietly, "Fifty thousand dollars."

After she hung up, Nancy sat at her desk thinking.

Fact one: the Sequoia Club was backing Birdsong with money.

Fact two: Birdsong was involved in something he didn't want found out, hence his elaborate precautions when he visited that east-side house.

Fact three: the girl from the house, Yvette, was scared to death about something.

Fact four: Nancy had found out earlier today that number 117 Crocker Street had been rented for the past year to a Mr. G. Archambault, about whom nothing was known.

Conclusion: the story was not ready to break. Nancy would have to wait until her meeting with Yvette six days from now.

NIM was at his desk working on his speech for the National Electric Institute convention, only four days away. His paper, entitled "Overload," was about future power demands.

The meeting was being held locally this year—in the Christopher Columbus Hotel. It would last four days. Because there were numerous social events, Nim had decided that it would be interesting for his family if they moved with him into the hotel for the convention. They were enthusiastic about the idea.

His promise to address the delegates had been made nearly a year ago, long before his removal as company spokesman. When Nim had mentioned the commitment recently to J. Eric Humphrey, the chairman told him, "Go ahead, but stay away from controversy." In fact, Nim's paper would be heavily technical.

GEORGOS Winslow Archambault was writing in his journal:

A day of glory nears! The valiant people's army, Friends of Freedom, fighting the vile capitalists who keep America in chains, will strike a blow to be acclaimed in history.

The people's enemies, consorting under the infamous banner of the National Electric Institute, begin assembling in four days' time. They are in for a grand surprise—and a deserved punishment.

Georgos smiled as he put the pencil down and surveyed the basement workshop, jammed tightly with new supplies.

Everything for the impending operation was knitting together perfectly—planning, equipment, logistics. The first set of bombs (containing high explosive) would detonate at 3:00 a.m. during the second night of the NEI convention, the firebombs from five to ten minutes later. Both sets of bombs, disguised as fire extinguishers, would be placed in position the preceding day.

The fire extinguishers had been bought locally, a few at a time from different sources. Birdsong had helped and now there were almost three dozen—ample for the Friends of Freedom plan. Georgos had emptied out their original contents, then machined the insides of the casings to weaken them. After that, in those which were to be firebombs, he inserted plastic bottles filled with gasoline, plus explosive charges and timing mechanisms. In the case of the high-explosive bombs, which would block off hotel exits, he substituted dynamite for the gasoline. Georgos had made three trips to the hotel to decide on the exact placement of the bombs.

With Birdsong's money Georgos had bought a used red pickup truck, now hidden in a locked garage adjoining a second Friends of Freedom hideaway—a recently rented apartment in the city's North Castle district—which only Georgos knew about.

The red truck was already lettered neatly on both sides: FIRE PROTECTION SERVICE, INC. A masterstroke (another of Georgos' ideas) was the choice of an open pickup. The vehicle's contents—seemingly fire extinguishers—would be exposed for all to see.

Georgos' own regular transportation, his old VW van, was in a private parking garage not far from the Crocker Street house and would not be used in the NEI attack.

Another masterstroke was Birdsong's diversionary scheme to stage an anti-GSP&L demonstration with about a hundred p&lfp supporters at the hotel at the same time that the fire-extinguisher bombs would be unloaded at the service entrance. The demonstrators would keep any security forces on the scene busy, permitting the red pickup to pass unnoticed.

For extra cover, in case any freedom fighter were questioned at the hotel, Birdsong had had some Fire Protection Service, Inc., work orders printed. These were now filled in. They instructed that supplementary fire extinguishers were to be delivered to the hotel and left in place for subsequent mounting.

As far as Georgos could see, they had thought of everything.

TWELVE

From the living-room window of a twenty-fifth-floor suite of the Christopher Columbus Hotel, Nim was admiring the panoramic view of the historic city, its busy harbor touched by the morning sun.

Bringing his family to the National Electric Institute convention, now beginning its second day, had been a great idea. Both children were excited when they had all checked in yesterday. Benjy had expressed a wish to hear his father's speech today, and Nim had arranged it. And there were other activities in which Ruth and the children would join—a harbor cruise, museum visits, movies.

From the window Nim could see some kind of demonstration taking place outside. Since he had an hour before his speech at 10:00 a.m., he left the suite and took an elevator to the lobby. He was curious to know who was demonstrating.

As Nim emerged from the hotel's main entrance, he realized it was the same old crowd—power & light for people. About a hundred persons of varying ages were parading, chanting slogans. He could see the ubiquitous TV cameras, and of course there was Davey Birdsong, directing it all. The driveway of the hotel was blocked by p&lfp-ers who had linked arms, preventing cars and taxis from moving in. Cordoned off by a second contingent was an adjoining service entrance. Two trucks were held up there—a milk delivery van and an open pickup with a load of fire extinguishers.

Several city policemen now appeared. They motioned the demonstrators away from both entrances, then escorted the two trucks in, and after that, the cars and taxis.

"Can you beat that for irresponsibility?" The speaker was another convention delegate, standing beside Nim. "That idiot bunch wants to cut off the hotel's protection and milk. Why?"

Nim nodded. "Doesn't make a lot of sense."

He returned inside the hotel and went up to the mezzanine. At the entrance to the convention hall, he bumped into Nancy Molineaux.

"Just picked up your speech in the pressroom," she said; she had a copy in her hand. "Pretty dull stuff. You planning to say anything extra that isn't printed here?"

462

"Even if I do, I'll be damned if I'd tell *you* in advance."

She laughed.

"Dad," a voice broke in, "we're going up to that place now."

It was Benjy, who had dodged through the crowd. Behind him Nim could see Ruth and Leah over by the stairway to the visitors' gallery. Both waved and he waved back.

"Okay," he told Benjy. "You'd better go get your seats."

Nancy asked, "You brought your family to the convention?"

"Yes," he answered curtly. "In case you consider making something of it, I'm paying their expenses personally."

"My, my," she teased. "What a terrible reputation I have."

"I'm wary of you," Nim said, "the way I would be of a cobra."

COMING here today was an assignment Nancy Molineaux had neither expected nor wanted. But the city editor, spotting Goldman's name on the program, had sent her, hoping she would find some vulnerability and thus continue what he saw as a newsworthy vendetta between Nancy and Nim. Well, he was wrong. She would report Goldman's speech straight. Apart from that, Nancy wanted to get out of here as quickly as she could. Today was the day she had arranged to meet the girl, Yvette. She hoped the girl would show, and would answer some of those puzzling questions.

Meanwhile, there was Goldman's speech.

AS NIM described the capacity problems—present and future—of GSP&L, the rapt attention of his audience showed that many of those listening shared the frustrations and fears which he was presenting under his title, "Overload." They, too, realized that a major electrical famine was a mere few years away.

Near the end of his prepared text, Nim reached into a pocket for a page of notes, which he would use to conclude the speech. "Most of us here," he said, "share two important beliefs. One concerns environment. The second concerns the democratic process. The environment we live in *should* be cleaner than it is. Therefore any who work toward that objective deserve our support—with certain limitations I will get to in a moment. However, some of those who call themselves environmentalists have ceased to be reasonable. This breed of environmentalist opposes *everything*. They are a minority. But by noisy, uncompromising, often uninformed fanaticism they have managed to impose their will on all of us—the majority. In doing so, such people have prostituted the democratic process—to thwart everything but their own narrow aims.

"But the fanatics among environmentalists are not alone. They have allies. The allies I speak of are the growing number of appointees on regulatory boards, put there for political reasons only." Nim paused, having sudden second thoughts. Then he plunged on. "There was a time when the boards and commissions regulating our industry could be relied on for reasonably fair, impartial judgments. But not anymore. Now a majority of them receive their appointments as political rewards. Seldom, if ever, do they get where they are through merit or experience. As a result, such commissioners and board members have little or no business knowledge. But all have political ambitions.

"That is precisely how our extremist critics find themselves with allies. It is the populist anti-power company stance which nowadays makes news, rather than balanced, thoughtfully arrived at decisions. I have no easy remedy. The best we can do is to let the public know that their interests are being undermined by an insidious alliance of fanatics and self-serving politicians."

Nim decided to leave it there.

While he was wondering what would be the reaction of his GSP&L colleagues, he found to his amazement he was receiving a standing ovation. Unexpectedly, incredibly, he was a hero.

"Congratulations!" "Took guts to say it, but all so true." "The industry needs straight shooters like you."

As delegates crowded around, congratulating him, Nim eased himself out of the hall. He took the elevator down to the main floor, where he had arranged to meet Ruth and the children.

"Watch it, please!" As Nim left the elevator, a figure in blue-gray coveralls moved past, maneuvering a trolley on which were balanced three fire extinguishers. "Won't be a moment, sir. Just have to put one of these in place." The man, who was young, lifted aside an unoccupied chair near a stairway, set down a fire extinguisher behind it, then returned the chair to its original position. He smiled at Nim. "That's all, sir. Sorry."

Nim remembered the man as the driver of one of the trucks which the police had escorted in during the demonstration. He noticed that the man's hands were badly stained. It occurred to

464

Nim that putting a fire extinguisher behind a chair was a strange arrangement. But presumably the man knew what he was doing. His coveralls were lettered FIRE PROTECTION SERVICE, INC.

Nim sat down in the chair to wait for his family.

NANCY MOLINEAUX had hurriedly phoned in her story on Goldman's speech, and now, eighteen minutes late, she entered the crummy bar where she had been last week. Yvette was at a corner table.

"Hi!" Nancy greeted her. "Sorry I'm late."

Yvette merely shrugged. She appeared to be in worse shape than a week ago—skin blotchy, hair a mess, clothes dirty. On her hand was the improvised glove which Nancy had noticed before.

Nancy decided to come to the point. "You said you'd tell me today what goes on in that house on Crocker Street."

Yvette looked up. "No, I didn't. You just hoped I would."

"Okay. Well, I'm still hoping. Why don't you start by telling me what you're afraid of?"

"I'm not afraid anymore." The girl made the statement in a flat, dull voice, her face expressionless.

"So what's happened to make the difference?" Nancy asked.

Yvette seemed to be weighing something in her mind. While she did, she used her left hand to rub the right. First with the glove on, then she slipped it off.

With shock and horror Nancy stared. What had been a hand was an ugly red-white mess of scars. Two fingers were gone. The other had portions missing. One finger was grotesquely bent.

Nancy said, sickened, "My God! What happened to your hand?"

Yvette glanced down, then, realizing what she had done, covered the hand hastily. "It was . . . I had an accident. They wouldn't let me go to a doctor." She choked back tears.

"Who wouldn't?" Nancy felt her anger rising. "Birdsong?"

The girl nodded. "And Georgos."

"Who the hell is Georgos? And why wouldn't they take you to a doctor?" Nancy reached out, gripping Yvette's good hand. "Kid, let me help you! I can."

The girl shook her head, her expression resigned.

Nancy pleaded, "Just tell me what it's all about."

Abruptly Yvette reached down to the floor and lifted up a battered brown purse. She took out two tape cassettes, which she put on the table. "It's all there," she said. Then, in a single move-ment, she drained her beer glass and stood up to go.

"Hey!" Nancy protested. "Why not stay and tell me . . . ."

Yvette had gone. There seemed nothing to be gained by going after her. Nancy picked up the cassettes. She would play them at home tonight and hope there was something worthwhile there.

WHEN Yvette told Nancy Molineaux, "I'm not afraid anymore," the statement was true. Yesterday Yvette had reached a decision which freed her from her overwhelming fear of arrest and life imprisonment. The decision was simply that, as soon as she had delivered the tapes to that switched-on black reporter, who would know what to do with them, Yvette would kill herself.

Walking away from that bar, Yvette felt peace. At last. It had been a long time since she had known any. There had been none with Georgos, though at first the excitement of being his woman, of sharing the important things he did, had made everything else seem not to matter. It was very much later that she began to won-der if Georgos was sick, perverted.

And yet Yvette still cared about Georgos; even now she hoped he wouldn't get hurt too badly or be made to suffer. About Bird-song, though, Yvette didn't give a damn. He was mean and hard. He could be killed or rot in jail and she wouldn't care.

Then she realized she would never know what happened to Birdsong, or Georgos, because she would be dead herself. Oh, God—she was only twenty-two! She didn't want to die. But she didn't want to spend the rest of her life in prison either.

Yvette kept on walking. She knew where she was going.

It was less than four months ago—after that night when Georgos killed the two guards—that she realized she was guilty of murder equally with Georgos. She was a hunted criminal. Some nights, lying awake beside Georgos, she had fantasized that she *could* go back to the rocky, dreary farm in Kansas where she had lived as a child. Which was rubbish, of course.

Yvette had left the farm and the fierce fights between her parents as soon as she was able. After coming west, she had gotten a job as a department store salesclerk, which she liked. What put her on the road she finally walked was being taken by a friend to some left-wing political meetings, where she met Georgos.

When Georgos had persuaded her to give up her job and go underground to form Friends of Freedom, Yvette had no idea of what she was getting into. At the time it sounded like fun.

Recently Yvette had sensed that her days as Georgos' woman were almost over; Georgos had become secretive about his work. Clearly he no longer trusted her. Then, without really knowing why, Yvette started to eavesdrop by making tape recordings of the conversations between Georgos and Davey Birdsong. It was not difficult. There was equipment available and Georgos had shown her how to use it. That was how she learned about the scenario of destruction and murder intended for tonight—or rather 3:00 a.m. tomorrow morning—at the Christopher Columbus Hotel.

The conversations were on the cassettes. So was a rambling account of it all by Yvette. Why had she done it? Even now she was unsure. Perhaps to save Georgos' soul (if he had one) from the terrible thing he intended to do.

Yvette looked about her. Her destination was a short distance ahead—a grassy knoll, high above the city. Its unofficial name was Lonely Hill. The final two hundred yards were up a steep, narrow path and she took it slowly. The top came all too soon.

She sat down on the grass and opened her purse. She lifted out a device she had removed several days ago from Georgos' workshop. It was a bangalore torpedo—a stick of dynamite inside a section of pipe. It had a five-second fuse. Long enough.

Reaching into the purse again, Yvette found a small cigarette lighter. Her hands were trembling as she tried to get it going in the wind. Finally it sputtered, then flamed.

Trembling even more, she managed to bring the end of the fuse to the lighter. The fuse ignited at once. In one swift movement Yvette dropped the lighter and held the bomb to her chest. Closing her eyes, she hoped it would not be—

"GOOD NIGHT, you characters." Nim kissed Leah and Benjy, then turned out the lights in the hotel suite's second bedroom, which the children were sharing. It was well past midnight, and the second day of the NEI convention was winding down.

In the living room, Ruth smiled as Nim returned. "Well, it certainly was a good day for you," she said, "and I'm pleased you got a fair press." She motioned to the *California Examiner* beside her.

"That was a fat surprise." Nim had read Nancy Molineaux's straightforward report of his speech. "Can't figure out that dame. I was certain she'd stick in the knife again."

"Don't you know by now that we women are unpredictable?" Ruth said mischievously.

He leaned forward and kissed her lightly on the neck, then sat down in a facing chair. "How are you feeling?"

"Normal most of the time. I tire easily, though, compared with the energy I used to have."

Nim reached out and took Ruth's hands. "You're sleepy and so am I. Let's go to bed."

They went, hand in hand, into the bedroom, where, just before turning out the lights, he noticed the time: 1:30 a.m.

A QUARTER MILE or so from the hotel, Georgos Archambault was seated alone in the red Fire Protection Service truck. He could hardly wait for the explosions to begin.

It was almost unbelievable how smoothly everything had gone. From the moment when the police cleared a way for the truck, only twice had the Friends of Freedom been stopped inside the hotel. Ute was queried by a security man, Georgos by an assistant manager. Both incidents gave them some nervous moments, but the work orders they promptly showed were passed back without further questioning.

Now there was merely the waiting—the hardest part of all. As soon as the hotel was well ablaze, with people trapped inside, Georgos intended to phone a radio station with the communiqué he had drafted. It contained his new demands. His orders would be obeyed instantly when the fascist power structure at last grasped the strength of Friends of Freedom. Only one small matter bothered Georgos. He felt uneasy about the sudden disappearance of Yvette.

Georgos checked his watch: 1:40 a.m.

JUST as a precaution, Davey Birdsong was giving himself an alibi. He was twenty-odd miles from the Christopher Columbus, and he intended to keep that distance until the action was over.

Hours ago he had delivered a lecture to an adult study group on "The Socialist Ideal." Now he was with a dozen tedious people from the group who had adjourned to the house of one of their number to go on gabbing about international politics. Clearly the whole deal could go on until dawn.

Davey Birdsong, too, had a typewritten statement he would issue to the press. A copy was in his pocket and it began:

> The popular consumers organization, power & light for people, deplores violence at all times, and especially the bombing at the Christopher Columbus Hotel last night.

Birdsong smiled as he checked his watch: 1:45 a.m.

COMING INTO HER apartment after a late night party, Nancy Molineaux remembered that she was going to listen tonight to those tapes the girl, Yvette, had given her. But it was 1:50 a.m. and she was tired. She decided that she had been working on that story a long time and one more day wouldn't matter.

She flipped on an FM radio, which she kept tuned to a mostly music station. While she was in the bathroom cleaning her teeth, the music was interrupted for a newscast:

> "Police are appealing for help in identifying the body of a young woman, apparently a suicide, discovered this afternoon on Lonely Hill . . . bomb fragments at the scene. . . . Although the body was badly dismembered, one of the woman's hands had two fingers missing, apparently from an earlier wound."

Nancy dropped the toothbrush. *Had she heard what she thought she heard?* Yes, she had absorbed enough to know they were talking about Yvette. Oh, God, Nancy thought, she had let the kid walk away. Could she have helped?

Suddenly Nancy was alert, her tiredness gone. She slipped on a kimono, located the cassettes Yvette had given her, and inserted the first one into her tape deck. There was a pause, then Yvette's voice came through. "This is about the Friends of Freedom, all those bombings and the murders. Where the Friends of Freedom are is 117 Crocker Street. The leader is Georgos Winslow Archambault. I'm Georgos' woman. I've been in it too. So is Davey Birdsong; he brings the money to buy explosives and the other stuff."

Nancy's mouth was agape. She felt shivers all through her.

The first side of the first tape ended. Nancy's tape deck had an automatic-reverse feature. The second side began at once. There was more of Yvette. She described the night on the hill above Millfield. The substation bombing. The killing of the two guards. Nancy's excitement mounted. She had the biggest news scoop of her career, and at this moment it was all her own. She continued listening.

There were two male voices—one presumably the Georgos whom Yvette had spoken of, the other unmistakably Birdsong. They were making arrangements. . . . Christopher Columbus Hotel . . . bombs disguised as fire extinguishers . . . second night of the National Electric Institute convention . . . 3:00 a.m.

Nancy's skin prickled. She glanced at her watch, then hurled herself at the telephone. Her hand was shaking as she dialed 911 for police emergency.

THIRTEEN

The duty lieutenant at the police department operations center made the only decision he could, and ordered, "Evacuate the Christopher Columbus Hotel." It was 2:21 a.m.

Half a dozen phones in the operations center went into use immediately. District police and fire units were alerted. Next, the police bomb squad. Ambulances were summoned, major law-enforcement, fire and city functionaries were notified.

Meanwhile, answers remained unknown to two vital questions. First, would bomb explosions occur at 3:00 a.m.? Second, could the hotel be cleared in thirty-six minutes?

BEFORE leaving her apartment, Nancy phoned the *Examiner*. As she gave the night editor a rundown of what she had, she sensed his excitement. She told him, "I'm going to the hotel, then I'll come in to write. One other thing. I have two tape cassettes. I had to tell the police about them, and they're sure to be impounded as evidence. Before that happens, we should make copies."

They arranged that a messenger would meet Nancy at the hotel, collect the tapes, and rush them to the paper's entertainment editor, a hi-fi nut who had his own sound lab. The copies of the tapes and a portable playback machine would be in the newsroom when Nancy got there.

Nancy made one more phone call before leaving her apartment. She dialed the Christopher Columbus Hotel and told the operator, "Give me Nimrod Goldman's room."

NIM SLEEPILY PICKED up the bedside telephone. "Yeah."

"Goldman! This is Nancy Molineaux. Listen to me!"

"Molineaux, don't you know it's the middle of the night?"

"Listen! You and your family are in danger. Get out of that hotel! *Now!* Bombs are going off."

Now Nim was wide awake: "Is this some sick joke?"

"It's no joke. Those Friends of Freedom bastards have planted bombs disguised as fire extinguishers. . . ."

The words Friends of Freedom convinced him.

"What about other people?" he asked.

"The alarm's gone out. *You* get moving!"

"Right!" He slammed down the phone and started shaking Ruth. Minutes later, with the children bewildered, still in night-clothes, Nim rushed them from the suite. He headed for the emergency stairs, in case the elevators should fail. They were three floors down when they heard sirens outside and the fire-alarm bells in the hotel began ringing stridently.

Evacuation of the hotel proceeded swiftly and, for the most part, calmly. Police and firemen moved onto every floor; they thumped on doors, shouted commands, hurried people toward stairwells. Few, if any, of the guests knew exactly what was happening, but they accepted the imminence of danger and moved fast, abandoning belongings in their rooms.

Agitated guests were already streaming from the hotel when the police bomb squad arrived. They poured into the hotel and, assisted by other police and firemen, carried out every fire extinguisher in sight to a quickly barricaded area in the street. Then they began working on the extinguishers.

By now every street leading to the Christopher Columbus was jam-packed with vehicles—fire equipment, police cars, emergency vans, ambulances, all with dome lights flashing. Representatives of press, TV and radio were arriving in growing numbers.

Nancy Molineaux was the center of a group composed of police detectives, an FBI special agent and a young assistant district attorney. She was evasive about the cassette tapes (which had already been collected from her as arranged), but promised they would be handed to the assistant DA within two hours. One detective, on orders from a superior, broke away to telephone two instructions. Raid the house at 117 Crocker Street. Arrest Georgos Archambault and Davey Birdsong.

Hotel evacuees were herded to a side street where more barricades had been erected. Nim Goldman and his family were among the early groups to reach this area. When he was satisfied that Ruth and the children were safe, Nim returned to the hotel, prompted by two recollections. One was Nancy Molineaux's reference on the phone to "bombs disguised as fire extinguishers"; the other, the young man who yesterday had placed a fire extinguisher behind a lobby chair while Nim watched. Nim wanted to make sure. Had that particular extinguisher been found?

It was almost 3:00 a.m. Nim managed to force his way back into the hotel. He headed to where he had seen the fire extinguisher.

"Mr. Goldman! Mr. Goldman!" Nim recognized Art Romeo, Harry London's deputy in the property protection department. Later Nim would learn that Romeo had been visiting the hotel, and was sharing a poker game with cronies from another utility when the alarm was given. He had promptly started to help.

"Mr. Goldman, you *must* go outside!"

"Forget that!" Nim explained about the fire extinguisher.

"Where is it, sir?"

"Over here." Nim strode to where he had been seated yesterday and pulled the chair aside. The extinguisher was there. Suddenly two brawny policemen seized Nim and roughly frogmarched him toward the main entrance. As Nim was thrust through, he glanced back. Art Romeo, with the fire extinguisher clasped in his arms, was following.

The policemen shoved Nim toward the evacuation area. At that instant there was the roar of an explosion followed by shattering of glass from almost every window in the block.

The bomb squad thought they had located all the bombs on the main floor and mezzanine. They had missed the one that Nim

remembered. By the time Art Romeo had bravely picked it up and staggered with it to the area where the fire extinguishers had been accumulated, all the bomb squad members were on upper floors, working frantically to disarm the firebombs. Consequently no one else was close enough to be hurt when the bomb exploded. Romeo was blown to pieces instantly.

Out of nearly twenty firebombs which the terrorists had placed on upper floors of the hotel, three were not located in time, and detonated a few minutes after the explosion outside. Fierce scattered fires resulted. Without the advance warning and evacuation the death toll would have been enormous. As it was, one policeman and two firemen died, and two more firemen were badly injured when the firebombs exploded.

By unanimous agreement the NEI convention was abandoned.

SOON AFTER the explosion which killed Art Romeo, Georgos Archambault was sobbing as he ran toward his parked Fire Protection Service truck. *It had all gone wrong!*

Some thirty-five minutes earlier, at 2:25 a.m., he had been puzzled to hear sirens, fire engines and police cars speed past the area where he was waiting in the pickup. All were obviously headed for the Christopher Columbus. As the activity increased, Georgos became thoroughly alarmed.

At 2:40 a.m. he could wait no longer. He got out of the truck and walked toward the hotel.

To his great dismay people were rushing *from* the hotel, many in nightclothes. He wanted to wave his arms and shout, Go back! Go back! Then, while he watched, some of his carefully planted fire-extinguisher bombs were brought out and disarmed, preventing what Georgos had so painstakingly planned.

He began to cry. Why had he failed? In what devious way had the enemy found out? As he pondered that question and watched the firemen and police, he realized that his own identity might now be known. He began to run.

No one seemed to notice him as he got into the pickup truck and started away. But when he turned into Crocker Street, he saw that it was blocked by police cars. A moment later he heard a fusillade of shots. Georgos knew that Wayde, Ute and Felix, who had stayed in the house, were trapped. Quickly he turned the truck around. There was only one place left for him to go: the apartment in North Castle, intended for a crisis such as this.

Georgos' mind worked quickly. If his identity was known, the police would be searching for him. In all probability the pigs would also be on the lookout for the Fire Protection Service pickup truck; therefore the truck must be abandoned. But not too close to the North Castle apartment. How near to his destination dare he drive? He decided: within one mile.

When Georgos estimated he was that distance away, he pulled to the curb and got out. The police might assume he had had a parked car waiting and changed vehicles. What Georgos did not know was that a drunk, recovering from a quart of cheap wine, was propped up in a doorway nearby. The drunk was sufficiently lucid to observe Georgos' departure.

In a quarter of an hour Georgos was unlocking the apartment door. At about the same time, a cruising police car spotted the red pickup, for which an alert had already gone out. The driver inspected the truck and called in that the radiator was still warm. The same officer noticed the drunk and elicited the information that the driver had left on foot, and in which direction. The police car sped away, but failed to locate Georgos.

DAVEY BIRDSONG was arrested shortly after 5:30 a.m. outside his apartment building. He protested bitterly to the two detectives who made the arrest. "Listen, you guys. I left my apartment at six o'clock last night and haven't been back since. I have plenty of witnesses to that."

Ironically, the alibi proved Birdsong's undoing. When he was searched at police headquarters, the p&lfp statement deploring "the bombing at the Christopher Columbus Hotel last night" was found in a pocket. The statement was later proved to have been typed on a machine kept in Birdsong's apartment—*the apartment he claimed he had not entered since 6:00 p.m. the previous evening, nearly nine hours before the bombing.*

Other evidence proved equally damning: Yvette's tape recordings, the statement of the cab driver Vickery, and proof of Birdsong's purchases of fire extinguishers. Birdsong was charged with four counts of first-degree murder, conspiracy to commit a felony, and a "shopping list" of other offenses. Bail was set at one million dollars, a sum which Birdsong could not raise, and he remained in custody pending his trial.

Of the remaining Friends of Freedom, Wayde, the young Marxist, and Felix, from Detroit's inner city, were killed in the gun battle with police. Ute, the embittered Indian, turned a gun on himself and died as police stormed the house.

Evidence of revolutionary activity was discovered at number 117, including Georgos' voluminous journal and other records, all of which were turned over to the district attorney.

AT THE *California Examiner,* they were already saying that Nancy Molineaux was a shoo-in for a Pulitzer. After leaving the Christopher Columbus and going to the paper, Nancy wrote continuously up to the *Examiner's* 6:30 a.m. first deadline. Through the morning and early afternoon she updated material for later editions.

Just as in a reporter's dream, almost the entire front page, under a banner headline, was Nancy's. But on the day during which her major story broke, Nancy went through a personal crisis of her own. It occurred shortly before noon.

Several times since 7:30 a.m., when the city editor came on duty, he had stopped by Nancy's desk with words of encouragement. And occasionally, when she glanced up from typing, Nancy caught him looking over at her. Though his expression was inscrutable, she had a notion they were both thinking about the same stark, grim truth: that for an entire week she had been in possession of information which, if shared, could have prevented the disaster.

The last thing Nancy had observed before leaving the Christopher Columbus was three shrouded bodies—the dead policeman and two firemen—being wheeled from the hotel. There were also two men outside the hotel, putting pieces of something into a plastic bag; it took her a minute to realize they were collecting the remains of the fourth dead man, the one blown to pieces by a bomb.

At 11:55 a.m., with two hours and twenty minutes still to go before the final edition deadline, Nancy felt she was ready to crack.

"Take a break and come with me." The city editor was beside

her. With unusual docility Nancy stood up and followed him down the corridor to a small meeting room. He motioned Nancy to sit.

"I've been watching you," he said, "and we've both been thinking the same thing. Right?"

Nancy nodded, suddenly unable to find words.

"Nancy," the city editor said, "as I see it, by the end of today you'll go one of two ways. Either right over the edge, which means a mental breakdown, or you'll get a grip on yourself and let what's in the past stay there. But you'll have to make a positive decision, not just let things slide."

Relieved at last to say it aloud, she told him, "I'm responsible for what happened last night. If I'd notified someone of what I knew, the police could have investigated."

"Nancy," he told her, "if you had known what would happen, you'd have acted differently. So my advice is this: accept what you did and didn't do, and remember it—for experience and learning. But otherwise put it behind you."

He went on. "Now I'll tell you something else. I've been a lot of years in this business, and in my opinion you're the best damn reporter I've ever worked with."

It was then that Nancy did something which happened only rarely. She put her head in her arms, broke down and cried.

The city editor went to the window, and with his back decently turned he said, "Take your time, Nancy. I promise that no one but you and me will ever know what went on in here today."

In half an hour Nancy was back at her desk, with her face washed, writing once more, and totally in control.

WHEN Nim Goldman telephoned Nancy Molineaux to express his personal gratitude, he added, a trifle awkwardly, "You pulled off a big story. Congratulations."

Nancy asked curiously, "What did you think of it all?"

"I hope Birdsong gets everything he deserves," Nim answered.

"How about the Sequoia Club?"

"Oh, I believe the Sequoia Club went too far. But it made us care about the environment." Nim paused, then went on. "I know the club is down right now, but I hope it isn't out. That would be a loss to everyone."

"Well," Nancy said, "sometimes a day is full of surprises."

IT WAS Friday, a week later, and J. Eric Humphrey seemed unusually perturbed. When Nim came in, the chairman was moving restlessly around his office, something he rarely did. He continued standing as he talked and Nim listened.

"There are several things I wish to say. The first is that I've received so many compliments about your NEI speech that I'd like to congratulate you. The second is that I would like you to return to your role as company spokesman. GSP&L needs people like you."

He paused, and Nim wondered what was coming next. "There's one more thing. For more than a year now," the chairman continued, "our company has suffered outrageous attacks by a ragtag band of terrorists. The FBI and police have accomplished absolutely nothing."

"They have Birdsong in jail," Nim pointed out.

"Yes—and why? Because one intelligent, determined woman reporter was more resourceful than a veritable army of professional law enforcers."

Humphrey's voice rose in pitch. Nim had seldom seen the chairman so openly emotional. "And I blame us, I blame myself, for not having been more insistent earlier that the law-enforcement agencies *do something*. Even now, that vile man Archambault is still at large. An entire week has gone by. *Where* is he?"

"I understand," Nim said, "that the police are still searching, and they believe he's somewhere in the North Castle area."

"Where he is doubtless plotting to kill or maim more of our people, and do our company more injury! Nim, *I want that villain found*. If necessary I want GSP&L to find him."

Nim was about to point out that a public utility was not equipped to perform police work, but he asked instead, "Eric, what do you have in mind?"

"I have in mind that we are an organization employing many high-caliber people with an abundance of brainpower. Judging by results, the law-enforcement agencies lack both. Therefore, Nim, these are my instructions: bring your own brain and those of others to bear on this problem. Call on whomever you require to help you. But I want results. I want that despicable blackguard Archambault caught and brought to justice."

The chairman stopped, then said tersely, "That's all."

IT WAS a coincidence, Nim thought afterward, that he, too, had been thinking about brainpower. Four months ago, largely because they seemed to be getting nowhere, Nim had abandoned the think-group approach to the problem of the attacks by the so-called Friends of Freedom. He had summoned no further meetings with Oscar O'Brien, Teresa Van Buren and Harry London. Yet, reviewing what was now known, the quartet's guesses had been uncannily close to the truth. Maybe now that the identity of X was known, and the man was believed to be hiding somewhere in the city, the think group could somehow penetrate that hiding.

"AS IT TURNED OUT," Nim said, consulting notes, "we were remarkably accurate."

It was Sunday afternoon. The members of the think group had assembled in general counsel Oscar O'Brien's home and were sprawled around an informal garden room. The house was high above the shoreline, with a magnificent view of sailboats running amid a flurry of whitecaps below.

Nim continued. "We hypothesized that one man—X—was the leader of Friends of Freedom, that he was masculine and vain, and that he had a woman confidante who worked closely with him."

"Right on target!" Teresa Van Buren interjected. The PR director was wearing a green caftan, as if she had come unchanged from a lazy weekend at home.

Nim proceeded. "Now that we know the identity of X and a good deal more about him, perhaps we can track him down."

Oscar O'Brien removed the cigar from between his thick lips. "I'm willing to give it a whirl," he said. "Where do we start?"

"I've prepared a memo," Nim said.

Opening a briefcase, Nim produced copies and passed them around. The memo contained a summary of all information published since the NEI convention about Friends of Freedom and Georgos Archambault.

Nim waited until the others had finished reading, then asked, "Do any of you know anything that isn't in there?"

"I might have something," Harry London volunteered, "from my friends in the law-enforcement agencies." In contrast to the others, who were dressed very casually, he had appeared in beige slacks and a starched bush jacket. "The newspapers mentioned that Archambault's journal was found. What wasn't let out, because the DA hopes to use it as evidence, is what was *in* the journal."

Van Buren asked, "Have you seen the journal?"

"I was shown a copy, and there are two things you can tell from reading what the guy put down. First, he has a compulsion to write. Also, he has very distinctive handwriting."

"Um." O'Brien was stroking his chin, drifting off into a reverie. "I have an idea, but it isn't ready yet." He motioned to the others. "Carry on."

"All right," Nim said. "Let's talk about North Castle. It's a rabbit warren. If anybody wanted to choose a place in this city where they could disappear, that's the district."

O'Brien queried, "Has anyone estimated the size of the area in which Archambault has apparently been swallowed up?"

"The police have," London said. "And the thinking is this: when Archambault abandoned that truck, he was in one helluva hurry. So while he wouldn't have left the truck close to his destination, it would not have been too far either. Say a mile and a half at the most. If you take the truck as the center, that means a circle with a one-and-a-half-mile radius, or a bit over seven square miles."

Nim said, "Which means roughly twelve thousand homes and businesses, with probably thirty thousand people."

"I know that looking for Archambault in there would be like searching for the proverbial needle," O'Brien said. "Just the same, we might smoke him out, and here's a thought."

Nim, London and Van Buren were listening carefully.

The lawyer continued. "Harry says Archambault has a compulsion to write. Taken with the other information we have, it adds up to him being an exhibitionist with a need to sound off. If we could circulate some kind of questionnaire in that area, he might not be able to resist answering it."

There was a puzzled silence, then Van Buren asked, "What would the questionnaire be about?"

"Electric power, of course—something to arouse his interest. Like, How do you rate GSP&L's service? Do you agree that continued good service will require higher rates? That sort of thing."

480

Nim said, "I suppose your idea is as the questionnaires come back, to look for the handwriting matching that in Archambault's journal."

"Right."

"But supposing Archambault used a typewriter?"

"Then we couldn't identify," the lawyer said. "If you're looking for a foolproof scheme, you won't find one."

"If you did get a questionnaire with handwriting that matched," Van Buren objected, "how would you know where it came from? You can be sure Archambault won't give his address."

"Wait a minute," London said. "There *is* one way a thing like that could be traceable. Invisible ink. We could put an invisible number on every questionnaire. You print it with a luminescent powder dissolved in glycol—any job printer can handle it. The liquid is absorbed into the paper so there's no trace of it. But when you hold it under a black-light scanner, the number shows up."

Van Buren exclaimed, "I'll be damned!"

Harry London told her, "Half the so-called anonymous questionnaires are done that way. Never trust any piece of paper which says you can't be identified."

"I don't see how we could distribute questionnaires widely enough," Nim cautioned, "yet keep a record of where each one went."

Van Buren sat up straight. "I do. Our own billing department."

The others stared at her.

"Look at it this way," the PR director said. "Every building in that area is a customer of GSP&L, and all names and addresses are stored in our billing computers."

"I get it," Nim said. "You'd program the computer to print out the addresses in that area, and no more."

"We could do even better," O'Brien put in. "The portion of the questionnaire with a customer's name and address could be detached so only the nonidentifiable part would be sent back."

"*Apparently* nonidentifiable," Harry London reminded him.

O'Brien slapped a thigh enthusiastically. "By Jupiter, we're on to something!"

"It's a good idea," Nim said, "and worth trying."

They talked for another hour, their eagerness growing.

FOURTEEN

GSP&L's computer center, Nim thought, bore a striking resemblance to a movie set of *Star Wars*. Everything on the three floors which it occupied was futuristic, clinical and functional. Security guards, operating inside bulletproof glass cubicles and speaking through microphones, scrutinized every arrival and departure. The company chairman himself was required to wear a visitor's badge.

The reason for this was simple. The center housed a priceless treasure trove: a computerized record of eight and a half million GSP&L customers, with their meter readings, billings and payments—all going back years—plus details on shareholders, employees and inventories, and technical data. Value of the computers was about thirty million dollars. Value of the recorded information was incalculable.

Nim had come to the computer center with Oscar O'Brien to observe the dispatch of a "Consumer Survey" mailing, which was, in fact, the trap in which they hoped to snare Georgos Archambault. Since the Sunday think-group session, many hours had been spent working on the questionnaire. Nim and O'Brien had decided on eight questions. The first few were simple:

Does Golden State Power & Light provide you with satisfactory service? Please answer yes or no.

Farther on, there was room for more expansive answers:

In what ways do you believe that Golden State Power & Light service could be improved?

And finally:

Golden State Power & Light apologizes to its customers for inconveniences as a result of cowardly attacks on company installations by small-time, would-be terrorists who act in ignorance. If there are ways in which you think such attacks could be ended, please give us your views.

As Oscar O'Brien observed, "If that doesn't make Archambault hopping mad and tempt him into replying, nothing will."

Law-enforcement agencies, when informed of GSP&L's idea, had reacted favorably. The DA's office had offered help in examining questionnaires.

Sharlett Underhill, vice-president of finance, whose responsibilities included the computer center, met Nim and O'Brien after they were checked through security. The smartly dressed woman told them, "We are running your survey now. All twelve thousand copies should be in the mail tonight. When I get the number which requires identifying, it will be entered into the computer along with a secret code, known only to one of our senior programmers and me. The computer will immediately tell us the address to which that questionnaire was mailed."

"We're gambling, of course, that we'll have a number to give you," Nim said.

Mrs. Underhill replied tartly, "Whether you do or not, I want you both to understand two things. I am not in favor of my department's equipment and records being used for what is essentially a deceitful purpose."

"Yes, we know that," O'Brien said.

"Please hear me out. When you have given me the number—*and I will accept one number only*—the information you want will be drawn from the computer. But *the moment that has happened,* the computer will be instructed to forget all the other numbers and related addresses. I want that clearly understood."

"Fair enough," the lawyer acknowledged.

RUTH GOLDMAN was in New York for two weeks of immuno-therapy at Sloan-Kettering. Other trips would be necessary later. "I can't make promises," Dr. Levin had told Nim and Ruth, "but the Sloan-Kettering people are cautiously optimistic."

Nim had taken Ruth to the airport early yesterday morning. "I love you," he declared just before she boarded her plane, "and I'll be doing whatever's the equivalent of praying."

She had laughed, then kissed him. "It's strange," she had said, "but even with all this, I've never been happier."

In New York, Ruth was staying with friends and would attend the institute several days a week as an outpatient. While she was

483

away, Nim had arranged—in fulfillment of an earlier promise—to take Karen Sloan to the symphony.

When Nim arrived at Karen's apartment, she was ready, wearing a becoming dark red dress and a single strand of pearls. The nails of her long fingers, which rested on her lapboard, were beautifully manicured. She greeted him warmly.

After Josie had disconnected the wheelchair from a power outlet so it could become more mobile, she said, "Mr. Goldman, I'll be doing the driving. If you'll come down with Karen in a few minutes, I'll go ahead and bring Humperdinck around."

"Ah, Humperdinck! How *is* your van with a personality?"

"Wonderful, but I do worry about my father."

"In what way?"

"Let's leave it now. I'll tell you later."

Nim marveled at the dexterity with which Karen, using only her sip-blow tube, piloted her chair out of the apartment and along a corridor to the elevator. On the way he asked, "How long is your battery good for?"

She smiled. "Tonight I'm fully charged. So, using the battery for the chair and my respirator, probably four hours. After that I'll need to plug in again to dear old GSP&L."

It fascinated him how tenuous was Karen's hold on life, and that electricity kept her living.

In the lobby, they met two children—a boy and a girl, probably nine and ten. "Hi, Karen!" they both said, as the wheelchair, followed by Nim, moved toward the entry.

"Hello, Philip and Wendy," Karen said.

The boy looked at Nim. "Who's he?"

"This is Mr. Goldman." She told Nim, "These are two of my friends."

"Karen," the boy asked, "can I touch your hand?"

"Of course."

He did so, moving his fingertips gently. "Can you feel that?"

"Yes, Philip," she told him. "You have gentle hands."

Not wanting to be outdone, the girl inquired, "Karen, do you want your legs changed, so they won't fall asleep?"

"Well . . . all right." Carefully the girl lifted Karen's right leg until it was crossed over the left. "Thank you, Wendy."

The children said good-by and ran off.

Karen smiled. "Children are so natural. They're not afraid to ask questions."

Outside, Josie was waiting with the van. It was a green Ford; a wide sliding door on the near side was open. Karen maneuvered her wheelchair so it was facing the door. "Now you'll see what Mr. Paulsen did to help me get into Humperdinck."

Josie lifted down two lengths of steel channel from the van's interior. Attaching both pieces of channel to fittings at the base of the doorway, she lowered the other ends to the ground. Between the van's interior and the ground there was now a double ramp, the width matching the wheels on Karen's chair.

Next, Josie stepped inside the van and reached for a hook on a steel cable; the cable was attached to an electric winch on the far side. She brought the hook to the wheelchair, snapped it through a steel eye under the seat, then returned to the winch.

"Here we go!" Karen said.

Josie pressed a switch down, and the wheelchair was pulled up the ramp. Once inside, Josie swung the chair around, the wheels slipping into two recesses in the floor, where bolts secured them.

Josie was a careful driver, and Nim, sitting beside her, relaxed during the journey to the Palace of Arts, where the city's symphony orchestra performed. At the main entrance, a uniformed attendant arrived. He whisked Karen and Nim through a side door and into an elevator, which carried them to the grand tier. There they had front-row space, and a movable ramp eased the way for Karen. It was obvious that the Palace of Arts was used to wheelchairs.

When they had settled down, Karen said, "This is special treatment, Nimrod. How did you manage it?"

"Dear old GSP&L, as you call it, has some influence."

It was Teresa Van Buren who, at Nim's request, had made the arrangements, and refused his offer to pay.

The program was heavily Brahms. Variations on a Theme by Haydn first. Immediately after, Piano Concerto No. 2 in B-flat Major. The piano concerto was among Nim's favorites and, judging by her rapt attention, Karen's too.

The music finished and lights went up. During the intermission Nim and Karen remained where they were. Both were briefly silent, then she said softly, "Nimrod, I sense something has changed in your life. What is it?"

Taken aback by her perception, he told her about Ruth, the malignancy which threatened her life, and how—because of it—she and Nim had found their way again.

Karen listened in silence. Then she said, "I'm glad for you in one way, Nim, and sad—of course—for your wife."

"We may get lucky," Nim said.

"I hope so. Some people do," Karen said quietly.

ON THE homeward journey in Humperdinck, Nim said to Karen, "You still haven't told me why you are worried about your father."

"There isn't a lot to tell," Karen said, "except Daddy is in some kind of financial trouble; he won't say exactly what, but it means that I won't have Humperdinck much longer."

Nim was shocked. "Why?"

"The monthly payments are too much for my parents."

"Look," Nim said, "I'd like to help. . . ."

"No! I said I won't ever take money from you, Nimrod, and I meant it. Besides, I managed without a van before and can do so again. It's Daddy I'm concerned about."

"I really wish," Nim said, "there were something I could do."

"Stay my friend, Nimrod. It's all I ask."

IN THE last week of March, a dramatic, suddenly erupting oil crisis overshadowed all else.

All members of the Organization of Petroleum Exporting Countries decreed that they would not take any more paper money. Only gold. The United States would not comply, so the OPEC nations came to a unanimous decision that no more oil would be dispatched to the U.S. until the dispute had been resolved.

Since more than half the oil the United States used was imported and eighty-five percent of that came from OPEC countries, America faced a severe oil shortage. Throughout the country urgent policy measures were being taken.

The president ordered immediate gasoline rationing. Additionally, all sales of gasoline were forbidden from Friday nights to Monday mornings. Also emanating from Washington was an edict closing national parks and halting all major sporting events and other attractions which produced large crowds. The objective was to reduce unnecessary travel, especially by automobile. In addition, schools in many areas were being closed, to reopen in the summer, when their electricity needs would be less.

More drastic steps, including three- or four-day weekends, were likely if the situation failed to improve. Meanwhile, all public utilities using oil were ordered to begin around-the-clock brownouts by reducing voltages five percent.

At Golden State Power & Light every discussion was overshadowed by the knowledge that the utility's stored oil was sufficient for only thirty days of normal operation. The question was no longer whether there would be blackouts, but how soon and to what extent.

Since some new oil, from tankers now en route, would still be coming in, it was decided that rolling blackouts would not begin until the second week of May. Initially the electricity cutoffs would be for three hours each day, after which more stringent measures might be needed.

WHILE blackout preparations went ahead, a sense of general disenchantment pervaded GSP&L. The disenchantment extended to the bogus Consumer Survey. It was almost three weeks since the questionnaire had been distributed in the city's North Castle district, and it now appeared as if the attempt to entrap Georgos Archambault had been a waste of time and money.

Hundreds of replies had poured in. A large basement room at GSP&L headquarters was set aside to deal with the influx, and a staff of eight clerks installed there. The district attorney's office had sent photographic blowups of handwriting samples from Archambault's journal, with which the clerks painstakingly compared every questionnaire. But the result was definite: nothing had come in which matched the handwriting samples. And to Nim, in any case, the project had become a lot less important than the oil-supply problem.

It was during an evening work session about oil in his office that Nim received a telephone call which disturbed him greatly. The call was from Karen Sloan. He knew she would be wearing the special lightweight headband, earpiece and microphone which enabled her to use the telephone without assistance. By arrangement with the phone company, Karen was able to reach an operator directly and have any number dialed for her.

"Nimrod," she said without preliminaries, "my father is in serious trouble. I'm calling to see if you can help."

"What kind of trouble?"

"You know that he has a small plumbing business. Well, Daddy has been questioned several times by people from your company, and now by police detectives."

"Questioned about what?"

Karen hesitated before answering. "Daddy has been doing quite a lot of subcontracting for a company called Quayle Electrical and Gas. Something to do with gas lines going to meters."

Nim said, "Tell me that company's name again."

"It's Quayle. Does that mean something to you?"

"Yes, it means something," Nim said slowly as he thought, It looked almost certainly as if Luther Sloan was into theft of gas. Though Karen didn't know it, her phrase "lines going to meters" was a giveaway. That and the reference to Quayle Electrical and Gas Contracting, the big-scale power thieves already exposed and being investigated by Harry London.

"Karen," Nim said, "if this is what I think, it's very serious. In any event, there's nothing I can do tonight. But in the morning I'll find out what I can, then call you." Realizing he sounded unusually formal, he explained about the meeting in his office.

Karen was contrite. "Oh, I'm sorry, Nimrod! I shouldn't have bothered you."

"No," he assured her. "You can bother me anytime."

As the discussion on oil supplies resumed, Nim's thoughts wandered. He wondered if life, which had thrown so many foul balls at Karen, was in the process of delivering still one more.

IT WAS almost eight weeks since Georgos Winslow Archambault had gone into hiding. He had not expected to survive so long, especially after the outpouring of descriptions and photos of him in newspapers and on TV that followed the Christopher Columbus Hotel bombing.

Georgos knew he was near the end of the line. He was being hunted by every law-enforcement agency and would continue to be for as long as he lived. Most critical of all, his money was

488

almost gone. Therefore, capture was unavoidable—unless Georgos chose to anticipate it by ending his life in his own way. He intended to do exactly that.

He would make one last fighting gesture and, if necessary, die as he had lived, doing harm to the system he hated. His plan was to blow up a critical part of a GSP&L generating station.

He had already moved partway toward his objective by a daring risk he had taken on the same day he went into hiding.

The first thing Georgos realized that day was the need for transportation. He had abandoned the red Fire Protection Service truck because he could not have used it without being recognized, but a substitute was essential. To buy a vehicle was too risky. Also, he had insufficient money. So the only possibility was to retrieve his VW van, even though he thought it might be under surveillance.

He had kept the van in a privately-owned garage not far from Crocker Street. Aware of the risk, gambling on being ahead of the police, Georgos walked to the garage that same morning, paid what was owing, then drove the van to North Castle. No one had stopped him, and by midmorning the VW was safely inside the locked garage adjoining the hideaway.

Retrieving the VW had been important because it contained several items essential to the daring attack he now proposed. In a secret compartment under the van's floor, packed in foam rubber, were five cylindrical bombs, each containing plastic explosive and a timing mechanism. Also in the van was an inflatable rubber dinghy and scuba-diving gear.

In the days that followed, Georgos left the apartment occasionally, but only after dark. When he had to buy food, he was careful never to use the same store twice. Also, he had shaved off his mustache and wore light gloves to conceal his hands.

From reading the newspaper reports about the hotel bombing, Georgos realized it was Yvette who had somehow learned of his plans and had betrayed him. He ought to have hated Yvette for that. Incredibly, though, he missed her and pitied her for the manner of her death on Lonely Hill.

The newspapers had dug deeply into Georgos' history. One reporter learned that his movie-goddess mother hadn't wanted to admit having a child, fearing it would destroy her youthful image, and that his playboy father had cared for nothing but avoiding responsibility. Georgos was therefore assigned to successive sets of foster parents, none of whom he liked. By the age of nine he had met his father once, his mother three times. After that he saw neither. As a child he had wanted, with a fierce determination, to know his parents, but they were equally determined not to know him.

Another reporter tracked down the former movie goddess in Athens. When asked if her own neglect of Georgos might not have been largely responsible for what he had become, the ex-actress spat in the questioner's face. And in Manhattan, Georgos' aging playboy father told the press, "My advice to the cops is to shoot the bastard on sight—to kill." Georgos read the reports of his parents' reactions. Neither surprised him, but they intensified his hatred of almost everything.

So now, in the final week of April, Georgos concluded that the time was near for action. The plan which he had worked out was to blow up the huge cooling water pumps at La Mission generating plant, the same plant where—nearly a year ago, disguised as a Salvation Army officer—he had placed a bomb which damaged the generator called Big Lil.

Georgos knew that there wasn't a chance of getting inside the main building at La Mission. It was now too well guarded. But with resourcefulness and some luck, he could get to the pump house and blow up the eleven massive pumps that were essential to the operation of *five generating units,* including Big Lil. In destroying them he would knock out the entire La Mission generating station for months.

It was a beautiful scheme. The only remaining question was—When? Today was Friday. Weighing everything, Georgos decided on the following Tuesday, after dark.

Now, the decision taken, he was restless. Once more, as he had done so many times, he roamed the apartment's three dingy rooms. On the kitchen counter top an envelope caught his eye. It contained a Consumer Survey which had come several weeks ago from—of all sources—Golden State Piss & Lickspittle. It had been addressed to one Owen Grainger, the name under which Georgos rented the apartment. One of the items on the stinking survey read:

490

Golden State Power & Light apologizes to its customers for inconveniences as a result of cowardly attacks on company installations by small-time, would-be terrorists who act in ignorance. If there are ways in which you think such attacks could be ended, please give us your views.

Georgos had sat down immediately and written a scathing reply which began, "The terrorists you presumptuously describe as small-time, cowardly and ignorant are none of those things. They are important, wise and dedicated heroes. You are the ignoramuses, as well as criminal exploiters of the people. Justice shall overtake you! Be warned there will be blood and death, not mere 'inconvenience,' when the glorious revolution . . ."

It was a truly splendid response. A pity not to have mailed it! But caution had warned, *Don't!* It might be a trap. So he had let the completed questionnaire remain where it was.

His reply, Georgos realized, was masterful. *Someone* ought to read it. Why not send it? After all, it was anonymous. He decided that he would mail it when he went out on Sunday night.

AT APPROXIMATELY the same moment that Georgos Archambault made his decision to bomb La Mission again, Harry London faced Nim Goldman. The two men were in Nim's office.

"No!" London said. "Not for you, Nim, or anybody else."

Nim said patiently, "All I've asked you is to reconsider launching proceedings and look at the extenuating circumstances. . . ."

A short time ago, remembering his promise to Karen the previous evening, Nim had telephoned Harry London to see if he knew of a theft-of-service case involving a Luther Sloan.

"You bet I do," had been the answer.

Now Harry London explained, "Your friend Sloan has been bypassing meters—lots of them—for better than a year."

Nim said irritably, "He isn't my friend. His daughter is."

"One of your many women friends, no doubt."

"Knock it off, Harry! Karen Sloan is a quadriplegic."

Nim went on to describe the Sloan family, how Luther Sloan had gone into debt to buy a special van for Karen. "One thing I'm certain of. Whatever he did with any money he made, he didn't spend it on himself."

"Nim," London said coldly, "in the Quayle setup, Luther Sloan was *the gasman*. They gave him most of the illegal gas work which came their way, probably because he was good at it. As far as we can estimate, what he did has cost GSP&L, in gas revenue losses, about two hundred and thirty thousand dollars. And unless you fire me, the Sloan case will take its course, which means a criminal charge is going to be laid within the next few days."

Nim threw up his hands. "Okay, Harry. You win."

London shook his head slowly. "No, I don't. Nobody wins. Not me, not you, not GSP&L and certainly not Luther Sloan. I'm simply doing my job." With that, he left Nim's office.

Nim dreaded calling Karen. But before he could pick up the telephone, his office door flew open and Ray Paulsen strode in.

Paulsen looked weary and haggard, his hair and beetling eyebrows grayer than a month ago. Dropping heavily into a chair, he growled at Nim, "You might as well know, we've lost Big Lil."

"We've what?"

"You heard me. We've lost Big Lil—for at least four months!"

Nim could understand Paulsen's distress, and share it. Big Lil, La Mission Number 5, supplied six percent of GSP&L's maximum load.

Nim asked, "What happened?"

"We've had Big Lil off the line for a week for routine maintenance," Paulsen said. "It was due back on today. And it would have been. Except for a damn fool operator."

Angrily Paulsen spelled out the sorry details. When a steam-powered, oil-fueled generator like Big Lil was started up, procedures were elaborate and precise. An operator, working in a control room, was trained to follow instructions carefully, step by step. Normally the process took several hours.

With Big Lil, the boiler which provided steam was activated first. Projecting into the boiler at various heights were rings of oil guns—burners which sprayed atomized fuel. The operator ignited the burners by remote control, level by level, starting at the bottom—for safety reasons.

Today the operator—failing to check his instruments—thought the lowest level of oil guns was alight. It wasn't. As succeeding levels of burners came on, the lowest level continued to pour out

492

unburned oil, which pooled at the bottom of the boiler. Eventually the accumulated oil and vapor exploded.

"I thought there was a safety interlock—" Nim began.

"Of course there is!" Paulsen sounded as though he were about to weep. "It's designed to prevent exactly what happened. But—can you believe this?—the damn fool operator overrode it manually. Said he wanted to bring the unit on line faster."

"Oh, God!" Nim could understand Paulsen's anger and frustration. "How much damage did the explosion do?"

"Plenty—to the internal boiler structure, much of the duct and flue work, more than half the water-wall tubes."

Mentally Nim was running over logistics. Big Lil was by far the most economical oil-fueled generator the utility had. Now Big Lil's output must be made up by other units which used more fuel. Therefore, suddenly, GSP&L's total oil reserves represented a great deal less electric power than before.

"Rolling blackouts will have to start within the next few days," Nim said.

Paulsen nodded. "I agree." He got up to go.

At a hastily called meeting that Friday afternoon, it was decided that rolling blackouts would begin the following Wednesday.

IT WAS not until late that Nim found time to phone Karen.

Josie answered first, then Karen came on the line.

"Karen," Nim said, "I made some inquiries to see if there was anything I could do about your father, but there isn't. I'm sorry."

"So am I," Karen said, and he sensed her dejection. "But I'm grateful to you for trying, Nimrod."

"The only advice I can give," he told her, "is that your father get himself a good lawyer."

There was a silence, then she asked, "Is it really that bad?"

There seemed no point in lying. "Yes, I'm afraid it is."

"The strange thing is," Karen said, "I've always thought of Daddy as the most honest person I know."

"Well," Nim acknowledged, "I'm not making excuses for your father. I can't. But I guess, sometimes, there are pressures which do strange things to people."

"But he didn't *need* to; that's what's so tragic. Oh, I've enjoyed the extra things my parents have made possible with money, including Humperdinck. But I could have managed without."

Nim didn't tell Karen that obviously her father had seen a way to expiate his guilt feelings and had taken it. That was something the courts would have to pass judgment on. Instead, Nim asked, "You still have Humperdinck?"

"Yes. Humperdinck hasn't been repossessed yet."

"I'm glad," he said, "because you'll need the van next week."

He went on to tell her that rolling blackouts would begin on Wednesday. "In your area, power will go off at three p.m. Wednesday and stay off for at least three hours. So, to be safe, you should go to Redwood Grove Hospital in the morning."

"It's truly wonderful," Karen said, with a flash of her normal brightness, "to be cared about so much."

"I REALLY do believe," Ruth Goldman observed, turning pages of the *Chronicle-West* Sunday edition, "that people are beginning to face reality about an electrical crisis."

The family had gathered in Nim and Ruth's bedroom. Ruth was still in bed, having recently finished breakfast, brought to her on a tray. Nim had got up early to cook poached eggs on corned beef hash for everyone.

Two days ago Ruth had flown back from New York following her treatments at Sloan-Kettering. There were dark circles under her eyes, and she had experienced some pain. It was still too early to know the effect of the treatments, and she would go back to New York in another three weeks. Ruth reported cheerfully, though, that the doctors were very hopeful.

"Listen to this," Ruth began reading an editorial:

"This newspaper, which tries to be honest and forthright, admits to having second thoughts about some stands we have taken in the past. We have, like many others, opposed increased development of nuclear electric power. We have, because of concern about pollution, aligned ourselves with opposition to coal-burning electric generating plants. We have supported wildlife-preservation groups who opposed building additional dams for hydroelectric projects, on the grounds that wildlife, especially fish populations, might be diminished. We expressed doubt about permitting more geothermal electric plants.

"We do not apologize for these stands. They represent our convictions in specific areas. But viewing the situation as a whole, we are forced—in fairness—to agree with the power companies of California, which argue that their hands have been tied while we have demanded of them what they cannot deliver.

"Instead of compromising here and there, as a give-and-take society should, we have said no to almost everything. Let us remember that when the lights go out next Wednesday.

"Perhaps we deserve what we are getting. Whether we do or not, the time has come for serious reappraisal of some long-held views—our own and others.

"There!" Ruth declared, putting down the newspaper. "What do you think of that?"

"It's a smooth piece of writing," Nim said. "Unfortunately that's all it is. Oh yes, and it's five years late."

"I don't care," Ruth said. "I suppose I should care, but I don't. All I care about now is being home, and loving you all."

THAT Sunday evening Georgos Archambault ventured out from his North Castle apartment. At a delicatessen he bought enough food to last him until his departure for La Mission on Tuesday evening. He also bought the Sunday newspapers and mailed the envelope which contained that stupid Consumer Survey.

FIFTEEN

Monday passed uneventfully, relatively speaking. Tuesday, in the early morning hours, did not. Nature, as if conspiring to embarrass GSP&L, mounted its own onslaught.

Deep in the earth beneath Old Desperado, the wellhead which had once blown out of control and was never capped entirely, a subsidence of rock and subsoil released new geothermal steam under enormous pressure. The steam rushed to the surface with the force of twenty locomotives, hurling hot mud, stones and rock high into the air and over the geothermal field.

By sheer good luck the blowout occurred at 2:00 a.m., when only a handful of workers was on duty, and all were under cover.

Consequently there were neither deaths nor injuries. But the geothermal field's switching and transformer yard was deeply covered in wet muck, as were transmission lines nearby. The muck was a conductor of electricity. As a result, everything shorted out and the flow of power from all geothermal-driven generators was instantly cut off.

No lasting damage was done. Old Desperado, its bout of mischief over, settled back to sporadic, harmless steaming. But for forty-eight hours, until the massive cleanup job was complete, GSP&L would be deprived of seven hundred thousand kilowatts and would need to find that power elsewhere. The only way it could be done was by bringing in more oil-powered generators and thus further deplete the utility's precious reserve of oil.

With the abrupt loss of Big Lil four days earlier, and now all geothermals, GSP&L's generating capacity—irrespective of the oil shortage—would be stretched thin for the next two days.

Nim learned of the geothermal failure and the potential capacity shortage on coming in to work on Tuesday morning.

He knew that until geothermal was back on line, GSP&L could not absorb another disaster. The realization made him decide to telephone Karen Sloan.

"Karen," Nim said, "I'd prefer it if you went to Redwood Grove Hospital today. Could you do that?"

"Yes, of course, Nimrod. But why?"

"We're having a few problems and it's possible there could be a nonscheduled power cut. It probably won't happen, but I'd feel easier if you were close to that standby generator."

"All right," Karen said. "Josie's here and we'll get ready. And, Nimrod, you sound tired. Take care of yourself."

THE SPECIAL STAFF which had been assembled to process the bogus Consumer Survey in North Castle had been disbanded two weeks earlier. The few questionnaires that still straggled in were routed to an elderly secretary in public relations, Elsie Young. When she had time and inclination, she inspected them.

On Tuesday, around midmorning, Elsie observed that one of the special Consumer Survey envelopes had been dropped into her "in" tray, along with a sizable batch of interoffice mail. She decided to deal with the interoffice stuff first.

SECONDS after Karen concluded her conversation with Nim, she remembered she had forgotten to tell him that she and Josie had planned to go shopping this morning. Should they cancel the shopping trip and leave for the hospital now? Karen was tempted to call Nim back, then remembered the strain he was under. She would make the decision herself. What was it he had said about a possible power cut before tomorrow's scheduled one? It probably would not happen. So, obviously, the sensible thing was to go shopping first, then leave for Redwood Grove in the early afternoon.

GEORGOS ARCHAMBAULT possessed a certain animal instinct about danger. Near noon on Tuesday that instinct warned him that danger was close.

Should he obey it and, taking a large chance, head for La Mission now—in daylight? Or should he disregard the instinct and leave after dark, as planned?

Georgos intended to make his approach to La Mission's pump house underwater. La Mission was built on the banks of the Coyote River, enabling the plant to draw water for cooling and return it to the river afterward. Getting to the river side of the plant was where the rubber dinghy would come in. After that, Georgos intended to make use of the scuba-diving gear—he was an expert, having learned underwater demolition during his training in Cuba.

He had studied maps and knew he could drive to within half a mile of La Mission and launch the dinghy on the river at a deserted spot. The current would take him reasonably close to the plant. He would submerge, and from then on the likelihood of being seen was minimal, even in daylight. In fact, daylight, filtering downward, would help him locate his underwater point of entry. But could he launch the dinghy and get into it, wearing scuba gear, unobserved?

The really horrendous hazard in daylight, however, was driving his van. If he were spotted, there was no way he could outrun pursuit. On the other hand, there were a lot of beat-up VW vans like his around.

Abruptly Georgos made up his mind. He would trust his instincts and go now, during daylight!

"THERE'S a telephone call for you, Mrs. Van Buren," a waitress announced, "and I was told to tell you it's important."

The PR director got up from the table in the GSP&L's officers' dining room, where she was lunching with J. Eric Humphrey and Nim Goldman, and went to the telephone outside. When she returned, there was excitement in her eyes.

"One of those Consumer Surveys came back," she announced, "and we've got a match on the Archambault handwriting. A half-wit in my department has been sitting on it all morning. She's on the way to the computer center now. I told her that we'd meet her there."

Minutes later the three who had interrupted lunch, plus Sharlett Underhill and Harry London, were gathered around a table in the computer center, examining the Consumer Survey which a chastened Elsie Young had delivered only a few minutes ago.

"Why on earth," Harry London said, "did he take so long?"

Without answering, the finance chief took the questionnaire over to a portable black light. She snapped the light on and held the form under it. The number 9386 stood out.

She led the way to a computer keyboard with a cathode-ray screen above it and typed in the project name—North Castle Survey—followed by the secret code which would release the needed information.

The computer signaled ENTER QUESTIONNAIRE NUMBER.

Sharlett Underhill typed in 9386.

The screen flashed back OWEN GRAINGER 12 WEXHAM RD APT E.

A LITTLE MORE THAN an hour later Harry London was reporting to Eric Humphrey and Nim. "Archambault's flown the coop," London said. "According to a neighbor, a man drove away in a Volkswagen van half an hour before the place was raided. The police have issued an APB for the van, and staked out the building. But"—he shrugged—"that guy has slipped through their hands before."

Eric Humphrey told Nim, "I want immediate notification sent to all our plant managers and security personnel. Instruct them to increase their vigilance and to report anything suspicious. He may decide to make us his target once again."

GEORGOS hummed a little tune. His luck was holding. He had been driving for an hour and a quarter and his van had attracted no attention. Now he was almost at the point where he planned to launch the dinghy. He turned down a gravel road and a few minutes later he saw the Coyote River through the underbrush. He stopped about thirty yards from the bank. No one was in sight.

As he began unloading the dinghy and supplies, carrying them to the river, his excitement grew. He pushed the dinghy into the water, tied the painter to a tree, and transferred the equipment into it. There was a compressed-air tank, a face mask, fins, a snorkel, a waterproof flashlight, a mesh belt and yellow wire cutters.

Last of all, Georgos loaded aboard the cylindrical plastic bombs. They weighed five pounds each and would be fastened to his belt. He had decided that eight bombs were all he could carry. As it was, they would destroy eight of the eleven water pumps—putting most, if not all, of La Mission's four operating generators out of action. He had read in Sunday's papers that Big Lil, the fifth generator, was already disabled.

When everything was in the dinghy, Georgos changed into a wet suit, got aboard, and untied the painter. Using a small paddle, he eased clear of the bank and began moving downstream. In less than ten minutes he could see La Mission's smokestacks and the big, functional building which housed turbines and generators. In another five minutes he decided he was close enough, and tied up in a small, shallow-water cove.

Now he donned the tank, mask, snorkel, belt and fins, and attached the remainder of his load. He took one last look around, turned on his air, then waded out toward midstream. Moments later he slipped into deep water and began swimming. He had already taken a sight on his objective—the pump house, a long low, concrete structure projecting into the river.

Georgos knew that the pump house had two levels. One—above the water—housed the electric motors which drove the pumps. The second level—underwater—contained the pumps themselves. It was this second level he intended to penetrate.

Soon he was halted by a concrete wall; he had reached the pump house. Feeling his way along, and guided by the pull of the water, he reached a wire mesh screen. The purpose of the screen was to prevent large objects from being drawn in with the water and damaging the pumps. It was a horizontal cylinder about ten feet across, which was rotated occasionally for cleaning. Georgos knew he would have to cut his way past it.

Snipping away with his wire cutters, he soon opened a large circle at the front of the cylinder. Georgos eased himself carefully through. Then he began working on the farther side. Soon that, too, gave way and he passed through. In the light filtering down from apertures in the pump-house floor above, he was able to make out the bulk of the first pump, directly ahead.

Georgos was not afraid of the suction of the pumps. From his textbook studies he knew that he would only be affected by it if he went deep, which he had no intention of doing.

He began looking for a place to locate the first bomb. Just as he found one—a flat surface on the housing—he sensed movement behind him and turned. The cylinder through which he had entered, and which had been still, was now rotating.

THE PLANT superintendent at La Mission was a bright, tough-minded young engineer named Bob Ostrander. He had been second-in-command to plant superintendent Danieli, who had been killed with Walter Talbot by the bomb which damaged Big Lil. Ostrander nursed a burning anger about terrorists in general and especially the misnamed Friends of Freedom. Consequently, when a teletype message arrived early Tuesday afternoon warning that Georgos Archambault, the Friends of Freedom leader, might make a new attack on GSP&L property, Bob Ostrander put himself and his staff on full alert. On his instructions the entire La Mission plant was searched immediately for intruders. Patrols were ordered to make continuous rounds of the fence, and guards at the main gate were told to admit no one, other than plant employees.

Bob Ostrander also telephoned the county sheriff, who diverted two police cars to search roads in the area for Archambault's van. Less than thirty minutes after Ostrander's call—at 2:35 p.m.—the sheriff reported that the van had been found abandoned close to the Coyote River, half a mile from the plant. An intensive search for Archambault was now in progress.

Ostrander at once sent patrols to the river side of the plant.

500

About ten minutes later the sheriff phoned again. An empty rubber dinghy had been discovered in a cove around a headland near the plant.

"It looks as if the guy has come ashore and figures to get in through the fence," the sheriff said. "Every man I have is over your way. Don't worry! We've got him bottled up."

As he hung up, Bob Ostrander wondered why Archambault would come through the fence in daylight. It did not make sense. Suddenly Ostrander said aloud, "Scuba gear! That's why he needed a dinghy. The bastard is coming underwater!"

He left his office on the run.

The assistant superintendent was among those patrolling on the river side of the plant. Ostrander, arriving hurriedly, asked him, "Have you see anything?"

"Not a thing."

"Come with me." They strode toward the pump house as Ostrander explained his theory about an underwater attack. At the forward extremity of the pump house, Ostrander stepped onto an open walkway. He leaned over and looked down into the clear water. The mesh cylinder was visible a few feet below the surface. "Go inside and turn the cylinder slowly," he told his assistant. There was an electric mechanism to do so.

Moments later the cylinder began to revolve. Almost at once Ostrander saw the first large hole. When the second hole appeared, his fears were confirmed. Running into the pump house, he shouted, "He's got inside! Keep the screen going!"

Ostrander's mind was icy cool as he assessed the possibilities. Somewhere underneath where he was standing, Archambault was swimming, undoubtedly with a bomb or bombs. There were two possible targets: the pumps, or the condensers farther into the plant. Blowing up the pumps could put all of La Mission's generators out of use for months. But a bomb in the condensers would be far, far worse. Rebuilding them might take a year.

Bob Ostrander knew about explosives. He had studied them at engineering school and since. A five-pound dynamite bomb, no larger than a loaf of bread, could pass through the pumps and enter the condensers. All Archambault needed to do was set the fuse and drop it; it would find its way to the condensers.

The condensers had to be protected. To do so meant shutting

down all generators. Now. Ostrander went to a wall telephone in the pump house and dialed 11 for the main control room.

A ringing tone and a click. "Chief operator."

"This is Ostrander. I want you to hit the trips on all units and stop the circulating water."

The operator protested, "You'll blow the rupture disks—"

"Damn it! Don't give me an argument!" Ostrander shouted, knowing at any moment an explosion might rip apart the pump house or condensers. "Hit those trips! *Hit them now!*"

As the cylinder continued to revolve, Georgos realized that his escape route was cut off. Not that he had really expected to escape, but he didn't want to die this way. Trapped. . . . In mounting panic he turned sharply to inspect the cylinder. Maybe he could cut two more holes.

With his abrupt movement the yellow wire cutters, which were fastened to his wrist by a cord, broke loose and fell. Instinctively Georgos kicked hard and dived, following the yellow. His hand was outstretched. He almost had them.

Then he felt a sudden rush of water and realized he had gone too deep and was being sucked into a pump. He let his mouth-piece go and started to scream. . . . The pump impeller blades, seven feet across, seized him and chopped him into little pieces. The bombs—unfused and harmless—disintegrated too. Seconds later, all pumps slowed and stopped.

Bob Ostrander had no doubt that his decision had been right. Blowing the turbine rupture disks was a small price to pay for saving the condensers, which he went immediately to inspect. No sign of damage or a bomb. Good!

Nor had anything happened yet in the pump house. As Ostrander was about to go down there, he noticed some pieces of debris which appeared to have come through the pumps and had collected on a condenser. He reached out to pick up one of the pieces, then stopped. It was a human hand, peculiarly stained.

Karen was shocked to realize it was well past 2:00 p.m. It scarcely seemed any time at all since she had promised Nimrod she would go to Redwood Grove Hospital, yet several hours had

gone by. The shopping had taken longer than expected. Then, when they came back they had had lunch at the apartment.

Now, with lunch over, Josie announced, "I'll go down and bring Humperdinck around. Will you be okay if I leave you?"

"Of course. While you're gone I'll make a phone call. Put my headband on, please."

Josie did so. Then she left.

A moment later Karen touched the telephone microswitch with her head. In her earpiece she heard a ringing tone, followed by a voice. "Operator. May I help you?"

"I have manual service, operator. Will you dial for me, please?" Karen gave the number of her telephone, then the number she was calling—her parents' house. There was a series of clicks, then the phone started ringing. To Karen's surprise no one answered. Early this morning she had talked with her mother, who was feeling unwell and did not intend to go to work today.

Karen broke the connection by moving her head against the microswitch and tried another number—Cynthia's. Again no reply.

She felt a vague unease. She was rarely alone and, when she was, liked to be in touch with someone by telephone.

Now she wished she hadn't told Josie she could go.

Suddenly several lights in the apartment went out, an air conditioner stopped, and Karen felt the slightest break in rhythm as her respirator switched from mains supply to battery. With a start, Karen realized that the battery on the wheelchair, which had been drawn on considerably during her shopping jaunt, ought to have been replaced immediately after she came in. Instead, Josie had plugged in the chair to the mains and switched the chair battery to "charge." However, the battery would need at least six hours of charging to recoup what it had lost; it had had barely one, and now, with external power off, the charging would stop.

There was a fully charged battery to the right of her chair, ready to be put on before leaving for the hospital. Karen could see it. But there was no way she could connect it herself.

Karen tried to telephone Nimrod. But she got a recording: "All circuits are busy. Please place your call later."

She tried again. The same result.

From her reading Karen knew that whenever there was a widespread power cut, phone lines became clogged because more people tried to use them than the system could handle. She began to be really alarmed. *Why was Josie taking so long?* And why hadn't the janitor, Jiminy, come in to see if she was okay, as he always did when anything out of the ordinary occurred?

Though Karen had no means of knowing it, a combination of events had contributed to her predicament. At 10:15 a.m. Luther Sloan was arrested and charged with sixteen felonies, under the California Penal Code, for stealing gas. Since that time, Henrietta Sloan, shocked, despairing, totally inexperienced in the matter, had been trying to arrange her husband's bail. Shortly before noon she telephoned Cynthia for help, and Cynthia left home to meet her mother. Cynthia's husband was at work. While Karen tried to telephone her mother and sister, both were shuttling between a bail bondsman's office and the jail where Luther Sloan was held.

They were in the visitors' section of the jail when the power cut occurred, but were unaware of it because the jail had its own standby generator, which had started up automatically. Neither the two women, nor Luther Sloan, would know about the power cut for another two hours.

WHEN the chief operator at La Mission plant responded to Bob Ostrander's order, "Hit those trips! *Hit them now!*" the GSP&L transmission system was deprived, without warning, of three million two hundred thousand kilowatts of power. The utility was already operating with a thin reserve, and because of warm weather and widespread use of air conditioners, the load demand was unseasonably high for a May afternoon.

The result: a monitoring computer, recognizing there was now insufficient power on line to meet demand, opened high-voltage circuit breakers, plunging a large portion of the GSP&L system into blackout. Karen's building was in one of the areas affected.

After Josie left Karen, she collected the van from a nearby service station, where it had been left overnight to be filled with gas and lubricated, and drove it to the apartment house front door.

Jiminy was touching up paint outside when Josie returned. He asked about Karen and, upon learning of the planned trip to the hospital, said he would come up to help. They were in the elevator, between the third floor and the fourth, when it stopped and its light went out. Both began shouting frantically for help.

Josie had long ago remembered about Karen's low battery, which made her cries more desperate. Though they did not know it then, they would remain in the elevator for almost three hours.

KAREN was now white with fear, and sweating.

She knew something serious had happened to prevent Josie coming back. She also knew, through calculation, that there was barely a quarter of an hour's life remaining in the battery.

She began to pray. She begged God to send Josie, or Jiminy, or her parents, or Nimrod, or *anyone!* She was still praying when she felt the respirator begin to slow. Frantically she tried the telephone again. "This is a recording. All circuits are busy."

Karen began to gasp, her skin turned red, then blue. Her mouth worked wildly as she fought to breathe. Then, as air ceased coming entirely, she choked; intense pain gripped her chest.

Soon, mercifully, the battery died and, with it, Karen.

SIXTEEN

In some ways, Nim thought, it was like the rerun of an old movie as he explained to the assembled press what had happened at La Mission to cause the latest blackout. . . . Was it really just ten months ago that Walter Talbot and the others died, and Big Lil suffered bomb damage which caused the blackout then?

Nim was aware of one difference today. It was the attitude of the press people, compared with ten months earlier. Today there seemed a genuine awareness of the problems GSP&L faced.

"Mr. Goldman," Oakland *Tribune* asked, "if you get green lights to build your plants, how long will it take to catch up?"

"Ten years," Nim answered. "But we need a lot of permissions before we can even begin. So far there isn't any sign of them."

He had come here, to a press conference in the observation gallery of the energy control center, shortly after the shutdown of all La Mission's generators and the resultant blackout.

Nancy Molineaux inquired, "Will you be able to restrict the scheduled blackouts to three hours a day?"

"It's unlikely," Nim said. "As our oil supplies diminish, we'll need longer blackouts—probably six hours."

A TV newsman asked, "Have you heard there's been some rioting—demonstrations against the Anti's?"

"Yes, I have. And in my opinion it doesn't help anybody." Nim had read this morning that stones had been hurled through windows of the Sequoia Club. It was predicted that there would be more demonstrations and rioting as unemployment increased.

Finally somebody asked Nim, "What's your advice to people?"

He grinned. "Switch off everything you don't need to survive."

Two hours later, at 6:00 p.m., when Nim returned to his office, he asked Vicki to call Karen Sloan at Redwood Grove Hospital.

She buzzed him a few minutes later. "The hospital says they have no Miss Sloan registered as a patient."

"Then try her home number," Nim said.

This time, instead of buzzing, Vicki opened his office door and came in. "I think you'd better take this call."

Puzzled, he picked up the phone. "Is that you, Karen?"

A choked voice said, "Nimrod, this is Cynthia. Karen is dead."

NIM left immediately in a company car for Karen's apartment. On the way, his thoughts were in turmoil. He had obtained no details from Cynthia, only the bare fact that the power cut had been responsible for Karen's death. When he arrived at the apartment, Cynthia came out into the corridor, closing the door behind her.

"You can't come in," she said. "It's too awful."

Nim could hear someone inside the apartment having hysterics— it sounded like Henrietta Sloan. Cynthia's eyes were red.

She told him as much as she knew about the series of misfortunes which added up to Karen's terrible, lonely death. Nim started to say that he blamed himself—for failing to check sooner that Karen had gone to Redwood Grove—but Cynthia stopped him.

"No, Nimrod! No one in a long time did as much for Karen as you. She wouldn't want you to feel guilt, or blame yourself. She . . ." Cynthia shook her head, unable to say any more.

"Is there anything at all I can do?" Nim asked.

Cynthia shook her head. "Not now."

NIM was back in his office. Despite Cynthia's words, his sense of guilt persisted. He wished there were someone he could talk to. But he had not told Ruth about Karen, and couldn't now.

He put his face in his hands. After a while, he knew he must do *something*. For an hour or two, at least. So, as much for mental relief as for any other reason, he settled down to work.

He had been concentrating for ten minutes when there was a knock on the door and Nancy Molineaux came in. As usual, she was dressed stylishly, though simply—tonight in a coral silk shirt-waist, a perfect complement to her flawless black skin. Her handsome, high-cheekboned face seemed to have become friendlier, Nim thought, since their meeting in the Christopher Columbus Hotel and the shattering events which followed it.

She sat down opposite Nim, crossing her long, shapely legs.

"What can I do for you, Nancy?" he asked.

"Sorry to barge over, but I'd like you to read this." She got up and placed a strip of paper in front of him. "It's a news story that just broke," she explained. "We'd like some comments from you."

Swinging his chair to where the light was better, Nim studied the story carefully.

WASHINGTON, D.C., May 3—In a dramatic move to resolve the current oil crisis, the United States is to issue a new currency, to be known as the new dollar. It will be backed by gold and be worth five existing dollars.

Some Washington officials have already dubbed the new currency "the honest dollar."

The OPEC nations will be asked to accept payment for their oil in new dollars, with price adjustments to be negotiated. Initial OPEC reaction has been cautiously favorable. However, OPEC spokesman Sheikh Ahmed Musaed stated that an independent audit of United States gold would be sought before any agreement based on the new dollar could be concluded.

The President is expected to inform Americans that they can acquire new dollars by surrendering their old dollars at the rate of five to one. The exchange will be voluntary at first but, under proposed legislation, compulsory within five years. After that, the old dollar will have value only as a collector's item.

Nim was aware of Nancy Molineaux, waiting. "I'm no financial genius," he said, "but I don't think you need to be one to know that what's happening here"—he tapped the sheet with a finger—

"has been inevitable for a long time. Unfortunately a lot of decent middle-class folk who've worked hard and accumulated savings are the ones who'll be hurt most when they line up to trade their dollars five for one. Even now, though, all that this does is buy us some time. Time until we stop purchasing oil we can't afford and begin developing our own untapped resources."

"Thanks," Nancy said. "That'll do nicely." She put away a notebook she had been writing in. "Over at the paper, by the way, they seem to think that you're Sir Oracle. Oh yes, and speaking of which, you might like to know that in Sunday's edition we're reprinting what you said at that hearing last September—the one where you blew up and got yourself in trouble. Suddenly it all makes more sense." A thought occurred to her. "Do you want to tell me—for the record—how you feel about it?"

On impulse, Nim opened a desk drawer and took out a folder. From it he extracted a sheet of blue stationery and read aloud:

> "*Be, at that harvest moment, forgiving, gracious,*
> *Broad of mind, large-purposed,*
> *Amused by life's contrariness.*"

"Not bad," Nancy said. "Who wrote that?"

"A friend of mine." He found he was having trouble speaking. "A friend who died today."

There was a silence, then she asked, "Was that the reason you looked the way you did when I came in here tonight—like you'd been swept up from a stable floor?"

Nim smiled briefly. "If that's the way I was, I suppose the answer's yes."

"Want to tell me about it? Off the record, if you like."

"Yes," he said. "It'll be off the record. Her name was Karen Sloan. I think she was the most beautiful person—in every way— I've ever known."

A pause, then, "How did you meet her?"

"Accidentally. Right after that blackout last July . . ."

An hour ago Nim had longed for someone to confide in. Now he poured it out. When he described Karen's death, Nancy stood up, moved around the room, and said softly, "Oh, baby! *Baby!*"

"So you see," Nim said, "I guess looking like something from a stable floor wasn't all that surprising."

Nancy had returned to the desk. She pointed to his spread-out papers. "Then why are you bothering with all that junk?"

"I had work to do. Still have."

"Rubbish! Dump it and go home."

Nim shook his head and glanced toward the rollaway bed that had been brought into his office. "Tonight I'm sleeping here. We still have problems, and tomorrow—remember?—we start rolling blackouts."

How to Write a Best Seller
from *I Married A Best Seller*   by Sheila Hailey

There is no such thing as a surefire best seller. Even a writer like my husband, with a series of successes behind him, can fall flat on his face. In my opinion, Arthur Hailey books have been best sellers for three reasons. First, Arthur is a cracking good storyteller. Second, through painstaking research, he gives people an unusual insider's view of institutions and technologies. Third, he has an almost uncanny sense when he begins planning a book of what will be topical at publication time.

The reason for this timeliness is simple. Arthur is a newsaholic. Every morning at our home in the Bahamas we get that day's *New York Times* and *Wall Street Journal*, along with the local papers. Then there are the news magazines, and the almost hourly news broadcasts from Miami which Arthur listens to. So the news never gets away from him. And he has an acute awareness of the forces shaping the world.

All this, along with that storyteller's instinct, seems to tell him what subject will make a topical novel three to four years from the time he chooses it. An example of this is *The Moneychangers* [a Condensed Books selection], which Arthur began working on in 1972. It was the story of a big bank, brought from success and power to near disaster. He believed the subject would be timely. What he didn't know was that prestigious banks would be toppling like ninepins when *The Moneychangers* came out, and that an international currency crisis would be grabbing headlines.

Once he has chosen the subject for a book, Arthur reads everything he can about it, then goes out to gather information. If he is researching a big organization, this may involve talking with chairmen in boardrooms, office workers in a cafeteria, disgruntled employees or retired executives. The research takes the best part of a year. Out of it will come hundreds of anecdotes, and a general theme that suggests itself to his storyteller's mind. After that it's pure imagination—creating characters and plot.

The next stage of a novel—writing a forty- to fifty-page outline—can take up to six months to complete. Arthur writes profiles for all his main characters. Their names he chooses with infinite care, so that the reader can easily identify them each time they come onstage. His first-name sources are a yellowed list I brought home from the hospital after our youngest child was born and *The Oxford Dictionary of English Christian Names*.

For surnames he keeps a Manhattan phone book handy—that massive two-and-a-half-inch-thick list of New York

Arthur Hailey

telephone subscribers. He may decide on a name beginning with K, for instance. So, depending on the types he has already used, he will choose a simple, one-syllable name (Kemp), a jawbreaker (Kouchakdjian) or a distinguished one (Kensington).

The actual writing of a novel takes Arthur roughly eighteen months. He scribbles a paragraph at a time, then types the passage cleanly. He then revises it, playing with a phrase, a word, and types the paragraph again and again until it is the best he can do. His target is six hundred words a day.

After the final delivery of his manuscript to the publishers, there is a long wait—another seven to nine months until publication day. It is a restless time. Arthur is impatient to see his work in bookshops. He's not quite ready to start a new book, so he wants something exciting to happen to fill the void.

It usually does. . . .

PUBLISHED BY MICHAEL JOSEPH AND SOUVENIR PRESS

THE MASTER MARINER. Original full-length version © Nicholas Monsarrat 1978. British condensed version © The Reader's Digest Association Limited 1979.

THE SNOW TIGER. Original full-length version © L. J. Jersey Ltd. 1975. Australian condensed version © Reader's Digest Services Pty. Ltd. 1977. British condensed version © The Reader's Digest Association Limited 1979.

ALONE IN THE WILDERNESS. Original full-length version © Mike Tomkies 1976. British condensed version © The Reader's Digest Association Limited 1979.

OVERLOAD. Original full-length version © Arthur Hailey 1978. US condensed version © The Reader's Digest Association Inc. 1978. British condensed version © The Reader's Digest Association Limited 1979.

Picture credits: THE MASTER MARINER: Pages 6/7: Detail from "Dutch ships running before a storm" by Willem Van de Velde the Younger: Cooper-Bridgeman Library, National Maritime Museum. Page 9: The Battle of the Armada: The Worshipful Society of Apothecaries of London; miniature of Francis Drake by Nicholas Hilliard: National Portrait Gallery. Page 53: Greenwich by Hendrik Danckerts; National Maritime Museum; portrait of Samuel Pepys by J. Hauls: National Portrait Gallery. Page 88: The Taking of Quebec: National Army Museum; portrait of James Cook by Nathaniel Dance: Greenwich Hospital Collection, National Maritime Museum. Page 122: The Battle of the Nile by Nicholas Pocock: National Maritime Museum; portrait of Horatio Nelson by Lemuel Francis Abbott: Greenwich Hospital Collection, National Maritime Museum. Page 169: photograph of Nicholas Monsarrat: Daily Telegraph Colour Library/Goddard. ALONE IN THE WILDERNESS: photographs on pages 5 and 359 by kind permission of the author. OVERLOAD: photograph of Arthur Hailey: The *Miami Herald*.